FATIMA'S SCARF

David Caute

FATIMA'S SCARF

❦

Totterdown Books

All characters depicted in this novel are fictitious
and neither represent nor are based upon real
persons except in the case of those public figures
who appear under their own names.

Copyright © 1998 David Caute

First published in Great Britain in 1998
by Totterdown Books
BCM Totterdown, London WC1N 3XX

A catalogue reference is available from the British Library

ISBN 0 9530407 0 4

Typographical styling by Tim Higgins

Typeset by Intype London Ltd

Printed in Great Britain by
St Edmundsbury Press, Bury St Edmunds

Distributed by Central Books, 99 Wallis Road,
London E9 5LN. Tel 0181 986 4854   Fax 0181 533 5821

For Martha

PART ONE

Bruddersford–*Nasreen*

෴

The Muslims of Bruddersford

ARAM, MRS ZAHRA, Headmistress of the Muslim Girls School

CHEEMA, ALI, lecturer

HAQQ, ISHMAIL, Muslim Independent candidate for City Council

HASSANI, HASSAN, Secretary of Maududi Mosque

HASSANI, NASREEN, his wife, community teacher, elder daughter of
S.B. Hussein, sister of Latifa

HASSANI, IMRAN, their young son

HUSSEIN, SADAR BAJ (known as S.B.), Labour Party veteran, father
of Nasreen Hassani and Latifa Hussein

HUSSEIN, RAZIA, his wife

HUSSEIN, LATIFA, their younger daughter, sister of Nasreen

HUSSEIN, ISHTIAQ, younger brother of Nasreen and Latifa

IQBAL, IQBAL, a pharmacist

JANGAR, MUSTAFA, imam to Islamic Council, Regional Guardian of
Muslim Youth League

KHAN, ABDUL AYUB, proprietor of Omar Khayyam restaurant and a
halal slaughter house. Muslim Independent candidate

KHAN, RANA, his daughter, member of police force

KHAN, KARAMAT, brother to Abdul Ayub Khan, Muslim Independent
candidate

KHAN, TARIQ, waiter, son of Karamat Khan

MALIK, HANI, Labour City councillor

MAROTI, MOHAMMAD, Labour Party member

QUDDUS, DR YAQUB, Chairman of Community Relations Council

SHAH, IZZA, Chairman of Islamic Council

SHAH, FATIMA, his younger daughter

SHAH, SAFIA, his elder daughter

SHASTI, IMTIAZ, car dealer, supporter of Haqq

SIDDIQI, TIGER, karate instructor, supporter of Haqq

ZAHEED, ZULFIKAR, Lord Mayor of Bruddersford

ZAHEED, WAHABIA, his daughter

ONE

In winter, even by mid-morning, the sun remains a sulking deity, shrouded by a densely sculpted bas-relief of cloud. Here and there a grudging beam of watery half-light illuminates some grim pensioner of a church tower or a shouting minaret. In winter Bruddersford is a city without shadows; the sky declines to offer the faintest indication of east or west. The bouncing mosques know Mecca by heart (129 degrees) even as the sullen churches grow blind to Jerusalem.

The Muslims gathering in the small square below the Lord Mayor's balcony keep their hands thrust deep into their anorak pockets, their shoulders tensed against the habitual chill by which Yorkshiremen recognize home.

'That's quite a crowd,' says Douglas Blunt, the City's Chief Executive.

'We might be in Karachi or Islamabad, Douglas isn't that what you mean?'

Lord Mayor Zulfikar Zaheed stands beside Blunt at the long window of his parlour in City Hall, his fingers tucked into the lapels of a gorgeous suit. Zaheed has dressed for the occasion: tricorn hat, red cloak, ermine collar, lace ruff and gold chain of office. Zaheed has replaced the old 'dressing mirror' in his parlour with a grander one, gilded and properly adorned by a riot of curlicues.

The Muslims are massing in the small square which lies immediately to the north of City Hall's imposing, late-Victorian, façade. The open space below the Lord Mayor's balcony is not really a square at all; the centre of the city is a tangle of irregular spaces, curves and loops, a testimony to the anarchy of commerce, the historic liberties of a pragmatic people who never suffered a Napoleon. The city centre is now rendered even more forbidding to visitors by a one-way traffic flow comprehensible only to natives. Douglas Blunt calls it 'snakes and ladders', not without a note of pride.

'Of course,' muses Zaheed, 'you are no doubt regretting better days, my dear Douglas. When this parlour was built, Muslims were

11

merely picturesque "Mohammedans" to be found in illustrated books written by intrepid explorers.'

'Aye: pyramids, camels and minarets.'

'But now you must suffer more than thirty minarets within sight of Woolworth's – though as yet no pyramids or camels.'

Blunt wonders whether the Lord Mayor is planning to display himself to the crowd in due course. No one steps out on to a balcony like Zaheed.

'And here you have a mob of wogs raising a riot over a book, Douglas. Did you tell me – I forget – whether you have yet read Mr Gamal Rahman's masterpiece, *The Devil: an Interview*?'

'Frankly, I can't see what all the fuss is about. That book's nowt but a long bout of wind, a pain in the arse.'

'A white Yorkshireman, a Christian, may not be the ideal judge of what constitutes an insult to Islam.'

'But an intolerable insult, Zulfikar?'

In easier times Blunt and Zaheed had been golfing companions – it had required Blunt's 'pull' to open the clubhouse to an Asian. Zaheed's golf is occasionally inspired but relentlessly erratic – no known handicap but terrific outfits, plus-fours from Boothroyd & Hill, tweed caps, co-respondent shoes. Zaheed hires a caddie to shoulder a vast white leather bag stuffed with every known club – you could have your dinner while he selects the right one for the next fiasco. 'Blast!'

The Muslims in the square below have begun to weld themselves into a congregation. Chanting begins, clenched fists are raised in unison. The Lord Mayor cannot take part; Zaheed cannot not take part. Blunt withdraws briefly to his own office to resume contact with the Chief Constable of West Yorkshire. Zaheed is the wrong man to overhear such conversations. When Zaheed is geering himself up for histrionics, torn between the conflicting loyalties and duties he loves to describe and suffer, then everything you do – or *they* do – is wrong.

'The police are invisible, I notice,' he remarks suspiciously when Blunt returns to the Lord Mayor's parlour.

'That seemed the wisest course.'

'Low profile for the time being, old chap?' The words are spoken with extravagant English-ness. Zaheed sighs and softens. 'Doug, where should a Muslim Lord Mayor stand on such a day?'

Blunt knows better than to answer that one – You'd have been wiser to have stayed at home, Zulfikar, worrying about the effect of frost on your gorgeous suburban rose-garden. But Zaheed needs every available Muslim vote to land him in the House of Commons, the nation's first Asian MP. Zaheed's political ambitions are not

12

properly Blunt's concern – only his dignity as Lord Mayor. A Chief Executive is an administrator, a civil servant, supposedly beyond political parties: Blunt believes he runs the City but would long since have been out of his job if ever tempted to say so.

Blunt will not forget Zaheed's first day in office. As the tricorn hat emerged from the vintage Daimler limousine, spit landed on the gleaming bodywork. White spit. The incident was much discussed (and denied) in the local press. Only after bitter debate had the Council's Tory minority agreed to Blunt's suggestion that the City should foot the bill for reinforced glass in the windows of Zaheed's expensive home in the white suburb of Snowhill. An alarm system was also installed, linked to the local police station, at public expense. And what a row about that! The correspondence columns of the local newspapers were full of it. Joe Reddaway had written one of his famous polemics in the *Echo*, arguing both ways with equal fervour. Visiting Snowhill police station, Blunt had picked up the resentment, the undercurrent of ugly jibes: according to one joke, Zaheed's chauffeur had been issued with a compass to ensure that the official Daimler was pointing at 129 degrees towards Mecca at prayer times.

At that time not a single Asian had been recruited to the Bruddersford police force. Now there are six.

The crowd beneath the Lord Mayor's balcony is packed tight, Sunnis mainly, a few Shi'ites, bearded mullahs and mustachioed youngsters, a densely woven quilt of collective indignation.

'Great dignity and restraint,' Blunt ventures, standing short and squat behind the tall, ermined Zaheed at the window.

'What do you expect?'

'Let's hope it stays that way. Book-burning is a small bit out of the ordinary round here.'

'Yes, Douglas, we "Ayshuns" are a bizarre bunch. We may play cricket but don't understand the rules.'

 solo

Nasreen Hassani observes the crowd from the top deck of a bus; the police are keeping the traffic moving at barely a crawl. Her husband Hassan has risen this Saturday morning even earlier than usual to intone his prayers and eat his breakfast – tea, cereal and white bread – with burning eyes. It's men's business, this jihad, fighting this Gamal Rahman book – though all Muslim women share and suffer the insults inflicted on the twelve wives of the Prophet when Rahman claimed that a thirteenth wife had turned up in Egypt in our own time – or something like that.

Nasreen is a community teacher employed by the Education

Department. She works for her beautiful, sad-eyed Director of Education, Rajiv Lal. She is not 'in love' with him because '*in love*' is not the sacred form of love, it belongs to cheap films and one-year marriages. She is married to Hassan for ever. She is a Muslim. Rajiv is a Hindu – by origin if not by faith. She wishes she knew whether he lives alone. She has tried to climb into his head; he is a gentle, serious, wise man but there are no windows into his head or heart.

Rajiv Lal is reluctant to discuss Gamal Rahman's book with her but she has pressed him for an opinion.

'This is an affair for Muslims, Mrs Hassani.'

'My husband will not let me read it.'

'For me, it is simply an allegory'.

She understood the word but coaxed him to explain. Sighing faintly, Rajiv offered a small, helpless gesture of his delicate hands.

'Who knows, Mrs Hassani? This book may seek to persuade us that we should always doubt the human agents of Divine Revelation.'

'But for a Muslim the Prophet is the one and only prophet.'

'As I've said, this is entirely an affair for Muslims.'

'I've heard that Gamal Rahman has led an immoral life in Egypt. He took money from Zionists and dishonoured the President's daughters and betrayed his own wife.'

'When people are upset they say things.'

Rajiv Lal's life beyond his neatly ordered office remains his own affair. Every evening his little red Metro emerges from the Reserved Parking at the back of Municipal House (observed from the second-floor window of Nasreen's office, if she is alone), merges into the rushhour traffic, vanishes. She watches him vanish, her warm breath clouding the winter window pane. Is he a Believer? Any belief would be better than none. Does he attend one of the city's seven Hindu temples? Rajiv is 'modern'. He uses terms like 'Euro-centric curricula' with a quiet passion. Nasreen fears he may be squandering his life on some 'modern' English girl who shares his hostility to 'Euro-centric curricula'.

Some English slut.

ര

Zulfikar Zaheed is surveying his enemies packed into the square below, the imams and Jamiyat fanatics from the Islamic Council, clustered round the unlit funeral pyre, closely observed by the television cameras and the telescopic lenses of the press.

Izza Shah

Mustafa Jangar

Hassan Hassani

14

Ishmail Haqq
Ali Cheema

Sir Tom Potter calls them 'the Prophet's luminaries' – though the last word, in safe company, can sound like 'loonies'. Potter is the veteran leader of the Tory minority on the City Council. He has held the reins of power and wants them back. Douglas Blunt plays golf with him, too. He wouldn't particularly want to be taking his instructions from Potter again, but it's beginning to look bloody likely, what with this Gamal Rahman book tearing Labour apart and City elections coming up.

Potter doesn't like to lose at golf or at anything. 'It all goes back to rifts in Pakistan,' he announced, weighing his chip shot to the deceptive sixteenth green.

'There's more to it than that, Tom.'

'Oh, aye. Frankly, Doug, ever since the great immigration of the Sixties, Islamabad and Lahore have often seemed closer to us than Bradford or Huddersfield. Even this book-palaver is nowt but a play-out of the fierce struggles between the Bhuttos and the Islamicists in Pakistan. Zaheed is definitely a Bhutto. His enemies in our Bruddersford Islamic Council are definitely Jamiyat, definitely pro-General Zia. They regard Zulfikar Zaheed as a godless traitor, a compromiser fired by personal ambition.'

'I'm fond of Zaheed.'

'Oh aye, he takes care to drink only British mineral water at official functions. Frankly, Doug, you made right fool of yourself over that Cricket Club affair.'

The comment stung. Yorkshire County Cricket Club, in its wisdom, had neither granted nor refused Zaheed's application for membership. On inquiry, it was always 'pending'. Finally Blunt had resigned his own membership in protest. No one seemed to mind, much. Resigning was the great tradition at Yorkshire CCC – and normally over bigger issues than accommodating the bum of a Paki clothes-horse. The big raging issue – families stopped talking to each other – had been the Club's refusal to open up the team to non-York-shiremen, all those brilliant, match-winning West Indian bowlers whom the other counties scooped up, leaving once-proud Yorkshire, the county of Len Hutton and Freddy Trueman, anchored to the doldrums.

'Rejected,' as he insisted, 'by a strategy of insupportable procrastination,' Zaheed had made political capital out of the 'insult' by travelling to Leeds and standing in line for the open enclosures of Headingley, wearing his full regalia of office and attended by photographers from the *Echo* and the *Yorkshire Post*. 'Zulfikar Zaheed's

world tour of Yorkshire,' scoffed Tom Potter. Embarrased but loyal –
admiring, too – Blunt had accompanied his Lord Mayor, to fend off
the hooligans' taunts and – when the sun swung to the western sky –
their empty bottles as well. Blunt knows how to silence the skinheads.

'So when were you last fighting in the Western Desert? Don't I
know your Dad, lad?'

Cricket was serious business but Blunt doubted whether this book-
burning was more than a cathartic gesture. Zaheed's involvement
should have ended when he rashly debated Rahman on the BBC's
'Final Call' following the Egyptian novelist's provocative decision to
visit Bruddersford and read extracts from his novel, *The Devil: an
Interview*, outside chosen mosques. Though capable of eloquence,
Zaheed had no defence against Rahman's personal mockery. 'Lord
Mayor, I understand your ambition to become Britain's first Asian
Member of Parliament, but frankly you are nothing but a peacock-
actor cut and tailored to play the hero in a TV mega-serial set in
the Raj.' Why, Rahman needled Zaheed, was the most secular of
Bruddersford's Muslim politicians suddenly posing as a Defender
of the Faith?

(And yet, and yet: hadn't a despondent Rahman visited Bruddersford not many years ago, begging Zaheed's help, and Blunt's help,
and everyone's help? Hadn't he been received with kindness? – all
forgotten.)

Driving to City Hall from Mrs Blunt's kippers-and-toast, Blunt had
heard Rahman getting in some further knifework on Pennine Radio
the following morning. No one was mealy-mouthed in Yorkshire and
political insults were as commonplace as toadstools, but Rahman's
acid commentary on Zaheed's political career was plain libellous!
Blunt anticipated a wearisome half hour persuading Zaheed not
to reach for his lawyers. 'Never leap into your own linen basket,
Zulfikar.'

Now Rahman's book is burning.

ᙣ

The yellow-and-brown bus inches forward like a rancid block of ice-
cream, its brown nether regions splattered in January grime. Trapped
by the demonstration, Nasreen's fellow-passengers on the upper deck
are growing restive.

'It's those Pakis again,' says a woman in the seat behind.

'Aye. Never satisfied, always grousing about summat,' her husband
says.

'It's that bewk,' the woman says. 'That Devil-bewk.'

16

'Nowt's ever good enough for them. You can bend over backwards but nowt will satisfy them. If it i'n't the one thing it's t'other.'

'Why don't they go back where they came from?' the woman says.

Nasreen's neck is prickling, stiffening.

'No one's forced to read nowt, is they?' the woman says.

'They want it proper banned.'

'We don't ban bewks here. They should know that.'

Nasreen turns in her seat. She cannot gaze straight into their faces because their faces repel her: that soot-grey, sullen look of ageing white people.

'Excuse me,' she says. And nervously adjusts her headscarf. The man leans forward in his seat. His voice is kindly.

'Don't mind us,' he says. 'No offence intended. We should have noticed you. I'll tell you this, young lady, I reckon we in Bruddersford knows how to get on wi' other folk.'

Nasreen nods and stares straight ahead.

Her regular Saturday-morning journey is to a special language-disability class for Asian kids – organized and funded by Rajiv Lal; she does it for him, not for the meagre pay. She's beginning to doubt whether she'll arrive in time, or whether any of her pupils will arrive at all.

'Tell you summat else,' the man behind is telling his wife. 'I reckon our Muslims here is the best in the country. No trouble at all, normally.'

Rajiv is wise and good and anti-Euro-centric. Nasreen would like to garland his slender neck in flowers, Hindu-fashion. Could she ever have become the wife of a Hindu? Rajiv is so understanding about the problems which arise in the city's classrooms – language problems, cultural problems, the inevitable suspicion and resentment of the white teachers when the community teacher, Mrs Nasreen Hassani, is called in to intercede. Why, they ask, do these community teachers speak to our problem-children in Urdu, Punjabi, Gujerati, Bengali? What is that Nasreen Hassani woman saying behind our backs?

'And still,' Rajiv Lal constantly complains, 'there are only 103 regular, full-time Asian teachers out of five thousand. We have to change that.'

ॐ

In the heart of the crowd stand the oaks of Islam, the elders of the Islamic Council: Izza Shah, President; Mustafa Jangar, imam to the Council; Hassan Hassani, Treasurer. And with them the Khan brothers, Ishmail Haqq and young Ali Cheema, intellectual-in-residence to Izza Shah.

17

The silence of three thousand tongues is awesome as the satanic book is held aloft by Mustafa Jangar. Intently the all-male crowd observes the fastening, the pinning (as if a wild animal has been trapped), the dousing in fuel – the sudden spurt of flame which brings a vast exhalation from six thousand lungs (though not every old mill worker can boast the complete pair). Mustafa Jangar supervises the burning of the book – indeed this is his personal fire. The flames seem to emanate from his nostrils, his eyes and his slightly parted mouth framed by the heavy lips of cinematic villainy. His beard is palpably on fire yet does not burn.

Pressing forward through the fringes of the crowd is a young man called Tariq Khan. He has arrived late, a night restaurant waiter who needs his sleep but cannot resist a crowd, excitement, a happening.

Hassan Hassani's soft glistening lips part as the book catches light. Inhaling the smell of burning paper, Nasreen's husband sighs with pleasure. But he is not at ease in dense crowds. He fears for his glasses in a fracas, and he often warns his colleagues in the Islamic Council that young Muslims (like Tariq Khan) may soon be tempted to act unwisely.

As the flames take hold and the devil's oily smoke rises from the blackening pages, so the breath of the crowd grows hotter. God is Great, Allah akhbar! Cameramen in Hong Kong trainers dance around the steps jostling for the perfect angle.

ᗥ

'The British are telling us to pack up and piss off,' the Lord Mayor remarks gloomily.

It doesn't look like that to Blunt: what he sees below is Saturday-morning martyrdom. A few white citizens are skirting the square, shrugging, heading for the shopping malls.

'I warned him in private,' Zaheed says.

'Who?'

'Rahman, of course! Egyptians have always regarded themselves as superior to "Pakis". I told him: "You will revive the dark images of a thousand years. You will create a million British Khomeinis – lunatics, fanatics stomping and chanting and waving hideous effigies." I told him.'

'It'll blow over.'

'Quite the contrary, my dear Douglas: it's a godsend to Izza Shah and Mustafa Jangar, not to mention Hassan Hassani and that scoundrel Ishmail Haqq. Not forgetting that ambitious pipsqueak Ali Cheema! They're all down there! The Islamic Council is on cloud nine. These men are dangerous. Biding their time. Rahman has given them the ball and they will run with it.' Zaheed sighs. 'I must join them, my people. They are looking for me.'

Blunt sees no evidence of that. In the square below not a single pair of dark eyes has bothered to lift its gaze to the Lord Mayor's balcony.

'I have seen demonstrations in Moscow, my dear Douglas. I have seen people gathering outside the Kremlin and raising their fists in anger against their oppressors. But their anger was understood by the British people. And why?'

'Why?' (This prompt-line is obligatory.)

'You ask me why, Douglas? You really want to know why? Because Russians have white skins, blue eyes.'

'Aye. And because their oppression is real.'

'If I go into the saloon bar of the Swan Hotel and shout, "All white women are whores, all white men are pimps!" that is a dangerous abuse of free speech! It's a breach of the peace. It's what's called "fighting words".'

'I'm no literary expert, Zulfikar, but I'm told that when Rahman's book first appeared, the reviewers scarcely noticed the Islamic aspect.'

'English reviewers, you mean, ignorant of Islam.'

'Even so, the critics were more interested in Rahman's "magical realism" and, er, dreams within dreams. What caught their attention was Rahman's high-wire act within the conventions of fiction.'

'So?' Zaheed's hands are gripping his ermine collar.

'I'm merely pointing out that it was the Izza Shahs and Mustafa Jangars who eagerly circulated selected quotations.'

(Blunt congratulates himself on leaving aside Zaheed's decision to join in the fury when Rahman visited Bruddersford.)

'But they did not invent the quotations. The insults are there! That Egyptian pimp knew exactly what he was doing.'

'And what was he doing?'

'In one book after another Rahman has struck at Nasser, at the Sharaf family, at Mrs Thatcher, at the Ayatollah. Our Holy Prophet and Almighty God were bound to follow.'

'And cannot Almighty God take care of Himself?'

'That, of course, is a profoundly Christian sentiment. Cannot Almighty God turn the other cheek, eh? Or am I just a simple-minded wog?'

Blunt watches the photographers prancing around the burning book, the funeral pyre; he knows that the 'photograph of the year' is the one he could now take, the back view of the dressed-up Lord

Mayor on his balcony, watching the burning. There might be difficulties of focus.

Abruptly Zaheed steps inside and tears off his robes, tossing his tricorn hat across the room (if Blunt is supposed to catch it, he declines).

'I shall resign!'

'From what?'

'From the Labour Party.'

'Ah.'

'Unless my white "comrades" agree to remove the book from the City libraries.'

Zaheed is of course powerless: the Lord Mayor is a strictly ceremonial office, a 365-day motion in the direction of superannuation, Douglas Blunt takes his policy instructions from the leader of the Council, Trevor Lucas, whose attitude is uncomplicated: 'We don't ban books in Bruddersford.' Thirty-five years ago Zulfikar Zaheed arrived in Bruddersford from Mirpur, the fifth son of a landless peasant, carrying five pounds and the address of a cousin. Now he's throwing his tricorn hat around the Lord Mayor's parlour.

'I spoke to Kinnock,' he complains, sprawled magisterially behind his mayoral desk. 'I told Neil: "You're pushing us to the precipice. Inaction is inimicable to the Party's interest, Neil. This could lose us the next General Election." '

'What did he say?' (Blunt knows what Neil said, he has heard this one before.)

'He listened attentively. He always does.'

'Frankly, Zulfikar, the real problem lies in Gamal Rahman's established literary reputation. Banning cheap porn doesn't count as censorship but – '

'Expensive porn is different? I shall resign.'

'Bruddersford needs you.'

'Bruddersford despises me. At the end of the day, just another wog in a flashy car.'

'The House of Commons awaits its first Muslim Member. Resign now, and it won't be Zulfikar Zaheed.'

ᢍ

When Rajiv Lal frowns there is no crease upon his brow. It is a spiritual frowning, a deep suffering – he cannot cure the world. Nasreen understands his suffering. Rajiv has so many silent enemies. The appointment of an Asian as the City's Director of Education had been widely resented. The flow-charts Rajiv produced on 'multicultural pluralism' went straight into the headteachers' waste bins.

Likewise the elaborate questionnaires he sent them inquiring into every detail of a school's 'ongoing multicultural policy and practice'.

Mrs Newman, Headmistress of Hightown Upper School, has said as much to Nasreen:

'Either we spend our lives filling in questionnaires or we run our schools.'

Mrs Newman drives her pupils, white and Asian alike, to what she calls 'attainment'. Attain, attain: 'I'm glad to say that this term Imtiaz (Nasreen's younger brother) has achieved a high attainment in English.' Mrs Newman is fond of Nasreen: more's the pity that this estimable young mother, previously dedicated to the three R's, to sound attainment, should recently have been converted to Rajiv Lal's 'ongoing multicultural policy and practice'. If not to Rajiv Lal's ghastly, 'politically correct', jargon.

Nasreen's most recent encounter with the Headmistress of Hightown Upper School had been an uncomfortable one.

'Now,' Mrs Newman began, severe but friendly behind her desk, 'what are we going to do about the dreadful Safia Shah?'

'Izza Shah's daughter? I don't know her well.'

'She's missing school regularly.' Mrs Newman flipped through the pages of her attendance register. 'No sighting of her for the past two weeks.'

'I know that Safia has caused her father much anxiety.'

Mrs Newman folded her hands over the closed attendance register. 'Frankly, Safia's less trouble when she's absconding. But until she's sixteen her father has a legal duty to bring her to school. So go and remind him, please. He's a magistrate, after all.'

'Me?'

'That's what community teachers are for, dear. And while we're talking of the Shah family, we're going to have to look out for young Fatima, too.'

'I thought Fatima was a model pupil?'

'Among my best. Didn't I take her to Paris last year? She was on her guard at first but soon fell in love with France. However: I'd better warn you that I've caught a glint in her eye since this wretched Gamal Rahman affair spilled all over us.'

'Oh – why?'

'She asked permission to wear a headscarf in school.'

'The hijab? Fatima must know the rules.'

Mrs Newman nodded. 'She told me that the Department of Education's rules are not Allah's rules. I'm expecting trouble. Have a word with young Fatima.'

The yellow-and-brown bus inches forward. The book is burnt. The elderly couple behind Nasreen have fallen into an apologetic silence they will not break until Nasreen leaves the bus. She is tempted to descend the stairs and sit on the bottom deck.

႙

Ali Cheema observes the proceedings with the air of aloof, perhaps disdainful, detachment which sets him apart in a small, unbrotherly vacuum among his fellow-Muslims. He stands motionless with his hands thrust deep into the pockets of the long blue overcoat he has recently purchased in London on the proceeds of a TV appearance. Zulfikar Zaheed's daughter, Wahabia, had dragged him to the Kensington Hyper-Market where, jostled by the tousle-haired Bohemian riff-raff of the godless capital, he allowed her to talk him into a coat marked 'Red Army Surplus – Made in Hong Kong'.

'It suits you, Ali. You look the part. You deserve something for defending the faith.'

Wahabia had learned to toss her head and laugh provocatively like the pagan sluts of the South ('the Christian community,' as Ali called them in print).

'My reward will be in Heaven,' he told her.

'Among all those houri-maidens?'

'Something like that.'

Has Wahabia jettisoned the faith of her ancestors?

Gamal Rahman's book is already propelling Ali Cheema from obscurity into features pages and late-night television – the dancing boy at the feet of the sphinx-like Izza Shah, President of the Islamic Council and lugubrious conveyor of the 'sorrow (*sorrah*) and wrath' of peace-loving Muslims. No one speaks English quite like Izza Shah – it sounds as if Yorkshire and the Punjab have collided in Jerusalem. Izza Shah knows his own limitations: Ali Cheema's mission is to engage in the more complex cultural confrontations currently burning the screens of the late-night intelligentsia. Ali's fluent English is free of the usual funny stuff, the awkward usages which make even a good idea – loving Allah, for example – sound like a mugging in the Baghdad bazaar. He has assembled all the known facts about Gamal Rahman's scandalous life as a lackey of the apostate Sharaf regime in Egypt. The Jewish money, the immoral relationships with the Sharaf women, the betrayal of good Muslims, spying for Israel, thrown into prison for embezzlement, the betrayal of a father and a wife. And more. With Rahman there's always some more.

'RAHMAN MUST DIE!' roars the crowd, a forest of raised fists jabbing upwards, towards God. Ali shifts his slender shoulders within his Red Army surplus overcoat. God's flames cannot warm a damp

Yorkshire winter morning indefinitely. What will the Bishop make of all this? Ali's thoughts are frequently magnetized by the Anglican Bishop of Bruddersford; the most urgent of his ambitions swings with the crucifix on the Bishop's purple breast.

'RAHMAN MUST DIE!'

Ali observes a timid smile of joy unfolding across Hassan Hassani's plump features; Mustafa Jangar's bearded countenance blazes; Izza Shah remains of stone in the shirt, tie and suit immaculately pressed by his daughter Fatima, the girl whose one ambition is to marry Ali Cheema. Izza Shah has never worn a thought on his face.

No one notices an obsure man drifting alone round the ragged edges of the dispersing crowd. He does not live in Bruddersford, he does not worship here, he has no friends here. Iqbal Iqbal wears a beard, wire-rimmed glasses and a fixed smile which is no smile. Like a dog in his basket, Iqbal appears to be dreaming of hares in the open. Furtively he glances up towards the Lord Mayor's balcony, unveiling his own sentence of death on the apostate, the make-believe Muslim, the masked traitor Zulfikar Zaheed.

TWO

⧉

The Ayatollah Khomeini issues a fatwa sentencing the apostate author Gamal Rahman to death. All 'intrepid Muslims' are informed that the author and his collaborators have been declared 'madhur el dam' – those whose blood must be shed. 'I call on all zealous Muslims to execute them quickly, wherever they find them . . . Whoever is killed in this path will be a martyr of Islam.' A huge monetary reward is offered to the assassin(s).

The press can talk of nothing else: first the public, ceremonial burning of a book outside a British City Hall – and now a death sentence on a British citizen (albeit naturalized) handed down by a foreign Head of State! Bruddersford is crawling with photographers and television crews cruising the modest, sensible streets of Tanner and Bellingham in search of turbaned fanatics, veiled girls – the dark and dangerous Orient. The telephone lines from London are jammed by reporters desperate to extract some blood-chilling quote, some bouncing cliché, from the lips of Izza Shah, Mustafa Jangar or Hassan Hassani. And they, for their part, are obliging: the more they see themselves on television, or quoted in the press, the more they like it:

'Mr Jangar, you are quoted in today's *Guardian* as predicting a violent uprising of Muslim youth throughout Britain if the Government does not ban *The Devil: an Interview.*'

'I was misquoted.'

'So what did you actually say?'

'I said that the Government would have only itself to blame if our indignant Muslim youth despaired of British justice and fair-play.'

'And resorted to violence?'

'I do not recommend that. I say it can happen.'

Hassan Hassani's video recorder is silently ingesting the Gamal Rahman Affair from channel after channel while his young son Imran steadily stuffs himself with chocolate bars and fattening Coke. Like his father, the boy is plump. Hassan Hassani's own father, meanwhile, is placidly absorbing the day's worldwide catastrophes – though he understands no English – while piling cigarette stubs into an overflowing tin ashtray. It won't get emptied until Nasreen brings the late-night cocoa to the sitting room. Her husband does not occupy himself with the smallest domestic task – unless it's a 'repair job'. The old man's Benson & Hedges are costing him two pounds a day. More since this Rahman Affair. What with the devil lurking everywhere, in the broom cupboard under the stairs, in the toilet bowl when the lid's down, Patel's corner shop sales of tobacco are soaring.

Nasreen is home late tonight. Occasionally Hassan glances at his watch with a slight frown.

ം

The wall calendar, below the tapestry of the Great Mosque, registers the year 1400. Christian Bruddersford, what's left of it, may be preparing to celebrate the 'second millennium', but Izza Shah's household is 589 years in arrears. Fatima Shah, his younger daughter, has come in from school, buying a Kit Kat at Patel's for 17p and taking care not to drop the wrapping paper in the street. Mrs Newman has more than once addressed Hightown Upper School assembly on the subject of 'litter louts' who drop greasy chip and kebab bags in classrooms, corridors, playgrounds and streets.

Muslim girls are not litter louts. To be fair, the Hindu and Sikh girls also use the litter bins. The white boys from the Council flats and suburban estates are the worst, but some of the Asian boys ape their bad habits.

Elbows on the kitchen table – no one is at home – Fatima opens the newspaper and gazes intently at the photographs from Iran. She sees a close congregation of Iranian girls, all dressed in black burkas and chadors, their faces clean of creams and paint, holding aloft photographs of the hated Gamal Rahman. Ink has been applied to his eyeballs: two satanic dots, intensely evil. A simple X across his face erases his right to exist. Below his features are some words in a script she does not know. Fatima studies the expressions of the Iranian girls – dignity, sweetness, discipline, faith – as they parade behind a forest of placards bearing identical portraits of the stern, bearded, black-eyebrowed Ayatollah. The message has been written in English: 'We Are Ready to Kill Shaytan Rahman.' Fatima enters into silent communion with her Iranian sisters in their burkas and chadors. She knows that Gamal Rahman is now hiding in England.

'He cannot hide for ever,' her father has said.

Nor, she vows, can Ali Cheema.

25

Five hours later Fatima's father, Izza Shah, and his usual late-night visitors are listening to Gamal Rahman's attempt at an apology on television. Fatima is asleep upstairs. All these men are joined by an exhaltation which buries fatigue. None of them doubts that Rahman's insults are Allah's blessing upon them. It is a rising from the dead. There he is, the author of *The Devil: an Interview*, published by Jews. There he is, eyes bulging and rolling, his lips shiny as worms, unrepentent in his repentence:

'Ours is a world of many sincerely held faiths . . . we should all strive to respect the [something] of others.'

Only one of the guests observing Rahman's performance in Izza Shah's front room catches that something-word. It's not a common English word. Mendacity and pride surge through every syllable. Only Ali Cheema hears it clearly: 'sensibilities'.

Mustafa Jangar leaps to his feet, his beard smouldering: 'He admits no errors! He does not promise to withdraw the book!'

Hassan Hassani's oval glasses gleam in accord: 'He has the cunning of the devil but we are not fooled.'

Izza Shah's rheumy sphinx-eye settles on Ali Cheema.

'Such a declaration is of no value at all,' Ali says.

Now the television screen flashes the Ayatollah's response through Irna, the official Iranian news agency:

'The imperialist mass media have been falsely alleging that if the author repented, his execution order would be lifted. This is denied, one hundred per cent. Even if Mr Rahman became the most pious man of all time, it is incumbent on every Muslim to employ everything he has got, his life and wealth, to send the apostate to hell.'

Fatima wakes up to the word 'hell'. Whenever she hears it, she imagines burnt food in the oven, smoke curling up the funnel of the stairs, blackened cakes. In her darkened room she sees Shaytan's face blackened like a burnt cake but his bulging eyes remain very bright, intense, staring.

Fatima's ear is cocked. She hears voices in the hall, men. She counts them out into the night, Mustafa Jangar, Hassan Hassani. She knows that Ali will always linger last, at her father's behest. A luminous love fills her. Covering her head, she creeps down the stairs to eavesdrop on the low murmuring of her father talking to Ali in Punjabi behind the closed sitting room door.

'And where is Safia at this hour? Night after night she's not coming home.'

Why is Ali silent? Fatima can imagine his grave expression, eyes downcast. She has always been convinced that she will marry Ali, although she is less than half his age. His special status as her

26

'brother' is a kind of betrothal, she is sure of it. Under English law she will not attain the age of marriage for a further 519 days. Tomorrow it will be 518 days. But what if he takes a bride in the meantime? As a Muslim she has no objection to being a second wife, but in England only one is allowed. Only very old men, born and raised in Pakistan, have more than one wife. Fatima isn't quite sure that she wants to share her husband anyway. The white girls at school sometimes tease her about the Prophet's twelve wives. Now that Ali is regularly travelling south to be on television and so on, she fears he will fall in with bad company, 'fast' women.

'How both Safia and Fatima could have sprung from the same union only Allah can explain,' Fatima hears her father tell Ali.

෮

Nasreen Hassani has told no one but her sister Latifa about her husband's rapid descent into madness. A djinn has planted a permanent rictus in Hassan's plump features. Day and night he thinks of nothing but Gamal Rahman. Within their common home Nasreen and Hassan now pass like ships in the night, neither at war nor at peace. Hassan has forgotten how to touch her – but he never did, much. She fears that if things go on like this, her husband may one day rise from his two hours' sleep so exhausted that he will crash his car on the way to the light engineering factory in Halifax where Hassan Hassani, B.A. (Leeds), has been marketing director for the past three years. This anxiety now competes with her habitual fear: he will get beaten up by white motorcycle thugs while praying in a lay-by.

Nasreen is occasionally permitted to borrow the Ford Granada after her husband returns from work – provided she has first prepared his dinner and fed Imran. Hassan doesn't like to eat unattended, and his wife's food doesn't taste the same without her hovering at his shoulder. Borrowing his car is never easy. Although Nasreen is now a 'named driver' on the insurance certificate, he worries about her driving alone at night – there are drunken motorists on the streets, altercations, you never know. Hassan wishes to be a modern husband within limits. These limits, he has explained to her, are a 'very delicate matter' for a Muslim professional couple living in Britain. He would do the washing-up if not invariably diverted by more pressing duties (like the television news); baby-sitting is 'no problem' (their son Imran can also watch the television news); and if Hassan is in the mood, father and son may settle down to the boy's train set or his chemistry kit or a game of chess.

'And you're not in bed yet,' Nasreen remonstrates on her return, running her hand through the half-awake boy's thick mop of black hair.

When she borrows the car she is always obliged to explain in detail where she is going. Inevitably Hassan will tell her which route to follow. But she has noticed in herself a growing temptation to deceive her husband in small ways – just for the sake of it, or to discover what she can get away with.

Nasreen is standing behind Hassan as he eats. 'Mrs Newman has asked me to visit Izza Shah's daughter, Safia. She has been missing school.'

'That girl is a disgrace to her father and to us all,' Hassan says, rolling food between tooth and tongue while scooping up the spiced meat with his fingers. 'I will call Izza Shah and ask him whether it is convenient to receive you.'

'I'm talking to Safia, not her father. Please do not trouble him. It only makes my difficult work harder. The girl will be waiting for me.'

But where? He does not ask. Presently Hassan wipes his mouth, pushes the last dirty dish from him, leaves the kitchen, and returns to the great male drama of blasphemies and fatwas unfolding on TV.

ᕲ

On the train south Ali Cheema re-reads the Bishop's letter. He has lovingly wrapped the crisp, crested envelope in a plastic sandwich bag, to protect it from grime, mishap and satanic spittle. Between Leeds and London Ali reads the brief, hand-scribbled message three times, probing every syllable, weighing every phrase, scrutinizing lacunae, hunting for oracular clues and watermarked signs of the zodiac. The Right Reverend Robin Goodgame, Bishop of Bruddersford, is fond of purple ink.

The message (surely?) is clear. The Junior Research Fellowship is yours for the asking, my dear Ali. What a pleasure to welcome you back to your old College. We all know how difficult things have been for you these last few years . . . The Master and Fellows join me in sending their greetings . . .

Actually, not even the gentle, sleep-inducing roll of the Inter-City Express can coax purple prose out of the Bishop's purple ink. What Ali holds between his fingers could be construed as a warning: 'fearsome competition', a 'formidable field of candidates, each more worthy of election than the other'. Ali knows perfectly well that the Bishop, as Visitor of the College, plays absolutely no role in the appointment of Fellows . . . beyond a nudge and a wink over the port. The Visitor's job is to expel Fellows whose moral turpitude can no longer be concealed from the press: bigamy is allowed but three

28

wives (concurrent) is one too many. Bishop Goodgame is writing to Ali – 'keeping you abreast' – strictly as a friend, a fellow-Bruddersfordian, a former tutor in Comparative Theology. Nothing beyond that. Merely a progress report 'strictly between ourselves'. The Bishop would regard young Ali Cheema as his protégé if that were not (he says) 'presumptuous'. That role, that honour, clearly belongs to Izza Shah. It is the Bishop's 'keenest wish' to carry his relationship with the esteemed leader of Bruddersford's Muslims to new levels of mutual accord, harmony and respect.

Ali aches for the Research Fellowship. A new post, and restricted to Islamic Studies, it offers him recognition, comfort, status, escape from Bruddersford. Already he can smell the wood polish, the old leather: dreaming spires are drifting upwards into divine mists. Bells tolling the half hours of timeless time. He can see the neatly italicized words – Junior Research Fellow of . . . – beneath his name on the title page of his forthcoming book, *Gamal Rahman's Dialogues with the Devil.* Frontispiece by Gustave Doré, illustrator of Milton's *Paradise Lost.* It was while tutoring Wahabia Zaheed in the subtle mysteries of that great Christian poem that Ali had first received a presumptuous kiss from the Lord Mayor's daughter. Can these television appearances damage Ali's academic prospects? Certainly not! The Bishop adores the media, relishes public disputation, revels in the higher gossip. How could the College turn down the most articulate, the most brilliant, young Muslim scholar in Britain? Ali can already smell the mellow wax of the long tables in Hall; already meet the unfaltering gaze of Founders, Benefactors, Alumni, as he – the slender young Muslim with the half-tonsured, prematurely bald patch, resplendent in his rented D. Phil. gown – is invited to sit and dine at the Master's right hand (after the Latin prayers, of course, the Christian prayers which Ali knows by heart).

Christianity: the non-believers' religion. How to explain True Belief to a corrupted television audience; how to convey the head-to-toe, dawn-to-dusk devotion of a Muslim who bends body and soul to Allah five times a day? So what is Ramadan? A real Lent. Why do our Christian brothers and sisters congratulate themselves on *trying* to give up some luxury during Lent? (Indeed the Bishop himself makes this joke, no offence given or taken.)

As the train approaches King's Cross, Ali dutifully reminds himself of Izza Shah's parting instruction: harness the book-burning to Islam's war against liberal decadence, pornography, homosexuality, alcohol, drugs, Aids.

The Bishop's crisp, crested notepaper is again under scrutiny. 'My dear Ali . . .'

A modest canvas bag rests in the rack above his head. A spare shirt, a second pair of socks, a Koran, nothing much else beyond a halal beef sandwich with pickle. He made it himself – no woman in his life. He lives alone, by choice, free of family ties, no grandparents, parents, uncles, aunts, brothers, sisters – that finely woven embrace which allows no one to be himself.

૭৶

Driving by night towards Knightley, Nasreen Hassani leans forward over the wheel to check the road signs under the weak street lights. Any woman would tell her that Hassan is a good husband. He is quite generous with money, pays all the main bills and outgoings, leaving her to spend her own salary on clothes for herself and Imran, household goods, odds and ends. Hassan wouldn't dream of excluding her from the sitting room if they had a 'modern' visitor, but that is quite rare since most of his friends and colleagues are ill at ease conversing in a woman's company. She often goes to bed early and by the time he switches on the bedroom lights and settles down to hours of paper intifada and jihad against Gamal Rahman she is sound asleep – the escaping sleep of the deserted. The double bedroom stands at the head of the first flight of stairs and contains an Amstrad computer, a printer and many neat boxes of discs on which Hassan inscribes his letters to the press, his pamphlets, the growing membership list of the Muslim Youth League. Mustafa Jangar, Regional Guardian of the League, has insisted that Hassan serve as local Secretary, because of his desk-top publishing skills. Hassan can never say no to anything – except a procreative cuddle. He makes love to card indexes and filing cabinets.

No copy of *The Devil: an Interview* is to be found on his desk when Nasreen retires for the night. Turning over in bed while he's absorbed in his work, she invariably catches sight of it, wrapped in plain brown paper. He keeps the book in a locked cupboard. Imran must never know that Satan does indeed reside in the house. Nasreen's desire to read Gamal Rahman's novel has grown acute; the ban on it whets her curiosity, but she is ashamed to request access to so much dirty language, so many blasphemous obscenities.

Nasreen had arrived in England from Mirpur at the age of eleven without a word of English, three years after her father, Sadar Baj Hussein, left Pakistan. In Hightown Upper School she had been placed in a class of immigrant children whose teacher, Mrs Hearst, constantly scolded them for talking in Punjabi. Her father raged at what he took to be a personal insult, but he paid heed. Sadar Baj Hussein (known to his Labour Party colleagues, Asian and white, as

30

'S.B.') was still working in the mills and patiently educating himself by night. He fought for his children every step of the way. 'Nothing must be holding them back.' He was a master of statistics, both real and less real; he constantly reminded the world that seventy-three per cent of Asian kids were leaving the City's schools without any certificate of qualification. Nasreen, the eldest, grew up without a television set, her head bent over her books, until she was finally granted a place in the technical college. With her father still behind her – and still raging – she went on to pass both parts of the Royal Society of Chemistry's GRSC examination – the equivalent of a B.Sc. But even then she couldn't find a job as a teacher. At the time of her marriage to Hassan Hassani she was travelling to Huddersfield every day, ninety minutes each way, to teach Muslim girls in a mosque school, unpaid, in order to obtain the PGCE teaching certificate. S.B. reckoned, and never stopped reckoning, that he had spent five thousand pounds over the years on Nasreen's board, lodging, books, travel: every item was written down in a black notebook. S.B. wanted to 'bloody some noses'.

Her marriage had been arranged. S.B. had known Hassan Hassani's father in Mirpur. When Nasreen was first introduced to Hassan in the presence of both families, he was a studious youth, solemn, unsmiling, with a soft-cheese face and a faint air of permanent vexation. S.B. Hussein regarded the Hassanis as ultra-conservative, Zia-fundamentalist, very anti-Bhutto, but politics had nothing to do with marriage (though in later years S.B. was not above making it sound as if Nasreen was to blame for her husband's reactionary attitudes). She had been content to be married to an educated man with good prospects and a comfortable home. The birth of Imran followed, but no further children, and soon there was clucking and chiding within the two families. The wife bore sole responsibility.

ॐ

Ali refuses television make-up and his hair is cut too austerely short to be tampered with. Despairing for her craft, the make-up girl attacks his small, bald patch with her powder puff. In the chair next to his own he observes the elaborate ritual grooming of 'Final Call''s handsome presenter, Inigo Lorraine, lazily submitting his famous jaw to powder, his thatch of wind-blown hair to laqueur. In the chair beyond Lorraine's crouches the playwright Rory McKenzie, probably brooding about Voltaire. A friend and vociferous supporter of Gamal Rahman, McKenzie has flown in from a Friends of Rahman rally in New York, organized by Rahman's strident American agent, Isaac Ben Ezra.

Isaac Ben Ezra is of course – of course! – a Jew. Ali remembers the owl-eyed Hassan Hassani gleefully laying the documentation before the Islamic Council. 'Who needs further evidence of the Zionist conspiracy, Brothers?' Unconvinced, Ali had held his tongue. According to Hassani, McKenzie himself was concealing a Jewish grandmother – a Rothschild, no less! – under the table. Granny Rothschild (Hassani wiping his glasses in excitement) finances the quarterly magazine *Prospero*, whose latest edition is entirely devoted to the Rahman affair. And who edits *Prospero*? Why, Rory McKenzie! With Isaac Ben Ezra's agile assistance, he has unloaded ten thousand copies on the Friends of Rahman in New York.

Ali regards McKenzie as an intractable atheist propelled by the usual love-affair with Voltaire and Rousseau – as Jewish as the sow's ear he physically resembles.

They file into the 'Final Call' studio. Ali invariably recoils from the brightness of the lights focussed on the three chairs ranged across the stage. Tonight's backdrop is a photographic montage showing Rahman, the Ayatollah Khomeini and the Bruddersford book-burning.

'Silence, please. Ten, nine . . .' At zero the red light flashes on the lead camera and Lorraine leans forward to his invisible audience with the expression of intense concern he employs for every occasion, whether genocide in the Sudan, starvation in Ethiopia, 'the fate of the novel' or the Royal Opera House's precarious finances.

'Good evening . . .'

Moments later Rory McKenzie is accusing Ali (and probably all Muslims) of rampant intolerance, dogmatism, and sexual neurosis:

'Isn't it the case that Gamal Rahman's novel stings you because modern Islam is suffering sexual confusion as it encounters Western norms of gender equality?'

Ali has anticipated this line of attack. 'Quite the contrary. It is the secular-Christian West which is in the grip of sexual confusion. Rahman's solution is to hurl the latrine bucket at the head of the Prophet Muhammad. The result is cheap pornography – and blasphemy by any definition.'

Inigo Lorraine intervenes. 'But surely Rahman uses the Prophet's twelve wives to question polygamy and the male thrust of the entire Islamic culture?'

'Which is why you burnt his book,' McKenzie adds.

Ali shrugs, almost. 'Gamal Rahman prefers to have his own ladies one at a time. That's his privilege. What he cannot be allowed to do is to demean Islam by hinting at the blasphemous heresy of a thirteenth wife of the Prophet in our own time.'

'He merely reports a rumour widespread in Egypt a few years ago,' McKenzie objects. 'He doesn't endorse it.'

Ali is unmoved. 'He puts it in the mouth of his own Muslim wife, whom he betrayed.'

'He did not! That's a lie and you know it!'

'Don't let's forget the uproar among Christians over *The Last Temptation of Christ.* As Muslims, we recognized that this film was deeply insulting to Christian beliefs.'

'Why,' McKenzie asks, 'should the Prophet Muhammad be allowed sexual desire but not Jesus whom you Muslims regard merely as a lesser prophet? Why defend a New Testament which the Koran claims to transcend? Isn't this a crazily perverse Puritanism?'

'When Christians feel insulted, outraged, we Muslims extend our sympathy to them. It's not a question of this particular theology, or that one. As the saying goes, you take off your shoes when you enter the other man's temple.'

'In other words,' says McKenzie, 'the great religious establishments of the world suspend their wars to confront the common enemy, the spirit of Voltaire. French cardinals who regard Muhammad as an impostor and polygamy as banned by Christian teaching, are now wringing their hands because Rahman may have added an extra wife to the Prophet's twelve.'

Lorraine turns to Ali: 'You want to come back on that?'

'The artist who shows no respect deserves none. The new deity, we are told, is this thing called the Imagination. But the underlying aim of the secular imagination is always to insult God, you see. That is why we need strong and active blasphemy laws – not to change the human heart but – as Martin Luther King reminds us – to restrain the heartless.'

'I'm not aware that Martin Luther King ever advocated censorship,' McKenzie says.

'Rahman's novel holds Muslims up to public ridicule. It also panders – very deliberately – to ancient prejudices in the Christian West. Why call Muhammad by the ancient hate-name of Mahmoud? In that sense Rahman's book is definitely racist. A godless takeover bid for the heritage of the Crusades.'

Lorraine nods. 'Perhaps we expect too much of immigrant communities.'

'We expect Muslims to cease to be Muslims whenever they step out of the mosque,' Ali says. 'Don't mix religion with "real life". In short, become a mutant.'

'Yet you are demanding that the host community abandons its own values – liberalism, tolerance – '

McKenzie cuts in on Lorraine: 'In Gamal's novel, the all-powerful Imam's muezzin calls down an anathema on history and progress: "Islam will conquer history, history the devil's harlot. We will amputate the satanic delusion called progress. We will guide mankind back to the single truth – the sum of knowledge was perfect on the day Allah concluded his revelation to the Prophet." '

Ali shrugs again: 'These are of course not the words of the Ayatollah Khomeini, but of our apostate author. And no doubt a Christian or secular audience is eager to swallow such distortions of the Islamic tradition.'

'And how would you sum up that tradition – in a very few words?' Inigo Lorraine asks him. (The red light is flashing.)

'Modern science constantly amplifies, expands and fulfils the sacred Koran. Fine. But when so-called modern knowledge is in conflict with the Koran, it is false.'

'Like Darwin's theory of evolution, for example?'

Bruddersford watches and listens. The Bishop of Bruddersford likewise.

❧

Knightley by night: Nasreen Hassani flinches, recoils in this ill-lit urban desolation where no passing stranger can be trusted. In an agony of hesitation she parks her husband's car a block away from the Bhangra. She knows the club only by ill repute and shudders to enter such a place alone. Although wearing a Western frock – Hassan does not object provided it's 'modest' – she decides to cover her head in the Muslim style. A broken neon light is flashing outside the discothèque. Two Asian youths manning the door nod to her with the respect due to a married woman who clearly doesn't belong here.

'Can we help you?'

'I am looking for Safia Shah.'

'She is inside. Shall we call her out?'

'No, I will go in.'

Politely they waive the entrance fee. A lady so ill at ease deserves free passage. As the inner door swings open she is deafened by amplified Punjabi folk music pulverized by a heavy rock-beat – this is the locally famous Shankaar band, which has just released its first cassette on the EMI label. A community teacher must know the scene (Rajiv says).

The room, or den, is crowded, dimly lit, thick with cigarette smoke and an odour she does not recognize. 'Pot,' she thinks – Rajiv sometimes speaks of 'pot' and 'hash' quite lightly, quite easily. Strobe lights, pulsing music, jiving figures – Nasreen feels like a plaster cast with feet of clay. She scans the room, deeply embarrassed, because no woman should be threading her gaze among young male strangers. But far more shaming than the strangers are the faces she recognizes. Word will get back! Hassan will hear of it! Who is that bearded young man leaning against a pillar and watching the dancing with slow-burning eyes? She remembers: Hassan had once invited Karamat Khan to the house in the company of his son, Tariq. How the boy has grown! He has a reputation, too, a wild lad, a member of the Muslim Youth League – rumour has it that all these lads have sworn to assassinate Gamal Rahman. Hassan says they took an oath on the Koran, with Mustafa Jangar presiding. Hassan wants nothing to do with assassination.

They won't find Gamal Rahman dancing in the Bhangra!

Tariq Khan's smouldering gaze leads Nasreen straight to Safia Shah. Tariq is staring at Safia as if poised to crack open the head of any boy who approaches her. But it's as much a look of contempt as of desire – both. Safia Shah is jiving frenetically, her long, lustrous, auburn hair flowing, her shapely bottom and legs clad in tight jeans. Nasreen takes note of the black roots of Safia's screaming red hair. Can this be Izza Shah's daughter?

The girls do not seem to be dancing with particular boys; even in this ultra-'modern' ambiance there is reticence about that; Nasreen has heard that if a Sikh boy makes an approach to a Muslim girl there can be immediate trouble. You can see that trouble in Tariq Khan's gaze. More than once the police have been called to the Bhangra, 'offensive weapons' have been seized, charges brought before Izza Shah and his fellow magistrates. Hassan once told her that Izza Shah always wishes to preside when Muslim youths are arraigned – not out of leniency but severity. Izza Shah believes in communal justice administered by the elders of the tribe.

The music ebbs for a break. Nasreen observes Safia flicking her fingers as she swings and sways back to her all-girl group, her gaudy features boasting a raging lipstick, heavy eyeshadow, a junkshop of bangles and ear-rings.

Nasreen touches Safia's arm and pumps herself up to a brave smile. 'Hullo, Safia.'

'Hell, what brings *you* here?'

'I want to talk to you, Safia.'

Safia takes a packet of Marlboro from her bag and lights a cigarette with a purple gas lighter which matches her lipstick. Tariq Khan is watching.

'Can we talk in my car?' Nasreen says.

'I'm here to have fun.'

'Just five minutes, Safia, and then I must go. Imran has got toothache.'

Safia shrugs sulkily, grabs her shawl and walks out into the cool, damp night, her high heels clicking sharply on the pavement. Not yet sixteen, she is taller than Nasreen. The two youths at the door shift their feet to let them pass.

Inside the car Nasreen turns on the engine and heater. Hassan's Koran lies above the dashboard. Safia lights another cigarette.

'Safia you cannot afford to abandon your education.'

'That bloody school! That bloody Mrs Newman! You can't wear this, you can't wear that – I suppose she wants me to walk about in a bloody burka. Listen, Mrs Hassani, Fatima may be the passive type but I'm not.'

'To throw away your education *is* passive. It may feel like rebellion but the upshot is – '

'Is what?'

'There will be nothing in your life except disappointment.'

Safia is flicking ash on the carpet of Hassan Hassani's immaculately clean car.

'They arranged *your* marriage, didn't they? And don't tell me you're happy, either.'

The scrutiny Nasreen encounters is charged with insolent female knowledge.

'I'm choosing my own husband, make no mistake,' Safia says. 'Listen, life here i'n't no bloody bed of roses. Bad vibes all round. I'm heading south soon as I bloody can.'

'Don't you think you owe anything to your father?'

'He calls me a modern slut. So what century is he living in?'

'Safia, the Holy Koran is our ultimate guidance. Nothing wrong with being modern – but we must follow the Book and the Prophet, peace be upon him.'

'I'd rather read Gamal Rahman.' Safia extracts herself from the car, slams the door and trots on clicking high heels back to the discothèque. Tariq Khan is waiting at the entrance, arms akimbo, barring her passage.

THREE

෨

A stranger entering the Omar Khayyam restaurant through its basement discothèque and bar will notice two fruit machines and several idling Muslim youths. Climbing the stairs to the empty restaurant, the visitor will observe a lone waiter in a white jacket leaning on another bar, studying the listings in the evening newspaper.

Tariq Khan's mission became clear to him when he joined the crowd outside City Hall to witness the burning of the book. No one was yet talking about assassinating the author but Tariq, observing Mustafa Jangar breathing fire from his dilated nostrils, then majestically offering the blackened pages to Hell, understood at that moment that he, Tariq, unemployed mill worker and part-time waiter, had been called. By cutting down the Apostate (a word often used by Mustafa) Tariq will win his cousin Rana's hand in marriage. It's as simple as that, no problem. He'd been sure of it ever since the grand old Ayatollah in faraway Iran offered a huge reward, millions of dollars, for Gamal Rahman dead or alive. Millions of dollars would do the trick with Rana's father, Uncle Abdul Ayub Khan, owner of the Omar Khayyam restaurant.

Tariq looks up from the local paper reluctantly, nodding to unwelcome customers. A rather handsome head of black hair is skilfully cut below his ears, but the short beard is less impressive, struggling and straggling to bless his chin. The eyes are tired, despondent, as his limp arm indicates any and every table.

'Sit where yer like,' he murmurs.

Chances are, the customers will soon find conversation impossible on account of Tariq's taste for local radio – Bruddersford City or Pennine – turned up to a high volume. His preference is for Urdu broadcasts peppered with commercials in English: cash-and-carry, fast-food, bargain-basement (visit it), top-of-the-charts, wholesale-bargains, electrical-goods: an urgent rush of hyphens is seeking out, in this heyday of Thatcherite enterprise culture, the modest money of a modest population. If requested to turn the volume down, Tariq settles for the most minor adjustment.

Tariq Khan was not born in Bruddersford but has barely glimpsed any other English city. His father, Karamat Khan, brought the family to England from Rawalpindi when Tariq was nine. After an uphill struggle with the English language and English kids, idle at school, too much telly, Tariq emerged with not a certificate to his name and dragged himself to Courtauld's mills, where he earned £130 gross, £100 net, as a converter minder. Evenings and weekends he watched videos, non-stop. His father, a socialist by conviction and a prominent figure in the local Labour Party, instructed him to join the General Municipal Boilermakers' Union. The slump came, and new machinery, the jobs disappeared, the union protested in vain. It was the Asian lads who were thrown on the street.

'Redundant, like.'

Redundant, Tariq stayed in bed for a year, drifting among the small ads, running up his father's phone bill. Eventually his uncle, Abdul Ayub Khan, took him on as a waiter in the family restaurant, the Omar Khayyam, in Bellingham Road. But a waiter's wage leaves you with nothing except Pennine Radio and dreams of killing Gamal Rahman.

Ramadan lies ahead, a good time for a holy killing on a fasting stomach: Tariq will not eat from 4.30 a.m. to 8.0 p.m., from technical dawn to technical sunset. Uncle Abdul has explained that whereas Christians wrongheadedly place their Christmas on the same date every year, the Ramadan calendar is scientifically based on the lunar month – in thirty-three years it passes through all the seasons of the year, spot on.

Feet are climbing the stairs from the discothèque but Tariq does not hear them; the restaurant is full of Pennine pop. The feet he likes best are the squeaking-squelching shoes of 'Big Joe' Reddaway, the famous *Echo* journalist who's partial to inexpensive tandooris and generous with beer and cigarettes (though he lights a pipe after a meal). Tariq wouldn't normally shame himself by drinking alcohol in front of a Christian, but Reddaway takes notes while Tariq sits at his table – it would be rude to refuse. In the company of Joe and a Carlsberg, Tariq becomes philosophical:

'This way of life, like, it's not right.'

'Way of life?'

'This mixing of boys and girls in the schools and the like. Don't get me wrong, I'm no "sexist", I mean, the Koran honours women don't it?'

'So how's your dad getting on with the business of his daughters?'

Reddaway knows that Tariq's father bears a great bitterness about his two younger daughters. The British authorities in Pakistan had refused to believe that they were genuinely Karamat Khan's, though Karamat had sworn on the Koran and produced birth certificates. After Joe wrote the story up, castigating the local Labour MP, Harry Flowers, for inactivity, Flowers had belatedly castigated the Home Office and the High Commission in Islamabad. 'But fat good it does.' Now there was this 'genetic-coding business, if yer can afford it,' but the two stranded Khan daughters were now past the immigration age limit, 'over-age, like'. Tariq sometimes shows Joe heart-rending letters from his sisters. He has recently seen a film on TV, a documentary about a young man in Pakistan who wasn't allowed to join his mother in the UK and (as Tariq puts it) 'suicided 'isself'.

Big Joe scribbles, eats, wipes korma sauce from his mouth.

'And how are things on the streets at night?'

'Not so bad.' Tariq immediately qualifies this by recounting how he and his mates recently got beaten up straying too close to the pubs in the city centre at closing time. Tariq has heard rumours of racist attacks in London's East End, but it's 'not so bad up here'.

Reddaway buys him another beer. 'What did you think about working for Courtauld's?'

'Aah, not bad. They took us by coach to visit a factory in Grimsby, they laid on food, a buffet, samosas, chicken legs, but they forgot about halal meat so that was that, the Indians ate the lot.'

'Indians? Hindus?'

'Yeah.'

'What about Gamal Rahman?'

'This Rahman bewk makes yer wonder, don't it? I mean, the British Government's supporting this apostate, a bewk full of swearing and foul language and the like. You have to ban a bewk like that so next time somebody'll think twice before hurting Muslim people. Otherwise you're a second-class citizen.'

Joe scribbles hard. Good stuff. As his friend John Fielding, lecturer in social psychology at Bruddersford University, had put it, 'Loss of potential integrationist impulses plus concomitant signs of cultural alienation.' Joe could translate that back into newspaper English: 'Angry Waiters Slam Blasphemous Book.'

Better: 'The Making of an Assassin.' What a scoop!

But this evening there is no sign of Joe Reddaway in the Omar Khayyam. Tariq is alone with his listings and Pennine Radio. A white couple have mounted the narrow stairs and entered the restaurant.

ତ

Driving home from his work as a marketing director in Halifax, Hassan Hassani's large, floppy ears are pinned to the tail end of the 'PM' programme on the car radio. News, current affairs, politics, diplomacy, economic crises, apostasy, famines, blasphemy, wars – all grist to his mill. Hassan's ears are on intimate terms with the regular newsreaders and presenters. Right now it's Valerie:

'Worldwide Islamic protests over Mr Gamal Rahman's book, *The Devil: an Interview*, claimed their first victims earlier today when five people were shot dead during a demonstration in the Pakistani capital, Islamabad. At least sixty others were wounded after police fired into a crowd apparently intent on ransacking the American Center.'

Hassan Hassani's heart swells with pride. We are the first to shed our blood. (On the dashboard of his Granada an amber light is breaking its heart trying to warn him that he has not fully released the handbrake.) Valerie's report is the usual Western propaganda – she just reads what they give her, he understands that, and a little smiling picture of her in *Radio Times* had excited him to send her a short message of support. 'Thank you on behalf of all British Muslims for your good work and fair play. Keep it up!'

It wasn't the Islamic protests which claimed five victims (may their souls go to Heaven) but the book itself! It is Gamal Rahman who killed them!

The male voice on the radio is now slightly blurred: our reporter in Islamabad, Steve Kenyon.

'The crowd, led by Jamiyat politicians hostile to the Government of Benazir Bhutto, were demanding the banning of Gamal Rahman's book in the United States. Several thousand men marched along the wide road which forms the spine of Islamabad, the Khyaban-i-Quaid-i-Azam. Some were carrying wooden staves. Police guarding the approach to the American Center are reported to have come under a hail of stones. In the National Assembly, which last week passed a resolution condemning Mr Rahman's book as an insult to Islam, Prime Minister Bhutto is now likely to face a twin-pronged attack, as Muslim activists who accuse her of heretical views form common cause with critics of the police. *The Devil: an Interview* was banned on publication. However, smuggled copies are being sold on the black market for up to 5,000 rupees, about 150 pounds.'

Hassan Hassani wants to hear more: more and more! But now Steve Kenyon has signed off with 'Steve Kenyon in Islamabad' and Valerie is chattering away about some report claiming that few magistrates' courts in England and Wales provide proper facilities for disabled defendants. In one notorious case, a wheelchair rapist was ordered to stand up for sentencing by a two-legged High Court judge. What a scandal to this 'liberal' society!

The traffic thickens where the Headland bypass merges with – or collides with – the A31. In Hassan's view – the amber break light has given up the struggle – wheelchair rapists should have their wheels cut off. His mind deserts the dead of Islamabad for an instant to dwell guiltily on the likely nature of the offence. He assumes that the victim, the woman, was also in a wheelchair and probably provoked the incident. The English courts are too quick to believe a woman's word. Under the Islamic law, the Shari'a, happily restored to Pakistan by General Zia ul-Haq, no less than four witnesses would have had to corroborate the wheelchair woman's story.

'PM' is followed by the national weather forecast. The 6.0 p.m. main news will bring him the whole story of the Islamabad martyrs all over again. With luck, the death toll will have risen by five past six – each martyr another nail in Rahman's coffin.

Parking his Ford Granada at his regular lay-by, Hassan Hassani removes a small prayer-mat from the boot, tenderly extracts his magnetic compass from the glove compartment, covertly scans the parked traffic from behind porthole glasses, climbs out into the York-shire wind, selects a relatively dry spot close to his car – and kneels towards Mecca. It's dark but the lay-by is lit by headlamps and partially illuminated by filtered light from the roadside café. A young motor-cycle couple swathed in leather pause from their ketchuped burgers to observe with mounting incredulity a man in a smart business suit on his knees, on his feet, on his knees, then bending to touch some kind of carpet with his forehead. A passing lorry driver might assume he was wrestling with a punctured tyre, and indeed on one occasion a mechanic from the Automobile Association had pulled in to offer Hassan his services.

At certain times of the year, March and October, Hassan Hassani must take care to consult his diary and avoid beginning his roadside prayers at the exact time of sunset: for this had once been the sacred moment for the pre-Muslim, idolatrous, polytheistic, sun-worshipping pagans of Mecca. Of Jahilia. And so it goes with sunrise, too.

Hassan begins as always with the nine lines from 'The Opening' of the Koran, speaking softly in Arabic:

> In the name of God, the Merciful, the Compassionate
> Praise belongs to God, the Lord of all Being,
> the All-Merciful, the All-Compassionate
>   the Master of the Day of Judgment.

41

Thee only we serve: to Thee alone we pray for succour.
Guide us in the straight path,
the path of those whom Thou hast blessed,
not of those against whom Thou art wrathful,
    nor of those who are astray.

જ

Hurrying home in his Red Army surplus overcoat from his job at the Community College, where he earns a modest living while dreaming of the books as yet unwritten, the university posts which have eluded him, Ali Cheema hears a heavy, squelching footfall gaining on him from behind. His slender shoulders already rounded by scholarship, Ali is always apprehensive of physical attack by young white thugs. At the junction of Bellingham and Tiptree, he pauses with cat-like caution, wary of secular-Christian van drivers sporting luminous 'I love Gamal Rahman' stickers.

The tall squelcher draws level with him, his breath noisy from exertion. The flushed, watermelon face belongs to the 'Plain Speaking' columnist of the Bruddersford *Echo*, Joe Reddaway.

'Saw you on the box last night, Ali.'

Ali nods, waits.

'I take it you don't deign to give interviews to the local press, Ali.' (Supercilious little bastard.)

Ali isn't inviting first-name familiarity. He reads Reddaway's daily column attentively, of course, and sometimes clips it as 'evidence', but keeps his thoughts to himself. Ali does not argue locally, only nationally.

'Izza Shah and Mustafa Jangar are the proper people to approach,' he says.

They cross the road, together yet apart. Reddaway has a mess of newspapers tucked under the arm of his shabby raincoat. An extinct pipe hangs from the corner of his mouth. They begin to climb Bellingham Hill.

'As a matter of fact I'm on my way to visit your colleague Hassan Hassani,' Reddaway says.

'Oh, yes.'

'I hear he's set himself the task of converting the British Isles to Islam by the end of the century.'

The very thought of Hassani fires a small but intense irritation in Ali. Reddaway probably knows as much. Hassani is a buffoon, a clown, his messianic messages filed into card indexes and computer discs. His nonstop letters to the *Echo*, gleefully printed, merely confirm the bubbling prejudices of the secular-Christian natives – Muslims are maniacs.

Reddaway is persistent, not too bothered by the steep gradient as they thread past knots of Asian youths idling at street corners – a new development in mid-winter, with a hint of menace to it.

'I gather that you're not universally supported within the Islamic Council,' he probes. 'Too keen on dialogue with atheists, is that it?'

Ali knows he should keep his trap shut.

'Did you get that from Hassani?'

'I never betray a source.'

'Hassani is a good Muslim with the soul of a tourist guide.'

Ali turns abruptly left into Sheffield Way, at the cost of extending his journey home by three hundred yards. Joe Reddaway strides on, his too-short corduroy trousers flapping round oak-tree legs, several shirt buttons missing, the least eligible bachelor in town, wild coils of reddish hair leaping from a beer-flushed skull. The lady he truly fancies is somewhat high on the ladder, the Headmistress of Hightown Upper School, Patricia Newman. Divorced, too, but definitely a Roxanne to his Cyrano – not that Joe's 'Plain Speaking' columns in the *Echo* rank as poetry, exactly.

'*This city's Muslims dream of distant lands while taking care not to live there.*'

'Yes, Joe,' Patricia had commented, 'but nothing is to be gained by saying so.'

Joe passes the Omar Khayyam restaurant and an enticing odour of tandoori. His stomach twitches, his stride falters: why not a couple of beers, some nan bread, chicken Madras, a chat with that charming, idle waiter, Tariq Khan? But duty (in the tedious form of Hassan Hassani) calls. As he hurries on, a flash LX Ghia convertible draws up outside the Omar Khayyam, disgorging a fat bloke who carries his suit jacket over his shoulder, and a blonde in a miniskirt. At a glance Joe fancies her.

ᘒ

Tariq, indolently bent over the evening paper, leaning on the bar, has his back to the white couple as they enter the Omar Khayyam restaurant. Pennine Radio is up full blast. The white bloke is touching thirty, with a stomach like two filofaxes and a swagger to match. He hasn't enjoyed the narrow stairs. The girl's hair is done up like a blow-dried cornfield, aggressively blonde. The bloke stares at Tariq's insolent-indolent back, just bloody typical.

Tariq is killing Gamal Rahman on the steps of some faraway mosque while the hafiz chants in Punjabi, praising the Prophet and how he looked, not too tall, not too short, a beautiful man with a black beard. You can't insult the Koran just like that, it's not the work of any ordinary man, it's the word of God.

'Well bugger this,' the white bloke says loudly above the din of Pennine pop. He is indeed buggered if he's going to walk across to this lazy coon, tap him politely on the shoulder, excuse me, could I have your kind attention?

Tariq looks up and makes an instant diagnosis: a married estate agent having it off with his secretary. The waiter drifts listlessly towards the unwelcome customers.

'Two, sir?'

'Ah, you can count.'

'Sit where yer like, sir.'

Tariq brings two large menu cards.

'A Carlsberg and a bitter lemon,' the bloke says.

'Yes, sir.'

'And turn that racket down. We want to hear ourselves speak.'

'Yes, sir.'

Tariq twiddles the knob but he can't bear to switch the radio off – must have something to keep you awake. He removes the bottles from the refrigerator and carefully pours them, tilting the glass to leave merely the thinnest film of foam cresting the beer. He places the full glasses on a tray and carries them back to the table. The blonde woman is wearing a mini beneath the table cloth. The bloke has hung his jacket on the back of the chair; he wears a boldly striped shirt, with fancy cufflinks, and two damp patches under his armpits.

'Will yer order now, sir?'

'Why not? For starters, two helpings of Gamal Rahman.'

The bloke is grinning up at Tariq; the woman is smirking, her hand over her mouth, holding back the giggle. The estate agent's mouth is flecked with foam from the beer. Tariq descends the stairs to the bar.

'Insults,' he tells Abdul Ayub Khan. Tariq's uncle would appear to be deep in his account books, but most often (Tariq knows) he is deep in political brooding.

'You're sure?'

'I'll kill him.'

Abdul Ayub Khan sighs and wearily mounts the stairs to the restaurant. A customer with two mouths is not to be lightly turned away. Give offence and the word can spread. Tariq trails behind, ready to slit the white bloke's throat. He's always been fond of Abdul Ayub Khan and spent much of his childhood mucking about with cousin Ahmed Khan in the friendly streets and alleyways between the two homes. On the wall of Abdul Ayub Khan's living room hangs a picture of English people haymaking, women and children, sunny and peaceful. Tucked into the picture frame are photographs of Her Majesty The Queen and His Royal Highness Prince Philip – in younger days. Abdul Ayub Khan had served in the British Army in Germany, BAOR, as a driver-mechanic. When he settled in Bruddersford he became a pillar of the Pakistan Association, always (Tariq remembers) reaching for his big Koran, chapter 84, line 18, to prove that the Prophet had predicted a journey to the moon long before the Jews and Christians got hold of the idea.

Wide-eyed to the unfolding mysteries of the universe, the two boys, Tariq and Ahmed, would perch on Abdul Ayub Khan's earthly knees.

' "When there is a full moon you will go there step by step," Allah told the Holy Prophet, peace be upon him.'

Lovingly Uncle Abdul would thumb through his beautiful, tooled-leather Koran:

> No! I swear by the twilight
> and the night and what it envelops
> and the moon when it is at the full
> you shall surely ride stage after stage.

Tariq's father, Karamat Khan, used to work a long day in the sheet-metal mill and then attend union meetings and Labour Party meetings half the night, so you never saw him much. But Uncle Abdul Ayub Khan was a businessman with the time to sit the two boys, his son and nephew, on his solid, spread-apart knees, and to tell them tall tales in a comforting blend of Urdu and English:

'The Jewish Christian Bible has been changed, more's the shame. The original Bible said nothing about the prophet Jesus being the son of God. That is blasphemy and was invented later . . . by a conspiracy.'

From an early age Tariq learned about conspiracies from Uncle Abdul. He knows that Gamal Rahman is part of a vast, worldwide conspiracy. The Jews paid him to write lies and send thousands of good Muslims to jail in Egypt. Even his own father would have nothing to do with him on account of Rahman's immoral dealings with the Sharaf women and then betraying his own Muslim wife, a noble lady whose name Tariq can't remember, to the Israelis.

Abdul Ayub Khan enters the restaurant a few appropriate paces ahead of Tariq. The white couple who'd ordered two helpings of Gamal Rahman are glowering now, sullen, unserved.

၆

Young Imran Hassani's gaze rests, glazed with exhaustion, on the television screen. His dad's fever simmers in his large, lustrous eye-balls. The boy will not sleep tonight, or any future night, until his father has looked under his bed and searched every cupboard for Gamal Rahman (whom Imran calls Gamal Shaytan). Imran's electric train-set lies spread out on his bedroom floor; its prettily fashioned miniature carriages and engines may spark to life and crazily de-rail themselves while the boy slumbers and the Devil's malign magnetic field drifts across the night sky above the Muslim quarter. Imran now demands that his bedroom door remain wide open, with the landing light on, but on several nights he has awoken in a panic to find the house in complete darkness. Responding to his son's cry, Hassan Hassani has been puzzled to discover the landing light extinguished; on a bad night this may happen three times. The house is haunted. Every Muslim home in Bruddersford is haunted by the book.

Rahman himself once visited this house, sat on this sofa, asked for help. Hassan has the exact date in an old diary.

The doorbell rings. 'Ah, that will be Mr Reddaway.' Hassan Hassani hurries to the front hallway.

'I see they're still not collecting your rubbish at the back,' Reddaway says.

'You are perfectly correct. Rats everywhere. I killed two last week. My boy hears them at night and thinks they are Shaytan Rahman.'

'Have you spoken to Councillor Hani Malik?'

'Malik is a socialist. He is too busy stitching up deals with atheists.'

'What about Lord Mayor Zaheed?'

'The same. These Labour people swallow the people's votes and leave them to rot. My wife is afraid to walk home from the bus in winter, so few street lamps are working.'

'How is your wife?'

'And we still have the white prostitutes and black-Caribbean dope gangs in the local pubs. We of the Maududi Mosque have repeatedly written to the breweries demanding the closure of all pubs in the Muslim quarter. Please come inside, Mr Reddaway.'

The demand to close pubs reminds Reddaway of the demand to ban Rahman's unreadable book, but it's not the moment to say so as he's ushered into the smoke-filled living room where neither the grandfather nor the plump boy accords him a glance. The telly holds sway. The room reeks of cigarettes, curry and odours too mingled to identify. Hassani makes no effort to turn down the television; indeed his own eyes are soon back on the screen.

'Hullo then, Imran!' Joe insists. No response. Oddly, the boy physi-cally reminds him of Rahman – the big, rolling eyes, the plum pudding features – uncanny! Joe studies the violently coloured tapestry of the Great Mosque of Mecca on the living room wall. 'There is no God but Allah . . .' Joe is familiar with these rainbow living rooms: the tapestries, the paper flowers on the mantelpiece, big wall-clocks, ornately designed emblems in gilded frames, some rectangular, some small and circular. 'A good Muslim with the soul of a tourist guide,' Ali Cheema said of Hassani. Joe has never penetrated the young scholar's own home, a small Victorian terraced house in Nuneaton Road. There have been rumours of late concerning Cheema's private life – some fancy bird seen coming and going.

Hassan Hassani's old father is chain-smoking steadily. The tin ashtray is overflowing so badly that Joe wants to empty it himself. It's the same with the uncollected dustbins: as rate-payers demanding their rights, these people have lost the old, village instinct for self-help. But you can't fault them on family solidarity; he remembers that Hassani paid six hundred pounds to send his father on the Hajj, the pilgrimage to Mecca, when the old chap was still strong enough to survive the arduous journey.

Joe hears the front door close softly. Nasreen enters the room with a shy smile, her head covered. Reddaway stands up but knows better than to offer his hand (not that Yorkshiremen are great hand-shakers). He has always fancied Nasreen.

'Working late, Mrs Hassani?'

She nods. 'A community teacher's work is never done.'

'So what's the latest gossip from the Department of Education?'

'Gossip? Will you have coffee or tea?'

The fact that she addresses him directly, almost looks him in the eye, and speaks English, marks her out as a member of the new generation. With the older women it's a timid knock on the sitting room door, the husband goes out into the corridor to convey the male guest's wishes, and then five minutes later another knock and the husband goes out to collect the tray. 'I'm no feminist,' Joe began a 'Plain Speaking' column, 'but every time I visit a Muslim home in this city . . .' But then he tore the sheet in two and binned it.

What he needs right now is a beer. A double whisky. Alcohol deprivation makes him twitchy, belligerent. Recently he read an article in one of the London tabloids, claiming that Gamal Rahman has a drink problem and spends his evenings raging at his minders because they're limiting him to one bottle of whisky a week. Joe reckoned that the source for such a story, true or false, must be a secret serviceman strapped for cash.

'How's things with Izza Shah's difficult daughters, then?' Joe asks Nasreen.

She flinches. 'Oh – so so.'

'I hear Safia's been skipping school?'

'These are private matters.' Her tone deflects the rebuke into a declaration of ignorance.

'Izza Shah has a national profile higher than Big Ben,' Reddaway says. 'If Safia skips school and Fatima insists on wearing the hijab in class, we may find it's no private matter.'

'Is that true about Fatima?' Hassan asks Nasreen.

'I believe Fatima may have spoken to Mrs Newman about it.'

'Rajiv Lal won't allow headscarves,' Reddaway probes, his eye on Nasreen. 'Will he?'

Her gaze slides away. 'I do not know Mr Lal very well.'

'But what about his multi-cultural stuff? I hear the headteachers are furious. If Labour loses its majority, and Samuel Perlman gets chucked out as Education Chairman, Mister Rajiv Lal could be looking for another job.'

'That I don't know,' she says softly.

'Your wife is very discreet,' Reddaway tells Hassan Hassani, desperate to get something out of someone for tomorrow's column.

'Nasreen, bring the tea,' Hassani says, half-wrenching his gaze from the TV screen.

ରୁ

Tariq has followed Uncle Abdul Ayub Khan up the stairs to the first-floor restaurant of the Omar Khayyam. The white couple are glowering, sullen, unserved. The bloke ostentatiously glances at a big, digital wristwatch.

'What was your order, sir?' Uncle Abdul politely enquires.

Clearly the 'estate agent' is in a dilemma. Alone, he might simply order his tandoori or korma or 'number 74'. But he cannot climb down in front of his blow-dried woman, inches from a mini-skirt as short as hers (which Abdul Ayub Khan has also noticed: no wonder they changed the Bible and never thought of the moon, these degenerates). The bloke has to stick it out or lose face.

'I asked for two helpings of Gamal Rahman.' He winks. 'It was a joke. It's April Fool's Day.'

Deeper waters still! By no means is it April Fool's Day and April Fool's Day, in any case, is no time for Christians and atheists to be mocking and insulting Muslim people. Tariq is definitely poised to slit the man's throat before hitchhiking south to kill Gamal Rahman. He has read about the 'safe houses' used by IRA terrorists when planting bombs in London, and he reckons there must be some Muslim safe houses down there, too.

'I cannot serve you, sir,' Abdul Ayub Khan tells his unwelcome white customer. 'I must ask you to leave.'

'It was a joke. Surely you can take a joke!'

'A true joke causes both parties to rejoice, sir. I am not rejoicing. You must leave.'

Tariq has always admired his uncle's English and his wit. Abdul Ayub Khan had driven 36-wheelers and walked the streets of Hamburg in British khaki with a corporal's stripes on his arm: you learn real English in English Army. He'd learned some German, too, not tourist stuff but real colloquial stuff with verbs at the end and so on. 'Every fraülein has her price, nicht wahr?' Things like that. He never forgot his German.

'Well, if we're not welcome . . .' the blonde woman says, reaching to the floor for her bag. The man drains his glass slowly, trapped, then bangs it on the table, while Abdul Ayub Khan writes out the bill for a Carlsberg and a bitter lemon.

'Fuck that!' The bloke is on his feet.

'You are required to pay for the drinks consumed, sir,' Uncle Abdul says. It's a matter of principle – everything is a matter of principle when Gamal Rahman is involved.

ഏ

'So what's next on the Gamal Rahman agenda?' Joe Reddaway asks Hassan Hassani belligerently. *Switch that fucking box off!* 'I hear the City Library has refused to ban the book.'

To his surprise, his host awards him full-frontal, owl-like attention, a refraction of the Great Mosque of Mecca dancing in his porthole lenses.

'You know something, Mr Reddaway? I grew up in this country without knowing who I was. The Jehovah's Witnesses were always putting their literature through the door.'

'Oh aye, but – '

'No respect, you see. No respect for us at all. We, the heathen, waiting to be converted.'

'So you learned about religious propaganda from the Jehovah's Witnesses? I must say, some of those leaflets of yours have been making quite a stir in this little city of ours. Even Bishop Goodgame is said to be murmuring to his boiled egg, which is some achievement.'

Hassan Hassani smiles uncertainly. 'The Bishop himself? Is that true?'

'Not to mention the Archbishop of York.'

'One does one's best. Of course, as secretary of the Jamiyat Maududi Mosque . . . shall I spell that?'

'I can spell it like I can spell Geoff Boycott. Fourteen mosques and madrasahs in Bruddersford, nine thousand followers.'

'Over nine thousand. When I was a youngster, you know, I always suffered from that nagging feeling at the back of my head that there was more to learn. One night I cried out in my bed, O God help me, where is the truth?'

Joe Reddaway isn't taking notes. There's a half-bottle of Scotch in his briefcase but it's out of the question. Instant ruin. Nasreen returns, carrying a tray with two cups of milky tea and a plate heaped with assorted biscuits. She leaves the room without a word, taking Joe's gaze with her.

'The more I read the Koran with an open mind,' Hassani is saying, 'the more I understand my mission in this world.'

'To turn books into ashes?'

Hassani sits up very straight.

'On August 1st last year certain Members of Parliament burned copies of the new Immigration Act outside the Home Office. No one was scandalized.'

Reluctantly Joe pulls his spiral-backed reporter's notebook from the carpet-bag pocket of his jacket. Rummaging, he finds a chewed pencil with a blunt tip.

'I'm listening,' he grunts.

'So why should Muslims not burn a blasphemous book which insults and reviles them? Who listened to us until we burned this book? Why are we on every TV channel tonight?'

'What will you burn next? W.H. Smith's? The City Library?'

'Burning a book is a non-violent act within the law. You must understand that we Muslims are hurt and sobbing.'

'And liberal values?'

'Liberals are interested only in spreading moral corruption, Aids, pornography and sexual anarchy. They invoke freedom of speech to conceal their base motives.'

'Would you agree, Mr Hassani, that the Islamic Council is exploiting this book to clamp padlocks on semi-liberated, modern-minded Muslim wives and daughters?'

'Every Muslim woman in Bruddersford is offended by this book.'

'How many of them have read it?'

'They have no wish to read blasphemies which can only scourge their Muslim hearts and souls.'

'Shall we ask your wife?'

Joe knows he's gone over the limit. All he needs is a drink.

Hassani turns to his son. 'Imran, go to bed.'

The boy is almost asleep. 'Naw,' he moans.

'Imran!' Hassani pulls the boy to his feet and leads him gently upstairs.

Joe and the old man are now alone in the room, watching the TV screen. It's an American soap opera; the old Pakistani peasant grins toothlessly whenever he hears canned studio laughter, though he doesn't understand a word. Joe takes himself and his briefcase up to the landing, catches a glimpse of Hassan Hassani and the boy crouched on the bedroom floor, searching for Shaytan Rahman under the bed, locks himself into the toilet, and pours whisky down his throat. His lust for the lady of the house eases as the fire scorches his happy gut.

∞

Behind Tariq's lazy, menacing movements around the floor of the Omar Khayyam restaurant are years of casual street fighting. He always goes tooled-up nowadays – though 'always' is a big word.

When younger, Tariq had asked his uncle why he, a Labour Party man, always sent congratulations to Mrs Thatcher after her election victories. Abdul Ayub Khan had smiled with delight at his clever nephew's penetration of his statesmanship. He'd informed Tariq's father that the boy would go a long way. But by the time Tariq became uncomfortably interested in Rana he hadn't.

'Mrs Thatcher is a fine Christian lady, very principled, very strong. That Neil Kinnock, the Leader of our Labour Party, is a confessed atheist.' Into English, now: 'Prime Minister never saying she not believing in God.'

All this talk of a female Prime Minister set Tariq's nerve-ends afire. He used to hang around in the street outside, prowling the cul-de-sac reserved for residents' parking, waiting for Uncle Abdul's daughter Rana – Woman Police Constable Rana Khan – to swing her blue Escort GX round the corner, two blinding headlamps. Rana owned a brand new car while Tariq was still desultorily tinkering with a clapped-out motor scooter; he wasn't at all sure it was 'modest' for a Muslim girl to drive a car. He'd invite her to the cinema, to see *Crocodile Dundee* or *Sammy and Rosie Get Laid*, but she usually pleaded fatigue. Rana's police uniform was covered in buttons he couldn't undo and she had four O Levels he couldn't undo either: Maths, English Language, Chemistry and Geography. Tariq knows her high grades by heart.

The blow-dried blonde woman is now stepping round the tight knot of grunting males – her escort, the 'manager' and the insolent waiter. Still at issue is the bill for the drinks. Uncle Abdul cannot risk an 'incident' or the police; but the 'two helpings of Gamal Rahman' constitute an unbearable insult and the frontiers of honour are not negotiable. Abdul Ayub Khan can feel Tariq at his shoulder, a steel coil waiting for release – whichever way the white man moves, so does Tariq.

Muslim waiter slashes throat of estate agent with meat cleaver. Claims he was insulted when asked to bring two helpings of famous author.

 و

Fatima's father comes home late, as usual: business, magistrate, Islamic Council, his plate is heavy, his body weary. She has his dinner waiting for him. Izza Shah takes his place at the table, alone; she serves him then withdraws a few paces, to await his needs, as her late mother had done. She stands behind her father while he eats, whatever the hour, however profound her exhaustion, in dutiful silence.

Fatima is about to say 'Dad' but checks herself. 'Father,' she says. He eats silently, preoccupied by the fatwa. The Muslims, he keeps telling himself, did not strike the first blow. They have been patient; written letters; protested peacefully; beyond the point of endurance. He takes his daughter's silent presence for granted; to talk to him she must request an interview.

'Father.' Fatima takes a half pace forward, behind his shoulder. His back is turned to her, his fingers are plunging into the bowls, he is eating intently, gravely, thinking, composing letters to the Queen, the Prime Minister and the Home Secretary, the letters of a good citizen, a Justice of the Peace, well respected by His Grace the Rt. Revd Bishop Robin Goodgame.

'Father.'

'Yes I must write some letters,' he tells her in Punjabi. 'I shall need your help, Fatima. Have you done your homework?'

'Father, give me permission to wear the hijab in school.' The word 'school' she says in English, the rest in Punjabi.

'Mrs Newman does not allow the hijab in school,' he says.

'Mrs Newman's no skin off my nose.'

Izza Shah half-glances towards her but his suited shoulder is in the way. Skin? Nose? – what does she mean? Constantly he has to remind himself that his children have grown up in England. Yes, Fatima has reached the age. It is wrong for men and women to mix. God makes rules to protect us from ourselves, to free us from the tyranny of desire. Izza Shah hates to contemplate his daughters exposed to the boys and male teachers without a decent, modest covering. As a father he is humiliated, demeaned, insulted by it; but Mrs Newman's policy is that of the City Education Board and Mr Rajiv Lal.

52

'Mrs Newman will send you home if you insist,' he says.

'Then I shall come home.'

'But you must do your lessons, child.'

He wonders whether her noble gesture is inspired by Safia's brazen rebellion – the daughter who has brought him nothing but shame and grief. Had Safia not said to him, in front of Fatima, that she would choose her own husband? That she wasn't going to be 'dumped into the lap of some peasant from the Punjab who will play the village tyrant'.

He continues his meal, forgetful of the pale, stick-thin girl standing behind him.

FOUR

ᚼ

Hassan Hassani is reporting to the Islamic Council concerning
his visit to Bruddersford's Central Library:

'I found no copies of the Rahman book on the shelves. I was told
that it is now kept "in reserve". The library has purchased ten copies
and there is a waiting list of two hundred readers. I put my name
down. The only way we can seize the book is to enter our names on
the waiting list.'

'They can buy more copies,' Ali Cheema comments.

Ali Cheema! Izza Shah's darling!

'Under the counter!' roars Mustafa Jangar. 'They are keeping
copies "under the counter"! This "under the counter" strategy comes
from the last war of England against Hitler when there was food
rationing for poor people and the butchers kept choice cuts of meat
"under the counter" for those women who had lost their faith in God
and were prepared to prostitute themselves.'

This information is gravely absorbed.

'Now,' announces their President, Izza Shah, 'I have some infor-
mations that passages of this blasphemous book are circulating in
our schools. White kids are reading passages aloud to torment our
Muslim children. They are pinning up these same offending passages
to notice boards.'

Resolved: that Izza Shah shall write to the Chairman of the City's
Education Committee, Councillor Samuel Perlman (a Jew of course),
to the Director of Education, Rajiv Lal (a Hindu of course), and to
the headteachers of all the City schools (not one of whom is a
Muslim).

Resolved: Not to support any party or candidate in the imminent
City Council elections unless that aforesaid party or candidate shall
be on record as demanding the banning of the Rahman book in all
City libraries. (Amended to 'all public libraries throughout the
United Kingdom'.)

The discussion turns to national politics, Izza Shah's province and preserve:

'The Foreign Secretary and the Home Secretary are telling us to mind our p's and q's and not step out of line.'

This is said in Punjabi, except for 'Foreign Secretary', 'Home Secretary', and 'p's and q's'.

'The Jews are behind this book,' Mustafa Jangar bellows. 'The British Government and the Labour Party dare not offend the Zionists. The Labour Party is in the hands of atheists! Michael Foot has publicly defended Rahman, his personal friend, and Michael Foot is a Jew!'

This brings Councillor Hani Malik to his feet. Bracing himself for an election campaign of unprecedented viciousness, Malik is in no mood to hear a word against the Labour Party for any reason whatever.

'Michael Foot is not a Jew. Frankly, book-burning is not my cup of tea. Nor is anti-Semitism. The non-Muslims of this city are shocked, outraged by all this uproar. They do not understand us.'

'Let them not understand us!' roars Mustafa. 'The Labour Party has dismissed our protests with contempt.' He offers a flamboyantly dismissive gesture, like a man sending away bad food from his table. 'As for our Lord Mayor, Zulfikar Zaheed, where is his voice in all this?'

'Zulfikar is working hard behind the scenes,' Malik says in English.

'Ach! We Muslims have five City councillors out of one hundred and one. That's the "scenes" you and Zaheed are behind. Don't offend the liberals! Pander to the whites!'

'Harry Flowers has expressed sympathy for our point of view,' Malik says, although without noticeable conviction.

'Ha! Flowers! Our Em Pee! Another atheist! All he cares about is thwarting Zaheeb's ambition to grab his seat and become the first Muslim MP! But when Flowers goes back to London, to meet the atheists Kinnock and Hattersley, they read him the Riot Act – '

Izza Shah intervenes in his slow, lugubrious monotone:

'This is not the language of brothers. We do not offer Shaytan a seat at this table. Brother Mustafa, you are not alone in sharing Allah's grief.'

Hassan Hassani always trembles throughout these political altercations. He recoils. His own furies work through his word processor, his pamphlets and letters to the press. But he knows what's at stake: three Muslim Labour councillors face the threat of breakaway, Independent candidates campaigning on the single Islamic issue of the Rahman book. As a result all three seats may fall to the Tories; likewise control of the City Council. Hassan Hassani is secretly quite happy at the prospect; it's time the Labour Party was punished for its opposition to the late President Zia and for inviting that bitch Bhutto to London. Indeed he is tempted to offer Malik's potential rival in Tanner Ward, Ishmail Haqq, the full support of his Amstrad word processor. But Hassan shrinks from politics.

⁊∾

Joe Reddaway steams up the pedestrian shopping precinct towards W.H. Smith's with the stride of a police sergeant, but twice the speed, his turn-ups flapping three inches above his ankles. His ear tells him that the white citizens of the city are on the boil; the previous evening his regular band of soaks in the Traveller's Rest had written his column for him:

—If Rahman gets done, every bloody Paki gets done.
—We're not going to take nowt from some Arab Ayatollah.
—Let's face it, they don't fit in here, never have.
Passing the bookshop's exit tills, Joe threads his way through stationery, greeting cards and diaries to the shrinking shelves of new books.

'I'm not seeing Rahman's novel,' he tells the young male assistant.
'We no longer stock it, sir.'
Flashing his card, Joe summons the manager. Five minutes later, with a quote in his notebook – 'The security of our staff must be our prime consideration' – Joe enters the *Echo* building and thrusts his wild carrot head over the subscription desk:

'I'd subscribe to anything for you, Sally. How about a film tonight?'
'Oh you!'
Joe reckons every jeweller in town should pay him a royalty; he no sooner looks at a woman than she rushes off to get engaged.

Upstairs, Joe begins to flip through his mail. Hassan Hassani – as usual! as ever! – takes strong and indignant exception to a provocative phrase from a recent Reddaway column: 'The mischievous posturing of the political piranhas who are now after their pound of flesh.' This, writes Hassani, is a 'calumny on the heads of all devout Muslims'.

Other correspondents strongly agree or strongly disagree with Joe's no-holds-barred attacks on City councillors who 'vacillate' (Trevor Lucas, Zulfikar Zaheed), City bureaucrats who 'fudge' (Douglas Blunt), churchmen who merely 'sermonize' (the Bishop), and politicians who 'posture' (Tory leader Potter).

He calls the City Librarian and is informed that the Rahman book is stocked only in reserve and now carries a new health warning on the cover: 'Members of the Muslim Faith are advised that this book may cause them offence.'

Joe gets straight through to Douglas Blunt. The Chief Executive makes it a point of principle to answer his own phone.

'Douglas, I hear that a health warning is now attached to the book in the public libraries.'

'Correct.'

'I assume that's a deal Trevor Lucas has stitched up with Zaheed and Hani Malik?'

'It's no secret that every Muslim wants the book banned. The majority of non-Muslim councillors in the Labour Group favour keeping the library copies in reserve, and carrying the health warning.' A pause. 'There is one notable exception – he wants the book on full display, open shelves.'

'Sam Perlman?'

'Ask him.'

'What about the Tories. What's Tom Potter saying?'

'Ask him.'

'Would you serve under a Tory Council, Doug?'

'Joe, I've got work to do.'

ᕗ

'Safia, what are you doing here? Why aren't you in school?'

Ali Cheema warily contemplates the heavily painted young woman sluttishly slumped in his living room sofa (an Afghan rug half-conceals the threadbare upholstery). A cheap pop star magazine lies in Safia Shah's lap; she has been reading about Peter Singh, 'Punjab's only rock'n'roll king'. A small pile of purple-stained cigarette ends have been crushed into the saucer he uses as a butter dish. He stoops to retrieve an empty crisps bag from the floor.

'Does your father know you're not in school?' he asks.

'Oh him! He thinks he can dump me on some peasant from the Punjab who'll play village tyrant. No thank you.'

In despair Ali has entrusted a front door-key to Safia. The alternative was to find her slouched outside, in full view of the neighbours, tossing cigarette ends on the pavement like a street walker.

'Safia, I have work to do.'

She shrugs her prize breasts. 'I'm not stopping yer.'

Safia knows that her father, President of the Islamic Council, regards Ali as the son he never had. It was Izza Shah who raised the money to put Ali through his A Level college – and then, more miraculously, through Oxford. This happened after Ali's parents went home to Pakistan to visit relatives and never came back – both killed in a car accident. Ali's father, Muhammad Cheema, had been Izza Shah's closest friend – they had both come off the same immigrant ship with scarcely a pound between them. Normally a Pakistani family would set great store on taking their only son back to visit relatives, to show him off, to ritualize his roots, but Ali had been studying for his A Levels and such was his seriousness of dedication that this intense, horribly ambitious bookworm scarcely lifted his head from his scribbling to bid his mother and father farewell. He moved in under Izza Shah's roof and there the orphaned youth stayed, adopted, as a 'brother' to Safia and Fatima.

When Ali's parents had failed to return from Pakistan, neither Safia nor Fatima had been of an age to register the event – indeed Fatima could not put a face to Ali's father and mother. As girls they merited no explanation and neither inquired: Ali's brooding, aloof presence in their home was a fact of life like the grey skies and mushrooming minarets of Bruddersford. But as nature fluttered within their dawning bodies, both girls had marked Ali down as a marriageable young man of prospects in whose unchaperoned presence a 'sister' loses no honour.

Then their mother died and the buffer zone of maternal vigilance was removed.

Did Ali mourn his own dead parents? Occasionally he would talk of Muhammad Cheema, a schoolmaster who had cultivated his only child's appetite for learning, his intimate communion with language, his questing soul – but a girl had to overhear such tokens of love since Izza Shah alone was deemed worthy to hear them. This was men's talk. Ali sometimes addressed Izza Shah as 'Father', but only as a token of respect, and when he deigned to address a word to either of the girls he said 'your father'. Neither Safia nor Fatima could lay claim to the smallest corner of Ali's attention.

After Ali graduated from Oxford with a very fine degree, one of the best, and immediately began to earn his first salary as a lecturer at the Community College, Izza Shah reluctantly accepted the brilliant young scholar's singular need for solitude, for a home of his own, a rare luxury for young men not yet married.

'I cannot work in peace here, Father. I need a proper space of my own if I am to write the books of which I am capable. The girls and their friends make too much noise. They cannot be blamed – children should enjoy their young years.'

Safia no longer considers herself a child. Ali warily contemplates the heavily painted young woman slumped in the sofa of his tiny house in Nuneaton Road.

'Safia, I have work to do.'

'I'm not stopping yer.'

To extract a front-door key from Ali, Safia has regularly pulled the tricks of her trade; Ali would arrive home to find half-a-dozen young white yobs revving their motorbikes in Nuneaton Road, Safia riding pillion.

'Hey! Delivered – one tart!'

Neighbourhood disgrace. Safia trades on his fear of disgrace. Is he already compromised? When will Izza Shah discover? Or – God forbid – the Bishop? The Rt. Revd Robin Goodgame has always admired Ali's tonsured celibacy: a married Muslim, with a string of brats to house, is not the ideal Junior Research Fellow. The older Fellows of an Oxford college, the bachelors, the widowers-Emeritus, covet the regular company at dinner of the young. The Bishop likes to quote the famous *obiter dictum* by the Warden of All Souls College, who had complained that young scholars were increasingly abandoning all souls for one body.

'The house stinks of your cigarettes,' he says. 'How can I work in this smog? And why don't you wear something decent when you come here?'

'I'm not expecting you to marry me, you know. That's little Fatima's big dream, i'n't it?'

'The heavens lie under your mother's feet,' he says, weary of repeating himself in front of this intractable bitch. At night he has been forced to drag a chest of drawers across his bedroom door.

'So how's your famous duel with Gamal Rahman going?' Safia rearranges her beautiful legs on the sofa. 'Oh, he had all the princesses of Egypt, didn't he?' she taunts. 'All those Sharaf girls.'

'Rahman lived off the Sharafs, purloined priceless antiquities and revelled in corruption until he was thrown into jail for embezzlement. He was also a Zionist agent who betrayed his own wife, a heroine of Islam.'

'I reckon that's all lies.'

'He sank so low that his famous father, the greatest of Arab novelists, disowned him. Please go home, Safia. I have much work to do.'

'Liar! You're just itching for it.'

'You should study the Koran.'

'Oh yeah? And what about the hadith that says the majority of people in hell are women hanging by their hair? And why are two female witnesses needed in business contracts, where one male will do?'

'This is for the protection of the women. Aisha, the favourite wife of the Prophet, peace be upon him, became a great stateswoman in the early years of Islam.'

'Yeah?'

He pulls his gaze from her breasts. 'Do not forget that Islam brought women the right to inherit property and keep their own earnings.'

'What property, eh?' A blob of bubblegum hangs on the end of her tongue. 'I do take precautions, you know. Too good for me, are you – a jumped-up telly star whose head has been turned by the smart set in London?'

She sounds the first 'o' of London – Yorkshire-fashion – like the 'u' in 'full'. London is the glittering prize, the dancing Shiva, and sex is the ticket she knows.

ॐ

Fatima is grey with purity and dedication; a moth to Safia's butterfly, she washes herself in ashes, clothes herself in black and grey, mostly black. She partly understands her father's distress over Safia, but she is a child, and children cannot dress wounds bleeding in Eden.

After her mother died, Izza Shah taught Fatima the hadith in which the Prophet was asked who was the person most worthy of respect. Three times the Prophet answered: 'Your mother'. Only on the fourth occasion did he add, 'Your father'.

Bereaved and deserted, Fatima understands, almost. Only in death has her mother become visible to her father.

'Thirty years ago,' Izza Shah is telling Fatima, 'everything here was very strange to us. We all worked in the mills. It was low pay but it was work. The white people were no longer prepared to do such work.'

'That was a hard time for you, Dad.'

She cannot beat back a cavernous yawn. He notices her fatigue but, having eaten his meal – her meal – he needs company.

'We could not find accommodations. Nobody was prepared to let us into their homes. We were living all cramped up, twenty to thirty people in a three-bedroom house.'

'Twenty to thirty!'

'The Council houses we couldn't get either. You go walking today around those Council estates, Buttershaw, Holmewood, Knoxburgh, Ravenscliffe, you'll see only white faces.' He grimaces. 'And what did Brother Zulfikar Zaheed succeed in doing about that? Another politician.'

Fatima knows that Zaheed is their Lord Mayor and that his no-better-than-she-should-be daughter Wahabia went south to some posh school. Beyond that Fatima harbours a forbidden knowledge.

'It was a state of siege in those days,' her father says. 'The mosques were our shelters. And then we lost our jobs. Cutbacks.'

'What is that?'

'Redundancies.'

'What is that?'

'They no longer need your labour. Our jobs were the first to go. They threw us out of the mills. Our younger men led some bitter strikes. I was on strike myself. And S.B. Hussein.'

'That's the dad of Nasreen and Latifa?'

'Of your community teacher Mrs Nasreen Hassani. Show respect, child. Then we had Paki-bashing. And we were fighting back always. In April 1976 we had twenty-four people arrested. Pitched battles it was, our youth confronting the National Front. S.B. Hussein was arrested. Karamat Khan arrested. But our children don't understand these things.'

Fatima takes the rebuke in silence, her hands folded across her lap.

'Our children were growing up "modern", despising our customs. They became angry, we could not reach them. Only now, with this Rahman book, are we reaching them.'

Rarely has he spoken at such length to her – but he has no son.

'Is Safia at home?' he asks. (As if he didn't know.)

'No, Father.'

'When was she last at home?'

'I cannot remember, Father.'

'So then,' he continues, 'we had all this Labour business. We Muslims made the big mistake of trusting everything in Labour. S.B. Hussein is a good man but in the thick of Labour and supporting that Bhutto woman. The Labour Party, they wanted only our votes, and men like S.B. and Zaheed kept promising us equal opportunities policies, race relations, money for our community centres.'

'Is that bad?'

'Our Muslim men forgot about God and worshipped Council jobs, Council grants . . . wheeling and dealing. But now Labour is showing its true colours with this Rahman affair. Our men know now that only Muslims can defend Islam.'

'I shall wear the hijab in school,' Fatima says.

'What does Mrs Nasreen Hassani say about that?'

Fatima shrugs her thin shoulders. 'She's frightened of Mrs Newman, isn't she? Everyone is. And Nasreen – Mrs Hassani – works for that Hindu, Rajiv Lal.'

'You have my authority, Fatima. We are invisible people until they stone us. But our martyrs, in Heaven, they are not invisible. I shall write a letter to Mrs Newman. You must help me write in English to Mrs Newman, the Queen and the Prime Minister.'

෨

Arriving home, Hassan Hassani crosses the square to the Maududi Mosque, two terraced houses knocked together, a Victorian yellow-brick building with large ground-floor windows, each divided by three sashes, plaster porticos and semi-circular window panels above the two front doors (one of which is now permanently locked, for security, though Hassan Hassani, as Mosque Secretary, has the key). A plaque on the façade warns, both in Urdu and English, 'Place of Worship – Jamiyat Maududi Mosque'.

Hassan is proud of the new mosque now under construction round the corner, in Peebles Place, a gift from Saudi Arabia: a rectangular, single-storey building crowned by a square brick tower and a modest minaret. But he will always feel more at home in the converted house where he and his family have worshipped ever since their arrival in Bruddersford. He himself has largely been responsible for the loving decoration of the interior: the board displaying rows of clocks, each indicating the time of day in one of the eleven Islamic centres of the world; the glossy wooden pannelling which covers not only the walls from the skirting to a height of six feet, but also graces the square concrete pillars which replaced the party-wall previously dividing the two houses, thus creating a larger space for prayer. The interior walls of the mosque sustain photographs, travel-bureau calendars and an ornate tapestry depicting Ibrahim's tomb in black, rimmed with a white 'halo' indicating an electric spiritual energy. Hassan Hassani's owl-eyes love strong colours: violently coloured paper streamers hurtle from wall to wall while more streamers in red and gold descend from the ceiling like the jet-streams of angels. Hassan is particularly proud of the big wall map, 'World of Islam – Dar Al-Maal Al-Islam', depicting the Islamic states clustered in green from Morocco to Afghanistan, with far-flung Malaysia and Indonesia lying further afield.

Hassan joins the rows of the faithful at prayer: himself – Hassan Hassani, B.A. (Leeds University), marketing manager, Secretary of the Maududi Mosque, local Secretary of the Muslim Youth League, faithful servant of Allah. Born in Pakistan.

Izza Shah, widower, magistrate, family dry-goods business, President of the Islamic Council, servant of Allah.

Mustafa Jangar, imam to the Islamic Council, Regional Guardian of the Muslim Youth League, servant of Allah, born in the Punjab.

62

Ali Cheema, M.A., D. Phil. (Oxon.). Lecturer, Grade II in the Community College.

Dr Yaqub Quddus, Chairman of the Community Relations Council (CRC). Labour Party member. Born in Pakistan.

Abdul Ayub Khan, businessman and owner of the Omar Khayyam restaurant and a halal slaughterhouse. Former soldier-mechanic, British Army of the Rhine. Labour Party activist. Born in Pakistan.

His brother Karamat Khan, ex-steel worker, trade unionist, Labour Party activist. Born in Pakistan.

Karamat's son Tariq, ex-mill worker, now a waiter. Born in Bruddersford.

Ishmail Haqq, employee of the CRC, Labour Party activist about to abscond as Islamic Independent. Born in Pakistan.

Hani Malik, Labour Councillor for Tanner Ward, insurance salesman (family business). Born in Pakistan.

Zulfikar Zaheed, Lord Mayor of Bruddersford, former mill worker, former charity organizer, former Chair of Housing Committee, aspires to be Member of Parliament. Born in Pakistan.

So! (concludes Hassan Hassani): our Bhutto-loving socialists have rediscovered their God at the eleventh hour! Where have you been, Brothers, during Labour's long dominion over our city? Hassan's forehead kisses the prayer rug, content in the knowledge that Allah's midnight will soon descend to obliterate the children of the eleventh hour.

Ali Cheema glances sidelong down the ranks of kneeling-swaying Muslims-at-prayer towards Ishmail Haqq, a born demagogue with a knack for being absent 'sick' from his municipal desk – though everyone knows that Haqq's 'sickness' amounts to roaring around the Muslim quarter in one of several loaned cars, scheming, plotting, lobbying, scattering promises like busted wheat seeds.

Ali is aware that his own version of moonlighting, his TV-trips to London, are as much denigrated as admired here, in this mosque, the spiritual cradle of his existence. Poor Islam! So eloquent, poetic and commanding in its own linguistic domain, so clumsy and tongue-tied in the land of the infidel. Coolies hauling an alien cargo from East to West. Revelation is the gift of tongues yet these pious men – with the exception of Izza Shah – distrust Ali's ability to think in simultaneous translation.

The faithful sit cross-legged on the worn carpets of the Maududi Mosque – even the old men can squat comfortably for an hour. Tonight, at Friday prayers, the richest and deepest moment of the week, Mustafa Jangar, imam to the Islamic Council and apostle of jihad, holy war, is the preacher. Ali now suspects Mustafa of a covert conversion to the Shi'ite branch of Islam – the tall, bearded warrior reveres the Ayatollah Khomeini as the 'Twelfth Imam', the alive-but-hidden imam of Shi'ite tradition. The Maududi is a Sunni mosque but Ali can predict that Mustafa will soon provoke dangerous divisions and crippling rivalries within the Islamic Council.

For Mustafa religion is politics and politics is religion. From the pulpit he curses Arab states wallowing in putrefaction, curses the godless President Saddam Hussein who wages criminal war on Iran, curses the Saudi royal family who terrorize Iranian pilgrims during the annual Hajj to Mecca, curses Cairo as the stewpot of corruption which spawned Gamal Rahman.

'And not a single Arab state has yet threatened sanctions against Britain for permitting the publication of the apostate's filthy book, *The Devil: an Interview!*'

The congregation nods with one head, one neck – traders, mill workers, taxi drivers, clerks, doctors, teachers, city employees, waiters. And now Mustafa Jangar brings his holy fire to Bruddersford as he embarks on his Khomeini-text: the Rules of Ablution. He rebukes everyone present, even Lord Mayor Zaheed, for lax habits in personal hygiene.

'Here the great Ayatollah warns us not to confuse total immersion with washing by stages. Let us pay close attention to what he teaches us. He says this:

' "One must first announce one's intention of washing oneself, then wash head and neck, then the right half of the body, then the left half. The right half one of one's navel and sex ought to be washed with the right half of the body, the left half of the navel and sex with the left half of the body. However, it is more prudent to wash them in their entirety with each half of the body . . ." '

Ali is listening and not listening. He's brooding about Gamal Rahman. He has seen no need to disclose his relationship with Rahman to Izza Shah and the Bruddersford elders. It began shortly before the assassination of President Sharaf, when an Egyptian writer unknown to Ali turned up in Nuneaton Road and spent the rest of the day sheltering from the rain and his own gloom under Ali's roof.

'One wonders,' the fat Egyptian had said, 'whether this kind of weather is the necessary condition of democracy.'

The visitor had later asked to watch the television news – was it a devilish prescience? Ali would never forget the barbarous rolling of Gamal Rahman's eyes as the extraordinary events were relayed from Egypt. Later, after Gamal settled in London, Ali had opened a correspondence about the conflict between faith and reason. Gamal was always slow to reply, charmingly apologetic, lots of jokes, puns, word-play. Casually he mentioned a novel he was writing which 'touched' (his word) on the nature of revelation, but when Ali asked to read the novel in draft he was met by cheerful evasions lathered in gossip about publishers and agents.

Ali persevered with the correspondence. 'How can one argue anything except through Philosophy and Reason? And what is the meaning of death?'

Gamal's responses tended to be evasive and flippant: 'God, I suspect, is less than satisfied with death. "And these wretched mortals turn to me from Fear, not from Love" – that is His constant lament.'

Ali had never before encountered a writer who had no compunction about scripting God's lines. He wrote again to Gamal: 'Is Reason the enemy of Revelation? Can a theologian be a philosopher and remain a theologian?'

A month later he was treated to another facetious response:

'Being neither a philosopher nor a theologian, I have to rely on my conventicles with the devil. He tells me that God regards every known religion – and religion *per se* – as merely a futile search for the divine postal code. Let me know when next you're in London – I shall always be delighted to see you and offer you my spare bed until the day you spit in my wine.'

Ali had availed himself of the spare bed – he couldn't possibly afford to pay for his pillow when visiting London. Gamal was always an exceptionally generous host, entrusting his house key to Ali, inviting him to the theatre, throwing parties attended by what Gamal called 'the glitterati' and 'the chattering classes'. What amazed Ali was the prevalent drunkeness – even the young women rapidly descended into inebriation, their speech slurred, their behaviour towards the opposite sex, himself included, undignified. 'Your friend is no fun at all,' a girl would complain to Gamal as Ali unfastened her arms from round his neck.

When the guest had finally departed, Gamal would allow himself a last drink before bed: 'One for the road to purgatory.' Slumped in his chair, burping and belching, he'd roll his bulging eyes.

'You'll not believe this, Ali Cheema, but the history of modern Egypt can claim no authentic existence outside my novels. It was I who settled the fate of President Sharaf and his family of headstrong women. It was I who invented the famous Virgin of Egypt, Hamida, by dextrous application of a small whip known in France as a fouet. The Virgin threw me into jail but she couldn't keep me there. And why? Ha! One day I'll tell you the true story of the Virgin's little sister, Huda, known to her millions of demented followers as the Prophet's thirteenth wife but known to me as mine.'

A signed copy of *The Devil: an Interview* arrived shortly before publication: *For my friend Ali Cheema with affection and gratitude.* When Ali published his first critical blast at the book he received a one-liner from its author: *There is no foe like the friend who is determined to become an enemy.*

FIVE

୭ঌ

At the gates of Hightown Upper School, the Muslims girls customarily remove and neatly fold their headscarves, their hijabs. Fatima
Shah crosses the yard, where the boys are yelling and kicking footballs
and bouncing them on their heads, scuffing their shoes; she enters
the classroom without removing her scarf. Excused attendance at
Religious Assembly, which under the Tory Education Reform Act
must now be 'predominantly Christian', she nevertheless chooses,
today, to attend.

'School stand!' cries the head monitor as the Headmistress enters
the Assembly Hall.

At the close of prayers, Mrs Newman steps forward to make the
day's announcements. Graffiti have appeared on the new paintwork
in the Science Block, mainly of the 'Rahman Must Die' and 'Rahman
Rules OK' variety. This will not be tolerated; those responsible must
report to the Headmistress immediately after Assembly. Pupils are
also reminded that they must not enter pubs on their way home from
school, now that licensing hours have been extended. Two thefts
from lockers have been reported and pupils are instructed always to
padlock their belongings.

Mrs Newman notices a gleaming white scarf on the head of Fatima
Shah – who normally does not attend Assembly.

'Fatima, you have forgotten to remove your scarf.' Some of the
white girls turn and titter. Fatima's fragile hands remain folded in
her lap. 'Fatima, come and see me immediately after Assembly,' says
Mrs Newman, heading for the door.

'School stand!' cries the head monitor.

Fatima is waiting outside the Head's office door when Mrs Newman
hurries up the corridor. The graffiti culprits have not turned up. No
one expects them to, least of all Mrs Newman. She will have to devise
some new collective punishment. Normally she favours loss of games
periods but Rajiv Lal has recently circulated a memo – another

memo! – to all headteachers reminding them that sport is essential for young people's health and physical development.

'Collective punishments,' the Director of Education's memo adds, 'are to be avoided on principle.' Mrs Newman closes the door behind Fatima.

'I see you are still wearing your headscarf.'

Fatima trembles – thin as one half of a wish-bone.

'It is my religion, Mrs Newman. There are boys in this school and male teachers. Islam compels me to remain covered in the presence of all men who are not of my close family.'

'If it compels you today, why not yesterday? Why does it not compel the 140 other Muslim girls in this school?'

'We have all been breaking the laws of our religion because of the school rules.'

'Have you spoken to your father?'

'He says he will support me. He has written you this letter.'

Mrs Newman takes the letter but does not open it. She has had many run-ins with Izza Shah: about halal dinners, about religious assembly, about girls' swimming costumes, about 'mixing'. About Safia Shah, truant and slut.

'Fatima, is this connected with the Rahman affair?'

Fatima drops her gaze. 'To wear the hijab is my religion. By our religion girls should attend separate Islamic schools but the Government will not let us.'

'I am asking whether all this agitation over the Rahman book may have affected you.'

Fatima's voice rises. 'Maybe it has! We have been insulted (*insoolted*). All Muslim females have been insulted. The Prophet never had a thirteenth wife. Rahman was doing immoral things with the Sharaf women in Egypt and the Jews paid him to send Muslim martyrs to prison and to kill his own mother and his own wife.'

Patricia Newman teaches French to pupils with no palpable interest in learning it; and the truly happy, fulfilling periods in her year are when she is in France attending conferences or caravanning in the Dordogne, in the Auvergne, the Ardèche or Provence (but steering clear of the coastal tourist traps). Mrs Newman is a divorcée; her two sons (whom she has sent to other City schools) have opted for universities in the south – and she has a Frenchman whom no one in Bruddersford needs to know about. She first met Jean-Pierre at a conference in London. He is a Professor of English Literature at the Sorbonne and married.

Fatima is standing before her in the white scarf.

Recently Patricia Newman has been much absorbed by the battle in France over Muslim girls' headscarves. Two girls had been barred from a school near Paris.

'And now you are missing your Shakespeare class,' she tells Fatima reproachfully, glancing at her watch. 'We don't want that, do we?'

A slight, defiant flick of Fatima's head. 'It's up to you, i'n't it?'

Mrs Newman stifles a rebuke. She cannot correct the 'i'n't' because even 'isn't it' would be impertinent.

'You are a very bright and promising girl, Fatima. We think you will do well in all six of your GCSEs. We have very high hopes. You really must not let your religion interfere with your education.'

'My father says the heart of a Muslim's education is her religion.'

'But Fatima, your religion is what you believe in. No one wishes to take away your beliefs. No one wishes to prevent you from studying the Koran. Religion is something we do outside of school.'

'That is a Christian view. I must obey Allah twenty-four hours a day. I must obey the Holy Book dictated to the Prophet, peace be upon him, by the Almighty Allah.'

Mrs Newman notes (as usual) the beguiling pronunciation of that strange version of God with which she has become so familiar at Hightown Upper. Whereas the English stress both syllables, contracting and hurrying through the word as if it were 'soccer' or 'better', Fatima lets the two l's roll from the back of her throat and then slowly releases the final 'ah' like a patient with a doctor's stethoscope to her chest.

Ahll-aah.

So two girls had been barred from a school near Paris after insisting on wearing headscarves. Uproar ensued. The Socialist Minister of Education, Lionel Jospin, had taken the dispute to the State Council for a ruling: did headscarves infringe the post-Revolution principle that all religious teaching and symbols were banned from state schools, the écoles laïques? Jospin himself, and his Prime Minister, Michel Rocard, advised that 'tolerance should take precedence over principle'. Fifty fellow-Socialists in the National Assembly promptly called for Jospin's resignation. The Communists vilified him. SOS-Racisme was bitterly divided. The President's wife, Danielle Mitterrand, spoke out in favour of 'tolerance', for which she came under fire from the influential feminist writer Elisabeth Badinter: scarves symbolized Muslim repression of women. The Minister of Education invited the head teachers of twenty-nine affected schools to lunch – fat chance of that happening in Britain! – and encountered unanimous opposition to any concession: multi-racial, multi-religious, multi-cultural schools require strict, uniform discipline to offset ethnic tension.

Precisely!

The stick-of-a-girl now standing in front of Mrs Newman embodies the stubborn intractability of a patriarchal culture which forces females to oppress themselves. Mrs Newman is quite clear in her mind about that. Indoctrinated to desire their own submission, they are doomed to an arranged marriage, semi-purdah, a career lost – why educate them? Why bother? Why try so hard?

'Fatima, don't forget that you are a girl of whom this school is extremely proud. You have the best command of French in your class. You made excellent progress during our visit to Paris last year. Genuine attainment. And I could see how much you enjoyed the trip.'

Fatima silent.

'Well answer me, Fatima – you did *enjoy* Paris, didn't you?'

Fatima silent. Mrs Newman's fingertips have begun a light tattoo on her desk.

'I am asking whether you enjoyed Paris, Fatima.'

'You did.'

Mrs Newman's drumming fingers are stilled. She smiles faintly. 'Of course I did. Now Fatima, I am hoping to arrange an exchange visit for you this summer with a girl from a Muslim family in Toulon. I only want the best for you. So please don't let me down.'

Fatima slowly shakes her head.

'Fatima, I shall have to send you home unless you remove your scarf.'

ଚ୬

The Islamic Council is in emergency session on a bitterly cold day, a northerly wind biting the city's bones. Wrapped in anoraks, pressmen and TV crews stamp frozen feet outside 4, Cornhill, the small Georgian building whose windows have recently been broken and front door daubed with taunts and obscenities. Attempts to erase the spray paint have enjoyed limited success.

—RAHMAN RULES OK

—PAKIS FUCK OFF

Mustafa Jangar has publicly called – in the name of the Islamic Council – for the death of Gamal Rahman.

MUSLIM LEADER VOWS TO KILL RAHMAN

The Bishop of Bruddersford, the Rt. Revd Goodgame, has urged an end to provocative statements from the mosques, which 'might lead to rising fear and anger among non-Muslims, endangering good race relations.'

Jangar hit back immediately: 'We Muslims have never enjoyed

good race relations in this country. Whenever we have stood up for our rights, the majority community has always reacted with contempt and hostility.'

'Jesus!' shouted Joe Reddaway as this pearl landed on his desk. 'Jesus F. Christ!'

He grabbed the phone and tapped out Izza Shah's home number. No answer. He tried Shah's dry-goods business number. Engaged. He glowered at a clever editorial in a London paper pointing out that the prophet Nostradamus had predicted a war between Islam and the West at the turn of the second millennium. Joe began to smash the keyboard of his word processor:

Who is this Mustafa Jangar? Does this fanatic in our midst speak in the name of the Islamic Council? Why does the City Council remain silent? Why does the Community Relations Council remain silent? Does it regard its valiant work over the years as wasted effort?

Joe tried Izza Shah again. Engaged.

Bruddersford has given and Muslims have taken. Bruddersford scrapped school bussing to placate Muslims, introduced halal meat into schools to placate Muslims, and excused Muslim girls from swimming lessons – to placate their parents. Bruddersford employs more Section 11 workers (most of them Muslims) than any other Council in the country. The statement from Mustafa Jangar is a nice way to say thank you. One feels like saying to Mr Jangar, 'If you dislike this country so much, why don't you go home?'

Entering the Islamic Council the following morning for the hurriedly convened emergency session, Izza Shah has made a brief statement to the waiting reporters in his uniquely opaque English: 'We Muslims was insulted. And we is continuing this campaign until we gets apology. We have support of Muslim states, all unanimous. Insulting Islam is depriving me of existence. It's wiping my face from Earth.'

The interior of 4, Cornhill is tatty: tatty brown linoleum, broken fold-up chairs, unshaded light bulbs, damps patches on the ceilings, cheap utility doors, and yellowing notices in several languages sellotaped to peeling walls. Copies of Joe Reddaway's 'Plain Speaking' column in the *Echo* are strewn about the conference room. City Councillor Hani Malik is demanding that the Islamic Council dissociate itself from Mustafa Jangar's statements.

'The Tories are hugging themselves,' Malik warns. 'This could be worth thirty thousand votes to them.'

Mustafa Jangar is serene behind his beard. He loudly clears his throat, as if purifying the channel before holy words pour down it.

'They are hearing us at last, Brother. Every British Muslim is bound by the Ayatollah's fatwa. This book of Satan has already spilled the blood of many Muslims martyrs. Yesterday ten people were shot dead in Bombay when police opened fire on ten thousand Muslims. Imam Syed Abdullah Bukhari stood up in the Jama Masjid Mosque in New Delhi, where my father once prayed, declaring his full support for the death sentence passed on the blasphemous dog Rahman. Our souls cry out for vengeance.'

'Frankly,' Hani Malik says in his curt, practical manner, 'we're in the soup. From here on in it's chicken-and-chips, with dollops of ketchup, for the Tories and racists.'

Huddled in his coat, hearing Mustafa Jangar's open call to civil war, Izza Shah knows he must conciliate. But Malik's version of Islam, like his ally Zaheed's, deeply offends the true believer in Izza Shah. After years of stable Islamic rule, Pakistan, the land of their birth, has been inflicted with a female Prime Minister who claims to be 'keeping religion out of politics' while blatantly attacking the Shari'a and the political authority of the mullahs. Yet Malik and Zaheed are shameless Bhutto-ites.

Mustafa Jangar has no appetite for conciliation. Schisms are his food and drink – always force the issue. He is now treating the Council to the supreme wisdom of 'the Sublime Guide, the Moses of our epoch, the Breaker of idols, the Exterminator of tyrants – the Ayatollah Khomeini. The Ayatollah has declared the final holy war, the jihad, the conquest of the non-Muslim world.'

'Conquest!' explodes Hani Malik, gripping his head in his hands as if struck by a meat cleaver. 'Are you mad, Brother!'

'It is the duty of every believer to bring the Koranic law from one end of the Earth to the other,' thunders Mustafa Jangar. 'The Ayatollah has clearly said that there can be no separation between religion and politics. Did the Prophet separate politics from religion? All secular power is the work of Satan. It must be wiped out.'

Izza Shah has been troubled by Mustafa's conversion to Khomeini's blatantly Shi'ite doctrines. He has consulted Ali Cheema in private. Ali is certain that Mustafa's texts were originally translated into French by Farsi-speaking scholars, then re-translated into English by the Islamic Foundation in London. Having carefully studied the French translations, extracted from Khomeini's *Valayete Faqhih* (The Kingdom of the Doctrine); *Kachfol-Asrar* (The Key of Mysteries); and

72

Towzihol Masa'el (The Explanation of Problems), Ali has advised Izza Shah that the English translations are of poor quality and seriously misleading.

'Khomeini's call for conquest refers only to the corrupt secular government of the late Shah. It may also extend to Saudi Arabia, Egypt, Algeria, Iraq and Syria. It does not apply to the non-Muslim world.'

'You're sure of this, Ali?'

'Yes, Father.'

Now, seated at the head of the table, Izza Shah studiously avoids theological debate. He must conciliate. Speaking slowly in Punjabi, he ponderously explains that the sentence of death on Gamal Rahman cannot be challenged, but. But:

'We all living under English laws,' he says in English, then reverts to Punjabi. 'The Zionist conspirators themselves will soon dispose of Gamal Rahman to lay the blame on us.' Back to English: 'And so, so, they will be killing him to blame us Mooslims, to prevent us from conclusive evidences from the horses' mouths.'

This is absorbed in respectful silence. It sounds about right. Ali is the only person at the table – with the possible exception of Hani Malik – who believes that Rahman wrote his novel entirely on his own initiative, without the collusion of the British Government or World Zionism. But Ali would never say so, not here, not even when alone with Izza Shah, the pale Fatima's ear pressed to the sitting room door. Ali can no more explain that the real conspiracy is a cultural one – Orientalism and the secular inquisition – than he can reveal that last night he again suffered Safia's night-long attempts to seduce him.

Hassan Hassani has plucked up the courage to speak. He is now able to reveal that one third out of two hundred writers who have signed a statement in defence of Gamal Rahman – are Jews. Ali Cheema remains silent. He alone in this room has met these writers at university seminars and London theatres – sometimes in the company of Rahman himself. He suspects that Hassan Hassani's ethnic 'information' comes from Yacoub Ishtaq, alias Dr Robert Bright, a white Muslim convert whose hobby is unmasking 'Jews'.

Hani Malik again demands a formal repudiation of Mustafa Jangar's call to assassinate Gamal Rahman. He isn't going to get it. The cold wind whistles under the recently vandalized door. The journalists outside continue to stamp their feet, hoping for another outrageously provocative statement from Mustafa Jangar. Tomorrow's tabloids want more. More! A good story runs and runs.

Isn't the world getting sick of the ranting that pours non-stop from

73

the disgusting foam-flecked lips of the Ayatollah and his British look-alikes? Clearly this Muslim cleric is stark raving mad. And more dangerous than a rabid dog. Millions of his misguided but equally potty followers echo every word of hatred he hisses through those yellow stained teeth. The contagion has now reached the famously sober English city of Bruddersford. Tory MPs have called for Mustafa Jangar's extradition to Pakistan. The *Sun* has a better idea – put him on the next plane to Tehran.

ର

Fatima is close to tears – perhaps she had half-believed that Mrs Newman would give way once she realized the depth of her conviction.

'What harm am I doing anyone?'

Mrs Newman knows the answer but dares not speak it: most of the other 140 Muslim girls will immediately follow suit. Contagion. The school will soon resemble a Middle Eastern kasbah. Once scarved, the Muslim girls will no longer talk to the white girls and the Hindu girls (which they now do, though not much). There will be mockery, taunts, from the white boys, followed by fights with the Muslim boys. Then more Rahman graffiti, more placards produced in classrooms, more tension. It's bad enough that kids can never quite forget the colour of skins, but at least a common way of dressing brings them together: they're all 'Yorkshire-England'.

But this is too complex to convey to a child, a pupil. Authority resides in not exposing one's reasoning. You don't get into an argument. Patricia Newman regrets this – but there it is.

'And how can you attend chemistry lessons in a long, inflammable cotton scarf?'

'I have thought of that!' With rapid, dextrous (and carefully rehearsed) movements, Fatima wraps and fastens her scarf into two tight knots at the back of her head. 'Like the factory girls during the war!' She beams with hope.

Mrs Newman summons her secretary and dictates a brief note to Mr Izza Shah, businessman, magistrate (like herself) and hero of local charities. It is her duty to apply the Regulations. She personally regards them as very sensible and in the interests of all pupils. It would be 'at this crucial time for Fatima' most regrettable if this 'sudden and inadmissible demand' were to harm her education. Yours sincerely.

Izza Shah! That man! Having so repressed his elder daughter, Safia, that she had kicked over the traces, hurled herself into a delinquent display of sex-obsessed Westernization – relentless absen-

74

teeism from school, punctuated by unacceptably flamboyant appearances in thick make-up and the kind of jewellery you could hear a mile away – having achieved that small miracle, Izza Shah is now turning his clever, dedicated younger daughter into a puritan fanatic. That man! Those absurd, lugubrious, elephantine utterances to the press about the Rahman book! Those medieval demands for apology and censorship!

'Please give this to your father, Fatima.'

'Yes.'

'And now you must leave the school. Go straight home, is that understood?'

'Yes.'

The door closes behind Fatima. 'Mr Rahman,' Patricia Newman says silently, 'you have much to answer for.'

She had met the Egyptian writer once, probably four or five years ago, right here in this office. She clearly remembers their brief conversation – and his rolling, lusting eyes.

Fatima finds herself catching the bus home at 9.30 in the morning. A strange sensation, the bus and the streets so empty. Like the time she suddenly went down with mumps during biology. She remembers the moment of sudden pain in her throat: the biology teacher, Mr Reading, had said, 'The reproductive habits and cycles of rabbits are, of course, rather different from our own.' Some boys had sniggered. 'Unlike most animals, most mammals, humans do not breed at any particular moment in the year. To make the point, why don't we all announce the month of our birth? In my case, it was January.' The next moment Fatima had gone down with mumps.

ଡ଼

Racial fever is on the rise. Guest of honour at a Rotarians' dinner, Douglas Blunt has lit his cigar and sniffed his brandy balloon when he hears himself introduced as Chief Executive of the first British city to have elected a wog as its Lord Mayor. Observing the smiles on the faces of the bloated, booze-flushed, self-congratulatory beef-eaters, Blunt – whom no portrait painter would have picked out from the rest – sits tight in his chair, refusing to deliver his after-dinner speech.

'You'll get nowt out of me, Sid, until you withdraw that outrageous remark.'

'It was just a joke, Doug, can't you take a joke, lad?'

'I'm sure sure Joe Reddaway would laugh his head off while shoving your "joke" into the *Echo*.'

Hearing the words 'Reddaway' and '*Echo*', Sir Tom Potter, the local Tory leader, rises.

'Doug,' he says, 'we are all of us proud of the fine job you've done in difficult circumstances. Working for a Labour Council is never easy, but I'd say you've kept this City of ours from falling apart.'

Douglas Blunt sits tight.

Potter tries again: 'Zulfikar Zaheed bowled me for a duck in a recent charity match. What more can I say for him?'

Blunt studies the man who may soon be his boss if the Gamal Rahman affair tears Labour apart. He remembers the uproar raised by Potter when the City had subsidized Lord Mayor Zaheed's 'goodwill' tour of five Asian States. The correspondence columns of the *Echo* had exploded on a scale unmatched since halal meat.

'The Labour Party,' Potter had told a packed City Council Chamber, 'are squandering the ratepayers' money on what is blatantly an exercise in pandering to a minority of our citizens. I have referred this matter to the City Auditors.'

Blunt is still sitting tight at the Rotarians' dinner. Although an old mate and golfing partner of Blunt's, Potter decides that Doug needs to be brought down a peg or two before he's summoned to Council Leader Potter's office the day after the election and told that the budget of the Community Relations Council is to be slashed by half. For starters.

'Gentlemen,' Potter addresses the Rotarians, 'let's ask Doug a question while he's hunting for his tongue. It's simply this: how many more of 'em does he want to let in?'

Blunt rises. 'If Tom Potter thinks immigration policy is decided by City Councils, I can refer him to the relevant evening classes at the Community College. They're free, too.'

ରୁ

Dr Yaqub Quddus teaches at the Community College. He is also Chairman of the Community Relations Council, described by Potter as 'a bunch of idle meddlers'. Quddus and Potter have frequently clashed in public; Potter once described Quddus to his face as 'a battery-powered hamster whose degree was no doubt awarded by the University of the Taj Mahal, where students customarily mark their own exam papers on pain of riot.'

Invited to address the Labour Group, Quddus arrives with his bulging brown briefcase and foghorn voice.

'Thanks for coming, Yaqub,' says Trevor Lucas, Leader of the Council. 'Personally, I found Rahman's novel impenetrable. Common sense suggests that the vast majority of British Muslims would find it unreadable.'

Dr Quddus removes his spectacles, wipes them on his sleeve, and replaces them with an air of showdown.

'Very well, Trevor, in my considered opinion what type of Muslims are currently getting angry? All Muslims are principled people, we are all fundamentalists on fundamentals. That's the bottom line, you know. The Islamic devil is alive and well in Christian mythology. Read Chaucer. Read Dante. What Rahman has done, very deliberately in my considered opinion, is to rub our noses in it.'

Zulfikar Zaheed sits very still, his elegantly tailored legs crossed. Samuel Perlman, Chairman of the Education Committee, has hoisted his feet on to the empty chair in front of him. Douglas Blunt, whom Lucas has invited to sit in on the discussion with observer status, knows what happens every time Sam Perlman hoists his feet. A sardonic smile surfaces:

'Dr Quddus, *in your considered opinion*, have not the imams and the Council of Mosques been circulating inflammatory passages from Rahman's book, most of them taken out of context? Isn't it all a case of Khomeini-fever?'

'Listen, Mr Perlman, I myself am a Sunni not a Shi'ite, but I too feel these insults deeply, here, here.' Quddus pounds his heart with (Blunt feels) dangerous vigour. 'The Christians are in power in this country, yes or no?'

'That's plain nonsense,' says Perlman.

Quddus doesn't care for Perlman – no Muslim cares for Perlman.

'Excuse me, sir, but the Christians are telling us Muslims, look, this is a secular society, you can say anything provided it's not against Christianity.'

'The blasphemy laws are medieval claptrap,' Perlman says.

'Yaqub is our guest,' Lucas rebukes Perlman. 'Let him finish.'

Quddus nods at Lucas. 'Thank you, Trevor. Now take this *Spy Catcher* book. The Government poured out money on tip-top lawyers to stop that book so why are they refusing to ban Rahman's book? Take the burning of Lady Chatterley's novel by Customs. They are burning filthy videos. Incinerators! Certain MPs were publicly burning a statute outside Parliament and proud of it!'

'Which of Lady Chatterley's novels did they burn?' Perlman asks.

Quddus is glancing at his fellow-Muslims among the Labour councillors, but he's getting nothing back from Zaheed, nothing from Hani Malik.

'OK, Yaqub,' Lucas says. 'That was very helpful.'

Quddus nods and gravely wipes his spectacles again. 'Any time.'

After the meeting Lucas talks to Blunt in the privacy of the Council Leader's office.

'The sub-text of this affair is the main text, Doug.'

'Agreed.'

'When young Ali Cheema said on television the other night that Rahman himself was already "irrelevant", it sounded daft but it probably wasn't.'

'Exactly. To Izza Shah and Mustafa Jangar, the book is a gift from God.'

Lucas sighs. 'It's the devil's gift for my unfortunate colleagues Zaheed and Malik – and for the Party.'

'Isn't this whole "affair" about seizing a place in the sun? Our Muslims are alert, intelligent people who haven't had a voice. They've felt themselves shut out. Ignored. The blacks go on the rampage in Brixton or Toxteth but Muslims and Hindus behave themselves. When Rahman answers his critics with a vast splash of words and photographs in a newly launched Sunday newspaper, or when famous writers and publishers are invited to contribute hundred-word opinions – then the medium is the message. The real contest is about fame, prominence, recognition – a place in the sun.'

'The real contest right here is for white votes, Doug. The Labour Party cannot be seen to pander to fanatics and censorship.'

'And what about the Muslim votes?'

'No problem.'

The response comes too fast – Lucas acknowledges as much with a twist of the mouth, then glances at his watch. Lucas doesn't play golf. He doesn't play anything. Trevor Lucas is made to measure, a computer-wise, gadget-conscious whizz-kid of local government politics. Bred in a test tube. Always on time, always neatly turned out, he earns his comfortable salary as Finance Director for Stenbridge Borough Council, then drives straight to the Leader's office in Bruddersford City Hall. Douglas Blunt has it on the grapevine from Westminster that Mrs Thatcher intends to scotch the musical chairs: senior local authority employees will be declared ineligible to stand as councillors – anywhere.

Blunt understands Lucas's present dilemma perfectly. The big battle, the key seat, will be in Tanner Ward. Traditionally, white Labour politicians and ward-heelers had been in complete control of Tanner, feeding off guaranteed Asian votes with a 'Thanks very much'. Almost all the Muslims, Hindus and Sikhs in Tanner Ward would vote for a white Labour candidate. But a Muslim, Sikh or Hindu candidate was 'ethnic' and 'divisive'. A Muslim candidate might lose the votes of whites, Hindus and Sikhs – and let the bloody Tories in! Very sorry about prejudice and backlash in the 'host community', we all regret it.

The ward's General Management Committee used to be seventy per cent white and not at all inclined to de-select 'proven' councillors with a 'track-record' and 'personal voter-confidence' in favour of 'inexperienced careerists' (Asians like Hani Malik). The white socialists also abhorred any hint of 'religion in politics'. Nobody in Tanner cared whether a white Labour man was Catholic, C of E, Unitarian, Methodist, Quaker – or Jewish even. Or nothing at all. But as soon as you had an Asian candidate he was a Muslim or a Hindu or a Sikh – you ran smack into the tensions which bedevilled the Punjab, Kashmir, Bombay and Bangladesh.

But the time had arrived when the Muslims of Tanner had been (as Malik put it about) 'buggered enough'. Why should they be represented on the Council by a Jewish atheist, Samuel Perlman, an intellectual with a careless attitude towards the ward's 13,083 voters and a tendency (closely documented by Ishmail Haqq) not to turn up to his weekly 'surgeries'?

It was Haqq who had masterminded the anti-Perlman campaign. Perlman's supporters accused the Malik-Haqq faction of 'anti-Semitism'. Two hundred Muslim citizens suddenly applied to join the Party. Few of them received a Party card. The Malikites accused the Perlmanites of deliberately not sending out the cards on time. They waved aloft brown envelopes bearing second-class stamps:

'Second-class stamps for second-class citizens' was Haqq's inspired phrase. Haqq then announced that he 'knew it for a fact' that white members of the local Post Office union had been 'got at' to deliver the notices of the Selection Meeting to Malik's supporters late. Threats of libel, corrected to slander, abounded.

The first ballot split 25–25. At the second ballot the District Party representative ruled that one of the votes cast for Malik was 'invalid'; he awarded the election to Perlman by 25 to 24. Uproar! This official then refused to display the 'invalid' ballot paper on the ground that every slip carried a number, which would allow the voter to be identified. Blows were exchanged in the street.

A new ballot was held and Malik's supporters 'carried the day late at night' – one of Malik's many jokes. Malik went into the election campaign against the Tories without a single white helper or canvasser; the Party was now in a condition of dismal racial schism. Haliq Haqq was elected chairman of the Branch, Karamat Khan as secretary, Abdul Ayub Khan as treasurer. Hani Malik had it sewed up. He took Tanner Ward by a margin of 713 votes over the Tory candidate. Energetic, resourceful, well-liked, he became Chairman of the City's Housing Committee, the hottest job in town. The defeated, de-selected Samuel Perlman was adopted, then elected, in a safe 'white' ward. The Chairmanship of the City's Education Committee followed – Lucas admired Perlman's gifts.

Three years later Gamal Rahman dropped from the sky, horns glowing, his sulphuric breath choking the city.

❦

Late at night Shaytan Rahman invades Hassan Hassani's living room. Hassan looks up from his pamphleteering and blinks. He has been listing all the things that The Authorities have ever banned in England, since the beginning of time, including a television play about a Saudi princess, a play about Zionists, and the live voices of Sinn Fein.

Shaytan Rahman is leering at him. 'I have invaded your wife,' he whispers, 'I can possess any woman. Why does Nasreen look right through you when you address her, why does she speak so often of Rajiv Lal's virtues, his multiculturalism, his deep-deep love of education? Perhaps you don't understand women, Hassani.'

Hassan Hassani trembles. His letters to the *Echo* have begun to provoke obscene, threatening telephone calls; he has forbidden Imran to answer the phone. Each night he must now search the boy's bedroom for the hidden Rahman not once but twice. He has sat at his desk far into the night, Nasreen asleep, sifting through his newspaper cuttings, labouring on his pamphlet, 'Satan Speaks'. His copy of *The Devil: an Interview*, wrapped in brown paper, is so thick with strips of marker-paper that it has begun to resemble an irritable potato sprouting roots. He sighs as his fingers race nimbly across the keyboard:

> In English the word 'bastard' is a filthy word. You would never use it in polite company. In Deuteronomy 23:2 it is written: 'The bastard shall not enter the congregation of the Lord; even to his tenth generation . . .' Yet Gamal Rahman uses the word 'bastard' 29 times. Sometimes it is the only word in the sentence! Rahman is capable of introducing three 'bastards' in a single sentence: 'That bastard, those bastards, their lack of bastard taste.' Could the publishers of this filth have paid Gamal Rahman a reported two million dollars in the cause of culture and literature (as the liberals tell us)? Not likely! They are Zionists with a shrewd business sense! That is why they allowed the Great Author to publish his filth about 'pig excrement', 'rotten cockroach dung', and 'This shit, you cunts', 'It's shit, it's fucking shit', 'shit dinner', 'white man's shit', 'black shit is bad'.

80

Tired yet elated, Hassan Hassani studies the luminous print, the doubly 'justified' lines filling his dark-green screen. By habit he begins to suck a ballpoint pen – then abruptly lays it down. Imran had picked up the same bad habit and once swallowed the cap of a pen. Only Hassan's resolute response to the crisis – Nasreen shrieking – plunging his hand down the boy's windpipe, saved his life. But Imran still does it:

'Imran, you must defeat Shaytan Rahman by not sucking your pen.'

'But he makes me suck it, Dad.'

This Yorkshire 'dad' never will never sound right to Hassan, but there's no conquering school and street: 'My dad can beat up your dad any day, wanker.'

Exhausted, Hassan climbs into bed beside his wife. Nasreen doesn't stir. He wonders whether she's dreaming.

SIX

❧

Izza Shah consents to receive Mrs Hassani in his office at the rear of his single-storey dry-goods store. Nasreen arrives wearing the hijab and a shapeless, ankle-length gown. She comes apprehensive and leaves petrified – that face cast of stone; the huge white beard; the bleach-white hair brushed straight back from his forehead; a deathly pallor. And that voice, those slow sentences, ponderous with patriarchal authority – he speaks English as if squeezing toothpaste from the bottom of a long tube. The conversation is brief and formal – deferential on Nasreen's side. Izza Shah is unmoved by anything she has to say.

'You must talk to Fatima, Mrs Hassani. I will support any decisions she makes.'

The old man politely conducts her out. She can sense, almost smell, his sickness. Hassan has heard that Izza Shah suffers from cancer of the prostate. Driving back to the Department of Education – she prefers to report to Rajiv Lal than to Mrs Newman – she ponders the enigma of Izza Shah, Bruddersford's senior Muslim. How could so venerable a personage have produced a wild and shameless daughter like Safia? Hassan calls her 'a slut'. Most women in the Muslim community blame Safia's condition on the sudden death of Izza Shah's wife.

Nasreen knows that after Izza Shah's wife died the old man went into mourning and was rarely seen. The respectable widows of Muslim Bruddersford patiently waited for a proposal, but a year later the patriarch shocked the community by falling into a headlong passion for a girl of seventeen and approaching her father for her hand in marriage.

The father whom Izza Shah approached was none other than Zulfikar Zaheed. The two men had little in common. Their mutual distrust was famous. Zaheed received the old man politely – of course! – then bided his time. When he finally announced his refusal, he gratuitously added to the humiliation by refusing not only on his own behalf, as a father, but on behalf of his daughter Wahabia. 'I do not intend to impose a marriage on any child of mine.' An outrageous insult, typical of that apostate, Zaheed.

But surely Izza Shah was at fault? Wahabia Zaheed is barely older than Izza's own daughter, Safia. And they say that Izza Shah had set eyes on Wahabia only once, and in totally unacceptable circumstances, before carrying his proposal of marriage to Zaheed.

Nasreen notices that her thoughts are becoming more conventional about other people's lives than about her own.

೬௨

Ali Cheema studies the boarded-up façade of Collett's firebombed bookshop in the Charing Cross Road. He sniffs as if testing the theological content of the incendiary odour.

'What are you thinking?' Wahabia asks.

'I'm not sure about this overcoat you imposed on me.'

'You look a rave in it. A dish.'

'Today's *Guardian* reports Rahman's hardback sales at 150,000. An unsigned editorial calls unequivocally for a paperback edition here and now – otherwise all British liberties are gone.'

Her arm lies comfortably in Ali's. Zulfikar Zaheed's lovely daughter has skipped classes at Sussex University to spend the afternoon with Ali before 'Final Call'. He hasn't yet told her about Inigo Lorraine's early-morning telephone tip-off before Ali caught the train south: his debate tonight will be with Gamal Rahman himself – provided Rahman's security minders sanction it.

'It may not come off,' Lorraine said. 'They're very jumpy. But Gamal is anxious to debate with you.'

When first absorbing this, Ali had imagined that he was being challenged to murder Rahman on the spot, to put his dagger where his mouth was – it took a moment before he grasped that Rahman would not be in the studio.

Entering Waterstone's, where selected new fiction titles are prominently displayed on shelves facing the door, he notes that fear, or its cousin prudence, has prevailed. He approaches the young man tending the till:

'Do you have the Rahman novel?'

The glance of appraisal is quick, discreet: Ali wears no beard, no profusion of dark Islamic hair, no funny clothes, merely a Red Army surplus overcoat bearing a Hong Kong label. The young man reaches under the counter and produces the big book in its richly decorated blue cover.

'Thank you,' Ali says. 'Full marks for courage. I've read it.'

The book is returned to the cardboard box at the assistant's feet.

Half-way down the stairs to the basement, Ali's stops at a shelf carrying the fifth anniversary edition of the magazine *Prospero*. 'Birthday Special!' the cover promises. *Prospero* is Rahman territory, edited by his master of ceremonies, Rory McKenzie, and distributed in the USA by Rahman's literary agent, the notorious Zionist, Isaac Ben Ezra. On page 7 Ali finds a poem; on the opposite page, a photograph of the poet-novelist, half in shadow, only one bulging eye visible, the visible eye wide open, replete with challenge, menace: love me or leave me. Ali scans the poem but is soon diverted by a statement printed in a smaller typeface underneath the satanic photograph:

> No part of this poem may be reproduced, stored in a retrieval system or transmitted, in any form or by means, electronic, mechanical, photocopying or otherwise without the prior permission of the copyright owner. No part of this poem may be reproduced, whether for private research, study, criticism or the reporting of current events without written permission.

The copyright owner is 'Gamal Rahman and Prospero Publications, Ltd.' The penalties for infringement are set out: 'civil liability and criminal prosecution'.

'Criminal! That's rich!' Wahabia exclaims.

'Here you see the Mammon-eye of the Liberal Establishment. Evidently the Holy Prophet isn't the only "businessman" in business.'

'Hm?' (Wahabia's response is guarded – she had found herself skipping the 'religious' sections of Gamal's novel, preferring the scandalous personal relationships.)

'Let us invent an extra line for the copyright notice,' Ali says. How about this: "No part of this poem may be learned by heart without written permission". How can I steal this copy of *Prospero?* – I need the exact text for quotation.'

'Oh, you mustn't do that! No, Ali, no!' Wahabia tussles with him as he slips it into his briefcase.

'We burn Rahman's book. No reason why we shouldn't steal his poem. I can't pay good money for this shit.'

'Think of my father!'

'Walk out ahead of me – nothing to do with you. I have no desire to thwart the parliamentary ambitions of the Bhuttos of Bruddersford.'

It occurs to him that it's odd to be stealing – on principle – a poem by a writer he may be debating on television that very evening. Wahabia Zaheed walks back up to the ground floor and out of the shop. He takes *Prospero* out of his briefcase and copies down the poem, the copyright notice, everything.

Wahabia waits at a discreet distance. Her thoughts settle on what Gamal Rahman had told her about Hamida Sharaf. The fabulous Hamida never waited for anyone. Wahabia kicks her heels impatiently.

❖

The General Management Committee of the District Labour Party is in session. Delegates hurry in from a bitter, late-winter night, signing their names into the register with freezing hands. Ted Francis, the party's salaried agent, stands guard over the register, alert to any hanky-panky, asking for membership cards in what he regards as a firm but friendly tone. The delegates are seating themselves in blocs – already the factions are counting heads. Two issues will dominate the agenda: the Council elections and the Rahman book. They are the same issue.

Resolutions have flooded in from the wards. Tanner's demands the outright banning of the book and the extension of the Blasphemy Act to protect Islam. Hani Malik could have done without this but Ishmail Haqq has rammed it through.

Alongside the Tanner resolution is one from the all-white working-class ward of Fendale – blocks of Council flats, rows of terraced Council houses, gardens, allotments, chicken and chips.

> This District Party condemns the recent burning in Bruddersford of a novel by Gamal Rahman; condemns calls for the banning of this or any work of literature; calls for the outright repeal of the Blasphemy Act; and reaffirms the Labour Party's traditional committment [sic] to freedom of expression.

Everyone knows that Samuel Perlman moved this resolution, though he may not have been responsible for the spelling. Zaheed is fond of pointing out to anyone who will listen that 'committment' [sic], like 'harrassment' [sic], is evidently a mental state demanding an extra consonant; Zaheed calls it 'the semantic equivalent of reinforced concrete'. Zaheed, of course, is too clever by half.

The District Party General Management Committee is a tower of Babel, many skins, many tongues, but dominated by the white élite which presently controls the City Council. Trevor Lucas, Leader of the Council and a close ally of Harry Flowers, MP, has been flogging his mobile telephone to secure agreement that both resolutions,

85

Tanner's and Fendale's, should be tabled until after the Council elections.

The room is thick with smoke – no environmentalist namby-pambies here! If a pregnant mum attends, her baby's chances are slim. But of fifty delegates in the room, only five are women, all of them white. The Sikh Chairman, Pradesh Singh, announces that he will take the Fendale resolution first. If Tanner wishes, it can move its own resolution in the form of an amendment to Fendale's.

Ishmail Haqq is on his feet: 'We protest! This is an outrageous fix! A motion which is wholly conflictive with another motion cannot be an amendment to it.'

Zulfikar Zaheed, an ace of procedure, smiles faintly. 'I must concur. The motion "the sky is green" cannot be an amendment to the motion "the sky is blue". An authentic amendment to "the sky is blue" would be to insert the phrase "in summer".'

Harry Flowers, talking to Lucas by telephone from Bertorelli's in Charlotte Street before a late-night sitting in the Commons, has mockingly predicted Zaheed's intervention word for word: blue skies and green skies and summer skies. Flowers knows that Zaheed wants him de-selected; Bruddersford West has sent a Labour MP to Westminster since the Norman Conquest and Zaheed wants it.

Hani Malik is waiting for Pradesh Singh's Sikh wink and gets it. 'Chair, on a point of procedure, I move that both these resolutions be held over until after the Council elections.'

'Objection!' shouts Haqq, furiously gesturing his supporters to their feet. 'That would be a flagrant breach of Party rules.'

Singh glances at Trevor Lucas. Lucas nods like an experienced dealer at an auction, seconding Malik's procedural motion. Haqq is bellowing continuously. 'Hypocrites!' The Chair instructs Haqq to sit down. Haqq does not sit down. A dozen other Muslim delegates, including the Khan brothers, are also not sitting down.

'We are confronted by a small clique of power-hungry opportunists!' Haqq shouts.

'Brother Haqq, I am ruling you out of order.' No one in the room can any longer doubt the thrust of his ambition: to take Tanner Ward from Hani Malik, to sit in the Council Chamber as the elected representative of Tanner's 13,084 registered voters, 42 per cent of whom are Asian. Haqq has patiently built himself a personal power base in Tanner while displaying every outward sign of loyalty to Hani Malik. Now he's about to strike; Gamal Rahman has provided the pretext. Haqq, Karamat Khan, Abdul Ayub Khan and perhaps a dozen other Muslim members of the General Committee are poised to walk out of the Labour Party and to run as Muslim Independents.

As a result, Tanner could fall to Sir Tom Potter's Tories. Potter's counting on it.

Zulfikar Zaheed is studying Haqq's bullyboy body language. More than once he has warned Hani Malik about Haqq but Hani wouldn't listen, he owed too much to Haqq's organizational skills. Haqq invariably fills in for Hani at the advice surgeries in the local Community Centre when Hani is busy. Haqq, Malik insisted, was doing 'an excellent job' as Chairman of the Centre

'Haqq entered this country illegally under a different name,' Zaheed reminded Malik. 'He claims he was later granted an amnesty but I don't believe it. He's a rogue elephant, Hani, he will tear down a fine old tree to pluck up a tuft of grass.'

Hani Malik doesn't altogether trust Zaheed. Haqq knows the doorsteps, Zaheed poses on the Lord Mayor's balcony. A fixer like Haqq is an indispensable aide: 'Your roof is leaking, Mrs Azram? Leave it to me, Ishmail Haqq.' Which means 'leave it to Councillor Hani Malik.' Malik is proud of his 'personal votes'. He counts them in his sleep, he knows every household, Muslim, Hindu, Sikh; he's even on good terms with the few remaining whites living in Tanner Ward. If a family has a problem – rents, repair grants, immigration – Malik is on their doorstep within the hour.

Malik and Haqq are both doorstep politicians.

Now Malik has the floor though Haqq hasn't sat down.

'Comrades, we must keep our heads or surrender this great city of ours to the Tories. Why hand it to them on a bloody plate? The racists are making hay while the sun shines, right? You pass the Fendale resolution and it's goodbye to our Muslim vote. You pass the Tanner resolution and it's goodbye to our non-Muslim vote. Why are we so anxious to shoot ourselves in both feet? Frankly, I'm as hurt and insulted as any Muslim by this Rahman book. I'd like to see it banned from our City libraries. But the Labour Party doesn't belong to any one religion or race, it belongs to the working people.'

Haqq is tenacious, he won't sit down. Unlike Malik, he carries nothing of Yorkshire in his vowels.

'Councillor Malik's motion is flagrantly out of order. Councillor Malik sits on this Committee as a delegate from Tanner Ward. He is constitutionally obliged to support a resolution passed by his own ward.'

Pradesh Singh is not impressed. 'Any member is entitled to put a procedural motion calling for the tabling of any resolution.'

Haqq again: 'This Party cannot bury its head in the sand. This book is what the people are talking about. The people demand to know the position of the Labour Party. They will not tolerate prevarication or equivocation!'

ஒ

'Gamal tells me you and he know each other quite well,' Inigo Lorraine drawls in the television make-up room. 'You haven't mentioned that.'

Ali shrugs slender shoulders under a flimsy pink apron lightly layered in talc. 'We had some correspondence.'

'Hm.'

'Does he intend to mention – I mean, is he going to make this personal?'

'Knowing Gamal, it wouldn't surprise me. His gut instincts remain those of a novelist.'

Ali's strives to disguise his apprehension. 'Don't expect me to join in any mud-slinging.'

Lorraine smiles his kindest smile as the make-up girl fusses over his hair.

'It's not easy to engage in life-or-death disputation with a famous face looming on a closed-circuit television screen. Admittedly the technique is commonplace during current affairs programmes but this is different: the face on the screen wants to know why you, Ali, would kill him if you could – and if you would.'

'The Prophet was indeed Allah's Messenger, his Message definitive. But to know why, to understand the singularity of that revelation, you must not only withstand – but welcome – pirate-raids of very clever mercenaries like Gamal Rahman. They are sent to test us: but they are *sent*!'

'That's a fine speech, Ali. Don't waste these pearls on the powder-puffs.'

ஒ

Council Leader Trevor Lucas is acutely alarmed by Haqq's calculated break with Malik. He knows that Haqq is now a focus for various personal grievances among Muslim Party members unrewarded for long and loyal service. In Lucas's view, Haqq couldn't care less about *The Devil: an Interview.* It's all about money and jobs. The problem with these Asians is that they expect to make a living out of politics and patronage. They demand the spin-offs. Haqq is discontented with his small-time municipal post in the Equal Opportunities Unit and bitterly disappointed by the rejection of his application for the job of Race Relations Adviser to the Council.

Haqq openly blames Lucas for his failure to obtain it. Who but the

Leader of the Council controls the patronage, the machine? Privately Haqq has been accusing Lucas of racism; but nothing is private. Haqq whispers through a megaphone. His invisible ink yells from huge hoardings. The Labour Party, he has suddenly discovered, has miserably failed the Muslims. 'It has swallowed our votes and then spat them out.'

Dr Quddus, Chairman of the Community Relations Council, has been half-up from his chair for the last ten minutes. The whites silently groan in anticipation. Following a ramble through various deities and world religions, 'all of them entitled to our respect,' a brief excursion to the Crusades and the expulsion of the Moors from Spain, plus a short(ish) report on the Palestinian Intifada, Dr Quddus comes to earth in Bruddersford:

'What we are demanding, Chair, in my considered opinion, is some two-way traffic in all this. The ball is in your court, sir. Otherwise we shall be into splits and schisms to say the least. So let us have some two-way traffic, kindly.'

Lucas takes note: Yaqub Quddus, too, is a discontented man; the chairmanship of the CRC is not enough; he coveted, but did not obtain, the well-paid post of City Equal Opportunities Coordinator. But Quddus is too timid by nature to leap with Haqq into the cul-de-sac of Muslim Independent politics. Indeed the good 'Dr' can regularly be spotted scurrying about City Hall whispering-down Haqq. Lucas himself had got an earful between his office and the Reserved Parking where a locked rectangle of space announces: Council Leader.

'In strict confidence and off the record, Trevor, Ishmail Haqq is not a good Muslim, he . . .'

Lucas is puzzled why Haqq's private life is subject to so many slanderous allegations. Hani Malik dismisses them as 'rubbish' and Haqq is patently a good family man, devoted to wife and children – though he is less often at home than they might like. But that goes for Lucas himself and practically every father absorbed by politics.

'You should know these things, Trevor,' Quddus is saying. 'Too much is under the carpet, frankly.'

'Aha.' Lucas walking, Yaqub Quddus pursuing, his voice a foghorn: 'Haqq recently gave an Urdu interview to *Daily Millat*: "Fighting for God". Already Haqq is printing leaflets giving no name and address of the publisher.'

'Aha.'

'Great pity Sadar Baj Hussein is still in Pakistan. He would be sorting out this whole caboodle. Zaheed recently spoke to him by telephone through the private office of Prime Minister Bhutto.'

'What did S.B. say?'

'S.B. said, "Don't panic, keep your hair on, Zulfikar." S.B. is a man of great wit, of course.'

'Aha.' Lucas could imagine one of those Third World phone lines which toss your voice back so that you seem to be answering yourself. You say keep your hair on and you're immediately instructed to keep your hair on.

ༀ

Inigo Lorraine's relaxed, assured screen-presence is under increasing strain. Gamal Rahman's bulging eyes are scorching the big screen dominating the studio as Ali Cheema launches one pre-emptive attack after another:

'I'd merely remind Gamal Rahman that his book has already caused more than forty deaths.'

'Caused? Caused!' Gamal shouts. 'Do you mean caused in the same sense that legionnaire's disease or the radioactive fall-out of Chernobyl destroy life?'

'Obviously a fatal disease of the soul operates according to its own laws of destruction.'

Lorraine intervenes with a calming joke about causation, but Gamal is not to be calmed.

'I say this to Ali Cheema, whom I regard as a small-time provincial shit and bully-boy trying to make his name on Allah's back. *The Devil: an Interview* was published four months ago in Britain and America. To date no one has died from reading it, holding it in the hand, smelling it – or quoting from it. What caused those deaths were particular traditions of agitation and riot long-established in Pakistan and India.'

'Ali?' (Lorraine)

'I won't respond to the personal insults. But Gamal Rahman knew very well how easy it is to cause a thousand deaths not only in Pakistan or India but also in Egypt. The Government of Egypt immediately banned the book. Yet Gamal Rahman wrote to the President of Egypt in the most arrogant, colonialist manner, insisting that the ban be lifted. In other words, Mr Rahman doesn't care how many people die.'

'And the agitators who stir up mobs bear no responsibility?' Lorraine asks.

Gamal Rahman cuts in. 'Ali Cheema and his friends keep warning us that if their demands are not met, if the book is not banned, if the blasphemy laws are not extended, then it is we, not they, who will bear responsibility for the violence that may follow. This is of course a rhetorical trick common enough in cheap, small-town, politics – to whip up hatred then to shelter behind it.'

 જ

Ishmail Haqq's hand is no longer up his sleeve. Here comes his five-trump trick, straight out of the tarot pack. If Hani Malik's motion is passed, then Haqq and seventeen other Muslim members of the General Committee will leave the Party.

'I never utter idle threats, Brothers!'

Malik is cocooned in gloom. His compact, hunched body seems to be composed of angry iron cubes lifted from some abandoned engineering project by the Iffley canal. He too wishes S.B. Hussein were here – the most respected Muslim in the Labour Party. Sadar Baj Hussein would know how to bring Haqq and his gang to heel. Perhaps S.B.'s daughter Nasreen Hassani has reliable information about his return; Malik makes a note to telephone her at the Department of Education, not at home: Hassan Hassani, an outright reactionary, always answers the telephone.

Pradesh Singh glances at Zulfikar Zaheed, whose gold-ringed hands have remained placidly folded in the lap of his pin-stripe suit. Zaheed's thumbs now rest lightly in the pockets of his waistcoat. You don't see many waistcoats around these days.

'In my experience Muslim voters are as good at recognizing political cowboys as anyone else,' Zaheed says. 'I'm sure that Brother Ishmail Haqq knows that better than any of us. He has dealt with Tory careerists and single-issue opportunists in his time. I ask Brother Haqq and his friends a simple question. If this meeting passed the resolution from Tanner, would they then loyally work for the Labour Party in the coming election – as they have done so heroically in the past?'

This is received with a heavy chorus of 'hear, hear'.

Haqq rises. He's on the spot.

'I cannot support this Party unless its national leadership embraces the grievances of Muslims.'

'Comrades, we don't want to bring Northern Ireland to Bruddersford,' Trevor Lucas interjects.

Haqq blazes. 'Hypocrites! Does not the Council Leader himself, Mr Trevor Lucas, send his children to a Church of England school? So why not Council grants for separate Muslim schools? Hypocrites! Double standards always!'

'This is not a debate on education policy,' Pradesh Singh rules.

Councillor Samuel Perlman has been silent so far but can no longer contain himself: 'Must I remind certain comrades who may

91

be newcomers to these shores what Neil Kinnock said in the Commons: "Mr Rahman is free, under the law of this free country, to publish; and no power has the right to menace or oppress his liberty to do so." '

Uproar. Just one phrase did it: 'newcomers to these shores'. And this from a Jew! A Jew!

'We will vote on Comrade Malik's procedural motion,' Pradesh Singh announces. 'The motion proposes that this meeting shall table the two substantive motions concerning a certain book. Those in favour?'

Malik's motion is overwhelmingly passed. Haqq, Karamat Khan, Abdul Ayub Khan and fifteen other Muslim delegates storm out. At the door Haqq turns to hurl the villain's line:

'You'll be sorry, all of you!'

∽

Inigo Lorraine's neck is twisted towards the big screen, Gamal Rahman's safe house:

'Very well. Now I'd like to raise the question of censorship. How can we usefully discuss the case for banning this book unless we have read it? And if *we* should read it, why not everyone else?'

'Don't ask me,' Rahman says. 'Ask the young censor from Bruddersford who used to beg me to show him chapters from my novel whenever he stayed with me in London.'

'Are you saying that Ali read the novel in draft?' Lorraine asks.

'He was shown those parts of it which he now wishes to ban and burn. He raised no sound or fury at the time – we merely discussed what he is fond of calling "theological puzzles" – over a glass or two of my wine, I may add.'

Lorraine is smiling gently at Ali.

'Muslims do not drink alcohol,' Ali says. 'As for Rahman's book, I was shown not a word of it until it was published. If he is accusing me of jumping on the bandwagon at a late hour, the suggestion is totally dishonourable. May I address the question you posed, Inigo – about censorship?'

'Please do.'

'This is of course a philosophical puzzle. To ban a book, someone must first read it.'

'But what I'm getting at is this: do *you* feel *corrupted* after reading this book?'

'Not corrupted but soiled, demeaned. Others less secure in their faith, less well versed in the Holy Koran, could also be corrupted. We are the poison-tasters with strong stomachs.'

'But how does one ban a work of literature in a democracy?'

'Just as one bans hard-core pornography – by legal seizure.'

'But we are talking about a work of art, surely. This is a writer whose novels, *The Patriots, The Crossing* and *Ra'is*, were heaped with literary prizes.'

'Western intellectuals grant a special license to fiction because they no longer take it seriously. They are interested only in commercial success. Frankly, the libels perpetrated by Mr Rahman would have been impossible in a work of non-fiction. Only fiction carries the capacity to pull a lethal snake from an empty hat. Only in fiction can Mr Rahman call the Prophet by the name of Mahmoud, then hold up his hands in protestations of innocence.'

Lorraine turns his fine, televisual chin towards Gamal Rahman:

'Why did you call Muhammad by that other name, Gamal?'

'My character Mahmoud is not the historical Muhammad. The events described in my fictional Mecca did not happen. But they might have happened. I am commenting on Revelation. My own source of Revelation is my father – whose name is Mahmoud.'

'But wait a minute, Gamal. You have surrounded your Mahmoud with a world and characters almost identical to Muhammad's. What are we to conclude? What are Muslims to conclude?'

'It is of course difficult to communicate with readers who neither read one's novel nor understand the traditions of imaginative literature. Take *The Last Temptation of Christ*. Kazantzakis does not issue a health warning: "My Christ is not to be mistaken for the real Jesus." '

'Ali?'

'The artist as forger is of course an interesting subject. Gamal Rahman is a licensed liar – but when he comes before judge and jury he pleads "imagination", "literature", "art" as mitigating circumstances.'

The big screen vibrates with pale anger:

'Cheema is a pretty boy making pretty speeches on behalf of the eternal spirit of the Inquisition. One might forgive embittered old men like Izza Shah, or crazy fanatics like Mustafa Jangar, who want to lock up their daughters by scything down every bud of Spring – but in so young a man of learning as Mr Cheema it's a tragic perversion, this craving for censorship and vengeance.'

'When the Liberal Establishment practises censorship,' Ali says, 'it calls it by another name. Imagine what would happen if I wrote a novel about Auschwitz, entrusting the narrative to a young German officer. The officer is unrepentant. It had to be done, he says. We operated the system as mercifully as possible. Frankly, the sight of naked women carrying their children to the gas chambers made me weep. I even helped a few to escape. I had to harden my heart, had to remind myself of my Führer's message: the Jews are a pestilence. In fact we gassed only half a million, not the six million of Zionist legend.' Ali pauses. 'So this imaginary novel of mine reaches readers too young to know the truth about the Holocaust. Would the Liberals ban it? Of course they would! And why? Because the Holocaust remains a question of burning moral concern to them – whereas the Holy Books of Revelation are just desert stories.'

Lorraine turns to the big screen. 'Would you ban Ali's Auschwitz novel, Gamal?'

'If he manages to convey, through empathy with his hero, that the Jews merited their fate, that they ought to be gassed, yes. May I point out that *The Devil: an Interview* calls for the death of no one.'

Ali shrugs. 'What we are really confronting here are the self-serving rules of the Liberal Establishment. They control publishing, the theatre, the broadcasting media. They don't have to ban anything – they can stifle it at birth. No one hears the cry.'

A moment later Ali comments that Western culture knows the price of everything and the value of nothing. 'Even the best lack all conviction.'

'Gamal, do you lack all conviction?' Lorraine asks.

'I am convinced that religious Revelation is at best a tragic illusion, at worst a hoax.'

'To my mind,' Ali says, 'Rahman's book enjoys no more reputable status than the Protocols of the Elders of Zion – it's a kind of forgery, but employing imaginative rather than documentary structures. The result is the same: fraud, defamation, anger.'

'And you would put the author to death?' Inigo Lorraine asks.

'I would not urge any British Muslim to do so.'

'Oh?' Gamal Rahman's eyes roll. 'But Mustafa Jangar does. You take part in demos with him, Mr Cheema, book burnings surrounded by a forest of banners demanding my extinction. Placards lauding my executioner, Khomeini. Kill, kill. God's assassins.'

Lorraine nods sympathetically at the big screen. 'It must be an odd sensation to open the papers, day after day, and read statements from strangers demanding your death.'

'Very odd. Only yesterday the imam of Westhall mosque, Hafiz Khan Rahman, apparently unmoved by sharing my name, wanted me beheaded. "If the apostate has a spark of decency in him," declared the imam, "he should give himself up now and accept his fate like a man." I wrote to the imam asking why Satan should have "a spark of decency in him".'

Inigo Lorraine thrusts his chin at the camera.

'Thank you, Gamal Rahman and Ali Cheema. Perhaps we can end with a thought from Heinrich Heine: "You begin by burning books, you end by burning men." '

∽

Ali remains in London overnight. The domestic arrangements involve delicacy and discretion. Wahabia is staying with her friend Jasmin Patel, a small, fizzing and very intense literary lady from a Hindu family – she addresses Literature with a capital 'L', as if a deity. Educated at St Paul's Girls School in London, and currently a short-term contract producer for 'Final Call', Jasmin possesses the Kimberley Diamond of the hour: Gamal Rahman's coded telephone number. According to Wahabia, Jasmin is also head-over-heels with her presenter, Inigo Lorraine.

Much as Jasmin detests Ali's fundamentalism, she respects his ability to argue on level terms with Gamal Rahman – indeed Ali alone can heat the famous writer's hide to lard. Ali is always welcome to an overnight sofa whenever Wahabia occupies the spare bedroom of Jasmin's sleek studio-flat in Knightsbridge.

'Coffee?' Jasmin screams from her space-saving kitchenette.

'If you have decaff – thanks, Jasmin.'

'*Did* Gamal show you his book in draft? *Did* he?'

'No.'

'Gamal told me you asked to see it so insistently that he finally relented.'

Wahabia is not sure who (or what) she should believe. 'I haven't forgotten the horrible things Gamal said about Daddy,' she reminds Jasmin.

'Not to mention the Prophet,' Ali says. But Wahabia is not much interested in the dead. Her sleek feathers gleam with family oil.

'Daddy's still hesitating whether to take on Harry Flowers,' she announces. 'Mummy is frightened of public life. She hates being Lady Mayoress. She doesn't want Daddy to become an MP. But I do. What we – you – have to do, Ali, is swing the Islamic Council firmly against Flowers and behind Zulfikar Zaheed.'

'The Islamic Council never endorses political candidates.'

'Not formally, of course – but the word goes out.' The Bhutto-curve of Wahabia's pretty mouth has tightened.

'You know I haven't the faintest interest in politics or politicians.'

'But you may have an interest in Wahabia,' Jasmin says with the air of cosmopolitan sophistication that Ali finds irritating. Jasmin always *knows*. She has to know. Even if asked the exact penguin population of Iceland, she wouldn't bring herself to confess ignorance. Hindu bitch!

Phone calls of congratulation for Jasmin pour in past midnight. Evidently 'Final Call' was 'fantastic', 'mind-blowing', and 'out of this world'. All of her friends without exception would like to strangle Ali Cheema with their bare hands.

The eastern sky is already rousing the birds of Knightsbridge when Jasmin retires to bed, tossing a duvet and pillow to Ali. He has settled himself on the sofa when Wahabia emerges from the spare room in her nightdress and carries him to her bed.

'I'm glad I didn't have to marry your father,' she murmurs. 'Is Izza Shah really your father?'

'By adoption – you know that.'

'I sometimes wonder. You look so much like him.'

They both remember the day two years ago, when the old widower had unexpectedly called on Ali in Nuneaton Road and found him in the company of an elegant young woman wearing tight jeans and nothing on her head. With no female chaperone in evidence, it was Izza Shah's duty to withdraw at once, to excuse himself – but he had lingered in Ali's little sitting room for the best part of an hour, bemused and besotted.

Educated at a posh girls' boarding school in the south, Wahabia was at that time studying for her A Levels, a conditional place at the University of Sussex already under her belt. Zaheed had engaged Ali as her vacation tutor to perfect her written English. Normally such tutorials took place within the confines of Zaheed's residence, but the precocious Wahabia, having learned to drive the family car before her eighteenth birthday, insisted on chauffeuring her tutor back to Nuneaton Road, to save him half an hour on the bus and – no doubt – to brush up on her comparative theology.

(This joke belonged to Gamal Rahman. On a visit to London, Ali had imprudently told the whole story to Gamal, whose bulging eyes had spun with delight:

'Let's say the old man found you and Wahabia Zaheed in flagrante theologico.'

'We were wrestling with Milton, actually.'

'But it was Izza Shah who spotted Paradise regained.')

Izza Shah had sat for an hour in Ali's sitting room, a bearded ramrod, speechless, while Wahabia gaily chatted about her smart girlfriends who regularly invited her to their parents' flats and houses in London.

'In fact,' she chirped, 'I first met Ali in London.'

'Ah,' murmured Izza Shah.

'My friend Jasmin Patel, she's really the friend of a friend, I mean she's older than I am, but she knows this lovely fat Egyptian writer, he's a scream, and – '

'Please, Wahabia,' Ali cut in.

'Gosh! Sorry! I'm beginning to forget how careful one has to be in Bruddersford.'

The following week Izza Shah formally asked Zulfikar Zaheed for Wahabia's hand in marriage. He would not live long and by marriage contract Wahabia would become sole heir to his small fortune. She would also discontinue her studies – immediately – and discard her Western clothes, and devote herself to her husband.

'But,' Izza Shah conceded, 'she will remain free to visit Ali Cheema, since he is my son.'

After a decent interval Zulfikar Zaheed conveyed not only his own refusal but – worse affront – his daughter's.

Now, two years later, Wahabia and Ali lie together in a small bed, each to his own thoughts. Ali does not know that Gamal Rahman has been Wahabia's lover; nor does he know that she wouldn't mind bagging Inigo Lorraine, too, if Jasmin were not a friend. As a student with the money to travel from Brighton to London whenever Gamal threw a party, she had been beguiled by his air of self-depreciating super-confidence, and by his exotic tales of life in Egypt under the Sharafs. Twenty-two years her senior, Gamal treated her with affectionate contempt; he offered no apology when the phone rang, as it constantly did, turning his fat back on her while he chortled, quipped, punned and generally bubbled like a roll of overheated pork sausage. What fascinated Wahabia was his intimate knowledge of the legendary Sharaf women and their famous fate – the wife and daughters of the President of Egypt, Celia, Hamida and Huda.

'But are your novels to be trusted?' she would ask. 'Tell me the truth, Gamal!'

'I have invented everything,' Gamal would insist, pushing her into a taxi – late as usual – and heading for a new Japanese film at the NFT, a new feminist art show at the ICA, a Tom Stoppard preview at the Aldwych: it was essential, Wahabia gathered, for Gamal to be among the first to see anything. 'I'm making up for forty years of cultural malnutrition,' he told her.

'Did the President of Egypt really treat you as a son?'

'He didn't have one of his own.'

'Is it true that your own father renounced you and forbade you to use his name?'

'Having a famous writer for a father has its drawbacks.'

'That's not an answer! And did you sleep with the President's daughters – Hamida and Huda?'

'Why are women interested in only one thing? My dear girl, you are the spitting image of Hamida at the time of The Crossing.'

'Me!'

'The same intensity, the same piety, the same absolute devotion to your father – the same ingrained sense of propriety.'

'But in your book – '

'Hamida was one of nature's aristocrats. And a great beauty. Like you.'

'Thank you. And Huda, was she beautiful, too? What happened to her? There are so many rumours. Is it true that – '

'One day I may write about the real Huda. That was quite a story.'

'A word of advice,' he said one evening on the way home from a party given by the Director of the National Theatre. 'Don't waste your thoughts on Ali Cheema. He's the kind of Muslim who means it. They're always bad news.'

SEVEN

❧

Nasreen chooses mid-morning to visit Fatima. By mid-morning
the poor girl will have dutifully returned home by bus after her daily
ritual encounter with the school janitor, who has been instructed to
turn Muslim girls away from the main gate unless they pledge
to remove their scarfs inside the school.

Standing at Izza Shah's front door – the house does not betoken
the wealth of this man whose origins were as humble as any – Nasreen
averts her gaze from the insulting graffiti spray-painted by white
hooligans. Fatima comes to the door swathed in black, opening it
cautiously, on a chain, a mere inch, as if expecting to be stoned or
sprayed. She resembles the defeated half of a wish-bone, shivering as
the cold wind penetrates her stick-thin limbs. At a glance Nasreen
can tell that the girl has not been eating properly.

'Hullo, Fatima!'

'Good morning, Mrs Hassani. Dad's not in.'

'It's you I want to talk to.'

Fatima leads the way into the kitchen – the women's room, even
though the sitting room is empty. She pours Nasreen a cup of thick,
milky tea which is far from fresh or hot. 'Please sit down, Mrs
Hassani.'

Nasreen sits but Fatima continues to stand.

'Fatima, I want to talk to you as a Muslim woman.'

'Did Mrs Newman send you?'

'She knows I'm coming to see you. We are all worried that your
work will suffer.'

'They threatened my life,' Fatima says.

'Your life!'

'Two white boys – youths – outside Patels' corner shop. One of the
boys grabs me from behind while the other shoves a knife under my
chin. They know I'm Izza Shah's girl who won't go to school, and if
we don't fuck off to Pakistan they'll come and murder all of us. Then
one boy spits in my face: "Rahman Rules OK." '

Nasreen rises and moves to embrace the girl, but Fatima draws back. 'It's not OK,' she says. 'Shaytan does not rule.' She opens the big kitchen drawer which holds tablecloths and mats, removes a pink plastic folder, extracts a letter and hands it with obvious pride to Nasreen:

Rt. Honourable Mrs Margaret Thatcher, MP, Prime Minister.
  Honourable Madam,
The Muslims of Bruddersford and all over the world are shocked to hear this novel attacking our beloved Prophet Muhammad PBUH and his wives using such dirty language which no any Muslim can tolerate. This author is either mad or thinks ruling hole world in which there are million of Muslims. As citizens of this great country we is now expressing to you our very ill feelings about such harmful novel and state that this vile book be banned imeediately.
  Most Respectfully Yours, Izza Shah.

Fatima is observing Nasreen intently, as when a pupil follows the expression in the eyes of a teacher scanning her essay.
'I helped Dad correct the English.'
'What a good daughter you are, Fatima, he must be so proud of you. And where is the corrected version?'
'This is the corrected version.'
'Oh . . . Has this letter been sent?'
'It must first be approved by the Islamic Council.'
'Would you like me to correct it for you, Fatima?'
'There are no mistakes, I was very careful.'
'It's very well written, Fatima – but there are serious mistakes.'
Fatima shakes her head stubbornly and lovingly puts the letter back in the drawer with the tablecloths. Nasreen experiences a new level of concern: has this child gone, perhaps, a bit mad under the stress?
'Fatima, Mrs Newman is very worried that you are falling behind with your work through missing school.'
'It is not me who's missing school. I turn up every day. Every day they send me away.'
'You know the rules about the hijab.'
Fatima's eyes register a single word: betrayal. Her accent changes gear into half-dialect, the accent of defiance, the cheekier chirp of playground and street. The younger generation of Asian kids, born in Bruddersford, speak two or three versions of English:
'She must change the rules, mustn't she? She's like the rest of 'em,

she thinks women have no rights under Islam. Well it's time someone set her right. The Koran forbids the killing of female infants, don't it? We have the right to education, to work, to own businesses, to buy and sell property. It were hundreds of years afore women in the so-called enlightened West got those rights. Know what Christians say about child-bearing?'

'Yes, but – '

Fatima reverts to standard English: 'They say the pain of labour is God's punishment on women for Eve's temptation of Adam. Whereas we believe that labour is woman's jihad, struggling in the way of Allah. If a woman dies in childbirth she becomes a martyr and goes to Heaven.'

How often Nasreen herself had taken part in such hot conversations, the Muslim girls huddled together in a corner of the classroom or playground, glancing over their shoulders, on the look-out for spying white girls pretending to be friendly. (The boys learned to keep their distance at all times.)

Nasreen says: 'Fatima, you are growing up in England, where certain customs are different. These rules were not made by Mrs Newman, Fatima.'

'Who by then – that Hindu Rajiv Lal? Or that Jew Samuel Perlman?'

'They are the rules of the City Education Department.'

But Fatima has seen Nasreen flinch at Rajiv Lal's name, and now the girl takes wing on the woman's recoil:

'That Gamal Rahman is urging every Muslim girl to get rid of the hijab and wear skirts above the knee and go swimming naked with boys!'

'I don't believe that's true.'

'How d'yer know? Read his bewk, have yer?'

'Your tone is very rude, Fatima. What would your mother say?' Nasreen is close to tears over this girl's confusion and distress. 'Is it Safia that's bothering you?'

'What?'

'The way she dresses.'

Fatima's gaze blazes, wetly, in defence of the family honour. 'Safia's nowt to do wi'it.'

Nasreen changes tack. 'Fatima, it is not safe to wear the cotton hijab in a chemistry class.'

'Is that what Mrs Newman told you, that I'm insisting on that? This woman is lying to you. She is a lying atheist. My dad wrote to her and said I would bring a special headcap of fireproof material for chemistry.'

Mrs Newman had most definitely misled Nasreen about that. And if so, Nasreen should say so; at some stage she has to cross the bridge into the girl's own camp in order to take her prisoner.

'Fatima, what would you say to Beaumont Girls' School? A single-sex school might be more your cup of tea.'

Fatima shrugs. 'There's male teachers at Beaumont. I must cover my head.'

'But you might be happier in general at Beaumont, a girl among girls? – though I admit it would be a much longer journey each day.'

'You're trying to buy me off, Mrs Hassani.' A pause. 'I'm not a complete innocent, you know.'

A motorcyle roars to a halt outside. Shouts, laughter, then the front door slams loudly. Safia swings into the kitchen wearing tight jeans, a black plastic jacket and a mauve crash helmet. Tossing it down, she shakes out her luxurious locks of black-rooted auburn hair.

'Tea time, lass?' she says to Fatima, pulling off a hunk of cake with her fingers and gaily stuffing it between her painted lips. She offers Nasreen no greeting at all, ignoring her presence. Nasreen notices that Fatima does not look at her sister.

'Any more dirty calls today?' Safia asks, perching her tight buttocks on the table, her boots on a chair. Suddenly she swings her attention to Nasreen: 'You don't know the half of it and I bet *she* didn't tell you. Any old hour of the day or night and what do we hear? "Paki cunt! Muslim slag! Black scrubber! We'll burn down your house and cut your throats!" '

Fatima emits a wail and runs from the kitchen. Her bedroom door slams upstairs.

Nasreen herself has begun to hear taunts directed at Asian children on the streets and in the buses. She has recoiled from the graffiti scrawled and spray-painted on walls, hoardings, shopfronts even the walls of mosques: 'Gas chamber! Rahman Rules OK!' And the swastikas. Nasreen does not know what they mean or what they are called, these ugly spider-shapes.

'Safia, you should be at school.'

'Mrs Newman has locked me out. She won't have me.' Safia lights a cigarette. 'I'm living with Ali Cheema, if you want to know. So what's that look on your face? He's me brother, i'n't he?'

Nasreen silent.

'Not that I'm hanging about for Ali. He's all posh now, living it up in London with his princess.'

Nasreen would like to know who the 'princess' is but with Safia any display of interest is a fatal sign of weakness. Nasreen turns to climb the stairs in pursuit of Fatima.

'Not very friendly, are you?' Safia says.

'Safia, I want to be your friend if only you would let me.'

'Did you see Ali on the box arguing with Gamal Rahman?'

'No.'

'I daresay your husband won't let yer expose yourself to Satan, is that it? He wouldn't win a beauty contest, that Rahman, but he fair laid into Ali. Known each other for years, he said. Regular get-togethers, parties, booze, the lot.'

'Is that what that wicked man said?'

'And I believed him.' Safia blows an expert smoke ring in Nasreen's direction.

'What did Ali Cheema say?'

'Oh Ali came over right pompous. "Muslims don't drink alcohol" or some such baloney. Then he comes straight back from London, with his head full of the princess Zaheed, and throws me out. Lovely chap.'

'Safia, do please go back to school.'

'Fuck school.'

Nasreen climbs the stairs and enters Fatima's room without knocking. Fatima is sprawled across the bed on her stomach, a loose faggot of sticks. Nasreen sits beside her.

'Fatima, would you like to go back to school if you were allowed to wear the hijab?'

Fatima sits bolt upright and rubs her eyes as if to bruise them. 'Fat chance!'

Nasreen hands her a paper hanky. 'Your nose is running, dear.'

'Want to play at mother, do yer?'

'Yes. I'm a true Muslim mother. And I'm very fond of you, Fatima. And you shouldn't be alone at home all day.'

'So?'

In despair Nasreen proposes a formula which she has absolutely no authority to offer. 'You will wear the special fireproof cap in chemistry and I will tell Mrs Newman and . . . Mr Lal . . . that you should be allowed to wear the hijab at other times.'

Fatima ponders this. 'Since when did Mrs Newman listen to *you*?'

ॐ

The brand-new Masjid-E-Noorul Mosque announces its name in green letters fastened to a white portico shaped as an Arabian arch over four glass doors. The older mosques, set up by the first generation of immigrants in deconsecrated churches, private houses, empty shops, tend humbly to carry local names like Thornhill Lodge or Sherfield Park. But the new, Saudi-financed mosques with their grand domes and confident minarets challenging the secular-

Christian skyline are a different kettle of fish – and not shy of 'sounding foreign'. The rectangular windows of the Masjid-E-Noorul are set into a severely box-like building in yellow brick – a Bauhaus mosque – topped by a bright green dome and a golden crescent. Behind the mosque, in streets of mixed cobble and tarmac, boys of nine and ten in colourful anoraks and white prayer caps play among puddled potholes filled with detritus.

The vast prayer room within the mosque is dark and stark. Steel beams cross the ceiling. Karamat Khan, sheet metal worker, has removed his shoes and steel-grey anorak, washed hands and face, and then brought himself to prayer – a handsome man whose black hair, as yet unflecked by age, is brushed straight back from his forehead.

Ishmail Haqq prays beside him. Karamat Khan, father of Tariq, has never much liked or trusted Haqq. Just the type to desert the Party for his own ends. Now Haqq is urging Karamat to do precisely that – 'for Allah'. Between prayers and genuflections, Haqq murmurs constantly in his ear:

'Brother, you must stand as a Muslim Independent against Trevor Lucas right here in Jericho Ward. Right here, where you are known and respected by the entire community.'

To his own confusion, Karamat is tempted. Because, as Haqq keeps reminding him, when it comes down to it, after years of loyal service to the Labour Party, what is a Muslim, an Asian, but a vote-collector?

'People like Trevor Lucas and Harry Flowers do not respect us, brother,' Haqq whispers. 'They throw us away like used condoms.'

Karamat is brooding about his years of canvassing, leafleting, lobbying, 'bringing out' the Asian vote. A self-taught man, and a strong trade unionist, he has expressed similar sentiments 'in confidence' to Joe Reddaway (though not in earshot of Tariq – Karamat wouldn't put up with a word against Labour from any youngster).

'Bloody indigenous characters who don't care about ethnic minority needs and just drop us down in it. I'm telling 'em that straight, on their faces,' Karamat fumed to Reddaway (whom he doesn't trust an inch).

Both Khan brothers had been nominated as Labour candidates before the previous Council elections but neither had been included in the District Party's official shortlist. Vetted out, no reason given. In twenty years only seven Asians have sat in the City Council Chamber.

'Frankly, Karamat, it's a real shame, a scandal in my view, but you know how it is.' This was the brotherly voice of Trevor Lucas after Karamat had yet again been vetted out. A black face, a soupy Indian voice, loses white votes. The Asian communities will vote Labour anyway. So it's a real shame, Karamat. But all that is changing. Hani

Malik and Ishmail Haqq had ousted Perlman from Tanner four years ago; in College Ward Zaheed had forced himself past an incumbent white councillor, going on to become Housing Chairman then Lord Mayor. The Labour whites are so brazen about plonking themselves in the juicy Asian wards that recently the Tories have got wise and begun selecting Asian candidates. Oh certainly! But the Tories don't dare show the faces of their Asian candidates on posters and leaflets; when Jafer Riaz (another embittered Labour man) runs for the Tories in Tanner Ward, his image on the posters bears an uncanny resemblance to Sir Tom Potter's – or even to Maggie Thatcher's.

'This racism is on the peak, like,' Karamat Khan mutters to Ishmail Haqq. (One always speaks English to Haqq.) 'I'm telling Lucas this straight on his face.'

' "*To* his face," Brother.'

'Aye.'

Karamat is not very religious, more likely to get heated about shenanigans in the General Municipal Boiler Makers' Union than to turn himself into toast over some bloody novel. But came this Rahman book and he'd realized how badly he felt about the young Muslim kids in his catchment area having to attend the local Church School.

'The parents are strongly objecting,' he'd told a Labour ward meeting, 'but Trevor Lucas and Samuel Perlman don't want to knowing nothing about it. If a Muslim child is being teached the Christianity he's going to become immoral because he's going home with no respect for his parents.'

He had written to Harry Flowers, MP, whose duties as one of Labour's 'shadow' Treasury spokesmen regularly prevented him from attending his scheduled 'surgeries' in Bruddersford – and from answering letters. But Flowers isn't so bad – he'd intervened with the Home Office about the two daughters they wouldn't let Karamat bring in from Pakistan, but when the new genetic DNA test came it was too late, the girls were 'over age' or some such dodge. Harry Flowers is a wit, with the populist doorstep touch on the white Council estates:

WOMAN: What a fuss those Pakis are making about this bewk, eh?

FLOWERS: A dog fusses about its fleas.

Karamat doesn't really trust Ishmail Haqq, and he himself could never stand against Hani Malik, a solid comrade, a fellow-Muslim, a good bloke. But against that bastard Trevor Lucas, yes. Haqq and he are now leaving the Masjid-E-Noorul Mosque, Haqq's cupped hand licking Karamat's elbow:

'They swallow our votes, they drink our sweat, they bathe in our blood. You can make Trevor Lucas do the sweating, Brother Karamat. The people trust you. The people don't trust Lucas. You can win.'

Karamat nods bleakly. He knows he can't.

An hour later he is at his brother's house. They discuss Karamat's son – what is to be done? Tariq has been involved in another street brawl, another confrontation between white and Muslims youths. The police refused to release him on bail because of previous convictions. After spending two nights in a crowded cell, Tariq Khan had been driven in a locked van to Hope Street Magistrates Court on the Monday morning and fined fifty pounds for affray and assaulting a police officer.

'I had no one to serve customers in the Omar Khayyam on Saturday night,' Adbul Ayub Khan complains. 'Frankly, Karamat, you must speak to him. There are many other young men who would like his job.'

Karamat sighs. 'He is hot headed.'

'Karamat, this Rahman business has got to Tariq.'

'Tariq has been listening to Mustafa Jangar – all that Muslim Youth League agitating, nothing good can come of it.'

Abdul Ayub Khan is lovingly turning the pages of his cloth-wrapped Urdu Koran with fingers wetted and whetted. 'I have discovered recently that the original Christian Bible did not claim that Jesus was the son of God. That story is a subsequent corruption.'

'But should I stand against Trevor Lucas in Jericho, Brother?'

'If you don't, I will! Why didn't Haqq ask *me*?'

But it's OK. Later that night Haqq calls round to invite Abdul Ayub Khan to stand as a Muslim Independent against Samuel Perlman in Fendale Ward.

'Dent his Jewish pride, Brother, make him do the sweating,' Haqq guffaws – even Haqq cannot pretend that a Muslim candidate has an earthly chance in a ward which is ninety per cent white. But there is always a heavenly chance and the Khan brothers, so long the fetchers and carriers, the dogsbodies, will at last be official candidates for election – their own names on the voting papers! You can't ask for more than that, unless you're a Zaheed or a Malik. Make them sweat!

And Zaheed? Why does Haqq not put up a challenger to the Lord Mayor in College Ward? The answer is constitutional. As with many northern City Councils, Bruddersford's electoral system is rotational, like the American Senate: in any one year only a third of the wards are contested. Zaheed is out of the municipal fray this year and can therefore concentrate his energies on ousting Harry Flowers as Member of Parliament for Bruddersford West. This has to begin with 'de-selection', the roughest game in Labour politics, not least when the sitting MP enjoys the confidence of Mr Kinnock and Mr Hattersley.

‿

'Zulfikar Zaheed is watching and waiting,' writes Joe Reddaway in his daily column, 'Plain Speaking'. 'He may wait too long. A politician has to know when to jump, even if he falls flat on his face.'

On a warm evening in early spring Joe is ambling through the streets of Tanner Ward in the company of his dog, Humphrey. Humphrey is some version of a mongrel, depending on Joe's mood of the moment, and invisible – a mythical dog who eases ethnic suspicions and neighbourhood tensions. The younger street kids dance around the tall, ungainly, carrot-topped Englishman, relishing his notoriety.

'Hoomphrey's lookin' poorly today, Joe.'

Joe goes broad. 'Aye, a pit bull terrier 'ad 'alf 'is tail.' Now he spots the bulky figure of Ishmail Haqq hurrying from door to door further up the street, distributing leaflets. Joe's stride lengthens, trousers flapping.

'Losing no time, I see, Ishmail.'

Haqq throws him a wary look, followed by an ingratiating smile, as friendly as a mud-smear on a windscreen.

'All we ask is a fair deal from the press, Joe.'

'All we can offer is an unfair deal for everyone. So what's this then?' Without ceremony he plucks a leaflet from the thick bundle in Haqq's hand. 'Urdu, is it?'

'You should learn the language, Joe. Very useful.'

‿

HAQQ ALLEGES CITY DRAGGING FEET ON HALAL MEAT IN CITY'S SCHOOLS

The leaflet lies on Douglas Blunt's desk. The Chief Executive has convened another crisis meeting. Trevor Lucas, Samuel Perlman and Hani Malik are staring morosely at a typed-out translation provided by Dr Yaqub Quddus.

'This is serious,' Blunt says. 'All three of you are accused of corruption.'

'It's fucking libellous,' Lucas says.

'This goes beyond party politics, Trevor. It questions the integrity of the City's administration. Haqq is not only alleging that you and Sam have in practice reneged on your promise to provide halal dinners to every Muslim child in every school, he's also claiming that the "halal" meat currently being dished up at Hightown Upper

107

School is not halal at all – it's straight from the "Jewish super-markets".'

'Haqq's a raving anti-Semite,' Perlman says. 'That's all you need to know.'

'I'll be the judge of what I need to know, Sam,' says the City's Chief Executive.

'Haqq's tactics are transparent,' Lucas says. 'He names three so-called "conspirators", each of whom happens to be standing against his own mob – himself and the Khan brothers.'

'Where is the halal meat for the Hightown School dinners actually coming from?' Blunt asks Lucas – who shrugs and looks to Perlman.

'Ask the Department's catering manager,' Perlman says.

'You don't know?' Blunt presses him. 'And what about this statement in the *Echo* from Abdul Ayub Khan, Chairman of the Bruddersford Halal Slaughterers' Association?'

'My opponent in Hightown,' Perlman snaps. 'That's all you need to know.'

'Is it? Khan swears that every tender for the schools contract by genuine halal slaughterers has been rejected.'

'That's bloody nonsense,' Lucas says.

'Is it? I'm only asking, Trevor. Perhaps I should call in Rajiv Lal? I always get the truth from Rajiv.'

'Listen, Doug, a Tory Government has forced us, year after year, into budgetary cutbacks. The prices demanded by the halal slaughterers are exorbitant.'

'Ah. Light at last. So Muslim parents and children have been hoaxed?'

'No. There's not a word of truth in it.'

'Is that your view, Hani?'

'It most certainly is – and I shall be taking legal advice,' Hani Malik says grimly.

'Haqq claims you knew and conspired,' Blunt presses him. 'Haqq has been your political sidekick for years.'

Hani Malik is kneeding his finger joints as if to crack them. 'I'm Housing, not Education.'

At this juncture there is a small eruption from a forgotten corner of the Chief Executive's office. Dr Yaqub Quddus, indispensable translator of Haqq's leaflet, has been itching and twitching to get into the conversation. He can no longer be denied. His voice is a chain saw:

'Frankly, gentleman, not mincing words, our Muslim parents are running out of patience. Now kindly let me be explaining the genuine halal principle – '

'We've been through all that!' Lucas explodes. 'Over and over! Conventional slaughter uses the electric stunning method which creates a high lactic acid concentration in the animal and lowers the bacterial resistance in the meat. By the halal method death is instantaneous, but the time required to process each carcass takes longer – which is why it's more expensive. Nothing more needs to be said.'

'Plenty more, Trevor, plenty more,' Quddus says.

Perlman loses his temper with Quddus. 'You know damned well that Abdul Ayub Khan has a vested interest in obtaining the halal contract for his own slaughterhouse. Not to mention his political ambitions.'

'Maybe yes, maybe no,' teases Dr Quddus, delighted to have these great white City potentates at his mercy (as he briefly imagines). 'But to be perfectly honest, the halal method is second to none. The animals must be fed and watered, they must not see other animals being killed, no blood either, nor the knife. The Prophet, peace be upon him, told us, "Do not kill any animal twice".'

'Non-Muslim opinion in Bruddersford is not happy about bleeding beasts to death,' Lucas says.

'No, no, with the halal method there is no pain at all providing the knife is very sharp and – '

'OK, Yaqub, OK.' Lucas holds up his hand.

'Many thanks for your help, Yaqub,' Blunt says. 'Much appreciated.'

Quddus knows he's being dismissed so that the conspirators can work out their strategy and rule the world.

'The CRC will be issuing an urgent statement,' he announces. 'Frankly, this could be quite a caboodle.'

'Yaqub, this is a delicate area,' Lucas says. 'Why not wait until the City has completed its own independent investigation?'

'Trevor, I cannot be seen to be saying nothing.'

Perlman laughs. 'Dr Quddus, you mean you cannot be seen to be saying that there are no genuine halal slaughterers in Bruddersford. And that includes Abdul Ayub Khan.'

Quddus bridles, stiffens: 'I deny that, sir!'

'Then we'll prove it,' Trevor Lucas says.

'Gentlemen, take care, this could be turning into outright racism and right up Ishmail Haqq's street! For that man, never forget, the worse the better!'

⁊

Mrs Newman has kept Nasreen waiting for almost half an hour.

Nasreen has been offered a chair in the school secretary's cramped office, where she is constantly trampled on by a stream of kids seeking appointments or answering summonses – you can always tell which, by their demeanour – from the Head.

'She knows I'm here?' Nasreen asks. Perhaps the secretary has reported to Mrs Newman that Nasreen Hassani has arrived wearing the hijab. Nasreen broods. Her appointment had been arranged by Rajiv Lal. By keeping her waiting, the Headmistress is in effect insulting the Director of Education.

Patricia Newman harbours ambivalent feelings towards community teachers. A linguist herself – and painfully conscious of English kids' inability to learn French or any other foreign language – she is convinced that Asian children master English only when, from the earliest age, not a word of Urdu, Punjabi or Gujarati is spoken within the walls and playgrounds of the school – neither to child nor to parent.

'Be cruel to be kind,' she often remarks in the staff common room, sustaining the morale of some teacher depressed or battered by tortuous negotiations with Asian parents over a breach of discipline, late to school, won't eat this, won't eat that, protracted absence in Pakistan. The English language and culture must prevail if Patricia Newman's Muslim and Hindu charges are to survive and prosper as adults in England. 'Throw them into the deep end and they will swim,' she tells her colleagues. Yet Rajiv Lal's team of busybodying Asian community teachers – women like Nasreen Hassani – send the opposite signal to Asian families. All too often the intermediary becomes an arbiter, then an advocate for the child or family: Fatima Shah, for example. Why otherwise should Nasreen be sitting next door wearing her hijab?

As for Rajiv Lal, his reticence on this 'scarf' issue amounts to an abject failure to support the schools and the Department's own regulations. Abject! Instead of imposing his authority on dissident parents and vacillating politicians – what, one might ask, is Samuel Perlman's position on all this, not a squeak out of him – Lal spends his time composing ambiguous statements of general principle for the Heads. Only this morning his latest circular flopped on to Patricia Newman's desk:

In general, I regard the 'supportive' function of education to be no less important than the 'pragmatic' – which too often damages our multicultural philosophy. The particular family circumstances, the particular learning disabilities and the particular cultural or religious pressures experienced by each child must be treated with sympathy and tenderness. The school must never become a frightening, alien place, because that in itself inhibits learning.

A Tory Home Office Minister had recently warned Asians to learn English 'if they are to function properly in society'. Fair enough. But the Minister had gone on to link the general rise in crime to the population's loss of belief in Hellfire. Rajiv Lal had triumphantly tossed this 'idiocy' at a meeting of Headteachers as if they had uttered it themselves. As if an emphasis on sound grammar, spelling and syntax went hand in hand with crazy Christian fundamentalism!

By the time Nasreen is finally admitted to Mrs Newman's office both women are braced for war. 'Well, how can I help you, Nasreen?' Mrs Newman says brusquely, gesturing faintly towards the chair placed on the penitent's side of her desk.

'You asked me to speak to Fatima Shah, Mrs Newman.'

'Did I? Fatima speaks excellent English. She is in fact a talented linguist. I'm really not sure why a community teacher should be needed on this one.'

'I think the problem with Fatima is cultural and religious. She has also lost her mother – you wanted a Muslim woman teacher to talk to her.'

'Did I?'

Nasreen's hands fumble in her bag for her diary. Opening it, she shudders to see that its pages are littered with Rajiv Lal's name beyond the call of duty.

'It rather depends, Nasreen, on that Muslim woman teacher's own attitude. Hijabs and even chadors are all the rage at this hour – I see you've come here, contrary to custom, wearing your own. Did Fatima convert you?'

'As you know, Mrs Newman, many Muslim families are now involved in this protest.'

'It's a fever. A contagion. An epidemic.'

'Mrs Newman, for a Muslim woman the hijab is a sanctuary against the "haram" of the streets. It is a message of chastity for the unmarried and of virtue for the married. It gives a woman dignity as she confronts the cheap, fashionable values of modern society. It is a token of withdrawal from the great beauty contest which ensures her subordination as a woman.'

'Nasreen, you know perfectly well that the hijab is a token of patriarchy.'

'No, no, Mrs Newman, the Holy Koran, 24:31 tells us "They the believing women must draw their veils." '

' "Over their *bosoms*." That's what is written down, Nasreen. "Let

111

them cast their veils over their bosoms." Anyway, it was meant to apply only to the Prophet's wives – and that was thirteen hundred years ago!'

'The pagan world of Jahilya is eternally with us, Mrs Newman. The hijab defends a woman against the society ruled by ungodly powers, by money and licentiousness.'

Mrs Newman is tapping a pencil on her desk. She is famous for drumming her fingers on the magistrates' bench while some defence lawyer explains that twice two is nought.

'Tell me, Nasreen, why do Muslims speak of "the shame of sex"? Why is the sexual instinct shameful?'

'Western women do not walk the street naked even on the hottest day. It's called "indecent exposure". Yet many Western woman appear naked even when clothed. The Prophet Muhammad, peace be upon him, said, "In later generations of my Ummah there will be women who will be dressed but naked. Curse them for they are truly cursed. They will not enter into Paradise or get a smell of it." '

Patricia Newman ponders the younger woman. There is something dutiful, mechanical, about all these quotations. Does Nasreen really believe what she says? Or has Mr Gamal Rahman turned one giant key which reaches into every Muslim head? Only this morning Patricia Newman had been reading about the death threats suffered by an author – a young woman – in Bangladesh who had dared to criticize Islamic law, the Shari'a. She had been forced to flit from one hiding place to another under cover of darkness, confined to rooms without light or air. Outside she could hear the mullahs shouting for her death.

'This Rahman novel is driving you all over the edge,' Mrs Newman says.

'For any Muslim this is a filthy, insulting book.'

'As it happens the book is not part of the curriculum at this school.'

'A group of white boys were seen flashing the dust jacket of the book around the school playground.'

'I deplore that. I have forbidden it. But those same boys would never have heard of Gamal Rahman if the Izza Shahs and Mustafa Jangars had not blown the issue up.'

Patricia Newman is congratulating herself on her tact – she has not mentioned Nasreen's husband, Hassan Hassani.

'My husband, too,' Nasreen says. This woman reminds her of a colourless lettuce recently taken from the ice-box.

'Migration is of course painful,' Mrs Newman says. 'But I always remember Heinrich Heine's words – they are inscribed on a mem-

orial stone at Dachau: "Wherever they burn books they burn people."
She is too proud to add, 'Or similar words.'

Nasreen can identify neither 'Hiner' nor 'Dakow' but she remembers Hassan telling her that Customs and Excise regularly incinerate quantities of pornography. Hypocrites!

'Nasreen: you yourself passed through our school system without wearing the hijab and without peril to your virtue.'

'But I was not happy!'

'You were perfectly happy. It didn't even occur to you. A girl cannot conduct chemistry experiments or work in the tool room or play netball properly wearing a scarf! Things are bad enough as they stand! I have Muslim parents who won't let their girls wear swimsuits in the presence of a male baths' attendant; I have parents who won't even let their daughters wear cotton jump suits because they cling to the body when wet. This is holding these girls back!'

Nasreen recognizes a famous phrase dear to the city's white schoolteachers: 'holding them back'. It's the opposite of 'attainment'. She knows how dutifully Asian kids and parents absorb such slogans: 'I'm never the father to be holding my girls back,' her dad, S.B. Hussein, used to tell her.

'You people will not prosper in Britain until you break certain taboos, however painful,' Mrs Newman says.

'Drink alcohol, you mean?'

'Nasreen, I don't appreciate that remark.'

'Mr Rajiv Lal feels that policies work effectively only when they command widespread consent.'

'Does he?' Mrs Newman greets this with the tight jaw of a colonel who has received a rebuke from a general by the hand of a sergeant. 'Tell Mr Rajiv Lal that if he wishes to issue a written directive allowing the hijab in school, let him do so.'

Mrs Newman nods in dismissal.

Walking to the bus, Nasreen is waylaid by a small group of Muslim parents carrying placards. On her way in, anxious to be punctual for her appointment, she had hurried past them, making her excuses, but now she stops to receive their protests. One or two of the fieriest tongues do not belong to Hightown parents; they are not local people, she has never seen them before.

A builder's van passes them at high speed, its radio blaring rock. A young skinhead leans out, two fingers raised, jeering:

'Fucking Pakis! Rahman Rules OK!'

'You must excuse me,' she tells the group of incensed Muslims, 'I am already late.'

The rain shelter at the bus stop is thick with insulting graffiti.

Her own memories as a pupil at Hightown Upper still rankle. She remembers the very sincere Muslim teacher who was dismissed by Mrs Newman's predecessor after white parents complained that his English was incomprehensible – dismissal was possible because, despite a Master's degree from Bombay, he possessed no O Level pass in English. Nasreen's dad, S.B. Hussein, had stormed down to the school to protest and stormed back again, his breath reeking of drink. He never smelt his own breath or observed his own bloodshot eyes; for years he'd imagined he was keeping the perfect secret. The bus comes; until recently she liked buses; liked thinking about Rajiv Lal on buses; liked being paid a salary while riding around the town and dreaming of Rajiv. But now she is afraid of insults, obscenities, straight to her face, from sneering youngsters, or snide remarks behind her back by the older people. Every day she sees Muslims lampooned in the newspapers read by her fellow passengers: 'mad mullahs', 'fanatics'. Pressing through the white crowds in the city-centre shopping precincts, she whispers to herself, 'I am a fanatic. I must not betray my faith, my heritage, my own kind. Nasreen, you must not. Your son Imran would never forgive you.' The city is now alive, or dead, with evil and resentment – like the ivy plant she had once cut down from the backyard, twisted, blackened, tenacious, an octopus of brittle, contorted branches clutching at thin air in their death, dragging down fragments of brick and rendering, emitting evil dust as she struck them. She feels a grim rictus settling across her mouth, her cheeks: this contagion.

Who or what is Nasreen Hassani?

And her beloved Rajiv Lal? No hatred, no prejudice in him: just tenderness and understanding. He yearns to turn school assemblies and classes into celebrations of comparative religion, with all the little children learning to understand, to be 'friendly communities', to study the Christian Cross, Shiva, Krishna, Buddha, a Mexican totem pole, an African ancestral spirit mask – dear Rajiv. 'Pluralism,' he tells her, 'is beautiful.' And so, she answers silently, are you. There are always invisible flowers in his hair. She can smell them. She has been reading a book about Hindu customs. Her friend Jyoti Devi Chand, also a community teacher, had lent it to her on request, but with a little laughing remark: 'There's a lot to learn, Nasreen – and why should you be so interested?'

'I'm a great learner, Jyoti.'

'These days, with all this Rahman fuss, I sometimes feel we Hindus have been forgotten. To be honest, we are lying low, pressing our noses to the ground.'

'He has a lot to answer for, that Rahman.'

'We are lying low, Nasreen. If a girl wants to wear a scarf and burn herself alive in the chemistry class, it's no skin off our noses.'

'It's not as simple as that, Jyoti.'

'But can Rajiv Lal handle it, that's what my father is asking. Every Hindu in Bruddersford is glad he isn't in Rajiv Lal's shoes, and that's a fact.'

'He's a fine man, don't you think?'

' "Too fine for the job," my father says, "how can he deal with all these cutthroats and fanatics?" '

'You wouldn't want someone spitting on Shiva or Krishna, Jyoti.'

'I'd pretend not to notice, Nasreen. These little fires die down, you know, unless you take a pair of bellows to them.'

From the borrowed book – which Nasreen read in the kitchen while preparing Hassan's dinner and put away in the linen cupboard when he sat himself down to eat his solitary meal – she discovered that some Hindus drop their family names, keeping only their personal name and complementary middle name. (She diligently checked on 'complementary' and 'complimentary' in her English dictionary.) Lal was a middle name, not a family name! A family name indicated caste (she read) and Rajiv was too sensitive and discreet to indicate his high caste (she felt sure). She further discovered that if she were a Hindu the polite way to address Rajiv would not be 'Mr Lal' but 'Rajivlal'.

'How do you address Mr Lal?' she asked Jyoti Devi Chand at the next opportunity.

'As "Mr Lal".'

'Not as "Rajivlal"?'

Jyoti laughed gaily. 'I warned you not to be reading that book, dear. The wrong end of the stick is always waiting to be grasped by the blind man – as we say. Rajiv is thoroughly Westernized, you know. He doesn't want any of what he calls "insider-talk". No "Rajivlal" stuff. He's not having his Hindu staff calling him one thing, and his white and Muslim staff calling him another.'

'Oh.'

Jyoti Devi Chand cheerily appraised the impact of this mugging on her Muslim colleague. There was definitely some gossip here to be passed around – real or imagined, where's the difference? Jyoti would surely mention it, in passing, during her next visit to Mrs Newman and to everyone else in earshot.

Reaching the Department of Education, second floor, Nasreen finds a typed message from the Director's secretary: 'Mr Lal asks you to kindly let him have a short written report on your meeting this afternoon with Mrs Patricia Newman. Please be as objective as possible about the current situation at Hightown Upper School and convey Mrs Newman's point of view faithfully.'

The implied rebuke from Rajiv scorches her heart. She falls into her chair and stares at nothing.

EIGHT

❧

'**V**ote Haqq!'

Robson Street, Speedwell Street, knock knock who's there. At ten a.m. many mill workers are still asleep. An old patriarch is shuffling on a stick five paces ahead of his wife. She is fat, old, slow. Ishmail Haqq stops his car, bows deferentially, tries Urdu. The whispered answer from the bent old man comes back in Gujarati. Haqq now speaks to them in English. He asks them what street they live in. Ah, yes, he knows it well. He once had a cousin, as a matter of fact, in that same street.

'I am Ishmail Haqq. I have worked for Labour all my life. I have worn my fingers to the bone for it, sir. I have given my sweat for the people, sir. And now we are betrayed, sir, we are all betrayed, the Prophet is betrayed.'

'Peace,' the old couple murmur.

The next house carries an estate agent's hoarding: 'SOLD – Subject to Contract'. Ishmail Haqq crosses the family off his canvass sheet. Two houses along, he glances up at the drawn curtains of the bedroom: this is Ishtaq, who works for Bruddersford Yarn by day and drives taxis by night – moonlighting indeed. Ishtaq has been a member of the Labour Party 'for donkey's years', has two kids in college, and would be a valuable defector. Haqq studies the drawn curtains; to wake up an exhausted man is not the way to win his vote. He drops a leaflet through the door and passes on. Further up the street the karate instructor, Tiger Siddiqi, wearing his gorgeous yellow-and-green outfit, is leaping gates and fences on Haqq's behalf, a species of daffodil the Lakeland poet never observed.

Tiger Siddiqi owes his manly job at the Community Centre to its Chairman, Ishmail Haqq. Judo, karate, kick-boxing – the Asian lads can now walk the streets with heads up.

Two white ladies are walking down Church Street. Haqq passes. He knocks again. A Hindu lady comes to the door; she wears a sari which

117

reveals a broad band of flesh at the waist. No there are no men at home except Granddaddy who is ill in bed.

'Will you please show your good husband these leaflets?' Haqq says, offering her the Gujarati version aimed at Hindu voters.

HALIQ HAQQ – INDEPENDENT MINORITY RIGHTS

Siddiqi has knocked up one of his karate pupils, a young feller in tracksuit trousers. No, his dad's at work but Haqq can count on his vote if he has Siddiqi's support.

'Don't forget yer mother,' Siddiqi beams.

'Right.'

Haqq puts two triumphant ticks on his canvass sheet.

Next door the window carries a 'HANI MALIK – LABOUR' sticker in red and yellow. Haqq has spent his 'life' distributing them. In the distance a megaphone van can be heard: 'Vote Hani Malik – Labour.'

Belmont Street is littered with rubbish. A group of Muslim women with small children are sitting on the wall of the Council flats, enjoying the sunshine. Siddiqi hurries towards them. Automatically their hands reach up to adjust their headscarves. 'Come and meet your Muslim candidate himself. He is really with us today, Ishmail Haqq!'

Haqq makes a speech to the shy ladies in Urdu:

'Look at this rubbish, this filth, what a complete disgrace after six years of Labour in power! Labour in power is rubbish! Look, pot-holes, rubbish, rats, houses in decay. Labour is taking your votes and eating them!'

A swirling, footballing, group of small boys suddenly gain male courage and start chanting: 'Leh-burr, Leh-burr.' After a moment's anger, Haqq realizes that the kids, having heard 'Labour' from his lips since the dawn of memory, are being friendly. And what of their smiling mothers – their stupid fucking Muslim mothers: have they come to the same disastrous conclusion?

Haqq beckons to his support car, a gleaming Toyota version of the Range Rover driven by Haqq's wealthiest supporter, the car-dealer (Toyota franchise) Imtiaz Shasti, who is truly happy only when lounging, cigarette in hand, behind the gleaming dials of his 'ship'. With a flick Shasti activates the public address system:

'ISHMAIL HAQQ, MUSLIM INDEPENDENT. Vote HAQQ. Vote against Gamal Rahman. Vote against the Devil. Labour loves the Devil Shaytan. ISHMAIL HAQQ. This is ISHMAIL HAQQ your Muslim candidate. ISHMAIL HAQQ vows to defend the honour of Islam . . .'

Later, after evening prayers, the imams of the Maududi, Upper George, Thornhill, Masjid-E-Noorul and Omar Mosques are scheduled to make announcements – but what will they say? The Islamic

Council has never endorsed any political party or candidate. Haqq has lobbied furiously, never missing an evening's prayers since the election campaign began, but Hani Malik has been active, too.

Imtiaz Shasti, proprietor of the Pool and Snooker Centre, drives lazily at the wheel of his Toyota. He likes the feel of politics. Form your own party and you are in the front line immediately. Shasti is Siddiqi's cousin: they are both handsome, sports-loving men, and Shasti is wealthy on the Toyota franchise. Some of his best friends are Japanese. Haqq will make sure his trucks pass their MOT tests. Shasti tosses away his cigarette before knocking on doors:

'Ishmail Haqq is a really decent bloke, he's never going to any bar places, he don't smoking or drinking, you know. All the Labour ones they are smoking and drinking and supporting Gamal Rahman.'

Mimosa Grove, Royal Avenue School and Sports Centre, the valleys stretch down and away: delapidated terraced houses with a central open passageway to the communal yard at the rear. Crumby stuff but rich in potential votes. If they bother to vote at all.

Moving on, Haqq discovers an old white couple sunning themselves at the gate of their neatly tended front garden. He hesitates: but every vote counts. The perky wife, it transpires, is pure Yorkshire, the bent-backed, cadaverous husband Latvian.

'Latvia demands its freedom from Soviet tyranny,' Haqq responds immediately.

The old Latvian nods. 'But vot of all zees Chinees comings vom Hong Kong?'

'I agree,' Haqq says 'Frankly, sir, they are too many Chinese.'

The wife addresses Haqq: 'I don't say we shouldn't take some in but where are they going to house them?'

The Latvian says: 'I cannot understanding that, vy vy vy?'

The wife says: 'He escaped.'

He says: 'No! Escapp-ed? Vot escapp-ed? I vos in Latvian-German army. We fight the Roosians. Then Americans catch you. We get to the West and not let the Roosians get. Not get. If they come you know where go, far away.'

'You're quite right, sir. We must keep the Russians out of Brudders-ford. Frankly, it's the Labour Party that will let them in.' Haqq smiles agreeably and offers them his non-Muslim pamphlet. 'True Christians can now be counted as a minority in this Christian country,' he adds. A Muslim family living next door are doing some repairs for the Latvian: ropes, ladders, piles of sand straddle the low garden wall dividing the two properties.

The wife says: 'I don't know, I don't agree with this poll tax, we'll have to pay more, the two of us.'

Haqq declares himself poised to abolish the poll tax. 'This street needs an Independent candidate. The big party machines are all the same.'

She says: 'And pensions. They should put up the pensions more, when you've paid stamps all your life.'

'Our pensioners are the victims of the big party machines,' Haqq says.

'It's a pity that some people don't do more to help themselves,' she grumbles.

Shasti catches the wind, moves in. 'Madam,' he says, 'I'm with you one hundred per cent. I'm in business, personally.' He gestures towards the Toyota festooned in green and yellow stickers. 'Car sales, road haulage, wagons, big stuff. Ishmail Haqq is trying to bring this community together, you know, Rahman book, school meals, housing grants, stuff like that.'

'Who is?' the woman says.

'Your candidate, here, Ishmail Haqq.'

'What are you, Labour?' she asks Haqq.

'Independent, madam. I am campaigning to persuade my fellow-immigrants to stand on their own feet. No more handouts from the taxpayer. And frankly, too many of them have wanted to change the way of life of the English people here. First come, first served is my motto.'

He knows he's wasting his time on this couple, yet engaging in dialogue with white householders affords him a curious sense of his own plausibility.

'Labour politicians, madam, promote their own private interests. People like Hani Malik and Zulfikar Zaheed.'

'Who's that?' she asks. (The Latvian has fallen silent.)

'Our Lord Mayor. He is planning to stand for Parliament, his heart is not with us local people. We are mere steps on his ladder.'

'I thought that whatisname . . . Flowers . . .'

'Exactly, madam. Harry Flowers is our Labour MP. But Zaheed wants his seat. That's the way these Labour men behave. They stab each other in the back. And then they call me, Ishmail Haqq, a "cowboy"!'

'Vot American?' the old Latvian comes to life.

'Listen, I know all these Labour types personal,' Shasti says. 'I know for a fact they're corrupt.'

'Like the Gang of Four,' Haqq adds, growing bored, glancing at his watch, his eyes swivelling across the street.

'I've no time for that whatsisname . . . Owens,' the lady says.

120

'David Owen, madam? I did not mean that Gang of Four,' Haqq says. 'I meant the Gang of Four in China.'

The woman says 'Owens' should go back to China.

'You are of course good Christians,' Haqq says. 'What I am seeking to put across to the Christian community is that the so-called writers like Gamal Rahman – '

'Who?'

'These atheists are going to have a go at every religion, believe me, they'll go for Christians if we let them.'

The Latvian is nodding to himself. 'Vot escapp-ed?' he says. 'The Roosians coming, ve going.'

⁊

Tariq Khan distributes a new batch of Urdu leaflets for Ishmail Haqq after his night's work at the Omar Khayyam, shoving them through letter-boxes then moving on swiftly, because the leaflets are 'illegal'. Haqq has warned Tariq never to mention his name when distributing them. Haqq knows the lad's impetuosity and how eagerly he has adopted the role assigned to him by Mustafa Jangar, Regional Guardian of the Muslim Youth League:

'You are mujaheddin, young brothers, you are guerilla warriors of Hezbollah, the Party of God, you are the assassins of the holy jihad.'

Receiving a consignment of leaflets, Tariq has shyly mentioned to Haqq his mission to assassinate Gamal Rahman.

'Young Brother, speak softly,' Haqq murmured. 'Whatever you said, I did not hear you.' Haqq took his arm. 'Frankly, Brother Tariq, we must use our heads. Election first, vengeance later. Nothing must happen to the devil Rahman until after these elections. Ask your father, Karamat, he understands. Gamal Rahman is the djinn in my bottle. I don't want him popping out dead just yet. I don't want the whole of white England up in arms just now. Leave it to the Iranians.'

'Aye, but – '

'But nothing. Mustafa Jangar is a dreamer, Tariq. Ishmail Haqq is the practical soldier who will crush the infidels at the ballot box.'

Shasti and Siddiqi agreed. They always agreed with Haqq. Having taken karate lessons with the brilliant Siddiqi, Tariq was impressed. But the desire to impress his self-possessed cousin Rana is paramount. Uncle Abdul doesn't believe a daughter – even one with four O Levels – should choose her husband, that isn't a proper marriage, that's this Western 'love-thing' and look at all these 'Royal-Family divorcings'. When Tariq had finally plucked up the courage to approach Uncle Abdul and ask for Rana's hand – Woman Police Constable Rana Khan! – he was merely shown more photographs of

121

various royal families. The television was on, as always. They watched the 'Nine O'Clock News', then they watched 'News at Ten', and then Uncle Abdul took out his great box of photos and said, in Punjabi:

'Rana must marry an educated man, a fully educated man. There is no good marriage in which the wife is better educated than the husband, she being more ambitious and earning the money.' In English he added: 'That's fatal. And if people are marrying for love and lust, they are soon divorcing for love and lust. Even the Queen's family now. You young people are wanting intercourse at the dropping of a hat but God knows what's best.'

By that time it was 'Late Night Line-Up' and Uncle Abdul had settled back into cursing 'the bloody Indians' over Kashmir. He never said 'Indian' without saying 'bloody'. Next on-screen comes Gamal Rahman, that bloody Rahman, interviewed in his hideaway and laughingly denying the facts of his own despicable life, though well known to Uncle Abdul and every Muslim across the globe. No, he'd never been an agent for Zionism; no, he'd never been thrown into prison for embezzlement; no, he'd never put his pen at the service of the corrupt Sharaf regime; no, his own illustrious father had never renounced or denounced – Uncle Abdul isn't sure about the difference between the two words – him; no, he'd never entered into unmentionable relationships with the Sharaf women.

'Yes, my agent and publisher are Jews. But the money I get paid is not "Jewish money", it's my readers' money. No one has ever succeeded in telling me what to write or what to write about. Here I must make one exception: the devil himself.'

Uncle Ayub sits up straight: 'He has confessed!'

'The devil I know,' Rahman adds, eyes rolling, 'usually appears to me in the guise of a Cairo donkey.'

ᘓ

A leaflet slithers through the front door of Ted Francis, the Labour Party's election agent. He peers at its suspiciously, then reaches Trevor Lucas on his mobile phone.

'What is it?' Lucas asks.

'God knows. It's written in Muslim. We're in a religious situation.'

'Does it give publisher and printer?'

'You tell me!'

'Get hold of Hani Malik.'

Working for Malik, Lucas and other Labour candidates, Ted Francis lives, breathes, eats and makes love to what he calls 'voting promises'. The Bruddersford Party can afford a full-time agent without having to collect part of his salary from the bingo fund-raising on the Council estates. Ted Francis knows how to gain entry to any locked block of flats; which buzzer to press. But now he's baffled. Malik cannot be located; finally Francis reaches Dr Yaqub Quddus at the CRC.

'We need some translating, Doctor.'

'Yes, yes, what language?'

'It's in Muslim.'

'No such language exists. Just spell me the first words.'

'It's in some funny alphabet which jumps all over the page.'

Quddus arrives like a whirling dervish.

'Urdu,' he announces. 'No publisher or printer given.'

A saloon car pulls up outside. There's no shortage of parking space in Culver Street and when a car stops outside you have a visitor. Harry Flowers, MP, saunters into the sitting room, wearing a very nice double-breasted suit, followed by Trevor Lucas in an open-neck shirt and jeans. Bruddersford's two most powerful politicians make a striking contrast. Flowers exudes waterfalls of confidence, Lucas secretes rivulets of worry. Flowers always looks as if he's just returned from the Riviera, a permanent suntan offsetting his golden moustache; Lucas might have escaped from a slave-labour camp. Flowers's hair has been set to music; Lucas's short black mat seems to be in hiding. You can hear the lolly jingling in Harry Flowers's trouser pockets; Lucas, despite his high salary, can never find a coin for a parking meter.

'You'd better translate for us, Yaqub,' Lucas wearily tells Quddus.

Quddus does so with relish, his voice a megaphone.

'Brothers of the MUSLIM NATION! Gamal RAHMAN has written his *The Devil: an Interview.* But Rahman himself is SHAYTAN. God and God's Prophet are insulted! For two months the Muslims of the entire world have risen up in protest. Thirty MARTYRS have died. We in Britain cannot rest until this book is banned BY LAW.

'We expected much from the Labour Party. But Labour politicians have displayed their enmity towards Islam. Local and national leaders of Labour have spoken up in support of SHAYTAN! The Labour Party is led by an atheist, Neil Kinnock.

'Our present LABOUR COUNCILLOR, Hani Malik, has betrayed his Faith in his greed for the votes of INFIDELS! Malik voted for this filthy book! Malik voted down our heartfelt protests! Do not trust Malik!

'Friends, they will try to bribe you, threaten your housing grants. They will try to confuse you and hoodwink you. It is better to die

123

than accept such SATANIC offerings . . . the type of food which stops you flying.

'Vote for your true Muslim Brother, ISHMAIL HAQQ! Brother Haqq is pledged to fight to his last drop of blood to ban this filthy, impious book! BROTHER HAQQ will fight for halal meat in schools! BROTHER HAQQ will fight for housing grants and good pavements and street lighting for our old people, women and children.

'Teach the enemies of Islam and especially the Labour Party a lesson! LONG LIVE ISLAM!'

Ted Francis's brow is furrowed. 'What's all this about a type of food that stops you flying?'

Dr Quddus beams. 'It's Urdu poetry. The kind of food that stops you flying. A very beautiful sentiment.'

'Haqq's a political cowboy,' Ted Francis announces. 'He's after jobs, a fixer. He's committing suicide.'

'Put a copy in the hands of the police,' Lucas instructs Ted Francis.

'So how's my friend Zulfy Zaheed?' Flowers asks everyone. 'The lad wants my job, you know.'

'Zaheed's resignation is permanently pending,' Francis says with a sycophantic wink.

'Is he out campaigning for Malik?'

'Lord Mayors should remain above partisan politics. That's his current line,' Lucas says.

'He's sniffing the desert wind from Mecca,' Flowers says.

Trevor Lucas glances at Quddus uncomfortably. They all wish their Muslim colleague would go home now that he's done his translating.

'Zulfikar was on local radio last night, slagging me off for my ill-judged remark about fundamentalism and corruption.'

'What did you say?' Flowers asks Lucas.

'I said that Haqq always alleges bribery and corruption because bribery is normal practice wherever Islamic fundamentalism prevails.'

'Spot on,' says Flowers, a popular mimic in the bars of the House of Commons and famous for his imitation of Ishmail Haqq: "It's not halal at all, Brothers! It's haram! It's a rip-off! They beg for our votes then throw us away like used condoms!" '

Yaqub Quddus can take no more of Harry Em Pee. At the door he shakes a fist at Lucas. 'Frankly, Trevor, you have kicked the bucket.'

'Jesus,' Ted Francis sighs as the front door slams. 'You'd think we were in Zanzibar.'

'Zulfikar and Hani are livid about my remarks,' Lucas admits. 'Hani's unhappy all round. Haqq's allegations concerning halal school dinners have stuck. Jewish supermarkets and all that. Now we have this bloody scarf issue.'

Flowers laughs. 'Fatima Shah, soon to be the most famous school-girl in Britain. How about a drink, Ted, now that we can no longer offend anyone present.' He settles back in his chair, Scotch in hand, with a contented smile. He has acquired a new mistress in London: his research assistant. His wife doesn't know as yet, no reason why she should find out, the girl's discreet. Coming north bores him. All those bloody 'surgeries' in the freezing Party rooms. All those hours and hours of incoherent complaints from old people who just don't bloody know the language. Drifting from the Tribune Group to the softer edge of the right-wing Manifesto Group, Harry Flowers has caught the Leader's eye. The job – Shadow Minister at the Treasury – suits him fine. At least four TV and radio interviews a week. His face on page 2 of *The Times*.

His thoughts zoom back to Zulfikar Zaheed, the prick who wants to take it all away from him, even the adultery. No seat, no research assistant, no sex.

'Wasn't Zaheed involved in some public transport fiasco?' Flowers asks.

'Harry, that was many years ago,' Lucas says. 'The City Auditors' report entirely exonerated him.'

'Aha. I hear Zaheed's daughter is having it off with Ali Cheema.'

Lucas and Ted Francis are looking uncomfortable. Zaheed is their ally in this Council election, despite the Hamlet performance.

بٹس

Driving down Lester Road in the rear seat of her father's car, Fatima Shah cries out in pleasure. She has caught sight of two Muslim girls also wearing the full burka, swathed in black, their faces fully covered.

'Look, Father!'

Izza Shah does not respond. She knows that his prostate and bladder now dominate his concentration, day and night. Although she'd made sure he'd visited the toilet before leaving home, she can tell that already he needs to go again. He is now visiting the Urology Unit of St George's Hospital, Clinic 6, once a week; after successive urine tests and x-rays during which they pour fluid down his throat and pump up his bladder, they have shoved a tube straight up his privates. She knows the details because she invariably collects him from St George's and the doctors now confide in this pale, grave, stick-like girl as if she were a wife rather than a daughter.

In her black burka she could be a widow.

'Father, stop at the shop,' she commands. 'Toilet business.'

125

Izza Shah abruptly pulls in outside his own dry-goods store. 'Wait,' he says, hurrying inside.

The two girls in burkas have now caught up with the parked car. As they pass, Fatima wants to reach out and seize their hands in sisterly love. They walk on. Her gaze falls on a crudely spray-painted slogan defacing the wall of the new Masjid-E-Noorul Mosque at the corner of Paradise Street:

RAHMAN RULES OK!

Her father returns, his granite face creased with pain, damp patches on his trousers (which he no longer notices). She wonders whether he should be driving a car, these days.

You could easily pass the Muslim Girls' School without noticing it. It's housed in an abandoned Victorian primary school, on three floors, with an outside iron staircase topped and tailed by fire doors. The janitor shakes Izza Shah's hand and mutters a few words of blessing before leading them to the Headmistress's office. Fatima walks behind her father.

Mrs Zahra Aram rises from behind her desk. Her head is covered. She motions Izza Shah to be seated – the girl will remain standing. Mrs Aram being a Bengali and Izza a Punjabi, they will converse in English.

'Thank you for seeing me,' Izza Shah says.

'It is an honour, Mr Shah.'

'I am glad to see your girls are wearing the burka.'

'Well, it is optional, of course. We insist only on the hijab.' She throws Fatima a brief, encouraging smile.

'I have come to see you about my daughter Fatima,' Izza Shah announces, as if Fatima were not standing behind him, her hands knotted together. 'The girl is in much distress. Mrs Newman will not permit her to wear the hijab in school. Fatima is being sent home every day.'

Mrs Aram nods. 'I have heard about this situation. And your daughter is due to take her GCSE examinations?'

'That is correct. Frankly, what is your advice? You are a B.Sc. from the University of Lancaster and an experienced Headmistress. Mrs Newman is saying that Fatima cannot wear a hijab in chemistry classes.'

'When I was a student I devised a kind of cap which fitted tight, no loose ends, and made of a non-inflammable material. In fact it is safer to wear this cap than to wear nothing at all. Some non-Muslim girls pin back their long hair but there is always some danger from Bunsen burners.' Mrs Aram pauses. 'Unfortunately we do not have the facilities to teach chemistry at this school.'

126

Fatima's spirits sink – chemistry is her favourite subject, almost.

'Mrs Newman says girls may not wear the hijab in any classroom.'

'Yes, I believe this is sadly the rule in all the City's schools.'

'Can you persuade her to understand our Muslim feelings, as one lady Headteacher to another?'

'I fear she would be offended. Our Muslim Girls' School is very much disapproved of by the Education Department. We are accused of living in the Middle Ages.'

'That means the time of the Prophet.'

Mrs Aram nods respectfully.

'I am asking myself whether I should much better be sending Fatima to your school, Mrs Aram. The Islamic Council has supported your school.'

'Without its support we could not have survived, Mr Shah. The generosity of the mosques and some private donations have enabled us to keep our fees down to 550 pounds a year – but that is of course beyond the means of many Muslim parents.'

'We have applied many times for Grant Aided status.'

'So please tell me what subjects Fatima is studying for GCSE.'

'English, Maths, Fraanch, Chemistry and Punjabi. Also Bahlgy.'

'She is very bright, then.'

'She is. But I have been complaining to Mrs Newman about this "sex education" during Bahlgy lessons.'

'I understand.' Mrs Aram lowers her gaze.

'They are also teaching evolution.'

Fatima has been working out whether she likes Mrs Aram. She knows that a Head can be very nice to your father but not so nice when he's gone home.

'Unfortunately,' Mrs Aram says, 'Fatima could not study three of her six subjects here. We do not teach French, chemistry or biology. Fatima would not benefit academically. On the other hand, she would become happier and more self-confident here.'

'I have no wish to sacrifice my daughter's future.'

'It is a hard choice, Mr Shah. I will take Fatima for a walk round our school. We always say here, "the decision is the father's, the choice is the daughter's".'

Izza Shah nods. Whatever he thinks of this dictum, his prostate is again playing up and he is content to sit quietly in Mrs Aram's office. As she ushers Fatima out, she places the Holy Koran in Izza Shah's hand.

Once out in the corridor the plump Mrs Aram squeezes Fatima's wasted cheek. 'You're thin, girl. You haven't been eating.' She hurries along, shorter than Fatima, and bursts into a classroom. The girls jump to their feet. 'Good,' she says and closes the door. Fatima has barely had time to catch a glimpse of the rows of girls bent over their desks. Mrs Aram leads her out to a small courtyard.

'Now Fatima, is the hijab the only problem you have at Hightown Upper?'

'Insults. Things written on the walls.'

'So you wouldn't really want to go back there even if Mrs Newman allowed you to wear the hijab?'

'I don't rightly know, Mrs Aram. I'd like to pass my exams.'

'How about this: you continue to turn up at Hightown Upper every morning to register your wish to attend. When sent away you come straight down here and we fit you in. English, maths, Punjabi. I will personally help you, after school hours, with your chemistry and biology, though of course we can't do practicals.'

'Thank you. But – '

'Yes?' Mrs Aram says rather sharply – her tone suddenly reminds Fatima of Mrs Newman's.

'What about the other girls? There's fifteen of us at Hightown Upper insisting on wearing the hijab and getting sent home. It wouldn't be fair on the others if I sneaked off here while they went home.'

'You don't need to tell the others. Your father is a very important man, don't forget that. And the others may not be able to afford the fees.'

Fatima is thinking of 'the others': Mustafa Jangar's daughter, Ishmail Haqq's daughter, a niece of the Khan brothers . . . She can already imagine a column by the horrible Joe Reddaway, 'All Muslims are Equal but Some Muslims are More Equal than Others.'

Mrs Aram bustles back to her office, her long black gown swirling, Fatima trailing behind, appalled by what the other girls will say when they discover. The Headmistress repeats her solution to Izza Shah.

He rises from his chair with difficulty. 'I will pay the full fees,' he says, 'and a special stipend to you personally.'

Fatima cannot contain herself. 'What about the other girls, Father?'

Mrs Aram walks them to the front entrance. The silent school is now alive with cheerful chatter. It's break time. Groups of girls in plum-coloured shalwar camise (trousers and tunics) lower their veils as the famous patriarch approaches. Fatima feels the isolation of the new girl – she's sure they're all gossiping about her.

'We will expect you tomorrow,' Mrs Aram tells Fatima.

On the way home, huddled in the back seat, she ventures a

thought. 'Father, I was thinking that maybe Ali Cheema could tutor me.'

'Ali has no time for that.'

Fatima remembers that Ali had time to tutor Wahabia Zaheed. And she got into Sussex University. But Wahabia Zaheed cannot be mentioned to Fatima's father.

ॐ

Tariq Khan's straggly beard has thickened of late, as if heightened communal tension, the Koranic oaths administered by Mustafa Jangar, and nights spent in police cells had boosted the supply of testosterone to his chin. After months of indolence, apathy, hopelessness, the bored waiter of the Omar Khayyam has found a mission in life – his feet are now leaving their print on the world. Only WPC Rana Khan's rejection revives his moods of dejection. 'I can't consort with a persistent offender,' she told her father, Uncle Abdul Ayub Khan, when she returned from plain-clothes duties late one night to find Tariq dutifully studying her dad's celebrity-photograph album in the living room. Not a word to Tariq – spoke right over his head and new beard.

Mustafa Jangar has summoned his mujaheddin. Trouble is coming, it's inscribed in the calendar, the invader must be repelled.

'Keep out of trouble,' Karamat Khan has warned his son. 'Your uncle is at the end of his tether with you.'

Police vans converge from as far afield as Humberside and Greater Manchester. The British National Party advances in convoy. Threading north through sleepy villages of limestone cottages and gloomy churches, the BNP heads for its chosen terrain for a Saturday 'steaming' – rampaging through the small towns of West Yorkshire, overturning Asian market stalls, terrifying shoppers. According to the well-informed Hassan Hassani, the Home Secretary has imposed an eight-day ban on marches under the Public Order Act but he has no power to ban rallies.

'They always lack the powers when it suits them,' Hassani has told Tariq and his brethren of the Muslim Youth League. 'They can ban any old book except Rahman's.'

In Muslim Bruddersford every shop is boarded up in anticipation of the onslaught. From up the road, just out of sight, the mujaheddin can hear the BNP's public-address systems launching the action.

'Pakis out, out, out!'

The local white lads have gathered at the Red Lion pub. In better times Tariq and his friends used to spend evenings there, playing pool and cards, blowing their earnings on a pint or two beyond the gaze of their fathers. But the white gangs, pimps and drug-pushers have moved in to the Red Lion, making it their own – even Tariq wouldn't dare venture in there now. A place selling alcohol in the heart of a Muslim neighbourhood has become an affront. The mujaheddin have decided to storm the Red Lion.

Angry knots of young men are swarming through the streets like wasps, shouting, chanting, hurling fist-sized rocks at shops, battering their own souls senseless on the hot windowpane of the sun. In Seville Road, half-bricks, rocks and staves are flying. Temporarily outnumbered, the white youths are in retreat. Smashing their way in to the hastily locked pub, Tariq's lads break up the bar, hurling tables and stools through the window of the tap room to erect a barricade across the street.

The landlord and his family have taken refuge upstairs, wedging a bed against the door.

'Let's fire the place!' someone shouts.

Tariq grips his arm. 'There are women and kids up there!'

'They have no raght to be in this street. This is a Muslim street! These people give us the shit-eye all the time!'

'We are not murderers of children,' Tariq tightens his grip. 'You are speaking like a man full of alcohol.'

At the approaching scream of police sirens, the mujaheddin decamp, scatter, regroup. The police release their dogs. A helicopter hovers above, its video camera turning. It will be a long game, without boundaries or umpires, before the ambulances dare to move in.

Tariq, arrested yet again, is angrily confronted by his father and uncle after his release on bail. Their wrath covers him like boiling foam all the way home from Central Police Station in Uncle Abdul Ayub Khan's new Toyota, acquired from Imtiaz Shasti at a discount after he promised not to disclose Shasti's financial stake in his halal slaughterhouse. Ishmail Haqq has tipped off Shasti that Trevor Lucas's Labour machine is in vengeful mood; the slaughterhouse may soon be 'under investigation by those Jew bastards'.

'Tariq, you will be driving me out of business!' Uncle Abdul cries. 'You will be breaking my back!'

ॐ

It was (our apologies) Gamal Rahman who once likened Mustafa Jangar to a wounded elephant trundling from village to village, wreaking havoc, unaware that his hide is riddled with slow-acting poison darts. 'Call the darts Reason,' Gamal added. Unheralded, Mustafa pays a call on Ali Cheema. Wearing turban and robe, the

Ayatollah's messenger carries leather-bound tomes in his hand, his trunk coiled to trumpet the truth about the truth.

'Please come in, Brother.' Ali's voice is soft, his manner feline; London media people frequently mistake his telephone whisper for shyness or (grave error) modesty. Writing to the Bishop of Bruddersford, Gamal Rahman described Ali as the 'obsequious assassin'.

My dear Lord Bishop,

What more suitable recruit to academia than the voice who would silence other voices by literal death. I hear that Mr Cheema is very much the front runner for the Junior Research Fellowship: allow me, therefore, to offer myself as a candidate. Your esteemed College is thereby granted the exquisite dilemma of choosing between the martyr and those who would burn him alongside his poor book.

I do however recommend Mr Cheema's High Table manners as superior to my own. He never belches or farts during a Christian prayer; he does not tell bad jokes in the loudest possible voice: he is an entirely obsequious assassin.

The Bishop had read this letter in *The Times* a few seconds before it turned up in his morning mail, south-east of the marmalade jar. Predictably, a telephone call from the Master of the College followed within minutes. The Governing Body, he reported, was unhappy. The Master himself had received a 'small storm' of anonymous letters concerning Ali's Cheema's private life.

'Tear them up,' the Bishop advised. 'But make photocopies first.'

'Frankly, Robin, the Fellows are not sure whether to be delighted or outraged by Cheema's television appearances.'

'He will put the College on the map.'

'It may be a map of Hell, Robin. One of my anonymous correspondents accuses him of transgressing with his own sister.'

'Ali has "sisters" only by adoption. There's no blood tie and I don't believe a word of it. It sounds to me as if Mr Rahman is the author of each and every letter.'

'We don't think so.'

The Bishop has felt it his duty to put Ali 'in the picture' concerning this exchange. In addition he suggested it was time for a 'confidential meeting' with Izza Shah – would Ali care to arrange it through the good offices of Douglas Blunt? Very frankly, the Bishop had found recent statements by Mustafa Jangar and Hassan Hassani 'deeply disturbing'. Did they speak with the full authority of the Islamic

Council? *In the meantime, my dear Ali, I still regard you as the ideal candidate for our Junior Research Fellowship.*

Mustafa offers no apology to Ali for his visit – brothers call on one another. He launches straight into his oration.

'And when will British Muslims enjoy justice? For an answer, Brother Ali, we need search no further than the divinely-inspired writings of the Imam Khomeini.'

'Please sit down, Brother.'

'Islamic justice is simple. It requires only a single judge setting up in a town, accompanied by two or three executors, a pen and an ink pot, to hand down his verdict on any case and have it immediately executed. Twenty cases heard in a day, while Western judges and juries take months to achieve a verdict hedged about by technicalities and rights of appeal. If one applied for a single year the punitive laws of Islam, one would uproot all the devastating injustices and immoralities befouling England.'

'That is not our tradition, Brother.'

'You must convince Brother Izza that the legitimate heir to the Prophet is the twelfth descendant of the Imam Ali, Muhammad's cousin and son-in-law.'

'You vastly overstate my influence on Izza Shah, Brother Mustafa. I am merely a son to him. I cannot convert him to the doctrines of the Twelver Shi'ites.'

'You must listen more attentively to the Ayatollah Khomeini, Brother Ali. The twelfth descendant of the Imam Ali, after whom you yourself are named, is still "alive", though hidden.'

'But Brother, this twelfth descendant disappeared without trace in the Islamic Year 252.'

'The twelfth descendant will reappear in his own time as the Mahdi, the divinely guided one.'

'Brother, this is merely the old monarchical heresy which passes the Prophet's role down the biological family. Islam is riddled with this pernicious doctrine of "descent". Muhammad was plucked by Allah out of dust and returned to dust; God needs no human family trees.'

Mustafa is silent – a display of patience. He and every good Muslim watching television had witnessed Ali's lowered gaze as Shaytan Rahman mocked the Prophet's successors, beginning with the Caliph Abu Bakr, one of the Prophet's many fathers-in-law. Third in line was Uthman, the Prophet's son-in-law twice over (married to two of his daughters). Then, fourth, came Ali ibn Ali, another son-in-law!

'God was certainly keeping it within the family!' Gamal Rahman had chuckled.

132

And no reply from Ali Cheema!

Mustafa stands at the front door, poised to depart. 'Brother Ali, your private life is giving us all much cause for concern. This house of yours smells like a cheap scent bottle. I see a saucer piled with cigarette ends stained by lipstick. Various female undergarments hang from the clothes line in your back yard. It is clear that you have not been able to resist the temptations of a godless society.'

NINE

❧

The steeply climbing streets of Tanner are still crawling with journalists from the national press. Photographers carefully marshal the children – boys in prayer caps and girls in chadors are preferred – against old mosques and new mosques and steel-girder-mosques-in-the-making. Old men in beards encounter zoom lenses when taking their morning amble to the corner shop.

Caption: 'The Shape of Things to Come?'

Here comes Hani Malik, bustling from door to door, a splendid red-and-yellow rosette in his buttonhole, his canvass sheets and window-stickers fastened to a clipboard, a wad of 'Sorry You Were Not at Home' leaflets in his pocket. What he's running up against, in dwelling after dwelling, is the refusal of young adults to include their names on the electoral register for fear that it can be used to check their poll-tax liability. The young are disappearing themselves, most of them potential Labour voters. Actually, this could hit Haqq, too. The Tories are laughing.

Hani Malik reaches the familiar home of S.B. Hussein. Definite news of S.B.'s return from Pakistan would be a comfort.

The younger daughter, Latifa, answers the door, her head uncovered. Malik has always liked her – she's straight and forthright, Latifa.

'Greetings, Sister. How's your dad?'

'Nasreen's fetching him from Manchester Airport. Want a cuppa?' He follows Latifa into the kitchen, his practised eye noting the dereliction, the large patches of damp on the walls.

'Take a good look, Hani,' Latifa says, banging the kettle down on the stove. 'We're in this street twenty years, no improvement grant, all run-down here. The white people are getting all the improvement grants up there.'

This sounds to Malik like the voice of Ishmail Haqq – you can virtually wipe Haqq's footprints off the pavement. Malik has already counted twelve Muslim Independent stickers in ground-floor windows. Haqq is dashing about denigrating Malik as the token Muslim Chairman of the overwhelmingly white Housing Committee. 'That's the Labour Party all over – stuffing Zaheed into the Lord Mayor's robes to fool poor Asian people.'

Malik takes out his notebook. 'You should be top of the list for a full improvement grant, Latifa.'

'Only before an election. After the election, goodbye.'

Her tone astonishes him. Is this really the voice of S.B.'s daughter?

'And you say you've had no grant at all, Sister?'

'Only an intermediate grant which is half the full grant. We need top-to-toe replastering, rewiring, a new roof. We have big rats jumping all over the place.' Latifa plonks milk and sugar on the kitchen table. 'Help yourself, Hani.'

ᧁ

'You will help Daddy, won't you?'

Brighton! The sea, the harsh cries of the gulls over the shopping malls, the wind in Wahabia's flowing hair as she gaily leads a shivering Ali by the hand along the promenade after enforced visits to the Palace Pier and the utterly fantastical West Pier. Mrs Newman's best pupil – until Zulfikar Zaheed despatched his daughter to a girls' boarding school in the South – is in high spirits:

'Tu as froid?'

'One comes south to get chilled to the marrow.'

'But you do want Daddy to be elected to Parliament, don't you?'

'I'm a yogi, Wahabia, a mandarin. I don't share Gamal Rahman's appetite for politics.' They walk on a few paces in silence. 'Who does?' Ali adds.

In Brighton there are more hippies, travellers, communes and 'alternatives' than he's seen in his life: ragged, unwashed young people with long, matted hair and the slow, dazed look of druggies.

'Shall I buy us some Brighton rock?' Wahabia laughs. 'You're a tourist, after all.' She leads him to the Royal Pavilion, a Mogul palace, which he at first mistakes for a mosque, or maybe several mosques. 'Regency,' she says, and drags him to a succession of posh antique shops – as if they were getting married.

'The University of Sussex has done you no good,' he says.

'A room in the Old Ship Hotel can cost seventy pounds a night.' Wahabia squeezes his hand. 'One quarter of your TV fee for proving that Gamal Rahman is a bad boy. Am I worth it?'

He scowls at the aggressively raked green-glass façade of the new Hospitality Inn. Reaching the Grand Hotel, she pulls him inside the front door.

'This is even more expensive. Shall we book a room?'

He hauls her out from under the gaze of uniformed bellboys into the salt-wind: is this a dream orchestrated by Gamal?

'Cheer up, Ali! Don't you know when you're in love – if only for a day?'

In Little East Street she leads him to the Blues Brothers, where live jazz is on offer Friday-Saturday nights and a table d'hôte dinner costs £12.90. Warily he examines the menu in the window. Starters: Boston Clam Chowder, Vegetable Arcadiana, Giant Buckaroos (flat mushrooms). She coaxes him inside and is greeted from almost every table: a royal tour of introductions. He is famous; everyone saw him debating with Gamal Rahman. Down here in the South, in Brighton, in the Blues Brothers, everyone is pro-Rahman and anti-fatwa, but any friend of Wahabia's is welcome and a genuine fundamentalist is a collector's item. A young woman touches his hand: 'Wanted to make sure you're real,' she smiles.

ॐ

Sadar Baj Hussein is due back from Pakistan! All will be resolved!

Nasreen is driving Rajiv Lal's car to meet her father and her young brother, Ishtiaq, at Manchester Airport. Rajiv Lal generously insisted on lending his sacred red Metro, knowing that her husband could not get to work without his Ford Granada. Rajiv gave her a full day's leave of absence, adding a gentle quip:

'If your father can resolve the scarf crisis, you can have a whole week off.'

These words filled Nasreen with guilt as well as gratitude. For several weeks she has been taking every opportunity – but there were few – to tell Rajiv Lal that the scarf crisis would have been quickly solved if Hightown Upper's most influential Governor had not been far away, in Pakistan. Her dad, the renowned S.B.: former District Party Chairman; former Party agent; former City councillor; friend and confidant of Harold Wilson, Jim Callaghan, the Bhuttos, everyone.

But now, as Nasreen took possession of Rajiv's car, his very own car, she wondered.

Hassan wondered, too. He wasn't keen on her driving all the way to Manchester alone. When S.B. and his youngest, Ishtiaq, had set sail three months ago, they had booked on to a weekend flight so that Hassan himself could deliver his father-in-law to the airport.

S.B.'s departure had not been an entirely happy one from Nasreen's point of view. She had begged her dad to talk to Mrs Newman before taking Ishtiaq out of school for three months.

'Am I going to be told which side of bed to lie in by that bloody woman?'

'But Dad! – you're a School Governor! You know how Mrs Newman feels about absenteeism!'

Fathers, husbands, grief.

Nor was Hassan keen on her borrowing Rajiv Lal's car.

'Is it properly insured, Nasreen? Is it in sound working order?'

'Of course.'

'You know these Hindu people – airy-fairy about details.'

'Mr Rajiv Lal is generous.'

'To everyone – or just to you?'

'To everyone, Hassan.'

'And what if you are assaulted while crossing the Pennines?'

'Why should anyone assault me?'

Terrified of breaking down while crossing the high, bleak Pennines, and being raped by white van drivers, Nasreen opts for a dark suit with the hem below the knee, nothing on her head. Hassan Hassani surveys this apparel with mixed feelings: to guard her virtue among barbarians a woman should shroud herself; and not drive about alone in a car belonging to a Hindu who has no business lending it to a married woman.

Hassan insists on personally filling the tank of Mr Lal's red Metro to the brim.

'You will need to refuel on the way back,' he warns her.

'I am not a complete fool, Hassan '

'The car must be returned to Mr Lal with a full tank.'

Tremulously driving up to the 'knobbly backbone of England' – she does not know Mr J.B. Priestley's work – Nasreen shudders as the high moorlands come into view. Inside the car, with the heater on and the radio playing, she feels safe enough, but the road is narrow, the culverts deep. Sadar Baj Hussein has never taken his family weekend-picnicking on Bodkin Top or High Grave or Black Moor or Five Gates End where, Priestley reflected, 'in summer you can wander . . . all day, listening to the larks, and never meet a soul'. Bruddersford's Muslims are not keen on never meeting a soul, and still less keen on the soul you might meet in that void. The djinns of the Pennines are not friendly to dark skins.

Most dreadful of these djinns are the dinosaur lorries carving along the narrow, winding roads at a great pace, driven by big, raw blokes who know every curve and press up close and menacing behind small saloon cars driven by female community teachers. Several times Nasreen feels so unnerved by the pursuing dinosaur

137

that she would gladly hurl herself into a lay-by or side road if there was one.

Manchester is the next nightmare: a menacing cityscape without escape, tangled in ring roads and fly-overs requiring the driver to make instantly correct decisions or be swept for miles into other hells. She pulls into a lay-by and opens the glove box in search of the road map she bought in W.H. Smith's the previous day. She feels sure she put it in the glove box (in fact it's lying on the seat beside her, but covered by her raincoat). With loving awe she probes Rajiv Lal's 'secret compartment', pulling out one sacred item after another (including three cassettes of Hindu and Buddhist mantras) until she comes upon a wallet of photos.

Sadar Baj Hussein's plane from Karachi is almost two hours late. Nasreen sits patiently in the arrivals hall, Rajiv's wallet of photos resting in her handbag. For ten minutes she resists the temptation to have a look. Then she has a look.

The two hours pass slowly. Finally, the flight from Karachi is announced. Pakistani families are pouring through the arrivals gate. She mustn't lose concentration – despite Rajiv Lal's photographs. As soon as she spots her father she knows from his tense, hollowed-out scowl that he's in desperate need of alcohol. He's pushing an airport trolley loaded with suitcases and parcels, gifts and rugs. Hours and hours aboard an Islamic plane in the company of his son have left him jangling. He barely recognizes Nasreen. His greeting is cursory, almost angry. His bloodshot eyes are swivelling desperately down the airport concourse in search of a bar.

She gives her little brother Ishtiaq a hug, which he isn't too keen on; three of his school friends have travelled on the same plane and may be watching.

'Ishtiaq, would you like to come up to the observation platform to see the planes landing and taking off?'

The boy shrugs, hesitates.

'Dad can have a cup of coffee,' she coaxes.

'Go with your sister,' Sadar Baj Hussein commands. 'I will look after the luggage. Back here in fifteen minutes.'

Has he understood her proposal or does he imagine himself the cunning exploiter of a naïve daughter's innocent affection for her brother? She doesn't know. Ishtiaq, who at twelve is old enough to profess mild contempt for plane-watching, perks up as soon as they reach the observation platform and see the jumbos coming in to land. He gives his sister a lecture on control-tower routines, radar and automatic pilots.

'How's Dad?' she asks, against the constant roar of engines.

138

'Wha'?'

'Has Father been well?'

Ishtiaq shrugs. 'He's always disappearing.'

'How do you mean?'

'Taking a leak or something.'

Driving back across the Pennines she feels more relaxed. The bucketing lorries have thinned out. She can no longer be raped. She has remembered to fill the tank of Rajiv's Metro, like Hassan said. She has replaced the wallet of photos in the glove box – keeping one for herself. Will he notice? Had he set a trap? No, no, Rajiv is without guile or malice. Her father's nerves have been eased by the several drinks she can smell on his breath. He talks nonstop, but less of Pakistan and Prime Minister Bhutto than of the other home to which he is returning, the city in which he is a big fish. Everything has gone to pot in his absence: a public book-burning, schisms within the Party, resignations, fratricide:

'A Muslim Independent candidate on my own doorstep!'

'Bruddersford is not a happy place,' she says.

'As soon as my back is turned.'

'Everyone has been awaiting your return.'

'I intend to puncture the whole tyre.'

Not once, between Manchester and Bruddersford, does he ask after his wife or his daughter Latifa. No inquiry about Nasreen's son and husband. Not a word about her job.

'I intend to puncture the whole tyre,' S.B. repeats.

ॐ

Back in London from Brighton, Ali and Wahabia are guests in Jasmin Patel's Knightsbridge flat. 'Gamal would be upset if he knew you were staying here,' Jasmin reminds Ali. 'I've sworn Inigo not to tell him.' With Jasmin, a nervy chain-smoker inclined to solemnity, it's always 'Inigo says this' and 'Inigo says that'. Her telephone rings constantly. Jasmin and Inigo have been filming a demo by the Southall Black Sisters outside the law courts in the Strand, demanding the release of Khadija Khalil, a battered wife who finally stabbed her husband to death, and not before time. The hallway of Jasmin's flat is chock-a-block with photo-posters of Ms Khalil and of Mrs Joshi, a social worker for the elderly who was thrown out of her home by her violent and adulterous husband only eight months after arriving in Britain, thus putting her in breach of the Home Office's notorious '12 month rule', which obliges immigrant brides of British citizens to remain married and living within the marital home for a year.

'I take it, Jasmin, that you are in favour of women leaving their husbands at the first opportunity.'

'What a chauvinist pig you are, Ali. You know as well as we do that the oppressive tradition of izzat forbids a Muslim wife to dishonour the community by reporting a violent husband or relative to the authorities.'

Ali studies Jasmin's wall-to-wall collection of Monstrous Regiment and Naggers wall posters. 'You should come to Bruddersford,' he says.

Jasmin bridles. 'And what news of your Oxford Fellowship? I hear that Gamal has declared himself a candidate.'

'No comment.' Ali has told nobody of the Bishop's most recent advice: 'Make it *abundantly* clear, my dear Ali, that you regard the fatwa as neither wise nor just.'

The phone rings. Jasmin runs to it like a Degas ballerina released from her frame. 'No!' she cries, 'it can't be true, I-do-not-believeeeve this!' She repeats the phrase. She loves deliberate repetition – copies of the *New Yorker* (in whose pages Gamal Rahman has practised the art) pile up on her coffee table. She regards Gamal Rahman as a 'master of narration' whose prose finally acquires an 'incantatory quality'. Jasmin and Wahabia both agree that you 'can't say no' to Gamal's prose. (In *The Devil: an Interview,* Gamal asks Satan to define the perfect female leg. Satan ponders this, while lazily water-skiing in his black wet-suit across the Venice Lido. 'A perfect leg,' he replies, 'must come in a pair. One perfect leg is not terribly attractive. You have to have the pair.')

'I don't believeeeve this!' Jasmin announces to Wahabia and Ali, replacing the receiver for its statutory ten-second rest period. 'More death threats!'

The target, it transpires, is a bookshop called Paper Clips, which has been suffering a 'concerted hate campaign' (Jasmin says, fluttering her hands and lighting a succession of cigarettes, one puff at each) because Paper Clips insists on stocking *Elsie Lives with Ted and Jason.*

'I don't know this book,' Ali says with mock gravity.

'Don't show it to him,' Wahabia warns Jasmin. 'Ali is homophobic.'

Jasmin tosses it into his lap.

'Is it Literature?' he asks. Can Inigo Lorraine really be beguiled by Jasmin's nonstop, quartz-battery animation? With mounting astonishment Ali turns the pages of *Elsie Lives with Ted and Jason.* The centre spread offers him a two-page illustration of a cheerful Elsie sitting up in bed between a cheerful Ted and a cheerful Jason.

'This is really for ten-year-olds?'

'Why not? Elsie is ten. Ted is her dad and Jason is Ted's black boyfriend. It's quite brilliantly done.'

'What happened to Elsie's mother?' Ali asks.

'She and Ted split up. She's the breadwinner so Ted is looking after Elsie, taking her to school, shopping, cooking, washing and ironing – dads can be loving, too.'

'Gays are abhorred under Islam,' Wahabia reminds Jasmin.

And now there has been a bomb threat to Paper Clips and 'everyone, the whole anti-censorship scene', is rushing to Jasmin's flat to confer. Their brochures are piled on her glass coffee table – Gay's the Word, Red & Green Books, Sisterwrite.

'Jasmin,' Ali says, 'you yourself are out and about pulling soft-porn from the shelves of newsagents. So you believe in censorship.'

'Pornography demeans and threatens us as women.'

'There is always a reason for censorship. Someone always feels threatened.'

'I was born female. No one should insult me for what I am.'

'Only for what you believe?'

'I think we've been through this argument before,' Wahabia says, in an effort to keep the peace.

'I am free to be or not to be a Hindu,' Jasmin says. 'That's why I'm not one. You and Wahabia are perfectly free to be or not to be Muslims.'

Ali is dismissive. 'Only under your laws of freedom – yours, Rahman's, Lorraine's – the Liberal inquisition. I am personally not free to become a champagne socialist repudiating the faith of my forefathers.'

'Ali regards Daddy as a champagne socialist,' Wahabia says.

'I'm going for a walk,' Ali says. 'To burn a few bookshops. The Bishop of Wakefield burnt *Jude the Obscure*, you know.'

'You're staying here,' Jasmin says. 'They all want to meet you.'

'I have no desire to rub noses with Ted and Jason. I do not believe that single-parent gay families give one a kick start in life.'

'Ali has lost both his parents,' Wahabia says gently.

'But Ali, I never knew!' cries Jasmin. 'What happened to –' Her last syllable is lost in a scream. Leaning over Wahabia, Ali has given her two sharp slaps to the face.

'I'm sorry,' Wahabia murmurs.

'Don't say you're sorry, Wahabia!' Jasmin cries. 'A man strikes you and you say you're sorry!'

The street door buzzer sounds.

'Perhaps Ali and I should go for a walk,' Wahabia says.

In need of comfort, Hani Malik calls on a local Party activist, Muhammad Maroti, Post Office clerk, originally from Bombay, take-home pay £150 a week. Malik has heard disturbing rumours about Maroti.

'Inshala.' Malik removes his shoes in the hallway. 'How are things, then?'

'Not bad. How are things?'

'Not bad. People are quite responsive.'

'That is good.'

'Yes, it's good. How are things, then?'

'Not bad at all.'

'And your good father and mother?' Malik inquires.

'My father will not last long, though we pray.'

'I pray for him.'

'I will tell my father that you are praying for him.'

There is a discreet knock on the door. Maroti opens it and talks to his wife in the hallway. She remains in the hallway.

'You will have some tea?' Maroti inquires of Malik.

'I must not linger, you know.'

Maroti's wife will bring tea and biscuits, anyway. Maroti closes the door.

'No, a man in your position cannot tarry,' Maroti says politely. Malik is beginning to find him too polite. 'Procrastination is the thief of time,' Maroti adds, beckoning to Malik to sit. The television is on: two young children are absorbed by the screen; Malik thinks they are sitting too close, bad for their eyes, so he says:

'I read today that doctors have discovered children are sitting too close to TV.'

Maroti tells the children to shift back across the floor, as if he had issued the same instruction a hundred times. The children shift back an inch or two. Not for the first time today Hani Malik attempts to banish his wife's recent comment that he might give his own children as much attention as everyone else's.

'I hope you will be with us in this election,' Malik says.

'I am a Labour man.'

'You are, Brother.'

'All my life in this city.'

'We need your help.'

'But this Gamal Rahman business is very bad.'

'We have tried to have this filthy book banned from the libraries.'

'But Neil Kinnock is supporting Rahman.'

'He has been misreported by the Tory press.'

Maroti doesn't buy that: 'He's not even agreeing with his own deputy, Hattersley. But Hattersley is another hypocrite – he has Muslim constituents.'

'Believe me, Brother, if we were the Government . . .' Malik can smell Haqq in this room, too.

'Now what about this poll tax?' Maroti says.

'It's a Tory, tax, Brother, you know that.'

'I know it. But Bruddersford Labour Council is setting the level. We used to pay 250 pounds rates here with four or five adults, and now each adult is paying 344 pounds each. Who can foot such a bill?'

'There are big reductions for the old people and anyone out of work, you know.'

'This isn't big bungalow with two people – they're sitting pretty now, those people up in Mount Pleasant. It's the last straw all round. We here will be running for dear life.'

'You have been listening to Haqq, Brother.'

'Yes, he was here. Frankly, what with this Rahman business, a Muslim candidate is quite an attractive proposition. To help people lift themselves rather than indulging in drink and drugs.'

'I'm a good Muslim.'

'But Kinnock is an atheist. He is supporting Rahman because Rahman insulted the Prime Minister. In the past we were all believing that Labour was for the Muslims but then that Jew, Michael Foot, spat in our faces.'

'He did not spit, brother. He was misquoted. He is not a Jew either. I have written to Kinnock. Lord Mayor Zaheed has written also. Did you not see our Ali Cheema debating with Rahman on TV?'

'Killing him is better than debating.'

'There are laws, Brother. Ali was killing him with words.'

'But Ali Cheema is not a Labour man. What are Labour people doing about this book? And what about the halal meat? That's an issue.'

'Soon all the City schools will provide halal meat. That is our policy.'

'I hear they are buying Zionist meat from the Jewish supermarkets. My children are still eating vegetarian lunches at Hightown Upper. We have protested many times.'

'I will speak to Mrs Newman.'

'Frankly, it is not in Mrs Newman's hands. That Jew Perlman will not give us halal meat. And now the Director of Education is that Hindu, Rajiv Lal. No hope for us Muslims there.'

'I assure you there is an agreed timetable for halal.'

143

'What about these "scarf" cases in the schools? I hear that these good Muslim girls are being sent home.'

'Unfortunately there are regulations.'

'They still want to send our daughters to the swimmings. I went to speak to Mrs Newman about it. That lady is frankly most intransigent. The Labour people are saying boys and girls must be the same. They are spreading homosexuality and Aids.'

A discreet tap at the door. Maroti brings the tea tray from the door to the table. Tiring cathode-ray lights bounce off the blonde heroine of the afternoon Western and on to the sombre browns and blues of the wall-tapestry depicting the Kaaba, the house of God first built by Ibrahim. Prior to the Islamic era, the pagan priests filled the Kaaba with idols – the great sin of Shirk, making partners to God, which God cannot forgive. Now the pagan cowboys are tumbling out of the saloon and galloping towards the Kaaba, shooting. Malik is restless; a man like Maroti carries influence.

'Brother,' Malik says, 'how many Muslims live in Britain?'

'They say one million. We know two million.'

'You can have the two million. We can achieve nothing by the road of separatism. If brothers like Haqq hoodwink our people, the Tories will be doing the laughing.'

'Gamal Rahman is attacking Mrs Thatcher. He is calling her Mrs Torment. The Prime Minister has said she regrets his book.'

'But she is refusing to ban it, Brother. She is refusing to extend the Blasphemy Act to protect Islam. Her Home Secretary is telling us to go back to Pakistan.'

Maroti nods. 'And now Comrade Lucas calls us all corrupt fundamentalists.'

Malik sighs. He's been waiting for this – if Maroti wasn't a good bloke, and tactful by nature, friendly, he'd probably have raised it earlier. Malik's neat, compact, Japanese transistor had been routinely tuned in to the usual ongoing local news chatter the previous evening when Lucas had decided to part company with sanity. There are no family conversations in the Malik household without Dad cocking his ear at the radio. Hearing Lucas's suicidal sentence while eating high tea, Malik had promptly found a reason to slap his elder son. 'Islamic fundamentalism thrives on corruption!' declares City Labour leader Lucas. 'Bribery is normal practice in the Muslim world!'

And sure enough BBC Bruddersford had Tory leader Tom Potter on a telephone link within minutes: 'Frankly, I'm disgusted. Trevor Lucas has insulted the entire Muslim community of this city. The Labour Group is in chaos. My advice to the voters of this long-suffering city is to get rid of them.'

Malik accompanies Maroti to prayers in the brand-new Masjid-E-Noorul Mosque in Paradise Street, off New Hall Road. As he approaches the mosque he sees a group of young Muslims grouped round a furiously gesticulating Tariq Khan. Malik decides to cut evening prayers. Cutting them is a habit of a lifetime, despite membership of the Islamic Council. He climbs into his car, offering Maroti a brotherly salute. At the New Hall Road intersection he crosses the invisible boundary between Tanner and Jethro Ward, entering tidy streets of nice 'white' houses, his blood pressure rising as he spots Trevor Lucas and Ted Francis lapping up congratulations on Trevor's radio performance.

'Don't let them bloody Pakis take you over, son,' Malik hears as he climbs out of his car.

Lucas lays a hand on his arm, leading him out of voter-earshot. 'Frankly, Hani, Haqq's Urdu leaflets blew my mind.'

Malik goes broad Yorkshire: 'That's a bit o' glad tidings, any road.'

'Trevor was misunderstood,' Ted Francis says aggressively – as if he were Lucas's personal agent and not the Party's.

Malik slaps him aside. 'Hey, Ted, I hear you told Yaqub Quddus that Haqq's leaflets were written in "Muslim".'

'When I first joined the Southend Labour Party twenty years ago, I didn't know I had to be a graduate in Oriental languages.'

Lucas is gripping the arms of both men. 'Cut it out, lads. My point, lousily expressed, is that Islamic fundamentalism thrives *in opposition* to social systems where corruption is endemic.'

'Pity you didn't say so, Trevor. I've been battered on every doorstep all day long. Frankly, I'm running out of card tricks.'

'The truth is, Hani, you, Zaheed and S.B. Hussein commonly use the term "fundamentalism" among yourselves.'

'Aye. Among ourselves. African politicians will murder you for using the word "tribalist" while freely throwing it at their opponents.' Malik leans across the bonnet of Lucas's campaign car. 'I am a fundamentalist. And I'll tell you why. Because I don't drink alcohol, I don't dress my daughter in a miniskirt, I send my sons to the mosque, and I don't condone a blasphemous, filthy, insulting book in the name of "freedom of expression".'

'I've issued a correction, Hani. Thirty thousands leaflets in Urdu and Punjabi. It'll all blow over.'

Malik doesn't want to prolong the quarrel. He does and he doesn't. Trevor's OK. But Malik has already seen too many Haqq stickers in cars, too many Muslim Independent posters in ground-floor windows. His conversation with Maroti has shaken him.

'Trevor, I am clinging to this Party of ours by the skin of my teeth.

Fifteen per cent of this city is Muslim, yet we have only five Muslim councillors out of one hundred and one. That's our problem. That's the wicket on which Haqq is bowling.'

෯

Asleep in Wahabia's arms under Jasmin's roof, Ali dreams himself down purgatorial corridors. Safia brazenly begs him to bring her south, to London, where her body may open its wares to money and – she insists – freedom. Slit-skirted, painted for battle, she pursues him to Bruddersford Central Station and hurls herself into his carriage, where every passenger is wearing an Oxford gown and reading *The Devil: an Interview*. The back jacket portrait of Gamal Rahman stares at him with bulging eyes for three hours while Safia perches herself on the knee of one don after another, like a bitch run amok in a vegetable allotment.

'Can't you put her on her lead?' Bishop Goodgame remonstrates from the High Table. 'Your position is rapidly becoming untenable, Cheema.' Flames flicker in silver candlesticks, Elizabethan mullioned windows shatter.

Reaching King's Cross at the end of the journey, Safia hands him a wad of banknotes: 'Take yer cut.'

He runs from her down the platform but cannot run. Safia is glued to him like a leg-splint. Finding himself in Trafalgar Square, he despairingly hauls her into the National Gallery but she immediately begins soliciting among the Impressionists and they are chased out by two dons claiming to be Manet and Monet. Emerging, they are enveloped by a party of French schoolchildren carrying colourful haversacks. Ali hears Bruddersford's most famous Headteacher, Mrs Patricia Newman, asking them to identify the figure on the top of the high column in Trafalgar Square, the man in the tricorn hat.

'Napoléon!' they shout. 'Vive Napolayon!'

Ali runs again but Safia rides his back, her gorgeous legs gripping his waist in black fishnet stockings. A few yards down Whitehall she pursues him into The New Chamber of Horrors, a waxworks museum presenting 'Holocaust' and 'Meet the Devil'. The Bishop is selling tickets.

'Ah,' he says, 'Ah. Is this lady your sister or your whore?'

Ali articulates a carefully considered reply but cannot hear it. He plunges through a curtain into a macabre tunnel of strobe lights, Safia clinging to his arm, and is immediately confronted by a talking head of the Ayatollah jerking his fatwa while his eyes roll. In the next cubicle a satanic Gamal Rahman is found cutting up the Koran with a giant pair of scissors, his oily voice repeating, at three-second intervals:

'Who – me?'

'Oooo,' moans Safia, 'I don't like it here.'

Move on: the waxwork Rahman jerks his hand back and forth, jabbing a needle into the eye of the Prophet (a handsome, bearded fellow who keeps getting his eye back again). The College dons are applauding: 'Do it again!'

Move on: the waxwork Rahman gloatingly rubs the dollars in his hands as back projections show Muslim demonstrators lying dead in the streets of Karachi.

Move on: the Last Supper. The twelve disciples all wear Oxford gowns (not a Cambridge man among them). Ali recognizes the Bishop in the guise of the Saviour, but it is Rahman's voice which comes at regular, metronomic, intervals:

'Which of you will betray me?'

Move on: the Bishop hangs on the cross, comforted by whores. Safia is masturbating him. His face jerks from an agonized grimace to a leering grin and back: grimace, grin, grimace . . . The strobe lighting is frenetic.

Ali and Safia pass through another curtain. The continuous din from the loudspeaker system is abruptly snuffed out: total silence. Green light, no strobe. Gamal Rahman is strapped into an electric chair. Place one pound in the waxwork Khomeini's mouth and you get an ear-to-ear smile, a display of teeth, before heavenly bolts strike down the author. Blood runs from his eyes and ears.

Safia is tugging at Ali's arm, demanding attention:

'Don't yer fancy me, then?'

Wahabia is stroking his brow. 'You've been dreaming,' she murmurs. 'What were you dreaming, darling?'

૭౿

Hassan Hassani sits alone far into the night, his family asleep, Shaytan Rahman chased out from under Imran's bed. Hassan labours on (and on) his masterly pamphlet, 'Satan Speaks', still sifting-searching Rahman's book for four-letter words. They crawl up at him like lice, maggots, cockroaches, peeling off this new-rich author's pages, wriggling their legs in the air.

Write, Hassan, write!

Because of the emotional (deleted: emotive) word 'fuck' Colonel T.E. Lawrence's autobiographical novel, Lady Chatterley and Her Lover, was banned in British-ruled South Africa for twenty years

147

even though the famous author was a born-again Crusader who had been flogged and worse by the 'Infidel' (Muslim) Turks in the Holy Land.

Hassan is sucking his pen again, uneasy about the spelling of Chatterley. His porthole lenses hover close over the page (at Nasreen's request he has installed a 60-watt bulb for the normal 100-watt). English spelling! No rhyme or reason, but what pride in mastering it! He glances in the direction of his recumbent wife and notices the curve of her hip beneath the covers. A perplexing desire invades him: to talk to her, to confide, to share his great work with her. Burning, he writes:

What grates me most is the rank hypocrisy of the one thousand and one Poets, Playwrights and Pimps; Editors, Essayists and Eunuchs; Novelists, Newspapermen and Nonconformists who signed and paid for adverts in the National Newspapers in support of Rahman's absolute freedom of speech and expression. Yet not a single one of those thousand will raise an eyebrow to defend Colonel T.E. Lawrence's Lady Chatterly and Her Lover.

Nasreen's dark hair is strewn across her pillow, spilling on to his own, as if inviting his embrace, her tender lips faintly parted as she sleeps.

He drags his attention to Rahman's obscene jibes at Mrs Thatcher. He admires Maggie. Her gender, as a Leader, causes him no offence because, unlike that Benazir Bhutto bitch, she is a great lady and a Christian. When she paid an official visit to Saudi Arabia she wore the correct clothes and he, Hassan, was gratified to observe, on television, the Saudi princes receiving her with full honours. Indeed Hassan's British heart had swelled with pride: she was his Prime Minister, she was Britain. She behaved correctly; she was received correctly; there was mutual respect; he was moved. He imagined this great lady calling at his own humble house: he would show respect; she would show respect; she would not be veiled; he would understand that it was not her culture. He would understand her bright make-up, like the Queen's. Benazir Bhutto's bright make-up is an offence against Islam.

And what does Gamal Rahman write about the Right Honourable Mrs Prime Minister? Carefully Hassan fingers through his 'Thatcher' markers. Nothing the least bit respectful. What can one expect from an author who drops 'fucks' into his paragraphs without the least

148

thought for decency? Diligently Hassani copies down the page references of his 'fuck' markers:

Seventy-one fucks and fuckings in what the Western world has called a literary masterpiece. List follows (for gentlemen readers only): Fucking Americans... fucking Argentina... fucking Beatles... fucking bedpan... fucking class... fucking creep... fucking clowns... fucking commandos... fucking diff... fucking dynasty... fucking dogs... fucking dreams... enjoy fucking... fucking guitar... fucking horny... fucking hellhole... fucking idiot... fucking tank... fucking pee aitch dee...

It's late. The house is at rest. His father, his wife, and Imran sleep unaware that Shaytan Rahman is perched on Hassan's bedroom desk. On the ground floor the kitchen is clean, cleared, washed, but pleasant odours linger, a family at home: this Rahman no longer has a family, no longer a home. He is Outcast. Hunted. Hassan again studies his sleeping wife through owl-eyes. Her beauty and innocence move him. These seventy-one fucks and fuckings have invaded his private parts. There is definitely a stirring down there. Now Hassan is standing over the bed, stroking Nasreen's lustrous hair, unaware of the absurd smile pulling at his damp mouth.

'Nasreen.'

No response.

'Nasreen.'

'Hm?'

'It is Hassan – your husband.'

'Come to bed, Hassan, you're tired.'

'This Gamal Rahman is the devil.'

'Hm.'

'Listen to what he writes, Nasreen. "Why you enjoy fucking with this one... You are fucking my woman... Don't holy men ever fuck?... God's own permission to fuck... Wild donkeys fucking wearily and dropping dead still conjoined... The sister fucking British." '

'Come to bed, Hassan. You are exhausted, so much driving every day.'

His heart lifts at her tender concern. And she's right! – those roads, lay-bys, prayers, the sneering motor cycle brigade in leather and ugly tattoos, poised to beat him up as he kneels – always imminent, on the cards. Any day now he will be delivered in an ambulance to his weeping family, battered – dead!

'The so-called Western World! Bastards!' he cries. 'Eighty lashes!'

'Hassan,' Nasreen murmurs. The most beautiful of bare arms is extended to him. Her soft flesh gleams modestly under the 60 watts.

'Do you know what he says about Her Majesty the Queen, Nasreen?'

Nasreen is sitting up in bed; her nightdress hangs tantalizingly on the softly sloping curve of her shoulders, drifting down across her full bosom.

'Come to bed.'

'Nasreen, listen to this. The British do not realize what their precious Egyptian idol, Gamal Rahman, is serving up.'

She yawns. 'I'm listening, Hassan.'

Hassan is dripping with sweat. His balding head burns with shame and desire. Nasreen is the defamed Maggie and the dishonoured Queen. He has his shoes off now, then his trousers.

' "Fine ladies are only good for discarding after fucking," Rahman informs us!'

He falls into the bed, covering her – and all the fine ladies of England – with wet kisses. It's all over in seconds, a sparrow's spurt, before he tumbles into snoring sleep.

Nasreen takes herself to the bathroom, unscrews a bottle of colourless surgical spirit, and swabs herself. If she has Rajiv's baby now, Hassan will never know it isn't his.

She eases herself back into her side of the bed. All she has from Rajiv Lal is the stolen photograph she cannot bring herself to burn.

TEN

⤷

Joe Reddaway heaves himself out of his car. The ragged ribbon of refuse dumps known as the Knightley Road is about to yield to the dismal mud patches and clumps of brambles which pass for countryside or 'green belt'. Some malign giant has layered the beautyspot in a film of grey soot – probably Gamal Rahman.

Abdul Ayub Khan's halal slaughterhouse is found five miles west of the city. The rusting iron gates are closed, padlocked. A vicious-looking dog strains at its chain, barking furiously. The stench would stop Joe in his tracks even if the Alsatian didn't. The slaughterhouse despatches cattle, sheep, lambs and, by repute, inquisitive RSPCA inspectors.

An Asiatic character with the contours of a wrestler is slowly approaching the gate from within, wiping huge hands on a blood-stained apron. He quietens the dog but makes no move to unlock the gate.

'I have come see Mr Abdul Ayub Khan,' Joe announces.

'Mr Khan with sick auntie Pakistan. You come back.'

The tin roof of the halal slaughterhouse is black with carrion crows. A vulture or two would be no surprise.

'Come back when?'

But 'when' is an obscure motion. The brute shrugs, walks away. The dog resumes its barking. Retreating to his car, pursued by the bellowing and screaming of the livestock within, Joe imagines the terrified beasts shackled by the hind leg and hoisted up high on a continuous overhead conveyor. Courtesy of Samuel Perlman, the *Echo* is now in possession of a report from the Department of Agriculture:

'The visitor can be in no doubt that the animals are driven to a state of panic and terror. The torrential flow of blood into a trough in full view of the other animals is both inhumane and contrary to Islamic rules.'

An interview with Abdul Ayub Khan would be easy enough to

obtain but what Joe really wants is a nice photo of the Muslim Independent candidate standing beside a dying beast in a pool of blood – preferably under a halo of carrion crows. A pity it has to be Abdul Ayub Khan. Joe has known him for years and has a soft spot for the ex-corporal's crazy interpretations of the Koran – a generous man, kinder to orphans than to animals, which is of course intolerable to the English. More than once Joe has been invited to the Khan household to inspect the celebrity letters, the signed photograph from President Ronald Reagan and his First Lady, thanking Abdul Ayub Khan for his good wishes, not forgetting the letter from General Zia himself (when still alive) on the subject of Kashmir. This was followed by the letter from the Acting President of Pakistan thanking Abdul Ayub Khan for his message of commiseration on the death in violent and suspicious circumstances of President General Zia ul-Haqq. But it was the Thatcher collection which took the prize: her *very personal* thanks for Mr Abdul Ayub Khan's congratulations on her election victories in 1979, 1983 and 1987, with more, no doubt, to come, well into the twenty-first century.

Driving back to town, distempered by a wasted hour, Joe is composing his 'Plain Speaking' column.

So this is the state of the halal art in Yorkshire. This is what Mr Abdul Ayub Khan and his puppet master Ishmail Haqq want to foist on the city's unsuspecting Muslims.

෧෨

S.B. is home. His telephone line hums. Harry Flowers, MP, once styled S.B. 'the deliverer', who could be counted on to deliver a branch meeting, a ward election, a parliamentary constituency, a handsome donation to Party funds from a local businessman. There was no nonsense about S.B., he was straight down the line, steady at the helm, always the first over the top – and no 'religious nonsense'. But all that was some time ago; no one knows how long, least of all S.B.

Now he will settle everything, puncture every inflated tyre.

S.B. calls Hani Malik: 'Why are you worrying about Haqq?'

'Things are frankly very bad, S.B.'

'And now they will listen to me. I am out on the streets already. Even as I speak to you I am out on the streets. I will wipe Haqq out. Wipe him.'

S.B. calls Haqq, gets no reply, leaves a message on the answerphone demanding a return call 'pronto'. None comes. S.B. calls again, summoning Haqq to a conference at S.B.'s home, Tuesday, 7.30, 'pronto'.

'Fail to attend,' S.B. warns the answerphone after the bleep, 'and I'll issue a bloody fatwa of my own.'

Hani Malik arrives first, followed by Yaqub Quddus out of breath. S.B. has not invited any whites: this is something for Muslims of the Labour Party to settle among themselves. Karamat Khan and his brother Abdul Ayub Khan come next, looking as happy as tyres facing imminent puncture, sheepish, reluctant to glance at Malik. S.B. forces them to shake hands with Hani Malik. What he can't impose is eye contact.

'So where's Haqq?' S.B. demands of the Khan brothers.

'We are hoping he will come,' says Abdul Ayub Khan.

'I am more than hoping,' S.B. says. 'I am bloody well hopping.'

S.B. embarks on an extended report of his visit to Pakistan, now under the progressive governance of Ms Benazir Bhutto. S.B. is general secretary of the regional branch of the Pakistan People's Party (600 members) – the plum in the pie of his power-base.

'Benazir is working very hard, you know,' S.B. tells them. 'She is an Oxford graduate through-and-through.'

'Extremely hard,' says Dr Quddus. 'But much to do, frankly. Unfinished business.'

Karamat Khan nods politely. 'I hear so.'

'But her enemies are active,' S.B. growls.

'She has enemies.' Abdul Ayub Khan concurs.

'The Jamiyat.'

Clearly the Khan brothers would rather be anywhere than in S.B.'s living room, but they feel bound by the habits and hierarchies of the years. S.B. tightens the screw:

'The Jamiyat are active here, too. You boys don't want to be playing the game of the Islamic Council. Izza Shah, Mustafa Jangar, Hassan Hassani, all Jamiyat, all pro-Zia fundamentalists. Not that I'm saying a word against my own son-in-law, he's merely a simpleton.'

'Haqq is making a clear bid for Jamiyat support,' Hani Malik says.

'That renegade, that turncoat, that hoodwinker!'

Everyone knows that if Haqq walked through the door, S.B. would embrace him warmly. Haqq's main crime is not to be walking through the door. Abruptly S.B. turns on Malik:

'And what is all this palaver over Brother Khan's halal slaughterhouse?'

'Frankly, S.B. – '

'They say you are up to your neck in this conspiracy to ruin my brother here, Abdul Ayub Khan.'

'Any days now I am in the dock, in handcuffs,' Abdul Ayub Khan adds. Neither he nor Karamat has made eye contact with Hani Malik since entering S.B.'s living room.

'This is a Ministry of Agriculture inquiry,' Malik says drily. 'Nothing to do with me.'

'When was I born?' S.B. bellows. 'You are running with that Jew Perlman.'

Malik's back stiffens. 'Brother, if you are now running with our Muslim Independent renegades against your Labour Party brothers, then the sooner we all know your position the better.'

S.B. is chastened. Malik normally shows him deference.

'Frankly, Brothers,' says S.B., 'Islam is protected by Allah and doesn't require us to make monkeys of ourselves.'

'Agreed,' the ever-forgotten Quddus chips in, 'wisely put. In Britain you don't mix politics with religion. You don't go running around the streets pretending to be the Hidden Imam.'

'But we Muslims have been driven into a corner,' S.B. says, changing tack again, mainly to teach Quddus to save his speeches for lesser mortals. 'I have spoken to Harry Flowers.' S.B. pauses impressively – he was once Flowers's election agent. 'Harry assures me that the Rahman book can be dealt with under the Race Relations Act.'

This is too much for Karamat Khan. 'No one worked harder for Flowers in '83 and '87 than me. Unfortunately he now marches in step with the atheist Party leadership in London.'

'Harry is no leftist,' S.B. rebukes Karamat – 'leftist' being a word that he customarily brackets with 'homosexual', 'promiscuous' and 'Aids'. 'Harry is pragmatic. He has not forgotten us. Harry is no leftist.' S.B. despises the London Labour scene with its gays and lesbians and feminists and atheists. All that 'flaunting' loses votes. S.B. once informed the general committee of Tanner Ward that Martin Luther had condemned sodomy, adding, 'Have you heard about Luther?'

Zaheed arrives late, aloof and patrician. S.B. offers him the best chair. S.B.'s wife taps on the living room door, bringing a tray of tea and sweets. S.B. steps outside to collect it.

'So what have we decided?' Zaheed inquires sardonically.

'We have decided that this should never have happened,' S.B. says.

'Very wise.'

A long silence.

S.B. had worked for years in the textile mills while hauling himself through five years of exhausting night study to a diploma in 'Social Analysis and Community Studies' at Bruddersford University. A fine man, a fine arbitrator, once famous for banging heads together

154

through a long night. That was before the drink problem crept up on him.

Zaheed reaches into his attaché case and distributes some sheets of paper, not moving from his chair, forcing the others to rise.

'I have this evening issued this statement to the national press.'

ZULFIKAR ZAHEED TO STAND FOR SELECTION AS LABOUR CANDIDATE, WEST BRUDDERSFORD PARLIAMENTARY CONSTITUENCY

As Lord Mayor of this City, and a Labour Party member for twenty years, I believe it is high time that the Asian Community of this country sent its first elected Member to the House of Commons. All Asians remain second-class citizens. Our anguished feelings and legitimate demands have been arrogantly ignored. We have encountered a breathtaking indifference at best, naked racism at worst. We have twenty nationalities and a dozen faiths in the Parliamentary constituency of Bruddersford West. Conciliation is always preferable to confrontation. It is time that the Labour Party represented the minorities whose votes it seeks.
Zulfikar Zaheed

Enticing smells from the kitchen. Will S.B. invite his guests to dine with him? His wife, Razia Hussein, mother of Nasreen, Latifa and Ishtiaq, is preparing a meal for six guests just in case. But djinns warn her that S.B. will any moment walk out of the house on some pretext or another, or his guests, observing his trembling hands, his rising temper, will leave. All this shopping and cooking has left Razia exhausted; her Nasreen and her Latifa keep telling her that she's too old to continue working in the textile mill, but where would the household money come from if she quit? Yes, too old to leave the house at seven every winter morning, but what can she do? If the Tories come in, that Sir Potter, S.B. could lose his job in the Community Affairs Department. Their home is poorly furnished and carpeted in odd rugs, mats, bits of cast-off. Mother and daughters know why: S.B. is spending ten, fifteen pounds every evening in that hotel bar for white people.

Latifa is weary too, but she cannot desert her mother with five hungry guests in the house. (Not that Zulfikar Zaheed would consent to dine with the family rats.) Her love for her father has gradually turned to anger; she can excuse his weakness and she can understand his pride, his delusions, but his refusal to confront her mother's exhaustion she can no longer forgive. A slender girl with small bones and a hollow chest, Latifa looks younger than her twenty-four years.

155

Unlike her sister Nasreen, she has only the LRSC in Chemistry, equivalent to part 1 of the GRSC.

'Oh!' she cries.

That giant rat! Right in the middle of the floor! Insolently staring at her! Would an improvement grant from the Council dispose of him?

The Hussein kitchen is plagued by rats as large as kittens. They have gnawed right through the skirting; Latifa no longer dares to come downstairs for a glass of water at night.

In the sitting room everyone is unhappy. Zaheed keeps glancing at his watch. He has thrown his hat into the ring. He has left no stone unturned for conciliation. He has carried the last straw on his back. He has constantly reminded his friends, more haste, less speed. But also: no use locking the stable door after the horse has bolted. A stitch in time saves nine. Zaheed recrosses his legs; the creases in the trousers of his blue suit are perfect. His good shoes gleam. Zaheed stands up. Stands up to stand for Parliament.

'S.B., you must excuse me. Much unfinished business.'

Zaheed's unfinished business coils like a worm through S.B.'s entrails. This pretentious bastard was once his humble protégé in the labyrinth of city politics. His pupil!

'In ten, twenty years there will have to be a dictator in this country,' S.B. announces.

Everyone has risen, anxious to leave.

'In ten, twenty years we will all go to the gas chambers here,' S.B. says. 'You can't say anything positive about Hitler here or you are killed. And they call this a democracy. Did Hitler kill six million Jews? Impossible. Zionist propaganda. One million maybe. He killed some.'

His hands tremble. He needs to get away, up the hill, past the pleasant landscaped park, to his exclusive saloon bar.

'S.B. Hussein will not be insulted by a Jewish pederast atheist who is in bed with Kinnock,' he declares.

No one is sure who he means. Zaheed has already departed. Everyone else is edging towards the sitting room door. Outside, on the street, Hani Malik will not speak to the Khan brothers. A failed meeting of reconciliation is worse than none.

'I have had enough of insults!' S.B. is shouting at the backs of his guests. 'When Nasreen was twelve a white teacher smacked her because she would not go into the swimming pool naked. Naked! I went down there to beat up that teacher but she was a woman. And now that Mrs Newman is carpeting me because I took my own son to the land of my forefathers. Me! – the longest-serving Governor of that bloody school.'

~

A crowd of people is pressing into the Royal Court Theatre. Two writers are posing for photographers, smiling and smiling. Their play will be performed tonight – world première! Rory McKenzie, editor of *Prospero*, wears a leather jacket and a face like Sunday dinner. The other writer is a mustachioed expatriate Indian dressed in a V-neck pullover and an elegant blue blazer. Jasmin flutteringly embraces them; they smile at Wahabia; they ignore her unwelcome, leprous escort, Ali Cheema.

Ali has read the Indian writer's advance self-promotion in *Time Out*. Evidently this famous champagne socialist had recently run into some Pakistanis at Heathrow airport. 'I am recognized and almost mobbed. They invite me to Bruddersford to talk some more. I invite them to the Royal Court.'

All around him Ali hears strange southern greetings and exclamations most of which boil down to 'Aaaaaah'. Everyone is greeting everyone. Jasmin keeps saying 'Hi!', and 'Aaaaah!', and 'I don't belieeeve it!' to people clad in the suede, leather and denim uniforms of the non-believers' banquet.

'Did you hear!' a young woman is yelling at Jasmin. 'Steve got married!'

'Steve! Married! Impossible.'

'Everyone's getting married! It's an epidemic! Steve even invited his parents to the wedding!'

For this, the press night, Jasmin had predicted a strong police presence but there isn't a uniform in sight. 'The Chelsea police wardrobe is a veritable théâtre de la complicité,' Wahabia murmurs in Ali's ear, pulling him through the jam-packed glass doors (which no one is bright enough to prop open – Southerners are not very clever after all).

Inigo Lorraine arrives. Heads try not to turn. It isn't done to stare at the famous at close quarters. Only the unfamous do it. Jasmin kisses Inigo dramatically.

'But where's Susan?' she cries.

'Susie is still down in the country but she may surface next week if she decides not to make her long-delayed famine-relief visit to Ethiopia.'

Ali notes the sardonic note, which sounds laboured. Wahabia whispers to him that 'Susie' is the rising young National Theatre star, Susan Gainsborough, the subject of a forthcoming documentary film

157

produced by Jasmin for 'Final Call'. Jasmin thinks Inigo has been seeing Susan beyond the call, or final call, of duty.

Jasmin's party, Ali at the rear, is trailing behind the two writers through the lobby. As they descend a flight of stairs lined with photographs of distinguished actors, Ali reflects that his last visit to the Royal Court had been in the company of Gamal Rahman, the main point of the evening being – as it transpired – a visit to the dressing room of Susan Gainsborough.

'She's a minor masterpiece,' Gamal had confided, eyes popping. 'She's built to hang – it's a short hop from the Nat Theatre to the Nat Gallery.'

Gamal Rahman will not be putting in an appearance this evening. His minders are not interested in minor masterpieces. As the audience settle into their seats, Ali leans across Wahabia to Jasmin.

'The Alhambra Theatre in Bruddersford has a great velvet curtain.'

'Curtains have been out since Brecht,' Jasmin says, tongue-swirling her chewing gum.

(At this juncture a bearded pharmacist slips unnoticed into a seat in the back row of the stalls. Iqbal Iqbal has made the journey from Bruddersford by train and spent the afternoon making sketches of the Reading Room of the British Museum – his next target. He lays his Koran on his knee and removes his false beard. The faint smile he wears bears an uncanny resemblance to Gamal Rahman's.)

The auditorium lights go down. The scene is a small front room in a northern town. There are two characters. The Father is a retired mill worker. The Son, who wears a smart business suit, rapidly resumes his life: so 'brilliant at calculus' that he attended Oxbridge University, he was one day walking with his English girlfriend when he was beaten up by the drunken Rugger Club, stripped, abused as a circumcised 'wog' and urinated upon.

'That night I vowed I would never again be treated as a "wog". I picked up my Koran after many years of neglect.'

Ali smiles sardonically: 'Allah akhbar,' he says loudly. Someone in the row behind hushes him.

The Son informs his dad that he has joined the 'Party of Islam'. It has 'five hundred secret members and ten thousand sympathizers waiting for the call of the imam.'

The Father looks sad and sceptical.

'This nation can be saved,' the Son says. 'The infidels of these islands must embrace Islam.'

'Protocols of the Elders of Zion reheated,' Ali announces. Heads turn in a fine blend of irritation and nervousness.

'Already they go in terror of us,' the Son tells the Father. 'A blasphemous book is immolated and the unbelievers cringe. Already members of the Cabinet have mumbled their apologies. Soon they will grovel.'

Ali is scribbling notes. He has already underlined the preface to the printed script-programme, which quotes W.H. Auden: 'Intellectual disgrace/Stares from every human face.' The Labour Party is chastised for its 'craven' failure to stand up to Islamic fundamentalism. Evidently Gamal Rahman is both the devil and the deep sea to this wretched Labour Party.

The Muslim Son, meanwhile, goes on strutting about the stage in his flash suit and platform heels, sneering at the infidels: 'A few threats, and liberty is discarded. Their scribes melt into blobs of jelly. They hasten to disown this troublesome punk poet, Gamal Rahman. They tear their own tongues out!'

Ali is wondering who, exactly, had torn their tongues out and grovelled. Certainly not the Ministers of the Crown who warned Muslims to obey British laws or 'go home'. Certainly not the Rt. Hon. Neil Kinnock – or Harry Flowers, Trevor Lucas and Samuel Perlman. Certainly not Joe Reddaway or the editorial writers of the national press.

A glance tells him that Wahabia is not happy with this play, either. The southern sun glows only so long.

Meanwhile, on stage, the villainy of the Son is growing arms and legs by the minute. This fascistic fundamentalist is also a capitalist crook! His good Father remonstrates: 'You talk like this yet you fly on Concorde to the Gulf every month.'

'Allah's work,' snaps the Son.

'Allah's work my arse. You're a racketeer greasing British arms sales to the Saudi monarchy. For you the green of Islam is the colour of the Great Satan's dollars. Your "Party of Islam" in the UK is a protection racket preying on honest shopkeepers.'

'Allah akhbar,' Ali says louder still, sending a current of tension down the ranks of the stalls. These people have all been very brave to come here; anything might happen – a bomb, a shooting, a dreadful massacre of the actors.

Wahabia is troubled, Jasmin glowing. Ali himself can think of no Bruddersford Muslim who flies to the Gulf – or anywhere – on Concorde. It takes them years to save up for a charter flight to Mecca. A 'tycoon' in Bruddersford owns a restaurant and a halal slaughterhouse – Abdul Ayub Khan, for example, but Abdul is hardly into Cadillacs, Concordes, and transnational crime.

'This is shit,' Ali declares.

A theatre attendant is shining a torch along their row, searching for 'the Arab'. Heads are anxiously turned. But Ali is seated in the middle of the jam-packed row and to get rid of him would bring the production to a halt.

Ali is counting the attacks on mullahs, imams, caliphs and ayatollahs, all of whom are evidently usurpers alien to the authors' vision of a libertarian 'true Islam'. He scribbles again: 'The champagne socialist version of the "true Islam" is an alternative, Channel 4-type Sufi Islam, wine, women and song. One is reminded of the degenerate Indian Mughal painting, c. 1700, "Woman Holding Wine Cup". The Mughals believed themselves to be Muslims, but were awash with Hindu pictorial lechery – call it pornography. Depiction of the human figure, not least bare-breasted and celebrating Bacchus, is idolatrous. Rules are essential, even if not always easy to justify (I mean explain).'

༄

Latifa's anger is accompanied by a physical recoil – you can smell S.B.'s breath at a mile. And her father no longer knows, cares, what she is doing with her life. Sometimes he calls her 'Nasreen'. Time is collapsing in his head – that once-handsome and noble head on whose devotion she had depended as a girl. Without his support she would never have gained her five O levels and her LRSC – Licentiate of the Royal Society of Chemistry. Now Latifa is studying computer programming but her father no longer remembers what she's doing. S.B. is now incapable of collecting her from the college by car on winter evenings.

Latifa's brother Ishtiaq slouches into the kitchen, frustrated that he cannot watch television in the sitting room. His mother serves him a plate of mildly spiced chicken.

'How many am I feeding tonight?' she sighs. 'What are they saying in there?'

'I hear only Dad's voice,' Latifa says.

'This Rahman business is driving your dad mad,' her mother says.

'All of us.' Latifa is nibbling vegetables, a young woman of small appetite occasionally punctuated by spasms of fierce eating. 'Did you hear about that silly bitch Fatima Shah?'

'She is now attending the Muslim Girls' School,' Ishtiaq announces.

'Silly bitch,' Latifa repeats. 'Ruining her education for a bloody scarf. Nas tried to help her. She tried to help Safia, too. But what can you do with a family like the Shahs?'

'Poor Nasreen,' the mother says.

'She's too good for her own good, your big daughter,' Latifa says. 'If

160

only she was happy! But how can you be happy married to Hassan Hassani?'

'Latifa!'

'He sits up all night reading Gamal Rahman and writing it down. Nas told me! She pretends she's asleep. I know she's in love with somebody, I can tell. I bet it's that Hindu bloke, Rajiv Lal, the way she keeps talking about him. He lent her his car, didn't he?'

'Latifa! Not in front of Ishtiaq.'

'Big ears,' Latifa rebukes her brother.

'I heard,' Latifa's mother murmurs, 'that Rahman's Jewish wife was behind this book. The Jews killed Jesus.'

'Mrs Newman says Jesus was a Jew,' Ishtiaq says.

'Jesus was a Christian,' Latifa corrects him. 'Rahman will attack Jesus and the Virgin Mary next thing. His own mother died when she saw she had given birth to a devil. He insulted his own father by casting off his family name. He had immoral relationships in Egypt with all the Sharaf women. He claimed he was married to the Prophet's thirteenth wife. Then he betrayed her to the pharaohs and the Jews just like Jesus was betrayed.'

'Mrs Newman says she once met Rahman,' Ishtiaq says. 'He came looking for the mother of the Queen of Egypt.'

'That's a likely story! We all know whose side *she's* on.'

Abruptly the rat begins gnawing at the wainscot. Latifa shudders. 'Why don't the Council send the exterminators?'

'Your dad has put down poisons,' her mother says wearily.

'Fat good!' Latifa's frustrations boil over. Her thin arm jabs towards the sitting room like a poker piercing dying embers. 'They all dream of power, those men. They're afraid of our generation. Listen, the Holy Koran says we are the caretakers of the world. We are polluting the planet, killing it, that is what we should be fighting about. And the rights of women. Each of those men there thinks he's a chip off the Holy Prophet . . . peace be upon him.'

Her voice dies away on the last words. A long silence in the kitchen. Occasionally S.B.'s voice rises above the murmurs from the sitting room. Eventually Razia Hussein speaks in a low voice: 'That Haqq never turned up.'

'Well he wouldn't, would he?'

Voices in the hall: the men are leaving. Finally the women hear the front door close and there is silence.

'Call your father to eat,' Razia whispers to Ishtiaq. But even as she says it, the front door closes again, in fury.

༄

161

The play is over. The audience is applauding; Jasmin is on her feet, ecstatic. Wahabia claps politely, for Jasmin's sake. The actors extend their arms towards the wings. Ali is expecting a walk-on by the two authors, but the tall, handsome man who strides across the stage to massive applause is recognizable as Joe Swahili, Black Africa's greatest writer. Hush.

'This is the great age of communication and its tempo cannot be halted by the Koran, the Bible, the Apocrypha, the Book of Ifa or the Bhagavad-Gita,' announces Joe Swahili. 'We will flood Iran with pastiches of Rahman's work by parachute. *The Devil: an Interview* will provide the text for the funeral obsequies of the Ayatollah. He must be punished for his arrogance, his hubris, and the implicit blasphemy in his arrogation of a Supreme Will. If Gamal Rahman is unnaturally and prematurely silenced, the creative world will launch its own jihad.'

Joe Swahili strides from the stage. The applause is uneasy; Ali concludes that terms like 'punished' and 'jihad' disturb the Liberal Establishment. They are not at ease with the notion that one fatwa deserves another.

Now follows a veritable procession of the good and the great in a long parade of liberal virtue. First comes the gay actor Roy Kilmartin (Jasmin wildly banging her small hands together, bracelets dancing):

'I support laws which ban written attacks on people's colour, race, handicap or sexuality – these qualities are inborn,' Kilmartin announces. 'Religious or political faith is a matter of choice, of free will, and should not be protected by blasphemy acts or other forms of censorship.'

Massive applause. Jasmin Patel on her feet.

Next to arrive is the best-selling yet always intellectually provocative writer Jilly Jumpers, whose numerous novels chart the freeways of modern love and are widely admired by experts in sexual politics. Jasmin adores her. A blonde bomber whose fiftieth birthday party is history – her extended report of it and the night following is legendary – Jumpers brings a tone of girlish innocence to her far from innocent questions.

'Why are we, the non-believers, so pathetically unable to stand our ground against the big, bullying battalions of brute Belief?'

Terrific! Jasmin is a live wire of excitement!

'I always distrusted muscular Christianity,' Jumpers continues, 'but I never expected to see our English churches handed over, wholesale, to this other, all-conquering desert religion!'

Ali glances towards Jasmin, who seems to be in two minds about this dubious emphasis on temple-snatching. Jilly could not be more loyal to Gamal but she does have a tendency to skid and spin when she hears her own tiny voice.

'And when we talk about "the Muslims",' Jumpers asks innocently, 'I suppose we mean the men. Half of Islam must be female but you'd never guess, would you? What comfort do we feminists have to offer all those poor, abused, sisters of toil who can be divorced and discarded as easily as you throw away a used bus ticket?'

Jasmin applauds loudly as Jumpers threatens to lead a Long March to greet and embrace 'the Sisters of Bruddersford'. Ali notes that Wahabia's lovely features are now set in a defensive scowl. She is not applauding as Jilly Jumpers bounces off the stage.

The auditorium is emptying. The pharmacist Iqbal Iqbal has departed, beardless. His ticking Koran lies neatly tucked under his empty seat.

Ali is already out in Sloane Square, determined to take the late train north after collecting his overnight bag from Jasmin's flat. Wahabia has a key. But Jasmin's little claw fastens on his sleeve. Firmly she leads him to the stage door, where Inigo Lorraine, surrounded by TV cameras, lights and pretty girls carrying clipboards, is preparing to interview the authors and selected members of the audience.

'Ali!'

Is the apparent warmth of Lorraine's greeting due to the affection of old campaigners, or, as Inigo charmingly puts it, because 'We need a Muslim'?

'You need two,' Ali says, drawing Wahabia to his side.

'Absolutely!' Lorraine smiles hugely at Wahabia. The cameras are rolling, Inigo's chin jutting:

'Wahabia Zaheed, you are the daughter of the Muslim Lord Mayor of Bruddersford. What did you – as a Muslim woman – think of the play?'

'It's a cartoon trading in ugly, racist stereotypes,' Wahabia says. 'Improbable dialogue stuffed into talking heads. (*Jasmin lights a cigarette.*) The Rahman case is of course a disturbing one for us all, but this play does not attempt to penetrate the real issues. (*Jasmin throws away her cigarette.*) Why, for example, is there not a single Muslim, representing two million British citizens, in our Parliament?' (*Jasmin lights another cigarette.*)

Lorraine nods. 'And your father intends to rectify that?'

'Yes he does. And he will.'

'Ali Cheema, you have taken part in live debates with Gamal Rahman. What is your reaction to the play?'

'What we saw this evening is straight out of a degraded music-hall tradition. (*Jasmin is now smoking two cigarettes.*) Foreign-born bullies with swarthy skins scorn the vacillating Brits – until, of course, the slow-to-anger Brits finally wake up and take to the skies. The authors of this play evidently regard themselves as Battle-of-Britain fighter pilots.' (*Both of Jasmin's cigarettes are scorching holes in Inigo's priceless suede jacket.*)

The camera swings to the author with the Sunday-dinner countenance, Rory McKenzie.

'I'm a pacifist myself and the machine guns in my wings are mere words, ideas, values. The Ayatollah's words are loaded with knives and bullets; they arrive among us supported by a huge reward in dollars for the murder of my friend and fellow-writer, Gamal Rahman. (*Smoke is pouring from Inigo's suede jacket.*) Do we have a writer under threat of death or not? Do we, like the Labour Party, sit on our hands and count the votes coming out of the mosques?'

Lorraine (*blazing like a book by Gamal Rahman*) nods in neutral: 'Ali?'

'None of the "votes coming out of the mosques" remotely resembles the sneering Muslim villain, the drug-trafficking protection-racketeer, depicted in this sordid little Royal Court pantomime. Moscow gold, Iranian gold, it's the same old canard. For a Muslim, his faith is the root and branch of his existence. The secular establishment cannot grapple with faith. I think you may be on fire, Inigo, by the way.'

'The secular establishment is on fire, you mean?'

'I advise you to take off your jacket while you can.'

Lorraine's fine jaw tightens. 'I understand – so you would censor this play alongside Gamal Rahman's novel?'

'As for censorship, we don't forget that this same theatre, the Royal Court, in effect banned its own production of Sid Felon's play, *Purgatory*. Felon had offended the powerful Jewish establishment. Yet his play was not anti-Semitic – unless you level the same charge against Hannah Arendt.'

At this juncture all dialogue ceases to make way for Jasmin's scream – the love of her life is a human fireball. A moment later Iqbal Iqbal's Koranic bomb explodes. Flames sweep through the theatre. Lingering patrons, trapped in packed bars and narrow stairways, panic, their bodies piling up at the jammed exit to Sloane Square.

But here the demon arsonist himself intervenes. Miraculously Gamal Rahman appears among the stampeding theatre-lovers, impishly flicking his forked tail.

'Friends! Enemies! Let us not lose our precious cast so soon! Let a post-modernist, magical-realist reversal cancel Iqbal Iqbal and his bomb. At this moment the pharmacist is in truth far away in Bruddersford, pushing his pamphlet, "The True Jesus and the False Jesus", through the letterboxes of humble dwellings where' – Gamal winks at a soot-black Jilly Jumpers – 'battered wives are being discarded like used bus tickets.'

ELEVEN

❧

'We are living in a secular society,' the Bishop announces, with no sound of regret.

Izza Shah and Ali Cheema are visiting the Bishop of Bruddersford, the Rt. Revd Robin Goodgame, accompanied by Douglas Blunt, the Bishop's good friend (with whom he plays a round of golf when their crowded calendars permit). Under a mild sky suggesting a provisional neutrality regarding the true Heavenly Order, the four men are strolling across the lawns of the Cathedral precints – the Bishop towering above the two Muslims at the regulation height for Anglican bishops, his crucifix swinging gaily across his purple shirt, his stride that of a golfer who relishes the long fairways and whose ball is rarely to be found where he'd aimed it.

Izza Shah is in a wheelchair. Ali pushes it.

The meeting is at the Bishop's request. The agenda is obscure: the Bishop may be weighing Ali's academic prospects, or merely the world's.

What Ali calls 'theological puzzles' the Bishop terms 'God's bunkers'. When an Oxford undergraduate, Ali had noticed that Anglicans can think only when walking on mown grass – probably the closest thing to Heaven they know. Perhaps it's the smell. Robin Goodgame carefully guides them round his special heaven, the croquet lawn (God's hoops). The Bishop seems quite happy about his 'secular society', as if a few Christians are better value than many – and less trouble. If he anticipates (as he does) that the Church of England will soon be blown apart on the issue of the ordination of women priests, this is not the company in which he will wish to discuss it.

'The Blasphemy Act is a redundant anomaly – in my view. I suspect that European Community Law prevents any privileged protection for the various Faiths. Brussels is now our Rome, you know. And while I absolutely agree with your distinction between legitimate criticism and insult, Izza, it's surprisingly difficult to make it stick in law. The

Rahman novel probably falls into the same category as the monstrous television puppets used by . . . by . . . Douglas?

' "Spitting Image," ' suggests Douglas Blunt, 'lampoons politicians.'

'But politicians are not Almighty God,' Ali intervenes. Having convinced himself that the Junior Research Fellowship hangs on this encounter, he has resolved to give no offence, to impress the Bishop by his tender knowledge of the road joining Mecca to Canterbury.

The Bishop offers Ali his heron-nod from an impossible angle. One would not guess that they have broken bread together in the past, ambled by the Isis, discovered a mutual passion for Milton.

'But history moves us on, Ali. For better or for worse. The sober questions raised by Tom Paine about the Virgin Mary were just as outrageous to Christians two hundred years ago as Mr Rahman's satire is to Muslims today. In my mind it is futile to pursue the blasphemy theme, since blasphemy offends ideas, beliefs. We must follow the modern practice – the Race Relations Act – which defends categories of *people* – women, black people, children – against the abuse to which they are specifically vulnerable. The buzz word is "communities", you know. I think the Prophet Muhammad, peace be upon him, can look after himself; it is not he, still less the Almighty, who is vulnerable to insult: it is people. You particularly. What Ali calls the "Liberal Establishment" – and I confess I am a paid-up member! – is sensitive to social damage. I would therefore suggest that we press for the Race Relations Act to be extended to insulting attacks on those religions which are particularly associated with ethnic minorities. Hm. How does that strike you?'

'Islam has the most followers in the world,' Izza Shah says.

'Oh quite. But not here, you see.' The Bishop smiles. 'Not yet.'

'My Lord Bishop, we are demanding equality not charity for second-class citizens.'

The Bishop almost flinches: in better times the President of the Islamic Council had been happy enough to call him Robin. This 'Lord Bishop' is bad news; but Goodgame is determined to rise above it. He has a head start, as they say.

'But equality with what, Izza? You behave as if the Church constantly invoked the Blasphemy Act to protect itself. But it never does. A dead letter. You say you are demanding an ancient right, but for whom? In reality the Blasphemy Act never extended to Catholics, Jews or Hindus either.'

Izza Shah's English meets the challenge: 'Islam, Christianity and Judaism have in common the one and only God (*Gahd*).'

'A special protection for monotheism, you mean? I must say I'm very fond of the Aztec sun and rain gods – wouldn't like to see them out in the cold.' This frivolous sentiment may be traced to the Bishop's time as a missionary in monotheistic Saudi Arabia, the least fruitful period of his life. Only this morning he has read a report from that land of oppression:

SAUDI HUMAN RIGHTS COMMITTEE BANNED
Saudi Arabian scholars and religious leaders who last week set up a human rights committee have been dismissed from their jobs and their group declared illegal by the supreme council of the ulama. Mohamed Mas'ari, a physics lecturer, was detained by the police and told to end his contacts with Western news media. The ban on the group was signed by Sheikh Abdul Aziz bin Baz, a long-time supporter of the Saudi ruling family.

'Demands for censorship and punishment offend the English spirit,' the Bishop adds. 'They seem domineering, intolerant, aggressive. Don't you agree, Douglas?'

Douglas Blunt agrees. 'The death threat to an author is profoundly shocking. People see "Kill Rahman" banners on the demos and they feel revulsion.'

Ali nods. 'Our people also see graffiti on the walls of schools and mosques: "Rahman Rules, OK." '

The Bishop jerks as if struck by Satan. 'Appalling! I am appalled. Let's face it, the worst in people is currently alive and well. I have seen swastikas recently. Swastikas! Does one forget that the Nazi stormtroopers also burnt books?'

Ali feels his self-control, his self-denying vows, ebbing.

'Hitler is not a pivotal point of reference for us,' he says. 'For us the Thousand Year Reich was the British Raj. Yet a Palestinian family which resists eviction from its farm on the West Bank in 1990 is accused in Brooklyn of laying the tarmac to Auschwitz in 1940.'

The Bishop declines to take offence. 'I assure you, Ali, that I have preached against Israel's military occupation of Judaea and Samaria.'

Ali cannot check himself. 'And East Jerusalem?'

'East Jerusalem is thorny one. Given the religious heritage of the Old City, I favour a United Nations mandate. I also take your point, Ali, that the symbolic burning of a single book does not turn our Bruddersford Muslim community into the S.S. But I do notice that your colleague Mustafa Jangar seems to want to extend the Iranian Islamic Republic to Britain – which of course is precisely what the Ayatollah's fatwa aspires to do.'

Neither Izza Shah nor Ali Cheema is happy with Mustafa's neo-

Shi'ite proselytizing – an embarrassment all round – but a colleague has to be defended.

'The aggressive dimension of Iranian policy should be understood as a response to decades of Western imperialism,' Ali says.

'My dear friend, Germany had been dismembered by the Treaty of Versailles. Hitler only wanted to restore the integrity of his country. Then came the call to blood, soil and Volk. And off we go! Every totalitarian dictator *needs* an Eternal Enemy. There's no shortage.'

'The fatwa,' says Izza Shah rigid in his wheelchair, 'is an inevitable function of Islamic jurisprudence. But we are British citizens living under British law (*lah*). Our demands are strictly legal.'

Ali says: 'May I quote the Chief Rabbi: "We should generate respect for other people's beliefs and not tolerate a form of denigration and ridicule which can only breed resentment to the point of strife." '

'I would guess that the Chief Rabbi is referring to conscience rather than law.' The Bishop sighs and inclines his chin to check if his crucifix is still there. 'The Prophet Muhammad, like Jesus, is the product of text, tradition and schismatic dispute. My theology is your heresy. We must not be too readily offended. I see so many of the old churches of this city sprouting minarets. Some of my communicants complain to me: "This should be stopped, it's not right." I say to them, "The curve of Heaven is infinite, fret not about spire, minaret or dome." But they do fret! I urge you, gentlemen, to remember the great communal riots and massacres in India, and perhaps to be a little more grateful for small mercies. I can only quote the Archbishop of Canterbury: "I understand their feelings and I firmly believe that offence to the religious beliefs of the followers of Islam or any other faith is quite as wrong an offence as to the religious beliefs of Christians." '

Izza Shah murmurs to Ali. He needs a toilet. Ali needs a Junior Research Fellowship. Wheelchairing his adoptive father across the lawn, he is gripped by fear: he has been too disputatious, too outspoken. Why has the summons to a formal interview at the College been so long delayed? Why has the Bishop said nothing about it?

ॐ

Mrs Newman receives Rajiv Lal in her office. Although Rajiv is nominally her boss, he does not like to summon Headteachers; he regards them as the 'front-line'; schools, not departmental offices, are the right place to discuss difficulties. Rajiv has however exercised authority by inviting Dr Quddus, Chairman of the Community Relations Council, to attend. Quddus bustles in with dew on his forehead, mist on his glasses, a fat briefcase, sighing and muttering as he wipes his lenses. Quddus is always bad news to Mrs Newman – a professional busybody. She approves of the CRC in principle because she holds progressive views; but Quddus is a meddler, a politician manqué, a whirling dervish rushing about the town, scheming, plotting.

She has not dressed for the occasion. Not dressed up. She gives special thought to her appearance only in the company of Jean-Pierre. His taste in women's clothes inclines to sharper-colour contrasts than hers. 'You go about camouflaged,' he says, 'like an infantryman of the Somme hoping to guard his life by merging into the mud.' At first she found such images hard to accommodate, but he added, sensing her chagrin, that Sartre had said as much to de Beauvoir.

She feels herself fully alive – fully 'herself' – only in his company. The 'Mrs Newman' she inhabits for most of the year is someone else – no, no, merely a remorselessly advancing crustation. Jean-Pierre is not handsome, not an homme couvert de femmes; he does not wear his raincoat like Yves Montand, he will not slip into Franco's Spain bearing dynamite, or even a dangerous message; he will not carry Gérard Depardieu's engaging scowl to Danton's death. He is a fat little man who likes his comforts. But even his lies and polite insults are what she craves. Not dressing like the Somme mud is entertaining. In Bruddersford no one could leave her office and give an accurate account of what she was wearing.

Dressed in good-quality mud, she confines her gaze to Rajiv Lal.

'Somewhat before your time, Mr Lal, Izza Shah was also the inspiration behind the so-called Muslim Parents' Association, which sought to buy five delapidated school buildings and set up all-Muslim, single-sex schools. That failed but Izza Shah is tenacious – if one thing fails, he'll try another. His own daughter is now the sacrificial lamb – halal lamb, a slow bleeding.'

Dr Quddus wails. This woman is not only a headmistress but a magistrate – where's the fair play? These English, can they ever resist an insult? For years halal butchers have been serving the Muslim community without fuss. But as soon as the school-meals issue arose the native whites instantly discovered that this method of bleeding an animal to death was an unspeakable cruelty. Dr Quddus is wiping his glasses:

'Muslim people are principled people, Mrs Newman. This scarf affair is political dynamite. Our Labour Council is already getting it in the neck for this Fatima-scarf business on top of the Rahman novel.'

'I am not interested in politics, Dr Quddus. I am interested in education.'

'Not separable in this city, most unfortunately,' Quddus says, his foghorn voice rising. 'Muslims are tax-payers like everyone else and therefore entitled to separate provisions. Christian and Jewish schools already exist on a denominational basis. We have Church schools, with Voluntary Aided status, getting eighty-five per cent of their funding plus capital grants.'

Rajiv Lal gently clears his throat.

'The issue of Fatima Shah's hijab is the immediate concern of all of us,' he says gently. 'But it is no longer a question of one girl. This gesture of resistance has spread. Twenty girls are now "on strike". Obviously it is symptomatic of a wider alienation. My colleague Nasreen Hassani's report makes it very clear that Fatima and her friends cannot be persuaded to abandon their demands.'

Patricia Newman has been expecting Rajiv Lal to capitulate all along.

'Mr Lal, when Nasreen presented herself on your behalf – I hope that's the correct way to put it – she herself decided to wear the hijab within the school. I took that to be an eloquent gesture of allegiance – and nothing she said disturbed my view. She has disqualified herself from any further role in this affair – as far as Hightown Upper School is concerned – so long as I sit behind this desk.'

Dr Quddus hears this challenge to Rajiv Lal's authority with keen interest. At last night's meeting of the Islamic Council, Mustafa Jangar had demanded Mrs Newman's removal. And Rajiv Lal's. And Samuel Perlman's.

'You can't score three bull's eyes with one shot,' Quddus had interceded. 'Ruling is dividing, the philosophers say. Resisting is also dividing.'

Now, closeted with Rajiv Lal and Mrs Newman, Quddus's suspicions are confirmed: the white Headmistress is the main stumbling block, the last straw, the Red Sea to cross. She is the et cetera. But of course Mustafa Jangar is less interested in practical solutions than in permanent ferment. He has now joined the mob of Muslim parents and agitators who picket the school gates and toss insults at Mrs Newman and other members of staff whenever they arrive or depart. Mrs Newman's car had been mildly vandalized while parked in its reserved space. The police inspected her car but hesitated to establish the permanent presence at the gate she called for; they don't like to enter jungles from which there may be no exit. Bruddersford's Police Commissioner, Friars, had consulted Rajiv Lal, Quddus himself, and Douglas Blunt. All three agreed that the sub-plot (the police presence) could rapidly supersede the main plot (the hijab) in 'these situations'.

Joe Reddaway had promptly come up with a 'Plain Speaking' column: HIGHTOWN UPPER TEACHERS HARASSED. POLICE STAND BACK.

At which Tom Potter had raised a voice as loud as the City Hall bell: TORY CHIEF SLAMS ANARCHY.

Delighted, Mustafa had redoubled his anarchic presence at the school gate, bringing with him a megaphone which penetrated classrooms and chemistry labs throughout the working day:

'For twenty-thirty years we poor immigrants have meekly accepted party politics on the Western model. But now the Ayatollah Khomeini has exposed the corruption of this secular trick called pluralism. Pluralism gives us Gamal Rahman's insults. God is not plural. The mosques alone, and the great teachers, are the Party of Islam.'

Dr Quddus is elaborately wiping his glasses.

'The least bad solution, Mr Lal, is to allow the girls to wear the hijab. I've never been in two minds about that. This city can blow up any minute under all of us. Defuse the crisis, take the steam out of the kettle. Otherwise I tremble to think. Education is not arm-wrestling, you know.'

Rajiv Lal nods gravely. 'Mrs Newman, I am searching for the gesture of compromise, of understanding, which would save Fatima's sense of honour while preserving our standards.'

'It may be time,' Mrs Newman says, 'for the Department to advise Izza Shah that he is failing his legal obligation to send his child to school. He is a magistrate, after all.'

'Fatima is now attending the Muslim Girls' School,' Rajiv Lal says.

Dr Quddus thumps his fist into his cupped hand but soundlessly. 'No prosecutions, please! Our Islamic Council is itching for prosecutions! Haqq is itching! Jangar is itching! They are all itching!'

Rajiv Lal nods again. 'Mrs Newman, when a community is in a state of principled civil disobedience, one can either play the Raj or seek a face-saving formula. If one plays the Raj – '

'I do find that phrase offensive, Mr Lal.'

'Time is our ally. Every fever subsides.'

'So what is your policy adding up to?' Dr Quddus challenges Mrs Newman, the wind in his sails. 'To do nothing? To sit on our hands? We have to take this thing on board, frankly, or the cat is out of the bag and no mistake.'

'Multiculturalism implies diversity as well as synthesis,' says Rajiv Lal.

Her jaw is set: this man is totally unfitted to administer a kindergarten let alone the Education Department of a large city. He's a dreamer, a theoretician, suited for a university chair where he can continue his cherished campaign against 'Eurocentric' curricula, undisturbed by the erratic behaviour of real children and real parents. Rajiv is a 'third-worlder' who regards all the cultures and religions as a glorious patchwork quilt, a tapestry of many colours. But now Mustafa's megaphonic sermon is unravelling the tapestry.

Mrs Newman has folded her hands. 'I shall of course require a formal directive from you, Mr Lal, suspending the rule forbidding the hijab.'

'I have not found any such written rule, Mrs Newman. It is merely custom and practice.'

'And a very good custom and practice.'

'Until it can no longer be applied.'

Quddus stands up, sits down again. 'People have a right to hang themselves,' he announces. 'If Muslims want to be separate but equal, that is their kettle of fish. Force-feeding makes the child sick.'

Mrs Newman opens her desk drawer and hands a sheet of paper to Rajiv Lal. It is a letter from his predecessor prohibiting the hijab in school.

'So,' she says, 'I must regard that as Departmental policy until you change it in writing.'

All three of them know that Rajiv Lal would rather avoid putting anything in writing; that he wants Mrs Newman to make his decision for him. She now hands him a second letter, this one from Samuel Perlman, Chairman of the City Education Committee, 'entirely endorsing' her stand in the Fatima Shah case.

So Patricia Newman has gone over Rajiv Lal's head! The 'arrival' of Perlman in the Headmistress's study throws Quddus into a wild state. He, too, has come armed. Trembling he removes a fat folder of documents from his briefcase.

'I quote: "All sections of the community have an equal right to the maintenance of their distinctive identities and culture, language, religion and custom." For example, I am quoting yes quoting not inventing, nothing invented by me: "The Sikh kara, a steel bracelet worn on the right wrist, and the Muslim tawiz, a string with a small bag or box attached, worn round the arm, neck or abdomen, are not counted as jewellery and children must be allowed to wear them if the parents so wish." Further! "Girls may wear suitable lightweight clothing such as the churidat-pyjama as an alternative to the swimsuit." '

'The hijab is not mentioned,' Mrs Newman says very drily indeed.

Rajiv Lal stands up. 'I feel we have all benefited from this discussion. Mrs Newman, I shall be glad of a couple of minutes alone with you. Dr Quddus – if you don't mind.'

Dr Quddus does mind; doesn't want to miss anything. His mission of reconciliation requires him to be a step ahead of everyone else, the universal messenger too adroit to be killed for the message. Reluctantly he heads for the door, lingers, leaves. Mrs Newman and Rajiv Lal are alone.

'I note,' he says, 'your remarks about Mrs Nasreen Hassani.'

'Yes.'

'I have found her to be a devoted and skilful community teacher, very much trusted within the Muslim community.'

'Mr Lal! We have a rule here against wearing the hijab in school. After years of compliance with this rule, Mrs Hassani comes here, to my office, wearing the hijab.'

'Most unfortunate. I shall ask her not to repeat the error.'

'I assumed she was doing so with your consent.' (Mrs Newman suppresses the word 'connivance'.) 'She seems, if I may say so, unhealthily devoted to you.'

'Unhealthily?'

Patricia Newman has overstepped the mark: womanly instinct leaves her in no doubt that Nasreen is head-over-heels with Lal, yet she is appalled to discover how anger has penetrated the seven skins of discretion:

'To be frank, Nasreen is labouring under too many conflicting loyalties. As you know, her father, Sadar Baj Hussein, is a Governor of this school. I shall have to carpet him for taking his son Ishtiaq out of school for three months without permission. Nasreen came here to beg me to let the matter drop.'

'I see. I see.'

ନ୍ଦ

'The rats are wearing my nerves out,' Latifa tells Nasreen. 'Only the other day one of them got stuck coming up – up! – into the toilet bowl.'

'I don't know why poor Dad can't get an improvement grant after all his years of service to the Labour Party.'

'Dad shouts at the rats and the rats shout back.'

'His temper has been terrible since his return from Pakistan.'

'Haqq's tyre has not been "punctured", that's why. Dad's summonses have been ignored. Now he can't decide whether to join the Muslim pickets at the gates of Hightown Upper School in defence of the hijab and the honour of Muslim females – '

'No!' Nasreen clasps her hand to her mouth in horror.

174

' – or to denounce the whole scarf agitation as a Zia-ite, fundamentalist plot to destabilize the Labour Party and hand the city over to "that bastard Potter".'

'Latifa, I want to leave this hating city!'

ை

Big-bellied, gleaming, solicitous, charming, Ishmail Haqq says anything that comes into his head on the doorstep:

'If some Tom, Dick or Harry calls my Prophet a bastard – '

Haqq's henchman, the karate instructor Tiger Siddiqi, is his ace card with the young, cruising the streets in his primrose-yellow jerkin with a broad-banded grey V, a golden amulet at his open neck. Tiger Siddiqi's sports club in the Community Centre is where the young Tariq Khan learnt to defend himself, to hold his head up on the streets.

Imtiaz Shasti's Toyota is parked outside the Community Centre, poised for an evening's campaigning. The rear window carries a sticker, green on yellow, 'Vote HAQQ Independent'. Another sticker shows a cartoon of a smiling car carrying a smiling family: 'Unleaded petrol at Tesco. It's kinder to kids.'

'The Rahman crisis raises all the issues shelved by the old political parties,' Haqq is telling a cub reporter as he strides out of the Community Centre. 'These issues are back on the agenda – sex education in schools, single-sex schools, the imposed Christian act of worship.' He nods happily as he boards Shasti's Toyota. 'You can quote me.'

The Toyota passes some white youths, one with a Mohican haircut, working on the entrails and gutted shell of a car. Lazily they offer obscene gestures. Equally unpromising are the Salvation Army building and Sikh Temple (Sri Guru Dadak, Sikh Sodgat), where a group of elderly gentlemen in turbans are seated on utility chairs in the forecourt, enjoying the sun, oblivious to Gamal Rahman.

Haqq plunges into a small shop, Sufi & Co, General Draper, in whose little window hang brightly coloured scarves and cloaks. A milk crate in orange plastic stands cheerily on the neighbouring front step, waiting to serve as cricket stumps when the kids come out of school. The Pakistan national team has arrived in England, bringing new fevers.

ை

Ali Cheema is studying the episcopal lawn beneath his shoe – not a clover leaf, dandelion or daisy in sight. The Bishop is merely trying to impose the passive fatalism of a defeated religion, a twice-a-year

175

religion, a birth-marriage-death religion, on a twenty-four hour religion in the ascendant. Although Ali himself no longer believes that the Blasphemy Act can be extended, he knows that Izza Shah's yearnings all reach in that direction. Poor, exiled Islam, forced to cry for justice in the Crusaders' tongue!

'What we Muslims complain of is double standards. Do you remember the case of Sid Felon's play, *Purgatory*?' Ali asks the Bishop. (They had once happily wasted a tutorial on Augustine debating whether the word 'impertinent' now meant 'too pertinent'.)

'Not off hand. Remind me.'

'The subject of the play is the failure of Central European Zionist leaders to resist the Holocaust tooth and nail. In some cases they even collaborated. British Jews and Zionists were offended. They brought pressure on the Royal Court Theatre to abandon the play before the first performance. These were powerful men within the British Liberal Establishment, household names – and names easier on the English tongue than ours. The play was cancelled.'

The Bishop nods. 'I take your point.' But he speaks in the tone of a man who would need to hear the other side of the story, the tone of a don suspending judgment on a Junior Research Fellowship. Ali cannot hold down the vomit of his own knowledge.

'Mr Dillon Watergate, who manages a major chain of bookstores, is on record that *The Devil: an Interview* should be published in paperback.'

'I am rather against that.'

'But Mr Watergate refuses to stock Jerome Racine's book, *God: The Futile Quest*, because it might offend Christians. Did you know that the founder of Rahman's own publishing house once burned his entire stock of a book because it offended some Christians?'

'Can you mean Victor Warlock? Really? I met him once or twice. Didn't strike me as a book-burner.'

'The book contained cartoons of a scatalogical nature, anti-clerical, some of them sexually explicit. Warlock took several accomplices to his main warehouse, filled a trailer with the remaining copies, and incinerated them. The next day his Trade Department reported the book to be out of print.'

'Very interesting. But isn't that rather like the BBC cancelling one of its own programmes in the public interest?'

Ali knows he should defer – just once! – to the Bishop's wisdom. Some token of a junior's respect!

'Banning or burning Rahman's book,' he says, 'is not "in the public interest" because the offended parties are mere immigrant Muslims.'

The Bishop says, 'Mmmm'. What needles Ali is Goodgame's

176

evident enjoyment of the duel, as if his Oxonian mind is too often put to sleep by choirboys, fund-raising to restore the fabric of the Cathedral, a parish priest caught in adultery, or thinking of something new to say on Armistice Day.

'I have a difficulty,' the Bishop announces. 'It's this. You, our Muslim friends, address us as if each of us was individually responsible for each and every damned odd thing that someone has done in this country. Follow? No? You speak to me as if I had banned that whatsit play about Zionists, or burned a trailer-load of scatalogical cartoons, or decided not to stock that whatsit book about God. *You* did this, *you* did that. But, my dear fellow, I spend half my day regretting what other well-intentioned Englishmen are doing! You might as well take me to task for the sauve qui peut philosophy of this awful Government of ours. It's not easy to twist the arm of a democracy – am I becoming pedantic? – because it's underlying cohesion resides in its diversity.'

Izza Shah's resentment now boils over. Unable to see anything of the Bishop strolling behind his wheelchair except his long shadow, he declares that Rahman's book is British society's deliberate insult to Islam, to God, to the Prophet. It didn't get published by accident. It was a decision at the highest level – though Mrs Thatcher herself is blameless.

Ali hears the earth strike his own coffin. Izza has declared Goodgame to be a hypocrite.

'Tea?' the Bishop suggests, swinging towards the open french windows.

Ali's mind veers angrily towards those upper-class English people who once convened every Sunday in the Anglican churches of Delhi, Cairo, Shanghai – Bishop Goodgame's natural congregation. The Sunday church for them was little more than a social motion, the hour when one wrapped in hymns the real passions of the club, the polo pitch, the fancy dress ball. The proof that Englishmen didn't take church seriously was the presence of women; where it mattered – school, club, profession – women were not admitted.

The Bishop calls for tea by inviting Douglas Blunt to press the bell. Blunt cannot think of anything more useful to do. He's lost half of a working day on this abortive meeting of minds.

Ali negotiates the wheelchair through the french windows. Izza Shah needs the toilet again.

By the time Ali brings him back into the drawing room, the Bishop is holding a small pile of Muslim pamphlets, around which he has wrapped two elastic bands, as if to restrain them. He and Douglas Blunt draw rapidly apart.

'These are all published by the Islamic Propagation Centre in

Birmingham,' the Bishop explains, placing them in Izza Shah's hand. 'They are all attacks on Christian theology – one need only glance at the titles to get the gist. "Resurrection or Resuscitation?"; "Who Moved the Stone?"; "Crucifixion or Cruci-Fiction?"; and so on. Your colleague Hassan Hassani regularly sends them to me, with an accompanying letter on Maududi Mosque notepaper. "For your better understanding," is his regular phrase.'

Izza Shah looks uncomfortable. 'Hassani is not *tahctful.*'

'Nor is Mr Gamal Rahman.'

Tinkling tea cups intervene; the housekeeper pours the thick, milky version of the beverage favoured in Yorkshire.

Ali is restless about the anti-Christian pamphlets. Hassan Hassani's tourist-guide soul is an embarrassment dwarfed only by Mustafa Jangar's mad-mullah flamboyance.

'Of course these issues are much debated in the Christian Church itself,' he says. 'Not a few Bishops, even, have questioned the Resurrection.'

'Oh quite so, Ali, quite *so*. And the Virgin Birth. I might have a few questions to raise myself. But this is not quite the same as Mr Hassani doing it for me.' The Bishop's smile is not genial. 'Since we are talking of "crusades and insults",' he adds.

The phrase leaves no empty place at High Table for a Muslim Junior Research Fellow.

Izza Shah now recognizes that they have touched rock bottom. Laboriously he reiterates Islam's respect for sincere Christians. He quotes the Holy Qur'an (Koran): 'And among them' – the Jews and Christians – 'are Mu'mins.'

The Bishop's teaspoon circles his cup. 'Allah also told the Prophet. "But the majority of them are perverted transgressors".' Silence.

'The God in whom I believe can take teasing and daily endure mockery,' the Bishop adds. 'And I too must endure it on His behalf.'

Ali is now reckless with rage. 'Perhaps excessive passivity is a sign of diminishing faith,' he says.

'It may be, Ali. The Church is a human institution and therefore imperfect. But our Lord Jesus Christ endured mockery and death. He was not a warrior or a statesman like the Prophet Muhammad.'

'And the Crusaders?'

'Holy wars are never wholly holy.'

Douglas Blunt passes the biscuits to the Bishop, whose need seems greatest. He wolfs them down with that show of greed which only nanny-raised children can display without shame. Blunt has seen the Bishop fill his own wine glass at dinner, then shove the decanter carelessly across the table – an aristocrat's boots up on the altar of decorum.

The Bishop is making a last effort: 'What we need is a new approach to national ceremonial, you know. We should even now be planning the Coronation of Prince Charles, with the Archbishop of Canterbury flanked by the leaders of all the religions of the Commonwealth offering their prayers and blessings. I'd call that positive action.'

Izza Shah is sitting erect as a Buddha, his trembling hands folded.

'My Lahd Bishop, I came here to discuss a satanic book, not the next *Carahnation*.'

Ali stares at the carpet. It's all over, finished.

The Bishop glances at Blunt; diplomacy has failed. Bridges have not been built. Minds have not met. God has not interceded, yet, among his warring children. Robin Goodgame now makes his offering: a letter signed by the vicars of St Barnabas, St Stephen's and Emmanuel, urging the withdrawal of the Rahman book from local libraries to help community relations.

Izza Shah inclines his head gravely; three vicars isn't a lot and the Bishop's own signature is conspicuously absent.

'Thank you, my Lahd,' Izza Shah says, 'for graciously receiving us.'

And graciously the Bishop walks them to Izza's car. His hand touches Ali's elbow. 'Don't worry,' he murmurs. 'You defended your corner.'

ൟ

S.B. enters the hotel saloon bar where he now spends his evenings. Here he drinks steadily with his friend, the Hindu, a giant of a man whose name he has no desire to know. It's a smart saloon bar with well-upholstered chairs and small tables, patronized almost exclusively by white people. S.B. and the Hindu can sit in a quiet corner and drink beer and whisky to the ritual refrain of 'my round'. This is S.B.'s precious other world and 'no one', not his wife, not his daughters, Nasreen and Latifa, knows about his hideout. Only the Hindu knows, a man with the physique of a former wrestler and a bald dome above a gentle, Buddha-face. Only the Hindu and the whole of Bruddersford.

'My arrows are out of my pocket,' S.B. confides to the Hindu.

'Quiver. Out of your quiver.' The Hindu raises his glass in salute to S.B.'s empty quiver.

'Yes, I quiver,' S.B. says. 'A man can only lick his wounds now. People are quickly poisoned.'

'So quickly, yes,' the Hindu agrees.

'This whole business has been whipped up, you know.'

'Whipped up,' the huge Hindu smiles angelically. 'My round.' It is not in fact his round but he wants a drink.

The Hindu comes back from the bar, perfectly balancing the froth on the beer mugs in his wrestler's hands.

'Cheers.'

'Cheers. My friend, I feel this Rahman business here, here.' S.B. thumps his heart. 'Here. This filthy book would never have been let out of the bag if I had been in the UK. But now I will puncture his tyre.'

'Cheers.'

'Harry Flowers is my friend but he is a bastard, did you know that? He is saying to himself, "These Muslims they are all monkeys in the tree." These Labour bastards like Flowers and Lucas have not listened to our Muslim .hearts. A lot of girls are deserting their homes now because of this Western permissiveness. When a daughter of mine is given to her husband she is bloody well a virgin.'

The Hindu nods deep assent. 'Signed and sealed,' he says.

'But this book insults Ibrahim.'

'Ah.'

'And you are my friend. My round.'

S.B. believes he walks to and from the bar steadily. But he does not. White customers reluctant to have beer slopped over their good suits move out of his way. S.B. believes he drives home from the bar in a state of perfect sobriety, believes that a few drinks sharpen his concentration, but Nasreen and Latifa know that his license has already been endorsed by the Bruddersford magistrates – the license might have been revoked had he not been Sadar Baj Hussein.

Returning from the bar, beer spilling on to the carpet and table, S.B. explains to the Hindu that the American raid on Libya, the invasion of Grenada, the support for the Shah, the *Spycatcher* affair, the TV play, 'Death of a Princess', and the 'muzzling of the Irish patriots', is all one and the same thing as 'this fucking Rahman book'.

'You can't be too careful,' the Hindu says.

'Mind you, I respect Honourable Mrs Thatcher. Not Kinnock – cheap atheist.'

It has never occurred to S.B. that the Hindu regards Islam as a rigid, arid, puritan single-text faith dredged out of Arabian sand; a desert religion, unsupple, fearful, ferocious. He has never thought of asking the Hindu why he is so brazenly content with the suspiciously elastic reach of his own faith: the erotic music, the libidinous dancing, the ungodly colours, the shameless belief in reincarnation.

'We are not going to be a Durex for the Labour Party,' S.B. tells him. 'I am not a condom.'

'High time,' the Hindu agrees.

S.B. occupies the comfortable municipal job that his long service to Labour merits, He works for the Community Affairs Department, but Tom Potter is promising to close down the Community Affairs Department, which he recently described as yet one more example of the Labour disease of 'throwing money at problems of their own invention.'

'My father died when he was 140,' S.B. tells the Hindu.

'A great age.'

'My mother died at the age of 109 or 115.'

'A great age. And yet you are only fifty-two, I remember.'

'Sixty-two.'

'Ah. And your mother was how old when you were born?'

'Sixty, maybe seventy.'

'That is indeed a great age.'

'Donkey's years.'

'Cheers.'

'Do you know the most famous philosopher in England?'

'I do not.'

'He has been converted to Islam because of Rahman's shameful book.' But S.B. cannot remember the most famous philosopher in England's name and the Hindu seems content not to know it. This indifference spurs S.B.'s memory. 'Yes, sir, I can tell you the most famous philosopher in England. His name is George Bernard Shaw. Only the other day he remarked that Islam is the only suitable philosophy for Europe.'

S.B. and the Hindu will never discover that their daughters are friends, colleagues, both community teachers in the Department of Education.

ॐ

Zulfikar Zaheed has embarked on his summer dream. Versions of this troubled idyll command his nights whenever the Pakistan cricket team visits Yorkshire; such dreams rarely end well – but one does not volunteer for dreams.

Wearing his robes of office, Zaheed travels from Bruddersford to Leeds by mayoral limousine, chauffered by his good friend Douglas Blunt. Reaching Headingley, they take their seats in the Northern Enclosure. Zaheed loses no time in reminding his companion that the eyesore which passes for Yorkshire's country cricket ground should be pulled down – not least the grim, high stadium where the Members refuse admission to Asian Lord Mayors.

Zaheed now scrutinizes the playing surface – the pitch, sometimes called the wicket, which sometimes means the three vertical stumps at which the bowlers aim, ah cricket – through binoculars.

'That wicket resembles a dubious virgin on her wedding night. It will display its virtue when your people are batting and turn into a whore when the England bowlers need help.'

'Oh aye. Gremlins and monkeys invariably surface in the pitch when Pakistan goes in to bat. Your team manager will protest, of course.'

This insult sets Zaheed brooding. Friendship with an Englishman is probably impossible during a Test match. Morosely Zaheed takes note of the advertising hoardings encircling the ground, pride of place belonging to the sponsors of the Test series, Cornhill Insurance, whose logo is also hugely printed on the grass at both ends of the pitch.

Zaheed's binoculars now focus on the Members seated in the Football Stand, smart lapel tags clipped to their suits, as they smugly enjoy the privileged view staight down the pitch.

'Bigots, Douglas, bigots to a man.'

'Well . . .'

'I see Harry Flowers and Trevor Lucas seated next to Neil Kinnock and Roy Hattersley. They are of course plotting how best to dish Zulfikar Zaheed.'

'Keep an eye open for Adolf Hitler.'

Zaheed decides to overlook this remark; clearly the prospect of defeat is driving his friend into a barely controlled state of hysteria. Douglas knows that England are going to be wiped off the face of the earth if they're lucky. Zaheed smiles contentedly. The previous day two famous Pakistani bowlers had visited Bruddersford to autograph copies of their new books. Lord Mayor Zaheed had hosted a special halal lunch for them in City Hall. An excited crowd of young Muslims had massed outside to greet their heroes as they stepped on to the Lord Mayor's balcony – in short, Harry Flowers, MP and adulterer, is doomed.

The England team is emerging from the Pavilion. Pakistan has won the toss, a good omen, not that omens are required when sublime genius confronts mediocrity. Zaheed's binoculars settle on the England players' shirts: a crown above three rampant lions, all in blue, plus the Cornhill Insurance logo in red – and a plug for Tetley's beer.

'Deplorable, Douglas, deplorable. Alcohol.' Zulfikar's heart swells as his binoculars discover the green and yellow stripes decorating the sleeveless jerseys worn by Pakistan's two opening batsmen. 'A pity that Gamal Rahman was not raised in a cricketing culture,' he adds.

Blunt chuckles. 'Maybe that explains everything.'

'A cricketing man could not have written such a book. Why did cricket take root in British India but not in British Egypt?'

'We had a rather longer innings in India.'

'Don't forget our native Rajah class, a local aristocracy with a military tradition and the necessary irrigation to maintain cricket and polo grounds in tiptop condition.'

'Aye. Nothing but dust and dates in Egypt.'

'You won't believe this, Douglas, but when I was a boy and England came out to play Pakistan in Lahore, I prayed for an England victory.'

'Surely not?'

'I believed that the game's creators should trounce the local upstarts to sustain the dignity due to them.' Zaheed sighs.

Soon the Pakistani openers are striking the ball nicely, no problem, wood-on-leather – smack! The scoreboard races to keep pace. Above the Pavilion roof, the red-and-white flag of St George wilts while, beside it, Pakistan's white half-moon and star flutters merrily in a breeze of its own.

'Frankly, this is no contest, Douglas. It's a slaughter.'

'Our bloody bowlers need to find a line and stick to it,' Blunt mutters.

'I'm afraid "sticking to it" has always been the Englishman's answer to talent.'

TWELVE

❧

Patriarch, Party Boss (erstwhile), senior School Governor, S.B. Hussein sits before Mrs Newman's neatly ordered desk with his knees pressed together like a boy summoned for punishment. Such is the set of the Headmistress's jaw that her mouth has vanished. How well he knows that grudging smudge of a mouth. S.B. has rehearsed his 'position' – would she deny him the first opportunity in ten years to visit the land of his birth, his forebears?

'A great moment in the history of my country, Mrs Newman.'

'Mr Hussein, Ishtiaq missed a whole term's work. You did not warn me of this before your departure, or seek my consent.'

S.B.'s eyes are rusting scimitars. Carpeted by this woman!

'I am his father. My son is my son. I am not seeking anyone's consent to be the father of my son.'

'As a School Governor here, Mr Hussein, I would have expected you to set an example to other parents. You have attended many discussions over the years when this perennial issue of family-absenteeism has figured on the agenda.'

S.B. needs a drink badly. She is blackening his name to his face! 'I am all for assimilation! But a boy must know his roots in order to maintain a proper dignity in this world.'

'The very parents who take their sons and daughters out of school for months at a time, and *without permission,* invariably come back complaining to the school when their children's work falls behind and they cannot pass their GCSEs.'

Mrs Newman pushes Ishtiaq's school report across her desk. 'Your Ishtiaq suffers from a lack of discipline and concentration all round.'

'Then smack him good. I authorize it.'

'We don't employ corporal punishment in this school – as you well know. The key to discipline invariably lies in the home.'

The mercury of S.B.'s temper is swelling against the glass. He is divided about everything; he resents what he admires, scorns what he praises. Ishtiaq reports that during breaks between lessons the Asian boys are constantly harassed by prowling teachers – white teachers, always! – stamping on conversations in Urdu or Punjabi. 'Speak English, Hussein!' Mrs Newman herself regularly patrols the corridors, playgrounds, toilets, smoking-holes, her ears cocked for alien lingos. S.B. knows how well this terror had benefited his own daughters' command of English.

And why this habit of lightly drumming her fingers on her desk? Why, over the years, have their conversations been so frequently interrupted by the telephone, which Mrs Newman grabs with a vinegary blend of exasperation and relief? S.B. clearly remembers the day that she put down the phone and began cursing the Islamic Council about halal meat. As if he, S.B., wasn't sitting the other side of her desk, a Muslim! He'd heard her cursing Rajiv Lal for foisting on her a dozen places for Asian children with special needs. A great Headmistress, Patricia Newman, no nonsense, gets results, top of the City league table in GCSEs, a real Mrs Thatcher, even if he'd have knocked a male Headteacher's teeth out within the hour for such lack of respect.

S.B. remembers the first halal meat crisis. Didn't the Muslim kids deserve a hot dinner? Must they eat cold sandwiches unto eternity? Mrs Newman promptly wrote a letter, an uproar letter, to the *Echo*, deploring the 'cruel' methods of slaughtering cows and sheep without stunning them first. 'Love of dumb creatures and respect for their welfare is one of this country's values.' She even enlisted the support of the RSPCA! According to a poll, ninety per cent of Bruddersford's non-Muslims were right behind her.

'And where do we get the money to redesign the school kitchens?' Mrs Newman asked during a Governors' meeting. 'And do I have to sack my non-Muslim catering staff?'

As a good socialist, S.B. Hussein was sensitive on the last point. A good union man, he. But here it became devilish complicated. The obvious solution was to contract out the school meals to private caterers: halal dinners from Abdul Ayub Khan, 'Christian' dinners from whoever. But S.B. didn't believe in dismissing union catering workers employed by the City Council, even though they were all white.

'I'm not going to yield to bigoted fundamentalism,' Mrs Newman told the Governors. 'I already have Muslim parents crashing into my office complaining that I allow boys and girls to sit facing each other at school dinners! Separate tables isn't enough! They mustn't even catch sight of one another!'

S.B. understands that Mrs Newman's working life is a continuous sheet of sandpaper. The narrow, linoleum-corridor outside her office is eternally packed with parental petitioners and litigants. From beyond the Pennines you could hear Mrs Newman chopping them into small pieces!

'Am I a doctor? Is this a clinic? How can I look after my pupils if I have to teach common sense to their parents all day?'

Take Mrs Choudhoury, for example, barging through the throng, dragging her delinquent son Nazokat by the scruff of his neck with one hand while carrying his shoes in the other.

'Here he is,' she'd yell at Mrs Newman's English secretary in Punjabi, 'now keep him here!' So saying, she'd hurl his shoes at her huge, delinquent son. Mrs Newman would steam out of her office in top gear:

'Mrs Choudhoury! I expect even the parents of proven criminals to be slightly better behaved than their children, but maybe that's too much to ask nowadays!'

Of course Mrs Choudhoury doesn't understand. Not a word of English. Mrs C. claims that her unfaithful husband is trying to kidnap the children and take them to Pakistan, in defiance of a court order giving her care, control and custody. Some control! More than once S.B. has found himself gripping the delinquent Nazokat by the shirt.

'You stay in school, boy! Liar! Thief! Bully! You're in trouble with the police already! Obey your mother! Obey Mrs Newman or I'll knock all your teeth in within the hour!'

So here he is, carpeted by Mrs Newman, staring at Ishtiaq's appalling school report, and needing a drink badly. So badly that he can't remember whether you knock teeth in or out.

ಲ

Evening. Ali is bent over an essay-review on 'theological puzzles' commissioned by the *Times Higher Educational Supplement.* Even as he writes he visualizes the neat columns of print being passed from hand to hand in the Senior Common Room of a certain Oxford college. Time to be conciliatory; to stress the Judeo-Christian heritage in Islam; a word of praise for the current Bishop of Rome – and the noble efforts of the Anglican Church to . . . build bridges. As for Gamal Rahman, a mere semi-colon, no, an ink blot, No!

No: Gamal Rahman's mission in life is to destroy Ali Cheema. He wrote his book in order to provoke Ali into a murderous exchange. Certain members of the Islamic Council – Mustafa Jangar, Hassan Hassani – have been openly accusing Ali of compromising, of 'swallowing too much soda water in the BBC hospitality rooms' (as Mustafa put it). Even the timid Hassani had stood up at the Islamic

Council to complain that Ali had criticized him for sending inflammatory pamphlets to the Bishop. Hassani had also discovered that:

'To obtain his Oxford Fellowship, Brother Cheema depends on the Bishop's high regard. I call upon Brother Cheema to renounce this devil-inspired ambition here and now!'

Hassani sweating, shaking, losing his wife.

'Here and now!' Mustafa Jangar had repeated.

And Izza Shah? Although bent double with pain, tremors racking his wasting frame, he had delivered a thunderbolt worthy of his prime.

'Brother Cheema accompanied myself to the Bishop's Palace. Faced with my Lord (*Lahd*) Bishop's obfuscations, he never wavered. He spoke for the Prophet, peace be upon him.'

Ali detects a faint knock at the front door. It could be some out-of-work youngster selling dishcloths or drain rods, but the knock is too reticent. Ali throws down his pen, subliminally relieved (like most writers) to be interrupted.

Fatima is standing on the pavement in full burka.

'Greeting to you, sister. You have a message from your father?'

'No.'

'Can I help you?'

She nods. He waits. She is silent.

'Do you want to come in, Fatima?'

She nods.

'Come in, then. I am working, you see. And how are things at the Muslim Girls' School? Mis Zahra Aram is a fine lady.'

Fatima is slowly absorbing the details of his workroom. It is her first visit. He feels pity for her – and impatience. These long, self-indulgent, anorexic silences; this new plaster-cast as the passive Victim.

'Sit down, then. Let me clear these books and papers from the chair.'

'Don't bother.'

'Fatima, we don't get to Heaven by standing up.'

She sits and stares into space, martyred.

'Well, you've certainly started something,' he says.

'It's not right, Ali, me going to the Muslim School and the other girls at home.'

'Well, there aren't enough places for all of them. And some can't afford the fees.'

'I've decided to go back to Hightown Upper. What's in a scarf, anyway?'

Of course she hasn't decided anything of the sort. She wants his

187

opinion. No, not his opinion, his attention. His love. A brother's love. No, more than that. A lover's brotherly love. She wants to create a new drama; to draw him in; he has remained aloof from this scarf business. Yesterday he drove past Hightown Upper while Mustafa Jangar was haranguing a small army of placards – Mustafa the Mahdi of Bruddersford's Twelver Shi'ites and their Sunni converts.

'What does your father say?' Ali asks Fatima, knowing the answer.

'I haven't told him.'

'Just me?'

She drops her gaze, fidgets with her burka. He returns to his desk and glowers sceptically at what he has written:

Too much human history is attached to Twelver Shi'ism. In the sixteenth century CE it became the state religion of the Safavid dynasty in Persia/Iran. In recent times it has served as Khomeini's weapon against the Shah's subservience to America and Israel. And this is the crunch: what the Europeans call 'the separation of Church and State'. Since the sixteenth century and the emergent doctrine of the 'divine right of kings', it was the European state, always the state, which repeatedly sought to encroach on that famous separation of functions. The Elizabethan Reformation created a permanent poodle in the shape of the Anglican Church; Napoleon took the imperial crown from the Pope's hand and laid it on his own head; the French Revolution went even further by chasing priests and monks into the nearest pond.

It was the American constitution which restored the ancient and necessary separation of church and state. Theocracy attempts to destroy that separation but reverses the equation: the church becomes the state. This was the dream of the Puritan sects, Calvinists, Brownists, Fifth Monarchists and Millennarians. And this is Khomeini all over! A Twelver Shi'ite who really means business.

Exiled to Najaf in Iraq, Khomeini began to insist that holy men are the only legitimate political rulers of an Islamic state, the true successors to the Prophet himself. The imam was the living agent of the hidden Twelfth Imam and governed on his behalf until his reappearance.

And now? Now Iran's entire power-structure is centred on the Wali-e-Faquih, the Jurist who deputizes for the Hidden Imam. This is Khomeini. Every personal obsession is elevated to a religious rule. If Khomeini decides that women should not peel more than five aubergines for fear of arousing erotic impulses, Mustafa Jangar passes on the instruction, gravely, to the Muslims of Bruddersford.

Mustafa makes no bones about his objective: to replace Izza

Shah and take control of the Islamic Council on behalf of Twelver Shi'ism.

Ali throws down his pen. He has almost forgotten Fatima's ghostly presence. The shrouded waif doesn't seem to mind him ignoring her. Perhaps it makes her feel at home, watching him at work.

'I could cook your dinner,' she says.

'What about your father's dinner?'

'He's in the hospital, isn't he?'

Ali jumps up. 'Hospital? I didn't know that. Tell me, girl.'

'It's just tests, they say. Overnight in St George's. I didn't want to be alone, what with the phone calls and things through the door.'

It is his turn to nod. 'Of course. You must stay here.' As he says it, he suffers a premonition of Fatima permanently on his hands if Izza Shah's prostate trouble should turn out to be malignant cancer.

'We can make some supper,' he says.

'I can do it.' She moves swiftly towards the hole in the wall which is his kitchen. Dirty dishes and pots are piled high in the sink. 'Just carry on with yer work, Ali. I'll manage.'

A motorcycle roars up the narrow street of terraced houses, stops, revs its engine, then guns away. Immediately there is a very loud thumping at his door.

Safia is done up to the nines, shimmering like a Christmas tree. She is as clearly No Good this evening as every other evening. A cascade of foaming auburn hair tumbles over her shoulders. Her heavy lips are aflame, her mouth an open wound. The street reeks of cheap perfume and motor bike.

'Well, are you going to invite me in or not?'

'To what do I owe the honour of this visit?'

'Just passing.'

'No one "just passes" along Nuneaton Road.'

'Don't be stuck up, Ali. Just because yer never off telly.'

He shrugs and steps aside. Her pointed breasts caress him as she passes into the narrow hallway stacked with books, magazines, boxes, his bicycle.

'Fatima is here,' he says, nodding towards the clatter in the kitchen (which has abruptly grown louder). With a flounce of her hips Safia makes for the kitchen. Fatima is staring into space, rigid.

'So what's this all about?' Safia says.

'Your father's in hospital tonight,' Ali says.

'So?'

'Fatima didn't want to spend the night alone.'

'Is that your story?' Safia taunts Fatima.

Safia is in permanent motion, pulling her hair out of her eyes, a step forward, a step back, examining herself in any surface which yields the faintest reflection. 'Well, great,' she says. 'Cosy, aren't we?' Taking a pack of purple chewing gum from her bag, she delicately inserts a piece in her mouth.

'Don't suppose yer got a fag?'

He has; under intellectual stress he sometimes smokes.

'Safia, I'm working.'

'So I see!' She tosses her head in the direction of Fatima, whose narrow, taut back is now bent over the sink. Safia's long nails flick at the pages on Ali's desk. 'I bet it's that Rahman book again. All that fuss about a bloody bewk! Couldn't understand a word o'it m'self.'

'You *read* it!' exclaims Fatima.

Safia shrugs. 'God, what a sight, that girl, black from head to toe.'

'And what sort of a sight are you?' Fatima cries.

'Shut it or I'll clip yer. Bitch. Listen, Gamal Rahman's no skin off my nose – though he's dead right about Muslim women. That's what all the fuss is about, i'n't it? Patriarchy in peril. Collapse of male ego. He never said the Prophet had thirteen wives, did he? So why does every Muslim woman in Bruddersford swear blind that he did? You can't blame him just because a lot of ignorant Egyptian peasants thought they'd spotted a thirteenth wife running around in the sand.'

'Safia, be silent,' Ali commands. 'You are trespassing on the terrain of divine providence.'

'Yeah, all very convenient for you men.' Idly Safia picks up a recent Sunday supplement in which Ali's smooth young face appears like a pixie peeping through columns of words. She jiggles her chewing gum. 'Me, I'm not spending my life wrapped in a dishcloth!'

'She wants to be a model in London,' Fatima says from the kitchen. 'We all know what that means.'

'Just shut it!' Safia yells, then swivels to display herself to Ali. 'Look – I've got what it takes. You're always hobnobbing with those media types in London, so why don't you take me along? I need a break, Ali!'

Fatima emits a long howl, drops all the kitchen pots on the floor and runs from the house.

౷

Joe Reddaway strides through the stone-terraced streets of Bellingham, 'Humphrey' on a tight lead, passing the tall chimney of Lister's Mill and City football stadium where fire had once consumed a crowd. He'd been there that winter afternoon, a day to forget. He knew families who'd never recovered – white families of course, even the toughest young Asians steered clear of the football. Men in pale brown tunics and square carpenter hats are hurrying, singly and in squadrons, towards the box-shaped Blenheim Mosque. In every street and cobbled alleyway kids are out to greet the pale, watery sunshine, girls in bright peasant costumes playing hopscotch on the pavements, shouting and squealing in broad Yorkshire. The boys play cricket in the street, using plastic milk crates as stumps; those prepubescent girls who've been enlisted as 'fielders' stand stiffly in faintly resentful postures, never getting to bowl or bat, and yelled-at when, daydreaming, they fail to stop the ball.

'Go on, Musarrat, chase it!'

Musarrat, Joe knows, means happiness. The girls move relucantly in their glinting, spangled trouser-suits, as if aware of impropriety in any female physical motion beyond a slow walk. Joe passes the entrance to the mosque: shoes are piled in the hallway. He can hear gargling and splashing from the washroom. And what does young Ali Cheema have to say about the gargling and splashing in today's *Times?*

Because God revealed himself to man, and through man, He can be understood by each generation only through human behaviour and human faith. The genuine philosopher must exist both inside and outside the human condition. Man is both captive (Satan) and free (God). There are no exceptions. This is the paradox and the puzzle we have to live with.

Thanks a lot, Ali. Joe prefers the dialogue from Brecht:

—We're all in God's hands.

—Things can't be that bad.

Glancing up the hill, Joe notices that the portly little Imran Hassani, Nasreen's son, is batting in the middle of the street. The fat boy swings his bat clumsily, misses, looks sulky. A stick-thin young woman – Imran's auntie – is approaching at speed.

'Hullo, Latifa.'

She half-smiles, her hand automatically reaching up to adjust her headscarf.

'How's your Dad?' he says.

'Fine. When are you coming to see him, then? Time you gave us a visit.' She stops, embarrassed: Joe probably knows where S.B. Hussein is to be found of an evening. 'I didn't read your latest piece,' Latifa says, 'but I hear it was diabolical. You may not be going to Heaven after all.'

191

'That's because I can't find a wife.'

She yields a full smile. He knew she would. He really enjoys Latifa, such a bloody bright girl – and no girl, either, probably twenty-three or twenty-four, not to mention a LRSC in chemistry. Funny the way the brighter Asian girls go for chemistry. Joe had always loathed the subject. Maybe that's the reason. Maybe it's easy to enrol.

'Any luck getting a job?' he asks.

'No.' She smiles. 'Mum says we've got ghosts in the house.'

'How many?'

Latifa laughs. 'Ever since the Rahman book there's been an out-break of ghosts. Our Ishtiaq is refusing to sleep at night in case Gamal Rahman's hiding under the bed. Dad called in the imam just in case. Dad says his own dad knew a man in Pakistan who protected the village by going out at night to talk to djinns.'

'Djinns?'

'Aye. They're bad news, so Mum says.' She shrugs. 'Anyways, the imam gave us these tokens to wear round our necks as protection.'

'Is Gamal Rahman a djinn – horns and cloven feet?'

'That's not funny. Dad was hopping mad about your book-burning article in the *Echo*.'

'I thought he was in Pakistan at the time!'

'Well, I kept it for him, didn't I?'

Again adjusting her headscarf, she throws him an impertinent look. Out of such moments are marriages made – but S.B. as a father-in-law isn't Joe's ticket or wicket.

'How's Nasreen?'

'Nas's OK. Worried about Fatima, of course.'

'What's your view on the Fatima affair?'

'Is this an interview? Well . . . I think she's a good girl and should be allowed to do what she feels is right.' Latifa is vaguely conscious of having expressed the opposite view to Nasreen and other Muslims. 'Anyways, that woman Mrs Newman is a right pig. She's even accusing Nas of immorality.'

'Meaning?'

Latifa is biting her runaway tongue. If only she had more people to talk to.

'I was kidding if you want to know.'

'About Rajiv Lal, is it?' Joe probes.

'You've got some cheek, Joe Reddaway.' Latifa glances sideways; a few words with a man in the street is one thing . . . 'Bye,' she says and walks on. As he passes Imran's cricket game the boys call after him, begging 'Big Joe' to bowl one of his famous googlies, and he can't

192

resist, though a rubber ball on hard tarmac isn't a cricket ball on a nicely crumbling grass pitch.

'I'll let Hoomphrey bowl this one,' he says. They love that.

REDDAWAY SAVES ENGLAND!

Joe's destination is the Three Anchors on the main Wittlesea Road, where he has an appointment with Harry Flowers, MP, no less. Entering the bar, he finds Flowers with the District Labour Party's young and cheerful Chairman, Pradesh Singh, who earns his bread in the City's Housing Department and is running Harry Flowers's re-selection campaign. Singh no longer wears the Sikh turban and has cut his hair.

Flowers buys Joe a pint. 'That should silence you for a month.' Bruddersford West's man in Parliament is wearing a Jaeger roll-neck sweater in sky blue and a tweed jacket from Aquascutum. His coiffeured hair is surf-boarding above his suntan.

'Cheers, Harry. So why don't you Sikhs and Hindus speak up?' Joe asks Pradesh Singh. 'You know you're pissed off about the Rahman affair. Your kids are getting as much abuse in the streets as the Muslims.'

'Abuse? Outright physical attacks. Bricks, iron bars, the lot. Listen, Joe, the city I want to live in is not the Ayatollah's Bruddersford, nor Mrs Thatcher's Bruddersford, nor Khalistan-Bruddersford either.'

'Then stop sitting on your hands, Pradesh.'

'The trouble with this overweight hack,' Flowers says, 'is that he wants to make the news he reports.'

'Someone has to make it,' Joe says. 'The Labour Party never will.'

'Ugly situations require cool heads,' Flowers says, ordering himself another gin and tonic with a wink at the barmaid. 'I've never known it worse. The BNP are coming back up out of the sewers. If the Labour Party loses control of this city I wouldn't like to think what might happen.'

'You mean an end to corruption, jobbing and ward-heeling?' Joe asks innocently.

'You're a bloody Tory at heart, Joe. The *Echo* has always hated socialists.'

'Socialists? There aren't many of those around. Anyway, no one tells me what to write.'

'Every Tory paper can carry one lunatic,' Pradesh Singh says.

'I'm fed up with this cowardly silence from the City Council – and all those do-gooders like Quddus carefully sitting on their hands. I've seen mullahs and imams out in the streets campaigning for Haqq!'

'It happened in Poland,' Flowers says. 'It's called Liberation Theology in South America.'

193

'Frankly,' says Pradesh Singh, 'I feel safer living among Muslims than in a white area. But I miss the songs and music of the Punjab in this austere, music-less, Muslim universe.'

'What became of those Sufi mystics who once challenged the rituals of the mullahs?' Joe says.

'Do you know the story of the Sufi who was rebuked for lying down with his feet, rather than his head, pointing towards Mecca? "Turn me anyway where my head is not pointing towards God," he answered.'

'I might use that,' Joe says.

'Well don't quote me,' Singh says.

'So what's today's Party line on Izza Shah's daughter's headscarf?' Joe asks Flowers.

'Looking after your daughter is important to all Asians.' Flowers smiles cynically. 'The Rahman affair is all about keeping the chastity belts locked. That's off the record.'

'The iron chastity belt is a Western invention unknown in the East,' Singh says.

'Well, it's good to see you, Harry, at long last,' Joe says. 'Been playing Greta Garbo recently, have you?'

'I'm better looking.'

'Better looking than Zulfikar Zaheed? I hear he's in London buying twenty new suits. And talking to Kinnock.'

'We're a democratic party.'

'How's your new research assistant in London, Harry?'

'If you want me to sue you for your boots, Joe, I'll do it.'

'Haqq's doing quite nicely against Hani Malik, I hear.'

'Hani Malik will wipe him out,' Flowers says. 'Lucas and Perlman will wipe out the Khan brothers. Storm in a teacup.'

'Give or take a riot or two?'

Flowers shrugs. 'Lot of kids in this city are now behaving like well-rehearsed extras in a film.'

'And what about Mustafa Jangar? Why hasn't the local Labour Party called for his prosecution: clear incitement to murder?'

'The fundamentalists are itching for prosecutions. Time will come when people will get stone bored with all this fuss about a book. Or a girl's scarf. So let's have some martyrs! Between you and me, the Thatcher Government's handling of the Rahman affair is diabolically brilliant. Who's laughing in Bruddersford? Tom Potter, the Geoff Boycott of City Hall. No strokes offered, content to wait for the no-balls.'

'And Zulfikar Zaheed – he's hot on your heels?'

'Hamlet Zaheed, you mean?' Flowers carefully surveys their neighbours at the bar. His voice drops. 'This is off the record, Joe. I have it from inside sources at the Home Office that Zaheed's daughter Wahabia was seen with Ali Cheema outside that bookshop in Charing Cross Road only minutes before it was fire-bombed.'

'It was fire-bombed at night.'

'Correct.'

'Who saw them? Who recognized them?'

'Anonymous telephone call.'

'Police enquiries?'

'Not a chance. They reckon someone's setting up Zaheed.'

ॐ

'May all Gamal Rahman's filthy lucre choke in his throat, and may he die a coward's death, mired in misery, a hundred times a day, and eventually when death catches up with him, may he simmer in Hell for all eternity!'

Mustaga Jangar is already in full flood at evening prayers when Ali Cheema arrives late at the Maududi Mosque – he's usually late. During the lunch hour he had visited Izza Shah in St George's Hospital, but was told that Mr Shah was under sedation. After work Ali called on Fatima, who had fled the previous evening, soon after Safia showed up, and was relieved to find her in the comforting company of Nasreen Hassani. But there the comfort ended. Ali's arrival seemed to hurl the ashen, sleepless Fatima to the verge of hysteria.

'He's fucking my sister,' she told Nasreen with an unnerving, lunatic smile. 'My sister wants to marry my brother.'

Nasreen's troubled gaze remained fixed on the Holy Mosque of Mecca hanging over the mantelpiece.

Fatima laughed nastily, a screech. 'And you, Mrs Hassani, are a whore living in sin with Mr Rajiv Lal.'

Then the brick came through the sitting room window and Fatima collapsed into Nasreen's arms.

Kneeling in the Maududi Mosque as if at prayer, Ali is pondering whether Gamal Rahman is eligible for full membership of Hell. Surely Hell is a divine space reserved for errant believers – can one go to Hell if one refuses to believe in it? The Koran curses the non-believer; but what determines faith? It's a puzzle. And what is really involved in the doctrine of free will? Such questions will inevitably come up during the formal interview at the College. Indeed an impressively letterheaded communication has summoned him to attend the following week:

You will have an opportunity to meet the other short-listed candidates, including Mr Gamal Rahman. The College believes that you should be accorded a unique opportunity to put your professed principles into practice by assassinating the devil's instrument in full view of the assembled Fellows. We have commissioned Señor Goya to execute the painting.

The letter was signed, 'Mahmoud, PBUH, Master of the College'.

ை

The Odeon offers *Warlock* (15) – 'He's come from the past to destroy the future.' Tariq is drooped across the upstairs bar of the empty Omar Khayyam, half-listening to Pennine Radio and half-reading the ads in the *Echo*. Rana might fancy *Warlock*. Then there's *Married to the Mob* (15) with Michelle Pfeiffer and Dean Stockwell. Then there's Arnold Schwarzenegger and Danny DeVito in *Twins* (PG). Then there's *Hellbound: Hellraiser II* (18) – 'It will tear your soul apart . . . Again.'

Tariq knows what Rana would really like: *Gypsy*, 'The Smash Hit Family Musical' at the Alhambra. Tariq cannot afford two seats at the Alhambra though Rana certainly can. Maybe she's sitting there right now, with some bloke, some off-duty police sergeant or the like. The last time he waited for her in the dark street outside Uncle Abdul Ayub Khan's house she didn't suggest a kiss-and-cuddle up near the Council estate. She told Tariq that she had been put on 'special duties'.

'Yes, Tariq. That means identifying potential troublemakers and anyone inciting Gamal Rahman's murder.'

'So?' (But he was shaken: Rana spying on her own people!)

'So I don't know yer, got it? Not until all this blows over.'

Tariq's most recent arrest occurred after he learned that white youths carrying RAHMAN RULES placards had gathered, mob-like and tooled-up, outside Hightown Upper to bait the Muslim pickets and throw beer over the Asian girls. When Tariq and his Muslim Youth League mujaheddin showed up, the iron bars and blades came out. Children ran screaming and parents cringed as youths with murder beneath their headbands tore across the streets. Five were carted to hospital and Tariq spent the night in a police cell for the third time in a month.

MUSLIM CANDIDATE'S SON ARRESTED AGAIN.

The front page of the *Echo* carried photographs of Tariq, Karamat Khan, and Uncle Abdul.

But even then Uncle Abdul did not send his nephew packing. When the moon is full and when the moon is asleep behind the curtain of night, in times of fasting and in times of feasting, the Prophet enjoins us to love our family. The morning after Tariq's release on police bail, Ishmail Haqq came storming into the Omar Khayyam and gave Tariq what Tariq later described to his mates as 'a terrific bollocking' – with Uncle Abdul hovering in the rear, sighing.

'Do you have a brain in your head? Does Islam deserve juvenile delinquents? Does Islam teach us to spit upon the father who begat us and the uncle who held out the hand of love?'

AI. What's 'AI'? Drooped across the upstairs bar of the empty Omar Khayyam, Tariq turns to the jobs columns and other 'Opportunities' in the *Daily Millat*. He's not familiar with this thing: 'AI'. He knows Aids but not this 'AI.' But he gets the message from the Burnside Clinic ad.: he is 'healthy', he is Punjabi (Bengalis and Gujaratis also required), and he could make a little money, enough to take Rana to the Alhambra.

Next morning he phones the clinic from a call box. A female voice answers.

'Burnside Clinic.'

'I'm inquiring about this ad.' Tariq hopes he sounds upmarket.

'Are you a potential donor, sir?'

'I'm thinking about it.'

'What racial group, sir?'

'Punjabi-Muslim.'

'Age?'

'Twenty-two.'

'Do you have a birth certificate, sir?'

'Definitely.'

'You can visit us any time between nine and five, sir.'

Arriving at the clinic, he is given a blood test, a cup of tea and a brief interview with a chubby man in a white coat, Dr Braithwaite, who shows him a (very) broad test tube.

'In there.'

'Ah.'

'You can either take yourself to the toilet here, if you're in the mood, or you can take it home.'

'Oh, no, 'ome.'

'Fine. Now this is a freezer-canister in which to deposit the test tube, when full. It has to go straight into the freezer, understood?'

Tariq realizes that he's going to have to deposit his own sperm either in his mother's refrigerator or the Omar Khayyam's. Dr Braithwaite wearily reads this dilemma:

'If that creates domestic problems, Mr Khan, just jerk yourself off here and now. Much simpler. We have some girlie mags in the toilet if you're feeling inhibited.'

Tariq doesn't know the word but knows he's feeling it.

'Whatever you do, do not attempt to run water over the outside of the test tube. If some semen spills on the outside, no matter.'

'Right.'

'Make sure you wash your hands thoroughly before you masturbate.'

చు

A cheque for 150 pounds arrives at Ishmail Haqq's address, made out to him personally, and signed Iqbal Iqbal. An enigmatic message, in Punjabi, seems to indicate that God's warriors are coming up from the grave – everywhere. Haqq decides to risk a phone call. Iqbal Iqbal sounds shy, not a warrior, not interested in politics. Evidently his car has recently been vandalized; he wants the hands of the villains to be cut off and posted to him by the 'High Court'. Hearing this, Haqq fears that Iqbal's cheque will bounce but readily agrees about the justice of sending the severed hands of criminals through the post. Haqq agrees about everything.

'Heavier penalties for rape,' murmurs the soft voice over the phone.

'I agree, Mr Iqbal, we all do. Your advice is taken most seriously I assure you.'

'The pederasts should be whipped to death.'

'Agreed.'

'Women taken in adultery stoned to death.'

'Long overdue, sir.'

'Rahman executed.'

'Every good Muslim feels as you do, sir.'

Iqbal's voice suddenly gains in volume: 'I'm not talking about feeling, I'm talking about doing. Doing doing, Mr Haqq. Why is this elementary step not in your party's manifesto?'

It occurs to Haqq that he is being set-up, framed, bugged by Hani Malik's Labour machine.

'Which mosque do you belong to, Mr Iqbal?'

'The Tabligh Mosque, Knightley. The Christians round here are quite active in the new St Peter's Church. They wear their best clothes for weddings and baptisms and so forth, but I want them to understand that Islam is not the enemy of Christianity. Islam is the perfection of Christianity.'

'Agreed, Brother.'

'I want them to know that I regret the recent changes in the Bible.

198

Now they have changed the Bible to claim that Jesus is the son of God. That is a recent corruption designed to prevent the hearts and souls of Christians falling to Islam.'

'That is indeed serious, Brother.'

'It is very serious. But it is not in your party's manifesto. I have written a pamphlet on the true Jesus and the false Jesus. I have printed this pamphlet at my own expense. I have sent you one hundred and fifty pounds. I want your party to distribute this pamphlet.'

Haqq groans. Another nut.

'We should meet,' Iqbal is saying. 'You must not come to my home. The Christian police are now watching my home. Round the clock surveillance. You must come to my pharmacy.'

༄

Hassan Hassani's cuttings are beginning to make unauthorized journeys. The floor under his desk is littered with them, some already ancient, yellowing, trying to lose themselves. He reaches for the glue bottle and carefully dabs the corners of a captured cutting, trapping it in his scrapbook, nailing the liberal-secular-Christian-Jewish Western World to its own infamy:

WILDING IN THE NIGHT. A brutal gang rape in New York City triggers fears that the US is breeding a generation of merciless children. Last week in Manhattan these six teenagers were indicted for the rape of a 28-year-old investment banker who was jogging in Central Park

Below, six pics, all obviously taken in police custody, with heads bowed in varying degrees: 14, 15, 16, 15, 15, 14. Hassan gazes at the young niggers. Baboons. Apes. That poor white lady jogger. He is bathed in sweat. It's getting to him. Soiled, befouled, he begs Allah to condone his self-lacerating labour. His forehead strikes the desk and leaves a damp patch. The house is full of ghosts. His plump fingers flutter at the keyboard ('Satan Speaks'):

Does it make the white ladies' mouths water, that Rahman wants them to be fucked by black people and thrown away? Gamal Rahman himself has already set the example, he has FUCKED AND THROWN AWAY the noble Egyptian ladies and . . .

Hassan rubs the dancing obscenities from his eyes: novelists and whores, where's the difference? Carefully he hangs his business suit and soaking-wet shirt on his bedside chair. Pushing open the bathroom door, he smells his wife's sandalwood cologne, the gentle fragrance of her love for Rajiv Lal. Hassan knows that she wishes to be rid of him, it's in her constantly distracted eyes – that Hindu! Hassan's drunken father-in-law, S.B. Hussein, had phoned him with an incoherent warning, some jumbled story, in which the name Rajiv Lal was the only constant. Hassan stumbles back to his desk in the bedroom, giddy with hatred:

Nobody has yet drawn the attention of Rahman's Hindu admirers to the obscene defamations he heaps upon the gods and goddesses of their faith, the 'lecherous' Rama, the 'flighty' Sita, the 'adulterous' Shiva . . .

Hassan runs out of Hindu deities and Hindu sins. Dutifully he clears away, stows his text, his notes – such things must never defile his family's eyes. I honour my wife, my family. He creeps into bed. Nasreen's back, as always, is turned, but Allah will replenish his soul. In the morning he will drive to work along the Headland bypass, his ear alert to news of roadworks and tailbacks on local radio, ready to plant his prayer mat in his favourite lay-by at 129 degrees to Mecca.

Motionless but wide-awake, her back turned to her snoring husband, Nasreen cannot forget the snake-venom in Fatima's accusation: *And you, Mrs Hassani, are a whore living in sin with Mr Rajiv Lal.* By what devilish telepathy are such secrets of the heart transmitted? Is Fatima possessed by an all-knowing djinn?

ॐ

Izza Shah has been released from hospital, brought home in an ambulance, Fatima at his side. Ali has had the broken window repaired. Leaving his shabby office at the Community College, and regretting the sacrifice of another uninterrupted evening's writing, Ali presents himself at the old man's bedside. Opening the door, Fatima averts her gaze. Nothing is said between them. Ali goes straight up. Izza's room is in semi-darkness, lit by one weak table lamp. It smells of urine.

'How are you?' Ali asks in Punjabi.

Izza is holding the Holy Book.

'Time will tell. I have been reading the Qur'an, 53, where it is said: "The goal of all things is God. He is the One from whom starts Reality. No other can ever intercede except as He wills." '

Ali removes a damp towel and a spare pair of underpants from a broken-backed wooden chair. He places it beside the bed.

200

'Mustafa Jangar has visited St George's Hospital, seeking a medical certificate to prove that you are no longer capable.'

This is slowly absorbed. 'Mustafa? Surely not.'

'Mustafa has been campaigning to depose you as President of the Islamic Council,' Ali adds.

Izza shakes his head in disbelief. His voice comes slowly, as if cranked out of a barrel organ. 'The Holy Qur'an tells us of the constant intercession of Satan in his many guises: "That He may make the suggestions thrown in by Satan, but a trial for those in whose hearts is a disease and who are hardened of heart . . ." '

'Yes, Father,' Ali says, 'but consider Mustafa's recent behaviour. Can we conclude that Satan troubles only evil minds?' The carved sphinx is impassive. An ugly clock, a gift from the Jamiyat in Pakistan, ticks on a prefabricated shelf above the boarded-in coal fireplace.

'Are you sure about Mustafa Jangar, my son?'

'Yes, Father.'

Izza Shah quotes again: ' "Many are the gates of Evil, but peace and dignified joy will be the goal of those whom the grace of God has made His own." '

Ali is helping the old man urinate into the heavy china chamber pot Fatima keeps under his bed. The shrunken genitals disturb him. Did we all drip out of something like this? Ali had never seen his own father's penis. Do we somehow, mysteriously, choose our parents? Had his father and mother really died in a car accident or had Ali himself somehow willed the independence he had inherited from their violent deaths? He forces his mind back to the eternal puzzle of predestination and free will. Choice, after all, is implicit in the constant prayer, striving and fighting incumbent upon the faithful. Why does God bestow his 'grace' on X but not on Y?

Izza Shah is back in bed. Ali fixes his pillows. Izza has never in his life said 'thank you' to any member of his family. Ali leaves the bad-smelling room to empty the bowl into the toilet. Fatima is standing at the foot of the stairs as if waiting to be summoned.

'Go to bed, Fatima,' Ali says.

'I can no longer attend the Muslim Girls' School,' she says.

Ali shrugs – she'll stop at nothing to command his attention, even by defaming him in front of Nasreen Hassani.

'The other girls are accusing me of betrayal,' she says. 'The other girls are missing school. Mustafa Jangar's daughter and Ishmail Haqq's daughter accuse me of betrayal. They are calling me a hypocrite.'

'Take no notice, then.'

'You must be my tutor.'

'Go to bed.'

She doesn't move. He returns to Izza Shah's bedside. Among Bruddersford Muslims, Ali alone – perhaps – has noticed the most recent statement by the Ayatollah. Addressing instructors and students of Iran's religious seminaries, Ruhollah al-Musavi al-Khomeini justified his fatwa on Gamal Rahman – 'this dangerous snake and mercenary' – and scorned its detractors:

> God wanted this blasphemous book to be published now, so that the world of conceit, of arrogance and barbarism, could bare its true face in its long-held enmity to Islam . . . part of the effort of the World Devourers to annihilate Islam and Muslims.

What can this mean? It can mean only that Satan, Evil, is not a force run amok, out of control, but is, on the contrary, God's instrument: 'God wanted this blasphemous book to be published!' Ali can hear Gamal's corrosive chuckle: 'Publish my book, ban my book, two rapid motions in God's will. To awaken the faithful. Is that it?'

'You are my heir,' Izza says. 'Fatima will be yours to govern and yours to protect.'

Ali sits down on the broken-backed wooden chair, folds his hands.

'And Safia,' Izza adds weakly.

The Jamiyat clock is ticking. Duty dictates that Ali should move in to the spare room, by night at least – a life of captivity. Goodbye to the modern world. Izza Shah is asleep. Ali reaches for his wrist to feel the old man's pulse. Is death days or weeks away? Then what? Mustafa Jangar and Twelver Shi'ism will ride triumphant.

On his way out Ali finds Fatima sitting like a broken stick on the bottom stair. *I should pack a bag and return tonight.* He passes her with a simple 'Goodnight'. Hurrying home to his desk, through the street-cricketing children of a summer evening, Ali composes an answer to Rahman: 'God sweeps up Satan's dung and turns it into fire and light.'

As he enters the kitchen in Nuneaton Road a scuttling mouse catches the outer rim of his sightline. Must put down more poison, lay more traps. Safia has gone, leaving the bedroom in a mess and a lipsticked message across the bathroom mirror: 'Fuck you.'

He has no sooner settled at his desk with a cup of milky tea than the phone rings.

'Hullo, Ali darling! It's me.'

'Yes?'

'Is that all you can say?'

'I was working.'

'Jasmin tells me that Gamal is about to publish a huge piece in *Prospero* – the story of his life.'

'Send me a copy.'

'Gamal hasn't let Jasmin see a proof yet but she got the gist from Rory McKenzie. Gamal wants the world to know how he came to write *The Devil: an Interview.* He's also keen to reveal the true nature of his relationship with President Sharaf and the Sharaf ladies.'

'The truth is not Rahman's currency. I've no doubt he engaged in disgusting practices – I've said so in a piece due to appear next Sunday.'

'Perhaps you should wait until we hear Gamal's version.'

'No good Muslim is obliged to wait for Rahman.'

'Apparently he claims to have had long conversations with the devil.'

'I expect he gives himself all the best lines.'

'Apparently Gamal's father, the novelist Mahmoud, appeared to him in his sleep, disguised as the devil.'

'Mahmoud renounced him, disowned him – it's common knowledge.'

'Jasmin believes Gamal hasn't concealed a thing. He even plunges into the hot water of his dealings with the Israelis and the true story of Huda el-Sharaf.'

'The so-called thirteenth wife of the Prophet. We can confidently expect another outburst of blasphemy.'

'Apparently Gamal insists that he never supported the Sharaf regime. They threw him into prison.'

'They threw him into prison for embezzling State funds and priceless Egyptian antiquities.'

'Jasmin says that isn't true.'

'For years Rahman worked with Hosny Hikmat, arguably the greatest of Egyptian newspaper editors – though in my opinion a time-serving atheist. Shortly before his death from cancer, Hikmat told Henri Chevalier, of *Le Monde*, that Rahman was the most corrupt journalist he'd ever employed or known.'

'Gamal's piece exposes Chevalier, Jasmin says.'

'As you know, I don't share your high opinion of Jasmin's intelligence. She grabs at anything that glitters – a Hindu trait, between ourselves.'

'Jasmin is hardly a Hindu!'

'Try and get me an advance copy of Rahman's apologia. Inigo Lorraine's bound to have one.'

Wahabia's tone becomes commandingly practical.

'I'm coming north next weekend to stay with Daddy. You and I are taking over Zaheed's campaign.'

'Apparently Benazir Bhutto does it.'

'Does what, Ali?'

'She invariably refers to her executed father as "Bhutto".'

Wahabia giggles. 'Gamal once told me I reminded him of Hamida el-Sharaf. Now it's Benazir. I'm not doing badly.'

'I'm not interested in politics,' Ali says.

'But you're interested in me. By the way! Who was that uneducated female who answered your phone?'

'It must have been Safia. Izza Shah has been in hospital. I felt it my duty to – '

'No need to apologize. Why do you sound so guilty about it? Now listen, I'm catching the early train from King's Cross on Saturday. Ali, are you listening?'

THIRTEEN

❧

Nasreen is now 'seeing things'.

'I can't concentrate from one moment to the next,' she tells Latifa. 'I don't know why. I really don't know why. And then, you know, I'm looking at one thing and quite another jumps at me from the shadows.'

'You should see Dr Khalil, Nas.'

Her younger sister's angular scrutiny is softened by concern but there are no flies on Latifa.

'Heavens, Latifa, are you a complete fool! Dad would hear of it in no time. I don't want Dad telling me to leave Hassan – do I? *Do* I?'

'You haven't been eating, Nas.'

'You should talk! You're nothing but skin and bone!'

'How much weight have you lost, Nas?'

'How should I know? What use is it talking to you? How can you know what's it like to be a married woman, what with Dad passing remarks about Hassan on a daily basis and Mother asking me why Imran has neither brother nor sister though he's nine years old. Honestly, Latifa, I sometimes think you'll never marry anyone, I mean any man who so much as looks at you is turned to stone.'

'Don't you want more children, Nas?'

'Heavens! Hassan is not interested in that.'

'What does it have to do with him? Just go ahead.'

'He is not interested in what makes children. Can a man conceive a child by prayer and writing pamphlets all night?'

Latifa unfolds the *Echo* which lies across the kitchen table, open at Joe Reddaway's latest 'Plain Speaking' diatribe against Islam. Timidly she points a chewed fingernail to a display advertisement under the 'Personal' columns:

Pregnancy Wanted? Seek Medical Advice. At the Burnside Clinic you can specify the sperm required: Pakistan, North India, Muslim, Hindu. Tested for HIV Positive and Hepatitis.

'Latifa, what do you take me for? Are you calling your sister a whore? I am shocked that you should even look at such things. Anyway, how could I afford something like that? Don't you know the prices they charge?'

Latifa shrugs meekly. 'There's a shortage of Asian sperm – only two donors for every twenty-five women requiring the service.'

'Don't be speaking to me in that disgusting manner.'

Latifa subsides on to a kitchen chair, her legs spread wide in what always strikes Nasreen as an unladylike posture.

'Oh I heard all about this Burnside Clinic and places like that,' Nasreen says. 'Some white doctor offers you a test tube which he claims is straight from a Muslim clinic in Bombay or Delhi, but how do you know the donor isn't some filthy Hindu Untouchable? Or some black-skinned Tamil from the South, a Christian even? Now kindly don't be telling me how to have children, Latifa, worry on your own account, you're not getting any younger. Now look, I'll be late for my meeting with Mr Rajiv Lal, I can't sit around here all day gossiping.'

Nasreen has no scheduled meeting with Rajiv Lal. Latifa's dancing eyes are insolent with knowledge.

'I suppose, Nas, that we all have to take it out on someone.'

Reaching the front door of S.B. Hussein's home – the house in which she grew up – Nasreen drops her leather briefcase to embrace her sister.

'I've become completely horrible, haven't I? You don't deserve such a sister. I'm even horrible to Imran. Sometimes I catch him looking exactly like his father and I can't bear it. I didn't mean anything I said to you – I only meant that you could have any intelligent Muslim in Bruddersford for a husband and – ' suddenly Nasreen smiles, laughs, 'and it's cruel to keep them all in suspense!'

Releasing herself from the embrace, Latifa smiles bravely. 'Now don't you be seeing things, our Nas!'

But once on the bus, Nasreen is back with her dancing ghosts, her jumping djinns. She has never felt like this before, though her work has brought her into contact with disturbed children and parents close to schizophrenia. Close! Don't speak that word! I want to be close to Rajiv! I want Rajiv Lal's baby. She feels sure, quite sure, though not always sure, that Rajiv has been cooler to her of late, since his visit to Mrs Newman. That woman had humiliated him. Why has he forbidden Nasreen to make any further contact on the Department's behalf with Fatima Shah and the other Muslim girls who have now carried the 'scarf' strike into its seventh week?

'You are better out of it,' Rajiv advised, gazing out of his first-floor window in Municipal House.

'Is it because I wore the hijab when I visited her?'

'You are better out of it.'

'I am sorry if I offended Mrs Newman.'

'This is becoming a bitter political struggle, Nasreen, and that woman has Perlman's full support. You are better out of it.'

If Nasreen had Rajiv's baby it would be half-Hindu, half-Muslim, a child of love and reconciliation. Rajiv – whether Mr Lal or Rajivlal – is not married. She wants to divorce Hassan and marry Rajiv. But she has no Islamic ground for divorcing Hassan and Rajiv Lal has never said anything, nothing at all. She keenly observes his expression, his behaviour, when there are pretty women in his office, students and young teachers and secretaries, but his gaze always remains neutral, limpid. You can look straight into his eyes, as women are trained not to do, and nothing happens. None of the young women she encounters in the Department of Education resembles the unknown female in the stolen photograph.

'I am going mad,' Nasreen tells herself as she gets off the bus. 'Latifa, I no longer know who I am. I am just bits and pieces of a woman.'

☙

VOTE ISHMAIL HAQQ!

Haqq's chauffeur Imtiaz Shasti prowls along a better-off street, his wrist on the wheel, smoking, proud of the Japanese dial which indicates the tilt of the Toyota (for campaigning in Tibetan villages). The terraced houses here are larger, the doors are of quality, the paintwork new, with potted plants, flowers, cypress trees; attached to a lamppost is an official notice: 'P. Permit holders only.'

'Slow down, Imtiaz. What the hell's this?'

The Latvian and his Yorkshire wife – Haqq never forgets a face capable of making a cross on a ballot paper – are deep in conversation with a very tall white gent dressed in an extremely expensive, double-breasted suit, and a regimental tie. A gleaming Rolls Royce more or less blocks the street.

Shasti whistles softly at the majestic hardware. But what brings him to a standstill is the Rolls's spectacular license plate:

ISLAM 1

'Holy smoke,' Shasti murmurs.

And more! Propped against the pavement side of ISLAM 1 is a cardboard-backed poster bearing the tall white gent's unsmiling portrait and the words:

ISLAMIC PARTY OF EUROPE
VOTE PORRIDGE

The woman, the wife, waves cheerily to Haqq.

'It's those Labour people again,' she tells her husband.

'Vot they come?'

The tall gentleman allows himself to turn, though reluctantly, for he is clearly not for turning by the Labour Party or anyone. Haqq climbs out of the Shasti Toyota warily.

'I am Ishmail Haqq,' he announces, offering his hand. 'I am the Muslim Independent candidate.'

'Really?' Reluctantly the gentleman offers a limp shake, glancing cursorily at the stickers festooning the Toyota. 'In that case I must be canvassing for you. Thought I'd tie up the English streets since you obviously don't have a hope in hell on your own.'

Haqq knows the English up and down, but he has never before encountered a fruit-cake accent so packed with genuine nuts and raisins.

'Sir, I regret that I do not know your name.'

'Muhammad Porridge.'

Haqq gapes incredulously, as if inviting the man to think again, to have another stab at it.

'Vot say?' the Latvian asks his wife. 'Vy Leh-burr man iss talking to Tory?'

Hearing this, Mr Porridge leans his huge frame back over the pensioners' wall, threatening to split the trellis which trails a meagre offering of honeysuckle.

'We are your Islamic candidates, sir.'

'Vot Ispanic?'

'You was telling us about pigs,' the woman urges Porridge.

'Ah yes.' Porridge adopts an expression of extreme earnestness. 'When you inspect the skin of the common pig, madam, you find that the pore pattern is in the form of a triangle or pyramid, the symbol of the unholy trinity. Some of the Children of Israel were transformed into pigs and apes. They worshipped the phallic obelisks at ancient On, now Heliopolis, in Egypt. Statues of baboons were traditionally placed at the bases of obelisks in the postures of adoration.'

Haqq glances at Tiger Siddiqi (who does his routine, 'Shall I kill him, Boss', karate-shuffle) and Shasti (who is calculating whether a bloke who can afford an ISLAM 1 Rolls might not stretch to an ISLAM 2 Toyota Mountainbreaker).

'If we eat pig we will lose control of our sexual desires,' Porridge announces.

The Latvian registers interest. 'Vot say?'

'You mustn't eat pork chops or you'll be runnin' amok,' his wife explains.

Muhammad Porridge straightens up and extends his hand to the old couple.

'So don't forget, Vote Porridge and er . . .' – he glances at the stickers on the Toyota – ' . . . Haqq.' He turns to Haqq, dropping his voice: 'I think we've just about got this pair o' grouse in the bag. Entirely at your disposal, Mr Haleeq, though I'll probably do better in the English châteaux on my own.'

'As you wish, sir. Perhaps you would care to distribute my election manifesto. To prevent confusion.'

'No need, old boy. One name at a time is quite enough.'

'But you are not the candidate, sir!'

'We don't want to be legalistic about this, Mr, er, Halif. If the Asians vote, er, Haleb, and the whites vote Porridge, we're home and dry, aren't we? You can't expect English people to vote Kebab, can you?'

'Sir, this is an outrage!'

'I shall be standing for Bruddersford West. Against Flowers or Zaheed. Frankly, it's in the bag. All the polls confirm that the Islamic Party of Europe will command a clear majority in the Commons.'

'Ah – you mean you're a candidate for Parliament?'

'Precisely.'

'In three years' time?'

From a great height Porridge accords Haqq a withering scrutiny. 'I hope I can count on your support, Mr Kebab.'

৩৩

Five days after Tariq handed in his test tube to Dr Braithwaite's secretary, and walked out one hundred quid the richer, Nasreen Hassani arrives at the Burnside Clinic for her appointment, her eyes darting fearfully beneath the black scarf in which she has swathed the aching, sleepless head which no longer, in moments of acute stress, seems to belong to her.

She is terrified of meeting someone she knows in the waiting room. She whispers her name to the white receptionist.

'How do you spell that?'

'H-a-s-s-a-n-i.'

'Status?'

'Sorry?'

'Married separated divorced or single?'

'Married.'

'Maiden name?'

209

'Hussein.'

'Children?'

'One. A boy.' She doesn't want them to think she is short of a son.

'Religion?'

'Muslim.'

'Ethnic group?'

'Sorry?'

The white receptionist sighs. 'Where is your family from?'

'The Punjab.'

'Please take a seat, Mrs Hassani.'

Nasreen thinks of locking herself in the toilet until her name is called, but she may not hear it, they may conclude she has bolted, may wipe her from their computer. *I have come to buy Mr Rajiv Lal's sperm.* She sits in a huddle, in a private pool of liquid self, hands fidgeting, oblivious to the hygienic modernity of the waiting room, the piles of bright toys for children, the women's magazines on the glass-topped table.

'Dr Braithwaite will see you now, Mrs Hassani.'

And there he is, plump, white, genial. He wears a white linen coat but otherwise you might mistake him for a commercial traveller in a hurry.

'It so happens, Mrs Hassani, that you are lucky today. By rare good fortune we have had a recent donor of ideal specifications: Muslim-Punjabi, good health, young – local resident.'

'He lives in Bruddersford?'

'He does.'

'Is he fair-skinned?' she whispers.

'A handsome fellow.'

'Can I please see a photograph?'

'We have to protect the donor's anonymity. Women may think they are going to behave rationally, a simple contract, but very often, particularly if things don't go well in their lives, they start bringing paternity suits and you-name-it against the donor – the natural father.'

'I wouldn't. Please let me look.'

Dr Braithwaite is studying the woman's lowered gaze, her trembling lip. He has seen it all before. Probably her husband is fair-skinned and impotent, or simply running around the town, playing the sheikh.

'We do however offer a high-quality colour print of the donor's skin-colour – the hand.'

Nasreen gazes at the print – at the big, male, alien hand which has masturbated for money. Can a photograph be trusted? Can anyone be trusted? Only Rajiv can be trusted!

'May I think about it?'

Dr Braithwaite sighs. This woman's five hundred pounds may be slipping from his grasp. Rising, he bangs opens his steel filing cabinet, rifles through his folders, shrugs.

'Mrs Hassani, do you want a baby by a fair-skinned Muslim of Punjabi origin? Or do you not? Such donors are rare. The demand from women in your position, I must tell you, is overwhelming.'

༄

Tariq is visiting Hassan Hassani's home with other ardent mujaheddin of the Muslim Youth League. Mr Mustafa Jangar has arrived brandishing a sheaf of press cuttings. Mr Jangar makes Tariq's blood boil by reading out the latest infamous speeches of the white politicians in London.

'They are touring the country, lecturing us!' Mr Jangar roars. 'Listen to this, young Brothers: "Threats of death, talk of arrows being directed at hearts, are vicious and repugnant to the British culture," the Home Office junior minister declared. "No one can pick and choose which British laws to obey." '

Mr Jangar's beard is quivering with rage.

'I'll kill this minister man!' Tariq mutters to Mr Hassani, who is looking rather nervous. Tariq realizes that Mr Jangar is fearless, whereas Mr Hassani belongs to the shadows of his own living room, blinking owlishly behind his porthole glasses.

Mr Jangar and Mr Hassani hurry off for evening prayers, the young mujaheddin following. Tariq, already late for duty at the Omar Khayyam, hangs back, slightly ashamed of missing prayers yet again.

Leaving the house, he encounters Mrs Hassani arriving home. She's wearing a long-skirted dress in the Western style, with a smart jacket-top, and carries a leather briefcase. Tariq notices that she comes home with her head uncovered and her hair untied. A very handsome lady, full-breasted, nice buttocks, educated too – Tariq wonders whether a caged rabbit like Mr Hassani could command the admiration of so good-looking a wife.

'Evening, Mrs Hassani.'

She raises one eyebrow. Obviously she hadn't noticed him.

'You are Tariq Khan, are you not?'

'Aye.'

'I've heard my husband speak of you.'

He shuffles his trainers as she slips her key into the latch. 'Aye,' he repeats as the door swings open.

'I can give you a cup of tea, Tariq. Imran is playing with friends so I am not so busy.'

'I've to go to work, like.'

'You can be five minutes late.'

Once inside the house, with the door closed, she tosses down her jacket, revealing fine breasts under a soft white blouse. He can tell that she's a modern lady, the kind that drives a car – hadn't she come looking for that slut Safia Shah at the Bhangra late at night?

She leads the way into the kitchen and fills the kettle.

'You don't have a beer?' he asks.

'And how would a Muslim house have beer?'

He grins, emboldened by her bantering tone. She folds her arms across her breast and appraises him. 'You are often in trouble, Tariq, so I hear.'

'Yeah.'

'Hot-blooded?' She smiles, splattering hot water from the kettle into a tea pot. 'I know you've been seeing Safia Shah.'

Tariq's hands dig restlessly into his trouser pockets. 'Naw. Just trying to set her right, like.'

Nasreen is pouring tea into two cups. 'It must be hard for a young man to resist a girl who lacks all modesty.'

'She's keeping bad company, Mrs Hassani.'

'Here's your tea.'

Tariq eyes it disconsolately then takes a noisy sip, to be polite. Mrs Hassani has seated herself beside him, very close. To his astonishment he sees her hand settle on his own.

'Would you like to make some money?'

'You know of a good job, Mrs Hassani?'

'Not a regular job. Just make some money.'

'How?'

'You're a virile young man, aren't you?'

He is abashed: his mind darts to the Burnside Clinic. Is that what she's suggesting? Even as this idea is clattering around his head she is handing him a small printed card from her handbag.

'You should be at this hotel at eleven next Saturday morning.'

'Why's that, then?'

'A lady will be waiting for you. A good friend of mine. Get the beer off your breath, Tariq. The lady doesn't care for the smell of beer. Just drink sweet tea from now till then.'

He stares at her.

'You'll be late for work,' she says.

Two minutes later, as Tariq Khan leaps agilely aboard a moving No 11 bus, Nasreen stands naked and trembling before the bathroom mirror, clutching her pudenda. But the mirror shows only the tears coursing down her cheeks: Hassan Hassani does not allow full-length mirrors.

ൠ

So here is Haqq, alone this time, very carefully alone, driving into Knightley, another of those strip-suburbs where the more prosperous Asians are buying houses and the retreating whites are selling them. Along Cumberland Road the shops, too, are visibly changing hands; Haqq knows how white residents curse their neighbours who sell to the 'Pakis' – before doing the same themselves. Such is the social pressure that the vendor often keeps the sale secret and does not allow a For Sale sign.

Haqq enters Iqbal Iqbal's pharmacy with a headache and some caution. Two white lady assistants in starched linen aprons discreetly observe him as he weighs the choice between pain-relievers. A bending head is visible through the small 'window' in the plaster-board wall which divides the shop from the dispensary. Iqbal Iqbal, B.Sc., is dispensing.

Haqq purchases a bottle of paracetamol. Headaches he will never be short of. 'Is Mr Iqbal available?' he murmurs discreetly to the prettier of the white ladies. He is about to give her his card when he thinks better of it. 'Ishmail Haqq,' he says.

Iqbal emerges from his lair, sporting a big bushy beard, shakes Haqq's hand, and leads him into the dispensary, a tiny space piled with cardboard boxes, the shelves loaded with pills and liquid medi-cines. The prettier white assistant – her buttocks in particular command Haqq's side-glance – brings Iqbal a new prescription and Haqq, on request, a glass of water for his paracetamol. She smiles, lightly perfumed. The hand which brings the glass carries a modest little wedding ring. Haqq would polish Hani Malik's brass door-knocker for a year to have this lady's undivided attention for one full night.

Iqbal, who wears wire-rimmed glasses, is emptying pills from a bottle and counting them through a drum-like machine. He then types the prescription on to a computer which automatically prints it out on a gummed label. Haqq wonders whether this can be the same Iqbal who wanted a vandal's cut-off hands through the post from the 'High Court' and pederasts whipped to death.

'I'm afraid this is a bad time of day,' Iqbal says in Punjabi. 'The Health Centre begins surgeries at four p.m. and then business builds up. Of course higher prescription charges create problems. People come in here with three separate prescriptions and then they feel

213

they cannot afford all three. So they ask me which one is the most important. In fact the three are medically interrelated: A may be designed to prevent side-effects from B. But if I don't agree to eliminate one prescription they'll go up the road to someone less scrupulous.'

'At least your conscience is clear,' says Haqq, a lifelong student of the conscience.

Iqbal turns from his pill-counting: 'White people come to me for medicines. Why do they not come to learn the true faith?'

Haqq feels relieved. It's the same Iqbal Iqbal.

A customer – a broken old white pensioner – has entered the shop with a hacking cough.

'In my opinion,' Iqbal continues in Punjabi, 'those who disease themselves by smoking and drinking should have to pay for their own medical care or not receive any.'

'That is an important point.'

'The Blasphemy Act must be extended to embrace Islam.'

'That is in our manifesto, brother.'

'The Bishop of Durham has said in the House of Lords that this would create a cluster of mutually blasphemous doctrines. He should study the Holy Koran.'

The prettier assistant with the buttocks returns to murmur discreetly in Iqbal's ear. Haqq observes Iqbal step into the shop and approach a young white woman who is huddling behind a rack of nail scissors, razors, combs. Iqbal stands stiffly, listening to her. He says a few words. The young woman turns and bolts.

'Pregnant,' Iqbal says in Punjabi on returning to the dispensary. 'She wants an old wives' remedy. I am obliged to direct her to the clinic next door. I would rather have her whipped. Do you have daughters, Mr Haqq?'

'One son, one daughter, still young.'

'Our young people today are in the grip of temptation.' Iqbal is measuring liquid through a pipette. 'Punishments are inadequate. Hell fire is not feared.'

'You are so very right, Mr Iqbal. And I must confide to you that the Labour Party will reduce the age of consent for homosexuals to sixteen. In London the Labour Party is planning to issue free travel passes to proven homosexuals. Even taxis will be free.'

Iqbal says a word to the buttocks. 'There is no conflict between science and the Koran,' he tells Haqq. 'You know of course about Louis Pasteur's discovery of microbes?'

'Pasteur, certainly!'

'The Frenchman discovered the underlying principle of what we call the "germ" of infection. But already in the Koran we find a verse about small things you cannot see.'

'I had forgotten that, yes. Small things.'

'Small things you cannot see,' Iqbal sternly corrects him. 'Why did Allah choose this way to reveal knowledge? That is what Louis Pasteur cannot tell us.'

'Indeed, the West boasts much but knows little.'

At five-thirty the white ladies take off their linen aprons, but unfortunately out of Haqq's line of view.

'Goodnight, Mr Iqbal,' they call gaily in chorus.

Iqbal locks the shop, pulls a blind down over the door – and removes his beard. 'Just a precaution,' he explains with a smile which – uncanny! – fleetingly reminds Haqq of Gamal Rahman's TV grin.

'Mr Iqbal, sir, please afford me the courtesy of a little more biographical detail. Were you born in this country?'

'In Singapore.'

'Ah. That's rare, sir, very rare.'

'But I was conceived at sea, on a passenger ship of the Union Castle line. My parents were returning to Singapore where my mother was a brain surgeon and my father a judge of the High Court. I am of course a Sagittarian – the ninth and highest sign of the zodiac.'

'Yet your first language is Punjabi . . .'

'Hindi, in fact, though my mother is a Bengali.'

'Ah. And where, sir, did you study?'

'I acquired my B.Sc. in Harare and my Pharmacological qualifications in Tokyo.'

'Ah! Ah. So what brought – '

'Allah brought me here – from Cairo.'

'From Cairo!'

'Gamal Rahman must be executed before Ramadan,' Iqbal announces, unlocking a safe to reveal neat bundles of pamphlets.

'Before Ramadan, most certainly, Mr Iqbal.'

'My pamphlet is called "The True Jesus and the False Jesus." What do you think of the title?'

'Spot on, sir. Nail on head. Fair and square.'

'You may take these and distribute them to every house in Bruddersford.'

'That's a lot of houses, Brother!'

'You have the organization, Mr Haqq. I am a lone warrior. The eyes of Christians must be opened.'

Haqq's jaw, or jowl, has dropped a fraction. The first page is a mass of quotations. The second page, much the same. And the last page, too. Haqq is calculating how many white votes this might lose him –

a gloomy subject all round, since there may be none to lose. So far he has a firm 'pledge' from only one white person in Tanner, but she is ninety-four and under the impression that she has already voted.

('I always votes for your lot,' she keeps yelling at him.

'Madam, perhaps you will require transport to the polling station? It can be arranged. My friend Mr Shasti – '

'Shifty?'

'Transport, madam. Car. Rrmrrm.'

'I told you, I voted last week.')

Haqq's thoughts have wandered from the task in hand, whatever that may be. Iqbal is smiling his smile. From the safe he removes a Koran. 'Open it,' he says.

Haqq obeys. There are no pages; it's a bomb. He sits down. He needs another paracetamol. Iqbal hands him a glass of water.

'I did the Charing Cross Road bookshop, Mr Haqq.'

Haqq flinches. 'You – '

'God's warriors are rising from their graves. Rahman must die – '

'I heartily concur!'

Iqbal smiles his awful smile. 'You could kill him here and now.'

'Here? Now?'

'Yes, here. Yes, now.'

'But – '

'I am Gamal Rahman. Or I might be. You never know. Shaytan lurks in all of us.'

Haqq attempts to absorb this useful information. 'Quite so. I've always said as much.'

'But first the apostate Zulfikar Zaheed must die.'

ര

All week Nasreen has experienced a giddy euphoria – an out-of-herself feeling. She had picked Tariq Khan up on her own doorstep, brazenly, and made the handsome young man eat out of her hand! She could do it! Like any Western woman! Just roll your eyes and you can have a baby. This evening Mustafa Jangar is Hassan Hassani's guest for dinner. Delicious odours fill the house from Nasreen's kitchen. She hears herself humming as she delicately, discriminatingly saffrons the rice. She's had her hair done and bought herself a jar of face cream called 'Passion'. She keeps wondering how much money Tariq will expect. She can hardly give him a cheque – too incriminating. She will have to withdraw cash from her NatWest bank account.

Imran is guzzling at the kitchen table before Mr Mustafa arrives. Hassan stands over his son, brimming with pride and severity.

'Abu Hurairah reported that the Prophet, peace and blessings of Allah be upon him, said: "The believer eats with one stomach, and the disbeliever eats with seven stomachs." '

The boy looks abashed and obediently stops eating, his plate still piled high in a delicious, creamy korma sauce.

'It will get cold,' Nasreen scolds her husband. ' "O you who believe, eat of the good things we have provided you with, and give thanks to Allah, if you serve him." '

The boy resumes his meal. His father beams indulgently.

Mustafa Jangar arrives. Nasreen plucks her headscarf from her shoulders and places it over her newly-done hair, but Mustafa does not acknowledge her existence.

Mustafa and Hassan will toil far into the night (while Hassan's old father stares at the television screen, filling the tin ashtray), preparing two new pamphlets to be issued in Urdu by the Maududi Mosque:

Holy Rules for Adult Male Persons
Holy Rules for Adult Female Persons

These (new) holy rules are, once again, the product of Mustafa's ever-closer study of the Ayatollah's three great works, filtered through an English translation from a French translation. Mustafa has enlisted Hassani's talents as a pamphleteer – not forgetting the financial resources of the Maududi Mosque, which its secretary-treasurer controls. It is Mustafa's aim to distribute these holy rules to every Muslim head-of-household in Bruddersford. In Britain.

Hassan Hassani is somewhat startled, indeed shaken, by the Ayatollah's teachings on questions of sex and hygiene, the holy imam's devoutly scientific interest in the female version of the human body:

If the woman sees the blood flowing from her vagina for more than three days and less than ten days, and she is not certain whether it is menstrual blood or from an abscess, she ought if possible to introduce a piece of cotton into her vagina and then remove it; if the blood flows from the left side it is menstrual; it if flows from the right side, the blood comes from an abscess.

Hassani has more than a vague feeling that perhaps this ought to be submitted to a local panel of Muslim doctors, but Mustafa does not trust any doctor who has been trained and qualified in a Western hospital.

'They fit women with Dutch caps and coils,' he declares, prowling Hassan's sitting room. 'They look at genitals.'

217

Hassani has always taken it for granted that a doctor might legitimately look at anything, if circumstances demanded, but Mustafa demolishes his objection by reading aloud a quote from Khomeini:

If a man or woman, in giving medical help, is forced to look at a person's genitals, it ought to be done indirectly, in a mirror . . . unless it cannot be helped.

'It often cannot be helped,' Hassan reasons, blinking behind his porthole lenses.

'Brother, we must seriously consider the position of Izza Shah and Ali Cheema. Sadly I must inform you that Izza should resign and young Cheema be expelled from the Islamic Council.'

'Brother Izza is . . . not well.'

'He is stubborn, Brother Hassan. He is set in his ways. And his family is riven with scandal.'

'Scandal? I don't think so. I've never heard that.'

'You have never heard that Safia Shah is a prostitute? You have never heard that she lives with Ali Cheema? That they fornicate – regularly.'

Hassan Hassani is blinking. 'Regularly?'

Mustafa nods gravely. 'Regularly, Brother. The doctors in St George's Hospital have registered Brother Izza as insane.'

'Insane?'

'I shall soon have the certificate. Now, Brother, take down these sacred words of the Ayatollah as I dictate them. Ready? "If a man washes the dead body of another man, or a woman washes the dead body of another woman, they are permitted to see the body of the dead person – except for the genitals . . . He or she who performs the ablution but transgresses this prohibition commits a capital sin." '

Hassan recalls Ali Cheema's insistence that Mustafa's texts have been inaccurately translated from the Farsi into English. Indeed Ali insinuated that the English version was a wicked hoax from start to finish, another Judeo-Christian plot. The more Mustafa draws Hassan into the Ayatollah's 'Rules for Devout Living', the more nervous Hassan becomes:

' "If a man has relations with a woman during the period of abstinence, the Fast of Ramadan, for example, he ought to avoid saying his prayers so long as he carries traces of the sweat resulting from his coitus." '

'This might apply in a hot country,' Hassani suggests, 'but our Bruddersford bedrooms . . .'

His protest withers on Mustafa's lustrous eye.

218

'Just write it down, Brother. And remember that, to my certain knowledge, these rules are not obeyed by Ali Cheema – whom Brother Izza has corruptly appointed his spokesman.'

'Corruptly?' Hassan blinks. 'Surely you do not mean corruptly, Brother Mustafa?'

Another Rule carries them past midnight.

၆౿

'Final Call' is once again staging a debate between Gamal Rahman and Ali Cheema, the only Muslim intellectual in Britain whose name is easy to remember and pronounce – a big plus in the opinion of the producer, Jasmin Patel. Research has shown that audiences are quickly excited and incensed by Ali's habit of expressing hateful opinions in tones of calm rationality. Mustafa Jangar could be an alien from Muslim Mars floating over the dead mills of Bruddersford, but Ali's soft, pretty features belong to an Oxford graduate who has absorbed everything that Western civilization can throw at him. He doesn't look like a Muslim – no beard, no turban, no flowing gown, just a black shirt open at the neck and revealing a sinister talisman.

'The resonances of your name deserve a study,' Inigo Lorraine remarks in the make-up room.

'To the English ear?' Ali smiles. 'Cheema, cheek, cheater, cheetah. Insolent, untrustworthy and uncomfortably fast-footed.'

Lorraine nods admiringly. 'Just so.'

၆౿

The restaurant of the Omar Khayyam has not seen a customer all evening. Listening to Pennine Radio – cash-and-carry, bargain-basement – Tariq Khan has been brooding about Safia Shah. Hearing that Safia had been 'involved in an incident' (Tariq has picked up this lingo from WPC Rana Khan) between Muslims and Sikhs at the Bhangra, he is contemplating making a late-night journey to the discothèque. Some Sikh wonderboy had called Safia a slut and boasted that he'd shagged her. Tariq is seriously considering a visit, tooled up and ready to front-out any Sikh lad who wants a bit of grief.

At ten o'clock Uncle Abdul Ayub Khan tells Tariq he can go home. 'And go straight home,' he adds. 'No beers on the way, nephew. You can watch Gamal Rahman on television with Ali Cheema.'

'Ali Cheema likes the sound of his own voice,' Tariq says.

Uncle Abdul's rebuke is fierce. 'He speaks for Izza Shah and the Islamic Council. He does not go brawling in the streets. He does not spend his nights in the police cells.'

Leaving the Omar Khayyam, Tariq sets off at a brisk pace, picks up

219

a pint at a pub frequented by young Asians, and resumes his journey towards Nuneaton Road, his heart alight with the new but certain knowledge that Ali Cheema is two hundred miles away, in London. Tariq's brow burns. He has overheard Mustafa Jangar in conversation with Uncle Abdul when the Guardian of the Muslim Youth League recently descended on the Omar Khayyam. Mr Jangar brought with him the teachings of the Ayatollah, which he insisted on reading aloud to Uncle Abdul:

'Now take heed, Abdul Ayub Khan: "A man who has ejaculated as a result of coitus with a woman other than his own, and who ejaculates again during coitus with his legitimate wife, is not entitled to say his prayers if he is still sweating; but if his first coitus is with his legitimate wife and only subsequently with another woman, he is entitled to say his prayers even if still sweating." '

Tariq had seen his uncle sweating. 'No, no, I cannot believe this – this justifies adultery, Mustafa!'

'So? The man can be punished – if there are four male witnesses. But when are there four male witnesses? In his wisdom the Ayatollah has anticipated that most of us are alone with the Almighty in our sins.'

Then Tariq had heard Mr Jangar speaking ill of Izza Shah. He had distinctly heard Mr Jangar say that Ali Cheema is committing 'sins' with Safia Shah. Uncle Abdul had told Tariq not to listen but Mr Jangar had said every good Muslim should listen, and know.

Tariq stands at the corner of Nuneaton Road, hands deep in the pockets of his big, broad-shouldered anorak. He can see a dim light in the sitting room of Ali Cheema's house and the blueish flicker from a television screen. He will be alone with that slut Safia and there will not be four male witnesses, there will be none. He crosses the road, cautiously peers through the ground-floor window, then taps on the pane. After some gesturing from Tariq and shouts of dismissal from Safia, the front door opens.

'What do you want?'

'That Rahman's on telly with Ali Cheema.'

'So?'

'I was just passing. Come on.'

Tariq follows Safia into the sitting room. She's wearing a tight bodice in some shimmering material and a scarlet skirt slit up one side to the thigh. She flounces into a chair and stares at the TV without another word to him. A blob of chewing gum pops to the tip of her tongue between ruby lips. Tariq forces his attention to the bulging eyes of the hated apostate, Gamal Rahman.

Inigo Lorraine smiles gently, tilting his fine chin upwards to the big screen in the studio. 'Gamal, we are discussing censorship tonight. Is that agreed?'

Gamal Rahman's eyes roll. 'Fine. And let's face it, sexual repression has been a long-running feature of both Christian and Islamic culture. Jesus had a miraculous conception but not a miraculous birth – yet Mary's pregnancy is nowhere depicted in the madonnas and icons. This Puritan fury over *The Last Temptation of Christ* defies logic and reason. When a holy monk or nun chooses a life of chastity in the service of God, it is an act of renunciation and self-denial – but without sexual desire Jesus's chastity is merely the indifference of the eunuch, a non-man sent to convert a world of men. He fears death, after all, he knows pain, he eats: why no desire? And that is what I found so moving in *The Last Temptation of Christ* – Jesus being pulled, fascinated, into a dark, glowing brothel in which a thick crowd of men intently observe the prostitute Mary Magdalene copulating with each client in turn behind a thin veil. Jesus emerges from the brothel still chaste, and full of pity, and all the more admirable for that. But Ali Cheema wants to ban this film as well as my book.'

'Is that the case?' Lorraine asks Ali. 'You want to deny *me* the right to see this beautiful film?'

'I am not overwhelmingly worried what you see or what Rahman sees,' Ali says, 'since you are both alien to the experience of faith. Whether Jesus did or did not experience sexual desire is not my concern either. But why do Rahman and the makers of this film insist on hurling our holy prophets into brothels? The good monks whom Rahman mentioned do not earn the plaudits of their superiors by hanging around brothels, wallowing in the odour of immorality, then bicycling home without a stain on their trousers. A Muslim who rejects alcohol does not sit with an unopened whisky bottle on his table – to prove his virtue and strength of will. The fact of the matter is quite simple: modern artists like Gamal Rahman have a shrewd eye for box office. The high-sounding philosophy comes later, when the shekels are in the bank.'

Tariq's attention has wandered – too much big talk and clever stuff. Safia is pretending to be following it all – the slut. She's gazing at her famous Ali-boy, her legs curled beneath her and that slit in her skirt wide open to show her thigh.

'A load of nonsense,' he says loudly. 'You don't argue with Satan, you put a knife through him.'

'Go and do it,' Safia says, without taking her eye off the screen.

'What's that supposed to mean?'

'It means no one invited you here, Tariq Khan.'

'And what are you doing in a man's house?'

'Ali's my brother – got it?'

Tariq ponders this. He's not sure. 'I've heard things,' he says.

'Oh yes, what?'

'I bet your dad don't know you're here.'

'Run and tell him then.'

ᏩᎦ

'Ali Cheema, why do you say shekels?' Inigo Lorraine pounces. 'Why not pounds or dollars?'

'Ali Baba is about to catch his forty Jewish thieves,' Gamal Rahman says.

'You will find,' Ali says, 'that the majority of commercial films which have caused deep offence to faithful believers have been produced by Jews. It's regrettable but there it is.'

'He's about to tell us that some of his best friends are Jews,' Gamal Rahman says. 'The bigot's caveat.'

'I am talking about a certain kind of hyper-Westernized, hyper-secularized Jew – and not at all about the deeply pious and admirable Orthodox Jews of the Hasidic tradition. The president of the company which published Rahman's book is also a secularized Jew.'

'And also under sentence of death,' Gamal Rahman cuts in. 'Perhaps Hangman Cheema can inform us whether my publisher is destined to suffer the same fate as my Italian translator, who was stabbed to death when leaving his apartment this week.'

Ali is unpeturbed.

'Let's not forget that Rahman betrayed the Palestinians by accompanying Sharaf to Israel. Rahman's record as a spy working for Mossad is now beginning to emerge – call it a parallel apostasy. A rehearsal.'

'I would draw Ali Cheema's attention to the forthcoming issue of *Prospero*,' Gamal Rahman says. 'It disposes of the myths concerning my life so assiduously propagated by Islamic Jihad worldwide.'

'We may have strayed from the question of censorship,' Inigo Lorraine says.

'I believe that even sincere atheists should be protected from insult,' Ali says.

Gamal Rahman laughs. His laughter is huge upon the huge screen.

'Protect sincere atheists from insult? By law do you mean? A further extension of the Blasphemy Act to protect "sincere atheists"? How does one "insult" an atheist – what is it that no one must be allowed to say about my godless universe?'

Lorraine intervenes. 'I want to know how far you would go, Ali. Would you ban Voltaire's *Candide*, Tom Paine's *The Age of Reason*, Russell's *Why I am not a Christian* – or Monty Python's *Life of Brian?*'

'Well here we must distinguish between serious argument, doubts gravely expressed, and the frivolous, obscene, commercialism of certain artists. *The Life of Brian*, like *The Devil: an Interview,* should be removed from the domain of public knowledge. Such works demean believers and hold up their convictions to ridicule.'

'But surely satire can be a serious intellectual weapon,' Lorraine objects. 'Major critics have placed Gamal Rahman in a respected surrealist tradition.'

Ali nods. 'Quite so, but I'm not aware that Magritte, or Breton, or Dali, or Buñuel even, ever called the Messenger of the largest religion on earth a charlatan.'

ᏋᏮ

'That bastard!' Tariq says, bored and infuriated by all these films, books and people he has never heard of. 'They're both bastards, the two of 'em.'

'You don't have to listen,' Safia says.

'Go on then,' Tariq says, 'you think he's great, i'n't that it?'

'Who's "great"?'

'You can't wait to hop off to London to leap into Gamal Rahman's bed! Tart! Slag!'

'Just fuck off, Tariq. No'un invited you here.'

'They say you've been shagged by your own brother.'

'Get out of here!'

'Only white guys, Sikhs and Hindus is good enough for you, is that it? The posh sort.'

ᏋᏮ

Inigo Lorraine announces a special treat: 'Final Call' is about to screen a new video produced by Evernew Studios of Lahore.

'We will then invite Gamal Rahman and Ali Cheema to offer us their personal reactions to this film which, as it happens, is already on sale in many British Muslim corner shops and general stores at the modest price of £8.99. Promotional ads can be found in the *Daily Jang* and the *Daily Millat*.'

The video begins with the Holy Koran shrouded in reverent smoke, then cuts to glasses laden with Chivas Regal and the sound of popping champagne corks. Next, a meeting of the worldwide Jewish conspiracy, whose boss sports a red plastic cowboy hat and a US cavalry jacket trimmed with epaulettes. He is constantly surrounded by over-plump Punjabi bimbos in tight red dresses.

Tariq sees Safia in all of them. He moves behind her chair and plunges his hands to her breasts. She stiffens, squirms, but she does not scream. Nuneaton Road is a white road, mainly, and she disdains to appeal to white neighbours against one of her own kind. She feels faintly ashamed of the disgrace she and her motorbike louts have already brought on Ali.

'Slut,' he growls, reaching for the slit in her skirt.

Rahman, Cheema and Lorraine are watching the video projected in the 'Final Call' studio.

A team of heroic mujaheddin sets out to kill Gamal Rahman, who is hiding-out on a lush island in the Philippines or somewhere, protected by hundreds of Israeli soldiers and further bimbos in tight red dresses. Rahmam occupies a luxurious palace, where he spends his time drinking and torturing captured mujaheddin. Invariably he executes a few before retiring to bed with a bimbo.

Tariq has pulled Safia to the carpet. She resists, struggles, scratches, but she does not cry out. The telephone is ringing.

'Gi' us a kiss, Safia.'

Momentarily both their attentions are diverted by what is happening on the telly. Divine intervention finally arrives as lightning strikes the satanic author dead, blood running from his eyes and nose, his body consumed by fire.

'Gamal,' Inigo Lorraine leans towards the big screen, 'we have showed this video only with your consent. Should it be freely on sale at corner shops or should it be banned?'

The bulging eyes roll expressively. 'I'm not too keen on emotive material which incites to murder – not least when I am the proposed victim. On the other hand, this video usefully exposes the sexual hysteria, the pathetic heroics, and the crass taste of my persecutors. It belongs to the uglier face of human history.'

'Ali?'

Pressing the struggling Safia across Ali Cheema's carpet, Tariq finds in her silence a confirmation that she's asking for it.

'Slut.' He flings her panties aside. 'Slut! Whore! Bitch! Slut!'

'What would Rana Khan say!' Safia cries, the only appeal to his decency she can think of. 'You should be ashamed, Tariq Khan!'

Tariq slaps her mouth, hard, bringing blood.

'Ali?' Inigo Lorraine's gaze is steady on Ali Cheema.

'This video you have dug up is obviously a grotesque cartoon. If you extracted certain elements from the ludicrous format and the melodramatic storyline, the deliberate exploitation of half-naked women under the guise of condemning them, and the simplistic vision of divine wrath in the *Don Giovanni* mould – then you would find that the video is not so wide of the mark.'

'What mark?' Lorraine presses.

Safia submitting, afraid of further slaps and blows – blood is seeping from the corner of her mouth. Tariq huge with lust, thrusting as if to split her in two.

'The Israeli connection and a rampant appetite for a hedonistic lifestyle have been major corrupting elements in Gamal Rahman's life,' Ali says.

Tariq pulls himself out and off Safia. He's in the clear so long as there are no male witnesses. Anyway, she'd asked for it – she doesn't even weep. He hears the front door slam, leaps up, fastens his trousers. He sees Ali Cheema walk into the room while still visible on the television screen.

The programme has been pre-recorded.

'Tariq Khan? Son of Karamat Khan?'

The muscular young man hangs his head, mute. 'She asked for it,' he mutters.

'Well, don't just stare like that!' Safia yells at Ali. 'What's it to *you*, holy man of Allah? Big meedja star! Look at him – butter wouldn't melt in his mouth!'

୶

The mid-summer issue of *Prospero* was entirely given over to Gamal Rahman's 'An Open Letter to my Friends and Others.'

Rahman began by listing the allegations levelled 'not at my book, but at my imagined life'. The true and only test of a book, he wrote, 'is what's in it, not who wrote it'. He complained of 'cultural immigration officers' feverishly checking credentials, exploring provenance, 'and deciding who can and who cannot cross the frontier today'. He remembered sitting on a jury set up to award a prize to a work of unpublished fiction. The identities of the authors had been erased from the typescripts. 'It was a damn good lesson.' He conceded, however, that if an interview with the devil could be proven to have been written by the devil, and copyrighted in hell, 'this might be of some marginal interest.' He therefore intended 'to abandon my usual modesty' by listing 'the most punishing ten of the three hundred charges currently levelled against me, though still counting.'

1. I am not who I claim to be. I am the Devil's amanuensis.

2. My life has been one long scramble for money, loot and the fleshpots. Only twenty-four *escargots* will do with the champagne.

3. I regularly passed off my own work as my illustrious father's. My father disowned me. My father has refused to speak to me since (fill in preferred date or incident).

4. I betrayed my mentor and patron, the illustrious editor of *Misr*, Hosny Hikmat.

5. My literary agent is Jewish and an Israeli spy. I have betrayed Egyptian State Secrets to Mossad, I have betrayed Palestinian freedom fighters to Mossad, I have betrayed the entire Arab world to the Zionists, and I retire to bed in a yarmulke loaded with shekels.

6. I betrayed scores of Islamic freedom fighters to Sharaf's prisons, torture chambers and execution squads.

7. I was jailed for massive embezzlement of State funds and priceless Egyptian antiquities.

8. I conspired with Egypt's Coptic Christians to subvert Islamic civilization.

9. I engaged in 'disgusting practices' (to quote Ali Cheema) with female members of the Sharaf family.

10. I betrayed my loving, faithful wife. As a result she lost her life along with the child in her womb, my son.

'These ten charges,' Gamal Rahman concluded his preface, 'will do for starters. So kindly bear with me while I meander back down the Nile to the year 1948. Historians can start laughing now.'

This was plain enough. Anyone could understand it. But no one could fathom his concluding sentence: 'My apologies to my Bruddersford characters for this brief interlude or entracte. Normal story-telling will, I assure them, resume shortly.'

PART TWO

Egypt–*Huda*

∽

Gamal Rahman's Egypt

AHFRAZ, Gamal's cousin
BEN EZRA, ABRAHAM, a rabbi
BEN EZRA, ISAAC, his nephew, later Gamal's literary agent
CHEVALIER, HENRI, a journalist
CHEVALIER, NICOLE, his wife
FARUK, King of Egypt
HIKMAT, HOSNY (the Toad), editor of *Misr*
HUSSEIN, ANIS, a poet and journalist
LEILA (LULU), Gamal's aunt, a writer
MAHMOUD, a novelist, Gamal's father
MIKHAIL, the Coptic Patriarch
NASSER, GAMAL ABDUL, President of Egypt
SADAT, ANWAR, Vice President and President of Egypt
SADAT, JEHAN, his wife
SCHEHERAZADE, a figure in the *Arabian Nights*
The SHARAFS, creatures of fiction:
    FAWZI EL-SHARAF
    CELIA, his wife
    HAMIDA, his daughter
    HUDA, his younger daughter

FOURTEEN

❧

O n a fine morning, when the air was clear of dust and sand, Gamal could see the tips of the pyramids of Giza from Mahmoud's shoulders in Mahmoud's garden. It was a large garden overlooking the Nile. At the age of two Gamal knew that the Great Pyramid was one metre higher than Kephren's – although they looked the same size from Mahmoud's garden. I, Gamal Rahman Mahmoud, was one of the first children in Egyptian history to learn to talk before I could walk. Any visitor, adult or child, who could not pass the test and accurately identify the higher pyramid was loudly ridiculed.

Guessing was cheating and forbidden. Any visitor, adult or child, who got it right was accused of guessing.

When three, Gamal noted in both his diaries, the Arabic and the English, that the real pyramids looked like toy pyramids from a distance of fourteen miles ('miles' being a colonial inheritance he was not yet ready to question). He could transfer the real pyramids to the floor of his cool, spacious playroom, setting them down among his toy camels, desert tents and fellahin. (Mahmoud did not allow his son to play with toy soldiers or tanks – but the boy never showed any interest in bang-bang, so the prohibition went unprotested.) Everything Gamal was given he moved around his floor, his domain of power, with restless impatience, searching for his own solutions. Quick to realize that Allah and the Prophet Muhammad would never be available as toys, he fashioned them out of plasticine and put them through a series of exacting, even humiliating tests:

—Move Kephren's pyramid
—Make it a metre higher than the Great Pyramid
—Make that camel fart
—Give that fellah a fatal dose of cholera

You could see the real pyramids above the trellised wall of Mahmoud's garden, between the dripping fig trees, from Mahmoud's shoulders. Sitting on Mahmoud's shoulders was a privilege conferred for good behaviour, or because Mahmoud had just won some long overdue literary prize. In truth, Gamal was less interested by the shimmering tips of the pyramids, al-ahram, which were frankly boring because always where they should be, than by Dad's transparent attempts to brush his thin, sleek, jasmin-scented hair over the bald patch on his crown – like the obfuscatory dust and sand which periodically hid the pyramids. Occasionally Gamal would dare to ginger-finger the bald patch, setting off a gentle remonstrance, but the fat little boy with the high forehead, helpless legs and large, revolving eyes had made his point:

I can see through – through you, Baba, Dad, through the pyramids, through the world.

Gamal had been an abnormally fat foetus whose outsize skull cost his mother her life in childbirth. Dad clearly blamed me for having swollen to eleven pounds in the womb – as if I had selfishly chosen to dispose of my mother rather than give up my own ghost. (I have always been vaguely anti-abortion on the straightforward premise that no woman would want to have me.) But Mahmoud's reproaches were indirect:

'From infancy, Gamal, you have insisted on being at the centre of things. Having successfully defied God, you were determined to rub shoulders with the pagan deities of our time. The drama of your birth set your heart beating at twice the normal rate. By the age of three you had filled a scrapbook with pictures of kings, queens, presidents, prime ministers, film stars, Olympic athletes (if they won), Generals Rommel, Patton and Montgomery, Hitler, Stalin, Gandhi, Churchill, Roosevelt, de Gaulle, Humphrey Bogart-and-Lauren Bacall, Chaplin, Garbo, Marlene Dietrich, Hemingway, Steinbeck, G.B. Shaw, Einstein, Himmler, Gracie Fields, Napoleon, Louis XIV, Jesus.'

(I was getting this earful in Mahmoud's half-lit study – he wore dark glasses, despite the venetian blinds – which reeked of sandalwood furniture polish and half-smoked Gitanes. How old was I? Any age will do. Wearing his long blue silk shirt, Mahmoud is pressing his fingertips delicately together:)

'Your earliest questions to me, Gamal, were about royal families, not only our own, but the British version, too; you knew exactly how many years months days hours Princess Elizabeth was older than Princess Margaret. Your first comment to me, after Nurse spanked you for wetting your bed, was that Mrs Simpson had acquired an "unbreakable hold" on King Edward VIII, so that he "became incapable of denying her anything, even abdication". At the age of four you were the world's leading expert on this event – which had taken place many years before you were born.'

'Twelve years.'

'Your earliest "novel" was one page and six lines long. It was entitled "First Lady of Egypt". The author gave his name as Gamal Rahman Mahmoud. I read it with interest.'

'You should not have read it.'

'You thrust it into my hand.'

'To show you. Only to show you.'

'The hero of this epic is called Gamal. He saves the First Lady of Egypt from a foreign assassin called Moshe – an Israeli of sorts, I gathered. But the First Lady is not grateful. She throws Gamal into jail, where she visits him in dead of night, with a secret key, declares her love for him, and insists that the luckless young hero, eight years old, give "immediate and tangible proof" of his ardour. We are now at page 2, line 3, with only three lines remaining for proof of ardour, escape from jail, overthrow of the First Lady's husband, the Sultan, the conquest of Israel, and a brief allusion to God's role in all this.'

Mahmoud's fingertips remain lightly glued together. He sits cross-legged in a rocking chair, his trouser creases immaculate, his dark glasses highly polished with the shammy he wears in the button-down breast pocket of his blue silk shirt. The collar is also button-down, although he has never been to America. The lecture invitations pour in but he never goes.

I don't want to give the wrong impression. Mahmoud wasn't talkative. A distracted, murmured phrase or two was the most that you could normally hope for – even though I tried every expedient to gain his attention, from hanging out of high windows and getting my fat stomach stranded up a fig tree to writing novels one page six lines long. The massive speech of his, quoted verbatim above, is probably culled from twenty years of brief, elusive remarks. My father did his talking on to paper; the dialogue poured out, while fat-I hid behind the heavy satin curtains – did I say venetian blinds? – watching him at work with my large, revolving eyes, hoping to see his lips move. His mouth was wide and narrow; at moments of intense concentration it disappeared. It swallowed itself. I used to practise this vanishing act in front of a mirror but my lips were too blubbery.

Mahmoud wrote in silence, as if the air had been sucked out of his half-darkened study. When I write it's a noisy affair, punctuated by shouts, shits, curses, guffaws, cries of 'Gotcha!' and 'Viva Gamal!' When I toss off dialogue, a pool of spittle has to be wiped from the page with my sleeve. I doodle little verses in English rhyming 'name', 'blame', 'shame' and 'Worldfame'.

ဘ

'What is the oldest living language in Egypt, Gamal?

231

'Coptic, Dad.'

Mahmoud's passion was Coptic Cairo, particularly the stoical rotunda of the Mari Girgis Church. 'There is no Egypt without the Copts,' he would say, then pause. 'And there is no Egypt without the Jews.'

Not forgetting the Muslims. My famous father would walk little-fat Gamal to the Mosque of Sultan Hassan, below the Citadel, then deliver a lecture on the Mamluks who (I gathered) were a good or bad thing rather depending on such contingent factors as the success of Mahmoud's latest novel in Paris or whether I had been dragging my fat feet and begging for fruit juice. The Old City of the Fatimids was familiar to Mahmoud yard by yard, and I had little choice but to share the yardage. He would predictably quicken his steps when passing the Mosque and University of Al-Azhar where (Dad said) 'the ulama lay prone and lifeless in its own shame'.

'What is that?' the boy asked.

'The ulama is the body responsible for religious doctrine. I told you that three Fridays ago.'

'Why did it lie prone and lifeless?' the boy asked.

'Al-Azhar University has always shined the shoes of the regime. Any action taken against the ruler, the ruling power, has been condemned by Al-Azhar as fitna, sedition. Even resistance to the occupying foreign power, the infidel, is not permitted. In 1914, after the British imposed martial law, the Al-Azhar ulama announced: "It is our duty to remain tranquil and silent." '

Gamal thought about this – a strip-cartoon of images hurtling across his matricidal mindscreen.

'What's martial law?'

If Mahmoud explained this, it was probably by way of a story. He told his stories in an eloquent murmur, with teasing pauses, inviting me to believe or not believe. Did I (the Sultan) believe the fantastical, beguiling stories spun to me by my captive slave girl Scheherazade? This was a very big question since I (the Sultan) would have to execute her next morning if I didn't believe her. *The Arabian Nights* was no place for the faint-hearted.

One day Mahmoud advised me that good writing is recognizable by its silences.

'Delete every other line. The imagination breathes between the lines.'

Between the lines! I went straight up to the big playroom I had all to myself – I had been my mother's first, fatal, attempt – and wrote a two-page novel without any lines and entirely composed of betweens. It was all about the Sheikh of Al-Azhar grovelling to brutal British boots, and when I'd finished there wasn't a single word on page one and just my signature on page two: Gamal Rahman Mahmoud.

I'd better explain about the brutal British boots. Dad was an ardent nationalist who, with inexorable cunning, attempted to fill me with rage and shame concerning our stolen heritage as Egyptians. (He didn't let on that the authors, painters and composers he most admired were Europeans, often British.)

'What are you, Gamal?'

'Gamal misriyyum. Gamal is an Egyptian, Baba, "first and foremost".'

'And second?'

'An Arab.'

'And what is our faith?'

'Islam.'

'And what is a Muslim?'

' "He who submits to Allah." '

Thus al waldu, the boy, learned to appease al abu, the father. I was hardly out of nappies – though Isaac is at this moment sneakily changing the word to diapers in the Madison Avenue premises of Isaac Ben Ezra, Inc., Literary Agents – than I was forced to sit on abu's knee and absorb-by-heart stuff like this:

'Our revered King is the great-great-great grandson of an Albanian, Muhammad Ali. We Egyptians have long since lost all sense of ourselves. Our literary language is French, our political language English, our operatic language Italian. Arabic literature has been despised, ignored. When I was a student one had to be reading Renan, Wilde, d'Annunzio. When Fuad came to the throne in 1917 he spoke French with a Corsican accent and knew only enough Arabic to reprimand his servants.'

Striding past the imperious minarets of Al-Azhar, my hand in Mahmoud's, Gamal did not know that one day his own sentence of death would be declared from these verysame minarets. (So *that* cat is now out of the bag and bouncing.) On the sabbath our journey might take us through the gate known as the Bab Zuwaylah, to the south of whose walls (the reader will be anxious to hear) the Sudanese militia of the Fatimids had been quartered until Salah al-Din very sensibly burned their barracks. In the narrow streets of the Old City, Gamal learned to jostle on even terms with overloaded horses, donkeys and yelling traders. Cocking an ear for the finger cymbals of the roving fruit-juice man, I would pester Mahmoud for a glass of the black, syrupy tamarhindy. Then a plate of fried bananas – I can taste them now, from my exile, forty years on – would usefully revive my thirst.

'Forty years on'? My father has always deplored my habit of time-jumping; he believes in the famous Greek unities of time, place and action.

Emerging into the painful sunlight of the ancient Kasbah, Gamal would be magnetized by sleek Levantines beckoning him into their gold shops, but Mahmoud traversed the bazaars without spending a piastre and muttering about 'tourist traps' – though he knew exactly how many shops were clustered in the Khan al-Khalili.

'Who counted them?' I asked.

'Baedeker. His great rival, John Murray, did not stoop to count anything. Murray bombarded the prospective traveller with scholarly information about the Sphinx, but did not deign to advise him where he could safely spend the night at Giza.'

'Why?'

Unlike the fathers of most of my schoolfriends (I had none), Mahmoud never dismissed a juvenile question as insolent or stupid. This, as you will see, probably ruined my character from the start and accounts for my present hot-water status worldwide. As a child I must have traversed every inch of Old Cairo, dragging my flat feet a reluctant yard or two behind Mahmoud's, absorbing the irregular flow of his murmured observations.

'What colour is the sky today, Gamal?'

'Blue?'

'One might say cerulean. And why are those kites floating above the flat rooftops?'

'Because the poor stack their rubbish on their roofs.'

'That sign above the barber's shop – is it in Greek or Turkish?'

'It's written in the Latin alphabet as adopted by decree under Atatürk.'

'And that old woman sitting on the steps of the mosque?'

'She's tired.'

'She will be dead within a few moments. She has wrapped her shawl around herself like a shroud.'

'Shall we stop to watch her die?'

Across the maydan, ice-creams and confectionery were being eaten on the terrace of a café. Mahmoud chose a table; the waiter, recognizing him, flapped his filthy cloth across it with extra fervour. I was halfway into my vanilla double-cup when Mahmoud touched my arm: the old woman on the steps of the mosque was dead. People were leaning over her.

Mahmoud unfolded a French newspaper and lit a Gitane. The creases in his cotton trousers were always perfect – the best in Cairo. He earned a sedate living as a civil servant in the Ministry of Education, returning to his Nile-side residence before or after a civilized lunch, followed by a siesta (no one must breathe in the house between three and four-thirty), a cup of sweetened lemon tea (despatched in beautiful red tins from Fortnum & Mason, London), a Gitane or two, and then a long, tranquil stretch of between-the-lines composition on thick, ivory-coloured paper, far into the night. The reading world sighed in pleasurable expectation.

'Gamal, you are in too much of a hurry.'

'Dad, I'm a journalist! The first law of journalism is Hurry.'

How old is this obese, mother-killing journalist? Eight, still? Am I monkeying with Dame Time to irritate Mahmoud, National Prize for Letters, Collar of the Republic, Prix Nobel? Am I guilty of time-tinkering because he (in my mother's enforced absence) gave me the name Gamal only five years before another of the same name gave us a Republic?

Dad is dandling fat-me on the dangerous knife-crease of his knee in a cloud of Gitane-smoke:

'What does your name mean, Gamal?'

' "Beauty". Furthermore, only in Egypt do we sound the "g" hard, as with the English words "good" and "gall". When I visit other Arab countries, they will call me "Djemal". The British will call me "Gamel" as with "camel".'

'Hm.'

☙

Cooking smells are wafting up from the kitchen. This ten-year-old Gamal – I'm in a hurry – invariably left his plate shiny as a hungry dog's. He spent much of his time in the kitchen on account of a new maid whose magical breasts I was allowed to fondle provided the cook herself was at the market; my first masturbatory reveries date from that time (since you ask), and I believe I can claim to have become a father at the age of ten-and-three-quarters, happily without consequences. I mean obligations: Mahmoud paid the girl off.

Let's take a long shot followed by a close up on Gamal's ongoing love-hatred for the Orientalists whose skins carried the pinkish tinge of King Edward spuds. (You can't beat an Egyptian potato, by the way, boiled fried baked or roast.)

EXT. DAY. Smart street in CAIRO. Fat Egyptian BOY with high fore-head and large, revolving eyes observes BRITISH OFFICERS and their LADIES seated in horse-drawn gharries on their way to Shepheard's Hotel, the Continental, the 'Umar Khayyam or the race course, polo fields and gardens of the Gezira Sporting Club. Beneath red tarbushes, little moustaches perch on the stiff upper lips of our tomato-faced rulers as they languidly observe donkey carts, bicycles and the barefoot thousands clinging to trams so loaded with humanity that they resemble a bee-swarm. Our protectors' LADIES' painted faces glitter with a condescension occasionally softened by a flickering concern at the sight of crippled children stretching begging hands to their gharries.

CUT to lawns of the Anglo-Egyptian Union, illuminated by the bright, greenish light from the windows of the Officers' Club.

CUT to beautiful English LADY with tennis racket (Wisden) across her white-stockinged knee. She does not notice fat Egyptian BOY up her skirt.

CUT to EXT. NIGHT. Barbed wire surrounding the British encampment, which stretches from Tahrir Square to the banks of the Nile. Close up of fat Egyptian BOY's bulging eyes.

MAHMOUD (*off*): The British, of course, are here to protect us against ourselves. They accorded us sovereignty in 1923 but they don't want us to misuse it. The Canal is precious to them. It's the corner-stone of all their policies. They are East of Suez, and to be East of Suez you must control the Canal.

GAMAL (*off*): We will throw out the imperialist bastards, Baba.

[To be continued . . .]

I must now reveal that the great nationalist Mahmoud was not averse to rubbing shoulders with these same imperialist bastards in the famous Opera House built to mark the opening of the Suez Canal. He actually shook hands with them – our oppressors!

'The first performance of Verdi's *'Aida* was staged there,' he informed me – as if that let him off the hook.

Ah, those English ladies, those Wisdens and Slazengers, the beguiling glue-whiff as they unsealed their vacuum-packed cylinders of new balls – but had these yet been invented? I ask myself – and nibbled daintily at cucumber sandwiches. A new short story bursts from Gamal Rahman Mahmoud!

The blonde beauty has lost her way in Old Cairo. Her grey Wolseley has broken down with a steaming radiator. Lady Fan is the lustful young widow of Colonel Sir Hubert Fan. He has recently perished in a duel – or while snipe shooting – or maybe he'd broken his neck while playing polo. The beautiful Lady Fan has been terribly plucky about it beside the swimming pool at Gezira Sporting Club. But now she is lost in the Old City while on her way to Groppi's for afternoon tea, and in every kind of peril. While thieves and worse wait to pounce or worse, she holds a dainty little handkerchief to her nose to fend off the smell of the drains, the animal droppings, the kerosene burners, and the street vendors who crowd around her, proffering

236

scarab rings, khelim rugs, a pair of leather slippers bearing a crude, could-be-anyone profile of Queen Nefertiti.

Lady Fan is about to be seized by kidnappers! Then rescue!

The lady is astonished to be led to safety by a gallant fat-boy speaking perfect English despite dubious-dodgy complexion. He displays his class by refusing her tip. 'Then you must ride with me,' Lady Fan insists. Pulling up her flowery dress she reveals the silky secrets I had discovered in fashion magazines stolen from street stalls – that Gothic cathedral arc formed by the pull of a suspender on a silk stocking.

'And what is your name?'

'Gamal Rahman Mahmoud, madam.'

'You are very handsome and fair-skinned for a Gyppo boy, Gamal. And you speak the most perfect English. Would you like me to adopt you and send you to Eton?'

[To be continued . . .]

God knows how Mahmoud got hold of this masterpiece. (Perhaps I left it on his desk. Why hadn't he married again? Did he remain celibate? Did he visit certain establishments while pretending to be watching 'Aida?') Anyway, his rage was quite something – gone was the sardonic urbanity.

'The British have yet to build a proper hospital in our countryside, where only half our children can hope to survive infancy, where blindness is at levels unknown in the civilized world, and where more than sixty per cent of adults carry deadly parasites from drinking Nile water. The British you so admire, Gamal, have not drilled a single well or given us a single rural school. They have propped up King Faruk, the owner of two yachts, is it a dozen aeroplanes?, and too many cars to count.'

'But you talk to them at the Opera, Dad!'

'Stop picking your nose, Gamal. It's a disgusting habit. Now go to your room.'

Justice? Like whisky, it's not for children. If you doubt this, or if you have difficulties with 'is' and 'ought', or your sense of reality was permanently maimed by a diploma in Cultural Studies, the following anecdote may convince you that Captain Dreyfus was never more than a candidate victim of injustice. (End of hectoring preamble.)

Gamal had burst into Mahmoud's venetian-blinded sanctum, crying pitifully, my stout aiya panting up the stairs in pursuit, after a sliver of a front tooth had been knocked out by my cousin Ahfraz during a literary discussion in the garden. (Don't expect much more about Ahfraz in these pages.) Dad surveyed my injury by allowing his dark glasses to slide expertly down his nose, then sceptically dabbed a paper tissue against my bleeding gum.

'What did you say to Ahfraz?'

'I told him [sob] that my vocabularly [sniffle] is more extensive than his.'

'Now tell me the truth.'

Who needs a father? (Actually, I'd told Ahfraz in three languages that he was Satan's arse-hole.)

'I may have hinted [sob] that his conception was a mistake.' [Huge, heartrending wail.]

'I see.'

Punishment followed. Mahmoud never raised his hand to me, he didn't need to. His blows came through a tight, thin mouth which disappeared itself in moments of anger:

'Arabic had once been the official language of Egypt since its conquest by the Arabs – when was that, Gamal?'

'The eighth century.' [Sniffle.]

'Later it replaced what tongue as the language of learning and science?'

'Greek.' [Sob.]

'By the eleventh century Arabic had become the vernacular of the masses. So why is this rich and magical language not good enough for the young Egyptian author who now calls himself – I notice – Gamal Rahman?'

Blood on the paper tissue pressed to my blubber-lips.

'English is up my street, Dad.'

Mahmoud pondered me through dark lenses, his fingertips lightly joined.

'But why "Gamal Rahman"? Why has the name Mahmoud been firmly crossed out on the title page of the short story you deposited on my desk yesterday?'

' "Mahmoud" is a bit of a burden for a young writer, Baba. I don't want to disgrace you, do I?'

'It seems you do.'

'What?'

'I find my own manuscript pages have been tampered with. Various negatives have been inserted in a young hand I recognize. Evidently my opening sentence should read, "Unhappily censorship is *not* still with us".'

Gamal's mind was whirring for a life-saving diversion.

'What do you think about atheists and God-haters, Dad? Do you really *believe* in Al-Lah?'

238

Mahmoud stood up. He was no more to be diverted than the Nile (peace be upon her).

'It seems, Gamal, that, [ten-megaton comma] not content with killing your mother, you wish to dispose of your father as well.'

And then the storm of my tears, my grief and shame, descended. I was taken to bed, the doctor was called, and a vile, syrupy sedative was administered. This was the first occasion that Shaytan invaded my dreams.

The devil was leading me by the hand into some huge Gothic palace – was it a hotel? – which I'd never seen before. Although we were walking quite firmly towards this hotel-place, we never got any nearer. It didn't seem to matter, I was perfectly happy holding the devil's hand, which felt exactly like Dad's.

'Dad, is your name really Satan?'

'I have many names – Satan will do.'

'Can we begin in the beginning?'

'There was none. My Master was Himself a universe without walls, without time and space – indeed the universe was nothing but His infinite consciousness.'

'So He grew bored – or lonely?'

'You have lost no time in turning God into man. God, I must tell you, is infinite Power in search of Knowledge. Utterly alone, He realized that Knowledge could not be achieved merely by contemplating a void. The notion of Action, of doing and making, was born – the radical leap which you call "the beginning".'

'What Action did God take?'

'He made Another – His creature, but endowed with a restless disposition. He glanced to His left and there I was, smiling and nodding happily. In making me He created a satellite consciousness hell-bent on the idea of Creation. He also created language.'

I thought about this. 'It takes two to talk, you mean?'

FIFTEEN

༄

Gamal was born too late to catch the post-war political fever. I was still in my ill-fated mother's womb when our students launched their demonstrations – Marxists, proto-Nasserites, the Muslim Brotherhood. The number of newspapers and journals tripled after the war; by the time Cousin Ahfraz treacherously broke my tooth, Egypt's contingent of journalist-scum had increased from 1,200 to 8,200. I have always hated to miss anything; to the young Gamal it seemed close to impertinent that anyone had considered life worth living, wars worth fighting, treaties worth signing, operas worth singing, in his absence.

At the age of seven I informed Mahmoud that one more journalist was needed. 'I shall know everything and report everything without fear or favour.'

'In that case you will be writing for a paper without a proprietor, an editor or a publisher.'

Many years later, when the President of Egypt, the Rais, was threatening me with imprisonment, and Mahmoud's health was breaking down under acute anxiety, Dad sightlessly gazed upon his son from behind dusky lenses:

'You were never content to climb a high tree and jump, Gamal. You always had to sit astride a stout branch and gradually saw it off.'

But there I go, time-hopping. Mahmoud wrote a regular column for the literary pages of our greatest newspaper, *Misr*. On the sixth floor of *Misr* – which means 'Egypt', no less – most of Cairo's senior writers and critics had a desk, constituting a liberal, secular ulama. A special desk was reserved for Mahmoud. He liked to sip coffee and smoke Gitanes while slowly composing some masterpiece for the literary pages. Hosny Hikmat, whom everyone called the Toad on account of his amphibian countenance, always hurried down to greet Mahmoud when news of his arrival reached the Editor's office.

The Toad used to pat my head. 'And what are you going to be, Gamal, when you grow up?'

'I have already grown up, Mr Hikmat, I am one of those children who are incapable of experiencing childhood. I'm precocious, highly gifted, impervious to other children, and entirely at ease in the adult world.'

'And your name is Mahmoud,' the Toad smiled toadily.

'My name is Gamal Rahman,' I announced solemnly. This was greeted by silence. I had disowned my father. I was guilty of patricide. 'I mean my pen name,' I mumbled sheepishly. 'Mahmoud is too much of a burden . . .'

At this Mahmoud stubbed out the Gitane-end which had been browning his brown fingers – let's say yellowing. He had decided to entertain the troops – the fast-assembling, mice-scurrying hacks, acolytes and sycophants of *Misr.*

'I will tell you why this young genius is unduly burdened by his father's name. Allow me to introduce you to the author of a short story, as yet unpublished, entitled *Lady Fan and I.* His name is Gamal Rahman. Immediately prior to composition, Mr Rahman had several times been caught reading his father's new novel, *The Alley,* which is not intended for children and which, as some of you may know, plays on our Arabic word "quqaq", meaning both "alley" and "blind alley". Mr Rahman then wrote *Lady Fan* by way of patricide. For what is his beautiful English heroine, Lady Fan, but a blatant social inversion of the heroine of Mahmoud's novel, *The Alley?* Some of you may remember Sayyida . . .'

(Sighs of appreciation from hacks, acolytes and sycophants. Ah, yes, Sayyida, what a masterly creation, et cetera – puke.)

Mahmoud places another Gitane between his thin lips, the assembled waiters rushing forward to light it.

'Some of you may remember my Sayyida, a handsome, angry, very proud young Egyptian woman, raised in poverty, fostered at an early age to a marriage-broker, and ambitious for a wealthy husband. In short, Sayyida is Egypt.'

Terrific pause. Puff puff. The spirit of Montparnasse alive and well in Cairo.

'Young Mr Rahman took it upon himself to reverse the agonies and humiliations suffered by Sayyida and her humble courtier, the honest barber Abdul, who daily pursues her through the streets, pouring out his compliments in the face of her stinging insults, pathetically clinging to the convention that so long as a woman consents to speak to you, however rudely, she is not utterly rejecting your overtures.'

Mahmoud pauses. No one understands what he's talking about

(except Gamal). But the maître grazes comfortably in the long grass that the sheep cannot find.

'Mahmoud's long-suffering Abdul,' continues Mahmoud, 'goes off to work for the British Army, after swearing his engagement to Sayyida on the Koran, duly returning with the required shabka, or wedding present, only to discover . . . only to discover what?'

Egypt waits, spellbound. Even the Toad has stopped glancing at his watch or snatching filthy scraps of paper exposing imperialist, anti-Nasser machinations from the telex machine.

Mahmoud resumes. 'Abdul discovers his beloved Sayyida in a bar, unrecognizable in thick make-up and garish clothes, surrounded by beer-drinking British soldiers, her legs stretched across their laps. In short, Egypt's degradation. Abdul flings himself upon them – and dies at the hands of the drunken Tommies.'

Long sighs from the assembled Abduls of *Misr*. Poor Egypt! 'Which,' says Mahmoud, 'brings me back to Mr Rahman's master-piece, *Lady Fan and I*. Here the young Egyptian hero rescues the English lady from the terrible fate awaiting her in Cairo's mean alleys – and achieves honour when she offers to adopt him, send him to Eton – and display her fine, widow's legs to him from time to time.'

All eyes are turned upon the cringing, leprous, fat-boy.

'Needless to add,' Mahmoud concludes, 'this exercise in patricide was written in English, or a version of English – the language of the higher civilization.'

Gamal slinks into a corner and extracts a melting bar of chocolate from his sticky pocket. But then, reader, a miracle occurs: the Toad comes to my defence, slapping a hand on my cowering head.

'Who needs a famous father?' he chuckles. 'There's no imperialist like an anti-imperialist patriarch.'

I don't know whether Mahmoud ever forgave Hosny Hikmat for this remark, but I do know that only once in my forty-fat years have I seen my famous father yield so starched a smile. Here a reluctant word about the Toad. Hosny Hikmat had made his name covering the Palestine war for another paper, *Akher Sa'a*. He was 'very close' (Dad said) to Nasser and the other young officers who had plotted the overthrow of the monarchy and fat Faruk. (Actually, if you really insist on knowing what Gamal looked like as a boy, any old photo of Faruk on his yacht at Cannes will do.)

The Toad patted my head again. 'You want to be an ordinary journalist or a great one?'

'The greatest of all time.'

'The greatest journalist of all time, Gamal, would be a man with no beliefs, no loyalties – and many friends.'

That was a set-back. How did one acquire friends?

Everyone would converge on Mahmoud's desk. His rare visits were special occasions. 'I hope we don't have a coup d'état while Mahmoud is talking his Chinese,' the Toad would chuckle.

Mahmoud brought his fingertips together as he explained, expounded, held court, relishing his celebrity status. Dad had been applying comparative linguistics to Arabic, proving that it was basically related to the Indo-European languages.

'This discovery revives the old controversy as to whether the Koran is coeternal with God, or merely "in history" and inspired by God at the time of Muhammad. The Sunnis have always maintained that the Koran existed in God's mind before the creation, and strictly in Arabic.'

The journalists of *Misr* listened in awe to the great writer so content to float on the slow Nile of wisdom. Yet Gamal was nagged by the knowledge that his father's work was known only to small circles in Cairo. His real audience was abroad, in translation. Gamal was definitely not interested in small circles. He was determined to catch the Toad's eye, even though the famous editor – trodden on by a camel during infancy, according to Mahmoud – had failed to publish a series of ground-breaking reports on recent Events by Gamal Rahman.

For example!

MUSLIM BROTHERHOOD ATTEMPT TO ASSASSINATE PRESIDENT – eye-witness report from Alexandria by GAMAL RAHMAN (6), *Misr's* front-line, fearless Chief Political Correspondent: A vast, happy crowd had gathered to welcome the Nation's Leader. Every word he spoke was greeted with tears of joy. Suddenly I heard a shot ring out from behind me. My heart stopped. The heart of the whole Nation stopped. Gazing up at the platform I saw a hole where the Sudanese Ambassador had been standing beside our President. Nasser barely paused in his speech as the angry crowd fell upon the assassin. 'My life or death is not important,' declared the head and heart of the Nation, as he disappeared behind a wall of security men, with only his monster-size hook-nose still visible. 'If I die a thousand Nassers will rise to take my place. Our Revolution is immortal.'

Two years later the Toad turned down another of Gamal's scoops:

The sirens are wailing over Cairo. The night sky is lit by British and French flares. The Imperialists can never forgive our great President's historic decision to restore the Suez Canal to its rightful

243

owners, the Egyptian people. I am out in the streets, fearless. The bombs are falling on Port Sa'id and the Canal cities of Suez and Isma'ilia. I am simultaneously reporting from all three cities. The invaders are being thrown back into the sea! Their aeroplanes are tumbling out of the sky! I have just witnessed a whole battalion of British parachutists surrender to our valiant warriors, the Sons of Al-Lah. I am interviewing a captured British Officer in fluent English. His name is General Sir Hubert-Humphrey Fan. His wife, the beautiful Lady Fan, begs me to spare his life.

ৰু

From earliest, tiniest, days, Gamal has been taken by Mahmoud to visit his Auntie Leila, known as Lulu. She is usually found in an insalubrious cafe called Flower of the Orchard, with all the charm of a provincial English milk-bar except for the hookah-smokers sitting cross-legged on the pavement, like a row of stoned clarinettists.

Crossing the city by taxi, the prospect of cream cakes in Auntie Lulu's company brought out my philosophical dimension. (My large, bulging eyes swivelling, my cherub-wet lips slack.)

'Dad, do you really *believe* in Al-Lah?'

'I would rather ask whether Al-Lah believes in me, Gamal.'

'Be serious, Baba.'

'We must always behave as if God exists,' Mahmoud murmurs, dabbing his high brow with one of those white tissues he liked to toss down to give the fellahin street sweepers a holiday from their notorious indolence. (Look over there, in that doorway, a barefoot chap in a long cotton galabiyeh, with full sleeves and a low-cut neck, fast asleep but clasping his broom in one hand and his white turban in the other.)

'Behave how?' I press.

'Behave as if every other human being also belongs to God and is loved by God. Scorn prejudice, Gamal; avoid tribalism; never allow this or that Holy Book to convince us that we are uniquely chosen. Never persecute those who hold a different faith. People speak of "tolerance" but I prefer "humility" – tolerance is an arrogant notion, full of condescension. It is *we* – every one of us, who must beg to be tolerated.' A pause, another paper tissue. 'What I say to you may be close to Christian doctrine, though not to Christian practice.'

'But Dad, you expect that sleeping fellah in the doorway to pick up your paper hankies.'

'So? He has his job and I mine.'

'We wouldn't want to be that fellah, would we?'

'No. But now you are talking about social equality, which is a different subject, Gamal. Did you know that the idle street cleaner over there hangs a little plate, or the horns of a sheep, over his doorway, to fend off the evil eye and djinn? Pure superstition. Did you know that his wife wears a charmed necklace of light blue beads and allows her long black shawl to trail in the dust, obliterating her footsteps and thus bamboozling Beelzebub? Equality with such people is neither possible nor desirable.'

I may have nodded.

'But I demand education for that sleeping fellah's children.' Mahmoud continued. 'I demand a living wage for that street cleaner; when he is ill the holes in his pocket should not exclude him from the doctor and the hospital.'

'But he's asleep! He's not working!'

'No one has ever shown him a good reason to work, but he has a hundred wise reasons for sleeping.'

Where was I? Ah yes, long-suffering Auntie Lulu is waiting for us in the Flower of the Orchard. She has just written another book challenging the imposition of the hijab on women permanently condemned to nursing and nurturing and awaiting the Caliph's pleasure. Mahmoud carries the nightmarish manuscript, scored and scorched by Auntie's innumerable erasures and whole paragraphs kangaroo-leaping from one page to the next. Wearily he wipes the plastic table-top with one of his tissues and places the masterpiece down in front of its author.

Gamal squeezes in beside his father (further offending the child-less Auntie Lulu.) His large, revolving eyes inform him that Auntie will not ask for her famous brother's verdict on the manuscript. It's invariable: Mahmoud diligently obliges by reading every word, whereupon Auntie 'forgets' to solicit his opinion.

'They want to cancel all the rights women have gained,' she addresses Gamal. 'To put the clock back. Here in Cairo no two clocks show the same time. In this city of fourteen million we inhabit many different centuries.'

'Yes, Auntie.'

'Some of these fundamentalists are reclaiming the old Islamic right to buy concubines!'

Gamal observes Mahmoud's gentle smile. 'Purely as a matter of principle, of course,' my father says.

'Exactly!' Auntie Lulu guffaws. She always has a packet of sweets for Gamal. Indeed he associates the taste of smooth, scented sugar on his tongue with chain-smoking Auntie's café-blasts against the 'misogynist hadiths'. But the peroration is liable to be punctuated by

245

a shrewd schoolmistress's sudden silence, a pointing of the finger across the classroom:

'What is a hadith, Gamal?'

'A traditional, extra-Koranic saying of the Prophet, Auntie.'

'My nephew is no fool,' she tells Mahmoud, who is placidly puffing at a Gitane.

Auntie Lulu never married. As Headmistress of an Islamic Girls' School she knows she would lose her job instantly if any of her scandalous writings were published. Mahmoud has explained this to Gamal, who understands.

—Then why does she write them, Baba?

—She would like to lose her job but no publisher will touch her work.

—Would you touch it?

Auntie is on the side of the angels. Unfortunately, there are too many of them. Their wings are tangled.

Auntie reaches across the table to grasp Gamal's wrist. 'Do you know what the sheikhs and imams are saying? "Copulate and pro-create! Allah shall gain glory from your numbers on the Day of Judgment!" Ha!'

Mahmoud lights another Gitane. It is now too late for Auntie to copulate or procreate. She no longer walks five times round the pyramid at Giza in search of fertility.

෨෪

Those were bad times for Jews – 'And when are the good times?' Mahmoud remarked. Dad never mentioned Jews without respect and even affection. Gamal knew his father to be a man whose views were rarely those on sale in the souk. Which brings me to the shrivelled walnut who used to visit Mahmoud, wearing a peculiar, broad-brimmed hat. This was Rabbi Abraham Ben Ezra. Normally a Nubian safragi answered callers, but whenever I knew that Rabbi Abraham Ben Ezra was due I rushed down to open the front door, thrilled at the prospect of seeing the miniscule old Jew glancing nervously behind him down the street. He would reach up, not down, to pat my head. I always hoped that a pogrom was immininent so that we could give him shelter and never reveal his whereabouts to 'them'. Rabbi Ben Ezra was from Gamal's earliest memories a fixture in Mahmoud's off-duty hours; diminutive, shrunken, lost in the furniture. When Mahmoud and the rabbi conversed there was never a lamp lit, just dusty light filtering through the drawn blinds of Dad's window. Out of all this was to come the most unpopular sentence in my second novel, *The Crossing*: 'Jews and women have one thing in common: they talk only about being Jews and about being women.'

(This was the only sentence in the novel on which the Rais himself offered a congratulation. But there I go again, in too much of a hurry, and having to restrain myself from leaping straight to my first meeting with the Rais's beautiful wife and daughter. Your money back if I don't get there soon.)

Occasionally Rabbi Ben Ezra brought with him his nephew Isaac, a lanky boy of Gamal's age who always wore a silk yarmulke during Sukkot, the Feast of the Tabernacle. During these sessions Isaac and Gamal avoided one another's gaze and said not a word, dangling their legs as the two men talked. Where Isaac went to school, or who his parents were, remained a mystery to me, though Gamal, fiercely attentive, picked up a clue from the rabbi's references to Damascus and Aleppo, his sighs and groans over the miseries suffered by the Syrian Jewish community which – I gathered – dated back to the destruction of the First Temple in 586 BC. Gamal and Isaac effortlessly identified each other as rivals and future enemies. Whenever Mahmoud gently urged Gamal to take Isaac to his room 'to play', neither boy moved an inch. Removed from their adult anchors, one of them would have to die. Gamal had known this as soon as Rabbi Ben Ezra mentioned that the silent Isaac spoke six languages fluently.

'Isaac is tongue-tied in six languages,' Gamal noted in his diary.

'Things,' Mahmoud explained to Gamal, when the rabbi had crept off into the dusk, leading the mute Isaac to their mysterious habitation which I imagined to be an underground cellar where light never shone – 'things have not been good for our Jews since the 1948 war in Palestine. They got worse after the Patriot Officers took power; and worse still after the war of 1956.'

'But worse is still to come?'

'I fear so.'

I was asleep before he replied – and here we go again, Dad leading me by the hand towards that huge Gothic palace-hotel we may never enter.

'Tell me what happened after God created you, Shaytan.' (Mahmoud always insisted on being addressed by his real name.)

'God had already split Himself into cosmos and satellite. And then came the stars and planets, a fever of experimentation, Knowledge seeking to expand itself through Action. My Master remained entirely absorbed in His own graphs and equations, a storm of speculations about atoms, molecules, electrons, ozone layers, lunar tides, speed of

247

light, entropy, time curves, particle physics, black holes and big bangs.'

'But surely He and He alone was all of these things?'

'Yes and no. In order to observe He had to create, but the act of creation – as He discovered – is more stimulating if it involves a potential loss of control. Unless He granted to the physical universe a measure of autonomy – laws of its own – He could not fulfil His own quest for Knowledge.'

'And you were involved in all this?'

'Very.'

'God likes to kick an idea around?'

'It was I who proposed that He should create a living creature to inhabit one of His planets. A creature with a soul.'

'Why?'

'I have always been interested in morality.'

'And God wasn't?'

'He didn't know the word. What He wanted to understand was why the square of minus-three is identical to the square of plus-three. Still not solved, by the way.'

'What did He say when you proposed the birth of Man?'

There was no answer from the devil. Waking abruptly, I reached under the bed for the latest copy of *Picturegoer*, where Gina Lollobrigida, star of *Bread, Love and Dreams*, was displaying her lovely, incomparable, never-to-be-equalled, boobs.

 confirm

Gamal is proud to be the son of a banned author. All of the writers and journalists gathered round Mahmoud on the sixth floor of *Misr* seem to be congratulating him, as if being banned is a terrific achievement, proof of World Class. These men keep pinching Gamal's cheek as if he'd been banned too; Gamal readily embraces the burden of persecution; in his still unbroken voice he announces that if any of his own books ever gets published in Egypt he will die of shame. The Toad smiles toadishly; *Misr* had already serialized Mahmoud's new novel, *The Children of Mustafa*, when Nasser granted the ulama of the University of Al-Azhar their consolation prize and banned the book. The fundamentalist weekly, *Al-Itissam*, then launched what the Toad called a 'splenetic attack'. Gamal read it eagerly:

In Mahmoud's pseudo-Koranic narrative, Moses, Jesus and the Blessed Prophet Muhammad, peace be upon him, are cynically reduced to mortal proportions. Mahmoud's message is clearly blasphemous: God is dead and man has awakened to recognize the new god, science.

Mahmoud holds court; Gamal notes that his every word is received with reverent sighs and admiring smiles:

'But let's be fair and accord the ulama of Al-Azhar at least the sincerity of a Savanarola. You will remember his view of Lorenzo de Medici's neo-pagan Florence.'

Gamal isn't sure he understands a word of this; he definitely doesn't remember Savanorola, who sounds like an Italian Land Rover. The Toad is pretending to understand, his hands deep in the pockets of the stylish tweed trousers he buys in London.

'Frankly, Mahmoud, your crime is obvious,' says Hikmat. 'You have given us a fictional God, your Mustafa, who falls asleep between bursts of activity; an old man never more irritable and capricious than at the moment of awakening, when he dishes out instant punishment.'

The young poet Anis Hussein intervenes (Mahmoud has described him to Gamal as 'brilliant but unscrupulous' – the Toad has already recruited him to his staff despite my silent protests. Anis Hussein has accordingly joined Isaac among those marked down for destruction).

'Mustafa's hibernations,' Anis Hussein addresses Mahmoud, 'suggest a divine artist escaping from his own botched brush strokes.'

'Then I have been misunderstood,' Mahmoud says. 'Mustafa is not God but a certain idea of God that men have made.'

This is received by a collective intake of breath, followed by a profoundly reflective silence. Time for my intervention: 'With respect, Dad, that's all very well but this "certain idea of God that men have made" is precisely the only idea of God available to us through the holy books. Jews, Christians and Muslims have never explained what God is doing when He isn't involved in textually recorded events. God speaks to Abraham and Moses; later He speaks to Jesus; six hundred years later He speaks to the Prophet Muhammad. God is a written text conspicuous for its enormous historical gaps. This is what your great novel says – or says to me. That is why it is profoundly blasphemous and profoundly wise.'

OK, OK – OK! I didn't say a word. It's what I might have said. In fact it's what Mahmoud said – he always slid into reverse very easily, no grinding of gears. Gamal's liquid eyes are fixed on Mahmoud. He yearns, aches, to be cleverer than Anis Hussein; he wishes his childhood could be cancelled here and now so that he could settle accounts with the worm.

'My novel,' Mahmoud goes on, 'shows that the people of the alley

– all mankind – have misunderstood God in terms of the earthly life they experience and suffer: they believe that in a world of warlords and tyrants, He must be the greatest, the most powerful, the immortal – tyrant.'

The Toad's tongue flicks. 'But consider, Mahmoud, the vital role of the prophets in your novel: Moses, Jesus, Muhammad. Do they not listen to Mustafa and believe him and labour in his cause? Are the prophets also deceived by this not-God God? Clearly they are! Which is why you are banned, Mahmoud.'

Mahmoud lights another Gitane. 'Moses, Jesus and Muhammad are not to be found in *The Children of Mustafa*. The characters called Yacob, Gawas and Nissim are not pseudonyms. There is no one-for-one correspondence. They are the creatures of allegory. It's always a mistake to attempt a literal translation of an allegory.'

'It's a mistake the talented allegorist invariably invites,' the Toad says. 'The uproar from our readers following serialization was quite catastrophic: circulation rose by sixty thousand.'

Laughter.

Gamal – twelve years old, give or take – is growing bored because hungry. There comes a point when you can no longer think brilliant thoughts if your stomach is banging away. The best part of these informal gatherings on the sixth floor of *Misr* is the great table regularly reserved for lunch in whatever local restaurant the Toad chooses to patronize – you never know, which adds to the anticipatory yum-yum in the tum: koufta, wara einab, meloukhia, taheena, kounifa – the odours have been with him all morning.

Over lunch Mahmoud turns the conversation to another author who, on his recommendation, has recently been serialized in *Misr*, Laurence Durrell. This has required courage on the Toad's part, nothing British being in good odour following 'Suez', but the Toad does not lack courage. The truth is that Gamal is far more excited by Durrell's exotic, ultra-modern world of European expatriates than he is by Mahmoud's dire struggle with God and Man set down in an utterly boring ancient desert infested by Arabs.

By night, Justine lies in Gamal's sticky bed. Durrell's enigmatic heroine is on the train from Alex to Cairo, racing towards passion, undeterred by the stench of rotting fruit, jasmine and sweating bodies. The express thunders through the Nile Delta, watched by small boys wasting their lives at water wheels. Gamal is enthralled by Justine: 'She took kisses like so many coats of paint.' Eagerly he has pursued her through the twisted warren of streets which crown the fort of Kom el Dick as she strides, swift and silent, impatient of her companion's habit of lagging behind and peering through doorways into scenes of domestic life which (glowing like toy theatres) seemed filled with dramatic significance. Gamal cannot quite imagine Justine beyond a pair of long, European legs topped by suspenders. Arab women are fat and waddle, blocking your path, blocking progress. Gamal is fat and cannot squeeze past. He's nibbling at a toffee apple as he reads. The sheets of his bed are sticky with toffee and thoughts of Justine; a familiar smell of almonds reaches him from under the covers. He shifts wetly.

ର

Mahmoud used to drag Gamal to Rabbi Ben Ezra's hidden-away synagogue, setting him to work on the English-language version of the tiny booklet which the tiny rabbi had published, dedicated to 'the Leaders of the Revolution' with a 'respectful hommage [sic] of loyalty'.

'Correct the spelling, the usage,' Mahmoud instructed me, 'and be honoured.'

Gamal was flattered. 'Hommage' lost an 'm' and Ben Ezra's 'exercing his mission' got a new lick of paint. Working on the rabbi's booklet, I was puzzled to come upon: 'This is the end of the matter; all has been heard: fear God and heep. His commandment for this is the whole duty of man. Ecclesiastes.'

'Look up your Ecclesiastes,' Mahmoud advised. 'You will find the words "keep His commandment".'

At the end of the booklet, Rabbi Ben Ezra had printed some impressive tributes to his labours from:

—Senior Service Champlain, Rome Area Allied Comm. CMF: 'Much impressed with historical date'

—J. Bateshnik, Major n.l.f. in E.F.: 'Throughs light on the Jews'

—H. Devonshire (otherhow Mrs R.L. Devonshire, author of 'Qample in Cairo'): 'Keep up the good walk'

—Dr Bahour Labib, Director of the Coptic Museum: 'Unutterably convincing'.

From Rabbi Ben Ezra's booklet Gamal learned that the synagogue – with its 42 Jewish families – was 'surrounded' by 29 mosques and 20 churches; by 133,000 Mohamedans and 10,000 Copts. Gamal whispered to the old rabbi that 'Mohamedans' sounded hostile, even offensive, to Muslims, and that 'surrounded' wasn't very good either. Could not the 42 Jewish families be 'living side by side with . . . [etc.]'? Rabbi Ben Ezra looked suspicious, as if the veiled indications of persecution were being carted away by the persecutor. Did this Arab boy bother himself why only 42 Jewish families remained – 'side-by-side,' haha! –

But Ben Ezra accepted Gamal's formula when Mahmoud endorsed it.

The rabbi was a teacher; his finger jabbed; like every damned Jew in the world he knew everything. One day he sat Gamal on his knee, though Gamal was twice his size and soon fell off, while Mahmoud smiled faintly in the bookish dusk he conjured for himself from first light. The rabbi told Gamal a fable in the slow, ponderous, self-loving style of a stupid old man, too long cocooned in the sluggish miasma of the Orient, who believes the wisdom of the ages resides between his ears. It was the old story of the fox who'd been eyeing some lush fruit in a fine orchard.

'There was one hole in the fence but it was too small for him. So the fox fasted for three days, then wriggled through the hole and feasted on the grapes and apricots. He then decided it was time to make his escape. But once again the hole in the fence was too small for him. So he had to fast for another three days! This time in great danger of the master of the orchard coming upon him.'

Gamal yawning and nodding dutifully.

The rabbi wheezed. 'And the fox said, "What avail has my cunning been to me?" '

It was too much. Something, as they say, snapped.

'Excuse me, Reverend Rabbi, but I beg to dissent. The fox said to himself, "It's better to have lived and died than never to have lived at all. One must live for the moment because life is only a passing moment. There is no truth on earth or in Heaven beyond that passing moment. Everything else is the lies that old men tell to children." '

Shock, horror, deicide, patricide, genocide.

'I beg you not to beat him,' Rabbi Ben Ezra finally whispered to Father. 'Man comes naked into the world, and naked he must leave it.'

Mahmoud said: 'Gamal will be a writer if he learns to smile up at the world rather than sneer down.'

This riposte seemed to satisfy the old Jewish dwarf's code of honour. He even started to reach up for the patting business but I was cultivating a Rock Hudson hairdo de l'époque and these pattings did it no good.

'Pat Isaac,' I said. 'He looks as if needs it.'

It was more than a shock when the mute nephew-boy emitted a shriek, leapt out of the shadows and tried to strangle me (thus establishing a lifelong habit – my perfect English he can never forgive). After the men had separated us Isaac screamed something curseful in one or other of his six savage languages. I'd always suspected they were a bunch of brigands up there in Damascus and Aleppo. God – Nebuchadnezzar – hadn't brought down the First Temple for nothing. Isaac began to weep. 'He's hungry,' I said and he flew at me again. After the rabbi had led him away into the night, glancing to right and left, Dad sent me to bed (and Justine) without food.

'There's always food for thought,' he murmured, burying himself in a French newspaper.

Even the exotic world of Justine paled on an empty stomach. I fell asleep.

'Shaytan,' I begged, 'give me food for thought.'

We were ambling, the Dad-devil and I, around some hideous upstart city of the new Egypt which seemed to have sprung out of the sand like a concrete cactus.

'Do you notice,' Shaytan said, 'that the geodesic dome of the Saudis' mosque has already begun to split?'

'Yes, Dad, but why?'

'And look at those new government buildings claiming the sky as they fall down.'

'What did God say when you proposed the birth of a living Man?'

'He invited me to define the word "living". And what did I mean by "soul"? This, of course, brought us on to the subject of death. To desire. By which I mean wanting to live and not wanting to die. It was a huge leap into the dark, since hitherto we – I mean He – had created nothing with a will or consciousness of its own.'

'God hesitated?'

'More than that. He cast me out. But don't imagine it in the banal terms described by Milton and the poets:

' "Nine days they fell; confounded Chaos roar'd
And felt tenfold confusion in their fall: Hell, at last,
Yawning, receiv'd them whole, and on them clos'd." '

'How should I imagine your fall?'

'Merely a temporary closure of dialogue. God no longer listened.'

'Why?'

'In my view – naturally we never discuss it – my Master experienced fear for the first time when He contemplated my blueprint for Man. I remember His disgust and fury when I suggested that Man should be a creature in His own image. "In *My* image, Satan? How can anything be in *My* image? I am the One and Only. I am infinity. I am Knowledge!" And so on. That was when He ceased to acknowledge my existence.'

'But He went on to create Man?'
'He botched it.'

෭

Gamal is brooding in a state of shock: the son has been punished for
the sins of the father. Leaving school last Thursday, Gamal was
attacked by a gang of young fundamentalists all fired-up for Friday.
Chanting in unison with clenched fists, they enveloped the blubber-
lipped fatboy as he drifted homewards on flat feet, eyeing the dusty
streets for fruit-juice vendors and the Western magazines – film,
fashion, 'porno' – for which he paid a high, 'underage' price to the
wily old itinerant fellah known to the schoolboys as Musa-the-News.
  'Son of Satan!'
  'Enemy of Allah!'
  'Reviler of the Prophet!'
He recognized some of his tormentors but 'tormentors' was not
the word – this was quite unlike the personal taunting and bullying
he suffered at school and knew how to buy his way out of. Even as the
spit flew into his large, revolving eyes he sensed the impersonal,
mechanical quality of their rage – and for once in his life he was
speechless. When wooden sticks and iron bars emerged from
beneath the boys' galabiyeh, he merely whimpered. A puddle formed
round his shoes.
  By the time a passing teacher intervened Gamal was lying in a pool
of vomit, blood and urine, barely conscious. What happened after
that he cannot remember. He lay in bed heavily bandaged and under
sedation. He overheard Mahmoud murmuring to the doctor that
three boys had been arrested – then released.
  Hosny Hikmat, otherwise the Toad, wrote and signed an editorial
in *Misr* denouncing 'fundamentalist barbarism'. He went further:
the Egyptian Constitution guaranteed freedom of religious belief
and expression. 'What are the police doing in this case?' he thundered in conclusion. 'Who is covering up?'
  Gamal adamantly refused to set foot again in the local school. Ever
since the ulama had denounced Mahmoud, Gamal's few schoolfriends had peeled away.
  'I've had enough of fucking Arabs! Those squalid, dirty, illiterate
sons of fellahin! What do they know about anything?'
He demanded to be sent to what had once been the British School,
now patronized by a medley bunch of wealthy expatriates. The prospect of being despised as an Arab seemed preferable to being beaten
to death. Mahmoud hesitated (as God had done), clouding his
thoughts in Gitane smoke and murmuring about 'a defeat for every-

254

thing I believe in'. But when he took his son's broken nose to a lawyer, he was advised to forget it: no witnesses could be found, not even the teacher who had intervened. A famous sheikh from Al-Azhar had visited the school to conduct prayers and to remind the faithful that the Sins of the Fathers shall be visited on the Sons.

Guilt forced Dad's hand: he, not Gamal, had published *The Children of Mustafa*. He, not Gamal, had licensed a Beirut publisher to import bound copies into Egypt after President Nasser had banned the book (which contains exactly as many chapters as there are Suras in the Koran, in case you imagine my dad Mahmoud was a modest man).

From day one at what had once been the British School, Gamal was baited as a 'wog swot'. He scored effortlessly in all subjects except the natural sciences despite patchy attendance and an inclination to abandon his homework in favour of unauthorized compositions. He made no friends at all. 'It's a pity,' he wrote, 'that one cannot cancel this whole demeaning thing called childhood.' The real world lay beyond the school walls; the real world was the sixth floor of *Misr*, where he was often found, even in school hours, attempting to flog 'ideas' and beg commissions from the Editor.

The Toad was more generous with advice than commissions – he enjoyed my company.

'Be warned, Gamal, times are changing. The independence movements of the Arab world have been led by modernizers, by political parties essentially secular in character, whatever the lip-service to Islam. But they are failing the people. Nationalism is a drug which wears off unless it delivers the goods to the masses. Religion is on the march.'

SIXTEEN

❧

The Toad commissioned my first professional assignment when I was fifteen, the day they shot Kennedy. My brief was to describe what I'd been doing, and what passed through my head, when I heard the news. I was granted 'fifty words maximum' and wrote 300, describing how I'd cradled the mortally wounded Senator's head in the Los Angeles hotel basement, before being arrested, tortured, and dragged before the court. NASSER PLOT! EGYPTIAN YOUTH HELD!

Imagine my shock-chagrin when the Toad's new stooge at *Misr*, Anis Hussein, published the moronic testimonies of a dozen other Egyptian schoolboys but not mine. It emerged that I had got the the wrong assassination: it should have been President Jack in Dallas not Senator Bobby in LA. (I was twenty, not fifteen, when Bobby went – no one later gave me credit for prescience, not even the Toad.)

Mahmoud took me on a trip up the Nile. White egrets hurtled across the water while lazy herons would occasionally flap heavily out of their hunched postures on the bank. Mahmoud pointed to a black ibis on a sandbank: 'Posing like a sculpture,' he smiled. I spent hours in idle contemplation of the toiling fellahin, their galabiyeh looped up to free their legs; the boat stopped frequently to take on board the huge loads borne by the camels and donkeys parked beneath the feathery palm trees. I fell in with a young fellah who informed me that the land-rent he was forced to pay was double what the Revolutionary Law allowed.

'Oh – why?'

'Why, young Pasha? Because the landlord, the maamour, the omdeh and ghaffir – they're all in cahoots.'

Let me translate: he's talking of the police commissioner, the mayor and the village policeman: all in cahoots. But he becomes vague, evasive, when I ask him where he lives. He moves away.

'He's not lying, he's afraid,' Mahmoud says.

Plunging down to my cabin – Mahmoud can afford separate cabins – I bash my typewriter until dinner time. WHOSE REVOLUTION?, by

Gamal Rahman, lands on the Toad's desk the day after we return to Cairo. Imagine my shock-and-chagrin to receive a note from the Toad's aide, Anis Hussein (the Anus):

'Dear Gamal, one peasant's story does not make a story. You have to get to that maamour, that omdeh, that ghaffir. You have to check it out. Greetings, Anis.'

A word about Anis Hussein: he was only twenty-two, fresh from Cairo University's Faculty of Anuses, the Toad's darling and – le tout Cairo knew it – the Toad's lover. (The Toad was even reputed to have anal-ized a dead Israeli soldier during the 1947 war; Nasser, on hearing this, was reported to have commented that there's nothing in the Koran against sodomizing the corpses of infidels.) I put it about that Anis Hussein had packed his bum with ice to achieve the corpse-like temperature which excited the Toad.

I wrote back at once: 'Dear Anis, Such high professional standards you set! No wonder not a single peasant has been heard to voice a single complaint against our Revolutionary Government in your pages. Kindly examine your conscience, if you can locate it, and show my article to Mr Hikmat.'

The Toad ran my article and sent me back up the Nile to become the youngest reporter to witness the famous, epoch-making diversion of our great river.

On this historic day Egypt hails its heroic Russian friends who nobly stepped in to build our Aswan High Dam after the Western Powers attempted to sabotage our Nation's future, following the frustration of their Imperialist designs on the Suez Canal.

Tall and serene, President Nasser stands on the heavily guarded tribune with his Distinguished Visitor at his side. The diminutive Nikita Khrushchev wears a panama hat and leers proudly – a kulak pretending to be a Chekhov hero taking the Crimean sun. He is surrounded by Soviet engineers with brick-red skins and an ill-disguised desire to return home.

After the ceremony I overhear Vice President Anwar el-Sadat chatting to his Russian guest. Khrushchev is lecturing Sadat about the inevitable triumph of Communism worldwide. Sadat politely replies that we in Egypt have built socialism in one country. Khrushchev displays his missing front teeth. 'Your socialism is one of "ful" (horsebeans) while ours is one of shish kebab.'

A curt note arrived from the Anus: 'Dear Gamal, the Editor wishes me to convey to you that the historic diversion of the Nile is not an occasion for juvenile facetiousness. And you weren't there, anyway.'

The Anus was right – I hadn't been there. I have lied to the reader (not for the first or last time): the Toad had declined to finance my brilliant project. 'Start where you stand, dear Gamal,' he had scrawled on a notepad letterheaded 'Hosny Hikmat, Editor'.

Oh really? My blood boils. Shakespeare himself – not idly invoked, as you'll soon see – could not conceive a rage the depth of mine. Placing myself in the Hilton bar, dressed for the occasion (Milanese sports jacket, London slacks, and a Brooks Brothers button-down collar), I slide into the vacant bar stool beside a bored American television presenter who's been covering the diversion of the Nile, otherwise known in the USA as 'the Soviet hegemony afflicting Nasser's Egypt'.

I address him by name; a flicker of interest is reflected in Bert Bradshore's bourbon-on-the-rocks.

'What would you pay for some unusual background on Nasser, Mr Bradshore?'

'Let's hear it first, sonny. How old are you – twelve?'

'Egypt is governed by twelve-year-olds, didn't you know?' I snap back in my practised Brooklyn accent. (I go to the movies, don't I?)

'I like that,' the famous, prime-timer concedes. 'Kick the ball.'

'The young Nasser went to the Ras el-Tin school in Alex, near the royal summer palace.'

'Is that the story?'

'When Nasser was seventeen he played Julius Caesar in a school production of Shakespeare's play.'

'He did? A story, son, is that the Soviets have five million personnel here, not the reported five hundred thousand.'

'Nasser's father proudly attended the production of *Julius Caesar*. When this honest postman saw Caesar being stabbed by the Roman conspirators, he leapt up from his seat to rescue his eldest son.'

Mr Bradshore nods slowly, a faint smile begging entry into his depressed countenance. 'Want a drink?'

'Dry martini.'

Mr Bradshore gestures to the barman and offers me a Philip Morris. 'Unfortunately the British tell that kind of story better than we do. They have an audience for it. It's just a bit élitist for Americans.'

'Thank you, sir. Cheers. Long live CBS. I suppose I'll have to sell the final part of the story to the BBC.'

'There's more?'

'It was Nasser's father who was far-sighted. His son became Caesar and in 1954 a real attempt was made to assassinate him.'

'Hm.'

'When Joseph Mankiewicz's film, *Julius Caesar*, came to Cairo, starring James Mason and Marlon Brando, the Egyptian censor wanted to cut the scene showing the murder of Caesar on the steps of the Roman Senate.'

'You're kidding!'

'None of our papers was allowed to mention that Nasser knew the play well and had spoken the words "Et tu, Brute!" when still a schoolboy.'

'Yeah? Wow!'

'At that juncture my father wrote a letter, published in *Misr*, pointing out that Caesar's ghost, Mark Antony's famous speech, and the great Battle of Philippi, would all be somewhat up in the air if Caesar had banged his head in the bath or died in a traffic accident.'

'I like it! Wait a minute – you're telling me they actually published your father's letter? Why?'

'Mr Bradshore, sir, honour forbids me to explain who my father is. But you are doubtless on good terms with Mr Hosny Hikmat, the distinguished Editor of *Misr* – he will vouch for me.'

At this juncture Mr Bradshore turns to his beautiful assistant whose long legs, draped across a bar stool, have hitherto been obscured by Mr Bradshore's bulk.

'What d'ya make of that, Celestine?'

'It's not a TV story,' Celestine says.

'It's not a TV story,' Mr Bradshore tells me. 'But it was certainly worth a martini.'

'Here is my card, sir. I am the most talented, well-connected young journalist in Cairo. I am prepared to work as CBS's stringer on the basis of results, sir, strictly results. Nothing up-front. I am also a most gifted translator – American English or English English, no problem. As I say – you need only call Mr Hikmat.'

Mr Bradshore looks to Celestine. They have both been examining my engraved card for signs of forgery.

'Call Hikmat,' Celestine says. 'There's fuck-else to do in this dump.'

'I'll call him,' Mr Bradshore tells me with a final, piercing eye-to-eye, as if to say, 'This is your last chance to back out, son.'

Off he goes, across that Hilton carpet, putting Celestine's legs into full view. Boldly I ask her why she isn't in the movies. 'You could put Cyd Charisse out of business,' I add.

'Wow! How old did you say you were?'

'Sixteen but I've stopped growing. Incidentally, I might get you an interview with the eldest daughter of our Vice President.

'You have five Vice Presidents,' Celestine reminds me. 'In the States we regard one Veep as one too many.'

'My own is Fawzi el-Sharaf. He's seriously anti-Russian, though of course he dare not say a word in public.'

'CBS is very public. Anyway, who's this Sharaf guy? I've never heard of him.'

Mr Bradshore returns, his expression noncommittal. Cyd Charisse's legs vanish again.

'Hikmat was out but his assistant, Anis Hussein, finally agreed he knew you. Of you. The best he could say on your behalf was that you probably are who you say you are – because no one else would want to be you. Martini again?'

'A double.'

'Basically, Gamal, I don't believe everything I hear in Egypt – or anything.'

ော

Did I refer to Fawzi el-Sharaf as 'my' Vice President? Did I mention his daughters? I never break a promise despite the nonstop lies, so here goes: enter the Sharafs, Fawzi, his wife Celia, and their daughters Hamida and Huda. Gamal is fatly heading for hot water, determined to make (you guessed) a splash.

Well below Mahmoud's sightlines was a politician as senior as he was obscure, one of Nasser's five – safety in numbers – Veeps and known (if known at all) to educated Cairo as a clown. Greetings to Fawzi el-Sharaf, who bore such a remarkable physical resemblance to another Veep, the hugely respected Anwar el-Sadat, that Nasser himself could not tell them apart. If Sadat stepped out of line, Sharaf was just as likely to get his face slapped at the next presidential encounter. The Toad claimed that to his 'certain knowledge' they were twin brothers and that Fawzi had changed his name to escape arrest after the British had imprisoned Anwar el-Sadat during the war.

Only when accompanied by their wives were Sadat and Sharaf safely distinguishable. Whereas Sadat's young wife, Jehan, was English on her mother's side and spoke the language perfectly, Celia el-Sharaf invariably addressed Gamal in Arabic or – when steaming through Paris's fashion houses – in a French more or less unintelligible to the French. Celia always strove to conceal her jealous admiration of Mrs Sadat, mainly by pretending the other lady did not exist, but she could not hide her envy of a woman who had given Sadat a son, as well as some fine daughters, whereas Celia herself had never managed to produce a male child, despite many clandestine visits to the seers and soothsayers of Giza. Gamal never stepped inside the Sadat household but all reports (i.e. the Toad) indicated a very different style of life from that of the Sharafs. Although the Sadat women inclined, naturally, towards the Western fashions long since taken for granted among the Egyptian upper classes, they invariably dressed themselves with decorum and good sense, nothing to offend the sensibilities of our great Arab-Muslim people. In this respect, as in so many others, the Sharaf women were a different kettle of fish.

A woman of notorious social and political ambition, Celia el-Sharaf was on the lookout for someone to teach her twelve-year-old daughter Hamida 'proper French'. Having tried a drifting student from Paris, whose head was full of revolutionary cloudbursts and who tended to leave a house wearing the owner's jewellery, his pockets stuffed with objets de vertu, Mrs Celia el-Sharaf concluded that 'proper French' would be better served by a well-bred young Egyptian versed in family decorum. The Toad happened to be dining at the Sharafs' villa in Pyramids Road when Mrs Sharaf asked whether he knew of anyone not too rich to scorn a few piastres but not so poor as to count them.

'Male or female?' the Toad's tongue flicked.

'Oh, heavens, that's such a dilemma!' Mrs el-Sharaf cried. 'As a feminist I know how badly our female students need teaching jobs. But poor Hamida meets only girls at school and I really do feel she deserves the company of an inspirational young man.'

The Toad made his rapid calculations and I found myself in the Sharafs' mansion vainly attempting to prevent young Hamida from showing me her silk knickers every time Mama's back was turned. Little 'proper French' was taught and even less learnt; the same applied after Mrs Sharaf informed me that, so impressive was Hamida's progress, she herself had decided to learn the language. If you refuse to believe a word of this, the Nile is not short of spots where you may conveniently feed yourself to the crocs. May I remind you that the life we lead in the Orient is not handcuffed by the drab probabilities which the English novelists of the realist school have stretched into a continuous yawn. When pursuing the opposite sex (or any old sex) we do not plod along, year after celibate year, squelching in the rain (we have none). We do not confuse courtship with wading through bogs, fens and puddles, or whatever it is that waterlogs the English libido. This is not Bruddersford that now engages my pen; I am no longer carving characters out of soot and the compost heaps of the cabbage allotments which cower beneath Ilkley Moor.

Ah Hamida, ah Huda.

೬ಎ

From what used to be the British School it is impossible not to gain entry to Cairo University (I'm ladder-zooming again). Gamal Rahman is the first highly educated boy to be turned down since the time of the pharaohs (or the Tudors, given that Egyptian history did not begin at the British School until the first Brit stumbled ashore crying 'Champagne! Champagne!'). Gamal dutifully sat the papers, finished each hour-long test in ten minutes, bowed fatly to an incredulous audience, then waddled out. The University authorities decided to fail him for 'setting a bad example' even though he scored close to 100 per cent or 101 per cent on each and every paper.

Gamal wants to go straight to Oxford, in Tudorland, but Mahmoud isn't having it – 'One step at a time' and all that.

Celia chides Gamal. Beyond the window of her downright-vulgar sitting room the feluccas with their swallow-wings glide up the Nile on the habitual northerly breeze or pass down-river on the current whose life-giving source lies in the mountains of Ethiopia (courtesy of the Aswan Dam).

'Your poor father.'

I bow my head.

'What a silly boy you are, Gamal.'

'Asif, hadritik – sorry, madame.'

'You don't sound sorry. And I've told you not to call me "madame" when we are alone. I spoke to the Vice President at breakfast this morning. He is very angry with you. He says you have made him the laughing stock of Cairo. How can his eldest daughter continue to receive private tuition from a young man who fails his exams?'

Gamal is now kneeling before Celia, though not permitted to place his head in her lap on account of his lightly greased Rock Hudson hairdo.

'It was a conspiracy, madame. The University administration is controlled by Nasserites determined to discredit Mr el-Sharaf.'

'Your head is full of conspiracies.'

'My head is the world.'

'Hamida is very upset, you know. She's saying that the French you've been teaching her must be wrong.'

'Does my divinely beautiful mistress agree?'

'I've told you not to use that word, Gamal.'

'But you are my queen! The first Elizabeth of England, though a virgin, was "mistress" to all her courtiers.'

'Hamida has made good progress with you but I don't like the way you've been looking at her recently. She says you've been calling her "princess".'

My Swiss watch is a gift from Celia. I never go away from a tutorial hungry. She has rapidly learned the full menu of my cravings and passed them on to her cook: taheena (a rich mixture of chick-peas worked into a cream with sesame oil); or ful medammes (croquettes of puréed beans strongly spiced). Oh tummy, tummy, target of young Hamida's pleasing taunts.

Carrying a wad of the crisp pound notes which comfort his pocket whenever he fatly slips out of the Veep's residence by the garden door, Gamal reaches the backstreet café where film music blares out from a cheap radio by the cash-till and broken-toothed men sit at formica-topped tables playing cards with drained eyes. Gamal is late – his preoragtive. Abdel Wahhab glowers at him from behind an empty coffee cup. Abdel Wahhab hates him almost as much as Gamal hates Anis Hussein. Abdel Wahhab has been hired by the State Tourist Bureau to put an end to complaints about the deplorable standard of English prevailing in the Bureau's brochures, maps and posters. Abdel Wahhab has a degree in English from the University – just the man for the job – but the complaints continue: derisive, pale-faced laughter can still be heard from the Hilton to the Sheraton. The more Abdel Wahhab corrects these English-language texts, the worse they get. He has reconciled himself (though he hasn't) to handing over rapidly increasing chunks of his miserable salary to this opinionated shit, Gamal Rahman.

'An expresso coffee,' Gamal tells him, heaping brochures from his briefcase on to the table.

Gloomily Abdel Wahhab studies his own text machine-gunned by Gamal's emendations.

Ancient Cairo! There stood a city which rejoined [rejoiced] at the daily birth of the sum [sun]. She [It] set up temples to him [her] and builded [built] for his sake [in her honour] the Ein Shams University.

Abdel Wahhab begins to argue; always does. He insists that a city is feminine and the sun masculine. As for 'sum', that was a printer's error he hadn't happened to notice. Gamal presses on to the next passage:

The name Cairo came into being [can be traced back to] 969 A.D., after [following] the Fatimid's [Fatimid] invasion of Egypt. 'Cairo' is in perfect [delete] fact the English for [version of] Al-Qahira – meaning 'The Triumphant', [named] after the planet Al Qahir (Mars), which was in the ascending [ascendant] at the time that

263

the labourer's [labourers'] buttocks [mattocks] first stuck [struck] the soil to found the city we enjoy [hate] today.

When Abdel Wahhab reaches the penultimate word, 'hate', he yells in triumph. 'Sabotage! I shan't pay you a piastre!'

'Got to keep you on your toes, Abdel.'

'You want me to lose my position! You want me in disgrace!'

Gamal tosses another brochure at him:

' "The saga of man's beginning of civilization" is no good. "A choice variety of unique Oriental Floor show" is no good either.'

Leaving Abdel Wahhab gloomily fingering through piles of emended tourist brochures and maps, two more pounds joining Celia's wad, Gamal begins his regular tour of the city-centre restaurants, pouncing on:

—kidneys and 2 soiled eggs

—witm inced meat

—bolled spageti and minteral warter.

More time-consumingly (but lucratively), he persuades the proud proprietor of a restaurant in Houda Shaarawi Street that 'Fatta and lamp' just doesn't sound attractive to your average English-speaking tourist. Nor does 'foul with linseed oil'.

'Why not say "ful", boss? Or "brown beans"?'

The proprietor snorts. 'The English don't understand "ful" – only "foul".'

Naturally I never hinted to my beautiful pupil Hamida, an immodest thirteen years of age, or her vigilant mother that I was earning a few piastres by this work – still less that I was often obliged to accept 'drought bear' in lieu of payment. Failing my entrance exams was bad enough, but in an honourable tradition (as I explained), whereas scootering from one tatty restaurant to the next would have wiped me from the Sharaf map. The Sharafs wanted as tutor the son of a prix Nobel, not a word-waiter on wheels.

'Do you know what "foul" means in English, Hamida?'

She nodded dreamily, then giggled.

'Tell me, then.'

'I don't know. Brown beans.' More giggling.

Celia scowled fondly, the ever-attentive chaperone flipping through fashion magazines on the sofa – I always begged a peep.

'It seems highly unlikely, Hamida,' Gamal continued sternly, that any cricket-loving Englishman would spend 12 piastres on a dish of "foul with linseed oil". Do you agree?'

Hamida studied me. 'Mummy,' she said, 'why is Gamal so ugly?'

('You stink of French perfume,' the Toad told me an hour later.

264

'Be careful, Gamal, these Sharaf women are dangerous. Hm. What are they telling you about me?')

ᘒ

Mahmoud always dined modestly but well: grilled lamb, fish or pigeon. This evening my own passions had been allowed to prevail with the cook: meloukhia (an opaque, purée-like soup made of greens and stock), followed by wara einab and kounifa (a pudding made of sweet batter, fried in butter, mixed with raisins, almonds and cinnamon – then drenched in honey).

Presently Dad resumed one of his favourite obsessions: Laurence Durrell's version of Egypt might belong naturally to the English language, but I would lose all 'authenticity' if I persisted in turning my back on Arabic.

'After all, Gamal, you write for *Misr* in Arabic. You are first an Egyptian, second an Arab and – '

'That ended the afternoon my fundamentalist friends greeted me outside the school gate.'

'But you were born only six years before Egypt finally achieved her independence. Your generation – '

'Baba, my generation regards our present leaders as clowns.'

He sighed. 'Perhaps you belong in Alexandria. It might be your milieu. One Alexandrian out of three speaks no Arabic. Under the palm trees of the Corniche, on the café terrace of Muharram, outside the Cecil Hotel, and in the port quarter – what does one speak? Greek if in business; Armenian if an artisan; Italian if one believes oneself to be a performing artist; English if one aspires to power; French if one is rich and anxious to make the fact known. Alexandria is like a ship moored to the land of Africa but eager to depart. Walking through the Egyptian quarter, the smell of flesh subtly changes to accommodate ammoniac, sandalwood, saltpetre, spice, fish.' Mahmoud delicately wipes his mouth with a starched napkin. 'Perhaps you belong in Alex. The city has been built like a dyke to hold back the flood of African darkness – right up your street.'

I am eating silently (i.e. noisily).

Mahmoud lights a Gitane between courses. 'Perhaps you would consider the University of Alexandria . . . and then go on to Oxford?'

'Only your wealth stands between me and Oxford, Dad. It's called a "means test". You failed it. Otherwise they'd grant me a scholarship, everything paid, tuition fees, maintenance, books, and one pint of lukewarm best bitter a day in the King's Arms.'

Mahmoud removes his dark glasses, replaces them.

'If you go straight to Oxford you will succumb to a fatal schizo-phrenia. You will no longer know who you are.'

'There is no good writing without schizophrenia. I mean the black hole, the space, the fissure of alienation, the sore point where one is not oneself. That is where writing begins.'

'I wish I had known,' Mahmoud murmured sardonically.

Stuffed with wara einab and kounifa, I fell asleep.

'No, this is not Cairo,' Dad-Shaytan was saying as we traversed the dusty streets, still heading for the vast Gothic hotel, 'this is a new city of pre-stressed nostalgia, form without function. This is the effigy of Islamic architecture without its heart.'

I asked again: 'But God went on to create Man and – you say – botched it?'

'Yes, with other angels whispering in His ear. Arrivistes and oppor-tunists! At that time my Master had developed a habit of blowing angels into the air like smoke rings.'

'Is this why you swelled with rage and envy when you first saw Adam in paradise, and vowed to ruin him and his posterity – merely to disappoint his Maker?'

'You have been reading Milton. Frankly, I was appalled by what I saw in Eden! What I had proposed to my Lord was a creature pos-sessing a moral faculty and free will. Hence a soul. This in turn demanded desire and the denial of desire; life and the denial of life – in other words the tensions without which free will and ethics cannot function. But what did I find in Eden?'

'God had no sooner granted free will to man than He had taken it away?'

'Precisely. The whole, ridiculous fable about the serpent was merely God's alibi.'

'For what?'

'For botching human sexuality. For laying down the law before Adam had even taken note of the fig leaf across his loins. For inventing sex as the only means of reproduction – then immediately banning it. In short, for turning the exercise of free will into sin.'

'And He blamed you?'

The devil nodded. 'As an afterthought.'

ତ୬

Neither Dad nor the Sharaf ladies must learn about my lucrative trade conducting tourists around the Citadel and the City of the Dead. A guide speaking such immaculate English is a rarity who receives huge tips not merely for his services but for his proud bearing. An educated man requires an educated tip.

266

Delicately I point to the kites wheeling above the flat rooftops where the poor stack their rubbish. The European ladies shudder, the American ladies moan. And when I lead them to the desert region beneath the Mokattam Hills, I explain that it was Napoleon who put a stop to the habit of burying the dead in front of the houses. More cries, shudders.

'Nowadays, ladies and gentlemen, as you can see, the dead enjoy their own city where the mausoleums are built like houses. The relatives of the dead bring food and bedding, keeping their dear departed company until the spirit becomes accustomed to the new life in paradise. Living in paradise is not easy, you know.'

My clients laugh. I have made a joke which bridges their culture and 'mine' – they are appreciative. The English are happy to be 'abroad', the Americans 'overseas', the French 'à l'étranger'.

'But here, ladies and gentlemen, I run the risk of shocking your Western sensibilities when I reveal that our dead are not at first buried but merely placed under the floorboards on which their families are sitting.'

The gharry horse stamps its feet as if warning the tourists to leave before they catch a whiff of unburied death in the suffocating air reflecting off the Mokattam cliffs.

'And there, ladies and gentlemen, you see the Muhammad Ali Mosque which may remind you of an alert white cat perched on the Citadel. Tomorrow, if you wish, we shall visit the elaborate tombs of the Caliphs and Mamelukes.'

'Thank you, Gamal,' the Americans say, their parting handshakes leaving my hands stained with dollar bills. They head back towards the cocktail hour, grateful to be among the living who will soon enjoy dust-cleansing hot baths and a faltering version of air conditioning.

By night I toiled on my novel. The annual khamseen rattled the shutters and blew layers of desert dust across my pages. My new patrons, the Sharaf family, knew nothing of my endeavours; if one page of *The Patriots* had fluttered through their window, Gamal Rahman would have made as dramatic an impact on history as a squashed fly. I was aiming straight for the head and heart of our nation! No one stood above my sightline.

Or beneath it: in idle moments I filled notebooks with pen portraits of my foreign tourists. One party of intrepid travellers arrived from Yorkshire. There was a Mr and Mrs Blunt: he, Douglas, was a junior executive in the City's Development Planning office, nice chap, totally gullible. A local-paper hack, Reddaway, caught sunstroke immediately and spent the next few days stretched out, vomiting. A schoolteacher called Patricia Newman – very attractive, we spoke

French for fun – was clearly not getting on with her husband; at the end of the day she pressed an extravagant tip into my hand. I wouldn't have given their marriage ten minutes but when I called at their hotel la Newman saw me off in rather severe English – evidently I had misunderstood her 'generosity'. Also in the party was a Muslim couple from Pakistan, she shy, he far from it and very upper-deck. Zulfikar Zaheed always wore a club tie whatever the heat but he didn't believe in tipping. He even informed me it was a matter of principle.

They all forgot me, of course, the moment they left Egypt. But they would be sorry, particularly la Newman and Zaheed. Invited to take his clients for a ride twice, the Gamal-camel never says no.

SEVENTEEN

⟳

From *The Patriots*, by Gamal Rahman

Where shall we haul our future Hero of the Nation out from between his mother's thighs? This, reader, is no detail. Heroes of our Republic are not born in Nile-side villas, idly observing the distant tips of the pyramids or the swallow-wings of the feluccas heading under the English Bridge. They do not begin their social life on houseboats nor do they hear the thundering hoofs of polo ponies, the swift thwack of stick on ball. Heroes of the Republic must be 'of the earth', even if that earth becomes, in due course, which is right now, dust kicked in our eyes.

After careful study of our national map from Alex to the High Dam, I'm plonking Fawzi el-Sharaf's birth down in the Nile Delta village of Muhi el-Din, forty miles north of Cairo. (The author's decision is final.)

Date of birth? Not known, but it must surely have been some kind of Christian holiday, otherwise the British would have come to slaughter our dangerous baby like so many Herods. Our patriotic astrologers insist that Fawzi was most auspiciously born during – or almost during – the year of Egypt's National Revolution, when British colonial police fired live ammunition into the crowds and pursued demonstrators into the Mosque of Al-Azhar. This Revolution, which forms a centrepoint to the early novels of our greatest writer, Mahmoud, also meant a great deal to Baby Fawzi.

And what can we say of Fawzi's father? Legend dictates a true peasant, a barefoot fellah, but unfortunately the Patriots to whom we all owe so much are classic petty-bourgeois to a man. We therefore bestow on Fawzi a father with a general certificate of education and a job as a small-time civil servant. In short, he worked for the Oppressor.

Imagine the young Fawzi taking the cows and water buffalo to drink from the canal – or driving the oxen pulling the wheat thresher

– or helping in harvesting the dates and cotton – and you will be spot-on. The boy learned to stuff bits of dried cheese into the pocket of his galabiyeh; he also loved treacle mixed with curdled milk.

One summer the future Hero of the Nation saw a party of British officers arrive in Muhi el-Din, wearing beautiful high brown boots and fierce moustaches. Fawzi observed the inborn arrogance written into their sun-blistered skins. The map of the world at that moment was just about as red as it would ever get. The officers had come to shoot pigeons at the invitation of the local village headman, or omdah. Bang bang bang, feathers all over the place, well-trained retrievers racing to load their jaws. But then things went wrong.

A wheat silo caught fire, apparently struck by a British bullet. The villagers went beserk, a Brit captain was killed and two other officers wounded. Serious! The villagers were arraigned before an Egyptian court, just as Joan of Arc was tried in Rouen by her fellow-countrymen, with the English standing just outside the door. The Egyptian court duly condemned four villagers to death and twelve to be flogged and imprisoned. Fawzi's Uncle Fawzi, after whom he had been named, was the first to go to the scaffold erected on the spot where the killing took place.

Many years later I myself was privileged to hear Fawzi el-Sharaf telling this story to his daughters before bedtime. Indeed I heard it forty or fifty times.

The story of the British officers' pigeon-shoot gained and garnished itself in the repeated telling; I could imagine how Rudyard Kipling might have related it, just-so, just-so, with the dead British captain's widow receiving a letter of condolence from all Egyptians on the last page. (I venture this digression only in the certain knowledge that our Censor will whip it right out.) 'I saw my Uncle Fawzi hanged,' the future Hero of the Nation would tell his sleepy daughters, 'and I wished to grow up like him. I hoped his story would grow into a ballad that would live in the hearts of posterity.'

But posterity – hold your breath – was almost denied its due. Young Fawzi fell into an irrigation canal and nearly drowned; as the muddy waters filled his protesting lungs a thought reached him like a lifebelt: Egypt was about to lose Fawzi el-Sharaf. 'Somehow I scrambled up on to the bank and lay there, thanking Allah on the nation's behalf.'

Fawzi el-Sharaf has been generous with his memories and our own function is merely to shine the shoes of his vast recall. But here and there he has not bothered us with trivialities, and your storyteller must humbly thread his laces through the empty holes before fleeing the country.

At the age of twelve Fawzi discovered another 'Uncle Fawzi' from far and foreign parts. Enter Adolf Hitler. Fawzi dreamed of marching on royal Cairo like Hitler marched on Berlin. However, as things turned out, it was not Hitler but Mahatma Gandhi who visited Cairo on his way to London – a rather different model of anti-British hero, one might think, but the Egyptian press was full of Gandhi and Fawzi's theatrical instincts were aroused: divesting himself of his black shirt and jackboots, abandoning the goose-step for a barefoot shuffle, the boy covered himself with an apron in honour of the 'half-naked fakir' derided by Mr Churchill – and equipped himself with a spindle of his own manufacture to engage in passive resistance on the roof.

Did I mention Fawzi's 'theatrical instincts'? Hitler and Gandhi, of course, eventually made their marks on Hollywood, and here we must mention a lady film producer who placed a talent-scouting ad in the Cairo papers. Fawzi responded: 'I am a young man with a splendid figure, well-built thighs, and handsome features. Yes – I am not white, but not exactly black either.' Arriving at the offices of the film company before first light, he found himself in competition with two dozen other Valentinos but whose complexions (we must guess) were fairer. This proves that History is mainly the work of unemployed actors – but here again your humble narrator is merely giving our non-existent censor a chance to ease his frozen arm.

And History – here she comes again! The Anglo-Egyptian Treaty of 1936, a new chapter in tutelage you may say, carried its hidden blessings. Faced with the rise of the Actor Hitler, the Brits shrewdly permitted the Egyptian Army to expand and open its élitist officer corps to the lower orders – to the Sons of the Dust. But how to gain admission to the Royal Military Academy? The beys and pashas still ruled that province; Fawzi's father was now a senior clerk in the Dept. of Sanitation but not acquainted with any bey or pasha. Learning that the Chairman of the Committee, which examined applications to join the Military Academy, was Major General Ibrahim Khayri Pasha, mentor in horsemanship to Prince Faruk, Fawzi's father boldly arrived at the Major General's palace in Al-Qubbah Gardens. He and Fawzi were instructed to stand in the hallway, waiting, waiting for the pasha to notice them (or not) on his way out. And here he comes, splendidly attired!

'Ah yes,' he murmurs, 'you're the senior clerk in the Sanitation Department and this must be your son who . . . I see . . . all right! all right!'

The great pasha shoots towards the door while Fawzi's father trots after him, mumbling his pleas. Now for the twist! Imagine the scene twenty years later, after our glorious Revolution, when the same

Major General Ibrahim Khayri Pasha calls on a Vice President of the Republic to humbly petition for restitution of his confiscated property. And who is the Vice President of the Republic? Fawzi el-Sharaf. (!!!)

(The Toad says I am confusing Sharaf with Sadat but the Toad is a boot-licker.)

Your humble scribe is again guilty of galloping. We must beat a chronological retreat to the year 1941. Britain is at war with Germany. Egypt and the Suez Canal lie at the heart of both Powers' global strategy. Lieutenant Fawzi el-Sharaf is twenty-two. The studio portrait shows him in a British-style tunic and Sam Browne belt, stick clasped in both hands, a plain fez upon his head. The Brits were easily fooled by studio portraits – in reality Fawzi was plotting Revolution and in dangerous contact with two emissaries sent by Rommel. However! – while seeking his expertise as a wireless operator, the unworthy Kraut agents sank into turpitude, living it up on a houseboat rented from Hikmat Fahmy, the celebrated belly dancer. Visiting the houseboat, Fawzi found himself in the Thousand and One Nights – indolence, voluptuousness, you name it. Observing the two Nazis helplessly drunk in the company of two Jewish women, Fawzi el-Sharaf duly made off with the powerful transmitter he'd promised to repair.

Next we find the Hero of the Nation buying 10,000 empty bottles in the glass market, his mind set on Molotov cocktails. For a difficult ten days, glass bottles were unobtainable in Egypt. British Intelligence began to follow the bottles – which brings us to an episode of such dazzling complexity that one must again raise one's hat, or fez, to Mr Laurence Durrell, the novelist who persuaded young Gamal that an Englishman's Egypt is more pleasurable than the real one.

Some years after these events, Hamida's diligent tutor attempted to reconstruct the episode in an effort to divert her attention from drawing up lists of prospective traitors whom 'Pappi' (our hero Fawzi el-Sharaf) must put down 'like vermin'. Hamida never saw much virtue, or point, in my variations of Mr Durrell's Egypt, though Huda did – ah Huda.

'Imagine, Hamida, an Egyptian officer, your brave father, in resplendent boots and tarbush, carrying under his arm a giant fly-whisk with an ebony handle, knocking on the door of an Alexandrine apartment occupied by a mysterious Englishman. Nearly perfect English falls negligently from Fawzi's earnest face fitted with a dazzle of small teeth resembling seed-pearls. The future Hero of our Nation is cunningly taking thirty-nine steps into the lion's den, so to speak. Courteously he conducts the mysterious Englishman by staff car to an unstated destination. After driving through a straggle of small streets and alleys near the rue des Soeurs, they stop before a great carved door, then cross a courtyard with a stunted palm tree, ascend some stairs, and enter an elegant, warmly-lighted room with neatly polished floors enhanced by fine Arab carpets.

' "Good God," exclaims the Englishman (who might be Mr Durrell himself, though probably not). "Scobie!" '

('What?' Hamida asks. She has just added the Minister of the Interior to her list of subversives. 'What's this "Scobie"?'

'Pay attention, Hamida.'

'Yes, Gamal.' She is sixteen, the year is 1970.

I continue with my story of her father in the year 1942:)

'Scobie looks up and gives a Drury Lane chuckle. "At last, old man, at last."

'Tarbush on head, whisk on knee, old Scobie now carries an extra pip on his shoulder. He rises quickly and glances outside the door, then the window, then up the chimney. The coast is clear. Scobie places a tea-cosy over the telephone before addressing Durrell (he appears to ignore the Egyptian officer with the pearly teeth).

' "Not a word to anyone, old man. They've made me head of the Secret Service." The words fairly whistle in his dentures. "This is Inside Information and not to be disclosed to anyone. There's a war on. It began three years ago, one gathers. Frankly, we need your help. The enemy is at work, right here among us."

' "A spy, you mean?"

' "Exactly. A character in one of your novels, Balthazar by name. He's been scribbling codes on postcards." Scobie opens a drawer and triumphantly lays two postcards on the desk. His visitor examines them.

' "Those are chess moves," he objects. "Balthazar used to play postal chess with Justine. And look at the postmarks – four years old."

' "Hm." Scobie looks grumpy. "Don't jump to conclusions, old boy."

'The Egyptian officer (Fawzi) clears his throat. "Mr Scobie, if you'll excuse me, I have many duties to perform."

'He salutes smartly, turns to open the door – and finds it locked. Scobie chuckles. "You're under arrest, Sharaf. You are the bogus Balthazar."

At this Hamida jumps up, fists clenched, unable to bear the thought of her Pappi's arrest, even twelve years before she was born.

'Another traitor,' she cries, 'this Englishman Scobie. Kill him!'

'But Hamida, this is history. The British did the arresting and killing in those days. And they had a habit of getting it right after getting it wrong – El-Alamein, for example.'

'What's that?' Hamida asks suspiciously.

'It was a battle. The British won.'

'Who against?'

'Hitler's general, Erwin Rommel.'

'I don't believe you. Pappi says Hitler never lost a battle. He was betrayed.'

'Either way, Hamida, your honourable father, Fawzi el-Sharaf, became a guest of the British in the Aliens' Jail, where he spent his time learning German and breeding rabbits.'

'Rabbits!' Hamida snorts disbelievingly and returns to her list of traitors. (The Toad is also disbelieving; he insists that it was Anwar el-Sadat who was bunged into the Aliens' Jail, and that Fawzi changed his name to avoid arrest. Sharaf himself disdains to discuss such malicious rumours.) But when little Huda's turn came, two years later, to hear my story, she not only rejoiced in it, her gentle dove-eyes sparkling, her tiny hands knotted, she even ventured an elaboration (though shyly – ah Huda).

'What were the chess moves written on Balthazar's postcards?' she asked. 'I think it was part of a Sicilian defence, warding off the dangerous lunges of Justine's queen.'

'Very possibly, Mademoiselle Huda!' I beamed with pleasure (I'm sure I did). I never beat Huda at chess after she passed fourteen, and our games were of necessity clandestine because her mother, Celia, considered chess 'unsuitable for girls', while Hamida, if she spotted us bent over the board, was inclined to sweep the pieces to the floor like so many fallen Ministers of the Interior or Chiefs of Police.

'Of course,' Huda continued gravely, 'Pappi didn't understand what Scobie was saying, did he?' It was a delicate probe, modestly delivered.

'Well, Huda, perhaps "Pappi", I mean your esteemed father, the Vice President, perhaps he – '

'Your character Fawzi el-Sharaf was a bit of a banana, wasn't he?' Her dove eyes grew wide, huge, with the question. Then she giggled at my discomforture and drew a finger across her lips. 'Ssssh or Hamida will put us on her list!'

Ah Huda – and they say I later betrayed you.

By 1946 Fawzi is back in prison on the usual trumped-up charges. No bed table chair. No books. Cold water oozing from the walls in winter, swarms of cockroaches. Digestion ruined. By grace of Allah a copy of *Reader's Digest* is smuggled into Cell 45 of Cairo Central Prison. God (Fawzi reads) sends us our crises as an act of friendliness, to teach us endurance: Fawzi is flooded by fortitude.

Today Cell 45 is regularly visited by parties of Cairene schoolchildren. Indeed they arrive at the Ramses railway station from all over Egypt if they can be accommodated – and particularly when they can't. Every one of our patriotic boys and girls has seen the famous photograph of Fawzi el-Sharaf on trial, penned in a wire-mesh enclosure along with a dozen lesser heroes, all standing, all laughing (at something). Every Egyptian girl and boy now knows that Sharaf's prison number was 2050.

Released from prison, Fawzi once again dreams of stage and screen – his thighs are still well-built. He places an ad in the Cairo quarterly, *Al-Fusuul*: 'I am a handsome youth, 1.69 metres tall, celebrated for my comic acting and am ready to play any role in the theatre or cinema.' Fawzi's appetite for any old role in any old clown-show carries him towards the Marxists; then sweeps him towards the Chabab Muhammad, the Youth of the Prophet; then hurls him into the arms of the attractively fascistic Misr el-Fatat, Young Egypt. He also falls in with a group of Free Officers led by the current husband of a famous belly dancer. (Even Celia confesses that he's very keen on belly dancers.)

Fawzi's problem is this: how to become an officer again. Cashiered, court-martialled, imprisoned – no chance! To be a Patriot but not an officer is simply haha. Only the army can overthrow Fat Faruk (Farouk). Marriage to the vivacious nymphet Celia only sharpens Fawzi's appetite for those shoulder-pips and for overthrowing Fat Faruk. But some grovelling must precede the overthrowing.

Look now, here is Faruk himself arriving at the Hussein Mosque for Friday prayers. Fawzi has been hanging about for hours, waiting for the royal cortège. The security men eye him with suspicion: is this comic actor, 1.69 metres tall, the long-anticipated assassin? As the King flops out of his Cadillac, Fawzi prostrates himself, kisses the chubby royal hand and begs forgiveness. The King merely nods because the width of his neck won't allow more. Sharaf is summoned by the Cdr-in-Chief and dressed down as a hooligan, an assassin, and a disgrace. By January 1950 he is again a captain. Newwife Celia fondles his dick and whispers ambition – her Fawzi should be, must be, a colonel like Nasser. Nothing less is worthy of her.

'To become a colonel I need a revolution,' Fawzi cries as Celia brings him to his captain's climax.

ର

Extracts from the notebook of Gamal Rahman (aged three):

Things are boiling up against Brits. Popular pressure forces Egyptian Govt. to abrogate aforement'd 1936 Anglo-Egyptian Treaty, due to run until 1956. Muslim Brotherhood declares holy jihad (again)

275

against Brit. soldiers in Canal Zone. Guerrilla commando infiltrates Brit. base at Tel el-Kebir and blows up munitions, leaving 10 (ten) dead. In Isma'ilia Gen. Erskine (bad) encircles barracks of Egyptian auxiliary police (good), whose complicity with aforement'd guerrillas is not in doubt. Jan. 26, 1952, Black Saturday, Isma'ilia. Seventy police die when Brits storm garrison with tanks and artillery. Next day mob in Cairo sacks Shepheard's Hotel, cafés, bars, cinemas, the Rivoli, the Metro, the Turf Club, where 8 (eight) leading members of Brit. colony perish in flames. Faruk is holding banquet in Abidin Palace; his Prime Minister is having blow-job at manicurist's. All Egypt is vomiting. Patriots' coup is coming.

Colonel Nasser gathers his conspirators. 'Twelve months ago,' he says, 'I spoke to all of you. Give the politicians one year – is that not what I said? Gentlemen, we have given them a year; the situation has become intolerable, and I am not prepared to tolerate it any longer! The Constitution is hereby abrogated! Central and provincial legislatures are dissolved! Political parties are forthwith abolished! Martial Law is now imposed!'

Your reporter, Gamal Rahman, is claiming – here and now – to have been been a fly on the wall of the Egyptian officers' conspiracy at the age of four (or did I say three?). The cabal caballed in the usual cinema where the officers normally watched Charles Laughton movies. I can distinctly remember, with stop-watch accuracy, wetting my pants when I heard Colonel Nasser overthrowing our King. 'Good idea!' I whispered, but even so there was that giveaway puddle on the floor. The rebel officers were all on their feet in the stalls, hands reaching for revolver holsters, the works.

But what of our future Rais, Fawzi el-Sharaf? Summoned to a rendezvous on the eve of the coup, Sharaf unaccountably takes himself to the wrong movie. Nasser comes in search, can't find him, then leaves a note at the ticket kiosk: 'The plan will be implemented tonight. RV at Abdul Hakim Amer's at 11 o'clock.' However, Lauren Bacall's mouth is now joined to H. Bogart's – hence delay. Eventually Fawzi drives to Nasser's rendezvous, finds no one at home, leaves note. (Revolution is evidently a kind of confetti trail of unread notes.) He speeds through the streets to Army HQ but is halted by a Free Officer and detained because he doesn't know the password. He tries 'Charles Laughton' but merely receives a slap across the face. Bogart and Bacall produce further slaps.

Anyway, these things happen. All was forgiven. Vice President Fawzi el-Sharaf has recently confided to this writer: 'I represented a force with experience and history behind it. I discovered that I had a natural inclination toward good. Love is the real motive behind my every action. He who is in need of nothing is his own master, Gamal.'

Now we must return to a super-hero who has been off-stage for too long. Fawzi had never allowed himself to be taken in by Allied lies concerning Adolf Hitler. In case you thought A.H. was dead by this time, Fawzi didn't – and sure enough, eight years after Adolf's 'suicide' in the bunker, news came through that the Führer had escaped incognito to Brazil. The Cairo weekly, *Al-Mussawar*, asked public figures what they would say to the resurrected Adolf if they ran into him in the jungles of Brazil. Fawzi remained true to his boyhood hero and sent this message:

'I congratulate you with all my heart. You were the real victor. There will be no peace until Germany is restored to what it was. That you have been immortal in Germany is reason enough for pride.'

Hitler never replied. Fawzi is still waiting. 'He cannot have received the message,' is all he will say whenever I ask him about this.

Gamal (no relation) Abdul Nasser, meanwhile, was much in evidence and the object of Fawzi's daily devotions. Hook-Nose regularly went to war with Israel (1948, 1956, 1967) and emerged triumphant from every defeat. The first President of the Republic was everything an Egyptian should be: he ate ful for breakfast and regularly listened to Um Kalthum's Radio Cairo concert on the first Thursday of the month. A word or two from Fawzi on this paragon:

'Gamal Nasser, O Lord, is your magnificent creation, your conquering genius, your true servant, your reliant one, your inspired one, the bearer to his people and his nation of the message of righteousness, dignity and peace.' (This I overheard in 1955, when seven years of age and monitoring Sharaf's turn to lead morning prayers in the National Assembly.)

By the time of the Six Day War, our President had become a paranoid chain smoker with shaking hands. And here a personal footnote: the Toad's acolyte, the Anus, alias Anis Hussein, is lying when he puts it about that Gamal Rahman was granted exemption from military service 'for reasons which do not bear scrutiny'. The reasons (like Anis Hussein) would merely bore the reader, so here they are:

Gamal Rahman's recent appointment as 'cultural adviser' to the wife of Vice President Fawzi el-Sharaf was of such critical-mass significance that it qualified as 'national service'. Anis Hussein can argue until he's blue in the face that 'Rahman pulled apron-strings to fix the Army Medical Board,' but their verdict was unanimous: 'regular heartburn', 'periodic trauma', 'paranoia', 'gross obesity', 'flat feet' and 'total incapacity to submit to normal discipline'.

And so to the true story of the Six Day War. First day: the early morning sky over Cairo is black with warplanes. Gamal waves patriotically until one of the pilots shouts 'Shalom!' while parting my Rock Hudson hairdo. I head for the cellar.

Mahmoud takes his normal morning walk, ignoring the wailing sirens, then returns home with his usual batch of newspapers, mainly foreign, looking faintly Montparnasse in his dark shirt and dark glasses and his sleeked-back hair greying at the edges after his customary shave, trim and manicure at Hamid's Barber Shop. Having sat down to his breakfast of French coffee and croissants, Mahmoud sends the maid down to the cellar with a laconic message: if his son aspires to practise journalism, today is not the one to spend in the cellar. A brief fling with the maid – another of those nubile, Upper Nile, wenches who had (had to) come to terms with my urgencies – calms my nerves and allows me to poke my head out of the cellar and take a close-up of Mahmoud smoking his third Gitane of the day. A thicker variety of smoke hangs over the military airfield recently barbecued in the desert outside Cairo by the Israelis.

Turning on the radio, I hear the famous broadcaster, Anis Hussein, reading out a succession of jubilant reports: 'The brave Egyptian Air Force has shot down 115 of the Israeli enemy aircraft.'

My father murmurs, 'So that's all right' and buries himself in *Le Monde*'s report of a new production of *Cyrano de Bergerac* at the Comédie-française.

Meanwhile, not so far away, Vice President Fawzi el-Sharaf, our future national hero, is appraising the situation with that remarkable sang froid we have all come to know and admire. As he later told me in an exclusive interview:

'I did not rush out to put on my clothes but entered the bathroom to shave and take a shower as I did every morning.'

Celia remembers: 'As Fawzi put on his uniform he said to me, "Celia, this time we will teach the Israelis a lesson they will never forget." '

For four days the Israelis swept over Cairo, shattering windows with their sonic booms – hence the Toad's joke about 'The Glaziers' War'. My father continued work on his new novel in between visits to Hamid's Barber Shop, unresponsive to phone calls from American and European magazines begging him for his first-hand account of our defeat (*Paris Match* was offering him 5,000 words and a fee I can't bring myself to mention). When I begged Mahmoud to allow me to write the piece under his byline, his reaction was somewhat negative:

'Never let me hear such cynicism pass your lips again, Gamal.'

My bulging eyes closed instantly.

At last we entered the great Gothic palace-hotel – after so many attempts! – to find a hall of soaring, flamboyant arches and a marbled floor graced by gleaming cuspidors and lackeys, half-man, half-monkey, in toy-soldier uniforms and red fezes. Dad was still wearing his Shaytan outfit but the head flunkey (or monkey), was too deferential to comment (or notice). We ordered iced lemonade all round. Dad lit a Gitane:

'My Master's great error, at the so-called Creation, was to stumble blindfold into something called Religion. This was inevitable as soon as the Great Scientist, fearful of His own experiment, hastened to clamp the notion of Sin on the exercise of free will.'

'Sin is strictly a religious notion?'

'Of course. I was interested in morality, in good and bad – which can be judged only in humanistic terms.'

'Why not in Divine terms?'

'As I explained, God had no notion of ethics. Man's capacity for ethical behaviour was meant to be strictly a byproduct of his free will. In other words Man would learn the meaning of good and bad only through his experience of other men. That, at least, had been my intention.'

'But God panicked, imposed the Fall, and – '

' – and lost His scientific detachment. Power became His only consideration – power over these naughty, two-legged creatures who constantly escaped His control. Hence the Fall. And sin. And religion.'

'When did He first blame you for the Fall?'

' "When"? There are no calendars in the divine cosmology. Sooner or later – let's say – He reminded me that I had been in too much of a hurry with my Book of Genesis, my "Seven Day Wondershow" (as He put it). He reminded me that He had wanted the full works – tadpoles, dinosaurs, primates, the whole evolution thing.'

'Tell me, Shaytan, why we Muslims are forbidden to believe in evolution.'

'We'll come to that.'

EIGHTEEN

ᐧ

June 9th: Nasser appears on TV, tears in his eyes, his voice thick and tremulous, that great hook-nose desperate for the comforting fumes of a fag. Our President is admitting that the war has been a nakba, a setback. 'I take full personal responsibility.'

'But not for long,' murmurs Mahmoud, in whose company I am watching this ultra-dramatic moment.

'I have decided,' says, or answers, the President, 'to give up completely and finally every official post and every political role, to return to the ranks of the public to do my duty with them like every other citizen.'

'But not for long,' my father repeats.

I rushed out into the streets along with nine million other Cairenes, half of them clinging to the roofs of buses caught in three-hour traffic jams, just as the sewers were overflowing from a violent rainstorm, and headed for *Misr*, composing messages to the Toad advising him to throw Anis Hussein from a sixth-floor window and appoint Gamal Rahman as Special Advisor to the Editor. I couldn't hope noticing, however, that two or three million of my fellow-citizens were already packing the five miles from the centre of the city to Nasser's presidential villa at Manchet el-Bakri. This vast concourse of stupidity was evidently set on keeping Hook-Nose in power, thus frustrating Gamal Rahman's mission to rescue Egyptian journalism from its supine subservience.

'Ya Nasser, Nasser, ihna ma'ak! Lan neqbal el-hazima! Nasser, Nasser, we are with you! We will not accept defeat!'

The streets and markets were jam-packed with male galabiyeh and female hijabs, as if Arabs in their hour of despair must each prove his or her closeness to Allah by erecting a personal tent. MOSQUE ATTENDANCE UP 600 PER CENT, announced the atheist Anis Hussein. Even the Copts got into the act (though without the tents): for more than a month hundreds of our deranged Christians flocked to see the Virgin Mary floating above a desert monastery of the Wadi Natrun.

As predicted by Mahmoud, Nasser no sooner had leapt from his camel than he was back in the saddle, stamping all over those who had betrayed him by accepting his resignation. I can now reveal that Vice President Fawzi el-Sharaf did not dare leave his house for three weeks. For twenty-one days Fawzi sat motionless in his chair, not taking phone calls and gazing at his beautiful garden. Meanwhile truckloads of wounded were brought in from Sinai suffering from napalm burns: men blinded, men without arms and legs. As Celia later confided to me on the Second Empire canapé where I was allowed to hold her distracted hand: 'I wanted to help our wounded, but others were too jealous of the privilege.'

Such was her own jealousy that she could not mention her rival by name. Mrs Sadat, Directress of the Red Crescent, had gone among the wounded with beds and medicines while Celia merely wept. The nation hailed Jehan Sadat as a great lady, Um el-Shuhada, Mother of Martyrs. No one hailed Celia – until I began to slip references to her many charities into my columns in *Misr*.

Purge coming up. The entire ruling élite sat at home waiting for the arrival of the removal vans. Field Marshal Amer locked himself into his luxury villa at Giza. 'Abdu' (as he was known to his friend of twenty-five years, Nasser) had advised the President to open hostilities at the end of May; by refusing to attack first Nasser had condemned Amer's army and aviation to extinction. So claimed 'Abdu'. Nasser ordered the Toad to drive to Amer's heavily guarded villa as an emissary. I was summoned to the *Misr* building by the dimunitive editor.

'You will accompany me, Gamal.'

'I'm very busy, Boss.'

'You will get out of the car first. You will approach Amer's paratroopers with both hands above your head. You will present my Letter of Credential, signed by the President.'

'I might have to lower one of my hands in order to do that. Unless I carry the Letter of Credential between my teeth.'

'This could be your big break, Gamal. I happen to know that CBS, NBC, ABC and the BBC have already set up long-range television cameras near Amer's house. They will be in competition for the inside story.'

'You mean we're going inside!'

'Wear your best suit.'

'Shouldn't you make a preliminary telephone call to the Field Marshal? Take his temperature?'

'Nasser has cut all the lines.'

So off we went. Three hundred yards from the fortress in which the disgraced Amer lurked like a wounded lion at bay, we were halted at a roadblock manned by the paratroopers who would have won the Six Day War if they had climbed out of bed. We had evidently reached the frontier between the Republic of Egypt and the Republic of Abdu – I remembered the piddle-puddle spreading between my feet when, aged four, I had observed the Free Officers plotting the overthrow of the monarchy. Fortunately I had on this occasion taken the mature precaution of absorbing no liquid since the previous sundown. My best suit and fat-I were casually roughed up for ten minutes while the Toad sat behind the smoke-tinted windows of his Chevrolet. The letter was delivered. After ten days' prevarication, Abdu finally admitted the Toad and me to his armour-plated, bomb-proof bunker beneath his home of reinforced concrete covered by vast camouflage nets. The man looked a wreck. His hand shook; he was incapable of lighting the mentholated Winstons he chain-smoked. The Toad addressed him with the kind of exaggerated deference displayed by foreign spies in British movies.

'These misunderstandings are a tragedy for the whole nation, Field Marshal. No one, and certainly not the President, regards you as anything other than the Republic's greatest military leader.'

'Yeah? So who fucking swings for losing the fucking war?'

'The President believes that all differences can be ironed out and amicably resolved.'

'So who fucking swings for losing the fucking war?'

'Nasser invites you to dinner at your convenience.'

Astonishingly, Amer kept the appointment, dining with Nasser in the presence of all five Vice Presidents. During the meal the Toad and I hung about in the kitchens, arguing about which of the Veeps to poison. Hearty laughter, then singing, could be heard from the dining room. Glasses klinked – the best French wines, no doubt. Then footsteps in the marbled hall. Then silence.

'Field Marshal, you're under arrest!' Amer was told by the Commander of the Presidential Guard. Amer promptly – i.e. after several weeks and one botched attempt – swallowed poison. I spent a week under the Toad's patronage documenting Amer's lifelong treachery as an Israeli agent. My father read this junk in *Misr* (no byline of course) in Hamid the Barber's, then walked home in his immaculately creased trousers to dip his croissant with extra finesse into his French coffee:

'Write a novel,' he said, 'but take your time.'

'This is a novel,' I told him. 'It will be called *The Patriots*. You and I already inhabit it.'

'And will you claim that your "Fawzi el-Sharaf" is both real and unreal?'

'Nicely put, Baba.' So saying, I felt drowsy with pleasure and fell asleep.

An old man pushing a dustcart paused from his desultory street cleaning to observe Dad-Shaytan and myself as we traversed the city which was not-Cairo. He stared at us without deference or inhibition (qualities which evaporate with age). On his forehead he wore the gatta, the permanent bruise acquired by the fanatics who press their brow to the prayer-mat five times a day. He seemed about to speak but we heard nothing as we passed.

'You said that God knew nothing of good and evil?' I pressed the devil.

'He is primarily a mathematician – though, of course, He is primarily Everything.'

'But do we not read in the Old Testament: "And God saw that the wickedness of man was great in the earth, and that every imagination of thoughts of his heart was only evil continually"?'

'That was written aeons later, by some Hebrew know-nothing hardhat. The voice of Religion. The fatal, philistine (if a Hebrew can be a Philistine) equation of "wickedness" with sin. In short, Man was "wicked" every time he got off his knees to pursue some comely wench. It had become a question of Power and Sovereignty. Only the pagans were capable of ethics – need I mention Socrates, Plato and Aristotle?'

'And punishment followed sin?'

'Of course. The Flood. A vengeful God of wrath. With the Flood He went all the way from nuclear physics to the nuclear bomb. Fear was the only rule – which brings us to Abraham and Isaac.'

'You say "fear" – but what about "love"? I mean Abraham's love of God.'

'Gabriel and the acolytes kept telling Him it was love. But God had neither loved nor not-loved before the Creation – how could He know the difference between love and obedience? "Thou hast obeyed My voice," He told Abraham.'

'Which brings us to Job.'

'Don't mention Job!'

Shaytan was gone.

෴

Do you remember the silent Jewish boy, Isaac, he so mysteriously from Aleppo and Damascus, the undeclared rival of my youth? Isaac and I had learnt to exchange conventional enquiries about each other's health, but without forfeiting our mutual premonition of a future showdown, of a world too small to accommodate us both. It was Mahmoud who 'lent' Rabbi Ben Ezra the money for Isaac's flight-for-life when war with Israel became a certainty. Imagine my surprise, therefore, when I received a letter from a midtown Manhattan address, letterheaded 'Isaac Ben Ezra, Inc. Literary Agents', inviting me to join his 'list'.

I duly sent him my account of the Six Day War and the arrest of Abdu – but under Mahmoud's byline. In high excitement Isaac passed it to the *New Yorker*: his benefactor, the great Mahmoud, had joined his list!

Two days later I was summoned by telephone. Mahmoud didn't explain (always a bad sign) and he'd never before put a call through to Celia el-Sharaf's boudoir. He was waiting for me in his study, close to the uncomforting Doré etching of Abraham asking God whether he must slit his son's throat. I noticed that Abraham's upturned eyes seemed on this occasion to be beseeching permission to go ahead. A typescript printed out on telex paper lay in Mahmoud's lap. He handed it to me without a word. A letter was attached from William Lawn, the famous editor of the *New Yorker*.

Dear Maître Mahmoud,
Your first-hand report of these epic events in the Near East is fully worthy of one of the world's great writers. Your description of the arrest of Field Marshal Amer is as brilliant in its detail as it is Shakespearean in its tragic contours. We in America have always heard that you refuse to write in English, and we are therefore doubly grateful that on this occasion you have broken your own rule. Thank you, Maître, for thinking of us here at the *New Yorker*. We are honored.

    Respectfully and gratefully yours, Wm Lawn

'I grovel,' I said. 'I am dirt.'
'Your forgery is not even passably written,' Mahmoud said.
'Baba! This piece has been accepted by the *New Yorker* – which sets the highest literary standard in the English-speaking world! Can't you understand what that means?'
'They saw the name Mahmoud. If it was written by Mahmoud, it was good. I despise those people.'
'Despise William Lawn? Dad, consider the authors he's published!'
My father's lips had almost disappeared. 'Never me. Not until Egypt was the hot subject of the hour. Many of my short stories have been sent to your Mr Lawn. He has rejected them all.'

Mahmoud lit another Gitane, inhaling tragically. We sat in silence. Occasionally he passed a hand delicately over his sleeked-back hair.

'Baba,' I said, 'I am of your flesh though unworthy of your spirit.'

'You killed your mother.'

I stood up (always an effort). 'I may not have been responsible for her pregnancy, sir.' This had no palpable effect. I did not understand – I do now – I was only nineteen, Reader – that those who control, mask, suppress anger all their lives eventually become its most help-less victims. Once a Muslim father, always a Muslim patriarch.

'You never went to university. You have lived in the gutter,' Mahmoud said. 'A tourist guide! My son begging for tips!'

'Or "singing for his supper". A roving minstrel, a strolling player – an honourable tradition.'

'I can forgive anything except you passing your work off as my own. That is where fatherhood stops, Gamal.'

'Right. Right! I apologize. We need never meet again, great Mahmoud. I'm going.'

Going was a bit inconvenient, with all my stuff upstairs. It wasn't clear how I'd make ends meet without Mahmoud's allowance. It had been OK to be naughty so long as the godhead had remained indulgent. When I arrived at the Sharaf residence in the guise of Mother Courage, the lady who so envied the Mother of Martyrs sighed consolingly while hearing an expurgated version of my patri-cide. She immediately telephoned Egypt's prix Nobel.

'Maître,' she said, 'This is Mrs Sharaf. Your son begs your forgive-ness. I, too, on his behalf.'

'How can I refuse you, madame?' Mahmoud said. 'He may return home tonight or whenever you can spare his services. Tell your young friend that I have sent the following message to New York: "Regret shameful case of fraud and deceit. Piece written by my son Gamal Rahman under my name. Profound apologies. However, piece better than anything I could have written, so take note that the baton of Egyptian good writing has passed hands. Feel free to publish under name of Gamal Rahman. Greetings, Mahmoud." '

But my version of the Six Day War never appeared. Week after week I haunted the newsstand at the Nile Hilton, shiftily leafing through the contents page of the *New Yorker*, occasionally sending bad-tempered telexes to Isaac Ben Ezra. Three weeks later I received a letter:

Dear Gamal,
A great start to my career in New York. Thanks to you, I begin with a monstrous deception and am told by the most prestigious literary

magazine in town to expect legal action. Don't you fucking Arabs know right from wrong? Get lost, Isaac.

I replied:

Dear Isaac,
Don't you fucking Jews know good writing when you see it? Every magazine in America will soon be eating out of my hand. Pity you won't be taking your pickings. Good luck! Gamal.

The Purge continued until it reached out for the purgers. Hearing that I was tutor in French to Hamida el-Sharaf and her mother, Nasser instructed the Toad to put me on a handsome 'retainer' – my new duty was to tease out the hidden dreams of the Sharafs by means of cunning exchanges in French. Of course I accepted: refusal was not an option: the Nasser restaurant was strictly plat du jour, with no à la carte. Tipped off, and quick to understand that she must provide me with some morsels of subversion, Celia would walk with me in her beautiful garden, murmuring into my tape recorder:
'Fawzi fears that our President is working himself to death for Egypt.'
'And what does Sharaf think of these constant arrests, madame?'
'He trusts our President's judgment – although it's painful to discover how many comrades have been guilty of disloyalty and subversion.'
I duly submitted my tape to the Toad who, scanning my single-page report, assumed the vile expression from which Hosny Hikmat derived his universally adopted nickname.
'This is no good, you twit. Nasser wants the dirt on Sharaf.'
'Sharaf is loyal.'
'Bilge and balls. No one is loyal to Nasser. Except me.'
Had I reported to the Toad half of what I heard in the Sharaf household, I could have sent our future Rais to the gallows – we don't hang women. From the garrulous Celia I learned of the Veep's grave disquiet about the hasty exodus of foreign nationals from our soil following the war. That the Jews should take to their heels was perhaps natural and wise; but Nasser's pogrom also sent Greeks, Turks and Armenians into flight. Sharaf was no friend of xenophobia.
'Fawzi says Nasser is seeking scapegoats while offering our Arab citizens rich pickings,' Celia confided.
What a good idea! At about this time the Sharafs rented a larger house on the Pyramids Road. Given my extensive knowledge of antique furniture, it was only natural that Celia should invite me to

accompany her to the Attariai, an old area of Alexandria where French antiques, crystal chandeliers, Gallet vases and jewelled troikas poised on marble ostrich eggs commissioned from Fabergé by the last of the Tsars were now to be had for a tenth of their international value. Evidently Nasser's pogrom had its upside. I had never seen such examples of sumptuous vulgarity, but Celia collected them with high-spirited abandon and (I suspected) little intention of paying: a Veep's lady cannot be refused credit. She was also partial to replicas of Egyptian antiques.

'What I can't accommodate right now,' she confided to me, 'I shall store away in our big basement for the dowries of my daughters.' Sadness then invaded her beautiful countenance. 'Poor Fawzi,' she whispered, 'he so wants a son. A man with no son feels himself less than a man.'

I had of course thought of that – so had all of Egypt. Was Celia afraid that Fawzi would divorce her? – Egypt's secular ruling class did not take more than one wife at a time. It wasn't kosher.

'Madame, why do you not try again?'

'Try! How I try, Gamal! The doctors say that Fawzi's sperm count has suffered from so much drinking.' Bravely she squeezed my arm. 'Perhaps a grandson would assuage Fawzi's grief.'

'Really?'

'Tell me, Gamal, do you agree that whoever marries Hamida will be a lucky man?'

'I would gladly slit his throat here and now.'

Celia's hand slid into mine. 'Hamida is very fond of you.'

Clearly it was my patriotic duty to entertain this youthful and vivacious lady at a time when her husband had responded to acute anxiety by embracing a daily routine of ten hours' sleep, ten hours' brooding, and four hours on his exercise machines. Celia deserved a little fun. Naturally Hamida accompanied us everywhere (almost) and my presence as tutor was perfectly in order. 'Entertain my wife,' Sharaf urged me whenever his eyes opened for a few moments.

And I did! The ladies loved my tales from the *Arabian Nights*. Occasionally even little Huda was permitted to sit in on them. Small of stature, demure, deferential, Huda's modest nature seemed in harmony with her diminutive physique. (Hamida was not above twisting her arm or dragging her by the hair when Mama's back was turned.) Huda would tuck herself into a shadowy alcove, listening unnoticed, her doe eyes glowing gently.

'How did the medieval burglars decide whether a house was empty?' I asked Celia and Hamida.

'How?' Both mother and daughter were observing me intently – in their lives and minds burglary was a very bad thing and worth a hand-chopping.

'The trick was this, ladies. You sent a tortoise with a lighted candle on its back into the house, and then – '

'I know!' cried Huda from her alcove.

Hamida's mouth curled impatiently. 'She always "knows".'

'Hush, Huda,' Celia chided her youngest, 'Gamal is telling the story.'

'No,' I said, 'let Huda tell it.'

(In retrospect, historians, I can certify that this generous gesture gained me a wife – though I have never felt in need of one.)

Huda gazed at me warily, unsure whose side I was on, and probably fearful of her own imagination, a quality, or faculty, deemed akin to impertinence in the Sharaf household.

'Well,' she said, 'the thieves used to send a tortoise with a lighted candle on its back into the house. If they heard the inhabitants cry out in wonder, the house was not empty; if they heard nothing, they knew they could proceed, cautiously following the tortoise from room to room – and grab the spoils!'

Huda giggled, clamping a hand to her mouth, and blushed.

'Exactly,' I nodded. Celia beamed indulgently. The beautiful Hamida assumed an expression of indifference. She was bored by stories, unless salacious. Hamida was her own story.

Meanwhile, we pursued our own forms of burglary, and by no means at the pace of a tortoise, loading van after van with hastily abandoned antiques while the victorious Israelis, apparently impervious to the joys of looting, toiled round the Judaic clock building their Wailing Sand Wall along the Canal.

Did I mention that a grateful Egyptian State had allocated the Veep a splendid house in Rosetta, outside Alex? The villa enjoyed its own private beach plus garden with en tout cas tennis court. The Nassers occupied a holiday home in Ma'amoura. While Sharaf played backgammon with our chain-smoking President, who might arrest him if the game went badly, it was fat Gamal's duty to play tennis with Celia and her daughter, suffering Hamida's taunts before clumsily pursuing my beautiful tormentors into the sea, observed by hulking bodyguards cross-eyed with jealousy. I had never learnt to swim but my body floated like a rubber dinghy in the Mediterranean brine. Hamida's laughter turned to squeals:

'Maman! Cette baleine méchante me mange!'

And so on – there are many routes to a Foyle's Literary Luncheon. The thing I enjoyed most was sniffing the new Dunlop balls fresh from their airtight canister – not unlike a mild glue-trip. Sparkling white gear was of course de rigueur; Celia ordered her own tennis dresses, and Hamida's, from Teddy Tinling in London, each modelled on the outfit favoured by the current stars of the international circuit, Yvonne Goolagong or whoever. A Syrian tailor was called in to rig me out in the kind of short-sleeved shirt and vast shorts found in daguerreotypes of the Cecil Rhodes era – though a white, baseball-style cap was allowed instead of a solar topee. Celia and Hamida both received regular professional coaching in backhand, forehand and service, with dubious results. In truth there is no tradition of sporting achievement in Egypt beyond swimming – some dusky hulk was always turning up at Dover and heading heavily for Calais. The Brits never laid a single cricket pitch in our dust; unlike the Indian princes, the sons of our pashas had nothing to emulate, no thwack of lin-seeded bat on leather ball across the verdant outfield, no tinkling of applause from the pavilion. As for our fellahin, few of them sought world fame by running up and down the donkey tracks of the Nile. Nature had not earmarked me for sporting achievement; there was no available space between my legs. My attempts to make contact with a moving ball provoked Hamida to vulgar, sexually derogatory fits of mirth. I retaliated by confining her to her room until she had translated the most licentious speeches from *Tartuffe*. She appealed to her mother, without avail; her appeals ceased; the day came when she offered me a kiss in return for clemency.

'A French kiss, Gamal.'

I pondered this – why had Celia, since our move to Alex, ceased to chaperone these tutorials? Was her ear, even now, pressed to the door? Noting that Molière had (as predicted) done his work well, I rebuked my pupil with appropriate severity. Halfway through my admonition I found her sweet tongue in my mouth.

'Don't tell Mama,' she pouted.

'You mean you want to tell her first.'

'How could I! She'd be so jealous.'

'Write me one hundred words in best French explaining the origin of the tennis term "love".'

'Ha! – invariably your score in any game or set!'

'Do it.'

'Make me.'

Aaah, oh dear. The term 'love', dear Reader, as I had more than once explained to Hamida, derives from the French word l'oeuf, meaning an egg, which aristocrats had humourously likened to the figure nought – an oblong nought. You didn't know that? Lazy Hamida is retaliating with a tirade against unmanly intellectuals who serve double faults and are hopeless lovers.

289

'Maman est folle de te prendre au sérieux,' she adds.

As punishment Hamida is ordered by her tutor to translate an English novelist's descriptions of pre-war Alexandria into French.

'Why does this Durrell write so much about foreigners?' pouts our republican princess.

'He describes a Europeanized Egypt populated by seekers and escapers who neither seek nor escape; a sort of cultured detritus.'

Hamida ponders this, sucks her pencil. 'We have to get rid of foreigners.'

This spoilt brat has divined that I despise Egypt and admire all (or most) things foreign; I who am forever wrestling with the greatness of a father whose dedication to Arabic is like a wealthy Fabian's commitment to the unlettered poor, a deliberate self-immolation inspired by the largeness of sympathy reserved to privileged talents.

Ah, Alex – a city for Sufis drifting on a magic carpet of happy evasion. Anything goes and everything went.

NINETEEN

☙

Ah, Alex. Ah, the never-ending Corniche, the Sunset Boulevard of my unforgivable ambitions, built by Alex himself in what Celia calls 'ancient times'. How she would have loved to play Cleopatra to that distinguished visitor. She has her antique-market eye on the great lighthouse; it wouldn't surprise me if it ended up in her garden at Rosetta. Here I should mention that Celia el-Sharaf has com-missioned – or requisitioned – me to trace her paternal ancestry back to Queen Cleo, proving a line of direct descent from the Ptolemy dynasty. As for her mother, Celia now tells me she was born 'of pure Yorkshire stock', née Gertrude Plum, in an industrial town called Bruddersford.

I happened to be strolling with little Huda, or she with me, while my pupil Hamida was engaged in drawing up lists of traitors for Pappi to put down like vermin when he became President.

'You hate Egypt, don't you, Gamal?' Huda said.

'Me?'

'You'd rather be at Oxford, wouldn't you? I know you would.'

Decorously we skirted a garden sprinkler – Huda had stopped trying to push me into sprinklers, ponds and swimming pools when her breasts finally announced themselves beneath the plain white cotton blouses in which Celia dressed her.

'That doesn't mean I "hate Egypt",' I reproached her.

'I'd like to go to London,' she said dreamily, 'or Paris.'

'For the nice clothes?'

'Oh, you would say that! I'm not Mama, you know.'

'You're Huda.'

'I'd like to play chess with the most brilliant student at the Sor-bonne all day long.'

'Because I'm not good enough?'

She giggled. 'You don't really try, do you? You let me win.'

'Why should I?'

'Because you can't help being nice, though you pretend not to be to impress Hamida.' Huda did a little skip and momentarily took my hand. 'Oh Gamal, I'm so glad we know you.'

'And I'm honoured to know *you*, mademoiselle.'

'Comrade. Call me "comrade" – it's an order.' Huda's laughter rang across the palatial garden, pinging against the elegant shutters which shielded the sleeping Pappi from the afternoon sun.

'I wouldn't shout that word,' I advised.

'Coward!' The girl's hand again stole into mine, like the thieves' tortoise bearing the candle. 'Do you know what "liberty" means, Gamal? I bet you do.' We walked on a few paces. Huda glanced up at me. 'Hamida's very beautiful, isn't she?'

'Yes. But who knows? she may grow ugly.'

'Let's hope,' Huda said gravely, 'and expect the worst.'

Soon after this exchange in the garden, the Toad assured me that Bruddersford did not exist except in the imagination of a middle-ranking novelist called J.B. Priestley, whose popular, war-time broadcasts invariably coincided with an air-raid alert – 'Are you sitting comfortably behind properly blacked-out windows?' As for Celia's mum Gertrude, thereby hangs another tale into which your ill-fated storyteller will in due course be dragged.

In search of the Ptolemy family tree, I accompanied Celia in the limo to Marsa Matruh, where Cleo had built the beautiful palaces in which she'd shared a slice of history with J. Caesar, M. Antony, etc. The Veep's lady regularly took her daughters Hamida and Huda to swim in the lagoon known as Cleo's Bath, myself in attendance, the usual figure of derision in my old-fashioned, one-piece bathing costume.

I want no misunderstanding here: my work for the Sharaf family was by now at such a level of statecraft that I am frankly amazed I can report it without breaching the Official Secrets Act. In everything but name I was private secretary to Madame Celia el-Sharaf. Hardly a week passed without her pic splashing across *Misr* – do you imagine that these things simply happen? Who was responsible for ensuring that our model 'orphan village' was publicized round the world as Celia's brainchild? – though pedants like Anis Hussein privately insisted that it had been set up by the famous singer Um Kalthoum, the Nightingale of the Nile.

Nevertheless, despite my labours, Celia continued to lag behind Mrs Jehan el-Sadat in popular estimation. The Directress of the Red Crescent remained the much-loved solace of our widows, orphans and limbless soldiers.

ᘌ

The Sharaf ladies, Celia, Hamida and little Huda, occupy a special VIP/VEEP compartment on the train from Alexandria to Cairo. This express is the pièce de résistance of Egyptian State Railways; it leaves Alex at 7.50 a.m. and 2.15 p.m., arriving in Cairo two hours and thirty-five minutes later, with only one stop, Sidi Gaber. All other trains take three hours ten minutes with yawning halts at Damanhour, Tanta and Benha. Today there will be no stops (precious human cargo aboard); expectant passengers can damn well stand on the platform and watch the train flash past. The Veep-VIP compartment is a suite equipped with private toilet, shower room, adjustable bunk beds, portrait of Nasser, gilded mirrors and deep, deep chairs clad in real Italian executive leather. Did I forget the vase of roses and the card of welcome from Celia's cousin, now Director of Railways? Blinds shield the ladies from the gaze of the security men guarding us in the corridor – though the security men would be happier about this Islamic tradition if the Sharaf ladies were not taking it in turns, squealing with laughter, to tug the wispy goatee beard (it didn't last long) sported by their upstart fellow-traveller, the fat and probably seditious slob, Rahman, otherwise known as Gamal the Camel. (Humps-humping: you have to understand Arabic.)

Gamal is in fact most dutifully conducting a tutorial in French history, thoughtfully devised to instruct and entertain both mother and daughters. (If little Huda wants to listen, as she does, she won't understand a word of it because, of course, everyone must speak in French.)

'Today, ladies, I am going to tell you about the famous Marquis de Sade, which is French for el-Sharaf. Like our distinguished Vice President, the marquis was unjustly imprisoned on trumped-up charges.'

'By the British?' Hamida asks, snatching again at Gamal's funny beard. 'Gama, you *are* a goat!'

Gamal now produces the bottle of champagne he has secreted in the picnic hamper. The cork thuds into the roof of the compartment, the froth spurts to shocked squeals. 'Just a little-little sip for everyone, the Marquis de Sade always insisted,' Gamal announces. Celia insists that the girls are too young but soon everyone is sipping a little-little and giggling.

'Now please pay attention, ladies, to the Marquis de Sade. Finding himself in a remote castle without his wife's consoling company, the marquis applied to a well-known procuress in Lyon for four servant girls, young and pretty. He took them home.'

'Hamida, you are not to listen,' says Celia.

'Six months later the four girls' parents turned up demanding their return. The Marquis de Sade gave the girls back but was charged with abduction and rape.'

'Oh poor man!' (Celia.)

'The beast!' (Hamida.)

'Hamida, you don't understand. The marquis was innocent.' (Celia.)

'You mean he'd never laid a finger on the girls?' Hamida cries.

The Tutor shakes his head: 'The marquis never claimed a platonic relationship. He argued that the crime was not his: by French law, he insisted, it was the procuress who was guilty of supplying virgin maidens. As the marquis put it, "Even if the male offender has requested a virgin he is not liable to punishment: he is merely doing what all men do." None of these girls had "cause for anything but self-congratulation" on the treatment they had received.'

'How disgusting he sounds,' Hamida says.

'The marquis seems to have enjoyed a very self-serving sense of sin,' Celia says.

'That was the opinion of his great enemy, his mother-in-law, Madame de Montreuil, otherwise known as Madame la Présidente. After the marquis was incarcerated in Vincennes, he lamented to his wife that her mother had falsely accused him of "abusing bottoms".'

The ladies giggle. The champagne flows as the train arrogantly hurtles and hoots through Damanhour and Tanta, kicking dust into the human detritus on the platforms, men who know not the Vice President's wife, nor the Vice President's daughters.

'Ladies, please observe out of the window. This green Nile Valley, whose shape resembles the stem and flower of the lotus, was in early times a jungle swamp; the sea flowed over much of the Delta. The ancients lived on the adjoining plateaux, which formed a savanna not unlike the plains of East Africa today. Just imagine – elephant, zebra and lion abounding!'

'You sound like a tourist guide,' Hamida says.

'Hamida – how rude you are!' (Celia.)

'I haven't told you everything about the Marquis de Sade's adventures,' Gamal continues. 'On Easter Sunday, 1768, he took to his petite maison at Aerceuil a thirty-six-year-old widow of German origin, Rose Keller, whom he'd seen begging in the Place des Victoires. He offered her a job as a chambermaid, made her undress, tied her to a bed and beat her, using alternately a rod and a "martinet".'

'What is that?' Hamida asks.

'A cat o' nine tails. Or a French military drill master. Or a strict disciplinarian.'

'Poor woman,' Celia sighs. 'She was probably asking for it.'

'The marquis then eloped to Italy with his wife's sister.'

Both mother and daughter cry out in genuine horror.

'I thought he was in prison,' little Huda accuses me, her white-stockinged legs drumming against the seat. 'Liar! Gamal is a liar! It's all lies!'

Huda is the object of our astonishment. She is never supposed to be there, unless convenient. She's not expected to understand a word of French, notoriously the language of sexual connivance.

'Hush, Huda,' Celia chides her.

'It's all lies anyway,' Hamida says.

Gamal is not interested today in this doe-eyed child, his lusts rage crazily for Hamida.

'Now, Hamida, you have been an insolent pupil, a disgrace to your father, and you have just likened your tutor to a tourist guide. Punishment must follow. I will show you the Marquis de Sade's way of bringing an untamed young lady to proper obedience.'

From my briefcase I produce a small whip or fouet. All the ladies gasp.

'Oh Mama, don't let him!' Hamida cries.

'You will become the Virgin of Egypt,' Gamal assures her. 'As a result of this chastening experience you will be better disciplined to help your father achieve his destiny. You will crush his enemies and set him high among the world's great statesmen.'

Hamida is definitely interested. 'Will he be President?'

'Only if you endure the fouet without cries or tears.'

Hamida hesitates: 'I'll kill you if it's not true! Mama, is it true?'

'No, it's not true, darling. Gama is merely teasing us.'

'Then we should beat him!'

She seizes my fouet and rapidly finds herself sprawled across my knee. 'Gamal!' Celia cries as the first lash strikes tender buttocks. I am beside myself with excitement. 'Un! Deux! Trois!' At three Hamida, a strong girl, wriggles free and crosses herself (she has of late been attending a convent school). 'You swine! You'll be sorry!' Heavy banging on the locked door from the guards in the corridor ensues.

'All is well!' Celia calls. Then she hisses at me: 'You are an insane degenerate!' Hamida is fighting back tears. 'I'll tell Pappi! He'll chop your hands off!'

The train glides into Cairo. I'd never known a journey pass so quickly.

Clearly this has been dangerous work at the highest level of vertigo. Do not shoot your fat steeplejack merely because the scaffolding of his credibility is swaying nastily in the desert wind. (Your anticipated rebuke about 'over-elasticated metaphors' is duly noted, Dad.) OK,

OK, I admit that during this and other such journeys the Tutor was confined to the camel-van at the rear of the train along with political prisoners, camels and a million fleas. This caveat apart, everything happened exactly as set down above (pages 2,099–2,101 of *The Patriots*, by G. Rahman).

Whatever version your prefer, I was undone; by my own sweet folly I'd made a private pact to remain the Virgin of Egypt's frustrated slave. It's a shortish step from Vesuvius to Pompeii.

Did I mention Jackie? If Celia had one obsession, it was to be introduced to the young widow of America's assassinated President. Jackie was the most photographed woman in the world and reported to be spending a million dollars a year on outfits. As Celia's cultural adviser, fatboy became an overnight expert on little shift dresses, boxy suits and knee-length trapeze coats. Gamal bombarded the upmarket secondhand shops on Madison Avenue with cabled requests for anything Jackie had discarded after wearing it once: maybe a cashmere cardigan or a fawn wool coat by Oleg Cassini? In Paris money poured out of Celia's Hobo handbag from Gucci; the Veep despatched me by Air Egypt to drag his wife out of Charles Jourdan and Ferragamo's, where I found Celia, in a pair of Jackie sunglasses, torturing herself into a pair of knee-length Jackie-boots.

'Madame, there is an urgent message for you at the Embassy.'

Celia dreamed of creating her own Camelot on the Nile, her own Martha's Vineyard on the Corniche. But she'd never met Jackie. All she got under Nasser was Russia's first lady in space, who didn't look a million dollars. Then Jackie fled America, landing on an archipelago of Greek islands owned by Sharaf's 'good friend', Aristotle Onassis. Jackie – Celia excitedly concluded – was heading downmarket and in our direction. The noble breakers of the Atlantic coast had yielded to the good old stagnant pond, the Med, where Greek tycoons and Egyptian Veeps knew how to do each other small favours. I spent half my life on steamers trying to negotiate an invitation to the Onassis wedding. Reaching yet another of the private islands owned by the man who'd jilted Maria Callas, I discovered what it's like to be worked over on the jetty by guards recruited from the James Bond films. Arriving back in Cairo without an invitation to the wedding, and two suits ruined, I was ambivalently received by Celia.

'You're a dog,' she told me.

Vice President Sharaf was also in one of his black moods; under stress the peasant patriarch surfaced out of the urbane, modern husband: he began yelling 'Ya sitt! – Hey, woman!' in the middle of diplomatic receptions. His wife was 'forgetting her duties'. But would he tell her himself? No. I was summoned to attend his daily fifteen minutes on the bicycle machine.

'Gamal, my wife is neglecting her home.'

'Sir!'

'My wife is neglecting her husband. If she wishes to visit her charities in the morning, fine. But I want her home pee em.'

'Pee em, sir?'

'Pee em.'

'But your Excellency, I – '

'You heard me. Pee em.'

Celia would receive these messages with impressive dignity.

'Go tell the Vice President that I am entirely at his command. If I must abandon my role as the Mother of Martyrs, if I am commanded no longer to tend to our wounded soldiers, if my name and face must disappear from our television and newspapers, if Egypt must conclude that Sharaf is putting his wife back in purdah – then so be it, I obey. Go and tell him!'

'But madame, I – ' Unable to conceal my astonishment at her galloping delusions – the title Mother of Martyrs belonged securely to another lady – I incurred a sharp slap across the face – Celia really could slap, too. Perhaps it was the tennis. The slap invariably carried a verbal sting in its tail:

'Hamida says you forced your tongue into her mouth after making her rehearse a whole scene in which you played Tartuffe. Hamida wants me to dismiss you.'

Back to the exercise bicycle (or the sauna bath, or simply the siesta).

'Your Excellency, I have spoken to Mrs Sharaf and she – '

'Frankly, Gamal, you are seeing too much of my wife. In future you will not approach her without my written permission. Nasser may be an atheist but Sharaf is a Pillar of the Faith, you know. I am told that you do not fast properly during Ramadan. I am told that you do not get out of bed at three in the morning for the suhur, the pre-dawn meal without which one cannot fast until the iftar at dusk. I'm told that you do not wash properly before praying. That you rarely wash and never pray.'

I fell to my knees. 'Excellency.'

'Let me remind you that "Islam" means submission, Gamal. A "Muslim" is one who submits. Do you submit?'

'I submit to him who shall be el-ra'is and achieve tahrir misr, the liberation of Egypt.'

Sharaf nodded and sent me to the kitchens, where I was granted a plate of my favourite pastry packed with pistachios, almonds and raisins, all topped by a delicious syrup of lemon and honey.

Then disaster. Sharaf and Celia, not content with their Nile-side villa, hankered after the more splendid residence adjoining. It became an obsession with Celia; she had to have that splendid residence adjoining. The very thought of it brought on orgasms of force 7 on the Richter scale. The Sharafs then offered a laughable price to the unfortunate owner of the splendid residence adjoining, General Ibrahim Gogi. Taking advantage of Nasser's absence abroad, Sharaf arranged for Gogi to be served with an outright requisition order.

A scandal, even by local standards. It was the first time I had seen Huda shaking under the adult version of tears – she was all of thirteen. We walked together in the garden beside the Nile.

'It's shameful!' she sobbed.

'But – '

'Such greed! Such vulgarity! Such abuse of power! Gamal, help me to escape to Paris! You allowed me to read Sartre, didn't you, and Madame de Beauvoir. I read Frantz Fanon's *The Wretched of the Earth* the very day you gave it to me – and all night! I didn't understand every word of it but – '

'I hope you didn't leave it lying about, Huda.'

'Coward!' Her little hand had fastened on mine. 'Of course I didn't. Just imagine if our beautiful Chief of Police Hamida got hold of that!'

'Huda, Fanon wrote a book. A book is not the world.'

'It is! Traitor! Oh you love Hamida, don't you? She does . . . things with you, I know she does, and I'm just the silly gamine of the family. And she's got long legs. She wears high heels while Mama keeps me in button-shoes suitable for an école maternelle. Hamida plays tennis. Swoon swoon. I'm just a bookworm.'

I was touched. It doesn't happen often.

'You're my best friend in Egypt, Huda.'

'But not violent or vicious enough to love. You're being patronizing.'

The Toad summoned me into the usual cloud of acrid cigar smoke, his tongue flicking. If I could make the Gogi story against Sharaf 'stick' I could have Anis Hussein's anus-job. Currently Editor of *Misr*, Minister of Information and (whenever he felt like it) Deputy Foreign Minister, Hosny Hikmat feared that Nasser was on his last packet of fags and that Sharaf would become el-ra'is – the Rais: exit Toad. The dim, under-powered streetlights of Cairo flickered beyond the window of the Editor's office on the sixth floor of *Misr*.

'I may have had certain confidential conversations with Madame Celia, Boss.'

'Concerning General Gogi's residence? Yes?' The Toad's tongue flicked happily. 'Go write, Gamal. Be back here by midnight.'

I rushed to Celia and told her everything. She embraced me, tears rivuletting into her rose-tinted face powder.

'That Toad! His time will come. When Fawzi embraces his destiny as Egypt's President, you shall sit in the editor's chair at *Misr.* Now go straight to Hamida and propose marriage to her.'

'Shouldn't I speak to the Vice President first?'

'No, no, you can speak to Fawzi "first" afterwards.'

I fell on one knee before Celia, clasping her hand to my cheek. 'But madame, it is you I adore.'

'Silly boy, such a romantic.'

'Madame, the Sharaf dynasty will survive the intrigues of its enemies only if Hamida remains the Virgin of Egypt.'

'I do wish you wouldn't use that expression – and I've never understood what you're talking about.'

We were still bickering when I fell asleep on Celia's Second Empire canapé. My lids had no sooner hooded my bulging eyes than Mahmoud made his entrance like a well-loved actor of the Comédie-française he had frequented in his youth, transporting me through the new, fake Cairo he despised.

The old dustcart man with the gatta on his forehead finally eased his toothless gums into speech.

'I know this young gentleman,' he said, nodding at me. 'I pray against him.'

Dad and I passed beyond the reinforced concrete monstrosities – 'our not-Cairo Cairo,' as he called it – into an alternative landscape resembling the tombs of the caliphs, wandering among Mameluke memorials and empty madrasahs, waterless fountains and Koranic schools without pupils. We gazed up at the patterned stone domes of Barkuk and Barbay.

'The end of the great tradition,' Mahmoud murmured.

'Which brings us to Job,' I pressed.

'Don't mention Job! That was *the* nightmare! My Lord was dragging me all over the Holy Land, demonstrating his version of "love". The faithful were getting it in the neck. So we arrive at poor's Job estate. "Behold," my Master says to me, "all that Job hath is in thy power." I tried to protest: "Lord, Lord, Job is a good man." That cut no ice: if I may employ a metaphor, the divine eyebrows had a tendency to climb at the word "good". So I had to do it. I had to move the Sabeans to carry off Job's oxen and his asses; I had to move the Chaldeans to carry off his camels and murder his servants; I made lighting flash upon his sheep. Then I took a deep breath and blew down his house, burying his children in the ruins.'

'I am puzzled here. Was it not you, Shaytan, who wagered with God that Job loved Him only because he feared Him as the Divine Protector of his prosperity? Was it not you who laid down a cynical challenge to the Lord, "But put forth Thine hand now, and touch all that he hath, and he will curse Thee to Thy face"?'

'You've been reading the Hebrew hardhats.'

'Do you deny it?'

'The devil's *divine* role is to play the devil's advocate. You have to ask yourself what kind of a Divine Being would allow Himself to be provoked into pure destruction by His servant, who was merely His fingernail, the sweat-stain under His armpit. Why does God allow Himself to get into a wager with Satan? I worked strictly to the divine brief: I was not allowed to lay a finger on Job himself. And when the poor fellow passed the first test – "the Lord gave, and the Lord hath taken away; blessed be the name of the Lord" – I was instructed to get to work on the man himself, sparing only his life. So I had to smite him with boils from the soles of his feet to his crown. Whereupon Job's wife most unwisely advised him to curse God. But curse *God*, take note, not curse *Satan*. Even Job's wife knew who was writing the script. But our Lord wanted it both ways – He accused me of moving Him to destroy Job "without cause".'

'But could you not express indignation?'

'Actually, I felt a glimmer of hope. That "without cause" suggested the dawn of a moral consciousness. There was also some satisfaction in Job's final affirmation of Faith: "What? shall we receive good at the hand of God, and shall we not receive evil." '

'Such words indicating that God is merely Absolute Power?'

'Precisely. Anyway, it was a false dawn. Two thousand human years later the synagogues, churches and mosques have side-stepped the wisdom of Job's wife – their versions of Divine Providence normally indicate some hidden sin on the part of the victims. It's a form of permanent schizophrenia born out of the pathetic but burning desire to believe that the Almighty is also Good. The pagans never had that problem. They happily endowed their gods with every known human virtue and vice. They propitiated them with offerings. They covered them in gold leaf. Call it protection money – their gods were gangsters. But when our wretched Jews, Christians and Muslims pray for this or that, victory in war or save this sick child, they are never quite sure what they *deserve* from this capricious and invisible judge. Pathetically they toss evidence of virtue at the high altar of Power.'

'In short, the disease is religion?'

The devil shrugged. 'We have to live with it. Dying with it is the easy bit.'

ॐ

Composition of *The Patriots* was complete – an unpublishable folly – when Nasser suddenly died of a heart attack brought on by violently trembling fingers stained nicotine-brown to the elbow. The crowds came out, frantically hailing the Man of the Hour – whoever would be Caesar after the inevitable scuffles on the Senate steps.

The two candidates were total lookalikes – no one could tell Sharaf and Sadat apart. The masses gathering in the streets were prudently placing bets on both horses.

'Yahya el-Sadat! Long live Sadat! Yahya el-Sharaf! Long live Sharaf! May God be with you, future President!'

I hurried to the Sadat residence to convey my priceless support and was turned away at the gate: 'No beggars!' I scuttled back down Pyramids Road to the Sharaf residence, where I was received by a sullen Hamida.

'Mabruk, mabruk, mademoiselle. Congratulations to President Sharaf!'

Which is how history gets written, if not made, and what's the difference, Mahmoud?

TWENTY

⟳

Hook-Nose lay in state at the Qubbah Palace. Sharaf and Sadat kept calling in to pay their respects as if fearful that Nasser would open one eye and punish all those who had believed him mortal. Celia and Mrs Sadat, meanwhile, were busy comforting the nation's bereaved women, although as far as I could tell their paths never crossed. My task was to soak up rumours of Sadat's intrigues and to convey them to Celia. Panicked by the departure of their supreme patron, the Toad and Anis Hussein had turned themselves into a rumour factory. If anyone knew which way Hosny Hikmat would finally jump, as he splashed brilliantly from one puddle to the next, it certainly was not the Toad himself.

On the day of Nasser's funeral, Anwar el-Sadat fainted from grief – more probably from a surfeit of rumours. Fawzi el-Sharaf immediately did the same, but he was too late. In the split second before his head cracked open, Sadat was nimbly caught by the American Ambassador, a top-ranking amateur tennis player (Wimbledon, Flushing Meadow). Sharaf's head went all the way down to the floor; 'sources' told me you could hear the impact in Alex; he lay unconscious for a week. The throng of astrologers crowding around Nasser's open catafalque – myself included – read the portents. I had taught French in the wrong household. I rolled my eyes endearingly in the direction of the Sadat family – nothing doing.

Celia was crouching over the political corpse of her husband: 'Oh Fawzi, Fawzi.'

Hamida didn't move.

The Higher Executive Committee of our only legal political party, the Arab Socialist Union, also took note: the ASU promptly nominated Anwar el-Sadat as its candidate for President. One hundred leading Nasserites and a large chunk of the Muslim Brotherhood were deposited in the Tora prison, for safe-keeping. The Toad was whipped off his 'vacation' flight to London at Cairo airport and, to

302

his astonishment, invited to carry on as editor of *Misr* while serving as Sadat's campaign manager.

This boiled down to fixing Sadat's beaming portrait to trees, lamp posts and the tails of donkeys – I spent many hot hours fiddling with nails and balls of string while supervising squads of fellahin hired by the Ministry of Information. The Sadat camp (and the Toad) had overlooked one detail: Sadat's portrait was identical to Sharaf's. Fawzi was still in the running although in no position to know it.

Hamida and I conferred urgently by night – such was her excitement, her joie de pouvoir, that she more than once commanded me to wield my Sadean fouet.

'Ow! Fat swine!'

'I am the marquis and you are the Virgin of Egypt!'

'You must think of something!'

'Bring in the Russians.'

'But Pappi hates the Russians! They're Bolsheviks! And Mama says their women don't know how to dress properly.'

We brought in the Russians. The true Nasserites – those not in the Tora – rallied to the conspiracy. They didn't trust Sadat and they didn't trust Sharaf but Sharaf was in a coma and therefore the better bet. An unconscious President suited them perfectly. I arranged for the conspirators to seek guidance from the late Nasser through a spirit medium at Ain Shams University. The late Nasser advised that Sadat would sell Egypt to the Americans – which was why the American Ambassador had caught Sadat (rather than Sharaf) as he fainted during Nasser's funeral. The tape-recording of the seance was promptly despatched to Moscow, courtesy of Aeroflot. We may therefore imagine the scene in the Kremlin late at night (it's always late at night in the Kremlin) as Brezhnev and Kosygin anxiously studied a translation from the Arabic of a voice from the dead – it must have taxed their faith in materialism. The reply came straight back: unlimited MIGs, rockets, tanks, artillery, etc., if Sharaf was elected President of Egypt.

Unfortunately, the reply came straight back to the Toad through his sources in the Kremlin (i.e. Brezhnev and Kosygin, who were now thoroughly confused by the identical portraits of Sadat and Sharaf reaching them from their Ambassador in Cairo, Vinogradov, a thickhead with a weakness for thumping his piano all night long). The Toad took the evidence to Sadat who promptly went on the radio and proudly read out messages of personal support from President Nixon and Premier Kosygin – which was no doubt news to them.

'We must all pray for my dear brother Fawzi el-Sharaf,' Sadat continued. 'The doctors have warned me that he may suffer permanent injuries to the brain. Our thoughts are with his family. Only yesterday his wife Celia warned me that he may never recover consciousness. I therefore declare that 90.04 per cent of the Egyptian people have elected me their President. My first Executive Order is to appoint Fawzi el-Sharaf as my Ambassador to Outer Mongolia.'

(This was to be the one and only occasion that Sadat settled for anything less than 99.99 per cent of the popular vote. The Toad penned an eloquent editorial in *Misr*, calling it a triumph for democracy.)

Rising from his hospital bed, Sharaf selected the most dashing of the several German-style military uniforms which Celia laid before him, ran an eye over the speech I had written, and strode into the National Assembly to embrace his 'dear brother' Sadat. However, as his (my) speech unfolded before a flabbergasted audience of foreign dignitaries and self-elected parliamentarians, it became apparent that Sharaf, suffering from the after-effects of concussion, believed he was accepting the presidency. In short, he kept calling himself el-ra'is.

Celia was radiant. Dressed in fabulous new Balmains, the Sharaf women sparkled like the diamonds of a single tiara. Even Huda seemed momentarily forgetful of her rendezvous with Jean-Paul Sartre and Karl Marx at the Sorbonne. The recurring leitmotif of Sharaf's speech was beautiful in its simplicity:

—My programme is Nasser's. My programme is democracy

—Our socialism is Egyptian socialism

—Our love embraces every Egyptian

—The Egyptian nation is the jewel of the greater Arab nation

—We seek war with no one but our patience is not unlimited

—Your Rais is but the humble servant of his people

—Our only President for Life is Allah, our only Power is the power of prayer

—Holy Prophet Muhammad, I am listening as you listened

—Dear Brother, Anwar el-Sadat, you have served your Nation with selfless devotion, and I appoint you my Ambassador to Panama.

To his credit, Sadat had heard this out in dignified silence until the Panama bit, when he fainted again. This time Vinogradov and the American tennis player both leapt forward to catch him, each impeding the other, the result being that the thud of head on floor could be heard across the world and Fawzi el-Sharaf ruled Egypt for the next ten years although everyone thought it was Sadat.

Everyone including Sadat. Indeed so close was the genetic kinship between the two presidents, and so similar the brain damage suffered in all this falling down, that each sailed serenely through a tumultuous decade believing himself to be his own brother.

(From page 74 of *The Crossing*, by G. Rahman, all rights reserved.)

ﻋﺞ

Hamida el-Sharaf, sixteen years old and utterly indifferent to her own beauty, sits cross-legged (jeans) on the polished boards of the Rais's bedroom, watching him climb in and out of his German-style uniforms: layer upon layer of Pappi, each offering Egypt a slightly different destiny. The past lies at the Rais's feet like a tossed-off galabiyeh.

'Pappi, you must move against your enemies.'

He catches a glimpse of her in his long dressing mirror. His response is fond, dismissive: 'You have been listening to your mother, child.'

'Pappi, I have a list of your enemies hidden in my clothing. I have brought it to you. You must strike tonight.'

He smiles. 'What can a mere girl know?'

'Pappi, Gamal says he wants to marry me.'

'It's no business of yours, Hamida, who wants to marry you.'

'Gamal says if I marry him he will be your Minister of Propaganda and National Guidance. He will be editor of *Misr*. He will befriend all the subversive poets in Egypt and betray them to me.'

'That snake Gamal Rahman has been poisoning your innocent young mind. I shall throw this bad boy into prison tonight!'

'Thank you, Pappi.'

Hamida withdraws gracefully, with a hint of a curtsy. The Rais is about to lift the telephone and throw Gamal into the Tora prison when his attention is arrested by a pair of doe-eyes staring at him from the shadows. They seem vaguely identifiable.

'Pappi, you must not imprison Gamal.'

'Huda, my child.' He pats her head. 'My child,' he repeats, as if uncertain. 'What are you doing, spying on me?'

'It isn't true that Gamal asked Hamida to marry him. He never said any of those things she said he said.'

The Rais chuckles indulgently. 'And how would a tiny creature like you know about such matters?'

'Because it's me Gamal wants to marry.'

'Did he say so?'

'Oh lots of times, yes.'

'So that bad boy has proposed to both of you!'

'Pappi, if you imprison Gamal I shall kill myself.'

'How old are you, girl?'

'Fourteen, Pappi. And I have stolen one of your sharp razors.'

(Mahmoud was later to comment that my 'fabrications' were normally 'buttressed by the authorial presence'. The Toad put it more bluntly: 'You were hiding under the bed?')

Anyway, Sharaf struck all the Red Conspirators down.

I was now the Rais's primary speech-writer. He promised (I promised) the Nation to bring the home front into line with the military front. No one knew what this meant of course (least of all the Rais, the Toad or I). The students of Cairo University became restive. Students like to know what things mean and to become restive. Insolent derision was directed at Sharaf's 'fog speech'. Sixty thousand demonstrated in Cairo alone, swarming across the Nile bridges into Liberation Square, then gathering round the plinth which awaited, and still awaits, Nasser's statue. Huda was spotted among the demonstrators and promptly rescued by a State Security van. It was hushed up, of course, but I was back in the doghouse. The Toad roasted me on the sixth floor of *Misr*. If I couldn't 'deliver' the students, not even the Rais's daughter, who the hell could I deliver? As punishment I was assigned the menial task of making sure that not a word of the students' petition appeared in the press.

I got through to Celia on the telephone: 'Madame, we need a single, killing phrase to damn the students.'

'Where have you been, Gama? I never see you.'

Ten minutes later I was summoned to the Rais's presence, with the Toad hovering in the shadows and flicking his tongue.

'We need a single, killing phrase to damn the students,' the Rais announced.

'The Committee of National Treason,' I suggested.

The Rais went straight on the nation's airwaves and denounced the 'Committee of National Treason', but he also tossed in some fanciful notions of his own, blaming the Palestinian students in Cairo – there were 20,000 of them – and the 'anarchic spirit of 1968'. Evidently the French student revolt of that year had been the work of Zionists and the USA.

Having calmed down, the Toad became philosophical:

'Whenever you overthrow a conspiracy, you must borrow its programme. Sharaf is convincing Brezhnev that he is a better friend to the Soviet Union than the conspirators. Soon he will be convincing Allah that he is a better friend than the Muslim Brotherhood.'

I nodded. 'Sharaf has already convinced Hikmat that he's a better friend of Hikmat than Hikmat is.'

'Our Rais, my dear Gamal, is a very great man.'

'That's a new line from you, Boss.'

' "Some are born great, some have it thrust upon them." Shake-speare.' The Toad grinned smugly and shouted to the coffee boy and lit another cigar and put his feet on the desk and eased his collar and made an appointment with his dentist. He then casually pulled the manuscript of my novel, *The Patriots*, from his desk drawer.

'You're pushing your luck, Gamal. Who else have you shown it to?'

'I've sent copies to London, Paris and New York.'

'Wise.' Abruptly he seizes his jacket and propels me out of the building (now bugged head-to-toe) into the hot street via the execu-tive car park. 'You're a fool,' he says, furiously sounding his horn at a donkey cart. 'I've drafted a disclaimer for you. Read it.' He pulls a crumpled piece of paper from his pocket. I read it: 'All characters, events and settings in this story are entirely fictitious and any resem-blance between them and real persons living or dead is strictly coincidental.'

'Let's simply say that my Egypt exists at an awkward angle to your Egypt, Boss.'

The Toad rams the donkey cart. Its owner shakes his fist in fury and curses us; I recognize the gatta on the old man's forehead.

' "An awkward angle!" Ha! That's rich! Ask the Sharafs what they know about "awkward angles"! Ask the character who is regularly described in your filthy novel as "the Toad".'

The donkey is dead in its harness, or pretending to be. Its owner is hammering on the car window. A crowd is gathering. A policeman surfaces. The Toad flashes his card. The donkey driver is arrested for cruelty to a dead beast. We drive on.

'Boss,' I soothe him, 'I'm only telling a modern fairy-tale, nobody should get upset, or take anything I write too seriously.'

'And I shall be blamed!' Hosny Hikmat yells.

৹৵

'The way to avoid action being taken against you,' Mahmoud murmurs, pressing his fingertips together in the dim, blind-filtered light of his Gitane-scented sanctum, 'is not to publish your novel – anywhere. Not in Paris, not in London, not in New York.'

'Burn it, you mean.'

'Gamal, if you insist on publishing works of this kind you must first leave Egypt.'

Picture my famous father's undisturbed daily routine. He rises at 6.00 as the Magnavoxed muezzins sound the first call to prayer. By half past six he emerges from Hamid's barber shop and begins his daily walk, crossing the Nile by the bridge in front of the fifty million dollar opera house – a gift from the Japanese people – wearing his habitual dark tunic suit and polo neck shirt; his hair lies sleek and black on the skull, helped a bit by the rare, brilliant green, henna powder from the Sudanese spice market which turns things more red than black. He's slightly deaf now and not always sure-footed. The askaris on traffic duty salute him. He buys a swathe of papers and magazines at a kiosk. By 7.00 he is crossing Tahrir Square and passing the headquarters of the Arab League (Sharaf has not yet closed it down). He settles at his window seat in the Ali Baba cafeteria, sips coffee through missing teeth, reads the papers, returns home, raises the blinds of his sanctum window, lowers them, ignores the worldwide royalty checks strewn around his desk. His son is in debt and a nogood.

'I am of course awaiting your literary judgment,' Gamal says. 'Or must I "leave Egypt" first?'

'Gamal, it's a terrifying business, showing one's first book to one's father – whoever he is. It's as if our lifelong project, our hidden agenda, is to placate the phallus from which we sprang. Poor loving, confused phallus – for of course, as you must have feared, predicted, I can rejoice in your rich talent but I can scarcely come to terms with this helter-skelter "new journalism" you practise. And what is fiction? Who knows, who cares? Let's not be prisoners of library-shelf categories. As you know, the young Mahmoud would have been horrified by the old Mahmoud's lapse from naturalism into what some call mysticism – though I don't.'

'Another glass of wine, Dad?'

'I'll sit this one out. You *do* drink a bit.'

'There isn't a bad habit I don't have.'

'Really? You're not lazy and vain, like your father. And for all your engaging attempts to be Young Nasty, you cannot help being kind to me.'

'I'd gladly sacrifice your precious love in order to see you hold my book up to your fictional deity Mustafa, saying, "Lord, Lord, all your powers and domains crumble".'

'Perhaps I will have another glass of wine after all.'

As I bend over his glass to pour, Mahmoud catches me by the neck and kisses me. The wine spills on his immaculate trousers. We embrace and agree that the trousers don't matter – particularly as there is more wine, more bottles, more trousers. Mahmoud is in tears – when did I ever see that? – but for whom, for what?

'Gamal, you and I are divided about one issue. A writer cannot wrestle down the gods by dining with them. Or flogging their daughters in VIP railway compartments. Did that happen, by the way?'

'Of course. Everything happened. It's still happening. When I leave you this evening I may be followed by a dozen Internal Security men. Or I may not. Egypt is not Nazi Germany or Soviet Russia. It's not even democratic France, where a surveillance order means a surveillance order. What I want you to understand, Dad, is that my quixotic narrative is a truer reflection of our society than your descriptions of Cairo street-life borrowed, very frankly, from Zola and Gorky. Or your great family trilogy of money, power and love taken straight from Thomas Mann. Or your recent frail attempts to bring Samuel Beckett to Egypt.'

'I see.'

'Baba, I beg you not to stand on your dignity. You are a great writer! The son is merely screaming.'

'I have to rise above my vanity, you mean?'

'Yes.'

Mahmoud is tired now. He says: 'I'm tired now. Come again tomorrow, or whenever the world can spare you, and let's keep at it.'

But it is I who fall asleep.

'Yes, I know the young gentleman,' says the old dustman with the gatta on his forehead. 'I pray against him. You are very welcome out in the open, sir, very welcome out of my head.' He wipes his hand on his filthy smock and insists on pressing Dad's. I recoil a step in case I should suffer the same greeting, but the old man disdains me. We pass on.

'So how do you explain the Ten Commandments?' I ask Satan. 'You claim that God lacked any knowledge of morality, of ethics.'

'His only notion of Holy was Wholly Owned.'

'Do not Moses's Commandments amount to a catalogue of good and evil described in almost humanistic terms?'

Dad shrugs. 'They were my work. It wasn't easy. I remember once asking Him whom He preferred: the adulterer who fears God or the faithful husband who does not. My colleague, the Archangel Gabriel, rushed in to remind our Master that no man behaved well except out of love for God. I asked whether there were no good husbands among pagans. Gabriel hotly accused me of daring to apply the devil's logic in the presence of the Almighty: had not Abraham deserted his wife out of love for God?'

'Sin is strictly the product of disobedience?'

'According to Gabriel and his acolyte angels, yes. In the end our Lord accepted the Ten Commandments even though He couldn't see the point in any of them. They were just another stick to flog the subject peoples with. I mean, only consider the behaviour of the royal houses of Israel. Samson! Saul! Amnon ravishing his own sister! And

Solomon – the greatest Seraglio of whores in the history of the world! And these were the Chosen People!'

Gamal absorbs this with bulging eyes. I notice that the old man with the gatta is following us again, demanding recompense for the donkey slaughtered by the Toad.

'Tell me why the Jews became His Chosen People. Why did the Egyptians not believe? It feels like carelessness.'

'Maybe my Master was simply experimenting with Red Sea tides.' The devil waits for my smile. 'The primal urge for universal obedience yields to a more subtle enjoyment of power. My Master's creative intelligence constantly prompted Him to diversify, to experiment. How does one explain the pagan gods? Why did my Master take a fancy to Osiris and Aphrodite? – whom He of course created – though I'd rather not be quoted on that.'

ॐ

The Toad took a gamble by presenting a respectfully autographed copy of *The Patriots* to Sharaf – but only when he could wrap the book in complimentary reviews clipped from the best British newspapers. The novel was published in England when Sharaf still felt insecure, suffered from little heart attacks, bouncing blood pressure, a swollen prostate, palpitations – all the usual symptoms of an Egyptian president preparing for war with Israel. 'Before he can start throwing writers into prison he has to cross the Canal,' the Toad told me with that slow wink which invariably signalled a magnificent error of judgment.

Mahmoud now made a rare excursion out of his beloved daily routine, and agreed to lead a delegation of writers and scholars to the Rais. Their joint cause was the ominous growth of fundamentalist censorship afflicting Egyptian literature, films and even scholarship. After keeping them waiting in a small, chairless ante-room for half an hour, the Rais strode in, flanked by clicking jackboots, and rudely inquired how many members of the delegation were Jews. This produced a reaction of utter astonishment: no Jew remained in Egypt, except under a desecrated tombstone. Then Mahmoud silently raised his hand; after a moment's agonized hesitation, several others followed suit. The Rais fell into a rage (or pretended to):

'You've come to lecture me about the Holocaust, no doubt!'

The issue of censorship in Egypt never got discussed.

'We couldn't have been more dérangé if we'd emerged with yellow Stars of David pinned to our lapels,' Mahmoud told me. 'The man is mad. Nasser was mad, too. God help Egypt.'

Shortly after this conversation with Dad – he'd ordered the cook to prepare kounifa, a dessert to which I'd always been partial – I was waylaid by one of the Rais's private secretaries on leaving Hamida's quarters in the Palace. I don't suppose I was looking my best because the coming Purge was working the Virgin of Egypt into a high, Sadean fever. Her Larousse was constantly flying across the room.

'The Rais wishes to see you,' Anis Hussein told me. (Describe an anus's grin in not more than three words.)

I found Sharaf watching himself on television, his fine legs – what a family for legs! – encased in jodhpurs and cavalry boots. (Must warn Moshe Dayan and Golda Meir to expect a camel charge across the Canal.) Finally the Rais deigned to notice me.

'How many Jews died in the Holocaust?' he asked.

'Six million, Your Excellency.'

'You were there, counting?'

'Sir, Mr President, at whatever risk, I insist that six million were murdered. Now have me banished from your home, flogged, imprisoned, throw me to the Aswan crocodiles.'

'You are of course Mahmoud's son,' the Rais said. 'You love rhetoric. I know your father to be sincere in his follies. Now I am telling you that Hitler was a great man. He gave the British a black eye, and who else did, apart from Gandhi?'

'Mr President, the British did not send us to gas chambers.'

'There never were any gas chambers. Now be silent or I'll have you for dinner.'

Gamal bowed stiffly and took a step backwards, head lowered, but still facing the Rais, as in any film involving a vain or fractious monarch.

'Sire,' I said, 'if you called my late mother a whore – '

'I have not called your mother a whore. Nor anyone's mother. The mythical gas chambers were not your mother.'

I waited for the nod which meant 'Go' but the Rais enjoyed my company. He was bored – and probably shitting himself about The Coming Purge.

'So what's this I hear about you and my daughter?' he said. 'Hamida keeps telling me you want to marry her. She has a hundred suitors, doesn't she? Why should she choose to marry a penniless scribbler who'd stop at nothing to make a name for himself?'

Sharaf promptly arrested two thousand dissident students (who might also be planning to marry Hamida) along with prominent defence lawyers, pretentious writers, and opposition journalists. Mahmoud himself was spared; Sharaf had no doubt been impressed by my report of de Gaulle's refusal to arrest Sartre. According to Celia, the Rais was frequently heard announcing, while dressing himself, 'One does not arrest Voltaire.' The universities were also closed.

The Toad and I worked late into the night on a hard-hitting editorial, 'The Rais Teaches Egypt a Lesson.'

But the gods were not be propitiated. Mahmoud was put under undeclared house-arrest. His telephone line was dead. Evidently our new Minister of Information, the genial Dr Hatem, hadn't heard about Voltaire. The name of Egypt's most distinguished writer could no longer be mentioned on radio and television. I was relieved of my Ministry of Information pass. Celia and Hamida were suddenly unreachable. French lessons lapsed. The Toad gallantly provided me with a desk in *Misr* but I no sooner reached for one piece of paper than I was distracted by another. By the end of a typical morning I had achieved nothing; empty junk food bags littered the floor. In despair I sent a personal cable to the Rais himself:

> Honoured Excellency, Guide of the Nation, may I humbly suggest that the First Lady of Egypt should henceforward be styled Sayidat Misr el Aula? Your faithful servant, Gamal Rahman

(After The Crossing I came up with Um el-Abtal, Mother of the Heroes. But there I go again, galloping ahead of myself like a drunken snail.)

I am summoned by Hosny Hikmat. 'I have a message for you from Dr Hatem,' the Boss informs me. 'You will no longer work as a clandestine source for the BBC World Service. Only I am keeping you out of jail,' the Toad adds. 'The Sharaf women can't even remember the length of your prick.'

Goodbye, Fred Hemmings and his ten-pound notes. Fred and I used to meet in the urinal of the Faculty of Letters, where we turned on all the taps and repeatedly flushed the toilets – usually a vain exercise. An excellent Arabist with a minor teaching post at the University, Fred worked as a clandestine stringer for the Beeb's World Service. After three minutes in the fitfully gurgling urinal we would each slide out into our separate lives.

But Dr Hatem's vengeance does not stop there (or anywhere). His message orders me to report to our own long-wave radio station, the Voice of the Arabs, where I must prove that the BBC is 'a factory of lies' – and denounce by name my contact as a spy.

The Toad is watching the sweat oozing from my collar, wrists and socks.

'I don't like this any more than you do, Gamal. It could never have happened when I was Minister of Information.'

'To betray a colleague is murder.'

'But Dr Hatem wants you to do it. Dr Hatem wants what Hamida wants.'

My only hope was divine intervention. At this juncture Jesus Christ made a timely intercession on my behalf (unmerited is OK with me).

We begin with the death of the Coptic Patriarch Kirillos. The Patriarch (our Pope) is an important figure in Egypt. A successor had to be chosen. The procedure was well established and scarcely less extended than the search for a new Dalai Lama in Tibet. The names of the three candidates enjoying the most support in the Coptic Holy Synod would eventually be placed in a box in a darkened room. A child would withdraw one slip of paper from the box.

The question confronting the Rais and Dr Hatem was not complicated: which slip of paper should the child withdraw? And (supplementary), how old should the child be? They studied the names of the three candidates nominated by the Holy Synod and they hadn't a clue. But you cannot leave such things to chance; the Rais was planning his big Holy War, his Crossing, and the Copts had to be kept in line.

Now it so happened that I had been stringing for the official Religious Affairs Correspondent of *Misr*, a notorious pederast and drunkard who was never at his desk – Anis Hussein no less. As a result my Copt-contacts were second to none – I could practically pin to a map every church and monastery in Egypt. Here my father's gentle instruction in the tenets of the Christian religion stood me in good stead. I could deliver a lecture on why the Catholic Crusaders had regarded the Monophysites as heretics. Further back, I knew why the Emperor Justinian had failed to persuade the Patriarch Theodosius to embrace the doctrines of Chalcedon (AD 451). You don't want the full lecture, so let's just say it was mainly about the single incarnate nature of Christ, as God and man, with serious implications for the Trinity – enough?

Don't let me be misunderstood here: the Rais was not bruising his brow about the Trinity, nor was this the issue within the Coptic Holy Syndod. The issue for the Copts was the predictable forthcoming 'Islamic Storm' when the Rais Crossed the Canal – if he did, and perhaps worse if he didn't. Either way, Christians were going to get it in the neck for want of surviving Jews.

As the life of old Patriarch Kirillos ebbed under Christ's tender wings, the Coptic factions had begun manoeuvering and lobbying. I knew the whole scene and could have made a fair shot as candidate for Patriarch myself. So here I am, sweating on to the Toad's carpet at the prospect of betraying Fred Hemmings, when he casually invites my opinion about the three patriarchal candidates.

'The Rais favours the oldest of them, the seventy-five-year-old monk Paul, on the ground that whatever he does he won't last long.'

'The Rais is wise,' I say.

'But Dr Hatem claims he can "guarantee" the youngest candidate, Mikhail.'

'Ah. Mikhail.'

'You know this priest?'

I shrug. 'Nothing much – I chatted to him for a couple of hours at Kairinios monastery. I may have talked to a dozen of his close associates as well. His recent trip to Athens and Nicosia was of course interesting – and the Israelis refused him a visa to visit Jerusalem.'

The Toad is studying me. 'You spoke with Mikhail for two hours?'

'It was off the record. He went through the various scenarios: war against Israeli – or not. An Islamic fundamentalist upsurge – or not. A Second Coming of Christ – or not.'

'Mikhail is hard or soft? Did he meet the Israelis secretly in Nicosia? Is he planning resistance or accommodation?'

'I would want to explain that personally to the Rais. There are nuances which could get lost in the messenger service.'

'It might be arranged.'

'I see no advantage in talking to the Rais while certain circles are hellbent on driving me to betray my sources and to broadcast lies over the Voice of the Arabs.'

'Dr Hatem might be persuaded to forget that,' the Toad said. 'I'll call him.'

And so it came to pass that I was received by the Rais, attired in his latest German military uniform and the Green Sash of Justice (awarded to him by Hamida). I could smell a rank odour gushing from every pore and orifice of my fatself.

'Gamal! Long time, no see! Where have you been? Up off your knees, my son, that's no way to present yourself to a modern Republican President.'

It was a pleasure to convince Sharaf that Mikhail, the most militant Copt in Egypt, a real, bloody-minded, fire-eating Thomas Becket, was a cringing sycophant. Mikhail's name was duly picked out of the box in the darkened room by a boy called Gamal Rahman. (*That* chicken was to come home to roost some years later.) Celia invited me to tea.

'Gama, why have you been neglecting us?'

'The Beast from One Thousand Fathoms returns,' said Hamida.

But her French lessons resumed and my father once again enjoyed a telephone line, though he scarcely used it and incoming calls rarely got beyond the maid, whose Arabic served as an iron curtain between Mahmoud and editors in London and Paris – you had to write to Mahmoud.

ॐ

And so to the war – The Crossing.

Monday, September 10th. The Toad is summoned by the Rais to one of his many rest houses, the one at Bourg al-Arab near Alex. We arrive just as the Rais is descending the steps of his villa and about to enter a brown Mercedes. 'Come and sit beside me,' he commands the Toad. The Rais loves to drive, his guards following in the rear car. We sweep behind motorcycle outriders along a desert road cleared of donkey carts towards the oasis of King Mariut. One hand on the wheel, Sharaf gestures expansively at the countryside beyond the bullet-proof windows while I scribble down every word:

'Look at all this green – all this new life coming up. After we've finished our battle I think I'll settle down here, have a small ranch with horses and spend the rest of my life between the desert and the sea.'

'Between heaven and earth,' Gamal says from the rear seat.

The Rais ignores the pearl.

'I'll tell you a secret, Hikmat. Have you strong nerves? Our battle will start one month from now!'

[!!!]

(Evidently this secret is to be a secret from nobody except the Israelis. Soon every waiter and plongeur in Paris will know it, but Mossad will remain in the dark.)

'We still have to be certain what to do about the Russians.' The Rais is sucking contentedly on his briar pipe. 'That is to say, what exactly to do.'

'Speak to Vinogradov in vague terms,' the Toad advises. 'But do not divulge the details of the timings.'

Sparks are flying out of my ears.

On arrival at the next Presidential rest house the Rais hustles us into his sanctum and loses no time in displaying two black files. For an hour the Toad and I are accorded a complete rundown on the coming battle plan for The Crossing. Every detail. By the end of it I could conduct the entire battle myself, playing both sides. Gamal concludes that this Ubu Roi-like breach of National Security can only mean that the Rais believes the Toad, or myself, or both, to be an Israeli spy.

My patriotic duty is clear.

Cut to the Prime Minister's office in the Knesset.

MOSHE DAYAN: We have acquired the Egyptian battle plan and timetable for thirty-four dollars.

GOLDA MEIR: Who from?

MOSHE DAYAN: Isaac Ben Ezra in New York. He got it from a fat journalist close to Sadat. Or Sharaf. A slob by the name of Gamal Rahman.

GOLDA MEIR: He may be a good boy. Does he love his mother?

MOSHE DAYAN: He has no mother.

GOLDA MEIR: Then don't believe a word he says.

Our gallant Egyptian and Syrian commanders are meanwhile locked in brotherly argument. The Egyptians want to start firing their guns in the afternoon, when the sun will be in the Israelis' eyes as they face west across the Canal. The Syrians want to kick-off at dawn when the sun will be in the Israelis' eyes as they face east across the Golan Heights. This is to be truly the Battle of the Sun. The Israelis have Phantoms and God knows what but evidently they don't have sunglasses.

The security governing these military conferences – as I reported to the Toad – was impressive. For example on the Wednesday morning I had observed eight senior Egyptian officers and six senior Syrian officers making their way, *one by one*, from the Officers' Club in Alex to the headquarters of the Naval Command in the royal palace of Ras el-Tin.

'That would certainly fool any Israeli spy, Boss! And the conference room in Ras el-Tin has been re-checked for bugging.'

'Have they found our bugs?'

'No. Everyone's bugs are still in place. The Americans', the Russians', ours.'

A Grundig slowly turning on the Toad's desk, he and Gamal spent an hour listening to the assembled generals again arguing about when to begin the battle. The Egyptians now suggested that the Syrians could begin at first light (when the sun was in the Israelis' eyes), with the Egyptians following in the afternoon (when the sun was in the Israelis' eyes). The Syrians objected that this would leave them alone on the battlefield for up to eight hours, by which time the sun could well be in their own eyes. The Egyptians then suggested that they, the Egyptians, could start in the afternoon of D-Day, with the Syrians following at first light on D+1 (when the sun would be . . . etc.). The Syrians objected that by this plan they would forfeit the element of surprise and also lose face politically. The Syrians wanted the Egyptians to begin at dawn, even though the sun would be in the Egyptians' eyes, not in the Israelis' eyes, because everyone knew it was sound strategy to attack at dawn (because of the sun). At this stage it became clear that if the generals were not going to win the war, it was up to us. The Toad instructed me to write a bogus report indicating that the Commander in Chief had opened a list for those officers who wished to embark on the lesser pilgrimage to Mecca, the Umrah. The Israelis would read this report when they bought their copy of *Misr* in Cyprus on the morrow.

MOSHE DAYAN: Clearly the Arabs cannot be contemplating war if all their officers are to be on their knees in Saudi Arabia. (*Pauses*) Wait a minute –

GOLDA MEIR: Funny-shmummy that their Umrah-thing should coincide with Yom Kippur.

DAYAN: When's that?

GOLDA: You never heard of Yom Kippur, you schmuck?

DAYAN: I heard of it. What is it?

GOLDA: The Day of Atonement. You need some.

DAYAN: You're sure it isn't Passover – when our planes pass over Cairo?

GOLDA: I like it! Passover! Suppose we get the Chief Rabbi to jiggle the calendar and change the story a bit?

DAYAN: Which Chief Rabbi? We have ten and still counting.

GOLDA: Try the one in Brooklyn.

DAYAN: Anyway – what story?

GOLDA (*sighs*): Passover commemorates the delivery of the Jews from the Egyptians, you one-eyed pretzel. The Angel of Death passes over.

DAYAN: Just let him try.

GOLDA: Supposing they make their 'lesser pilgrimage' across the Suez Canal?

The Rais, meanwhile, strolls in one his many gardens with the First Lady and the Virgin of Egypt.

'Celia, I know I am going to win this war!'

Abruptly he swings – his aides swinging with him – to flick his fingers at me. Clutching my notebook but dropping my pen, I scuttle fatly across the smooth turf in my off-white suit.

'What is a Jew?' he asks me. 'What did Adolf Hitler say about Jews?'

'Rais?'

'Tell Hikmat I want *Misr* to begin publication of *Mein Kampf* – tomorrow.'

Either Sharaf wants Gamal Rahman to argue him out of this obscene madness or he's setting me up for a show trial when Egypt, as usual, loses the war. After Dr Hateb temporarily seconded Anis Hussein to anus-edit the obscure religious magazine *Al-Noor*, the Toad and I had concluded that pre-battle Jew-bashing was to be a specialist affair, visible to our leading cadres but almost invisible to the Americans. Holocaust Hussein reminded his readers that according to the Sira, the traditional biography of the Prophet, Muhammad expelled two out of the three Jewish tribes living in Medina, then inflicted collective punishment on the third, the Banu Quraiza, who were found to be conspiring with his enemies in Mecca. Females and children were enslaved, the males beheaded. From this mini-holocaust it was a short step – as Anis Hussein explained – to Adolf Hitler.

'It's for domestic consumption only,' the Toad had assured me. 'After the war we can rediscover Einstein, Mendelssohn and anyone you like.'

The next day the entire American press began reading my translations of Anis Hussein. I picked up a thousand bucks from the TV networks operating out of the Nile Hilton. I also sent copies to my old enemy and former agent, Isaac Ben Ezra. The reply was rapid:

Send me anything which documents rabid Arab anti-Semitism. Jewish press here is paying a buck a word. Agency is going places with a staff of ten. Isaac

The Rais knew the score. He knew what I had done. Anis Hussein had told him. Dr Hatem had told him. Even the Toad may have told him, as insurance. That was why I was being ordered to fill the whole of *Misr*, from the sports pages to the recipe and fashion columns, with a right-to-left version of Hitler's masterpiece. That was why brown-green stains which would be impossible to remove now covered my off-white trousers at the knees as I crouched on the lawn before the Rais and his ladies, licking the ants from the royal turf like an aadvark.

The signal for The Crossing would be the fat splash as I was fed to the Nile crocodiles.

ର

'I have to say,' Mahmoud murmurs, fastidiously fingering the sweat-stained manuscript pages of my novel-in-progress, *The Crossing*, 'that I find your Celia marginally more credible than your Hamida.'

I wait.

'Of course,' he continues, 'I suffer from conspicuous disadvantages, symptoms of senility, no doubt. The President of Egypt I daily read about is called Anwar el-Sadat and the First Lady who recently shook my hand at a literary reception bore a remarkable resemblance to Mrs Jehan el-Sadat – a lady of the utmost propriety, whom one might be so obsequious as to admire for her good works. The well-

318

mannered son and daughters to whom she introduced me were, I suppose, figments of my imagination.'

'Dad, we inhabit different Egypts, you and I.'

'Hm. The resemblance of the portrait to the sitter is not, however, my point. It did not trouble Gainsborough or Reynolds. I fear that Mademoiselle Hamida el-Sharaf has been sculpted out of the fantasies peddled in the so-called Underground magazines which are regularly mailed to you from Amsterdam, New York and London. I have a pile of them in the cellar, by the way, awaiting your kind disposal.'

I'm heaving. 'So you don't like my novel?'

'Like it, Gamal? Is one supposed to like it?'

TWENTY-ONE

❧

Operation Badr! The Rais himself had chosen the operational code name, in honour of the Prophet's famous raid on the Meccan caravan in the year AD 624. On that occasion three hundred of the faithful and one thousand angels had overcome one thousand unbelievers. But how to breach the Bar Lev Line, the 'impregnable' rampart 47 feet high and 110 miles long, erected on the East bank of the Canal by the Israelis after the Six Day War?

DAYAN: Believe me, it can't be done.

GOLDA MEIR: If forty million Egyptians pass water simultaneously on our big sand castle, what happens?

As usual Golda had got it. The Rais's brilliant-secret plan was indeed to pass water: the Engineer Corps would cut passes in the sand earthworks of the Bar Lev Line using high-powered German water pumps, then lay pontoon bridges for the tanks and trucks.

The crowds gathered outside the Sharaf residence. 'We crossed! We crossed!' they chanted. 'God bless Sharaf!' Celia moved into the el-Tahrah Palace 'to be with Fawzi'.

'All those who died for our country, who sacrificed themselves, are my sons,' the Rais announced on television. A message from the Toad advised me that my talents were urgently required by the Army Information Service – a leaflet was to be distributed to every hero, son and brother.

'Your "text" is as follows: "In the name of God, the merciful, the compassionate: the Prophet is with us in the battle." You've got ten minutes.'

I was already scribbling:

The first Hero to cross the Canal saw the Prophet, PBUH, dressed in white and pointing his hand. 'Come with me to Sinai.' Many of our Heroes who have crossed the Canal have seen the Prophet Muhammad, PBUH, walking among them with a light all round him and a benign smile. Those who reached out to touch the

320

Prophet felt a glow in their hands, as when we warm ourselves before a fire. Those who have fallen in battle now dwell in the perfumed gardens of Paradise, to be waited on for all eternity by four gorgeous Houris, untouched by man or djinn.

This gem was no sooner off the presses than Sharaf began to lose the war. The Toad's spirits sank – no gorgeous Houris for him. 'And you!' he jabbed a finger at Gamal. 'Why do you think Sharaf showed us his secret plans, those black notebooks, a full month before the battle?'

'So that we could pass on false information to the Americans, Russians and Israelis.'

'Exactly. The Rais thought he was giving us false plans, but as it turned out his false plans became his real plans. Lucky neither of us passed anything on, eh?'

'Extremely fortunate.'

'Eh?'

'Don't look at me like that, Boss. You know I'm a patriot.'

'Sharaf is running the war single-handed! He keeps dressing up in new uniforms, with ever-more ribbons and sashes. He does nothing but rebuke General Saad Shazly, our Chief of Staff, for offering competent professional advice! And you are to blame!'

Disaster followed. Goodbye, 250 Egyptian tanks. The Israelis under Sharon now crossed the Canal in our direction, the Double Crossing. In vain General Shazly urged the Rais to withdraw tanks from Sinai to confront the Israeli bridgehead on the West Bank.

'Not one of our tanks withdraws!' the Rais bellowed. 'If you persist in these defeatist proposals, Shazly, I will court-martial you. I do not want another word!'

By October 23rd the road to Suez was in Israeli hands. Two Egyptian divisions, 45,000 men and 250 tanks, were cut off.

'Write me one thousand words on the horrors of the Holocaust!' the Toad shouted at me.

Having snatched defeat from the jaws of victory, jettisoning his Syrian allies between lunch and dinner, the Rais embarked on 'reconstruction' and the free-market jamboree known as Infitah. All economic controls lifted! Let the money flow! Beat back the glacier of state control! As a gesture in that direction the doe-eyed Huda el-Sharaf, now seventeen, was engaged to be married to Andreas ('Andy'), the notoriously dissolute, playboy son of the Greek billionaire contractor Plato Popodopoulos ('Poppy'). Poppy had of course wanted Hamida for Andy, but she was not on the market: as the

Marquis de Sade had foreseen, running the secret police was worth a harem of husbands.

The Virgin of Egypt's true passion was for intelligence reports; Gamal's occasional duties included reading to her the latest telephone taps and secret service summaries of public opinion.

'Mama herself isn't above suspicion,' she told me.

'Your mother!'

'She's too busy cultivating ladies of the old aristocracy and the wives of officers of the Presidential Guard. They're all plotting with the Saudis. Or with the Libyans. Or the Syrians. Or the Palestinians.'

'But – '

'They're all plotting!'

'It seems a fair division of labour.'

This earned a sharp slap. Ah, Infitah – something for everyone, especially those who lived in the villas of Garden City and Heliopolis where Chivas Regal was now served from behind private bars to Gamal Rahman and other jet-setters sprawled in Louis XV (Luigi Khamarshtashr) chairs. Everyone was talking of Huda's wedding to Andy Poppy. It was goodbye Nasser and the land reforms which had (notionally) abolished the largest private estates, distributing the land in two-feddan plots. Peasant rents were doubled, real estate was once again sold by auction, and an estimated 53.5 per cent of state lands around Alex passed into private hands without payment. A miniscule percentage came my way – say twenty feddans plus a few peasants, fellahin, thrown in.

'It's time to start reading Karl Marx,' the Toad cackled.

'How much have they given you, Boss?'

'Not a feddan.'

The Rais was forever brooding about Nasser, as if the promised but never-erected statue in Republic Square was haunting Sharaf's private Elsinore. The Toad warned me: a campaign of denigration against the late Hook-Nose was imminent; sure enough the Rais summoned Gamal to his country retreat at Muhi el-Din. Now styling himself Ibn-el-Hayy, the Son of the Neighbourhood, Sharaf was found on his latest exercise bike, a gift from a grateful Japan.

'What did Nasser ever achieve? Eh?'

I waited.

'Arab unity! Ha! Nasser turned Egypt into a loudspeaker for all the fucking Arabs!'

I scribbled.

'We did better than Gamal Abdul Nasser, we fought the October war. We crossed. Eh?'

'We crossed, Rais!'

Sharaf patted my head. 'You're a good boy, Gamal. I'm dismissing Hikmat as editor of *Misr*. The paper needs a younger editor – someone not secretly obsessed by the "greatness" of Gamal Nasser.'

'But Rais,' I protested, 'Hikmat has been seventeen years in the job! He's made the paper the finest in the Middle East.'

'I admire your loyalty. Hikmat has come to believe he makes the news. I make the news. In due course I shall transfer ownership of the paper to my own party, the Arab Socialist Union. Legislation is being prepared.'

'Rais, may I venture an opinion?'

'You may.' He smiled wolfishly. 'So long as you agree with me.'

'Your Excellency, I know Hikmat to be entirely loyal – '

'Kefaya! Enough! When you are appointed to replace Hikmat you will make sure that *Misr* remains the pride of the Middle East. Now run and see Celia; she grows bored with country life.'

I ran. Celia looked up from her fashion magazine and embraced me in a swirl of perfume.

'Congratulations, darling Gama. Mabruk.'

''Aid sa'id, hadritik – happy holiday, madame.'

'But I am not happy, Gama, and I don't know about any public holiday. I have been having terrible dreams. Fawzi won't listen. He's too good a man, too much a sufi, to believe the worst of others. Gama, even my own private telephones are now bugged. Djinns can be heard laughing whenever I make a call.'

'Have you mentioned this to Hamida?'

'What?'

'Your daughter now operates the switchboard known as Egypt. That "Allo? Allo? Allooo" we all suffer until we give up. No one is above Hamida's suspicion.'

Celia looked very pale. 'But I'm her mama,' she whispered. My head was by now in Celia's lap, for fondling; my oiled hair had recently been restyled aux Beatles – goodbye Rock Hudson.

☙

Gamal's new post as Acting Deputy Editor carries him to Hikmat's farm, twenty minutes north of Cairo, in a chauffeur-driven Merc. He finds the Toad smaller than ever, glowering moodily at his mango crop, and plotting. The Toad is taking one of his 'sabbaticals' – which means spending hours on the phone trying to find out what the Rais will do next, which way he'll jump, and how best the Toad should jump when the Rais jumps.

'Why are you looking so cheerful?' he glowers. 'Believe me, Gamal, your fate is tied to mine.'

'Boss, I shall never forget what I owe you.'

'That's what I'm afraid of.' We are in the thick of Hikmat's goats, some of which are tethered with good reason. 'I'm considering a trip to China at the invitation of Chairman Mao,' the Toad reveals. 'Go and sound out Sharaf.'

Over a lunch of hard-boiled eggs (butter, meat and fats no longer agree with his stomach), the Toad unveils various schemes simmering in his bullet-head, including an old obsession he has been wet-nursing for years: could he blackmail the Rais by proving that Celia did not originate, as she claimed, in the Yorkshire city of Bruddersford, née Plum, but in Malta, née Paletta? The Toad is a bore on this ridiculous subject not least when there's nothing to eat except hard-boiled eggs.

'We have a Rais who conceals his Sudanese mother and a First Lady who conceals her Maltese mother!'

'But Mrs Jehan Sadat has an English mother, Boss.'

'Of course she does! I've met the lady, she's real. But who has ever set eyes on Celia's English mother? And tell me why, never once in her life, Celia has paid a visit to Bruddersford to make contact with other members of the "Plum" family.' The Toad waves part of a crumbling egg under my nose while constantly brushing off swarms of flies with the other hand – giving the impression of a mad conductor who's lost his way in the score.

'Has she ever visited Malta?' I ask.

'You'd better find out.' The Toad's mouth splits open right across his face, ear to ear, and he begins to cackle: 'Ha! Ha ha! Knowledge is power! Ha ha ha! Ha ha ha ha!'

Chauffeur-swept back to Cairo with the murderous Rolling Stones on the stereo, I ponder the method behind the Toad's madness. He wants to get me into hot water again. Reaching my apartment, I lose no time in telephoning the First Lady.

'Oh Gama, I'm so lonely. Come at once.'

She receives me in a dramatic new outfit from Cardin. 'Let's talk about Huda's wedding.'

She burbles on about Huda's wedding.

'Perhaps she and Andy should honeymoon in Malta,' I suggest.

'Malta? Why Malta, darling?'

'Oh . . . Crusaders . . . you know. I've always wanted to take a peep. Ever been there?'

'I may have been but I don't remember. Sometimes a boat will stop at an island and maybe it's Malta, or Cyprus, or Crete, or Sardinia, or Sicily – how does one know unless one has an intelligent, handsome escort who understands about these things? Hmmm.'

'I've got a better idea!'

'Oh Gama, what would I do without you?'

'They could honeymoon in Bruddersford.'

'Bruddersford!'

'I'm sure Huda would love to discover her maternal roots. And you'd have a nice excuse for joining Huda and Andy – after a decent interval. Wouldn't that be fun?'

'I'm not sure Andy would think so.'

I settled my head beside Celia's on an Aswan Dam of scented silk pillows and took her hand. 'Tell me about your mother, madame.'

'Oh, you'd be bored.'

'Never bored by you.' (Squeezes hand.)

I believe I may have dozed off during Celia's long, involved saga of Mummy and Daddy, but occasional pinches and slaps enabled me to retain enough to convey the gist to the Toad (who immediately launched into his 'Ha ha!'). Evidently Gertrude Plum first met Ahmed Fayek on some kind of faintly naughty Mediterranean cruise. Ahmed, I gathered, was studying accountancy at the University of Cairo; Gertrude, for her part, 'fell head over heels, like me and Fawzi'. The young lovers then corresponded for two years while Gertrude's parents dug their heels in. When she and her tin trunk finally set sail for Egypt, her mother and father refused to accompany her to Bruddersford railway station, let alone to the boat.

'And she never saw them again, madame?'

'Never.' Celia began to weep a teeny bit – at least I remember twice picking her hanky from the carpet in between bouts of snoozing. I gathered that Mummy Gertrude, having thrown herself at Daddy Ahmed, quickly adapted to married life in Cairo and taught the Egyptian ladies how to make Yorkshire pudding.

'Did she convert to Islam, madame?'

'Well, yes and no. It was Mummy who taught me how Western women behave. It was quite a shock to Fawzi when we became engaged.'

'What was?'

'Gamal, are you asleep?' (Slap.) 'Fawzi was shocked that I would offer tea to male visitors to our home without a chaperone present.' (A giggle.) 'Even when he was the male visitor.'

Celia smiled fondly for Fawzi. I smiled fondly for Fawzi. Had Mummy Gertrude never returned home to Bruddersford?

'Just once, I believe, soon after I married Fawzi. Or maybe it was after he became Vice President. She discovered that both her parents had died. The house had been sold to strangers. She put a notice in the local newspaper. A cousin turned up at her hotel that very afternoon. They had so much to talk about! When she came back to Cairo, Mummy showed me a cutting from the Bruddersford paper – they thought it was quite a story!'

'I'd love to see the cutting.'

'Don't be silly, Gamal, I haven't seen it for years. Anyway, why are you so interested in my mother?'

'I never had one myself.'

'Poor Gama.' (A squeeze.)

Not for the first time, I found myself moved by a kind of love for Celia – for all her pretensions, her thirst for wealth and power, what a nice, cheerful woman! Loyal, courageous, energetic and always generous, she was la bonne bourgeoise. She certainly deserved an English mother if she wanted one, and it was more than likely that she wanted one because she'd had one, and not merely because Mrs Sadat had one. Celia and Fawzi never spoke of the Sadats, of course, but I knew she suffered from terrible jealousies every time that other First Lady, that other Mother of Martyrs and Heroes, came up on the television screen with her nice smile and modest wave. More than once I caught Celia smiling and waving in one or other of her long mirrors.

I saw no reason to doubt Celia's story, though I'd slept through most of it. On the other hand, the Toad was no fool. I could not forget his devastating aperçu as the last hard-boiled egg struggled past his Adam's apple: 'It's ten-to-one that a Maltese adventuress of suspect provenance called Giletta Paletta boarded the cruise boat at Valetta and seduced Ahmed Fayek before they dropped anchor at Haifa.'

෨

The city of Cairo was now a swathe of shimmering concrete and protruding steel rods: drills snarled incessantly beneath huge cranes and gantries; everywhere dusty labourers hung, and sometimes fell, from half-finished buildings. Beneath the hard hats white faces coated in dust made calculations, issued directives, sighed. Korean building teams began to appear. The urge to start a building was evidently greater than the need to complete it – all manner of tax dodges, depletion allowances and covert subsidies were at stake. And Huda's prospective father-in-law, Plato Popodopoulos, who had grown rich removing huge quantities of rock and debris during the construction of the Aswan High Dam, now grew wealthier by the hour. One of our less mature reporters, Gamal Rahman, picked up evidence that 'Poppy' had not charged for minor improvements to the Sharafs' private residence in Pyramids Road; Gamal duly slipped an item into *Misr* without a byline. The Toad (unaccountably back at the helm) flew into a rage, accused me of patricide, or bosscide, and began to repack his Mao tunics, but the Rais, who was currently negotiating a big loan from the World Bank, immediately insisted on paying Popodopoulos for the work 'as a matter of principle'. Poppy duly sent in a bill for £E80. He then renovated the Sharafs' house at Muhi el-Din without charge: air conditioning, wood panelling, the works.

A further seven million Egyptian pounds were spent on the Muntazah Palace, Alex. Much of the money arrived in Poppy's pocket, though he took care to divert a proportion into the Rais's overseas bank accounts. From the Muntazah, Celia frantically prepared for Huda's wedding to Poppy's playboy son Andy.

I have been, and had been, neglecting Huda. Perhaps I saw her less often than she saw me – those expressive doe-eyes gazing out of what had become a rather beautiful, almond-shaped face. I offered her passing smiles but Egypt was now my chessboard and Hamida was pharaonic Egypt – there is no other. Asking little of me, Huda got little beyond routine French lessons. Her engagement to Andy had been arranged; the girl had barely been consulted; the sight of the greasy slob made her shudder. Huda was simply bankable. She made no attempt to solicit my sympathy. 'She is buried in her books,' Celia would sigh, 'she dreams of studying at the Sorbonne and wearing dirty jeans in the company of riff-raff. Oh that girl.' Huda's pride was discounted; no one cared what it might one day amount to.

When the engagement was officially announced I sent Huda a flippant message: 'Félicitations, mademoiselle. Did you know that Andy, although a Greek Christian, is directly descended from good Islamic stock in the shape of Sultan Othman I (1258?–1326), who gave his name to the Ottoman Empire? I hope your Andy will be content with fewer wives than his illustrious predecessor.'

Very witty. I am not proud of this effort. I'm not even proud of having kept a carbon copy for my novel-in-progress. That night Huda made an attempt on her life, slashing her wrists with one of the Rais's cut-throat razors. They patched her up, hushed it up, fed her sedatives.

Celia was shaken but not very. The Sharafs now believed that anything they wanted was bound to happen.

'We shall erect a huge green and blue tent in the garden of the Muntazah Palace for the wedding,' she told me. 'Green for Egypt, blue for Greece. Or would the Qubbah Palace be better? Perhaps the Abdin . . .'

'Or the zoo?'

'Silly boy! And the tablecloths will be blue. No, Green.'

'How many guests will madame invite?'

Celia began counting on her fingers. 'Five thousand.'

'In that case many will be disappointed and unfairly accuse you of parsimony. I mean the "no no people" who never miss an opportunity to denigrate the Sharafs.'

'Well, those people are never satisfied. Perhaps ten thousand guests would be better. And we will command the best singers, dancers, acrobats and clowns in Egypt to perform.'

'I could tell a few jokes . . .'

'Silly boy!'

'And don't forget the wedding cake, madame. I suggest a perfect replica of Cairo's Citadel.'

'Oh Gama, how marvellous. What would I do without you? I shall need you every minute of every day as my cultural adviser'.

Celia concluded that nothing would be 'right' unless she and I flew to Paris on a vast shopping spree.

Huda made the second attempt on her life, pitching herself from the balcony of her bedroom. Two passing flunkeys caught her as she fell, no damage was done. Celia attributed it to Huda's 'time of the month'. When I presented myself at Huda's quarters within the Palace I was not admitted. Reflection could no longer be avoided.

'Did anyone arrange your own marriage to the Rais?' I asked Celia. 'You always told me it was a love match.'

'Gamal, what are you saying?'

Here Hamida chipped in impatiently. 'Mama was not the daughter of the President of Egypt.'

'Does the President of France tell his daughter whom to marry?' I asked. 'Or even the Queen of England?'

'He's been talking to Huda!' Hamida screamed. 'Huda has always believed herself to be in love with this slab of whale.'

There was no more to be said – the Toad rebuked me for having said so much. Huda was spirited away to a private sanatorium, no one would divulge where. The President's wife and her cultural advisor flew to Paris and lodged at the Ritz.

Ah, Paris! The First Lady was on a private visit, of course, attended by the fashion magazines, society magazines and women's magazines of the world. Europe simply didn't have a royal wedding coming up so Egypt would have to do. Celia's entourage poured into boutiques called Tendre Caprice or Les Folies d'Elodie to consider whether Huda should embark on married life wearing scarlet knickers by Scandale or a see-through bra by Ravage. Nor must Hamida's wardrobe be forgotten – I was treated to a lifetime's haute cuisine while desperate women journalists begged me to reveal why Hamida, the elder sister, had never been engaged. Did I not know her well – very well? As her erstwhile tutor, what could I reveal about her tastes, desires, inclinations and dreams? My London and Paris publishers reported a sudden spurt in sales of *The Patriots*; serial rights were being sold and re-sold all over the place. In New York Isaac Ben Ezra was merchandizing my frivolous, tantalizing, now-you-see-her-now-you-don't pieces as fast as I could cable them.

Gaily and memorably, Celia told the press that 'a woman is as young as she feels'. Despondent if the journalists allowed her five minutes' peace (neglect), her playful obsession was 'to give them the slip'. I suggested enlisting Monsieur Feydeau in this enterprise but she merely asked whether he was trustworthy. Now I must escort her, incognita, to the leg-show at the Crazy Horse, now to dinner at the Georges V. She wore a variety of blonde wigs and sported Jackie-type dark glasses which she kept taking off, to see who was watching. The French and Egyptian security men for starters. Day and night Celia bubbled with loudly Dionysiac thoughts about bridal sheets and bridal times of the month. We held hands in taxis.

'Oh how lovely to ride through Paris in a taxi again, Gama. Oh, the city of love!' (Love was a tall order with three Citroën-loads of armed goons hurtling after us.)

It was in the Georges V dining room that I conceived my most preposterous conceit for Huda's wedding, the pièce de résistance:

'At the moment Huda and Andy cut the Citadel cake, we must release a hundred white doves to soar over their heads, each with a band of green-and-blue ribbon round its neck.'

'Oh how divine, Gama!' (Celia, tipsy.)

'And we must make sure they have been well fed before we release them. They tend not to fly otherwise.'

'Are you sure about that, Gama?'

'Quite sure. Ask any French colombophile.'

Alas: green-and-white pigeon shit was not destined to rain down on the cake and ten thousand guests. Abruptly the wedding was postponed. The bride was said to be 'indisposed'. She was 'resting'. She needed 'privacy at this time'. Rumours, the routine offspring of censorship, abounded. Celia would tell me nothing. Her doors were closed to me. The Toad confidently reported that Huda had been sighted in Paris. In London. In Baghdad. She had joined the banned Egyptian Communist Party. She had sought sanctuary with Islamic fundamentalists in Upper Egypt. She was in Rome preparing for induction into the Holy Roman Catholic Church.

Isaac Ben Ezra telephoned from New York. 'Huda is the news, Gamal. Go find her. It's worth money.'

৩

Sharaf followed IMF directives by cutting subsidies on bread meat sugar oil rice soap. The workers – myself included – had had enough and took to the streets:

'Ya Batl al-Ubuur, Feen al-Futuur – O Hero of the Crossing, where is our breakfast?'

Anis Hussein published a diatribe in *Misr*, 'The Communist Agitators Must be Crushed.' I had no doubt that he'd received clearance – and more – from Dr Hateb, and in an effort to thwart this lunacy I, as Acting Deputy Editor, appealed directly to the Palace. Five minutes later Anis Hussein strode into my hot, smelly little cubicle to hand me my dismissal. It was signed by Dr Hateb. As things turned out, I was lucky to be fired. Massive rioting ensued, thirty-six hours of fury directed against nightclubs, boutiques, police stations, the offices of the ASU – all symbols of sulta, of Authority. The *Misr* building was gutted, top to toe, by fire. The city was littered with burnt-out cars. Sharaf had fled from Cairo just in case, disguising himself as a fellah, and travelling to his helicopter pad in an old taxi. To reassure the world, he left his women behind. Poor Celia!

'Al Sha'ab ga'an – the people are hungry,' cried the mob (myself included).

The Toad came through on the telephone from some undisclosed safe haven. Huda el-Sharaf, he reported, had been 'sighted' among the mob ransacking the *Misr* building.

I laughed sceptically. 'Who by?'

'Anis Hussein,' Hikmat conceded.

'In Egypt, Boss, women are not allowed to participate in violent mobs. It would cripple the mob's self-esteem. Every underclass is desperately conservative about gender. Just look at the American Blacks and the American Muslims.'

'The regime's days are numbered,' the Toad croaked. 'This is a family at war with itself. Don't underestimate your little pupil Huda.'

The rioting subsided. The Rais bravely returned to Cairo. Celia later confided to me that she had received an anxious telephone call from her good friend, Queen Mia of Omah: 'Are you quite safe, Celia? We are praying for you.' Queen Diba of Qatar also called, from Geneva. 'It will soon blow over, Celia. You are in our prayers.' All the Marie Antoinettes of the Middle East were jamming the lines.

The Rais restored the food subsidies. Anis Hussein (who'd escaped the mob by donning a galabiyeh) was exiled as Deputy Ambassador

(His Anus-Excellency) to the Yemen. I learned of my own appointment as Deputy Editor of *Misr* during a tense interview with Hamida at the Palace.

'Deputy Editor of a gutted building?' I asked.

She pouted fretfully, a young woman barely twenty years old yet so infected by the Medician intrigues and Machiavellian calculations of the Sharaf dynasty that she could no longer tolerate argument, let alone opposition.

'You are always raising difficulties, Gamal. The Rais does not need Doubters.'

No point in explaining to her that I was at that juncture totally absorbed in completing my masterwork, *Al-Crossing* (in which this Hamida-creature underwent a storm of mutations, depending on my phallic temperature at the moment of writing). I took the finished manuscript to Dad, returning a week later for his verdict. We opened the usual (sic) bottle of French wine. Mahmoud's gentle smile carried no sardonic undercoat.

'I have never needed to fornicate with my fictional characters. It's more a matter of temperament than of theory; compare Faulkner to Hemingway; a question of chemistry. You, Gamal, need to be in medias res, I do not. It's a pity when monomania – the bullfighter – displaces irony – the fly on the wall. The greatest danger to literature today lies in the American commercial notion of "superstar".'

Our discussions were always amicable. Unlike his son, Mahmoud continued to smell good, a mysterious, barber-blend of the Orient and Montmartre; always so tranquil and growing deafer. He didn't like me or my novel any more than you do.

TWENTY-TWO

❧

Isaac Ben Ezra cables a commission from *Esquire*. Things are apparently 'crunching up' in the Middle East – it's news to me – and a photographic interview with Sharaf is urgently required. Gamal meets the assigned Magnum photographer, Henri Chevalier, in the lobby of the Cleopatra Hotel. Henri also doubles up as *Le Monde*'s newly appointed correspondent in Egypt, a handsome fellow whose eyes change colour throughout the day.

I had first met Henri in Paris during my jamboree-jaunt in preparation for Huda's never-never wedding. Henri professed to adore his wife Nicole, though he seemed reluctant to spend much time with her; we passed two agreeable evenings in the cafés around the Odéon, then drifted down the rue St Antoine, eating overspilling kebabs bought cheap at Kurdish kiosks. Henri was definitely pro-Kurd and now I had brought him to the lobby of the Cleopatra Hotel, the threshold of the President himself.

'I know where Huda is,' he murmurs. 'I have a message.'

'I thought you might.'

The Rais is a moving feast; on this occasion he is to be found (or not found) at Maamourah, near Alexandria, a hermetically sealed camp with barbed wire barricades extending far into the water. To reach the Rais's Secretariat, one must pass through three guardposts – on a bad day, four. Gamal fritters away hours in clammy waiting rooms, watching belly dancers in stiletto heels performing on poorly tuned TV screens. Hours of belly-belly, then pacing about, then coffee, then last year's Grand National at Aintree, then a 1940s Western.

Gamal is making himself unpopular with loud remarks about the delays: 'The Rais's press secretary knows the length of a piece of string. Or does he?'

Gamal and Henri are finally hustled through the guard posts as if they've had the impertinence to arrive late, pushed into a vast reception room festooned with chandeliers, and firmly placed next to two caged chimpanzees. The Presidential cavalcade can be heard outside, sirens wailing, all those Sam Brownes and high burnished boots and ceremonial swords and engraved blazons. The Rais stages his entrance with Celia and two music hall figures, their guests, the Ambassador of the Congo and Mrs Congo. Celia is wearing a blue gym suit and a red baseball cap – her chimp-outfit. Henri begins leaping and clicking; the chimps look uneasy.

'Aren't they two beautiful chimpans, Gamal?' Celia smiles. 'The boy is called Togo and the girl Toga.'

The Rais feeds a banana to each chimp. Click click, smile smile. Ambassador and Mrs Congo smile smile proudly at their chimps' good table manners. Exit Rais-and-party. Gamal and Henri are left alone with Togo and Toga. No interview today. It's very hot: I fall asleep.

 લ

Togo and Toga are now dressed in the toy-soldier uniforms and red fezzes of the Gothic palace-hotel. The screaming memsahibs who are part of the furniture stare at us with disdain – they never let us down – when I notice the filthy old dustman with the gatta standing just inside the entrance beside his dust cart. He's pointing at me.

'And what about the miracles performed by Jesus?' I ask.

Shaytan delicately marries his fingertips. 'What are you asking?'

'The loaves and fishes. The healings. The walking upon the water – were they real? Or just metaphors?'

The devil groans. 'It was as close as I ever came to offering a rebuke to the Almighty.'

'Why?'

'I said: "Lord, Lord, how can poor mortals understand human love if Your mortal son constantly pulls Divine magic out of his pocket? Lord, Lord, an ethical Jesus must not inspire awe through displays of supernatural power. Your son is a *man* and should be as powerless as other men. After all, Master, You are not planning to whip him off the Cross by means of an earthquake!" '

'Perhaps He was! Did He answer?'

'He said, "Quite a speech." The Almighty is not exactly what the Americans call "a First Amendment Liberal". But, frankly, this whole issue was forgotten in the big wrangle between Gabriel and myself over the Last Supper.'

'The role of Judas?'

'Gabriel insisted that only I could inspire Judas to commit the ultimate "sin" – yes, yes, "sin" again. As usual I had to be the fall-guy. Once again the Divine Plan had to succumb to hypocrisy.'

'What was Jesus's view?'

'Jesus never had a view about anything. A very beautiful fellow. Good all through. In fact, if I had to chose a religion, I'd be a Christian. When they sat down for the Last Supper, I whispered desperately in his ear, "Lord, only give your most loving disciple, Judas Iscariot, a wink and a nod." '

'No response?'

'Worse than that – he said, "Get thee from me, Satan." It was hard to forgive. Fifteen hundred human years later I was urging the painters of Christian Europe to endow Jesus with that wink. Their hands shook! What temptation! Art wrestling with the tyranny of Divinity! Botticelli, Bellini, Leonardo – each longing to be the first. They masturbated with excitement but they couldn't do it. I told Leonardo that no one had ever captured the true anatomy of a Divine wink. He was trembling with ambition – another break-through, another first!'

'But no luck.'

'The devil has never been lucky. I was just a bum reduced to hissing like a bat and poisoning babies – the usual sitcom.'

⁊

Gamal returns to Cairo, tries to rewrite *The Crossing* (like a hen pecking at a few desiccated grains in a dusty farmyard), sits through a Danish movie in a downtown bar – but where is down and where up in Plato Popodopoulos's shapeless city? – and listlessly listens to the BBC World Service broadcasting in Arabic from Bush House. His old pal Fred Hemmings is anticipating a peace deal between Egypt and Israel. Thank you for not mentioning your source, Fred.

The phone sounds. 'The interview with the Rais is definitely on,' the press secretary assures me. 'Come at ten thirty p.m.'

'Ten thirty p.m.! You know what happens at ten thirty p.m.'

As it turns out, Gamal is not admitted to the Presence until near eleven. The Rais is adjusting the creases of his slacks while settling down for the hour before midnight which makes the expended day worthwhile. Egypt's overburdened ruler deserves his ninety minutes with Clark Gable and Carole Lombard (*No Man of Her Own*); or with Clark Gable and Vivien Leigh (he has viewed *Gone With the Wind* ten times); or with Elizabeth Taylor and Richard Burton (*Cleopatra*); or with Fred Astaire and Cyd Charisse (*The Band Wagon*). Sharaf – unlike Stalin – has rarely seen the end of any privately screened film; sleep and vodka inevitably claim him after an hour; his servants dare not carry him to bed while the spools are still turning, whirring, humming; indeed they dutifully change the reels even after the Rais's mouth hangs wide open.

'Good evening, Your Excellency. May we talk of the prospects for a permanent peace with Israel? There are rumours in the wind.'

'I am the wind.'

Carole Lombard has turned her beautiful, stand-up-straight, back on Gable: when she says no she means yes.

'And what does the wind wish to tell the world?'

'I have won every victory over myself,' the Rais declares. 'Let others eat, drown in alcohol, slide under the table with six whores or fool around with the domestic servants. But I can still shatter a glass tumbler with an oath from Muhi el-Din.'

The Rais is asleep. Carole Lombard has removed all her clothes, but off-screen. Her shoe falls to the floor (Hayes Code). Gamal contemplates the slackening features of Egypt's sleeping ruler as he dreams of being Clark Gable. A rustle; a fanfare of approaching perfumes; Celia and Hamida enter the Rais's cinema-room. Each takes me by an arm. I am led upstairs to Hamida's quarters. The arm-holding continues as I am firmly sat down on Hamida's bed; legs press into mine.

'You have been neglecting us, Gama,' Celia pouts. 'Such an ungrateful boy you are.'

'Who is this handsome French photographer you have been consorting with?' Hamida wants to know.

'His name is Henri Chevalier.'

'And he brought you a message from Huda?'

'No.'

'I wish to meet him. Is that understood?'

ର୬

Henri was certainly a handsome fellow. Having covered the Vietnam War and the emergent civil war in Lebanon, he had been despatched to Cairo in the expectation of an imminent peace deal between Sharaf and the Israelis. Sceptical and unhappy, his literary idol was Albert Camus; indeed the physical resemblance between them was striking. Henri inhabited Camus's novel, *The Plague,* with bitter joy; he even called Cairo 'Oran' and sniffed the stifling dust drifting in from the desert for a hint of the great wind carrying the plague.

'The plague,' I tell him, 'needs no wind here. It is permanently in residence. We wouldn't know how to live without it. Now tell me where Huda el-Sharaf is.'

We are dining in the Nile Hilton, observed by Hamida's spies.

Henri is after an interview with the great writer who cultivates the false reputation of a recluse, Mahmoud.

'My father is a difficult man to reach.' I roll my eyes expressively.

'Huda is in Paris,' Henri says.

'Don't forget that every waiter in Cairo is moonlighting for State Security.'

'But do they speak French?'

'Bugs up their sleeves. Hamida isn't short of translators.'

'You're one of them?' Henri asks with a hint of j'accuse.

'Autrefois – I used to be. So Huda's in Paris?'

'She travelled via Beirut with the help of sympathetic doctors and nurses from Médécins sans Frontières. They don't believe in arranged marriages.'

'You knew this when I was in Paris?'

'You were with Huda's mother.'

'Not when you and I were eating Kurdish in the rue St Antoine.'

'You were followed – always.'

'Point taken.'

'Huda is living with a groupuscule révolutionnaire – Maoists, Trotskyists, North African fundamentalists.'

'Aha? Does she play chess with them?'

'Chess?'

'You don't know much, Henri – or anything.'

This insult sends my friend into an elaborate engrenage mainly involving his beloved wife, Nicole, a lecturer at the Nanterre campus of the University of Paris who – I gather – had quit the Communist Party not when the Soviet tanks rolled into Budapest, not when the Soviet tanks rolled into Prague, but when the CP falteringly embraced the 'parliamentary road to socialism' in France.

'You know the old joke, Henri. They rejected the parliamentary road until they could find it on the street plan of Paris.'

Henri has no sense of humour. Camus's hero, Dr Rieux, did perfectly well without one.

'Nicole has Huda under her wing, is that it?'

Henri nods. 'The groupuscule is blamed for recent bomb attacks on the Egyptian and Algerian embassies. They are hunted by the police. Many of them face imprisonment or deportation if arrested.'

'You're telling me that Huda is mixed up with Islamic fundamentalists? That's not the Huda I know.'

'Call it an alliance of convenience. They all hate Sharaf.'

'It sounds as if an introduction to my father might earn me an introduction to your exciting wife, Henri.'

'I am the worst of husbands,' Henri sighs. 'Wherever I am, I am

336

soon overcome by the urge to be somewhere else. But Nicole would not be herself without her work. As Dr Rieux remarks, "L'essentiel est de bien faire son métier – the important thing is to do one's job well." Our love can breathe only in that tight space where chance brings us together.'

'I've never been much good at "love".'

'Do you know what Huda told Nicole? She said you are a writer who believes he'd never write another word if he rescued a kitten from drowning. Huda also said, "The best books about theft are written by adoptive thieves." '

'I smell more of Henri than Huda in these lines.'

'No, I swear, Gamal, I am quoting the woman who loves you. She calls you the Jean Genet of Egyptian literature.'

'OK, I'll take you to Mahmoud.'

Henri opens his wallet and passes me a sealed envelope. It carries a one-line message in a neat, diligent hand which evokes gentle doe-eyes gazing from a delicate, almond-shaped face: 'We can do so much for Egypt, you and I together, Gamal. Your loving friend and comrade, Huda.'

☙

It has been quite some time since I have been alone with Hamida. I dream of her lying across my knee in the pink underwear Celia had brought her from Paris while shopping for Huda's never-never wedding. All my desires flow together between those beautiful breasts and those firm globes of alabaster which cry out for the Marquis's ministrations. I even dream of Celia handing me the fouet like a nurse servicing a surgeon, while coaxing my dick to split its sides, the sharp diamonds of her imperial rings bringing blood from my foreskin. I have waited too many years to have the Virgin of Egypt!

Hamida receives me in the Muntazah Palace, a creature of rumour and scandal. Every time she persuades her father to sack a minister, or dismiss a Supreme Court judge, or humiliate a general, or fling a journalist into the Tora prison, she relishes the male-chauvinist backlash, which normally takes the form of faked photomontages in the exiled opposition press, pictures of a naked Hamida lying on a rock while another naked woman caresses her breasts, pictures of a drunken Hamida, wearing a slit-up Armani ballgown and jewelled anklets, drinking champagne on the knee of Andy Popodopoulos. The pictures are invariably forgeries, fakes, her head superimposed on the body of some dolce vita film starlet. Nothing shakes Hamida; she now controls all access to the Rais's private office; it is said that every cabinet appointment requires her approval.

Hamida is pacing back and forth beneath Titian's famous painting of her father-on-horseback, knee-deep (the horse) in the Canal. Gamal receives a sharp lecture on the responsibilities of the novelist in a Time of Crisis and is urged to model his future endeavours on those of the best-selling author, Ayn Rand.

'What the nation needs,' declares the Virgin of Egypt, 'is more optimism, more faith – and less filth.'

I incline my head respectfully. She's on automatic pilot but I never mind what Hamida says provided I'm close enough to touch her if I dared.

Her tone changes. 'Your bald patch is growing larger, Gamal. The Rais is about to launch a new political campaign, which we are calling "The War of the Slogans". Pappi thinks you have a gift for slogans. Let's hear one.'

' "Queen Cleopatra discovered America." '

'That's not a slogan!'

'It is when you add: "Fly Air Egypt".'

Hamida tries not to smile.

'Why don't you sit down right here,' I suggest. 'I had a bath only this morning. I used a deodorant stick in your honour.'

The war of the slogans is forgotten. Seated beside me, she takes my hand.

'Oh Gamal, who can I talk to except you?'

'No one.'

'Gamal, it was you who coined the phrase Virgin of Egypt. I thought it was a joke. It's no longer a joke. I want to enjoy a normal life but I can't! If only I could walk out of here and lead the life of an ordinary woman for a week!'

'Easy to arrange, Hamida – though you'd have to give up ruling Egypt for a week.'

'But then you'd want . . . want to . . . you've always wanted to, haven't you, Gamal? Oh, Gamal, I am in love with someone. I am driven mad by longing!'

'So am I, Huda!'

'Huda? Why did you say Huda?'

'I didn't!'

Up on her feet, Hamida slaps me. 'So you love Huda! You've been seeing Huda, conspiring with Huda!'

I grab Hamida and kiss her. She fights, scratches. 'You have the most gorgeous legs in the world,' I pant, pinning her to the sofa, 'the most gorgeous breasts, the most beautiful mouth . . .'

She is staring up at me. Her hand has found my prodigious, record-breaking erection. 'Gamal.'

'My princess.'

'You can come in my hand, Gamal – but only if you promise to show me everything and tell me everything you know now, or will ever know, about Huda.'

'No. I want to possess you.'

'But do you promise?'

'Yes. Yes!'

'Then we can take a bath together. In ass's milk. Would you like that?'

Reader! I have her pinned to the sofa. Her lovely thighs are stretched out beneath me, helplessly parted. I've dreamed of this! It's real! The Virgin of Egypt! Ass's milk, she says! I only have to heave myself off her, step back, struggling with my flapping shirt tail, and she'll be gone! That will be it! Reader, I serviced her! But I didn't! Toujours la politesse. (When very small, I had once announced to Dad, 'Toujours l'étiquette', unaware that this meant 'Always the luggage label'.) I was assailed by totem and taboo – even tabu: I wanted to be a gentleman worthy of Lady Fan, I wanted her to send me to prep school-Eton-Oxford: a gentleman worthy of admission to the Athenaeum.

When was virtue ever rewarded? The guards of the Muntazah Palace kicked me down a flight of thirty-two steps. As I hit the final one – the pain! – I realized that *The Crossing*, like *The Patriots*, could never be published in Egypt.

ௐ

To earn Mahmoud's good opinion, Henri must first take on Auntie Lulu, who currently lays claim to the powers of Isis, the goddess of knowledge, and Ma'at, the goddess of justice. She believes herself to be the repository of their immortal dreams. She has also recently developed a habit of telling me I'm not a good Muslim.

'Not a Muslim at all, Auntie.'

'In Islam there is no door marked "exit", Nephew.'

So here we are, at Auntie's, two gentlemen callers. She wastes no time in taking me apart for Henri's benefit.

'I used to dandle him on my knee and tell him stories but Gamal's hardly a dream writer for a feminist,' she chuckles, 'though I shouldn't judge him since I've never been able to get to the end of his famous, hot-water novel.'

Henri is diligently scribbling in a notebook. He is notionally interviewing Auntie Lulu for *Le Monde littéraire* to mark the banning of her new novel, *The Story of 'Aziza*, successor to the banned *Story of Zhina*. No Arab publisher will touch her work, in which the same autobiographical heroine invariably recounts, no holds barred, her emotional deprivations. Each novel contains its hysterical window-ledge scene but the heroine never quite jumps. Mahmoud has regularly protested to the censor on her behalf, but to no avail. As is well known, Egypt has no censor.

Lulu does bake nice cakes. She offers Henri, but not me, another. He wolfs it with a moan of Gallic appreciation. '*The Story of Zhina* is banned in twenty-one Arab countries,' he murmurs admiringly.

Gamal sighs fatly. 'Auntie, your daddy never beat your mother or made you wear the veil.'

'Ha! Nephew would know,' she snorts. 'He was still in his nappies at the time. And what does my brave, hot-water Gamal do when I receive all these death threats? Does he publicly offer me his support like his father does? Oh no, he's too busy tickling the vanity of his fictional Madame Celia. Have another cake, monsieur, don't let Nephew grab them all. He was always a grabber.'

Henri is scribbling like mad, though with a puzzled frown. Egyptian literary life is not without its complexities.

'We writers of conscience,' Auntie tells him, 'consider it our duty to expose the politicians, generals and imams. But your friend here has the soul of a rope climber. Eventually that broad bum will sit astride all the thrones and minarets he pretends to be toppling. It's the old male game of buggery.'

'So now you know,' I tell Henri.

'A cockroach,' Auntie says. 'Not satisfied with earthly conquests, Nephew is now poised to take on the Almighty.'

'Not many cockroaches have pulled that off, Auntie.'

'Oh, he always has the last word, does Gamal. One day he'll learn that there's no door marked "exit" in Islam.'

Trusting moron that I am! I should never have relaxed my hold on Henri by granting him the one privilege he sought from our 'friendship' – a meeting with the illustrious Mahmoud. It was easy enough to arrange; Dad's toes began to itch if not frequently tickled by some visiting sycophant, preferably of Gallic provenance. No sooner introduced to the venetian-blinded sanctum, Henri fell into a disgusting display of feet-washing. Did I too generously suggest that Henri resembled Camus? – forget it! More like Alain Delon playing James Dean in a B-movie. Maître, maître! How he lapped up the old rogue's elaborate stories of meeting the dadaists and surrealists in post-war Montparnasse.

'You actually met Proust, Maître? And Joyce! Gide!'

Spotting my fixed smile, Dad redirected his langour to the pleasures of infanticide.

'I suppose you know who's been writing the latest official slogans?' he asked his new foot washer. 'My worthy son. Of course he achieved his literary zenith when correcting English-language brochures for the Egyptian tourist industry. You didn't know about that, Monsieur Chevalier? He never told you how he used to conduct tourists around the Citadel? And now we must all gain inspiration from the slogans he churns out for Mademoiselle Hamida el-Sharaf. "Purging the power centres"! Hm? "Science and faith"! Hm? "Total confrontation and Zero Hour"! Hm? "Everything for the battle"! And best of all, "No peace no war"!'

My noble friend Henri did not know where to fix his gaze. Dad, however, was by no means finished:

'And surely you have heard of Gamal's brilliant new propaganda ploy – to associate the Rais with George Washington's log cabin? Oh yes. The Ministry of Information and the Ministry of Tourism are currently consuming whole Scandinavian forests of high-gloss paper explaining to the world that our President's greatest joy is his birth-place, the good earth from which he sprang, Muhi el-Din, where he enjoys "hours of infinite purity and repose . . ." Oh yes, how well your friend loves those long, paid-for journeys through narrow-strip cotton fields, bright green in winter, pale-yellow flowers in summer.'

Fatly I rose. 'Since you are both getting along so well, let me relieve you of my felonious presence.'

I probably banged the front door on my way out, like Ibsen's Nora leaving Torvald – for ever. Worse was to follow. Left alone with this ingratiating Camus-lookalike, my infinitely vain father allowed himself to be inveigled into writing a diatribe for *Le Monde*. What a scoop! Mahmoud's polemic appeared in Paris a week later under the title, 'The Mannequin Who Crossed'. Within twenty-four hours Egypt was threatening to break off diplomatic relations with France.

Dad now referred to Sharaf as the Khedive (after the extravagant Khedive Ismail, who had reduced Egypt to bankruptcy and European tutelage a century before). Mahmoud pointed out that the Italian Chamber of Haute Couture had dubbed Sharaf one of the world's ten best-dressed men: Sharaf rarely wore the same outfit twice; his clothes were designed by Balmain, by Cardin, by God; his dress uniforms were foreign creations involving a riot of sashes, sequins, fancy breeches, riding boots. His honour guards and galla-galla men had obediently decked themselves out to fill the stage of a vaudeville show which lacked nothing but a script. 'And we, the citizens of

Egypt, are the audience,' Mahmoud concluded in *Le Monde*. 'When shall we decide to hoot this rabble off the stage?'

I sent my father a short missive. 'A man is entitled to burn his own boats. Only God can burn other people's.' I then deposited my novel-in-progress and various documents in the vault of an American-owned bank where I had a small dollar account under the name of Walt Whitman, vacated my apartment, filled a suitcase with galabiyeh, and resumed my career as a tourist guide.

Near the tombs of the Mamelukes a stranger slipped a note into my pocket: 'Come soon, my dearest. Egypt groans under the tyrant's heel. Your adoring Huda.'

ھ

—If you rise early tomorrow, ladies and gentlemen, you will witness an extraordinary spectacle – the sun burning the mist off the Nile.

—And now, ladies and gentlemen, we stand in the shadow of the world-famous Colossi of Memnon.

—And now is the time for a short explanation. In the absence of rain, ladies and gentlemen, the economy of the old Egypt was entirely at the mercy of the Nile. The river and its annual flood were mother and father to the entire population. Torrential rain falls in the distant highlands of Abyssinia – yes, madam, that is the same as Ethiopia. The resultant Nile flood reached our great city of Memphis about mid-June. The river continued to rise until mid-September. The timing was unique and providential.

—Yes, madam, the notorious khamseen blows the sandstorms from the south during the spring. It is very painful to the eyes, I assure you.

—No, sir, our feluccas move upstream under sail and downstream on the current. (Gamal smiles.) Nature is wise. Nature is beneficient – provided we pray regularly.

—No, madam, I am myself a Christian. In our country Christians go by the ancient name of Copts – which means, in effect, Egyptians. You didn't know that?

—And now, my friends, we pause to allow you to take your snap-shots of the eternal Egypt. Notice the blindfold oxen toiling at the creaking sakias, or water wheels, whose wooden cogs are never oiled. You ask why they are never oiled, sir? Because, sir, the oxen would stop in their tracks and never move another inch without that familiar creaking tribute to their labours. (Smiles.) They would go on strike. Now over there you see an ass. You will notice that Mr Ass is no fool – he seems always to be cocking an ear for the next instruction.

Gamal slept under palm trees and in luxury hotels. His fitful sleep was plagued by dreams: Hamida and her secret police were combing the entire country in search of him. Seized while guzzling marinated lamb kebab at the dinner table of some beneficent Texans he had picked up in Luxor, dragged from the dining room by Hamida's Iron Guard, Gamal was forced to conduct the royal ladies to the Valley of the Kings, where he was threatened with instant death if he made the slightest error.

—Sing to us, Gama (Celia).

—Yes, madame. Very well. The dead pharaoh, who was regarded as both a king and a god, lay in state, stuffed with balsam, cassia and myrrh.

—Who else is both a king and a god? (Hamida).

—The Rais, your father, mademoiselle.

—Keep talking (Hamida)

—Very well. The dead pharaoh would then enter the New Kingdom cut out of solid rock. We will now follow the passages to the tomb as they creep into the darkness through numerous chambers and antechambers – yes, extremely numerous. Madame, I feel sure I would provide better service if relieved of these chains round my ankles.

(Slap from Hamida.)

—Thank you, Princess. Here in the last chamber of all the mummy was laid to rest in its double casing, splendidly decorated with lapis and gold. Even the pharaoh's wife might not lie, when her own time came, beside her consort – tomorrow, perhaps, we will visit the Valley of the Queens.

Celia's scented hand brushes mine.

Hamida kicks my shin.

Celia lies dead, wrapped in gold leaf.

—Then, Your Excellencies, came the robbers, the vandals, the scum of an ungrateful earth. The great stone trap doors were forced, the thieves' lanterns cast their long, sinister shadows, plebeian feet echoed through the vaults. Everything was taken – the gold, the jewels, the alabaster vases . . .

Celia sighing. Hamida's heel pressing into my manacled foot.

—Dreadful to relate, Your Highnesses, the shin-bones of a pharaoh would be sold for a few piastres in the bazaar – the revenge of the common people.

Oddly, these words came from another voice, whispering ardently in my sleeping ear. Huda! And there, flitting through the chambers and antechambers of the tombs are the grave robbers, armed brigands, led by a small, shrouded woman whose almond-face and doe-eyes elude me.

'Huda! Seize her!' The voice is Hamida's. 'Traitor! Conspirator! Enemy of her own father!'

Cut to Giza. Reaching the pyramids, Hamida insists on making the ascent. She chooses the most dangerous, Kephren's, whose base lines are shorter and angles steeper. In the cold air of the dawn we begin our climb, she and I, without a stitch of clothing – by her command. I shiver, she does not. Only the lowest courses are visible below the hanging carpet of mist. The blocks are friable, dodgy. I stumble frequently, moan that my flat feet are killing me, beg for a short halt. Slap. 'Climb,' she says, her bare breasts swaying above me. Now both the top and the bottom of the pyramid are lost in mist: I suffer agonies of vertigo, breathlessness, agoraphobia, asthma, bulimia nervosa, you name it.

'Climb!'

We reach a sinister region of habitation littered by the bones of chickens, the skins of rats, the castings of owls, the feathers of a falcon. A jackal slithers away along a narrow ledge.

'What are you afraid of? Climb!'

Higher still, towards the apex, we encounter a new danger, the smooth ashlar casing which originally clad the whole fucking pyramid. Here on a narrow ledge, which falls away, and away, and away into nothingness, Hamida chooses to stretch herself out in a pose worthy of Ingres – though you won't find *him* up here, and we only have Flaubert's word for it that he lugged his own syphilis, contracted in Lebanon, up here to the top.

'Now, Gamal,' Hamida commands. 'Now.'

'But mademoiselle, we might fall to our deaths!'

'Now!'

(To be continued.)

TWENTY-THREE

⁊

Perpetual motion was now Fawzi el-Sharaf's drug. His ceaseless movements became a logistical nightmare. The Presidential Guard had been raised to brigade strength, with one battalion assigned to follow him in perpetual motion from Giza to the Barrage to Muhi el-Din. For short hauls he now employed a flight of three Westland helicopters – so that no rocket-launching fundamentalist should know which one he was travelling in.

This week Sharaf is 'in retreat' at Muhi el-Din. Along the Nile road portraits of the Rais in primary colours are posted at irregular regular intervals, his eyes focused on God.

On arrival at the first security gate, Henri and I display our special passes and are promptly flung against a wall with arms raised while frisked from armpit to groin by guards in blue berets. Firearms and pistol holsters drip in the heat as bountifully as the Rais's pears and avocados. (They say the Nile has been diverted to feed his water sprinklers.)

'Are you Jewish?' Henri is asked.

'No.'

'What was your maternal grandmother's maiden name? Rothschild? Jabotinsky? Herzl?'

'Frankly,' sighs Henri, 'I can't even remember my own maiden name.'

'This is not the place for jokes,' I mutter. 'Even Cabinet Ministers are frisked on arrival here and required to remember who their grandmothers were.'

We wait. Henri seems immune to heat, thirst, hunger; he is content to play with his lenses and filters. This year Ramadan falls in the hottest season, July. Thank you, Ramadan. Tempers are short because smoking is forbidden until sunset. Here at Muhi el-Din majors, colonels, brigadier-generals, still sporting British-style uniforms, are all suffering from nicotine-starvation. Lifting Gamal's Camels from his pocket, the Security Chief's big hand slowly, s-l-o-w-l-y, crushes them. Only when Radio Cairo announces that the sun has set may the coloured gas lighters emit their flames with that familiar, comforting whoosh, transforming Egypt into a smiling democracy until sunrise.

Finally we are led out (let out) to the lemon orchard and briefed by a colonel:

'In three minutes the Rais will appear. He will walk towards you. He will offer you his hand. You will walk beside him and whenever he turns you will turn. Here is your tape recorder.'

And here the Actor comes, wearing a short-sleeved terrycloth shirt with a zip, a breast pocket for tissues, matching beige shorts of incredible brevity – clearly these lean, wiry, sixty-two-year-old legs ending in white socks and American tennis shoes are set to dominate the photo-opportunity. The Rais clasps a gnarled cane under his arm. Extravagant sunglasses and a straw hat complete the picture.

The Actor shakes my hand as if we had never met before. 'I am pleased to meet you,' he says.

The Rais carries his stick in his left hand along a paved path slightly raised above the richly manured earth of the lemon orchard. After a few paces, he turns. Then turns again. Gamal and his tape recorder are already in arrears. The path simply isn't wide enough to accommodate us both. The Rais, of course, knows as much. Gamal can imagine him giving meticulous instructions to the contractor: 'A path wide enough for one-and-a-half people.'

'Yes, Rais! One-and-a-half, Rais!'

Removing his dark glasses, the Rais wipes the perspiration from his head with a red tissue, reveals his plans to meet the Queen of England, then tosses the used tissue into the bushes. Gamal suspects that the Queen of England would never toss a tissue into the flower-beds of Buckingham Palace, Sandringham or Balmoral – nor would her tissue be red. Nor would she be displaying her legs in obscene beige shorts.

'A man must keep the body fit to keep the mind fit,' the Rais says. 'President Carter goes jogging. Recently he fell down and suffered a heart attack. I am content with my exercise bicycle.' Sharaf fingers his hanging lemons, which will be sold on the trees to a local merchant before they are ripe. He then displays one of his prayer-aids, a Swiss watch, inscribed in Arabic.

'With the help of one of the hands and this disc which displays the main cities of the world, I can accurately determine the direction of Mecca wherever I find myself.' The irregular but very white teeth flash. 'Only by finding a balance between the three God-given elements can a man become a creative thinker. The soul must be nourished through faith. A well-nourished soul rescues us from doubt.'

Gamal asks the Rais whether he finds himself able to fulfil his extraordinary duties while fasting.

'During Ramadan my mind achieves maximum clarity. When I fast I am closer to God. I see the Light and know what He expects of me. I know what path I must follow. I first discovered my mission in cell 45. All my greatest decisions have been taken during Ramadan – I made The Crossing during Ramadan.'

'And was not your Crossing of the Canal also a metaphor for the many Crossings that Egypt has achieved under your presidency?'

'That is for others to judge. For posterity.'

The Rais notices that one of the garden spigots is leaking and gestures to the corpulent bodyguard ambling behind us. The bodyguard turns towards the house and shouts – a chain of shouts follows and Gamal guesses that the spigot will be mended before the next red tissue flies into the bushes. The Rais resumes his perambulation:

'I am a trinity, as the Christians say. There are three Sharafs, the fellah, the citizen and the soldier. In fact I wear a uniform only on special occasions but the ministry decided that the public portraits should show me in uniform. The Egyptians need a leader, a man they can trust.'

It is very hot and getting hotter. Every twenty paces the Rais wheels round and Gamal wheels with him – like leopards in a cage. Henri is now gesturing to Gamal to get out of the way; he wants the Rais alone in his orchard because no one is more alone than the Rais. Gamal steps back off the path into the richly manured red earth.

We return to the house. The Rais's masseur, a hero of The Crossing who parted the Bar Lev Line with his bare hands, is poised to rub down his master after the fifteen-minute stint on the exercise bicycle, which stands expectant on a gleaming parquet floor. Henri leaps around murmuring 'Terrific, wonderful'.

The interview is over – but we are promised another photo-opportunity later in the day.

'How about the village?' Henri suggests. 'Wasn't he born here or something?'

'He was. Or something. I have visited this bloody village scores of times. You don't need me in order to find half-blind fellahin beating their donkeys and barefoot boys tearing along sandy paths honking wildly in "cars" made out of wire. "Baksheesh, baksheesh, mister." '

'I'll be off then. Ah – I almost forgot, I have a letter from Huda.'

I glance wildly around. 'Jesus! You've been carrying it in your pocket! Here!'

Henri is lazily searching his clothing. He shrugs. 'It will turn up.'

Henri strides off to the village while I settle for a snooze (Orientalists, take note!). Dinner follows at sunset – the ladies now make their entrance. The table has been set on the veranda, mainly Sèvres and Dresden, the true G. Washington homestead touch. Waiting for the Rais, Gamal and Henri are entertained by the First Lady and the First Daughter of the Nation, both done up to the nines, posing and pirouetting for the handsome photographer for whom Hamida is on heat. The princess is wearing a long-sleeved Afghan blouse over her designer jeans, every inch the Virgin of Egypt. Every inch shows.

'You must find it very annoying to be travelling with so ill-informed a journalist as Gamal,' Hamida tells Henri.

'Gamal is an excellent fellow, mademoiselle.'

'And what has Gamal told you about us?' Celia asks, throwing me a gentle, apologetic smile. Nice woman.

'He . . . well he . . . nothing really.'

'Nothing! He didn't mention that my daughter and I are both mature students at Cairo University, fighting for the modern status of women?'

'I believe he may – '

'Mr Rahman prides himself on his ability to predict the future,' Hamida says. 'Recently he informed the readers of *Misr* that my mother and I will fail our exams on the first occasion to prove that Egypt is a democracy – but pass them on the retake to prove that the Rais Rules OK.'

'Ah. Ah well.' Henri shrugs diplomatically.

'Well what?' Hamida asks him sharply, her pharaonic mask luminous with desire.

'I must say, Egypt is an extraordinarily beautiful country.'

The Rais joins us, a beaming searchlight of hospitality. I am seated next to Hamida, who promptly presses her high heel deep into my shoe.

'Pappi,' she says, 'Huda has been sending messages to Gamal, urging him to assassinate you.'

'I won't hear a word against Huda,' the Rais announces. 'Not in the presence of guests. She is a loyal daughter to me, she visits me often, and she is currently serving as my Ambassador in Zanzibar. Is that quite clear?'

Hamida sulks. Her heel works its way through the leather of my upper, then my foot, then the sole. I drape a napkin across my tumescence.

'I am proud of you,' the Rais informs me. 'You are my son. And what will you write next before I have you cut into small pieces and thrown to the crocodiles?'

'Excellency, the next novel will be called *Ra'is*.'

'It will be another scurrilous and obscene satire portraying me as a buffoon and a cuckold?'

'As Egypt's modernizing Führer, Your Excellency.'

'Good. But don't spare me. I am an exceptionally tolerant and liberal man. Anywhere else in the Middle East and I would be having you for dinner.'

'But you can only eat a man once, Your Excellency.'

'Exactly. I am very fond of you. You will accompany me to Jerusalem. In fact you will arrive before me. You will be my advance guard.'

'May I ask when this will occur, Your Excellency?'

'When God wills it.' The Rais chuckles. 'God and Prime Minister Begin.'

Hamida is fuming. By way of diversion, Celia asks Henri whether he is married.

'Yes, madame. Elle me manque.'

'The arrogance of men!' Hamida blazes. Henri looks surprised, unaware that this particular French construction baffles foreigners.

' "Elle me manque" means "I miss her",' I explain to Hamida. 'Your esteemed parents may think I was not a diligent tutor to you.'

'Oh yes, and Huda speaks perfect French! Is that it?'

The conversation happily ceases with the TV news. The television screen casts a magical glow over the table. News of the Rais – though there is none – arrives by the minute, the Rais this, the Rais that. A light breeze brings to the veranda smells of horse manure, mangoes and millennia of dust, all mingling sweetly with French perfumes and fat-floppy Gamal's sweat, which no deodorant can conquer. The Rais eats little, his attention morosely fixed on the magical rectangle where the Ayatollah Khomeini is addressing a small but fanatically fired-up crowd of Muslim males outside a mosque in Paris. One small woman wearing the traditional hijab stands close to him; as he moves to his car, the Ayatollah pauses for a moment to speak to her. We glimpse her serene smile.

'Huda!' cries Hamida.

Celia is trembling. She, too, has recognized her daughter.

'Nonsense,' the Rais snaps angrily. 'Huda is my ambassador in Zanzibar.'

At this juncture a servant enters, bows, and presents an envelope to Henri. 'Found under your bed, pasha,' he says in Arabic. Henri thanks him casually, pockets the envelope, and addresses the Rais in English:

'The whole world will be making the journey to Jerusalem with Your Excellency.'

The Rais beams. Hamida fumes. The Rais retires for his hour with Carole Lombard and Clark Gable.

ଡ଼

Here we must pause to consider two letters, either of which could have made a gift of Gamal to the Nile crocodiles. The first went straight down the toilet that night, though God knows Hamida was capable of draining every septic tank in Egypt.

Dear Gamal,

It has now become incontrovertibly clear that the Rais is preparing for a capitulation to the Israeli oppressors of the Palestinian people and the Arab Nation. You always taught me that the language of politics is befouled by partiality and bad faith (mauvaise foi). But we can still talk of 'justice' and 'liberty', surely? I have never believed that you served the Sharafs for ignoble ends, indeed I hope I have understood that a writer must know intimately those about whom he writes, however distasteful to him, and indeed my faith in you has been sustained by your writing, your novels, which pitilessly reveal the ruling family of Egypt, to whom I no longer belong, for what they are.

Yet word reaches me that you will perhaps be intimately involved in the Rais's ignominious journey to Jerusalem. Dearest Gamal, I cannot believe this but please, I beg you, lay my fears to rest with a simple assurance: you will not set foot in Jerusalem until the Palestinian flag flies over the Temple Mount. Strengthened by such an affirmation from you, I could set aside all personal feelings, the emotions of a foolish woman, and bear the burden of your indifference.

Your 'little' friend,
Huda

'How could she know this?' I asked Henri. 'I've only just heard it from the Rais.'

'This is the Middle East.'

No less considerate of the Nile crocs is my dad. Mahmoud chooses this moment to publish an Open Letter to Amnesty International on behalf of Egypt's political prisoners. Extract from text follows:

Sharaf fits our uniquely Egyptian concept of a fahlawi. A similar term, bahlawan, is found in general Arabic: it means clown, rope dancer. The Egyptian fahlawi is happy-go-lucky, a blusterer, full of pomp, jovial, pleasure seeking, always looking for the short cut, likes sudden excitement, displays violent audacity, then fizzles out into listlessness. 'Consider the matter solved, my dear fellow,' he says, 'I'll put it to the minister myself. Consider it done!' That of course is how Sharaf is currently dealing with Israel, notwithstanding that country's shameful oppression and dispossession of Sharaf's fellow-Arabs, the Palestinians. One hears that the Rais is poised to fly to Jerusalem – Jerusalem! – in his Boeing 707, paid-for by the Saudis at a cost of $12 million and as fully equipped as America's Air Force One. That includes the vodka. Sharaf believes vodka to be not only indistinguishable from water but also odour-less. He drinks two or three before the day's appointments begin. After a couple of hours he complains of overwork and the serious drinking begins. It is during these 'off-hours' that his daughter stuffs our jails with political prisoners. The nation's antiquities, meanwhile, suffer wanton pillage at the grasping hands of the entire Sharaf family.

Thank you very much, Mahmoud! And who furnished you with all these intimate details? Your much despised son!

Mahmoud was right, of course – the Sharafs were plundering the nation's heritage. Precious antiquities were dished out to Tito, to Brezhnev, to the Empress of Iran (a marble perfume pot which had belonged to Nefertiti), to Kissinger, to Mrs Nixon, Onassis, Giscard, Carter, Franz-Joseph Strauss. When Hamida attended a women's congress in Mexico she presented the President's wife with a wood and bronze statue of Throth, twenty-three centimetres high. I was delegated to carry it (and write Hamida's Viva Zapata! speech).

Many of these treasures I 'borrowed' – under the Presidential seal – straight from display in the Cairo Museum. It was particularly painful to see the exquisite 'Isis suckling Horus' sitting beside Hamida's bed. On one occasion Hamida had commanded me to seize twenty-six pieces in a single day. I protested in vain that I had become the most hated visitor to the Department of Antiquities. One distinguished curator spat at me:

'And to think you are Mahmoud's son.'

Such was Mahmoud's fury against the Sharafs that he was moved to write his open letter and to take the lead in organizing a public protest by the nation's leading scholars and writers. The genial Dr

Hatem, our long-serving Minister for Information and Culture, immediately summoned me to his Cairo office.

'You will appear on TV this evening to reveal that Mahmoud has been a lifelong Communist.'

'He is a lifelong liberal.'

'So we all thought.'

'Dr Hatem, the Government will gain no credit by setting son against father. Has the Rais authorized this attack on the sacred Egyptian tradition of family unity and filial loyalty?'

'Ha! Ha! The Rais has better things to think about!'

The following day the Rais hectored two hundred editors and journalists, denouncing Mahmoud as 'a cosmopolitan high-wire artist with black hatred for Egypt in his heart'. Foreign correspondents raised their paws to ask whether a man who protested the pillage of Egypt's historic treasures was displaying 'black hatred' for his country.

'I am not your "wog",' Sharaf shouted. 'I am not your "kaffir".' (Hamida, seated beside him, was busily noting down the names of the journalists who had called Pappi a wog and a kaffir.) 'It is tragic,' continued the Rais, 'that Mahmoud, a man whom Egypt had raised so high, should have sunk so low out of "black hatred" [again] for his country.'

The Rais sipped the glass of water which was seventy per cent vodka. In the bars of Cairo the joke that evening was whether the Rais would hold a plebiscite about his generous gifts of Egyptian antiquities. Any minute now the Rais would amend the Constitution to grant himself an unlimited number of antiquities and six-year terms of office.

Instead the Party declared him President for Life. It was less complicated. A week after the national celebrations Celia telephoned me in some agitation.

'Gama, everyone is accusing us of dictatorship. But how can Fawzi plunge all his sons into anarchy?'

'Madame, he cannot.'

'I never wanted to be First Lady.'

'Madame, you are now Wife for Life. You are married to a bas-relief.'

'People are saying horrible things about Fawzi's negotiations with the Israelis. Huda has been issuing the vilest pamphlets in Paris.'

'She is of no account – though I understand your feelings. As Huda's tutor I sometimes feel betrayed, but I soothe myself with the thought that I was also Hamida's.'

'But Huda is threatening to whip up such a storm in Palestine that Fawzi won't be able to set foot in Jerusalem!'

'Madame, please remind His Excellency that he once promised to send me to Jerusalem as his advance guard.'

She took no notice of this. It was Huda Huda. Fawzi was seriously considering asking the French Government to extradite Huda on charges of terrorism, a scandal from which he had hitherto recoiled. Thousands of posters bearing Huda's portrait had surfaced overnight in Cairo, Jerusalem, Tripoli and Baghdad.

Later that night Isaac Ben Ezra put through another call from New York. 'Gamal! Why are you sitting on your ass? Huda el-Sharaf was seen in conversation with the Ayatollah Khomeini! Gamal, did you open your eyes long enough to absorb that moment? You do have television in Egypt? Gamal, am I talking to a writer or a banana?'

The following week I left for Paris. 'Everything is arranged,' Henri told me, 'with Nicole.'

૭૦

I slept soundly throughout the flight.

'Ya Allah, Ya Allah!' the old dustman was shouting at his donkey as Dad and I walked past the mansions once occupied by the British along the banks of the Nile – imposing monuments to wealth and power, with gabled roofs and capriciously crenellated turrets. Their new, Egyptian, owners had not tampered with their names: Fontainebleau, Sandringham Villa, Balmoral, Giza.

'But when the Egyptians moved in,' Mahmoud smiled, 'they found no water pot near the toilet. The infidels wipe their bottoms with paper only.'

'We come to the birth of Islam,' I pressed Shaytan.

'Well, that's complicated. As the Almighty recovered His own assets in the great urban civilizations of Greece, Byzantium and Rome, He became absorbed with aesthetics. With beauty as an aspect of the greater physics. He took measurements of the Parthenon. He built Santa Sophia. He revelled in marble pillars, mosaics, alabaster, bronze horses, graven images. His once-Chosen People became His Forgotten People. The word "universal" was now glued to the lips of Gabriel and the acolytes. They decked themselves out like popes and patriarchs, their status determined by the weight of gold leaf on their wings.'

'Ethics forgotten?'

'Unless you take seriously a puritan bullyboy like St Paul, the Hammer of God, the Anvil of Jesus – everything right or wrong because the Lord said so.'

'What about Pelagius and Augustine? The debates about free will?'

'No progress. How could there be? The Almighty, my Master, simply would not grant Man his freedom – though I begged.'

'But this "freedom" you often speak of as the precondition of morality – how could it be real? As Job said, "What the Lord grants, the Lord can take away." '

The devil sighed. 'That's the problem in strict logic.'

'Is there any other kind?'

'Even if freedom is provisional it can be persuasive. The French existentialists made one vital error when they informed mankind that God was dead but urged their brethren to behave as if God existed. Can you define their error?'

'In your terms?'

'Yes.'

'God is not dead but men should behave as if He were?'

'Exactly. My Master has to be persuaded to put the "free" back into free will – He has to be converted! Euripides and Aristophanes, after all, were writing behind God's back because He let them do so. Offered them a free zone. He was delighted by the results – until Gabriel turned up to remind Him that these geniuses were nothing but "pagans".'

'I asked you about the birth of Islam.'

'Tread carefully, Gamal. Do not trespass upon yourself.'

'I am not a believer.'

'Islam is not a club one is free to leave – not until all men are free. Islam, my boy, is where God exercises His ancient appetite for severe penalties.'

⁊

At Charles de Gaulle airport I had no problems at all. I went straight through with a 'bon séjour en France'. I didn't like the smell of it; a wog with eyes like mine is almost invariably detained, even if entering Holland for the tulip festival.

'Are we being followed?' I asked my driver as we sped down the autoroute towards Paris.

'Don't worry, mon gars, France protects its guests.'

'What's your opinion of Jews for Jesus?' I shrewdly asked him.

'I read your last novel, *Le Trajet* [*The Crossing*]. Not bad, not bad. How's Henri? A good lad, that, we were at the Ecole normale together. Shall we speak Arabic? Mind you, I learned mine in Syria, I'd be inclined to call you Djemal, as your illustrious father once predicted.'

We picked up Nicole from one of the narrow streets where they had erected barricades in May '68. Her disapproving eyes conveyed the contempt of Left Bank radicals for the human beings whose causes they have decided to adopt. It occurred to me that Henri may have exiled himself in our plague-zone to get away from her, despite his constant sighs of love. Apparently our good-humoured driver was a member of her 'cell' and a professor at Nanterre.

'Henri isn't jealous,' she told me.

'But I am,' I said rolling my eyes all over her.

This was ill received – apparently 'Arab comrades' arriving in Paris found it hard to distinguish (as she put it) between une femme libre and une femme gratuite.

'Particularly when they emerge from English-speaking colonies where "free" covers both conditions,' I added. 'Are you Jewish?'

'Why do you ask that? What right have you?'

Nicole remained frosty and short-tempered as I was whisked from one 'safe house' to the next in search of the elusive, mobile Huda. These verminous rabbit warrens struck me as far from 'safe'; in one a staircase collapsed under my weight, in another the roof fell in when we hammered on the street door. The refuges of the clandestine groupuscules stank of kebab, chilli powder, garbage, low-grade hash and paranoia. Wild-eyed North African enragés kicked AK 47s into cupboards while offering us tea from filthy cups. Grenades hung from kitchen ceilings like onions. This was not the Paris that Mahmoud had known and certainly not the Paris to which Madame's cultural advisor was accustomed.

And still no sign of Huda. Just coded messages and occasional photos of the Muslim heroine drawing-pinned to peeling, damp walls.

I finally protested to Nicole. 'What is this, a novel by Simenon?'

We were stuck in a traffic jam, a magnificent embouteillage stretching (at an informed guess) from the Bois de Boulogne to the Bastille. A demonstration of lycée students was the cause of the trouble; they kept hammering on our windows and accusing us of 'accommodationism'. Finally Nicole leapt out of the car and seized one of their banners:

'Up your arse, fils à papa!'

Evidently this insult was deadly; we were immediately reintegrated in the proletariat and our windows were safe. Nicole leapt back in the car, flashing scorn.

'Whose novel do you want to be in, monsieur? Proust's?'

'Done! A château or a hôtel particulier would do very nicely. Failing which, just dump me at the Hotel St Antoine and I'll wait. Though I might go out to see the latest Catherine Deneuve, it's bound to be set in les beaux quartiers among the very rich, bourgeois people I like.'

'God, he's absolute scum!' Nicole cried to her professor. 'What does Huda see in him! What does Henri see in him?'

'Djemal merely enjoys the gift of honesty which we lost sight of when we decided to replace all existing worlds with ones not yet invented.' The prof. winked at me through his driving mirror.

'Shut up, Jacques.'

(So that was his name. On returning to Cairo, I'd be able to inform Henri that he wasn't jealous of Jacques.)

I opened the car door. 'I'm going for a walk. You can deliver my exhausted suitcase to the Hotel St Antoine.'

Nicole grabbed me. 'You're staying with us. Are you such a complete fool that you can't understand what we've been doing?'

'Yes.'

The professor winked at me again. 'We've been losing our tail, Djemal. Shaking off les flics. Trouble is, they're all off-duty today at the Parc des Princes. PSG are playing Marseille.' He sighed eloquently. 'I'd happily join them.'

An hour later the revolution caved in. I was deposited at the Hotel St Antoine. Settled in a chair in front of le télé, where Marseille were running rings round the local heroes, PSG, I flipped through *La Semaine à Paris* and soon found Catherine Deneuve at ten cinemas.

The nastily thumbed little mag was suddenly lifted from my hand by someone standing behind my chair.

'What has Catherine Deneuve got that I haven't?'

Huda was quite alone and beautifully dressed – Mama would have approved. Her hair had been redone – I hadn't seen her for two years – splashing bountifully around her delicate, almond-shaped face. A pair of dark glasses was her only concession to Egyptian State Security and Mossad; when she lifted them off, with the most exquisite, beguiling smile, I saw that the doe-eyes now belonged to a woman who'd graduated.

'Do you recognize me, Gamal?'

I didn't rise from my chair (always an effort). 'The Ayatollah Khomeini, I presume?'

She froze. Perhaps I wasn't going to be friendly. In Huda's life unfriendly Egyptians were dangerous. 'Gamal?' she said.

'You Sharafs are all cut of one cloth, do this, do that – or else.'

Huda stood aghast. 'I have never threatened you, Gamal! I pleaded with you not to go to Jerusalem!'

'Or else.'

The doe-eyes brimmed with tears. 'Aren't you going to kiss me,

Gamal?' She took the chair next to mine and lifted her hand to the hotel receptionist.

'Gaston, two cafés crème and one Cognac for monsieur.'

'Oui, Mademoiselle Huda.'

She sat gazing at me steadily. 'Gamal,' she said, 'I can see you are hurt and frightened. But I too.'

Up on the screen, Marseille's expensive Dutch striker, Wyp van der Wyp, casually blasted a fifth goal into the roof of the PSG net. All the off-duty Parisian flics were on their feet in the Parc des Princes, whistling derisively and demanding their money back.

'Have you missed me, Gamal?'

Gaston brought the drinks and banged my brandy down. He'd picked up the tone of our exchanges. I could see he was crazy about Huda but what was really getting to him was PSG 0, Marseille 5.

'Are all your friends in Paris racists?' I asked Huda.

'Oh Gamal, who do you mean?'

'Nicole for one. Can't you tell she despises Arabs?'

'Gamal, I'm so sorry about what you've been through. Please don't blame poor Nicole. Sadly, these byzantine precautions and absurd detours through a *roman policier* are strictly necessary.'

'Though here you are, alone and undisguised, in the centre of town. The Sharafs are great performers.'

'The question isn't who's following me, but who's following you.'

'Who is?'

'Me!' Oh, what a smile. 'You haven't kissed me yet, Gamal.'

Huda took me to a Matisse exhibition at the Musée d'Orsay and a production of Sartre's *Altona* at the TNP. We discussed each member of her family perfectly rationally. Indeed Huda was unnervingly rational – she had a theory about everything. Her father's power-mania she ascribed to the humiliations inflicted on him by the British, particularly 'Scobie'; when I tried to remind Huda that 'Scobie' was a Laurence Durrell character whom I had injected into the story of the young Fawzi el-Sharaf, she demurred calmly:

'No, Gamal, that was real. I remember it clearly.'

As for 'Mama', Huda continued gravely, Celia's problem all along had been the knowledge that she was of extremely humble birth on both sides, the Egyptian and the English.

'The result was an imagination irretrievably bourgeois. The bourgeoisie is incapable of distinguishing personal profit from liberty. Money increasingly deforms an honest woman into false consciousness and mauvaise foi.'

I listened to all this with extreme interest, reclining comfortably in a pavement café on the Champs-Elysées and sipping Cognac (Huda didn't touch alcohol, on Islamic principle, but was indulgent about my habit).

'All this sounds very French,' I ventured.

'Is that bad?' She smiled. 'I merely put the question to my former tutor.'

Next came Hamida. Huda loathed Hamida but wouldn't say so. Apparently Hamida could be understood in 'all her tortured complexity' if one made a thorough study of the films of Luis Buñuel.

'Ah. *Belle de Jour*? But that's Catherine Deneuve.'

'*Tristana*. That's the Spanish version of Deneuve.'

'She loses a leg? Hamida has lost a leg?'

'Ethical amputation under the force of inverted sexuality.'

'Well, Huda, it really sounds as if none of your family is to blame. And yet you are planning, I gather, to assassinate the lot.'

'Not Mama. As for Pappi and Hamida, one doesn't blame the crocodile before one shoots it.'

'So how does Huda explain Huda?'

Huda smiled sweetly, stretched her little legs, and gazed up the Champs-Elysées towards the Arc de Triomphe.

'I was rescued by love,' she said. 'I mean the power of love which flows through literature. You want to be bad, Gamal, but you cannot help being good. And why?'

'Why?'

'It's simply a question of intelligence. I no longer believe that Sartre was correct about le mal, about evil. It is not an existential or phenomenological choice. You regularly commune with the devil and – '

'What gives you that idea?'

'Oh I inhabit your dreams, Gamal, you have no secrets from me. You chose your father as your devil, ensuring that he would speak only the truth, the truth being le bon, the good. You allowed yourself to fall into the clutches of Mossad, those Israeli demons, precisely in order to transcend the banality of evil.'

'Mossad? That's news to me.'

'Your literary agent, Isaac Ben Ezra, works for Mossad. Didn't he tell you to go in pursuit of me?'

'All Sharafs have one-dimensional minds.'

'Gamal, I wrote begging you not to go to Jerusalem but of course I was wrong. You must go. You will do much good there pretending to be bad.'

'Hm. Don't go, must go – you're certainly a Sharaf, Huda.'

'I think you've already said that three times.'

'Revolutionary movements are packed with disappointed princes and princesses.'

'Gamal! How can you go through with our marriage if you think such things?'

My eyes rolled slowly, I'm sure they did. 'Eh?'

'It has been a very long engagement,' Huda said gravely. 'Happily, all is arranged for tomorrow. The mosque which will receive us belongs to the Gama'at brethren of Upper Egypt.'

'You've really embraced Islam?'

'Oh Islam! What else is there? I ran around with Maoists and Trotskyists for a while. What impact could the Little Red Book have in Upper Egypt or the streets of Cairo? You have to talk to people in a language they understand.'

'But do we love one another, Huda?'

'I love you. That is sufficient. I humbly hope that, with time, you will come to discover qualities in me which may merit your love.'

'That is touchingly put, Huda.'

'Oh Gamal! And I know your father would approve – your Auntie Lulu guaranteed his approval to me.' Huda smiled sweetly. 'I only wish I had known your mother.'

'So do I – though I'm not sure.'

'Gamal, I must confess something to you. I have money. My money pays for all the leaflets, pamphlets, manifestos, guns, bombs and logistical backup of the Gama'at. Andy sends me money. He still lives in hopes, you see, he swears he will divorce his wife if I will only change my mind.' She laughed. 'So he is not, despite your warning, like the Turkish sultan Othman.'

'You mean Andy knows where you are while the entire Egyptian security apparatus doesn't?'

'No, no, don't be silly. The money is lodged in Switzerland, that's all. Collecting it is no problem.'

'Huda, what makes you so confident that every table on this pavement is not packed with Hamida's goons and Mossad agents dead set on putting you in a body bag?'

'France is not a pawn of Zionism, Gamal. The Government here could have handed me over to Cairo long ago. It is through the Palestinians, the PLO, that France plans to resurrect its lost colonial influence in the Middle East. Paris maintains a guarded relationship with the Sharaf regime but doesn't expect it to survive.'

'You have grown prettier, Huda. Exile suits you. But I advise you not to trust Nicole.'

'Because she rejected your proposition?'

'My what!'

'She was afraid she'd offended you – she has a sharp tongue but a heart of gold. She's having an affair with Jacques but Henri doesn't mind terribly, just a bit, because he and Jacques have always been good friends.'

'Is Nicole Jewish?'

'Jewish! Of course not. How could she be? She is heart and soul for the Palestinian cause. She has even visited the Fatah military camps in Lebanon. If Nicole was less friendly to you than I would have wished, it's because we know that you are to accompany Pappi to Jerusalem. She does not understand, as I do, that tu fais le mal au service du bon.' Huda issued her 'so that's all right' smile.

'Huda, I'm not sure I want to be married to a woman who always spells everything out. My dad taught me about the necessary silence between the lines.'

'Gamal, I will learn to be silent between the lines.'

'Hm.'

'Do you find me desirable?'

'Oh, I always did!'

'But not like Hamida?'

'One couldn't love Hamida. Not even Hamida could.'

This comment restored Huda's brightest spirits. She ordered me another Cognac, her gold bracelets dancing in the eye of the waiter. He knew her. They all knew her.

'I remember, Gamal, when you first whipped Hamida in the train from Alex to Cairo, you and your stories of the Marquis de Sade. I'll always remember Mama's face when you solemnly told her that de Sade is French for Sharaf.'

Huda laughing. I could hear a camera clicking regularly somewhere near at hand.

'None of that ever happened,' Gamal said. 'It was merely a scene in *The Patriots*. Huda, you don't exist either.' I was drunk on brandy. I have no recollection of Huda paying the bill, only of Jacques and Nicole dragging me into a car.

ॐ

Boarding his Air France flight for Beirut, Gamal Rahman is convinced that he has been dragged and driven, dead-drunk, across Paris to a squalid northern banlieu and there hurled into an airless mosque smelling of bare brick and bad breath, and there married to Huda el-Sharaf, with the elders of the Gama'at standing in for her necessary but absent fathers and uncles. Convinced? Every detail of the ceremony evades him in recall. His only impression of his bride is of a small figure shrouded from head to toe and refusing to speak anything but Arabic. And what of the consummation? Nothing on that, either. Of Huda's naked-nuptial flesh he has no impression at all. Settling into his seat and ordering a double whisky as the plane rises over Charles de Gaulle, Gamal can find no trace of post-coital ease in his loins. Perhaps, contrary to the received wisdom, it does not take two to make a marriage.

But he would always treasure the moment when Huda lifted Catherine Deneuve from his hand – if not from his head.

TWENTY-FOUR

୭ଦ

We enter the 'magic carpet' phase of Sharaf's diplomacy. But decorum here demands a word about Anwar el-Sadat, whom an ill-informed world stubbornly insisted was the President of Egypt, the real and only President of Egypt – in short, el-ra'is. From the basement cellar where I sketched the global skyline, Sadat's pretensions (I don't deny that he honestly believed himself to be President of Egypt) looked no more credible than those of Ubu Roi. The author in Gamal had always had one, big-big problem about Sadat: I didn't know him. I didn't know his lady-wife. I didn't know his children. I'd never got a foot inside the Sadat door. In short, the Sadats were a washout.

Fawzi el-Sharaf agreed. In recent years he had completely forgotten the existence of his 'dear brother'; he contentedly pursued a parallel presidency and flew all over the world in his Boeing looking exactly like Sadat. I can now reveal that it was Sharaf who made the heroic-historic journey to Jerusalem, and if everyone – Israelis, Palestinians, CBS television crews – suffered from the delusion that he was the lookalike Sadat, he was too much of a gentleman to stigmatize the error. He had, after all, always done what Sadat would have done had he done it, so no one need get too upset, no treaties need be torn up, no pledges of lasting peace need be thrown in the bin.

I hope that clears the air as our President Sharaf hurtles above the Sinai desert on his way from Abu Sweir airbase to Ben-Gurion, Tel Aviv, accompanied by the American television networks and half the world's press. I reached Jerusalem two days ahead of Sharaf and insisted on taking up residence in a fine old hotel in the eastern, Arab, quarter of the city, where Salah el-Din Street runs down to Herod's Gate, a stone's throw from the Dome on the Rock. (Salah el-Din was none other than Saladin, known to bored English schoolboys as Safety Pin.) My Jerusalem hotel had, as they say, known better days and those days had ended in June 1967. Scarcely a tourist had set foot since that time and the air of decay was palpable. The Israelis warned me they could not guarantee my safety in East Jerusalem. Every step I took and didn't take was shadowed by Sephardis from Mossad, indistinguishable from Arabs except to Arabs.

My first morning I awoke to the scream of police sirens. Salah el-Din Street was plastered in blown-up photos of Huda. The Sephardis were tearing them down.

My old friend Sabri Mansour, once a fellow-student in Cairo – I had haunted the university rather than attended it – arrived at the hotel with a company of Palestinian journalists and intellectuals bristling for a fight. Huda's doe-eyes arrived with them – more leaflets. They shook my leprous hand with loathing.

'Why,' they crowded in on me, 'is Sharaf doing this?'

'Four wars have got you where?' I asked.

'We Palestinians,' Mansour said, 'have suffered the wretchedness and bitterness of being displaced to solve a European problem, the persecution of the Jews.'

'You are exactly right.'

'A problem for which we Arabs were in no way responsible.'

'In no way, Sabri.'

'We have watched in anguish as the State of Israel has used, exploited, the historical suffering of the Jews, to justify our own suffering.'

I nodded. 'If Sharaf does not get peace with honour, there will be no peace.'

'There will be no honour! Sharaf would sell his "honour" for a pile of sand in Sinai. You should listen to his brave daughter, Huda.'

And why, they demanded, was the Egyptian press now describing Palestinians as parasites and wheeler-dealers who had sold their land to the Zionists?

'Anis Hussein is not the Egyptian press,' I said.

I was loudly reminded that when Sharaf arrived to address the Knesset, he would be flanked by Itzhak Shamir, former Stern Gang leader, and by Menachim Begin, former Irgun terrorist – the two men who had supervised the massacre of Deir Yassin. My friends insisted on driving me to Deir Yassin; an Israeli hospital now occupied the site where, at 4.30 on the morning of April 9th, 1948, a combined force of Stern and Irgun had attacked the sleeping village. Two hundred and fifty Arabs had been slaughtered. Some twenty-five survivors had been loaded into lorries and taken on a victory parade through Jerusalem – then shot in a nearby quarry.

'And now Sharaf will break bread with these men!'

'Sharaf cannot chose the leaders of Israel,' I said. 'The PLO itself would negotiate with Begin and Shamir if given half a chance.'

'Never! Never!'

'Then who do you negotiate with?'

'We do not negotiate. The State of Israel has no right to exist. You should listen to Huda el-Sharaf, Gamal!'

'Do not,' I advised them, 'allow Sharaf to become the focus and scapegoat for your frustrations.'

'And what,' I was asked, 'does Mahmoud think of all this?'

☙

'Huwwa geh, he's arrived!' Trumpets sounded, spotlights played as Egypt 01 touched down at Ben-Gurion.

'I'm seeing it, but I don't believe it,' a famous Israeli radio commentator yelled into his microphone. This was my new friend Moshe Aronson, who was standing next to me as the Rais descended from the Presidential Boeing wearing a smart grey suit over a bullet-proof vest. Moshe suddenly hugged me. 'Right here beside me,' he went on yelling, 'is my Egyptian colleague Gamal Rahman, the distinguished journalist who is now assistant press officer to President Fawzi el-Sharaf.' Moshe switched from Hebrew into English: 'Gamal, tell our listeners in Israel how you feel at this historic moment!'

'Moshe, I wish I could say it in Hebrew, but Allah akhbar, God is great, and this God is our God and your God, the same God.'

'Bravely spoken, wisely said,' cried Moshe.

And yet! yet! – only a moment before the Rais's plane arrived, Moshe, who wore a white cotton shirt with sleeves short enough to reveal biceps and triceps which had been up to no good in several wars, had been inflicting the usual belligerent lecture on me.

'Are young Egyptians aware, Gamal, that during the nineteen years of Jordanian rule in East Jerusalem, the holy places of the Old City were barred to Jews of all nationalities, and to Israelis of all religions, except for one day in the year, Christmas, when Israeli Christians were allowed across the line for a few hours?'

'I'm not the King of Jordan and never was.'

'They destroyed the Jewish quarter of the Old City! They desecrated every Jewish cemetery!'

Eight thousand newsmen plunged into the temporary Press Centre, the Jerusalem Municipal Theatre. Among them was my 'colleague' Anis Hussein, Hitler-fan and Holocaust-scoffer, now poised to reveal that, 'The Israeli in no way resembles the image of the puny, bald, hook-nosed Jew who would sell everything, even his honour, for a profit.'

After trailing behind the Rais through the Yad Vashem memorial to the Holocaust, I was glad that a crowd of jeering Hasidim, half-

364

blind from generations of futile study, deadly pale under their broad-brimmed black hats – I spotted Isaac among them – had been safely corralled by the police in a patch of trees planted in honour of the 'Righteous of the Nations'. Hoping to be included among the Righteous, I paid one dollar for a stick bearing both flags, and $3.50 for a tee-shirt depicting a grinning Sharaf and Begin clutching a bright red heart: 'All You Need is Love.' Journalists crowded round for background briefings! What's Sharaf like, what does he eat, how often does he pray, what are his dreams?

I was a man inspired: 'Sharaf embodies the enigmatic wisdom of the Sphinx. Politician, philosopher, prophet, peasant – Sharaf is all four sides of the Egyptian pyramid. This is hard for the Western mind to understand – a geometry as strict in its logic yet as religious in its inspiration as the Pyramids. And is one ever sure which side of a pyramid one is looking at?'

'How do we know that Sharaf doesn't mean war when he says peace?' I was asked.

'In the year 628 the Prophet Muhammad, peace be upon him, signed the Hudabiya Treaty with a Jewish tribe, the Banu Kurayza. Why should we do less?'

I didn't add that the Prophet later massacred the Banu Kurayza in what I suppose must have been broad daylight or dead of night. The Hasidic crazies who regularly turned up outside my hotel didn't need to be reminded – most of them had been alive at the time.

'Huda!' they chanted viciously, 'Huda el-Sharaf, assassin!'

಄

Huda! Celia increasingly suffers from psychic disturbances concerning her runaway younger daughter. Frequently she chats by telephone with a phantom, congratulating 'Huda' on not having married the disgusting Andy Poppy, whose Faruk-like lifestyle in the pleasure-holes of Europe filled every glossy mag. I am enlisted as an audience to these bizarre, one-way conversations. 'Darling, I was always against your marrying Andy, it was your father who insisted.'

Celia misses Huda, she grieves over Huda, she reproaches herself – Hamida offers her nothing cosy, nothing a mother can mother.

'Yes, darling, but when shall we see you? I hear you met Gamal in Paris recently though he denies it. I've even heard rumours that you and he were married but that's just a silly story Hamida picked up from her agents in Paris, isn't it?'

Celia turns to me. 'Isn't it, Gamal?'

'Yes, madame.'

'Huda' has rung off. It's uncanny. I can almost hear the click at the other end.

'And what about Hamida?' Celia cries. 'No one can have her. Bahrain went home in tears; Abu Dhabi threatened to kill himself; Qatar did. She tears the hearts of men in halves.'

'Before eating them.'

'You have no feelings at all, Gamal. And you're always borrowing money. Hamida says you now owe us one hundred and seventy-five thousand dollars. She calls it fifteen years of spongeing. It's lucky for you I've never cared about money.'

Gamal tenderly kisses Celia's hand. 'Queen of Egypt, my Cleopatra.'

'Now do slip away, dear, the Rais is due back any minute.'

'He's in Omah, madame, trying to bail out the King, the last of the Rais's allies.'

'Liar! Is he? *Is* he? My dearest friend, Queen Mia, will be heart-broken not to see me.' Celia stares into space, distraught; she happens to be wearing a dressing gown adorned with royal oryx, a gift from Mia. 'But the Omah Empire dates back 3,000 years! It's almost as old as our own! It must never get out that I was not invited! How could Mia not invite me? This must never get out, Gamal. I am in Omah with Fawzi – is that understood?'

'Madam, you are wherever you wish to be. I would however point out that Queen Mia was until recently a Lebanese air hostess, the daughter of a belly dancer, and the King a Bedouin bandit.'

'It must never get out that I was not invited!' Celia screams.

I pick up the telephone and dictate a report to the news desk at *Misr.*

The deep personal bond between the Rais and the King of Omah, two statesmen of world stature, was movingly conveyed today when the King and Queen Mia royally entertained our Rais and our First Lady. The King invited the Presidential couple to drive in his Cadillac convertible from their hotel in Yahar, on the Red Sea, to the Imperial Oryx Palace. The King took the wheel – he is also a keen deep-sea diver – and drove at such speed across Omah's new suspension bridge, a gift from the Shah of Iran, that a train of mules landed in the water, along with the Rais's toupee and the First Lady's eyelashes.

'Keep your hair on!' the King joked.

Afterwards, in an exclusive interview with this correspondent, the First Lady described her day as 'enormous fun' and expressed her admiration for the social reforms undertaken by the royal couple. Three per cent of Omah's children now attend the Kingdom's only primary school.

Later the Presidential couple attended a farewell banquet of rare magnificence. The steps leading into the Oryx Palace are built upon the skulls and severed limbs of convicted criminals (i.e. the King's critics). The special national delicacy, the pièce de résistance, the eye of a live sheep, was offered to Mrs Sharaf, who swallowed it without hesitation and to loud applause – the story of her life. The Rais and the First Lady are due to fly on to a secret destination tomorrow. It is unlikely to be an Arab capital, since every other Arab nation has broken off diplomatic relations with Egypt since the Rais was seen embracing Golda Meir in Jerusalem. Despite the snarls of Communist malcontents, Egypt's worldwide diplomatic prestige has never been higher.

Celia sits on her Second Empire canapé and cries. She has the jitters and is tossing a pharmacy of little pills and capsules on to a dry tongue. Bravely she insists that she will attend the Women's International Conference in Oslo, though State Security (Hamida) have warned her that the Palestinian delegation are planning to stage a disgraceful scene and disrupt her scheduled speech. Worse yet, Huda may be among them: 'Madam Sharaf,' she will yell across the floor of the conference hall, 'you have betrayed your Arab sisters to the Zionist oppressor! The women of Jerusalem, Hebron, Nablus, Jericho, Bethlehem and Ramallah will never forgive you. I am ashamed to be your daughter – I am no longer your daughter!'

Celia wants me to accompany her to Oslo. Normally I would have jumped at the opportunity to view the Munch collection, that inspired madman, but unfortunately Hamida had set me to work preparing a judicial indictment of Hosny Hikmat.

The Toad – you have missed his mordant company? – had embarked on nonstop unauthorized globetrotting. Messages I received from Mao's Model Farm, or the Central Africa of the cannibal Emperor Bokassa, indicated an ongoing dementia. A surreal account of an all-night banquet in the Kremlin – Brezhnev had apparently confided to the Toad the exact date and time of World War III – ceased only when the line went dead and the voice of a Russian woman operator announced, 'You have been discontinued, please.'

Hikmat should never have gone to Moscow. The onion domes of the Kremlin were strictly out-of-bounds. Signing unauthorized treaties with Amin of Uganda or the Emperor Bokassa was tolerable – Sharaf was a slow-to-anger man – but when Hosny Hikmat returned from Moscow carrying contracts for two nuclear power stations, to be paid for in hard currency, the Toad landed in a pond drained of water.

'Your boss is to be charged with High Treason,' Hamida warned me from behind her shimmering, glass-topped desk in State Security. 'The Rais suspects you of plotting with Hikmat. So do I. Your own evidence against him will be essential to the prosecution.'

'But, Princess – '

'Don't call me that! In the Republic of Egypt I, and I alone, am addressed as Mademoiselle.'

'With a capital M from here on in?'

One of Hamida's braided, bemedalled State Security colonels moved as if to beat me to death with his white gloves, but the Virgin of Egypt abruptly commanded her aides to make themselves scarce.

'Gamal, you're not going to disappoint me?'

'I am your adoring slave, mademoiselle. Oops – capital M.'

'We have definite proof that Hikmat has been in contact with Huda. Her terrorist cells in Upper Egypt are now funded by Libya and the Soviets.'

I shrugged: it sounded more plausible than most of Hamida's shots across the dark night of tyranny's tormented soul.

'When did you last meet Huda, Gamal? I want the truth.'

'Many years ago – before her engagement to Andy Poppy.'

'You met Huda in Paris.' Hamida tossed a file of snapshots at me, most taken at the pavement café in the Champs-Elysées, but some, blurred and impenetrable, inside what might have been a mosque.

'Your wedding to Huda, Gamal.' Hamida is pacing her torture chamber. 'Why did you lie to me, Gamal?'

'Everyone does it, Mademoiselle.'

'You gave me your word of honour about Huda, remember?'

'It was a pact of union between us which you promptly broke by promising a bath full of ass's milk, before having me kicked down the stairs.'

'You had the impertinence to make demands beyond your station! Be grateful I never told Pappi! Snake! Traitor!'

'If the Sharafs had treated their younger daughter with genuine affection and respect, they would not have created a dangerous rebel.'

'Ha! Huda was always Mama's darling. Mama never makes imaginary phone calls to *me*! Do you know who Huda really hates? Me!'

I nodded. 'She may be jealous of your beauty.'

Hamida scrutnized me. 'Did she say that?'

'She constantly asked me whether I found you more beautiful than her.'

'Oh? And what did you say?'

'I said yes.'

'Is that true? Liar! I do not believe Huda married you. No Sharaf would ever stoop so low. Huda deserves the firing squad, but she is still my father's daughter.'

'Quite so.'

'How do you explain these pictures in the mosque? They come from one of our most reliable agents.'

'She may have married me. I'm not sure that I married her.'

'Your disgusting conceit! Shall I tell you what's wrong with your unreadable novels, which Huda so admires – I know she does – or do you despise the opinion of someone who never studied literature in Paris?'

'I shall pay close attention.'

'What's wrong with your novels, Gamal, is nothing to do with why they're banned in Egypt. Nothing to do with your vile, libellous portrait of the Sharaf family. No work of fiction, however "intellectual", can survive unless the author actually cares about the characters he creates or describes. I don't mean paint them in glowing, romantic colours, I mean *care* about them. *Believe* in them. You only believe in the author – yourself.'

'Technically – '

Hamida smiled, a rare thing. 'Your illustrious father is my source.' Hamida's smile had now become part of her – I'd never seen this before. She lifted her feet high on her glass-topped desk. 'Want a drink, Gamal? There's a bottle of brandy in that cupboard. Bring two glasses.'

I did so.

'Gamal, I wish to discuss my forthcoming visit to the Maison française.'

'Of course. A very special occasion to mark the opening of the exhibition 'Egypte en France, France en Egypte.'

'Your friend Henri Chevalier will attend?'

'I might intercede.'

'Make sure you do. Inform Monsieur Chevalier that I may be disposed to grant him an exclusive interview.'

'Jawohl.'

'Now get out.'

❧

Summoned back to State Security, I found an exhausted Hosny

369

Hikmat in the Prosecutor's office, confronted by the whole of his career, file after file. How ill he looked.

'Ha!' cackled the Toad as I was dragged into the windowless interrogation chamber, 'Ha! Judas arrives!'

Also on display was a large folder of yellowing newsprint – the 'treasonous' articles he'd written twenty years earlier. The Toad flicked his tongue across the cracked lips of his broad mouth and laughed:

'At that time I was Minister of Information, Acting Minister of Foreign Affairs and editor of *Misr.*'

The Prosecutor nodded – our old friend Dr Hatem. 'Therefore, Hikmat, you were already a foreign agent when you held positions of the highest national trust.' Dr Hatem then produced the black files which the Rais had shown us a month before the war of October 1973 – The Crossing.

'Mr Rahman, you were present when Hikmat stole these Top Secret files from the Rais's residence? You protested, of course, but Hikmat threatened you with instant dismissal?'

The Toad chuckled nastily. 'The Rais himself insisted on showing us every detail of the military plans.'

'Silence, Hikmat! I was addressing Mr Rahman.'

I did my jellybaby shrug. 'The Rais showed us the black binders, just as you are doing, sir, and laughed, and slapped us on the back, and slammed us in the ribs, and said, "I bet you'd give your right eye to see inside these, Hosny." Naturally Mr Hikmat was shocked and urged the Rais to lock the files away.'

Prosecutor Hatem's fist collided with his desk on a downward trajectory. 'You're lying! The Rais clearly remembers Hikmat stealing the entire War Plan.'

The Toad guffawed. 'You mean I just grabbed it and ran off into the night?' A bad bout of tubercular coughing followed this guffaw – an own-joke had always been the most likely cause of the Boss's demise.

'Take the defendant to the washroom,' the Prosecutor instructed an aide. 'Now, Rahman – enough fooling. The Rais clearly rememers that you telephoned his office next morning to warn him that Hikmat had stolen the War Plan and sold it to the Israelis.'

'The Rais has a better memory than I.'

'Under Article 34 of the new Constitution, the President for Life's memory is infallible.'

'Agreed. But I distinctly remember passing the War Plan to the Israelis myself. It was merely my patriotic duty. As soon as Mossad's agents in New York and Cyprus informed Moshe Dayan that I was the source of the leak, Dayan didn't believe a word of it – for which I deserve the Order of the Nile.'

The Prosecutor stood up, sat down, stood up. 'But you are not the accused, Rahman!'

'Quite. And now, sir, if you will excuse me I have pressing business on behalf of Mademoiselle.'

༄

Mademoiselle Hamida el-Sharaf, Daughter for Life of the President for Life, is the guest-of-honour of the Maison française. The occasion (as you already know) is the opening of a most splendid exhibition called 'Egypt in France, France in Egypt.' The sale of a dozen Mystère combat aircraft to Egypt is at stake. This being so, the French Ambassador has naturally invited Madame Celia to do the honours and has sent several nervous cables to Paris after Mademoiselle Hamida accepted on her mother's behalf. Could this mean only six Mystères – or none? Or is the Rais about to divorce his wife?

Henri has been badgering me for inside information about the Sharafs but I see no reason to disclose that the Rais had confined Celia to private life after she confessed that she'd inspired my bogus report about her visit to Omah as his consort.

'You have made me the laughing stock of the world,' Sharaf had reprimanded her. 'My father warned me not to marry a foreigner.'

'And maybe you will deign to explain why you sneaked off to Omah without me, making me the laughing stock of the world. The Empress of Iran and the Queen of Omah herself, my dearest friends, telephoned in tears to ask whether you intended to divorce me. The shame! The humiliation! First Lady of Egypt! Oh!'

'As for your fancy boy, Gamal Rahman, he will go on trial with Hikmat!'

'No! I ordered him to do it!'

But it was Hamida who intervened on my behalf; her agents were convinced that Huda was back in Egypt and set on claiming her husband. Huda's fundamentalist terrorists threatened the Sharaf regime no less dangerously than the Ayatollah Khomeini threatened the Shah's. G. Rahman must remain, all sixteen stone of him, at liberty.

Mademoiselle Hamida arrives in a cortège of limousines at the Maison française. She is dressed by Pierre Cardin in shocking pink for the occasion. The French Ambassador kisses her hand. The Director of the Maison kisses her hand. Her dark, threatening eyes swivel coolly along the ranks of assembled journalists. There is the thunder of Eros in her diplomatic smile. She is shown the prize exhibits: Léon Cogniet's 'Portrait de François Champillon', 1831, specially imported from the Musée du Louvre; then Champillon's book, *Des Hieroglyphes phonétiques employés par les égyptiens*... The Director is chattering away to her about the 'seminal significance' of this bloody frog, Champillon, but she moves on restlessly, in a heat of her own. As for Maxime du Camp's treasured photograph, 'Flaubert en Caire, 1850,' it diverts her not at all. Nothing does.

Abruptly she halts. Everyone halts.

'I believe there are several distinguished French journalists present today,' she addresses the Director.

'Certainly, Mademoiselle.'

'I wish to convey to them my father's personal greetings. The Rais has a great respect for the French press, as you know.'

'Indeed, indeed, Mademoiselle.'

'My father regards French newspapers as a model to the world.'

'Why yes, Mademoiselle – certainly!'

'My father particularly asked me to converse with each of your invited correspondents individually. Perhaps you would kindly place your own office at my disposal, Monsieur le Directeur. Yes? Thank you. My friend Mr Rahman will introduce them to me in turn. He is such an excellent interpreter. My family has relied on him for many years.'

Duly conducted to the Director's office, Mademoiselle commands her aides and bodyguards to remain outside. Chairs are hastily placed in the corridor for the Ambassador, the Director, and their wives. Everyone else – the staff of the Maison, the curators of the exhibition, Hamida's retinue and the Egyptian journalists more or less hang upside down like fruit bats in a reverential hush.

I lead the surprised correspondent from Agence France Presse into the Diretor's office, closing the door behind us. I introduce him to the Princess.

'Please tell me about your work, Monsieur Louvain,' Hamida says in Arabic. Louvain registers surprise – Mademoiselle has been speaking perfectly good French up to this moment. Three minutes later the man from *Le Figaro* is put through the same routine. The interview is even more rapidly concluded.

'I am unfortunately behind time,' she tells him, 'but it would not do to disappoint your distinguished colleague from *Le Monde* – would it?'

'Of course not, Mademoiselle.'

'Gamal, kindly bring him to me.'

Henri steps into the Director's office and suavely kisses her proferred hand. She appraises him head to toe, as men study women.

'We have never met,' she informs him. Henri is too much the gentleman to argue. 'I have heard much about you from Gamal,' she says. 'I cannot imagine why you should wish to keep such dubious company.'

'Friendship follows no rules, Mademoiselle.'

'I am told that you admire Camus. We all admire Camus here in Egypt. Ours is a very ancient civilization, you know.'

'But also modern, progressive, egalitarian – '

'Gamal tells me that you are married. What a pity that your wife has not been able to accompany you to Egypt. We in Egypt very much admire French ladies. My mother and I frequently visit Paris. We have visited the Louvre and the Galéries Lafayette many times.'

Hamida is prowling the Director's office as she speaks. The voltage is fantastic. Now she passes the official portrait of President Giscard d'Estaing over the Director's desk. 'My father greatly admires your President,' she says. Now she passes an etching of 'Napoleon on the Nile', now the profiled, non-Nubian bas-relief of her own father, now she insolently swings herself into Monsieur le Directeur's ultra-modern swivel-chair of black leather.

'Tell me, Monsieur Henri of *Le Monde*, who is the most powerful woman in Egypt?'

'You, Mademoiselle. And – forgive me – the most beautiful.'

'So why should she suffer the odious attentions of this fat, obsequious, evil-smelling "friend" of yours? Why should she not be free to entertain, at her private pleasure, handsome Frenchmen who graduated brilliantly from the École normale supérieure?'

Henri is struck dumb.

'And what do you say, Gamal?' Hamida asks.

'I say, Mademoiselle, that you are experiencing – and not for the first time – the sensation of living inside a text written by me.'

But even as I utter this imbecility the Virgin of Egypt is throwing off her shocking pink costume by Pierre Cardin. From the Director's swivel-chair her gaze never loosens its grip on Henri's.

'You would not insult the daughter of the Rais by doing less, Monsieur Henri of *Le Monde*?'

'Mademoiselle!'

Henri's jacket and trousers lie on the Director's very clean, very priceless, Persian carpet. Hamida's high heels surface on the Director's desk. With a helpless moan Albert Camus's hero, Dr Bernard Rieux of Oran, kneels beside her.

'Mademoiselle,' I interpose, 'we are all of us inhabitants of the *Arabian Nights*. You surely remember the captive virgin whose name is difficult to spell, Scheherazade?'

373

Hamida's long, tapering fingernails are excavating the roots of Henri's helpless hair.

'I remember everything,' she says.

'As you recall, Mademoiselle, Scheherazade was the virgin whom the Sultan condemned to die for the most capricious of motives – a form of revenge for the infidelity of his own wife. And how did Scheherazade sue for her life? By spinning stories which the Sultan could not resist.'

'Like fat Gamal.'

'Like fat Gamal, Mademoiselle. And he, like Scheherazade, when confronted with power, the absolute power of the state, has only words with which to defend himself.'

'Himself? Poor Scheherazade found herself singing for her life rather than for her supper. You are a free man, Gamal, free to leave, free to remain and chronicle Egypt's enduring love of France. Is that not so, Monsieur Henri – perhaps your friend has suffered from too much freedom under our benevolent rule?'

Henri resembles a dug-up Dordogne truffle which had expected to live out another winter. 'Ontologically speaking, Mademoiselle, I – '

'Gamal knows the difference between his supper and his life.' Hamida wraps her stockinged thighs around Henri's neck under the bleak gaze of President Giscard d'Estaing.

'All narratives are treacherous, Mademoiselle,' I beg-plead. 'One could say that Scheherazade – '

'I am not interested in the *Arabian Nights*. They took place in Baghdad. We Egyptians are not primitives.'

Dr Rieux's shirt tails are now rumpled around his waist as the Director's chair swivels giddily.

'Mademoiselle,' I exclaim, 'the *Nights* seethes with a hidden text – Cairo during the reign of the Mamelukes, the medieval capital of Islam, a city in which more than half the streets ended in a cul de sac – the blind alley, the zuqaq, of Mahmoud's most popular novel.'

The Maison française is shaking at its foundations. Is it an earthquake? The prize exhibits, the 'Portrait de François Champillon' and Maxime du Camp's 'Flaubert en Caire, 1850', fall from the walls to the sound of splintering frames and cracking glass. Ah, Max, licentious travelling companion to Gustave.

'Flaubert was besotted with Egyptian dancing girls,' I shout in Henri's ear. 'And what did he get? The pox!'

This does the trick: literature is Henri's gendarme. The most famously unruptured hymen in the Middle East remains (for the moment) intact.

'You remember Flaubert's girl Kulchuk?' I press him. 'She wore a large tarboosh with a blue tassel and a small spray of artificial flowers. Her breasts were shaped like apples, Flaubert reports, not the usual pears, not tangerines or figs.'

'Apples?' Henri is clearly thinking again. Hamida laughs.

'And my breasts, Monsieur Henri, how would you liken them?'

'Orbs of joy,' he moans. His mouth fastens on her left nipple. (All is lost.)

I throw my last card: 'Flaubert copulated with Kulchuk for a second time after staining the divan during a coup with Safia Zugairah – little Sophie. Flaubert's shame is our chastening heritage, Henri.'

Alas! Henri evidently remembers the great writer's concluding observation: 'Her cunt felt like rolls of velvet as she made me come.' Henri is now unstoppable. Into the velvet tunnel he plunges, wild-eyed. And out he comes. Hamida, as I'd suspected, has her price: Cairo is worth a cock.

'Would you betray your wife for me, Monsieur Henri!'

'No never! Yes!'

'Would you betray your "friend" here for me?'

'But he is my copain. Yes!'

'Betray your "copain" now, Monsieur Henri. Did he marry Huda in Paris? Were you present at the ceremony?'

'Yes! I conspired. My wife conspired. Gamal conspired. He knows where she is. Torture him, Mademoiselle, pump him full of water, jump on his stomach – he carries a photograph of her covered in kisses, his kisses, her kisses.'

Hamida seems delighted by this confession – or by her power to extract it – and Henri is duly rewarded. No one in the farthest slum quarter of Cairo, not even the deaf, could be in any doubt about the moment Henri came. Indeed all the city's clocks stopped.

The courtesy extended by the Rais's daughter to the man from *Le Monde* has now – all watches in the corridor tell the same story – run to twenty minutes. Yet Hamida's bodyguards, beserk with anxiety, dare not enter or even knock. (And so it had been, ten years earlier, during the famous train journey from Alex to Cairo.)

The Director knocks. He is a man of action, after all, when the action is over.

'Mademoiselle?'

'Attendez un instant, monsieur.' The voice is Gamal's, faithful to the last. Hamida is straightening her hair with fast, efficient motions and fixing her make-up in the faintly reflecting glass covering President Giscard.

The following day Egypt confirmed its intention to purchase twelve Mystères from France.

ௐ

His entretien with Hamida has turned Henri into a penitent pedant. He now wears hair shirts in the heat of the day and scourges himself (and me) with a torrent of self-castigation. He has embraced Islam. Disguised as fellahin and swathed in brown galabiyeh, turbans and beards, we enter the twisting alleyways of Zawiya el-Hamra, that other Cairo where the streets are barely passable to the occasional motor vehicle lurching between the pits, cracks, gullies, ravines, heaps of garbage and cesspools. The sheer density of humanity, the unplanned outcome of massive immigration from the countryside, has brought Henri's naïve Marxism back from hibernation – although it is now an Islamic Marxism heading (I gather) for the sanctuary of the hidden-away mosque of the Gama'at Islami (heaven help us).

'The brethren will shelter us.'

'From what?' I ask sourly. 'From the brethren?'

'From the State, the oligopoly.'

A few steps on and I am addressed by Camus himself: 'Les gens sont meilleurs qu'ils ne paraissent – people are better than they seem.'

'But, as Rieux points out, all victories of the human spirit are provisional.'

'Have faith, Brother.'

It's Friday prayer time and the overflow of worshippers has spilled out of the Gama'at Islamiya Mosque into the alley. The emir's attendants are lovingly spreading awnings across the street to protect those at prayer from the sun. Henri salutes the emir, a slender, mild-mannered young man, in the name of Allah. Despite our grotesque disguises (Henri's bright idea), the emir embraces him as an old friend.

'Allah is great!'

'Allah akhbar!'

We are invited to wash hands and feet then sit cross-legged on the matted floor of the mosque. I have difficulty, as always, in crossing my legs. After the prayers, when the congregation has evaporated through a myriad of adjoining alleyways, a group of devotees gathers round the young emir, eager to hear the full details of Henri's 'persecution' by the forces of Shaytan. The Koran lies in the emir's lap.

'You are very young for so responsible a vocation,' I address the emir.

'I am thirty-one. I was a graduate from the Al-Azhar University. Then I was without work. No jobs for graduates.' He smiles. 'I began to work among the poor.'

I ask the emir what he thinks of Sharaf. This question provokes consternation, indignation, among the faithful; they warn the emir that I may yet be a police spy. At this juncture Henri wisely reinjects himself into the conversation, stressing his Catholic upbringing in Charente – this wins the hearts of his audience; no one has anything against home-grown French Christians, only the stubbornly Egyptian Coptic variety.

'We are from one family tree, the tree of Ibrahim,' Henri tells the emir. 'We Catholics have also suffered insults from the State in France. I would happily assassinate the President of France, who is an atheist.'

I gaze at my friend with profound admiration. Only yesterday (having secured his country's aircraft industry by way of the velvet tunnel) he was telling me about his loathing for the French politicians currently campaigning on behalf of the Catholic écoles libres at the expense of the secular schools.

'To spill the blood of an infidel ruler is God's work,' the emir declares. 'Our mission is to restore the sovereignty of God on earth. The caliphate is His instrument.'

'And does Sharaf know the devil?' Henri asks.

'He knows the devil. Sharaf wears a mask. "Who so ruleth not by that which Allah revealed: such are the disbelievers." Sharaf is a pharaoh.'

'Is there a truly Islamic society in the world today?' Henri asks with the air of one who knows the answer.

'Nowhere. The Muslim world today is in a state of jahiliyyah, by which we mean pre-Islamic ignorance.'

Bloody priests! The Muslim faith as established by Muhammad ibn Abdullah required no imams, sheikhs or emirs. The faithful communicated directly with God through the Koran and through prayer. And what do we have now? The usual take-over, or should I say take-away, since Islam is now served up like fast food by mullahs and ayatollahs, all demanding their tarif. No longer allowed is the anguished confusion suffered by the Prophet when he heard voices, saw visions, plucked divine messages from his heart. It's all tied-up.

Only art can know Revelation.

This may not be the moment to leap up the minaret like a muezzin and seize the loudspeaker system. I have no desire to see Death

377

bending over me with his calling card, his sleeked-back hennaed hair white at the roots.

But what now! The cross-legged faithful in the Gama'at Islamiya Mosque are interrupted by a sudden commotion at the side door. A posse of bearded men in cotton trousers run in, guns slung from their shoulders. The young emir nods to them and rises. We all rise. She has come. Three women, shrouded in black and completely veiled in a style unusual in Cairo, have appeared in the doorway – a moment worthy of Ingmar Bergman.

The emir bows to Huda. We all bow.

Huda appraises my friend. 'Vous êtes très bienvenu, Monsieur Henri.'

She turns to me – what a sight I must look! – inclining her head with due respect. Clearly I have a wife on my hands. Worse, Huda is deferentially waiting for me to address her. I try to remember how ordinary, reliable Muslim-Egyptians speak to their wives, and rapidly conclude that I don't know any.

'Your presence, lady, does honour to the faithful.'

This seems to go down well. Everyone, starting with the emir, is regarding me with a new respect. For the first time in my life I'm a man. If this is what Islam brings, I'm all for it.

'With your permission,' I address the emir, 'I wish my wife to read us a passage from the Koran.'

This goes down *terrible*, which means terrific not terrible. I can't put a foot wrong. We all squat again while Huda turns the pages of the holy book with quick, confident hands until she finds the chapter known as 'The Table Spread'. She reads in a clear, confident voice (a woman reading to men in a mosque! – you can tell she's a Sharaf!), beginning with verse 33:

' "Those who make war on Allah and His Messenger will be killed or crucified." ' She then turns the pages to 'The Spoils': ' "Surely the worst of beasts in God's sight are unbelievers . . . they cannot frustrate My will. Make ready for them whatever force and strings of horses you can, to terrify thereby the enemy of God and your enemy, and others besides them that you know not; God knows them." '

Henri is wrapped in heavenly smiles but I have my doubts about the strings of horses and their punishing hoofs. This mosque, however, is clearly no place for doubters and I deflect my misgivings into the gravitas of a husbandly tutorial:

'So, wife,' I ask sternly, 'who will make ready the strings of horses?' (I can see the emir nodding: it's OK.)

'Some of us serve God by the word,' Huda replies serenely, 'some by the hand.'

'So there will be much blood?' I ask.

'Islam, husband, is a tree which must be nourished by the blood of its martyrs to spread its branches wide.'

Henri's eyes are now blazing with the joy of a pilgrim who has climbed Mount Ararat. At this moment he would gladly perform the Hajj on his head. And indeed here he goes, banging his forehead on the prayer mat, striving to work up a gatta worthy of our old friends the dustman and his donkey. I join in, there's no two ways about it, what with the emir and his brethren banging away.

The women, Huda's serviteuses, eventually lead husband and wife to a strikingly clean little room in an alleyway behind the mosque. I don't know what happened to Henri, I expect his masters in Mossad found him a little room of their own. Water is brought and then the door closes on man and wife. This may prove to be the sober version of my wedding night.

I sit on the bed while Huda kneels to unfasten my dusty shoes and peel off my rank socks. She washes my feet while my hands drift through her unveiled hair.

'Are you pleased to see me, Gamal?'

'Ilm.'

'Might I one day be beautiful to you?'

'Isn't all this a bit, well, risky?'

'Gamal, it's time to take our destiny in our own hands.'

Before we can do that, however, the narrow street beyond our alley is filled with the diesel-snarl of Hamida's State Security vehicles and the thud of steel-tipped boots.

Huda vanishes through the wall. One moment she's stroking my Judas-beard and the next she isn't there. I decide to sit tight, lacking the divine gift – and perhaps the physique – for wall-vanishing. I fall asleep, vaguely content to have evaded my wedding night for the second time.

ॐ

Those gardens! I suppose the British had a genius for it – Mahmoud said as much as we passed Sandringham Villa and Balmoral, whose previous, infidel owners had wiped their bottoms without resort to water. The old dustman, his donkey and bits and pieces of the Gothic hotel, swathed in bougainvillaea, came into view; overfed cats gazed at glittering carp lazing in lifeless pools. 'I know the fine gentleman!' the dustman of the gatta shouted. 'I pray against him. He's keeping bad company today. Stay out of my head!'

Shaytan was addressing me in his usual, leisurely way.

'You want to understand the birth of Islam, Gamal? Our friend

Gabriel – or Gibreel as you Arabs prefer – was an imperialist of the first order, for ever tapping the Almighty's elbow with alarming news of dissident rain-gods, sun-gods, totem poles and ancestral spirits. Gibreel was the Alexander the Great and Julius Caesar of monotheism.'

'You are not too keen on Gibreel?'

'To poison my Master's ear, he had cunningly stolen the vocabulary of ethics – my life's work. I had always insisted that true Morality is strictly the province of mortal men, but Gibreel convinced the Lord that Religion is the fountainhead of Morality. Pagan gods were therefore not the Lord's experiments but impudent servants of my diabolical Rebellion against the One and Only.'

'And there was no truth in that – you insist?'

'I admit that I felt at home among the easy-going deities of the Graeco-Roman world, Dionysus and Aphrodite, fun-loving creatures with no pretensions to being anything more than jumped-up humans. And what art they inspired, what philosophy, what poetry! What freedom of the spirit! Yes, yes, of course it was well known that I revelled in the sun-kissed pluralism of the Mediterranean and the Arabian desert. Gibreel's winged acolytes constantly reported my visits to Mecca and Medina – claiming that I had been caught copulating with the local goddesses of Jahilia.'

'Ah!'

'Call it harmless fun. The human species was my idea, after all. I deserved a little something from time to time.'

'So you do indeed possess the power to manifest yourself in human form?'

'Do not lapse into base superstition. My earthly powers are analogous to those of the Holy Ghost. You wanted to know about the birth of Islam, so let us concentrate on Gibreel. Imagine him on one of his spying missions to Arabia, when he spots a muscular fellow of mature aspect on his knees, deep in prayer and cursing the satraps of the local deities for his business difficulties. Gibreel bends an ear. "Talk to me, Muhammad," he murmurs. "I come from the One and Only. I am the archangel of Al-Lah." '

'And Gibreel promptly reported back to Al-Lah?'

'Yes yes. He had found just the chap, illiteracy no problem, probably an asset, a natural rebel well disposed towards Ibrahim, Moses, Jesus, and nicely fired up. Strong leadership potential, well endowed with camels, and capable of organized violence on an impressive scale. Susceptible to strong guidance.'

'In short, the Messenger? Arabia in the bag?'

'The Lord summoned me. A rare event. Did I have any objection to the liquidation of my – *my!* – pagan deities in the Arabian peninsula?'

'Did you?'

'There was Gibreel perched on my Master's lap in his latest Byzantine finery – his puffed sleeves were specially tailored to display his gilded wings – the patron of all the power-hungry popes and patriarchs who now littered God's Church. My anger rose beyond the bounds of discretion. Did the Almighty really desire to create a third human version of His Divinity – each in rampant conflict with the other? Had the Jews accepted Jesus as the son of God? Would this upstart Muhammad be likely to gain acceptance? Did the Lord desire to see His armies engage in ceaseless, bloody civil war across the face of the converted world?'

'And the Lord replied, "Quite a speech"?'

'Gibreel immediately offered a pledge: Muhammad desired only to be God's Messenger – a messenger of renewal. Christ's status as the Son was not in question.'

'And off Gibreel went to Mount Ararat?'

'Off he went. He had a field-day. Rules for everything – how to wash, what not to eat, how to clean one's arse, rules about halal slaughter and allowable sexual positions – even the sleeping camels suffered nightmares of guilt. It was the Old Testament updated, the whole desert survival-kit. That's Gibreel all over.'

'Gibreel was shrewd? The Prophet Muhammad's trances were remarkably user-friendly? He was allowed twelve wives instead of four?'

'That was certainly convenient but in my opinion a relatively trivial point when compared with Gibreel's betrayal of his pledge to the Almighty that Muhammad would acknowledge the divinity of Jesus.'

'And you – what were you doing?'

'I washed my hands of it.'

'Did you? How do you explain the legend of the Satanic verses, as mentioned by three respected early Muslim commentators, Ibn Ishaq, Ibn Sa'd and Tabari?'

'Sheer fantasy. You'll find no mention of the so-called Satanic verses in any of the six collections of hadiths assembled during the centuries after Muhammad's death.'

'But look at the Koran itself – chapter 53, lines 19 to 22, where you are clearly shown to be whispering your mischief in Muhammad's ear, encouraging him to make his peace with the pagan deities of Jahilia.'

The devil shrugged. 'According to Tabari, I wanted to make it easier for the pagans to accept the single God, Al-Lah. I therefore

inspired Muhammad to flatter the deities when addressing the idolators in the Kaaba. But why should I wish to do Gibreel's dirty work for
him? If anyone was whispering in the Prophet's ear, it was Gibreel.'

'But how can you blame Gibreel when you yourself are clearly
blamed in the Koran? I quote:

' "We sent not ever any Messenger
or Prophet before thee, but that Satan
cast into his fancy, when he was fancying;
but God annuls what Satan casts, then
God confirms His signs – surely God is
   All-knowing, All-wise – .
that He may make what Satan casts
a trial for those in whose hearts is sickness . . ." '

The devil shrugged his shrug. 'You must ask yourself in what
circumstances the Koran was assembled. The scattered fragments
were collected together from scraps of parchment and leather, tablets
of stone, ribs of palm branches, camels' shoulder blades and the
breasts of men. Only during the reign of the third caliph, 'Uthman,
was the definitive version agreed upon by a panel of editors who –
frankly – were guessing.'

'You disappoint me. I would have expected you to fight for your
principles.'

'And if I were to "confess" what would you make of it? My Master
triumphed – as always – and Gibreel's wings now cast their shadow
from Arabia to Africa. My beloved pagan goddesses of Jahilia, my
swans, died their death – like Dionysus and Aphrodite before them.'

TWENTY-FIVE

⁊

It so happened – historians – that I counted Elizabeth Taylor and Frank Sinatra among my closest friends. It went back to the time, early sixties, when Liz and her then-husband Richard came out to Egypt to shoot Cleo, though film-buffs insist not a camera set foot on Egyptian sand. How I got to know Sinatra I simply can't imagine – invent any story you like. Anyway, Liz and Frank: both great friends of Israel. Shortly before the *Playmate* disaster, I happened to be sharing a pizza with NBC's frontman, Walter Primetime, when it occurred to me that Walter was the man to get a message through to the two superstars.

I scribbled the message on the back of a napkin, stained somewhat with paprika and mozzarella: 'Dearest Liz and Frank, Whole Middle East peace process depends you contact me soonest. Gamal Rahman, c/o Madame Celia el-Sharaf, First Lady of Egypt.'

CUT.

DAY. EGYPT. NILE VALLEY. PYRAMID. SPHINX.

Liz is taking tea with Celia and half of the world's photographers. I stand between them in a new, outsize suit.

'It's crazy that Gamal turns out to be a mutual friend,' Liz tells Celia.

'Gamal is one of our most talented writers,' Celia says.

'Hey, I never knew that.'

The following day my byline reappeared in *Misr.* FIRST LADY CONFERS WITH LEADING LADY. At Celia's suggestion I was given the honour of escorting Miss Taylor by Presidential helicopter to meet the Rais in Isma'ilia.

'Welcome, Queen!' he greeted her, beaming.

This conjured a total blank from Liz.

'Have you forgotten?' the Rais guffawed. 'You are Cleopatra, Queen of Egypt!'

Then his eye fell on me. I certainly wasn't Antony.

So much for Liz but what of Frank? What a talent! And a very nice man! It was I who persuaded Frank and his musicians to fly to Egypt and perform at a charity gala for the benefit of Celia's cripples and orphans. Foreign businessmen dished up 2,500 dollars a ticket. Celia and Hamida attended a fashion show at the Mena House Hotel, featuring half-naked models parading Pierre Balmain's new collection of gilded fig-leaf bikinis. It was I who proposed an 'ivoire' theme for the fashion show and persuaded the Sharaf ladies to be made up to look like elephant's tusks by the international cosmetics firm, Passion, which was looking for an 'outlet' in the Arab world. The gala dinner was staged – at my suggestion – in the shadow of the pyramids. A $30,000 ticket secured a table for six and an Egyptian minister in attendance to advise on local markets. Philip Morris, Pan-Am, TWA and Mobil Oil payed up. Frank duly serenaded the Sphinx before I introduced him to the Rais. Gamal Rahman reports:

The two men hit it off from the first handshake. An instant meeting of minds. The Rais congratulated the great singer on his worldwide work for charity. 'We all serve one God,' the Rais told his guest. 'I am like a sufi,' the President explained to the great singer. 'Death is always close to me and I am at ease with my mortality. My life, by God's grace, has made its contribution to destiny.'

Mr Sinatra said he would like to make a feature film about the Rais's life and work. Would the Rais object if he, Mr Sinatra, played the part of the Rais in the film?

The Rais laughed heartily. 'No objection. Come and make it in Egypt. We have real pyramids here. I hope the world will be misled into believing I am as handsome as Frank Sinatra!'

The First Lady smiled and said she was very glad that her husband was not as handsome as Mr Sinatra, otherwise she would have had a hard time. Mr Sinatra then said, 'Well your husband is a great cat, Mrs Sharaf. God bless you all.'

It is understood that Mr Sinatra has been invited to visit the Rais's new rest house on Mount Sinai, plus the ten-ton tomb originally constructed for him at Muhi el-Din and subsequently moved to the Sinai desert at the Egyptian taxpayers' expense. In Saint Catherine's monastery, the Rais's American guest will be introduced to a Greek Orthodox community leading a centuries-old hermetic existence and more or less oblivious whether the soldiers wandering about in the sand outside are Ottoman Turks, British, Israelis, Egyptians or Sinatras.

Gamal Rahman (syndicated)

Here I must reluctantly unfasten the fiasco dubbed by Anis Hussein as Rahman's Revenge. Excited by the Sinatra episode (and by my agent Isaac Ben Ezra), the American magazine *Esquire* decided it urgently needed an illustrated interview with Celia el-Sharaf, working title 'The Arab Woman Who Wishes to Live in Peace with her Jewish Neighbours.'

Ecstatic, Celia took wing for fittings chez Balmain and Dior, appeared in the Pompidou box at the Paris Opéra, returned to Cairo for the first of our interviews, then flew by presidential helicopter to Luxor for tomb-photographs. Hospitals and hospices came next, hours and hours of orphans and crippled ex-soldiers expressing their gratitude to the woman who now styled herself the Mother of Heroes, although that title properly belonged to another. Finally I sent off my text. A fortnight later a cable arrived from the ineffable Isaac: 'Regret *Esquire* not interested. All other quality magazines also negative. *Playmate* will pay five thousand dollars.'

'Accept,' I cabled back without consulting the First Lady.

The interview appeared in truncated form and interspersed with nude male pinups, ads for sex aids, and cleavage-building scaffolds. Uproar ensued from Suez to Port Sa'id. The minarets reverberated with the muezzins' curses; Islamic students burnt the First Lady in effigy; the sheikhs thundered.

Tethered to a donkey cart, I was dragged barefoot to the palace. Through marble hallways I was kicked by janissaries, whipped by Nubians, sjambokked by Boers of the Presidential Guard. My smooth brow was banged on the floor by imams as punishment for my missing prayer-scar. Celia and Hamida confronted me in veils and dark gowns of mourning which touched the floor.

'You have dishonoured the First Family. This is nothing less than 'aib (shame) on the Rais, on Egypt, on Arab womanhood,' Celia said.

'You are a pimp and an atheist,' Hamida said. 'You are a Coptic Jew.' (She may have meant our old friends, Jews for Jesus.)

'You have defiled our daughter Huda,' Celia sobbed.

'You and Huda provoked the recent bread riots,' Hamida informed me. 'We can prove it.'

'You do not wash before praying and you do not pray,' Celia said.

'You have never been on the Hajj,' Hamida said. 'You are an apostate – and the Sheikh of Al-Ahzar will announce during his Friday khutba that apostasy is punishable by death.'

'The lizard on the wall has run out of shadows,' I sighed. 'Madame, the American public is now expressing boundless admiration for your unique work on behalf of Egypt's women. You and you alone can achieve miracles in this respect. A woman's right to request a divorce if her husband arrives home with one or two new wives was your idea! One day, rest assured, the President will grant your dearest wish, probably on the anniversary of The Crossing. "I, too, have crossed!" he will tell the National Assembly, "and my wife showed me the way!" Please believe me, madame, a large American public is now, for the first time, aware of your campaign on behalf of loops and coils among our rural women. Indeed, permit me to liken you to our intrepid Air Force pilots who loop the loop in our skies on the President's birthday. You are the Aswan High Dam of birth control! As for the obnoxious law which attaches to a man's testimony in court twice the weight of a woman's – if anyone can abolish such bigotry, it is Mrs Sharaf!'

And it was true: Celia had been inundated by messages of support from American women's groups since *Playmate* banged her passionate appeal for a Truly Modern Egypt up against an ad for vaginal jelly. Nor had she lacked the human touch when I asked her how she ensured that her husband invariably enjoyed, despite pressing concerns of state, of war and peace, a good night's sleep until ten in the morning.

'I always make Fawzi drink a glass of warm goat's milk before he retires for the night. This is a secret I am happy to share with other wives, though there are some little secrets that every woman likes to keep to herself.'

The *Playmate* episode precipitated a reign of terror on the university campuses of Egypt. The Student Union elections in Cairo and Alexandria resulted in sweeping gains for the Islamic Association, which immediately demanded sexual segregation in classrooms, laboratories and cafeterias. Rectors, deans and professors were held hostage. Boys and girls seen walking together were beaten up unless waving aloft a marriage license. 'Show us your license!' Galabiyehs and hijabs were distributed free: Cover Yourself! The human body was in flight from itself.

And everywhere portraits of a veiled Huda el-Sharaf.

In Cairo hundreds of young men appeared on the campus, carrying identical knives, shaped like the horn of a gazelle, burst into the Student Union, smashed the juke boxes and banned as sacrilegious any music beyond the chanting of the Koran. They then invaded the streets, insisting that Korans be displayed on dashboards, and distributing obligatory bumper stickers: 'There is no God but God and Muhammad is His Messenger.'

The jihad stormed radio and television. Whatever the programme – news, thriller, romance, comedy – it had to be interrupted by the five-times-daily voice of the muezzin. One radio station was now broadcasting the Koran nonstop. People wondered how these mullahs had got stuck inside their TV sets.

Huda was everywhere but State Security could not find her. Bearded youths brandishing sticks were regularly beating the legs of girls whose gowns did not reach the ground. By rumour a Presidential Decree was in the pipeline prescribing the death penalty for those who renounced Islam. Anis Hussein wormed back into the pages of *Misr* with a glowing account of a draft bill allowing for the amputation of thieves' hands. My wrist began to ache every time I heard the word Shari'a.

Mahmoud remained silent. Foreign journalists who solicited his comments on the crisis got nothing. Even Henri. Was Mahmoud turning his chamois'd dark glasses towards Islam out of cumulative detestation of the Sharafs' vulgarity, their opportunism, their secret police, their crammed jails, their purloined antiquities – their occasional patronage of his rotten son? Had it all got too much for Dad, creator of the God-tyrant Mustafa?

I asked him.

'I admire your brave wife,' he said, 'though I cannot imagine why she married you.'

Equally brave, Celia continued to attend classes on the university campus in Western clothes, her head uncovered. One morning a large gathering of black chador-shrouded women gathered to hiss the First Lady as she entered the campus. Although no one dared beat her legs, the shrieking women reviled her as 'modern', as 'Allah's enemy', as the apostate who sold herself to American pornography. From beneath her chador a woman produced a camera – thousands of prints were later released – at the moment Huda stepped out of the crowd to confront her mother.

'Madame Sharaf.'

Celia stood paralyzed.

Huda silently presented her with a black chador. But Celia did not take it.

Huda moved to drape the chador over her mother, then vanished back into the crowd.

Cheap reproductions of this encounter littered the city streets the following day. The most popular one was of Celia stepping back, fending off her saintly daughter's gift.

The Rais had had enough. I was summoned: 'Where are we?' he bellowed. 'In Saudi Arabia? In Libya? In Qatar? In Kuwait? This is Egypt!' After more bellowing, Sharaf suddenly put his arm round me. 'You're a good boy, Gamal. I have a job for you, as a matter of fact. We have decided to fund a Chair of International Literature –

Celia is very keen on the idea, very keen. Of course we plan to advertise the post, and there will be competition from all manner of ambitious rascals, but I believe you are the ideal man for the job. Ideal.'

'I'm flattered, sir – but may I mention that I don't even have the most humble degree.'

'Ideal. And let's hope your esteemed father will agree to serve as Chairman of the Assessors.'

'But – '

'No "buts", Gamal.' I found my arm interlocked with the sleeve of Sharaf's German-style tunic. We embarked on the familiar leopard-prowl, back and forth in an invisible cage of the Rais's imagination. 'Now, what I shall need from Professor Gamal Rahman is reliable lists of the subversives, the ring-leaders, the hard-core agitators – the scum. Staff and students. Names names names.'

'But Mr President – '

'I've always regarded you as a son, Gamal. Your mission is to hurl the filthiest kind of modern Western writing at the students – and let the fanatics expose themselves. Let them disrupt your classes. Then it's names names names.' Our interlocked leopard-prowl halted abruptly. The Rais lifted his German-style jackboot. 'Now look: I, Fawzi el-Sharaf, am stamping out the fundamentalists. Stamping. I want the arrest of 620 members of Al Takfir wa Al Hijra by the end of the lunar month – no, the calendar month.'

'But, Rais – '

'And Hamida expects you to lead us to Huda. Understood?'

'Huda is no longer Your Excellency's ambassador in Zanzibar?'

'Now go and talk to your father. Tell him that the First Lady has decided to forgive you for dishonouring her before the whole Arab world. She is merciful by nature. But I am not a woman.'

Dad finally agreed to see me. Mahmoud and I sat behind drawn blinds in uneasy silence. Once I had explained my candidacy for the new Chair of International Literature, Dad refused to have anything to do with it.

'We have enough nepotism,' he murmured. 'You are, in any case, not my candidate for such a post.'

'Baba, when will you stop looking down your nose at me? Just as cinema is *the* art form of our century, so journalism is *the* cutting edge of modern literature.'

'I fail to see the connection or the analogy.' Dad recrossed his immaculately creased legs. 'Your Auntie Lulu intends to apply for the Chair. She needs and deserves the post. This is her last opportunity.'

'Because her heroine 'Aziza could never quite throw herself from the window?'

'I deplore your cynicism, Gamal. Auntie does not hobnob with the Rais and his women. She is not a courtier or a placeman, she is not a slave to patronage. You are her nephew and owe her deference. It's even possible that you owe me deference, but that is no doubt the obsolete perspective of a mandarin.'

'I suspect Auntie Lulu is about to embrace Islam.'

'For that you must thank our "royal family". You may care to know that I myself have begun to attend Friday prayers in the Al-Azhar. I am currently in conversation with the ulama about certain matters.'

'On what terms you should renounce *The Children of Mustafa* and embrace their ban on the book?'

Mahmoud nodded.

'You would be betraying a whole generation, Dad.'

'And happily.'

'Well done the kids who beat me up outside my school, is that it?'

Mahmoud and his son sat behind drawn blinds in an uneasy silence. How happy we had once been in each other's company, me and my dad. The infant who had sat on his father's shoulders, examining his bald patch and measuring the Giza pyramids, had later perched on the great man's mental shoulders, begging knowledge, striving to write between the lines. Addressing the Swedish Academy in acceptance of his Nobel Prize, Mahmoud had laid stress on a long Muslim tradition of tolerance. After winning a famous battle against Byzantium, the Muslims, he pointed out, had exchanged their prisoners for books on the ancient Greek heritage in philosophy, medicine and mathematics.

Toleration was the burning issue. To ease the tension I raised it. 'Taking the Islamic tradition as a whole, Baba, a tall order I agree, does it indicate tolerance or not?'

'I've considered that often enough. Start with the Koran – it speaks with many voices. We are told, "O believers, take not Jews and Christians as friends; they are friends of each other. Whoso of you makes them his friends is one of them." Yet there are other more conciliatory voices – or, lest I blaspheme, messages – in the Koran. Jews, Christians and Sabeans are assured that "no fear shall be on them, nor shall they sorrow".'

'Take your pick?'

'Islamic law and practice have tended to distinguish between the monotheistic Children of the Book, the family of Ibrahim, and outright idolators. The former were generally eligible for the dhimma – which meant paying a poll tax, the jizya, and accepting certain legal disabilities as a condition for practising their religion and regulating their own communal affairs. For polytheists the choice was conversion, enslavement or death.'

'Ha! Will large numbers of idol-worshipping Aztecs, Africans and South Sea Islanders kindly step forward to take the heat off the churches and synagogues!'

Mahmoud lit a Gitane.

'There is nothing in Islamic dominion to compare with the forced conversion or mass expulsion of Jews and Muslims from Spain. Nothing to compare with the crimes perpetrated in the heart of Christian Europe.'

'And the conquest of the Balkans by the Turks?'

'If you look into it, the forced conversions at sword-point were not numerous. The majority of Bosnians who converted to Islam had belonged to the semi-Protestant sect known as the Bogomils. The best example of fanatical religious genocide in our times is the behaviour of the Catholic Church in Croatia and Bosnia during the second world war. And if we are reserving seats in hell, the Franciscans of those unhappy lands have already purchased most of the available tickets.'

'Yet Rabbi Ben Ezra – '

'May he rest in peace – '

'He used to tell us about the pogroms suffered in Syria, Iraq and Iran. He once sat me on his knee and described how Jews in Iran are not supposed to leave their houses on rainy days lest they pollute the earth . . . though I believe he said "choke the soil".'

Mahmoud allowed himself the ghost of a smile. He was still supporting Auntie Lulu for my Chair.

ᨀ

My International Literature course was packed out by grim young men in beards and shrouded females resembling walking coffins. The males sat on one side of the room, the females on the other. No one the least bit interested in Int. Lit. dared to attend, except Mrs Celia el-Sharaf who arrived without bodyguards and placed herself in the front row every Tuesday morning. She came bare-headed and wearing a two-piece costume modestly tailored, nothing visible above the shin. But she had to sit in the female section, a defeat.

Scared stiff, I hastily abandoned my announced curriculum. Goodbye Madame de Beauvoir and the second sex. Goodbye Henry Miller. Adieu, Jean Genet. Tempted to present *Waiting for Godot* as a 'profoundly religious text', I lost my nerve again and escaped into the arcane but delightful magical realism of Isabel Allende's *The*

House of the Spirits (which I'd picked up in the Charing Cross Road, rather remarkably, almost ten years before it was written – but that's magical realism for you).

I spoke in Arabic – any fooling about with English would be suicide in this company.

'So there was this terrible plague of ants,' I began – and immediately my audience was attentive, scribbling notes. 'The village people fought the ants with fire and water. They even buried sponges soaked in honey in the hope of attracting all the ants to the same spot . . . all in vain. They tried sprays and sprinklers, powders and pills. The ants merely multiplied and became even more impudent. They crawled into the children's beds, finished off the winter food reserve, started on the cows and horses.'

My peasant audience was spellbound. It's a short hop from Egypt to Latin America if you catch the right kangaroo. Only Celia in the front row looked puzzled: how could 'International Literature' be about peasants?

I continued:

'Finally the peasants brought in old Pedro Garcia. He had a reputation for arcane wisdom. The old man listened to the villagers with his hat in his hand, looking down at the ground and chewing the air with his empty gums. Then he asked for a white handkerchief. He entered the orchard followed by the villagers. The old man squatted down with difficulty and collected a fistful of ants, put them in the handkerchief, knotted its four corners, and placed the little bundle in his hat.

'Pedro Garcia addressed the ants: "I'm going to show you the way out, ants," he said. The old man mounted a horse and slowly disappeared, with the ants in his handkerchief in his hat on his head. By next morning there were no ants.'

The expressions of my male students varied from bemusement to rank suspicion. As for the females, one could only guess what was going on behind the chadors – their timorous eyes conveyed that they would not speak first, if at all.

'Now you must tell me the meaning of this story,' I said.

Silence. Then a male hand was raised.

'Was Pedro Garcia a Muslim?'

'There are very few Muslims in Latin America.'

'Was he a Christian?'

'The author does not tell us. She is silent about that.'

'Then Pedro Garcia was practising Shaytan's witchcraft.'

'But why should Shaytan wish to remove the ants?' I asked.

'To demonstrate his power, his witchcraft. That is why you have chosen this story to read to us.'

'Why – please explain.'

'You have chosen this story to undermine our faith in the one and only Al-lah.'

Celia raised her hand, a fractional, delicate gesture.

'Yes, madame?'

'I think that the villagers called in Pedro Garcia because they realized the importance of wisdom and tolerance. Pedro Garcia does not stamp on the ants, he cups them in his hand, he talks to them as if they were his friends.'

A loud murmuring in the room grew to the force of the khamseen – the wind from the desert that chokes eyes, ears, throat with stinging dust. Friends! Ants!

Celia spoke again, louder: 'Professor Rahman, can we conclude that this beautiful little story is an allegory – and therefore not really about ants?'

At this juncture I realized that Celia's presence in my class, though noble in its intention, would prove fatal. Nothing fruitful could transpire under the sweet curse of her patronage. Everything the Sharafs touched was poisoned fruit to these fired-up youngsters. And more than that: the brittle baked mud of the fundamentalist mind can be cracked only by questions – questions, questions – not by quick answers shoved down like the castor oil administered by Hamida's State Security goons.

Dear Madame [Gamal wrote], I fear that your intellectual power, which of course also represents that of the Rais himself, leaves Gamal Rahman with less professorial authority than he needs if he is to conduct this course successfully in the face of the intransigent hostility in evidence today among the students. Fully aware that your withdrawal from the class might initially be construed as a 'triumph' by the fanatics and as a 'defeat' for the liberal cultural values we both share and cherish, I therefore humbly propose that you issue a statement denouncing my course as subversive to the State of Egypt and designed to foster disaffection towards the Rais, the First Lady and Mademoiselle. This might do the trick – frankly, I cannot imagine what else will.

Your Humble Servant, et cetera

I was immediately summoned by the Rector of the University and told that the Chair of International Literature had been 'discontinued'. I was further instructed to transport myself to the Headquarters of State Security 'within the hour'.

Now, Reader, how good is your memory? Do you recall my long-ago role in another episode of magical realism, the election of the Coptic Patriarch Mikhail? Had not Gamal Rahman, in circumstances of not inconsiderable stress, recommended this young priest to the Rais, the Minister of the Interior and the Toad as the most dove-ish and sycophantic of the three papal candidates? One lives for the moment. One regrets it later, particularly when later is now.

Patriarch Mikhail was now up in arms. His churches were being bombed and burnt. The Islamic Shari'a might any moment supplant the nominally secular constitution of Egypt. The Copts did not fancy their chances under an Islamic State. Get caught in any Cairo traffic jam and a muscular young Copt with a crucifix tattooed on his arm was likely to plaster a portrait of Mikhail on your front bumper; at the next traffic jam muscular young Muslims would then put a stone through your windscreen.

Mikhail was uttering one loud blast after another. He declined the traditional Easter greetings with the President. Cancelling all Good Friday church services, the Patriarch and his bishops ostentatiously withdrew to a desert monastery of the Wadi Natrun to pray for deliverance. Sharaf ordered him to stay there.

At State Security I find Hamida nibbling a takeaway hamburger and wearing a designer-uniform of hermaphroditic severity – it's the new 'vampire-effect' much in vogue in New York.

'The Rais has a long memory,' she says. 'Since you claim to know the Patriarch Mikhail and his entourage so well, you have twenty-four hours to bring this mad priest to heel.'

'Mademoiselle, may I suggest the slogan of the hour: "No politics in religion and no religion in politics." '

She slaps me, twice, the second one a backhander loaded with heavy finger-rings. Bleeding from nose and mouth, I am chauffeur-driven into the desert, in the general direction of Patriarch Mikhail. Passing through the slums of Cairo's Zawiya el-Hamra, I count the corpses on display: communal rioting has reached the city. Thirty miles out of town we pass a ring of armoured cars and sand-bagged machine-gun emplacements surrounding a police station. My driver slows, then puts his foot down. Here is my report for *The Times* of London:

Dehan is now a ghost village. 'The police are protecting themselves first and last,' Kamel Azmi, treasurer of the local Evangelical Church, tells me. 'The police had plenty of warning that Gama'at

Islami was about to attack us. I warned them myself but they did nothing.' Kamel Azmi hobbles on crutches and carries both arms in splints – his legs and arms had been broken by a gang led by the local emir. Later Gama'at Islami returned, gunning down ten Christian farmers as they walked to their fields at dawn. The Muslim fanatics then burst into a church and shot the Christian teacher in front of his class of ten-year-olds.

When a stranger arrives in Dehan, eyes are quickly averted. 'For centuries there was harmony between Christians and Muslims in our village,' says Kamel Azmi. 'Please pray for us.' Prayer may not be enough. Asked awkward questions, officials of the Ministry of the Interior are invariably 'home for lunch'. Lunchtime now lasts the entire day.

Gamal Rahman

My driver was wise not to stop in Dehan. 'Kamel Azmi' would not have risked an interview. Ten miles beyond the village a huge, shimmering crucifix tattooed in the sky beckons us towards the Coptic Pope's monastic retreat. But hope is a shortlived commodity in Egypt. Ahead of us the road is blocked by an improvised barricade manned by militants of Gama'at Islami toting AK 47 rifles with magazines curved like sharks' fins. They recognize a Government car when they see one. Fortunately Gamal has jettisoned his letter of credential from the Rais to Mikhail and is merely carrying a 'To Whom It May Concern' from *The Times* of London.

'I'm an English journalist,' I hiss in my terrified driver's unhearing ear. 'Got it? Englizi.'

All four doors of the car are torn open simultaneously – a powerful reek of sweat, gun oil and garlic greets me.

'English,' I say in English, 'English journalist. Englizi.' I am pulled from my seat, leaving behind my usual puddle, and relieved of my watch, wallet and small change. 'English journalist,' I repeat as the chief guerrilla examines with squint-puzzled eyes my very English letter in English from the English *Times*.

'London,' I say.

'L-o-n-d-o-n,' he reads.

'L-o-n-d-o-n,' I say.

'You don't look Englizi,' he says in Arabic.

I shake my head uncomprehendingly. 'Speak only English.'

My driver meanwhile, sprawls in the dust, sobbing; they have discovered his identification papers hidden under the front seat of the car: he works for State Security. They have found his gun, too, right under his armpit. According to custom, they will slit our throats rather than waste ammunition – it's the halal method. Life, I have enjoyed knowing you: what a shame it's not reciprocal.

The steady clop of a donkey is heard on the road. A young woman resembling the Virgin Mary sits side-saddle, a haloed baby swaddled in her arms, while a despondent cuckold with Joseph written all over him leads the donkey into Egypt or out of it. Instantly recognizing the chapter and verse, the Islamic terrorists rush to take the Holy Family prisoner, though it's Good Friday.

The Virgin lifts the soft brown shawl covering her head. Joseph greets their captors in the Arabic of Upper Egypt: 'Allah is great,' he says. The baby in Huda's arms is packed with dynamite.

'Greetings, husband,' Huda addresses me. The Gama'at fighters furrow their brows: can this slug be Huda el-Sharaf's husband? My poor driver is picked up, dusted down, given water and generally treated as a freedom fighter, a Son of God who has penetrated State Security.

'So we are all heroes,' I say to Huda in French. 'You set this up. You terrorize me in order to liberate me.' She recoils from my anger, her doe-eyes widening; she is not used to being husbanded. 'A chip off the old block,' I continue, 'you and Hamida, nothing to choose between you, born to rule. By any means.'

My little wife takes me by the arm, draws me aside. 'There is no other way, Gamal. Marxism means nothing here. Not here. Yet still people are trodden down in poverty. Whom do the people turn to for food and medicine and schooling, if not the Gama'at Brethren?'

'The Brethren are simply fascists.'

I notice that the Gama'at fighters keep their backs turned to us, even at a distance, such is their deference.

'With respect,' she says, 'my husband is mistaken.'

'They slaughter Jews, they slaughter Copts, they even slaughter poets. I'm on my way to meet the Coptic Patriarch. Will he be telling me lies?'

'I have instructed the Brothers they must not harm the Christians but they have been told that the Copts are conspiring with Israel to subvert Islam.'

'So let me hear you, right now – right now! – tell them that the Copts are equally God's children.'

Huda is trembling. 'I cannot,' she whispers.

'Do you believe in God, Huda? In Allah?'

'Oh Gamal, dearest one, do not attack God!'

My driver is back behind the wheel of our car, desperate to leave and desperate not to leave: the Virgin Mary may not turn up again at the next bend in the road.

'Sharaf's soldiers will kill you, Huda. Go back to Paris – I'll take you.'

She kisses my hand as it holds her face. 'I have always loved you, Gamal.'

Three days later *The Times* carries the following report:

The Coptic Patriarch Mikhail received me in his desert hideout. 'You are a good Muslim,' he began, 'and all good Muslims know that Islam forbids forced conversions.' He then nodded to one of his muscular monks. A few moments later a young woman was brought to join us. Her name was Maria. Shyly, with lowered eyes, she was persuaded to show me the scar encircling her wrist. Although it might have been mistaken for a birthmark, the Patriarch Mikhail told me that it had been inflicted by Muslim zealots using concentrated sulphuric acid to remove the cross tattooed on Maria's skin.

The daughter of a Christian school teacher, Maria had been abducted, raped by fanatics of Gama'at Islami, kept in confinement for six months, compelled to wear a veil, and forced to memorize parts of the Koran. 'Then they took me to Al-Azhar University, where I was made to sign the papers of conversion.' Maria escaped after armed police stormed the house in search of Islamic terrorists. 'She is now in the care of the Servants of the Cross,' the Coptic Patriarch gravely explained. 'We fear what her father might do to her if he discovered that she had been raped by Muslims.'

Relations between Church and State have never been worse. 'The police and magistrates refuse to help the families of abducted Christian girls,' one of Mikhail's acolytes told me. 'The Government is a willing partner in this conspiracy. Sharaf's aim is to weaken the Christian community. We are treated as infidels – although we were in Egypt long before the birth of Islam.'

Gamal Rahman

I slept all through Easter Sunday – why not? – as the guest of the Patriarch Mikhail, while the bells of the monastery tolled mournfully in memory of Christ's Passion, Crucifixion and, hey presto, Resurrection. Dad arrived, disguised as Shaytan, and was hospitably offered a meal of dry bread and water. One of the monks neatly trimmed Dad's bald patch into a perfect tonsure.

'The devil was always a Christian,' Mahmoud murmured in my sleeping ear.

'What happened after Muhammad?' I asked.

The devil sighed his sigh. 'No sooner had the Arabs been awarded their One and Only than they were off into Persia, Syria, Spain – in His name. Jihad, jihad. Then came the Christian crusades – in His name. The question of the individual soul had long since flown out of the Divine window: a man was nothing more than the motto on his shield. Even a writer as intelligent as Daniel Defoe fell for it.'

'I can quote him.'

'Enjoy yourself.'

' "The Devil, finding it for his interest to bring his favourite Mahomet upon the stage, spread the victorious half-moon upon the ruin of the cross." '

'Yes, indeed. According to the wise Defoe, "And all Asia and Africa is at present overrun with Paganism or Mahometanism . . ." – all my work.'

'But you admit a soft spot for the pagans?'

'Oh certainly! A very peaceful, tolerant bunch on the whole. You don't catch them instructing you how to wash your groin, how to slaughter a cow, or why pork is off the menu.'

'The Hindus treat cows as sacred.'

'Granted. I'm making a case, not writing a doctoral thesis.'

'But you have nothing to say in favour of monotheism?'

'There is only one God. I should know. The damage is done by Religion. Observe the monotheists carving themselves into sects – Muslims splitting into Sunnis and Shi'ites, Christians burning each other for heresy. That was Gabriel's era par excellence – forever defining new heresies, burning witches, cutting off ears, building new versions of the Bridge of Sighs.'

'Your humped back was to the wall?'

'I was on all fours. My forked tongue was licking the shit of human folly off my forked tail. My life was a permanent pantomime of Gothic-revival castles in Transylvania, of owls and bats swooping on tame mice; my plat du jour was raped nun or roasted babe. Never was I so famous, yet so inactive.'

'Who but yourself inspired the Humanism of the Renaissance and, later, the Enlightenment of the philosophes?'

'My dear boy, that was God's work. The Divine Physicist resurfaced – He who had wanted to write the dinosaurs and primates into the Book of Genesis, now decided to experiment again with human freedom.'

'Religion was out?'

'My Master decided that the Divine Empire of Infinity had been plundered, pillaged, raped by the greedy gnomes of Dogma.'

'No hint of a mea culpa, I assume?'

'The Lord told Gabriel that Religion was a fraud perpetrated by priests and imams on Man. Heaven and Hell were now banned. Angels were abolished by decree – likewise all Scriptures and Holy Books. Gabriel's punishment was, I must say, spectacular: he was instructed to collaborate with Charles Darwin on *The Origin of Species*. At a stroke the Unknowable yielded to the Not Yet Known. I was awarded a new name: Reason. Academies with classical porticoes mushroomed. Stipends were lavished on Descartes, Newton, Diderot, Darwin. Rousseau and Robespierre sent me birthday cards after I rescued them from outright atheism by proposing a Supreme Being as Reason's natural companion. Virtue married knowledge. Morality ousted faith and sin. Good and evil were what men did to other men.'

'And you were now happy?'

I hear no answer. The scene seems to be shifting. Here comes the Patriarch Mikhail – no, it's Dad emerging from Friday prayers at Al-Azhar, shouting 'Ya Allah!', having renounced his novels and promised the ulama to stop wiping his bottom with paper, in the Western manner. 'Yes,' he announces, 'the boys who attacked my son Gamal were fully justified. The sins of the fathers must be visited on the sons.'

Dad is leaning on my arm as we walk unsteadily home from the mosque of Al-Azhar. 'I must wash my arse and forked tail in water,' he says in a voice cracked by age, 'I must not wipe them with paper.'

'Quite so, Dad. You were telling me how the European Enlightenment of the eighteenth century brought you much happiness? – not least in the company of William Blake.'

'It was I who talked him into his denunciation of the banal duality of body and soul. The churches were furious, of course. It was I who taught Blake that bodily energy is not evil – that the body is a portion of the soul discerned by the five senses.'

'*The Marriage of Heaven and Hell* – as Blake called it.'

'Man is both Reason and Desire. If the doors of perception are cleansed, everything would appear to man as it is, both finite and infinite.'

'And you met Tom Paine, too? You were responsible for his famous epithet, "My own mind is my church"?'

'It was a struggle to persuade Paine to remain faithful to a single God and Creator. He was sceptical but finally yielded when I proved to him that God regards science, philosophy and mathematics as the key to a true theology.'

'His original position before He created Man?'

'Certainly. My Master was still searching for a mathematical point of infinite density and infinitesmal extent, the true fons et origo of

Himself. This quest carried Him into general relativity and the uncertainty principle.'

'Uncertainty?'

'Oh yes. By now He was questioning His own existence. "How can I be sure of anything?" The "great conundrum", I was told, lay in the contradiction between relativity and quantum mechanics, that is to say the electromagnetic and nuclear forces which hold the familiar world together.'

'And maybe hold God together?'

'Nothing less than a "theory of everything" will satisfy His need for a "theory of Me". He tried N=8 supergravity, but that, too, didn't work out. Next it was this Black Hole idea – an object so massive and dense that nothing, not even light, can escape its gravitational pull. Lately one hears Him likening Himself to a "superstring" living in ten dimensional space – I can't claim to understand much of it.'

'And Big Bang?'

'Oh yes – the Lord strives and strives to remember whether He heard anything at the time.'

'At what time?'

'That's His problem!'

'So why is the Party of God, the Party of Allah, so potent in the world today?'

There is no answer.

∽

Wearing a new Paisley cravat, a birthday present from Celia, I am seated beside a bed which, attributed to the Empress Eugénie, enjoys a perfect view of the Mediterranean, give or take a few security walls, watch towers and steel helmets. Celia is enthroned in the bed, having her hair done and dictating her memoirs to Gamal Rahman. I notice that I am getting mixed up with the tycoon Andy Poppy in her narrative – another fatso – while Huda herself is vaporized under the hair-dryer.

The bedside telephone rings. 'You take it, Gama.'

I take it. It's the Rais. He's in a hurry. 'Tell my wife that the King has only hours before he must flee Omah.'

Celia gasps. 'Oh, poor Mia!' She grabs the red telephone and gets straight through to her friend, Queen Mia, in Omah. The Marie Antoinettes of the Middle East are at it again. I pick up the extension.

'Mia, dearest, I am so terribly concerned for you and your husband.'

'Celia, dearest, the King is confident it will all blow over.'

'Please don't forget, dearest Mia, that you and the King will always be welcome in Egypt in case of difficulty.'

'And please remind the Rais that you and he will always be welcome in Omah – in case of difficulty.'

'Goodbye, dearest Mia.'

'Goodbye, dearest Celia.'

Two days later Gamal stood not many paces behind the Sharafs at Aswan airport as the King piloted his own silver-and-blue jet, the *Oryx*, to a stop. The King looked ill. The following day the Sharafs took the King and Mia for a river trip along the Nile. Celia had prepared a bumper royal picnic, but Mia suddenly realized that the King had forgotten to bring his poison-taster from Omah.

'That fat fellow will do,' the Queen declared, pointing at me. 'Come here, boy, and taste this caviar.'

I prostrated myself at her imperial feet. 'Your Royal Highness, I beg mercy. Spare my miserable life!'

Mia was looking daggers at Celia. 'This ugly pig knows something.' Sulking, she declined to eat a thing and wouldn't let the King eat either. Protocol dictated, of course, that the hosts also had to go hungry. As the boat approached the serene waters of Lake Sharaf (formerly Lake Hook-Nose) above the High Dam, Hamida sought me out below deck, found me scoffing poisoned caviar, and fastened a claw of steel on my ear.

'Get this straight into tomorrow's *Misr*, Gamal. Word for word.'

'Word for word, Mademoiselle.'

'We are going to offer the King asylum.'

'Brave but unwise, Mademoiselle.'

'Egypt has always offered asylum to refugees from the time of when?'

'Jesus Christ?'

'And who else?'

'Hm? I believe your esteemed father would have welcomed Hitler if the exiled Führer had not preferred Patagonia.'

'The Rais has even allowed members of King Faruk's family to return. How could we close our doors to the King of Omah, who is now hounded by the whole world, even his so-called friends?'

'End of quote?'

TWENTY-SIX

⁂

Having spared the Reader for many years (and chapters) the presence of Isaac Ben Ezra, I must now offer a glimpse of my literary agent in the flesh as he zigzags neurotically across the polished boards of the million-dollar apartment overlooking Central Park which he shares with his partner, the famous ballet dancer Harold La Guardia. Did I say 'in the flesh'? Isaac and Harold between them could not tip the scales against a pound of butter (not that butter would ever gain entry to their vast refrigerator, which is filled with bottles of mineral water). On Isaac's desk lies the typescript of Gamal's latest novel, *Ra'is*. Isaac has been reading it, or pretending to, during the week since the despised Gyppo author's arrival – and never a kind word, merely variations from the Big Apple repertoire of howls.

'OK, Isaac, what does it all add up to? You hate my novel.'

'Did I say that? Did I say that, Harold, did you hear me say I "hated" Gamal's wonderful new novel?'

'Never, Issy,' Harold La Guardia purrs solemnly. Harold is incredibly elegant and due to dance Romeo at the Lincoln Center this very evening; his dark curls now kiss his ears, as befits a Montague of Verona. By contrast, Isaac resembles a length of frayed grey string.

'OK, OK,' Gamal says. 'You liked *The Patriots*, you "just loved" *The Crossing*, but the final volume of the trilogy is too "discursive", it "sprawls", minor characters "keep entering and exiting for no apparent reason", it "mistakes melodrama for drama", it's "paranoid", it's "fatally libellous", it sprawls – '

'You already said "sprawls", Gamal.' Isaac sighs. 'Harold, we have a difficult author here. We have an author who earnestly solicits criticism of work-in-progress, then accuses the critic of stamping on his head. We have an author who believes that being difficult is the obligatory club-card for the Big League. Harold, you never knew the young Gamal Rahman – that was my privilege. You never knew the Gamal who used to arrive in New York by charter flight, with one change of clothes and no return ticket, the Gamal who invariably spent his first night in the care of Immigration, the Gamal requiring a five thousand dollar bail deposit to guarantee his eventual departure from the United States. Harold, this was the Gamal who came in search of garments and accessories cast off by Jackie Kennedy after first use. While in town he would wear his shoes out up and down the Avenues, offering his cut-price services to the travel agencies. He used to stay in the YMCA on 33rd Street at risk of gang rape. He used to write to obscure state colleges offering a standard lecture called, if I remember, "Mahmoud My Father". He would tag along to the literary parties as the friend of a friend of an invited guest, invariably embracing his faintly surprised hostess with the words, "You don't know of me but you soon will." But now, Harold, we have an author who flies Business Class, excess baggage no problem, his diary dripping with appointments, lunches, interviews and background briefings for the benefit of trade department sales reps eager to learn why the "Egyptian experience" should prove deeply meaningful in Ohio, Maine and Arizona. We have an author, Harold, who is invariably accommodated in modest luxury by his long-suffering agent but is demonstrably looking for a pretext to dump that rotten, lousy, pederast-Jew-crook of an agent in the East River.'

'Issy, give over, will you,' Harold says.

'OK! So I mentioned libel. I just mentioned it, didn't I, Harold? Is it my fault that we have libel laws in the USA? Am I the murderer of the muse because I felt duty-bound to explain to Gamal that demonstrable malice is an important component of our libel laws? Did I write these laws? So I showed Gamal's chapters to our lawyers – and they came back screaming. Screaming! Gamal, will you kindly take a deep breath before you utter the word "censorship" yet again. And kindly stop rolling your eyeballs, they give me vertigo. Have a Diet Coke.'

'Whisky is preferable.'

'And one is preferable to five.'

'I brought you a 1.5 litre bottle from Duty Free.'

'You brought *me* this treasure? Do I drink whisky? Does Harold drink whisky?'

'Issy, you're not making our guest feel good,' Harold says. 'You can see he's gravitationally challenged.'

'I can indeed see! Gamal, when I met you at JFK after waiting two hours for your Middle East Airlines donkey cart to fall out of the sky – *must* you always fly Middle East Airlines? – do they give you two seats for the price of one? – we could scarcely squeeze you through the turnstiles. You promised me to lose three stone within a week. And yet! Only yesterday you were spotted in an Eighth Street delicatessen, loading up with pastrami and rye, all by yourself.'

'Cruel, Issy, cruel,' sighs Harold.

'You and Harold have a fine collection of lettuce leaves in your icebox,' Gamal says.

'OK, Gamal, I'll let you have one more whisky with mineral water. I will fetch it. Die in your prime if you must. Harold, kindly observe: the Rabbi Ben Ezra's "neurotic nephew, currently cult-leader of anorexia nervosa for Manhattan's gays", is now pouring his guest, the author of this flattering bio-byte, a large – Harold, are you watching? – dose of deathdealing calories and liver-destruction.'

'I thought you understood that literature is an en soi not an en dehors,' Gamal says.

'Gamal, observe closely. I am no longer pouring your whisky. I have relapsed into an en soi. I am pausing to ponder everything I know and don't know about literature. While pausing I am observing your hands trembling. I see you sweating into our best chair because of the whisky.'

'Because of no whisky.'

'How about "because of the whisky-factor"?' Harold suggests. 'Issy, why not give – '

'Why should I take offence, Gamal, when I read in your *sublime* pages that I once took you to the Russian Tea Room, ordered myself lemon tea, then mounted vigil over your plate in case something edible landed on it? Should I take offence, Harold?'

'Give him the whisky, Issy. If you don't give him the whisky I'll give him the whisky.'

'Maybe he should give himself the whisky.'

'Cruel, cruel,' Harold sighs.

'OK, so who's cruel? Me? The guy who finds himself described in his own client's pages as "a stick-thin Levantine rug merchant currently sharing an arriviste luxury apartment" – arriviste! – arriviste! – "in the Dakota Building with the Gentile ballet dancer Harold La Guardia and two early Matisses, probably fakes, all three." '

'Tell me, Gamal,' Harold asks, 'do you seriously hate us?'

'Harold, you should know by now that our distinguished guest speaks only with a drink in his hand. Does he hate me, you ask?'

' "Us", I said, Issy, "us".'

'Harold, our guest is an Arab or he isn't? Didn't I personally fling the Arabs out of Palestine? Didn't I build the Bar Lev Line along the Suez Canal with my bare hands, in between sodomizing the camels? Didn't I tell him that I don't believe a word about Liz and Frank travelling to Cairo at Gamal's instigation? Wait, wait – '

Isaac has moved away from the drinks trolley. His fingers are flying through the pages of my typescript, *Ra'is*, which bristles with coloured (colored) marker stickers, each vibrating with expletives.

'Harold, please get me the whisky,' I beg.

'I might be a fake, Gamal.' Harold has turned nasty.

'I'll change your name in the novel, Harold.'

'How about keeping Harold's name,' Isaac yells, still rifling through my pages, 'and substituting the words "Balanchine's most brilliant protégé" for the word "fake".'

'I'm not sure we want the Matisses to be fakes, either,' Harold says.

'I won't change a fucking word about either of you.' I burst into tears and begin to crawl across the polished, see-your-feet boards towards the drinks trolley. With a small motion of his million-dollar toe, Harold sends its wheels spinning away.

'I've got it!' Isaac cries. 'Here-it-is. Right here. I quote. Harold, am I quoting or making this up?'

'You're quoting, Issy, but maybe it's not wise.'

'I'm quoting: "It occurred to Gamal to ask an American client of Isaac Ben Ezra, Inc. what percentage of his earnings the agency was taking. The American writer looked surprised. 'The normal ten per cent,' he said. When informed that the same agency was purloining twenty per cent of Gamal's earnings, he looked stunned. 'See a lawyer tomorrow,' he advised." End of quote.'

'Terrible,' Harold sighs. 'Just terrible.'

'Do you hear what Harold says, Gamal? Harold is the friendly one of the family, remember? Harold is so upset now that he may not be able to perform tonight. If you were Galina Narina would you want to dance Juliet to Harold's Romeo tonight? If you were Galina Narina, who fled the Bolshoi in Paris at risk of her life, might you not be seriously tempted to skip the aerobatics tonight and play the Nurse? I'm asking you, Gamal, whether Harold, in this mood, can be trusted to catch a paper cup let alone one hundred and twelve pounds of priceless ballerina from Kiev.'

Gamal is crumpled in the middle of the floor, sobbing, an unmeasurable glob of melting porkfat.

'Harold, have I ever made one cent of profit on the Gamal Rahman account?' Isaac asks.

'Not a cent,' Harold says. 'Gamal, please get up off the floor.'

'Any primitive Bedouin understands the sanctity of hospitality,' I sob.

'Any Bedouin will offer Colonel Lawrence a whisky,' Isaac says. 'Do you hear that, Harold? – any Egyptian camel driver could teach us a few lessons in hospitality.'

'Perhaps we should give him his whisky, Issy.'

'A better idea, Harold – perhaps our eminent guest would care to look through the company accounts. Maybe he wishes to send in teams of hardened fraud-sniffers from Arthur Andersen International? Jesus, Harold, look at the time.'

'The time, my God!

'Your shower, Harold.'

Harold springs out of the open-plan living room with a single bound. Isaac casually hands me an inch of whisky blended with an inch of mineral water.

'Harold showers three times a day,' Isaac says, his voice down several decibels due to loss of audience. 'Frankly, Gamal, Americans *care* about hygiene. Didn't Celia el-Sharaf ever teach you about hygiene? You'll find a new deodorant by your bedside. It's a spray. It may work better than a stick. It may not. We shall have to await your next chapter to find out. Where is it?'

Ah that easing whisky, whisky, whisky, that atoning fire in my nervous system.

'The next chapter is on your desk.'

'I hope I didn't leave any hundred-dollar bills lying on it,' Isaac says, seating himself in a cross-legged, cross-sticked, I-can-do-it yoga posture on the highly polished floorboards of the apartment overlooking Central Park, where Isaac goes jogging in the required kit every Sunday morning. (Harold of course 'rests in' or 'rests up', his million-dollar limbs banned from the vagaries of Central Park by a battery of insurance clauses.)

'You are no longer obliged to read anything I write,' Gamal says, 'since I bring you no profit.'

'And all the Western world will know that I, Jewboy, screamed at you, "Get out of here, black bastard!" Is that the next scenario?'

Gamal shrugs. 'Another whisky, please. Shall I help myself?'

'Gamal, we are due at the Lincoln Center.'

'I'm perfectly sober.'

'That's what worries me! Gamal, Gamal, mens sana in corpore sano. Have you ever thought of leaving Egypt for a while – get away from all that corrupting hedonism? You have close to fifty thousand dollars sitting in your Chase Money Market account.'

'What would I write about?'

'You have a point. Who are you wheeling in for the next libel action? Can I hope that it will be a humble Cairo street cleaner who was kind enough to die yesterday?'

Isaac glances at his watch, squeals, and scampers to peep inside the bathroom. 'Harold, it's a quarter after.'

'It *is?*'

'It definitely is, Harold.'

வை

By the time I arrived back in Cairo, Reader – though Isaac complains I'm overdoing 'this "Reader" stuff' – it was clear that the exiled Shah of Iran would be returning to Egypt from the Americas to die. The Americans would no longer shelter the Shah because some fifty diplomatic hostages were held in Tehran by Khomeini's young fanatics.

'Mademoiselle,' I said, 'allow me to arrange maximum press coverage, worldwide, of the funeral.' I advised the Rais that his own instincts were, as always, close to God's: the Shah deserved the full works. (Mahmoud had once remarked, 'When he retires, Sharaf can take over at the Cairo Opera.')

'Your Excellency, students from the Military Academy must lead the procession, all playing instruments and dressed in white, yellow and black according to rank. Then, Sire, come soldiers carrying wreaths of roses and irises. Then officers on horseback. Then a squadron bearing the Shah's military decorations on black velvet pillows. Then the coffin, wrapped in the Iranian flag and drawn by eight Arabian horses on a military caisson.'

'This could be expensive,' the Rais muttered as we leopard-prowled round his retreat on Mount Sinai.

'This is your answer to Khomeini, Rais. You and Khomeini are now engaged in a struggle-to-the-death for the soul of the Arab world, Excellency. The funeral cortège will march three miles from the 'Abdin Palace to el-Rifa'i Mosque. This will be the most spectacular funeral that the world has seen since the time of your predecessors, the pharaohs.'

'You read my mind well, Gamal.'

'Excellency.'

Though I say it myself, the Shah's funeral was a huge success and the affecting tears of the veiled royal ladies were seen by millions worldwide. Despite a boycott by the world's heads of state, I per- suaded ex-President Nixon and ex-King Constantine to attend – though attempts to locate ex-King Zog of Albania sadly failed. I was privileged to enjoy a long chat with Mr Nixon (who seemed reluctant to depart). 'Take care to shred all evidence of your life as you go along,' this maligned statesman told me.

But now Andy Popodopoulos bounced back into our lives. A crazy construction engineer, Dr el-Khalid, who happened to be a Member of the National Assembly, imagined himself defrauded both by Andy and his father-in-law, the Rais's brother Hassan el-Sharaf, who had married his daughter Sabina to Andy after Huda took her own version of the veil. Having abused parliamentary immunity by revealing what he knew about various overseas bank accounts, notably those held in the names of the Rais and his brother Hassan, Dr el-Khalid had reportedly fled by camel into the Libyan desert.

Bon voyage. However, the el-Khalid file had now turned up in the hands of the BBC Arabic Service in London.

Summoned to State Security, I found Hamida in jackboots and fingering an Iron Cross, a gift from her father.

'Our Embassy in London reports that the BBC is planning to broadcast a summary of the documents.'

'I feared as much, Mademoiselle.'

'I don't care what you feared! It's no coincidence that the traitor Hosny Hikmat is currently in London. His role in this attempt to subvert the State cannot be doubted. Take the next plane to London.'

My fat heart bounded about. The Rais had set his own heart on receiving the Prince and Princess when the honeymoon couple's royal yacht, *Britannia*, entered the Suez Canal – a splash prelude to Sharaf's visit to London and Washington. Utterly isolated in the Arab world, threatened by rising Islamic fundamentalism at home, the Rais could not afford a scandal embarrassing to his British and American friends. Hamida's hand was a steel claw fastened on my sleeve.

'When did you last see Huda?'

'Don't be boring, Hamida. Huda Huda Huda.'

The face-slap was more than usually powerful. The Iron Cross really danced on her breast. 'I suppose you realize that Huda's scum helped the traitor el-Khalid to escape.'

'I'm short of money, by the way. Have five thousand dollars waiting for me in London.'

I was at the door when Hamida asked after Henri. 'Where is he?'

'In Paris.'

'Bring him back.'

'Have a further five thousand dollars waiting for me in Paris.'

I flew to London. The BBC hack masterminding the el-Khalid operation was none other than my old angel-of-the-urinal, Fred Hemmings. I hadn't betrayed Fred but he believed I had when they stripped him of his post at Cairo University, closed down the World Service studio, and deported him. He continued to claim that I had helped myself to his valuable collection of Arab literature after I (very helpfully) took over his apartment.

Fred Hemmings received me in a Bush House office crowded with exiled Arabs and moonlighting university Arabists browsing through Middle East newspapers and drinking machine-coffee from paper cups. The floor was carpeted in fine flakes of baclava pastry. Photographs of Huda lined the walls. These were men, and a few women, who had fled not only from Sharaf, but also from Qaddafi, Assad, Saddam Hussein, Hassan of Morocco, Bourguiba, the Yemen – not forgetting the Palestinians. On hearing my name they confronted the ugly, sweating visitor with indolent expressions of contempt.

Fred perched himself on the edge of his desk, long legs swinging.

'I take it you're representing the Sharafs, Rahman.'

'The documents belong to Dr el-Khalid. You have no right to publicize their contents. To do so is to condemn him to death.' This was greeted with derision all round Bush House. Even the portraits of Huda smiled. Beyond the windows grey pigeons were fluttering and farting on to the stonework of this massively imperial building.

Gamal said: 'I'm sorry that the BBC now obtains its material by theft.'

Cruel laughter. Gamal sweating.

At that moment Fred took an internal call. His expression tightened, darkened. How well I knew that tightening and darkening in the faces of journalists from my years on *Misr*. The entire staff of the Arabic Department had fallen silent. Each of them was learning yet again that the BBC World Service broadcasts – whether by long wave or medium wave or short wave – under the elegant shadow of the Foreign Office. My first call from Heathrow Airport had been to the Egyptian Ambassador in London.

Fred and I shared a lift to the top floor of Bush House in sub-zero silence. In the Director's suite several tall gentlemen from the Foreign Office were waiting in languid poses, like dehydrated lilies. There were no introductions, no handshakes. The Director brusquely reminded Fred Hemmings that the Royal Yacht was due to pass through the Suez Canal in two weeks time. The honeymoon of the heir to the throne was not the occasion for hitches. If the el-Khalid documents were broadcast there would be a hitch – the Royal Yacht would be turned back at Port Said. President el-Sharaf's subsequent State Visit to Britain would be cancelled – a mega-hitch.

I went and bought myself a kilo of Turkish baclava.

಄

A Royal Honeymoon! The Prince duly invited the Sharafs to dinner on the Royal Yacht as it sailed down the Canal – it was I who pressed the royal couple's aides to persuade the reluctant HRH to allow the banquet to be televised. Celia ordered my tenue à soirée from Kilgour

French & Stanbury – a cable came back asking for an update on my measurements. Before the speeches I was summoned from the staff quarters below deck – there's no harm in leftovers – and invited to tell a story which had delighted Celia and would undoubtedly please the Prince and Princess.

'Gamal is my minstrel,' the Rais guffawed.

'He would require a strong balcony,' the Prince quipped.

I then related how another Prince and Princess of Wales had, in 1869, progressed down the Nile as the guests of the Khedive Ismail:

'The royal party travelled in six blue and gold steamers whose interior decoration illustrated the story of Antony and Cleopatra. Each steamer towed a barge carrying four riding horses and a milk-white donkey for the Princess. Not to mention 3,000 bottles of champagne, 4,000 bottles of claret, four French chefs and a laundry. When the royal couple made the return journey, they brought with them thirty-two mummy cases, an immense sarcophagus, and a ten-year old orphan boy, Ali Cheema, who was destined to serve coffee in native dress at Sandringham.'

I admit I had deliberately not told Celia all the details. Her proud smile soon vanished. The Prince looked aghast, the Princess profoundly embarrassed, the Rais thunderous. I was hustled out by two Royal Navy officers and thrown in the Canal.

∽

Gamal returned to London with the President. Dignified as a member of the Rais's official entourage, I paraded myself fatly and (by one of those tricks of fortune which are no mystery to astrologers like myself) found myself right bang next to Mrs Tory as she waited – and waited! – for the Rais in the courtyard of the Foreign Office. (He being a Head of State, it was her duty to arrive first.) Mrs Torment was seething. If I'd offered to take the salute of the assembled Grenadier Guards myself, she would probably have accepted. It was Gamal's first encounter with Mrs Tory at close quarters – who could guess that one day he would have to place himself under her suffocating protection? That heavy make-up! that perm'd hair! the beige calfskin gloves! the plum-dark voice – a straight caricature of herself. A talking head. While waiting for the late (though alive unless assassinated while driving up Whitehall) Rais, she joked with anyone who would listen, including a cathedral spire of a Guards officer and the fat, young-old Arab who'd planted himself behind her shoulder.

'Are you from Egypt?' she asked Gamal.

'I am indeed, Prime Minister.'

She liked the 'indeed' as he'd known she would. 'Do you Egyptians keep African time or European time?'

'We keep the Rais's time.' Gamal smiled as demurely as he could imagine. 'It is not sunset until he says so.'

She gave me an appraisal: I was just a little too fresh and fat for her taste. She turned away. Then she examined her watch. Then she spoke to Gamal again (or perhaps to herself).

'Receptions and more receptions,' she murmured like dark chocolate. Momentarily he was overwhelmed by her matronly attractions, the nice set of her frock on her heavy flanks, what a mother to have, all that lipstick and powder and money, the laquered sweep of her hair, all done-up at an early hour when the Rais was still dreaming of God. Gamal found himself looking for the nuclear warheads among the orchids decorating her summery suit.

'I am ready to inspect the Guard of Honour,' Gamal heard himself say, 'at your command.'

Her eyes said hush hush much much too far you go my boy. Withering! The Rais got later and later. Again she ostentatiously looked at her watch. Any minute she'd send the Grenadier Guards back into the Canal Zone. Gamal prayed for her revived attention but she had wiped him off her map. He swore revenge: he would get her. He would get them all, the princes of Heaven and Earth.

When the Rais emerged from his Rolls-Royce in his super-starched whiter-than-white collar, he shook Mrs T's hand and discovered that he was in danger of setting light to her with his smouldering pipe; a bodyguard came running to relieve him of it. Gamal suspected that greeting any oriental wallah was a bit of a ha-ha business for Mrs Torment. Now the Rais was standing to attention yards away from him, the PM two or three inches back in pantomime deference to a Head of State. Inspecting the tall Guardsmen in their busbys, the Rais looked smaller than usual. No sighting of his wiry brown legs.

Gamal showed up at the Egyptian Embassy for the cocktail hour. The Rais was in exuberant form.

'I am told I arrived late for the inspection of the Guards. I have explained what happened to the Prime Minister. Before I left to see Mrs Thatcher I had an appointment with some photographers from Madame Tussaud's waxwork museum. They had already made one model of me, and I had sent them one of my suits to put on it, but I was astonished to see they had made me look exactly like Dracula. Anyway, they destroyed that first waxwork.'

Laugh now.

Ask now.

'Please tell us about Your Excellency's visit to Buckingham Palace?'

'The Queen graciously postponed her visit to Scotland so that she could meet with Madame Sharaf and myself. The Palace had been notified that I never eat anything during the day, only in the evening. "We shall serve you only juice," the Queen said. A glass of orange juice was placed before me. I could hardly explain to Her Majesty that I can't stand citrus fruit because of my gastric stomach, so I drank it.'

There is barely time to wing these pearls – and news of Madame el-Sharaf's costume changes throughout the day – to Cairo before rushing to L'Artiste Affamé, where I am dining with my British publisher and agent. But wait wait wait. A message from Isaac is waiting for me at the Strand Palace Hotel, two words:

CALL ME.

'We're in the money,' Isaac announces. 'Karl likes your novel. He's buying *Ra'is* and he's getting right behind it. Do you know what that means, Gamal?'

'Who's Karl?'

' "Who's Karl"! Jees-us! Karl is the man who's making all the big hits in New York *and London*. A tennis ball in Karl's hand is an ace before it leaves the racquet. You're with me?'

'Does Karl extend to a second name?'

'Gamal, where have you been? Does God need a second name? Now when are you scheduled to meet with Trevelyan and Bennett?'

'In England you meet, you don't meet with. Ten minutes ago.'

'Gamal listen. Could I just say something to you without you correcting my grammar or straightening my syntax? Trevelyan and Bennett don't know about the Karl-deal yet. They're out and they're not going to like it. Just be very very nice to them.'

'I thought Bennett was your "British end". You foisted her on me, remember? The best agent in London, you said. And what has she ever done for me, that off-blonde seedless grape who'd win second prize at the West Sussex sparkling wine competition? Bennett has probably never read a manuscript from end to end in her entire life. Her maximum attention span is two hundred words spread over a dozen intervening telephone calls.'

A long sigh from Manhattan. 'Just be very very nice tonight, Gamal. Very nice to Trevelyan, very nice to Bennett. Could you be very very nice for once in your life?'

Half an hour later a steaming Gamal is emptied into L'Artiste Affamé, where he finds his publisher and his agent half-way through the main course.

'Ah,' says Trevelyan, 'we'd almost given up on you.'

'Sharaf wanted to brief me privately,' Gamal says, wiping the dew

411

from his forehead and neck with a crisp napkin. Bennett is offering him her cheek.

'What will you eat?' Trevelyan asks.

'Two dozen snails and the steak, very rare.'

'Two dozen? Are you sure?'

Gamal helps himself to wine. 'The sales figures for *The Crossing* are a fucking disgrace,' he declares, revolving his bulging-accusing eyes from one to the other, then settling on the wine bottle.

'We are quite pleased with them,' Trevelyan says. 'Our marketing and publicity people have done a remarkably good job.' Trevelyan refills Gamal's glass, orders another bottle. 'For a foreign novelist, your sales are remarkably good,' he says.

'Must I be foreign? I write better English than the English. I'm expecting a knighthood.'

'When do you hope to finish *Ra'is*?' Trevelyan asks.

'It's pronounced "rayyis", not "race".' Gamal's eyes are bulging in limitless accusation. He drains another glass of wine.

'I think we should consider alternative titles, frankly.'

'I'm afraid I agree,' Bennett says.

Gamal grabs the new bottle. 'Muhammad's next in my sights, if you can bear the excitement.'

'The Prophet? Is that entirely prudent?'

'P.B.U.H.'

'Pardon?'

'Peace be upon him.' Gamal's high, domed forehead smacks down among the empty dishes.

'Oh dear,' Bennett sighs, 'it always ends like this.'

'But he's only just arrived.'

'Gamal was an only child. He's terribly spoilt.'

'Frankly, darling, if you can place this unsaleable genius with another imprint I'd be grateful. I don't suppose Karl would be interested?'

'No chance.'

ରୂ

A Gitane between his invisble lips, Mahmoud shares Gamal's taxi back to the Strand Palace.

'Baba, tell me why the Party of God, the Party of Allah, is so potent in the world today? Even you have rejoined it – you! Is it because the majority of men remain poor, ignorant, oppressed? Is it because Man continues to seek solace from death? Is it because prayer remains the only refuge for those who can never control their own destiny?'

'God lost His temper,' Shaytan says. 'I'd seen it coming, of course.

My great fear since the time of Newton was that one of these cheeky, cocksure savants would break through to the zero option: "I spit in God's eye. Let Him come and get me if He can." '

'Enter Marx?'

Shaytan nods. 'Marx it was – with apologies to Feuerbach – who first portrayed Man as an alienated god struggling through history to recover his human divinity.'

'A very grand portrait! – not diptych, not triptych, but megatych!'

'The Almighty took it in His stride – to begin with. "It's a logical conclusion," He said. "No need to panic. Let human experience itself overturn Marx's error. If the Pope insists on denouncing Marxian Atheism, so be it – but no word from Us." '

'But full-scale Bolshevism followed? God was burned in effigy across the world as the apologist and alibi for human oppression?'

'Eventually it was too much. I was summoned and instructed to prepare a sermon, to be read in all the churches, synagogues and mosques of the world – denouncing Atheism.'

'Goodbye, ethics?'

'Good morning, Religion – again.'

TWENTY-SEVEN

❧

State Security arrived at the Toad's fourth-floor flat on the Alexandrian Corniche shortly after 2.15 in the morning. I had answered a summons to 'debrief' Hikmat following his latest outbreak of subversive toadtrotting to all points on the compass. Sharaf's foreign enemies – there was no shortage – easily persuaded the Toad that his puddle was a pond of Homeric proportions; his columns continued to be widely syndicated abroad, enraging President Fawzi el-Pharaoh.

—How Long Can Sharaf Hold Out?

—Sharaf: the Writing is on the Wall

—Last Days of a Dynasty

Back home, 'convalescing' (I didn't realize how ill he was), the Toad contented himself by defecating on the Rais down the trousers of gullible acolytes. But few were prepared to risk the Rais's wrath; Anis Hussein had published a long portrait of 'Hikmat, Pervert and Pederast' in *Misr*, and been duly rewarded with a senior post in the Foreign Ministry. Egypt had become Hosny Hikmat's cell of solitary confinement – but he would always be Boss to me: a mensch.

I knew that his apartment was under constant surveillance but, as Mahmoud once remarked, 'You are never happy unless under surveillance, Gamal.' By the time State Security arrived at 2.15 in the morning, we had drunk too much vodka, the Toad eagerly absorbing my latest stories about the Sharafs with flicking tongue and a storm of violent snorts conveying accumulated contempt for 'The Clown' and for my own gullibility.

'Boss, I really believe Sharaf would like to be a First Amendment liberal if he could. He doesn't enjoy repression.'

'Haha!' – snort, flick – 'achya, haha!'

The Toad's floor was littered with shell-crumbs from a week's hard-boiled eggs, which he invariably discarded half-eaten. A massive shouting and thumping on the door of his apartment cut short our colloquy. The Toad hesitated but the door was immediately rammed off its hinges and locks. As the uniforms poured in, I was already

414

syndicating my eyewitness account of Hikmat's third arrest in two years.

'You are Hosny Hikmat?' a young officer of State Security grabbed me by the collar.

'Don't you know anything!' the Toad yelled. 'Don't you recognize the most famous journalist in the Middle East? Haha! Who coined the famous phrase "Sharaf's visitors of the dawn"?'

The officer almost saluted this display of authority, then turned back to fat-me with compensatory contempt.

'You must be Gamal Rahman?'

The State Security boys laughed as a puddle formed at my feet. We were given five minutes to pack a bag and change my trousers. The Toad, an expert in the protocol of the gulag, asked whether he needed a big bag or a little bag.

'Are we staying in Alexandria or heading for Cairo?'

'You will remain in Alexandria, Mr Hikmat.'

The visitors of the dawn were already rifling through the Toad's shelves and drawers in search of atheism, Islamic fundamentalism and Toad's spawn. His fish tank received close attention. I imagined my own flat in Cairo simultaneously jam-packed with uniforms: goodbye to my priceless collection of *Playboy* centre-spreads, and farewell to my unique collection of *Mad* magazine. Were the Guardians of the State even now wrestling the captions into non-mad Arabic?

The Toad came out of his bedroom to make an announcement:

'All my important papers are stored in UK banks. Return my passport and we'll take the first plane to London.'

When this brilliant idea met with no hoorays, the Toad lifted his shoulders in my direction as if to say 'lunatics', then launched into a terrific cackling and snorting.

'I suppose you realize, Officer, that the arrest of Hosny Hikmat will not only precipitate a diplomatic crisis with Moscow and Peking – but almost certainly with Washington as well. I was with Ronald Reagan only last week.'

'Please pack your bag, Mr Hikmat, we are in a hurry.'

'I also have in London,' the Toad announced, 'an 8mm movie and still photographs of a certain young lady with a certain gentleman, in flagrante delicto.'

'In what, Mr Hikmat?' The young officer showed a faint interest.

'In the Maison française. Hard at it.'

The State Security men moved into a corner to confer.

'Who is the lady, Mr Hikmat, and who is the gentleman in the French delicatessen?'

'The young man? – ach, who cares about some obscure foreign correspondent with more ambition than good sense?'

'And who is the lady?'

'Start at the top,' the Toad cackled. 'Go as high as you can go.' But here his nerve failed him; his 'ultimate insurance policy' suddenly resembled an unsigned death certificate without post-mortem. 'I have nothing further to add,' he declared, as if this sordid subject was altogether beneath him.

'Time to go,' the officer said.

The landing and stairway were swarming with soldiers carrying automatic rifles and walkie-talkies. From the radio-chatter I gathered that the Toad and I were 'Operation 8'. We were bundled downstairs and into a Peugeot van. Arriving at State Security headquarters, we found ourselves among former Cabinet ministers, journalists, lawyers, imams and Coptic priests, many of whom cheerfully greeted us as we were herded into army trucks which immediately sped away along the rough agricultural road towards Cairo.

'So they lied to us,' the Toad announced. 'This is a big-bag occasion.'

It soon became alarmingly apparent that the soldier at the wheel of our truck was in constant danger of falling asleep as the vehicle swayed about the narrow road, attempting to keep pace with the motor cycle escort. His neck twisted and his head rolled as he struggled to remain awake. The Toad began to shout about the Universal Convention of Human Rights with particular reference to his prostate problems.

'I shall be dead on arrival unless allowed out to pee!'

That did the trick – we Egyptians are a compassionate people. Everyone was granted a life-saving pee while the peasants cowered in their huts, wondering what this unexpected irrigation was all about.

It was all about the Tora prison, Egypt's newest gaol, a triumph of American penal technology (minus the civil rights). On arrival everything was taken from us: books, papers, wallets, money, clothes, even medicines and toothpaste. The Toad and I found ourselves reduced to our underclothes – mine badly stained by now – in a small cell whose floor was covered by filthy rubber mattresses strongly impregnated with DDT. Each new arrival was warmly greeted; finally ten of us were stuffed into the concrete box. The stench from the hole in the floor left no doubt about its function. There was no paper.

A soldier arrived with a bucket of disgusting-looking molasses and a basket of bread covered in flies. The Toad refused to eat on account of the notorious stones in his kidney and gall-bladder (he was convinced the Rais had been poisoning his special, fat-free soups for years), so I grabbed his bread as well as my own. No tea, no coffee, only tap water. Flies attacked by day, mosquitoes by night. Defecating was an agony for body and soul. We stank.

'I demand a copy of *Misr* to discover what my crime is,' the Toad constantly shouted at the guard.

'No newspapers, Mr Hikmat.'

No visitors, no lawyers, no doctors. No letters in or out. And no charges – merely other men's nightmares to add to my own. But most of my fellow-prisoners had served in the army, some in battle – two had been prisoners of the Israelis; Gamal was the gutless softie, the baby of the cell, though not the youngest, always moaning.

'I'm seriously hungry, Boss. My stomach is a trampoline, throwing up everything that lands on it.'

'I've never seen you in such good shape, Gamal.'

'But – '

'Put it all down to experience,' the Toad consoled me with one of his acidic cackles. 'And if you don't live to report it, someone else will. As Sartre said, the world is someone else.' The Toad's tongue was flicking like a viper's.

We were of course an articulate bunch, familiar with prison-literature from Solzhenistyn's gulag to the Latin Americans. Clinging to sanity, we fell into a routine of formal discussion groups, with a chairman du jour, hoping to ensure that the most talkative (Hikmat), or explosively unhappy (Gamal), did not entirely dominate. Each of us took it in turn to explore his own history, ambitions and philosophy. This was a qualified success until it came to my turn. My self-proclaimed mission – 'to get on level terms with God' – was too much even for the non-believers among us, all of whom regarded me as utterly unworthy of my progenitor, Mahmoud.

We played a game called 'First Out'. If we were allowed to release one of our number each week, how would we set the priorities? The younger prisoners insisted that the heads of families should be the first to gain their liberty; the heads of families argued that the youngsters had lives ripe with promise to enjoy. We were all steeped in honour and nobility because the real choices were not ours.

At night the rationality and altruism of the day gave way to the groaning demons of self-preservation. The djinns were out. Those terrible dreams we were forced to share! The heartrending pleas for privileged treatment! The Toad was a noisy and melodramatic dreamer, constantly issuing threats to someone he addressed as 'Chairman'. My own nightmares lacked the brevity of Uncle Vanya's: whereas Chekhov's character merely dreamed that 'my leg belonged to someone else', both my legs belonged to my only hope, Isaac Ben Ezra.

Gamal is dragged by Isaac and Harold La Guardia into a crowded Flatbush, Brooklyn, apartment chock-a-block with Jewish refugees, mattresses and cardboard suitcases. These people are from Damascus and Aleppo. They are Isaac's people, Isaac's charges, Isaac's conscience. Patiently they have been waiting for the emissary of the aliya to arrive in a limousine loaded with toilet rolls, bagels, cream cheese and forged travel documents.

'Hi. Hi Ben. Hi Rebekah. Hi Lina. Hi Batya. Hi Yosef. Hi Moni. Hi Zacky.'

Isaac circulates beneficently among the warm-warm women, offering a pederast's ribs to the flesh-pressing daughters of Ruth. Brother Isaac! Isaac the messiah!

An old man with blackened gums grabs Gamal's sleeve:

'I from ghetto of Damascus, young man. I having one hundred members of family to feeding. Half my people still in Syria. If I sending any sons and daughters here from New York to Israel, pfftt! – I never again seeing ones who in Syria remaining. Pfftt!'

'That's the Arabs for you, sir,' Harold says, bad-eyeing Gamal.

'It's the deal between Assad and Washington,' Isaac says, snapping a celery stick in his teeth. 'Congregation Beth Torah is working for a better deal.'

Gamal has seen the raw-concrete brute-Zionist apartments these people dream of, hideous havens of hope called Bat Yam, Yad Eliahu and Holon. The old man is tugging his lapel.

'Rabbi Ben Ezra my uncle. He leading young Isaac here to Promised Land.'

'But they ending up in Egypt,' Gamal says. 'Maybe they following wrong star.'

'Our hearts always wailing at Western Wall.'

'That's just beautiful,' Harold says.

'Syrian Mukhabarat catching me,' the old man says proudly. 'They giving me electric shockings. Then they pulling out all nails. Then they breaking back. I spending next forty years paying baksheesh to Mukhabarat for everything.'

'Terrible.' Harold throws a glance of bitter reproach at Gamal. 'Terrible. Don't you feel ashamed to be an Arab, Gamal?' Eventually we tearing ourselves from aliya. Harold (whose precious toes are due for a foot powder commercial in midtown Manhattan) touches my knee as the limousine crosses Brooklyn Bridge (Isaac is busy fixing further deals – Washington-Damascus-Tel Aviv – on his five mobile telephones).

'Gamal,' Harold murmurs, 'you don't *need* to feel *bad.*'

'Bad? Who saying I feeling bad?'

'As an Arab. OK, OK, so your people have oppressed our people for centuries but . . .'

'Tell Isaac I want him to get me out of the Tora, Harold.'

'The Torah. You want us to send you a Torah?'

'Out of the Tora, Harold. It's a prison in Cairo. It's bad news.'

'Gamal, you should never have married Huda. Isaac thinks that was your gravest error. That woman is dangerous, a fanatic, she dreams of the Palestinian flag above the Temple Mount, of dynamiting the Western Wall. How can we trust a man who chose to marry a Nazi?'

'A Nazi! Huda! My sweet loving angel!'

'Issy, shall I kill this Arab bum or is that your prerogative?'

ை

Mornings brought no sweet skyline of Manhattan, no Tora-Torah, merely hunger, illness and apathy. Our peasant-jailers, who hated the regime, though diligent spies on its behalf, brought excited news of a million Hudas defacing the public buildings of the city. The regime was running out of gum-solvent. Innocent of my own claims on her, our jailers reported that Huda could soar above any bullet, could dissolve into pure spirit if seized, and regularly flew from the apex of Kephren's pyramid to Mount Ararat – and back – bearing messages from the Prophet.

Indeed she was now revealed to be the thirteenth wife of the Prophet.

The Toad cackled in his delirium. '*He'll* never let you out, Gamal!'

News filtered in that an assassination attempt on Sharaf, involving his most trusted bodyguards, had narrowly failed. Each of 'the martyrs' was revealed to have carried an undamaged portrait of Huda over his torn-apart heart. Senior officials and army officers were rumoured to be turning up in Damascus, Tripoli and Baghdad carrying only a tube of toothpaste.

The interrogations I suffered in solitary confinement became more ferocious. Sometimes Hamida herself took part, and always Anis Hussein, done up in the uniform of State Security (rank of colonel). The crouching of a prisoner whose rags are worn-through at the knees, whose hair is thick with lice, whose stomach can hold nothing down, was not, Reader, fatboy's theatrical crouching of yesteryear.

They wanted one thing from me: Huda.

'Gamal,' Hamida said, pacing the interrogation cell (three steps, three steps back), 'you may not know where that serpent is coiled, but you can lead us to her.'

'Yes, yes, Mademoiselle, but first you must release me.'

'And what would you do then?'

'Nothing, absolutely nothing. I would resume a normal life and wait.'

'Until she comes to you?'

'Exactly, Mademoiselle! She always does . . . sooner or later.'

'There's a quicker method,' said Anus Hussein. 'We could lay this scum out among the tombs of the Mamelukes and wait for the widow to claim the corpse.'

'Very dodgy!' I objected. 'She would send servants.'

But my hopes were invariably dashed. Metal gates clanged and I was thrown back into our communal cell to service the Toad's obsessions. Hosny Hikmat's health was deteriorating rapidly. His mind was going. An old fantasy resurfaced and festered in confinement: our 'only hope' was to expose Celia's brazen claim that her mother was English.

'Boss,' I whispered, my arm round his shoulder, 'I thought your only last hope in the world was our famous, 8mm pornshow of a French journalist with more ambition than good sense pleasuring a young lady called Start at the Top.'

'No, no, that was always a foolish idea of yours.'

'Of mine!'

'You must hurry straight to Bruddersford, Gamal, travel via Tibet and Romania, go on now, why are you hanging about, I want you back with the evidence by morning!'

౧ఌ

The muezzins were summoning the faithful to morning prayers when I was pulled, half-asleep, from the cell, given a bath and fresh clothes – my own, taken from my apartment – then led to the office of the Deputy Prison Governor.

'You have a visitor,' I was told.

Who could it be? A small pile of my personal belongings lay on a table: money, house keys, my address book. I signed for them, resisting the impulse to scribble 'No passport!' across the document. A door opened and a very thin but expensively outfitted person of anorexic aspect was conducted into the Deputy Governor's office. He looked me over through wire-rimmed spectacles as if weighing whether I was the man he'd come for.

'Let's go, Gamal,' Isaac Ben Ezra said.

And we went. No one stopped us. Emerging from the Tora, I was blinded by the sky.

'Hungry?' Isaac asked as his chauffeured limo traversed the Nile, the comforting profiles of the great hotels visible through the smoked glass windows. From virtually every wall portraits of Huda smiled gently back at me, replete with trust.

I described the Toad's condition to Isaac. 'Can you do anything for him?'

'Hikmat isn't my client.'

'He's my Boss. The Toad has shown me the way for twenty years.'

'All the way to the Tora.'

'He's ill. He's dying. They won't let him see a doctor. I need a drink.'

Isaac handed me a handsome hip flask. 'We think of everything,' he said, 'for our twenty per cent.'

ʒ

Mahmoud made an effort to extend his arms to me. Not a full embrace – he'd never attempted that – but more than a routine greeting. His stick arms trembled as he lifted them stiffly, like a blind man double-testing a void. Receiving my touch he withdrew quickly – recoiled – as if burnt. Dad moved slowly and – far worse – spoke slowly; talking to him was like making a very long-distance phone call to Central Africa – two voices echoing back at one another, with awkward collisions in the pauses. Isaac had forewarned me about the rheumatoid arthritis. Dad now leant on a stick with an ivory elephant head, inherited from his father and waiting its moment for years in the umbrella-stand. Each brittle-thin limb performed its remembered duties in isolation, as if piastres were being fed into a meter hidden at the base of the spine. He had difficulty lighting a Gitane and heard only what he wanted to hear.

Mahmoud understood that I was his Gamal, but the knowledge of it could no longer animate the crinkled parchment, the old Sufi manuscript, surrounding the absurd sunglasses. His sanctum was now illuminated only by shy oil lamps whose glasswork had been spun on the Venetian island of Murano in the days when Verdi was composing 'Aida for the opening of the Suez Canal.

'Thanks to the immense kindness of Isaac,' Mahmoud murmured, 'whose late uncle, the Rabbi Ben Ezra was my closest friend . . .' Nothing more came. He couldn't remember what was thanks to the immense kindness of Isaac.

Isaac's distress surprised me. This was not the mannered, camp, obligatory 'stress' of Manhattan's professional élite, but a dark, haunting echo of an orphaned childhood spent scuttling through alleys in the grip of the rabbi-uncle who would not let him hide his yarmulke in his pocket. Stretched tight across his cradle of nails, Harold La Guardia and the Lincoln Center far away, Isaac solicitously ushered Mahmoud into the limo carrying us to dine with Auntie Lulu.

Auntie greeted us in the full Islamic paraphernalia, refusing my embrace and turning her back on Isaac's outstretched hand. Only Mahmoud did she consent to embrace. A huge portrait of Huda hung from her wall. Goodbye, 'Aziza, martyr of modernity.

'Brother, your poor, neglected sister hears that le tout Cairo is buzzing with Gamal's comings and goings – this "son" of yours.'

'Not much coming or going recently, Auntie,' I said.

'Rumours reach her that the loyal nephew who deprived her of her due at the University will not rest content until he has proven that the Prophet, peace be upon him, was a phoney.'

'Auntie, art never proves anything,' I said.

'Cool it, shithead,' Isaac hissed in my ear.

'Brother, kindly explain to your "son" that we Muslims do not regard art as sacred, that's a Greek ideology.'

'Auntie – while I was in the Tora an imprisoned sheikh proudly informed me that you now write regularly for our respected religious weekly, *Al-Noor*.'

Auntie Lulu's hands rested on her hips, an Islamic washerwoman pitching for a fight. 'And why not?'

I appraised Mahmoud. He had been sat down. There was one chair he always favoured when he visited Auntie and she never let anyone else sit in it, even in Mahmoud's absence.

'Did you know that Auntie has been writing for *Al-Noor*, Dad?' I shouted.

Isaac leaned towards my ear. 'Give over. This is a family reunion.'

I kept shouting. 'You must be aware, Baba, that for months, years, decades *Al-Noor* has been pillorying Mahmoud, Egypt's Nobel laureate. Remember all those crude cartoons depicting you burning in hell?'

Mahmoud crouched in his favourite Auntie-chair in his darker-than-ever glasses under his aura-halo of Gitane smoke, searching stiff-necked for the source of his son's alien voice.

But I was not to be stopped. 'You were once a famous liberal, Auntie – but now a member of our esteemed board of censors. The spearhead of a campaign against "immorality" in the arts!'

'Yes! And none more immoral than Gamal Rahman! When it comes to Islam, we don't give a fig for "art" or "literature" or this great thing of yours, "the imagination".'

'We agree about that,' Isaac moaned loudly, throwing despairing gestures at an absent Harold. 'We all agree that Gamal is no good at all.'

'You keep out of this – Jew,' Auntie spat at him. 'Jew.'

Isaac's demeanour changed. The spirit of Camp David fell away. 'You're right,' he addressed me, 'this old woman is non-negotiable. Let's go. I can send the car back later, Honoured Mr Mahmoud, to take you home.'

Mahmoud sat paralysed, understanding everything but no longer able to intercede. Many years before I first discovered Alexandria, he'd told me how he had been introduced to the great Greek-Alexandrian poet, Cavafy, for whom a particular café-chair was reserved each night by his expectant admirers. Cavafy – and here Mahmoud was quoting E.M. Forster – stood 'at a slight angle to the universe'. This memorable meeting had occurred in the autumn, when the quail fly in over Alex from the Mediterranean, heading for warmer climates. Fifty years later 'slight angles' were no longer available. Even we prisoners of the Tora had heard Huda's latest pronouncement from the wilderness of Upper Egypt: the Ayatollah Khomeini, she declared, was the Living Imam.

'Rank heresy for a Sunni,' the Toad had cackled in his delirium, 'but who cares?'

ᕥ

Isaac had booked me into the Nile Hilton, sparing me my ransacked flat. Over dinner he ate nothing and made a heroic effort not to notice me cleaning out the cellar and the brasserie. His mood was melancholic – he hated Egypt, a 'land of tombs and lies'.

'As for this "wife" of yours, Gamal, she's crazy. She was sighted in Upper Egypt, Cairo and Jerusalem all on the same day. Entering Hebron, she put the Zionist settlers to flight. They're calling her the Prophet's thirteenth wife. Steer clear of her.'

I nodded sleepily. 'The Prophet's family is ahl-al-bayt, the first family, and his wives are always 'zawjat mutahhardt – sacred.'

Isaac leant across the table. 'The next attempt on Sharaf may succeed. Under Islamic law you could be held responsible. The husband governs the wife. Leave Egypt, Gamal. Leave now.'

'Without a passport?'

'You're booked on to an Air France flight for Paris tomorrow. Your passport will be handed to you as you board the plane.'

'On whose word?'

'I had a ninety-second telephone conversation with Hamida el-Sharaf. They want you out – for ever. You can call yourself the Alexander Solzhenitsyn of Egypt if that helps.'

Isaac, of course, was lying; he'd made a deal with the Sharafs. Huda, no doubt, was in Paris fixing arms, fixing the money. I was to lead them straight to her. Mossad would make no mistake this time – let the French break off diplomatic relations with Israel for a token ten days if honour dictated.

I sank into sleep in a beautiful bed with crisply laundered sheets and the gentle hum of air-conditioning, but it was a sleep more painful than any I'd experienced in the Tora. Shaytan hovered over me but I did all the talking while he puffed his Gitanes – I now knew all my lines.

'Dictators, prophets and imams are my special province, Dad, my safari park. You've awarded me the hunter's licence, Dad! I have them all in my sights!'

With joy I observed my pen racing across the parchment, describing the Prophet's closest companions in the most demeaning terms. Then I paused to listen to my young, doe-eyed Huda caustically questioning her other husband: 'Will Allah stop short at thirteen wives for you if some other comely wench crosses your horizon?'

As these blasphemies poured forth – I could not stop! – the veiled women sat in a circle, sewing my shroud.

The devil's deep silence is the measure of his contentment.

We part at the dockside, Dad and I. I am embarking on some huge ocean liner carrying tall, old-fashioned funnels and the name 'Titanic' inscribed beautifully at the bow. I remember Dad telling me about this ill-fated ship when I was four, and now I'm striving to convince him that I don't want to go aboard. 'Baba,' I cry, 'I'm only four!' But there's no way back. Dressed in gorgeous furs, Celia and Hamida take me by the hand. 'We'll look after you,' they say. 'Huda is waiting for you.'

∽

'Huda is waiting for you.' Henri takes my suitcase as I emerge into the futuristic concourse of Charles de Gaulle airport.

'We have to hurry,' Nicole seizes my arm. 'Your plane was late.'

(As if it was my fault.) This is my first sighting of Monsieur and Madame Chevalier together; I like her even less in the flesh than by recall. As for Henri, all easy charm gone, he keeps grinding cigarettes under his heel after one puff.

'I need a café crême,' I announce. 'And a ham sandwich. Two ham sandwiches.'

Nicole is not impressed by my needs. 'Huda must leave Paris within a few hours. We have no time to lose.'

I sit down stubbornly. Even after the dietary regime of the Tora I'm not for lifting. 'How did you know I'd be on this flight or any other flight?' I ask.

'Ah merde,' Henri fumes, glancing at his watch. 'Don't you yet realize that virtually every pair of eyes in the Arab world now belongs to your wife?'

'Where are we to meet her?'

'Huda's security men will decide the rendezvous. But first you must telephone this number,' Nicole says, handing me a slip of paper. 'Huda will not come until she hears your voice.'

Huda: love finally has me by the throat. I'm asking myself about the day Henri and I drove to interview the Rais at Muhi el-Din. Why had Henri refused to divulge his grandmother's maiden name to the bad-tempered officer of the Presidential Guard? He never was a Catholic! Nicole never was a revolutionary, a Fanonist. The Chevaliers are Jews! Mossad.

Now I notice a group of 'Arabs' observing us across the concourse. They are not the usual, overalled sweepers and poubelle-emptiers from Algeria, Tunisia and Morocco, but smart businessmen dressed in identical, ready-for-anything imperméables. There are five of them. Five's a lot.

It's an odd spot to be fighting for the soul of Egypt, among all these high-tech escalators and tubular elevated passageways, this great clean sweep of modernistic concourse adorned with gleaming ads for cars, liqueur brandies, banking savings accounts and agences immobilières. And the women on the hoardings! Those long legs encasing themselves in fine-mesh Pretty Polly stockings, all ripped down in Cairo as the Rais desperately strives to appease the fundamentalists.

'Who are those gentlemen?' I ask Henri.

'Which gentlemen? Those? I have no idea. They are probably selling oil.'

'Now please make your telephone call to Huda, she's waiting,' Nicole snaps.

'Ham sandwich.'

Nicole sits beside me, placing (with palpable loathing) her hand on mine. 'We know how you have suffered in prison, Gamal.'

Henri lights another cigarette. 'When a political prisoner emerges into the daylight, Gamal, he trusts nobody.' This tormented shell of a man is no longer the Camus-hero I'd known.

I make my way to the battery of public telephones, choosing one out of earshot, and dial the number given. A man answers in thick French. 'This is Gamal Rahman,' I say.

'Who?'

'Gamal Rahman.'

'Wait.'

A woman comes on the line. 'Where are you calling from?'

'Charles de Gaulle.'

'Who is with you?'

'Nicole and Henri Chevalier.'

'Wait.'

Nicole and Henri are observing me intently, likewise the five Arab oil salesmen. I roll my eyes at them.

'Hullo? Gamal?' Oh, sweet voice.

'Yes, Huda, it's your Gamal.'

'What is the French for Sharaf?'

'De Sade.'

'How does Scobie come into it?'

'1942 and very complicated – a question of whether Balthazar was playing chess by postcard or transmitting state secrets to Justine.'

'Oh Gamal, Gamal, they've let you out!'

'You didn't know?'

'How could I know! Nicole called early this morning with news from a contact in Cairo. Oh Gamal, you're here, in Paris, they let you out, they released you. How clever of Nicole to find you. How I value her friendship. And Henri, too. They made it up between them, you know, despite her professor, they were brave and good about it, both of them.'

'Does Nicole have your address?'

'No one does. Just a contact number, the one you phoned. I'm now surrounded by the most Byzantine security. It would make you laugh, you sceptic, you terrible novelist.'

'How are you, Huda? Your face is all over Cairo. I hear you've married the Prophet.'

'Peace be upon him. Oh how superstitious our simple people are. One cannot blame them, such is their suffering.'

'I also hear that you hailed Khomeini as the Hidden Imam.'

'Gamal, I cannot discuss these things on the telephone, really not. You will find out everything about your faithful wife in half an hour, beloved Gamal. Oh how I feared for you. Did they torture you? Now, Gamal, please be patient and hold the line for a moment until you hear the voice of an Arab who will tell you exactly where and when to be. A nice hotel – for us.'

'No.'

'No?'

'I am not alone, Huda.'

'You mean Henri and Nicole? Naturally they will leave us to be together. They are both very tactful people. They understand love.'

'I think the situation is rather more complicated. The Sicilian defence is involved: queen's knight to pawn 6 takes bishop.'

A fractional pause. 'Mossad?'

'They're building the Third Temple on the Dome of the Rock right here in Charles de Gaulle. You ought to understand assassination, Huda, you practice it often enough.'

'But you cannot suspect Henri and Nicole!'

'Perhaps their grandparents were arrested during Le Grand Rafle.'

'The what?'

'The round-up of Jews which took place here in 1942.'

'Gamal, you must return to Cairo immediately. Understand? Take the first plane out.'

'Hamida wants your skin. I'm the bait.'

'Hamida! I'm smarter than Hamida!'

'You mean who, in the end, shall be queen.'

'How I love your cruelty.' The phone goes down. I shuffle fatly back to the Chevaliers and relieve Henri of my suitcase.

'Huda has to leave France,' I announce. 'Apparently the next assassination attempt on Sharaf is due during Friday prayers at the Al-Azhar Mosque.'

Henri and Nicole are regarding me with bafflement and anger. The five 'Arab' oil merchants from Mossad are watching us.

'Next Friday?' Henri says. 'You're sure?'

'Quite sure. I expect Hamida would accept a reverse-charge call about that, Nicole.' I honour her with the Gamal Rahman 'special', the huge eye-roll which adorns the back flap of my books. 'If not, Jerusalem will pass the message.'

The Chevaliers vanish. I squander my life's savings on a sliced baguette, stuffed with ham. At the Air France desk I book myself on to the first plane to London. The clerk looks at me pityingly when I ask whether there is a direct flight to Bruddersford. She checks her computer screen then a directory.

'Bruddersford does not exist, monsieur.'

TWENTY-EIGHT

❧

Observing the fat fellow with the swivelling eyes approaching hesitantly across the open-plan editorial floor of the *Echo*, Joe Reddaway was reminded of a teddy bear searching for a picnic. Medium height, tyres of flab, early to mid-thirties, heavy lips, pale-skinned for an Arab – and those eyes! This must be the chappie from *Misr*. A large packet of Kit-Kats protruded from the pocket of his sagging jacket

'Take a pew,' Joe gestured him to a chair, offering his hand without rising. 'Tea or coffee?'

'Is the coffee real?'

'It's unreal.'

'I'll try it. Three lumps of sugar, please.'

'Lumps?'

'I thought British sugar came in cubes, otherwise known as lumps. I could hardly ask for "three cubes", could I?'

The Egyptian laughed affably, trying to be likeable.

Joe extracted some filthy brownish water from the machine into a paper cup and tossed a couple of packets of sugar alongside it. His visitor looked at it with recoil. Joe guessed that food was important to this bloke. Amazing eyes! – like the revolving beacons of a lighthouse. Accent like a fruit cake.

'At school in England, were you?' Joe asked.

Abruptly the bulging eyes were hooded. 'Eton or Winchester – but I can never remember which.' A pause. 'I am the genuine article, Mr Reddaway. A Gyppo.'

'No offence intended, just a simple question. People call me Joe, by the way.'

'Gamal.' They shook hands again. Joe noted the thrust on the second syllable. Gam-ahl. Like Al-laah. It was Hassan Hassani who had tutored Joe out of 'Aller' – by sheer, maddening persistence.

'You're the straight-talking columnist here, I believe.'

Joe nodded. 'You write for *Misr*?'

'I used to. I worked for Hosny Hikmat.'

'How do you find Bruddersford?'

'It comes in shades of grey. We have two inches of rain a year in Cairo so I'm not used to dripping like a used teabag.'

'Nothing ever happens in Bruddersford.'

'It will. The fundamentalists are coming.'

'I keep hearing that word. It can mean anything.'

'Not to Khomeini.'

'Khomeini? Here? You're joking. The souls of our Pakis are securely padlocked to Yorkshire pudding and medium-pace bowling. Anyway, Khomeini's a faraway Shi'ite. Most of the lads here are Sunnis.'

The visitor raised his eyebrows. Joe began to bridle: here we have the knows-everything-on-arrival type. Joe made a show of looking at his watch. 'So what can I do for you?'

'My former boss, Hosny Hikmat, is in the Tora prison. I want him out. Any chance you've heard of Hikmat?'

'We have a saying here: "If it happens in Lancashire, put it on the foreign page." ' Joe waited, shifted his long legs. 'I've never gathered how Hikmat fell foul of Sharaf, apart from the Nasser-connection, of course.'

'You could talk to Sharaf for ten minutes about Hikmat. You could talk to Hikmat for ten hours about Sharaf. You'd end up none the wiser. Nor they.'

'You want me to know that you're well-connected?'

'Hikmat is a newspaperman. He's in jail and dying. They won't let him see a doctor.'

'If I had the keys to Cairo jail, Mr Rahman, I'd catch a plane tonight. I can write a polemic, of course, but it won't get further than the fish and chip shops of Bruddersford.'

'Mrs Sharaf claims that her mother was born and raised in Bruddersford. We don't believe it.'

'What difference does it make?'

Pearls of sweat were spreading across the Egyptian's high, domed forehead. He hadn't touched his unreal coffee.

'Mrs Sharaf says her mother's maiden name was Plum. I've searched the Registry of Births in London but not discovered a single person called Plum born in or near Bruddersford between 1890 and 1910. The English mother may be a fabrication.'

'You want to blackmail the Sharafs into releasing Hikmat?'

'According to Mrs Sharaf, her mother returned to Bruddersford just once, many years after settling in Egypt, in search of her family. She put an advert in the local paper, which produced one surviving cousin and a few lesser relatives. They all had tea together. The local paper recorded the occasion – remarkable story, mother-in-law of Egyptian Vice President, et cetera.'

'Do you have the date of the mother's visit?'

'No. I don't believe it ever took place.'

'You want to search through how many years of the daily *Echo* in our Black Hole?'

'As many years as it takes.'

Joe scratched his fiery head. 'Forgive me if I'm getting this wrong but isn't it difficult to prove a negative? If I understand you, you don't want to find that story, you want not to find it. You find something, it's evidence; you don't find something, maybe you were asleep that afternoon.'

'Hikmat is in jail and dying.'

'I'll see what I can do. By the way, steer clear of Plum Lane. The whores up there don't always wash behind the ears.'

℞

Douglas Blunt received the Egyptian in the Chief Executive's Office of City Hall after a call from Joe Reddaway.

'Tea, coffee?'

'Tea with three packets of sugar, please.'

' "Packets"? We have lumps here.'

Blunt made the tea himself, using a pot and strainer, the proper way.

'I haven't read much Egyptian literature myself, apart from Mahmoud.'

'My father.'

'Really? Milk? Is Rahman a pen name?'

'I was born Gamal Rahman Mahmoud. Rather early in my career, at about the age of six, I decided to cut myself in half – the worm anticipating the gravedigger's spade.'

'So how do you find Bruddersford?'

'Fascinating.'

Blunt chuckled. 'That's a new one!'

'I used to write brochures for the Cairo Tourist Board. The trick was to be able to spell "fabulous". I gather you know this town and its history better than anyone, Mr Blunt.'

'This "city" we say here – very proud of that. We have a Lord Mayor and a cocked hat. So how's things in Egypt? – not so good, I hear.'

'Not so good.'

'We have the same problem of fundamentalism in Northern Ireland. I reckon I know every prominent Muslim in this city and I'd give my life it couldn't happen here. A fellow called Ishmail Haqq raised a fuss about one of Mahmoud's novels being available in the City Library – I forget the title.'

'*The Children of Mustafa?*'

'Aye, probably. Anyway, the Council of Mosques firmly reminded Ishmail Haqq that banning books is not the British way. Joe Reddaway tells me you're looking for Plums.'

'Did you ever know anyone of that name?'

'Only in Sheffield – which isn't a million miles away. I gave Sid Plum a call – without saying why – I realize you're running risks, Mr Rahman, I'm not keen on Sharaf myself, by the way. I asked Sid if any distant relative was known to have married an Egyptian. He just laughed. "It may have been Cleopatra Plum," he said. You're looking depressed. May I ask why Mrs Sharaf should claim to be half-English if she isn't? The Brits were hardly the most popular folk in Egypt in Nasser's day – or any day.'

'Snobbery. She's very proud of her fair skin.'

'Aye, aye, but I can't help thinking you're chasing a short straw. Don't forget that in the 1950s and early 1960s there were no less than three local newspapers here. And there's always the mother of us all, the *Yorkshire Post*. Are you sure Gertrude Plum placed her ad in the *Echo?*'

'No.'

Douglas Blunt glanced at his watch. 'By the way, steer clear of Plum Lane. The whores up there don't always wash behind the ears.'

☙

The Egyptian moves hotel every other night. It's a sweat and a bore never to be reachable by telephone – not that you can be reached in the damp, eight-pounds-a-nighters he can afford – but it only needs the Egyptian Embassy to catch wind of his enquiries and he could end up with his throat cut in one of these cold, soiled little bedrooms used by travelling salesmen. He doesn't trust anyone in this benighted town which styles itself a city and is crawling with mosques. There are no touch-me-not plants huddled beneath tamarind trees in Bruddersford; nothing smells good. Far away the swallow-sails of the feluccas glide up and down the Nile.

Gamal talks himself to sleep over a bottle of whisky. Mahmoud sits opposite him (though there's only one chair):

'With you, my son, literature finally aspires to rule the rulers and, thus, the world. To you my Master and I are what Jupiter and Saturn were to Virgil – mere verses.'

'Kiss my feet, Shaytan.'

431

'You smile but you mean it! I've heard this before. Dante demanded that I kiss his sandals; Shakespeare insisted that I kiss his wife's tight vagina; Milton, his sightless eyes; Goethe, his conscience; Dante, his inferno; Dostoyevsky, his morning turd. Yes, I auditioned them all – and you are not the only contemporary writer under consideration.'

'Who else?'

'These things are confidential.'

'Who else?'

'Never mind. So I put to you a test: what is it you really want me to kneel-and-kiss?'

'My fame! My everlasting fame! Let my name and my face be known across the world!'

The devil nods. 'But nemesis invariably follows hubris.'

'Let it! Any other tests? – why not urine tests for writers? I may have boosted my talent on steroids.'

'Very well. What is truly blasphemous – Jesus cursing God on the Cross or Jesus begging God to grant him one night with Mary Magdalene before ascending the Cross?'

'Your point is taken.'

'And what is my point?'

'Religion has tortured us poor men into an agony of guilt and self-loathing. By the way: the level of blasphemy should be assigned a tariff, like the different dives into a swimming pool, or like the pirouettes undertaken by ice-skaters, or like – '

'What will you call your novel?'

'*The Devil: an Interview.*'

'Sounds harmless enough.'

'I'm glad you think so.'

'I would have made an ideal insurance actuary if I had not been called to lower things.' Shaytan smiles faintly. 'Life insurance is our speciality.'

'When insurance men speak of life they mean death.'

Mahmoud's fingertips come delicately together – but how his hands tremble! 'You will be wise to settle in London,' he murmurs.

'So tell me, Shaytan, what is your purpose in all this? – that is what you have never quite explained.'

'My purpose now, as always, is to discredit the Party of Religion, which calls itself, falsely, the Party of God, and thus I hope to persuade the Almighty to grant Man his freedom.'

'And Woman?'

'Every Holy Book is of course a blueprint for the eternal oppression of Woman – but that is not my concern.'

432

Immaculately attired, Councillor Zulfikar Zaheed received the Egyptian journalist in the office on the second-floor of City Hall which he shared with five Labour colleagues.

'Douglas Blunt asked me to see you. I should say straight away that some of my Muslim colleagues regard Sharaf as the betrayer of the Palestinians. That is not, however, my personal position.'

'Thank you for finding time to receive me, Councillor Zaheed.'

Zaheed shook his smart white cuffs down the sleeves of his grey, pin-striped suit, fingering the lacquered links.

'The City Council has passed a resolution calling for Hikmat's release. We sent it to the Egyptian Embassy in London.'

'He'd be grateful if he knew.'

'All pressure counts.'

'He doesn't have long to live.'

Zulfikar Zaheed began to pace the room. 'Very frankly, Mr Rahman, and I'm speaking off the record here, in my personal opinion the Sharaf family is the only force now standing between Egypt and a fundamentalist uprising.'

'It's a point of view,' the Egyptian said.

'Strictly between ourselves, Mr Rahman, some of Bruddersford's Muslims are beginning to cock an ear to the Ayatollah Khomeini. I put my faith in twenty years of religious tolerance in this City – but sometimes Zulfikar Zaheed has his doubts.' Zaheed glanced at his watch. 'Now how can I help you?'

People did not glance at their watches in Egypt – not even the Rais did it. With the Rais you always knew when you were dismissed; he would fall to his prayer mat and close his eyes; he would say, 'I'll throw you to the crocodiles!'; he would pick up the phone and start talking to the Shah – but he would never glance at his watch! Gamal hated cold, damp Bruddersford: so smug, so inviolable.

'Councillor Zaheed, have you ever heard a rumour about Sharaf's mother-in-law having been born in Bruddersford, née Plum?'

Zaheed sat down, carefully crossing his legs.

'We are all migrants, immigrants, exiles here, Mr Rahman. Many of us go home to visit our relatives. It's perfectly normal. I can go further. It's my personal belief that Mrs Sharaf's courage in modernizing the status of Egyptian women is clear proof of English blood.'

Showing Gamal out, Zaheed issued a caution concerning Plum Lane – apparently the whores up there didn't always wash behind the ears.

Being kept waiting by a Headmistress was not so bad: plenty of posters and leaflets to examine – language problems, religious diversity, cultural tolerance. Gamal assumed that this was the post-sixties progressive package now under fire from the 'back to basics' disciplinarians.

Two parents, Pakistanis, were sitting in the secretary's office when Gamal arrived. Gamal nodded in their direction. The husband responded. The wife, who wore a hijab, stared into space, eyes averted from the male stranger. After a while there was a brief and rapid exchange between them in (probably) Punjabi, but it could have been Urdu. Finally the couple were called in to the Headmistress's office. The wife followed the husband.

Gamal wanted to say 'Good luck'.

When he was finally shown into Mrs Newman's presence he found a woman who was younger than he'd expected and surprisingly attractive. He was glad he'd worn a tie.

Mrs Newman didn't offer him tea or coffee. The issue of sugar lumps therefore never came up.

'Douglas Blunt asked me to see you, Mr Rahman.'

'You will have seen many families pass, so to speak, under your bridge, Mrs Newman.'

'My secretary has checked the school register but I'm afraid she found no Plums. There are of course many other schools in this city.'

'Of course.'

'I very much admire your President's wife, Celia el-Sharaf.'

'I know her well.'

'I'm told she's half-English. Is that correct?'

'It's a rumour.'

'I thought you said you know her well.'

Gamal wouldn't care to be one of Mrs Newman's delinquent pupils but he would care to take her out to dinner. He had never known such loneliness. She was standing now – the interview was over.

'Please convey to Mrs Sharaf my congratulations on the wonderful work she has done to raise the status of Egyptian women.'

'I will indeed.'

'Whether she can beat off your fundamentalists you will judge better than I. We have our own problems here in Bruddersford. You may have noticed the couple who came to see me. They want their daughter to wear a headscarf in school. It's out of the question, of course.'

'Obviously you – '

Mrs Newman offered her hand. 'Keep calm, be reasonable, that's our motto.' She smiled pleasantly. 'Good luck with your quest.'

Walking out past the humming classrooms, the multi-cultural posters, the rainbow of smiling 'ethnic' children, he wished he'd invited Mrs Newman to dine with him. To discuss Celia el-Sharaf. The worst thing about Bruddersford was the evenings alone. Gamal had hoped that Joe Reddaway would propose a pint of Tetley best bitter in a pub but he never did. Gloomily Gamal plodded up Plumb Lane, whose silent final 'b' had eluded him, in search of a whore called Plum.

໑

'Try Hassan Hassani,' Reddaway advised when Gamal telephoned to report 'morale at zero'. 'It won't do you any good but it may give you an insight into Muslim Bruddersford.'

Visiting Hassani's modest, terraced home, Gamal quickly lapsed into catatonic boredom. A gas fire sustained a stupefying level of heat in the small living room with its garishly tinted photographs of the world's great mosques. Gamal marvelled that so educated a man could be so superstitious. Hassani was as obsessed about djinns as Laurence Durrell's fictional simpleton, Hamid. Admittedly Hassani's djinn did not inhabit the kitchen sink or waste pipe, but there was one lodged behind the refrigerator (of all places!). Gamal wondered whether Hassani sat himself on the WC and groaned 'Permission O ye blessed ones!' to appease the djinns, who might otherwise have dragged him down into the sewage system.

'Satan is alive and well, you know,' Hassani told him, one eye fastened to the television news. Gamal heard female voices in the corridor outside the closed living room door, but they passed straight to the kitchen.

'A great struggle is being waged in our country and yours,' Hassani said, his watery eyes alight.

'Pakistan, you mean?'

'General Zia is our best hope. But your President el-Sharaf is a wicked man. You're a Muslim, Mr Rahman?'

Gamal nodded faintly. Hassani's porthole glasses glinted.

'Yes, I am a Muslim,' Gamal said.

'You can pray with us. I shall take you to our mosque, the Maududi.'

Gamal's visit to the Maududi mosque – all those fucking Pakistani peasants banging their heads – was followed, at Hassani's suggestion, by a call at the home of Izza Shah who, being a magistrate and everything, might easily have come across a Plum or (as Hassani put it with a damp smile) 'sent one to prison – there's no shortage of white whores up Plumb Lane.' Izza Shah received his visitor with an almost morbid gravity. He shuffled through the dark corridor

435

towards the dim, yellowish light of the sitting room as if Islam was a war against the electricity meter. He knew of no Plum and predicted the imminent fall of 'that atheist Sharaf'.

On his way out Gamal was surprised by a glimpse of a girl who didn't belong here and knew it. Chewing gum, she tossed rivers of lustrous auburn hair, black at the roots, as she slinked-slunk up the stairs in tight jeans; he felt convinced she'd been listening at the door. At a glance he could tell that she yearned for pulsing music, an amplified existence. For this young lady Mecca was a ballroom. A younger girl, perhaps nine or ten years old, was standing in the shadows, watching intently as Izza Shah showed the visitor out. Gamal noted the gravity in her eyes, the covered head.

'Go to bed, Fah-ti-mah,' her father said.

෮

It was back to the stifling Black Hole in the basement of the *Echo*. The woman who grudgingly admitted Gamal to her archive clearly believed that back copies of the newspaper were to be preserved, not read. She kept fussing, sighing and asking him what he was looking for (at Gamal's request, Joe Reddaway had not explained his research). Gamal's evasive murmurings she took for 'downright rudeness'; the tension in the Black Hole reached lockout proportions: 'I suppose yer think I got nothing better to do.' Had the teeth-grinding Gyppo relaxed and had a chat over a nice cuppa tea, he might have learned the woman's name and life-history: Mabel Rowlands, widow, born Mabel Plum, first cousin of Celia el-Sharaf. She could have told him about the tea party when Aunt Gertrude arrived from Egypt, and how they'd been photographed for the old *Examiner*, now deceased.

Gamal sometimes forgets which hotel he's staying in tonight. By night he walks past the city centre pubs fearfully avoiding groups of young whites, steering clear, backtracking, losing his way. His imagination is working overtime: already he hears the gangs running through the streets, the madness burning on their brows, setting fire to shops, hurling bricks at police cars. Passing across the open space in front of City Hall, Gamal halts abruptly; some tramps, or 'travellers', have lit a fire right outside the police station. He wakes up sweating in a very cold hotel room with thick condensation on the grimy window panes. He groans: the prospect of that grim harridan in the Black Hole is too much.

He falls asleep again.

Magic carpet to Cairo – and a curious (do I mean 'peculiar'?) invitation to dine at the home of a man describing himself as a 'junior civil servant of peasant stock and of single-minded but thwarted ambition.' Gamal immediately recognizes this person as the principal character in one of Mahmoud's minor novels. The junior civil servant of peasant stock lives precisely where Mahmoud had accommodated him: on the third floor of a block in al-Bahr Close in the Bab al-Shaerriya quarter. He is fatter than Gamal, repulsively ugly, and old in a timeless, Methuselah-like way. The supper he has personally prepared for his guest – every item – is known to Gamal in advance: ox tongue, ox brain, ox cheek, ox eye, along with sausage, bready beef soup, fried onion, raddish and pickle, melon. They settle down to eat.

'I will tell you,' the ancient junior civil servant muses, 'something.'

'Yes?' The eye of the ox pauses between Gamal's open lips.

'The wisdom of Omar al-Khayyam is more beautiful than all of Al Ma'arri's poems. You know of course the Raba'iyyat?'

Gamal nods. 'Of course. Each day of Omar's life was swifter than a fleeting thought.'

'And are you familiar with Al Ma'arri, the eleventh-century poet dedicated to celibacy, solitude, austerity?'

'Of course. Each day of his life was longer than the parabola of a comet through the heavens.'

'Please swallow the eye of the ox, Mr Rahman. It is the best thing on the table.'

Gamal's host is now wearing his (familiar) dark red tarboosh over his bald crown, although the guest has no recollection of him putting it on.

'Tell me about your friends, Mr Rahman. I take it you have many friends?'

'A successful artist will soon find himself barnacled by every kind of parasite and hanger-on and groupie. Misplaced loyalty is ultimately to the advantage of neither party – one may appear to have cut a knot which has in fact been unravelling quite steadily.'

'So much for your friends. Shall we talk of your enemies?'

'Talent, you know, is always resented. I have received my share of death threats.'

'Death, even? Here in the Arab world, the Islamic world, these are unquiet times . . .'

'Between ourselves, I have become addicted to these threats – the intimate knowledge of whom I am.'

His host inclines his dark red tarboosh. 'That is why I send them to you so punctiliously.'

'You?'

'But this small bureaucratic service will soon be discontinued. It is merely one of my minor departmental responsibilities, like the laying of water pipes and electric cables.'

Gamal lifts his wine glass. 'No problem.'

'The only item on the agenda is now deicide.'

'Agreed.'

'And when will you leave Egypt?'

'Leave? Why leave?'

'In Egypt you are no more than a 50-watt bulb hanging from the wall in a village latrine. Just another petty-pharaoh propitiating local gods to green the Nile Valley.'

Gamal slowly wipes his mouth with the freshly laundered napkin. He feels its stiffness, its starch, faintly harsh against his mouth; he studies the greasy smear upon it while making a small speech to his host:

'Exile comes, like your good self, in many guises. Are we talking of James Joyce the wanderer, or Marcel Proust the hermit crab of the cork-lined room? Do we mean Dostoyevsky the debt-ridden fugitive or Mayakovsky the love-haunted gambler? Must I scurry across continents and seas, a dark-skinned Brecht ever-pursued by the Gestapo of Islam? Or should I set up house in the comfortable safety of England, like Victor Hugo and Karl Marx?'

Mahmoud – for it is who else? – ignores these questions.

'I see you, Gamal, some years hence, buried alive in Mustafa's desert – and waiting for a letter from your father. Waiting to read these words: "I warned you." '

ຄ∿

The next day it rained again. The clouds scudded in from the Pennines, discharging their load on the rows of terraced flats, the Council houses, the city centre. Bruddersford gleamed dully, without conviction. Gamal decided to spend the day warm and dry chatting to a new friend over endless cups of sugared Nescafé – although 'friend' was perhaps premature. Gamal had sought out Ali Cheema on hearing from Joe Reddaway that the young man was Muslim Bruddersford's only student of philosophy to have gained entry to Oxford. It was disappointing to discover that this alert, baby-faced theologian had read neither of his novels.

'In general, I read very little modern fiction,' Ali had explained without a trace of apology. 'Belief may not be the same as the suspension of disbelief.'

'You have never read Mahmoud's *The Children of Mustafa*?'

'Mahmoud is the Egyptian apostate? No.'

'It's essential reading for a theologian. Mahmoud took as his text

438

Meister Eckhart's nostrum that it's not enough that God is good. He should be better.'

A steady rain was beating pleasantly on the window. Gamal felt warm and comfortable in Ali's little terraced house. The gas fire hummed nicely. He'd made it up about Meister Eckhart: the sober towns of West Yorkshire seemed to demand make-believe.

'What do you think of the New Testament?' Ali Cheema asked.

'That's a big question.'

'I have been rereading it. The Christians claim that it's God's work. But it's full of errors, naturally. I don't suppose the liberty to get things wrong extends to God.'

'Oh but it does.' Gamal's eyes rolled hugely. 'May I lend you Mahmoud's novel? I always carry a copy wherever I travel. It brings me luck.'

Ali smiled. 'Can one borrow another person's luck?'

Gamal watched the rain splashing in small puddles beyond the window. 'I was once in Oslo,' he said, 'and – '

'Yes, I was there for a conference,' Ali said.

'Did you not fall in love with Munch, and the aura he painted over Ibsen's head, and the extraordinary watery light of mid-afternoon, the woodsmoke kippering the sharp-sharp air, the smell of leaves and earth and oncoming Arctic night?'

'I was there in summer.'

'One wonders,' Gamal said, 'whether steady rain and buttered crumpets is the necessary condition of democracy.'

'Necessary but not sufficient,' Ali replied.

'May we watch the television news?'

'Of course, feel free.' Ali seemed surprised, faintly disdainful, as if the daily news should be of no interest to intellectuals. Perhaps he suspected that his worldly visitor was bored by his company.

The TV set stammered to life. The newsreader's voice came up before the image clarified. Sharaf dead. Sharaf assassinated during a great military parade to commemorate The Crossing, the storming of the Suez Canal. Gamal's eyes rolled.

'Egypt has finally lost the boy who fished himself out of the Nile in order that Egypt might not lose him.'

Ali Cheema kept his gaze on the screen, which showed American-built Phantoms weaving aerobatic trails of vapour across the cerulean sky, above the stadium.

'And we may surmise,' Ali's visitor went on, 'that a new uniform had arrived from the Rais's London tailor, cut in the preferred German style. We may even offer an educated guess that Sharaf had refused a bullet-proof waistcoat because it disturbed the slim set of his uniform. Celia once confided to me that Fawzi never got over the shame of appearing vest-swollen in Jerusalem – every camera caught the telltale scaffolding.'

No response from Ali, who was liking his guest less and less. Now came the military parade, Sharaf on his feet in the reviewing stand, capless and beaming. Then the pictures cut out into a blur.

'Egyptian film,' Gamal commented. 'The American networks must have skipped the occasion. Heads will roll in New York. What happens to the Middle East peace process now?'

'The "process" of capitulation is dead with that godless dictator,' Ali Cheema said.

The newsreader was now reporting that the late President's younger daughter, Huda el-Sharaf, had been detained at the scene of the assassination. 'Official sources allege that she masterminded the conspiracy to kill her father.'

Gamal Rahman's eyes opened very wide. 'Huda! You have turned Lear's Cordelia inside out!'

'You know her well?' Ali asked.

'Evidently not.'

Celia el-Sharaf came on-screen, grave, dignified, her eye-shadow unsmudged. 'My husband gave his life for his people.'

෧ঌ

Cairo Airport had been reopened for less than an hour when Gamal Rahman belly-flopped down after a journey involving three hours' delay on a sweltering tarmac at Beirut. The national airline was still refusing to serve alcohol on-board, Sharaf dead or not.

'Don't you know anything!' Mr Rahman kept yelling at frightened stewardesses of Air Egypt.

They didn't. No one was taking the risk of knowing anything.

Night had fallen when the Boeing reached Cairo. Soldiers, police, tanks swarmed hysterically round the plane. Eventually the dehydrated author was bundled (without his baggage, of course) into some kind of Government car and driven through interminable road-blocks manned by fear-crazed soldiers in steel helmets to an isolated villa surrounded by multiple fences of barbed wire and vast steel barriers designed, presumably, to fend off further coups and Islamic suicide bombers. A familiar, lifelong odour informed him that the villa was situated on the banks of the Nile; a few crocs could be observed monitoring his stinking feet. Coup d'états were up their street.

The night reeked of soldiers, raw concrete, and the barely controlled panic occasioned by unpredicted eclipses of the sun. Despite the blazing arc lights, most of which had failed, this was a night which might last forever. I was led into a cramped guardroom where the sweat of men mingled with the sweating of the walls. I noticed a portrait of Sharaf lying on the floor, its glass shattered, its commanding posture crumpled – the dead dictator looked as if he was crying. I was ordered to sit down, stand up, sit down. When I demanded whisky I was slapped by a colonel who – you could guess – hadn't dared touch a drop since the assassination. It reminded me of Ramadan while waiting for sunset, except this time the sun had already slid into the Nile and might never resurface.

Eventually a braided army officer and a brace of soldiers led me to a small room whose sole occupant was Hamida. The officer saluted her smartly. The Virgin of Egypt remained the princess although the Acting President, a nonentity hitherto beneath the elevated sightlines of these pages, had lost no time in relieving her of her official functions. She had been 'detained for her own protection' but tomorrow, who knows, the Acting President might be detained by Hamida for his.

'You may leave us,' she commanded. They obeyed but the turn of the key in the door could have been heard in Vladivostok (not a bad place to be at this juncture, it struck me).

'Thank you for coming, Gamal.' She was wearing the black chador of mourning, her head covered, but her beauty and ill-concealed contempt for this fat bum set me blazing with my usual devilish designs. However, having Hamida does take time – twenty years so far – not least in a black chador, and my attention was swiftly diverted by a large bottle of Johnny Walker, a jug of water and a couple of glasses on her bedside table. It wasn't the moment to stand on ceremony.

'Say when,' I instructed myself, pouring and gulping. 'Cheers,' I said. 'How about you, Mademoiselle? Just a drop in honour of Pappi?'

'No, thank you.'

'You can lose your temper with me if you like. It might be more fun.' I poured myself another mega-tot, felt better, allowed my marbled gaze to settle on Hamida. 'How is your poor mother?'

'As brave as ever, but her heart is utterly destroyed. She wishes you well.'

'Please thank her.'

'I will convey your message. It was kind of you to come from England. We realize that you didn't have to.' Hamida was clearly struggling to keep her rage in check.

'I came under the Acting President's protection after several hours of haggle-haggle at the Egyptian Embassy.'

'Then you are an honourable husband.'

441

'Huda, you mean? Where is she?'

'You will be taken to your wife very soon.' Hamida stood tall and erect as ever – the chador could not compete with her famous breasts. 'Gamal, you once told me that you invariably lied to me because everyone did. But now you must answer truthfully when I ask whether you and Huda are in fact married.'

'She's married to the Prophet, I hear, but I don't mind standing in.'

'Gamal!'

'OK, OK, if a Sharaf tells a chap she's his wife, then she's his wife.'

'My sister is with child.'

'Whose?'

Hamida's imperious features were glazed in something akin to hatred. 'I am waiting – and my poor mother is waiting – for you to honour your wife, and her family.'

I sighed, poured myself another tot, and pondered my rising lust – a lifetime's thwarted desire! – for Hamida.

'Huda's a nice kid, that's all. We all make little mistakes during a civil war.'

'Are you accusing your own, faithful, devoted wife of adultery?'

Hamida knew and Gamal knew that according to custom and practice she should by now have slapped me senseless, torn my blubbery lips apart on her pharaonic finger rings, and summoned her janissaries to hurl me down several flights of marble stairs. The extraordinary restraint which brought her itching hands into a tangled knot of self-denial was proving rather disappointing.

'By the way, I'm hungry. Where's the menu?'

Hamida was probably assessing whether the fat slob would be more compliant, a better family man all round, on a full stomach: or just fall asleep with any wife who cared to claim him. She evidently concluded that I would be more likely to sign the document on an empty stomach.

The 'document', Reader? Out it came from beneath the black chador, several pages of stiff creamy parchment bearing the seals of the Acting President, the Supreme Court, and the ulama of Al-Azhar over and under parallel texts in Arabic and English. Gamal's morose eye skimmed the lines, right to left, left to write – either way someone called 'Huda el-Sharaf Rahman' had done what she had done only in obedience to the dictates of 'her lawful husband Gamal Rahman Mahmoud, known as Gamal Rahman'.

Who was hereby and thereby granted Immunity from Prosecution on condition of Permanent Exile from the State of Egypt (Misr).

I remembered the interrogation sessions in the Tora prison, where the dying Toad, the finest Egyptian editor since Ptolemy, was denied access to a doctor. I remembered a decade of pillage, repression, censorship and the constant fanning of the peacock's tail.

Hamida may have read my thoughts. 'You made your bed, Gamal, now kindly have the good grace to lie in it. This is the only way to save Huda's life. You want to save Huda's life, don't you?'

'Who's making the rules at this moment in time? And who will remake them tomorrow morning?'

Out from the chador came a second, shorter document, an affidavit written in French and signed by Monsieur and Madame Henri Chevalier. They reported a meeting between Huda and myself in Paris, at the Hôtel du Nord, attended by themselves. I had advised Huda that the Rais could be assassinated the following Friday when Sharaf would attend prayers at the Al-Azhar Mosque. (The Rais had been in the habit of constantly changing mosques like Westland helicopters.) The plan, claimed the Chevalier affidavit, had been agreed, and Miss Huda el-Sharaf dutifully followed her husband's instructions, sending word to her network of Gama'at assassins, but the Rais altered his prayer plans at the last minute (as usual) on the advice of the security services (as usual).

I studied Hamida, my lust rising: barefaced feminine mendacity is worth a powdered rhino's horn.

'What else did Henri and Nicole tell you?'

'They confirmed in private what they could make public, that you and Huda engaged in conjugal relations while in Paris.' Pause. 'In the Hôtel du Nord.'

' "Engaged in"? You mean she and I brought the ceiling down and made a baby even while I was on a plane to London in search of your mama's "English" ancestry?'

'It remains a mystery to me why my dear sister should have married a man of your unequalled vulgarity and coarseness of spirit.'

'I'm hungry.'

'You will dine at your wife's table tonight.'

'And what happens to *you*, Mademoiselle, if I don't sign this surrealist document?'

Hamida did not deign to answer; she merely opened the 'locked' door of her room and imperiously flicked her finger at the platoon of colonels smoking in the corridor. They clicked their heels and jerked straight in the old manner; having survived under Nasser and Sharaf, they had no intention of betting on anything.

'Conduct Mr Rahman to his wife.' To me she added, touching her veil, 'You may take the document with you.'

'What about the whisky?'

Hamida contemptuously handed me the Johnny Walker bottle, or what was left of it.

Three colonels conducted me down a windowless corridor reeking of naked breeze block and raw concrete. I was led into a small, shuttered room lit by a single bulb hanging by its wire from a ragged hole in the ceiling. Iron bars covered the small window; a pretty vase of dried flowers beside the narrow bed was the only visible concession to the prisoner's femininity.

The prisoner was dressed in a plain white – not black! – cotton gown and headscarf. Her little stomach yielded no indication of my future son's presence, or anyone else's future son. I saw at once that Huda was as always enjoying being Huda, neatly tucked into herself in that infuriatingly humble way much favoured by servants of God after a killing spree. Her delicate, almond shaped features retained their trademark serenity – she smiled at me like a little boat fresh from a repaint. Kneeling to unfasten my shoes, she washed my stinking feet in an enamelled bowl of warm, soapy water.

I lifted her up – serious drinking seemed indecorous while she was on her knees.

'So you're with child, Huda?'

'Oh yes, Gamal, isn't that wonderful? I shall bear you a son.'

'Hm. What does the Prophet say?'

'Please do not blaspheme, Gamal.'

I sighed fatly (as fathers do) and allowed a little Scotch to ease my paternal burdens. 'Frankly, I don't see how we can have a sensible conversation with bugs and cameras peeping through that hole in the ceiling.'

'Oh there are none, Gamal, we are entirely alone, I assure you.'

I took her hand. 'When do you face trial?'

'That is up to you, Gamal. Already I am losing track of time. My baby – our baby – is my only clock.'

'Ask him when dinner is.'

She smiled. 'It's coming, everything is being prepared, your favourite dishes.'

I sat on the small bed, which groaned, perhaps in anticipation. 'Hamida showed me this bizarre "confession" I'm supposed to sign.'

'Yes, I wrote it myself.'

'*You* wrote it! It reads to me like the work of a thousand sheikhs and mullahs from the ulama of Al-Azhar – with additional script by Hamida, Anis Hussein and Auntie Lulu.'

'Gamal, as a novelist you have taught me that the truth often lies buried.'

I ran my eye down the document again, both texts.

'So, Huda, for many years you have obeyed me without question, first as my pupil and later as my wife?'

'Yes, Gamal, and such obedience brought me much happiness.'

'It says here that I once told you a story about thieves in ancient times who sent tortoises bearing lighted candles into the houses they intended to rob.'

'Yes, Gamal, you did.'

'And you later came to understand, as a mature woman, that you were the tortoise and I the "divinely inspired thief"?'

'Yes, Gamal.'

'It was I who instructed you to break off your engagement to Andy Poppy?'

'Gamal, you warned me against accepting a lifetime's unhappiness.'

'Did I?'

'Yes.'

'It was I who arranged for your flight into exile?'

'Through your friend Henri Chevalier.'

'It says here that it was I who constantly masterminded your terrorist activities – which you wrongly and weakly shrank from out of misplaced family loyalty.'

'I shall always be grateful to you for your firmness of purpose, Gamal.'

'And here I read that I protected you by deceiving the Government of Egypt as to your whereabouts.'

'And at terrible risk to yourself!'

'I discover in this document that I summoned you on numerous occasions to Cairo, to Upper Egypt, to Paris. As my "wife" you felt obliged, under the Islamic law of the Shari'a, to obey my every command. Finally I drove you to the "God-hated crime of patricide".' I took her chin in my hand. 'Isn't there some contradiction here?'

Huda's serenity was unshakeable. She was now seated beside me on the bed, her knees pressed together, her small hands folded – far more relaxed than Hamida's writhing claws.

'I understood you, Gamal, even when you did not speak in so many words.'

'Huda, it strikes me that in subscribing to this phrase "God-hated crime of patricide", you are in effect renouncing your own faith and the final battle cry, "O Jerusalem, Caliphate of Death, the Muslims are coming." You are tying God's knot in Satan's obfuscatory ribbons.'

'Hamida thought it was a good idea.'

'So it was Hamida who wrote this!'

Huda nodded – give her credit, she did nod!

'Gamal, I care nothing for my own fate. But if I die, then our child dies. Gamal, no Islamic court is going to accept my signature to this document as sufficient. I am merely a woman, a wife. Only you can decide, Gamal, whether you wish to condemn your own son to die in his mother's womb.'

'Supposing it's a girl?'

Reader! Not in my wildest booze could I solicit your forgiveness for that remark. But I was hungry – hadn't eaten properly since I tucked in, courtesy of the Acting President, to an Air Egypt dodgy-sandwich over the English Channel. Huda was silenced at last: a girl is no good. Anyway, what evidence was there of a child, male or female, in this little Sharaf womb? And, anyway anyway, it was ten-to-one that it would bear a striking resemblance to Henri, alias Dr Rieux. All evidence to the contrary, I'm no fool.

'I don't believe they'd hang a woman,' I said.

'I have been promised the firing squad.'

'And if I sign this document, if I "confess" to this tale out of the *Arabian Nights*, what will they do with you?'

'Your son and I will merely suffer imprisonment, with the prospect of presidential clemency at an appropriate time.'

'Huda, no one in the Western world will believe a word of it! I will be an object of derision! Entire audiences attending Verdi's version of the death of Desdemona at the Paris Opéra will suddenly howl with mirth. Horses competing at Ascot will roll over and split their sides. At the State Opening of Parliament Her Majesty the Queen will begin to giggle just as she's announcing, on Mrs Torment's behalf, the closure of the National Health Service. The Pope will step out on to the balcony of St Peter's to address the Easter pilgrims and then find himself leading them in laughter rather than prayer. Angels will fall out of the heavens helplessly flapping their wings. Surgeons will struggle to steady their hands during heart transplants. Hamlet will declare himself to be in a comedy – "Who cares who killed my dad?" The minaret of El-Hanafi Mosque will fall to the ground, chuckling, and the poor people of Shubra el-Khaimah will be reduced to laughing destitution.'

'Yes, Gamal. Mama always said you had great wit.'

I took Huda's little face between my hands and kissed her. 'I'm a no-good bum, Huda, a scribbler carrying a hitman's contract. You're right and I'm wrong about everything.'

'The worst thing you ever did, Gamal, was to make me wonder whether I was just another of your jokes.'

'This child of yours cannot be mine. You bloody well know that.'

Huda looked stricken. Her sweet little almond-face tucked into my hungry shoulder, my hungry neck. 'Oh Gamal,' she whispered, 'the Prophet came to me while I slept.'

'He did?'

'Oh yes, I'm quite certain. I had a dream.'

'Remember how we used to play chess under a shaded bower of the Muntazah Palace? – your dear mama always worried that you'd suffer sunburn on account of your English blood. You used to cheat when I snoozed off.'

'It's a long time since we played chess, Gamal.'

'Is it? Prophet takes author's wife, checkmate.' And here I lost my temper on a yearning stomach. 'Damn it! Are you telling me that the pupil I tutored in the tenets of the Enlightenment is really claiming to be the thirteenth wife of the Prophet? Look at me, look at me! And is his name, peace be upon him, Henri Chevalier?'

Huda let loose a cry of anguish, then hurried to the door, skipping frantically like the white-stockinged child I'd first known, and summoned my dinner.

'Yum-yum in the tum-tum,' she said with desperate jollity, avoiding my marbled eyes, 'that's what you used to say when Mama's cook was preparing something special for you . . . kufta . . . or meloukhia . . . or kounifa.'

A turbaned servant entered wheeling a silver trolley laden with steaming, fragrant, extravagant adjectives and dishes. There was even a bottle of Burgundy, Gévrey Chambertin, one of my favourites. It came with a note from Hamida: 'Your novels deserve publication in Egypt.'

It would have been churlish to say no to so much solicitude. We Egyptians are a hospitable people, as I had never tired of reminding tourists from Texas. Huda proudly watched me gobble and burp through the feast (as a good Muslim wife should).

A final belch as I pushed the empty dishes aside.

'Tell Hamida I command her attendance. She must witness my signature to this document.'

'As you wish,' Huda whispered.

'Yes I do wish, little tortoise.'

And Hamida came – entered! – in her black chador. I had not seen the two sisters in the same room for seven years. I noticed that neither would look at the other – they were like separate paintings in a single gallery, by different artists, neither wishing to hang beside the other.

'I hope the food was to your liking,' Hamida said.

'I've never been a fan of post-coup cooking, it tastes of sweat. The wine was at room temperature but it was the wrong room. However. Yes, however. If I am to be Huda's husband, we need a witness to our wedding night.' My eyes rolled. 'Third attempt by my abacus – I recall that Mademoiselle's State Security forces interrupted the second one.'

Hamida was staring at me with heaving breasts while Huda shrank into herself, mute. I wiped the grease from my mouth on my sleeve, though napkins had been provided, then bit into a ripe peach, squirting juice down my now-several chins.

'So undress yourself, little wife. Well go on, history calls, the Prophet demands it, undress!'

Huda turned her back on husband and sister, covering her face with both hands.

'And you too,' I nodded at Hamida, reaching for the wine. 'I'm taking a second wife. Double wedding.'

Both sisters cried out together. 'No!' It reminded me of the last act of Wilde's *The Importance of Being Earnest* – any minute now they would start addressing each other as 'Sister'. I sighed expansively and glanced at my watch.

'This habit of female submission I hear so much about seems to be confined to documents.'

Eventually they submitted, though this was the smallest bed in Egypt. Happily (Reader) I was in good form, despite the whisky and the bottle of Gévrey. I suppose every man hopes for the moment when he will be swallowed whole by his own penis – ears, eyes, nose and mouth subsumed by that single, inexhaustible, slit. Ghastly to report, not even Hamida could fake virginity – her vigorous style and vicious expletives, which I cannot repeat in a family novel, suggested varied encounters with the captains of the Presidential Guard. My Sadean tutorials had been in vain. If I wanted a soft and sensuous Molly Bloom, if I needed to hear 'yes I said yes I will Yes', I would have to settle in Dublin, where there are no crocs. But who knows? Who can say what I would have discovered had I turned to the crumpled, neglected and weeping Huda? But the taming of Hamida finally knocked your hero out, dropping me into the sleep of the Orient. So Gamal failed, yet again, as a husband. Blame the devil.

೧೦

Reaching London, I settled into the top floor of a comfortable Victorian house in Hampstead and resumed work on *The Devil: an Interview*. Isaac telephoned from New York frequently. Karl, he reported, ardently hoped that my new novel would contain a detailed account of my role in the assassination of Sharaf.

'Let Karl wait and see.'

'Gamal! Karl's talking in six figures.'

'Frankly, I prefer to sell books I've written.'

'Gamal! Unwritten books are the money! Nothing you write will be – can be – as good as what you're going to write, or might write. Gamal! Editors don't care for books! They like *ideas* – isn't that so, Harold? Harold, come out of the shower, I'm talking to Gamal. Gamal, editors adore *ideas* for books because an idea is only two-and-a-half pages long and because editors can later give themselves credit, and even share options, for the original *idea*. "We worked on this together," they say. "We kicked it around." To hurl a finished novel at a publisher is a slap in the face!'

'We've always done that.'

' "Always"? Am I hearing this, Harold? Am I talking to an Egyptian peasant, a clod of Nile silt who believes things will always be what they have been?'

'Maybe,' I heard Harold's voice, off, 'maybe he wants you to earn your twenty per cent.'

The trial of Huda and her fellow-conspirators at a high-security military installation outside Cairo was now only a week away. It was clear that the new regime meant business. Thousands of members and suspected members of the Gama'at had been rounded up. The official Egyptian press (Anis Hussein again) had published Huda's 'full confession' – it bore no resemblance to the one I had signed and indeed did not mention me at all. It was a ringing affirmation, eloquent and defiant, of the Koranic duty to execute godless tyrants. 'Who so ruleth not by that which Allah revealed, such are the dis believers. Our mission is to restore the sovereignty of God on earth. The caliphate is His instrument.'

Not a word about Gamal Rahman!

I hurried to the Egyptian Embassy in London to deposit a text of my own, explaining that Huda had imagined herself to be the character I depicted in my trilogy. I sent copies to the Acting President, the Acting Minister of Foreign Affairs, the Acting Editor of *Misr*, the President of the Special Tribunal (a military court) and Huda herself. But had she received it? Repeated attempts to telephone her failed. She was 'unavailable'.

As the world knows, Huda el-Sharaf stood before the firing squad on the second Friday of May. She was twenty-six years old. Doctors pronounced the four-month foetus to be male. I'd never had any doubt that it was Henri's. Hamida died in childbirth a few months later, victim of another boy, a whopper, twelve pounds, sporting truculently bulging eyes. I suppose it must have been the kufta or perhaps the kounifa.

I have written a letter of commiseration to Celia. Her baby

grandson is said to be a great consolation to her – or so the Toad claimed, in his last letter to me before the cancer took him. At least I assume 'that Maltese woman' referred to Celia. And there, Reader, I conclude my 'Open Letter to my Friends and Others'.

PART THREE

Bruddersford–*Tariq*

TWENTY-NINE

ɢ⌢

Young Tariq Khan has not forgotten his pledge to Mrs Nasreen Hassani: he had promised to present himself at the Taj Mahal hotel at 11 a.m. on Saturday. Tariq remembers Mrs Hassani drawing her chair close to his and asking him if he'd like to make some money. 'You're a virile young man, aren't you?' She'd also said something about himself and Safia Shah: 'It must be hard for a young man to resist a girl who lacks all modesty.'

'She's keeping bad company, Mrs Hassani.'

'A lady will be waiting for you at the hotel,' Mrs Hassani had said. 'A good friend of mine. Get the beer off your breath, Tariq. The lady doesn't care for the smell of beer. Just drink sweet tea from now till then.'

Whatever Tariq has been drinking the past week, it isn't sweet tea. His subsequent encounter with Safia has left him riddled with shame – though that slut had been asking for it, dressed like that and all alone in Ali Cheema's house.

'You're a virile young man, aren't you?' That remark had jolted his thoughts back to the Burnside Clinic, jerking off for a hundred quid. That test-tube business had wounded his self-esteem, what with having to help himself along with a pile of well-thumbed mags, *Mayfair* and the like. He'd been on the edge of coming when Gamal Rahman had winked at him from the pages of *Playboy*. 'Sexual Repression in Muslim Society,' Tariq had read. Rahman had even mocked Mustafa Jangar – an insult Tariq took personally – for 'running around Bruddersford' distributing leaflets laying down the Ayatollah's teachings on sexual conduct. Tariq had torn out the offending page of glossy paper and pocketed it.

Mustafa Jangar instructs the faithful that 'if a man sodomizes the son, the brother or the father of the woman after his marriage, the marriage remains valid.' It may remain 'valid' to you, Mustafa, but what is the poor wife to think? According to the Ayatollah of

Bruddersford, a man who commits adultery with his own aunt ought not to marry her daughters. How many of the Bruddersford brethren need to be warned off their own aunties, Mustafa? And then the sublime Jangar advises us that 'If a man commits adultery with his wife's daughter, the marriage is not annulled.' In Jangar's bizarre universe, women clearly get whatever comes to them.

Filling the test tube hadn't been so easy after reading that – bloody Rahman kept leering and winking at Tariq. It had stayed in his mind when talking to Mrs Hassani about Safia Shah: 'women get whatever comes to them.' The slut. Safia had put up a show of resistance, of course, but it wasn't real, he could tell she was shamming, she didn't cry out or anything. But then Ali Cheema had walked in while you could still see him on the telly screen, in London, and every day Tariq expected his father Karamat to summon him, or his uncle Abdul Ayub Khan. Nothing has happened – Tariq reckons that Ali Cheema has something to hide. Plenty.

'*A lady will be waiting for you. A good friend of mine.*' What did Mrs Hassani mean? She couldn't mean herself, that was obvious – though the way she'd sat close to him and spoken to him it wasn't obvious at all.

And then Mustafa Jangar had turned up again to address the mujaheddin of the Muslim Youth League at the Omar Khayyam restaurant. Uncle Abdul had told Tariq that Mustafa Jangar was swinging the Islamic Council behind the Independent Muslim candidates in these Council elections. That meant behind Ishmail Haqq and the Khan brothers, Tariq's uncle and father. Mr Jangar had said there was to be a big anti-Rahman demo and every member of the Muslim Youth League had to be outside City Hall on Saturday morning, 10.30 a.m. sharp.

'I might be a bit late, like,' Tariq had told Mr Jangar.

'You do what Mr Jangar tells you!' Uncle Abdul had shouted at him.

☙

Nasreen hasn't slept a wink, apart from one miserable descent into nightmare when she strove, but failed, to prevent her beloved Rajiv Lal from being lynched by a howling Muslim mob led by Mustafa Jangar. She could hear – but not see – her husband Hassan urging them on from the minaret of his precious new mosque. 'Kill him!'

She awoke with a cry. Hassan, gently snoring beside her, didn't stir. He'd forgotten to remove his glasses before going to bed after another long session with Gamal Rahman: ludicrously they dangled from the tip of his nose.

All night long Nasreen has told herself she can't go through with something so shameful. Why am I doing this? Rajiv, please! Only look at me, just once. Am I mad to besmirch my own honour irreparably? Do I really need a second child so badly? Yes. I want a baby to love. Rajiv's baby. Hassan, of course, will guess – know – that it isn't his. And you will have to live with that knowledge, Hassan: you will have to keep silent; may your everlasting shame choke you.

Nasreen's trembling hands explore her dry, dormant genitals. Like her head, they don't belong.

She makes the journey to the Taj Mahal hotel by bus, heavily made-up and wearing her most fashionable Western summer frock. She carries one hundred pounds in her handbag plus a little extra to pay for the hotel room. She has dithered and agonized over the amount. As a waiter in the Omar Khayyam, Tariq might earn fifty pounds a week. Or perhaps he earns one hundred pounds with tips. Without tips. But he may have earned more when he worked in Courtauld's mills. Am I made of money? Isn't he lucky to spend an hour with me? An hour? She has heard that some young men get it all over with in two minutes. Am I made of money? – apparently it was a Jew who first used that expression. She had overheard Hassan telling Imran that when the Jews were at their wits' end in ancient Egypt they had offered money to their God to get them out. 'It was hidden in a golden calf,' Hassan explained to the wide-eyed boy. 'Their Pharisees secretly hoped that God would never find it. They wanted to cheat Him if they could.'

Nasreen had timidly repeated this story to Rajiv Lal without mentioning its source. Rajiv had smiled his oblique smile.

'Apocryphal, no doubt.'

'Oh, what does that mean, Mr Lal?' (Anything to hold him in conversation.)

'The best way to understand any religion, Nasreen, is to listen to its own stories – not those of its detractors.'

'But then, surely, we would each of us have to believe in every religion?'

'You may be right, Nasreen.'

Oh, Rajiv!

Why am I counting pennies? A test tube of sperm from an unknown male person at the Burnside Clinic would have cost five hundred pounds – and you wouldn't be sure of what you were getting, you can hardly sue them when you find a dark-skinned, Untouchable baby at your breast, you can hardly go to court in front of your husband and family and say 'I don't want my own baby, I want my money back.' So here you are making calculations even though Tariq Khan is a healthy Punjabi Muslim who you can see with your own eyes and –

– and touch. Nasreen's heart freezes. Is she not insulting herself to be paying a man for the privilege of dishonouring her? But she is stuck with her own words: 'Would you like to make some money?' She can't go back on that. Maybe she can. Maybe she can say, 'Tariq, I know you would not consider it honourable to take money from a lady. I do not wish to insult you.' She has placed the money in a sealed envelope. She had found a brown envelope but then she began to think that the father of her future child deserved a white envelope. She prays that Tariq won't open the envelope in her presence.

The Taj Mahal hotel is situated immediately opposite the bus stop. Nasreen falters as she sees a group of young men, Hindus at a glance, lounging insolently in the shabby entrance hall. They don't look like the kind of Hindus who would know Rajiv Lal, but she isn't sure of anything when it comes to Hindus, they're very free and easy people. The young men are all smoking. One of them flicks ash on the floor and lazily asks what he can do for her.

'Insurance? Driving lesson?'

'I booked a room by telephone.'

Reluctantly he drags himself behind the reception desk and opens the register. 'Name?'

Her heart pounds. 'Hassani.'

He nods. 'Room 17. Who's paying?'

Shame floods her. 'I can pay.'

'Twelve pounds fifty.'

She hands him the money, fifteen pounds, three five-pound notes, but he doesn't have the correct change. Evidently 'the boss' holds the key to the cash register. The boss may or may not return 'later'. She longs to escape the insolent scrutiny of these young Hindus. 'Never mind. When Mr Khan arrives, please ask him to come straight up.'

'Will do.' The young Hindus are grinning behind their impassive expressions.

She climbs the narrow stairs. The floorboards creak in mockery. Nothing – walls, doors – has been redecorated in years. The carpets are moth-eaten and worse. A cockroach scuttles along the skirting. A toilet flushes angrily as she passes. She reaches the appointed room. At first the key seems to be the wrong one but the tag says '17' and the door says '17' and eventually the door swings open. The sun is blazing through a south-facing window, penetrating layers of grime. The room smells. She stares at the bed.

By eleven in the morning the buses are arriving from Bradford, Halifax, Blackburn, Bolton, Dewsbury and from as far afield as Newcastle and Leicester. Bareheaded youths in trainers and headbands pour out, followed by cautious elders in headcloths. Once disembarked, they kneel on the hard tarmac of the municipal car park (coach section), to pray. Then the banners are raised – a thousand scowling Ayatollahs. Under a light police escort they march to join their Bruddersford brothers in the irregular 'square' outside City Hall. Mustafa Jangar leads the procession.

'Bruddersford's Reverend Ian Paisley,' Zulfikar Zaheed comments, gazing down through layers of melancholy from the big window of the Lord Mayor's balcony, Douglas Blunt at his shoulder. Once again Zaheed is wearing his full regalia with the tricorn hat. Blunt suspects that he is planning to address the crowd, but won't.

By 12.15 the Muslim Youth League are already showing impatience with their stewards' exhortations to discipline. Roads leading to the square are blocked, traffic at a standstill. The megaphonic voice of Hassan Hassani is urging patience, restraint, discipline – but Tariq and his brothers are wearing Intifada headbands, a girding of the soul for war. Surrounding a stranded yellow city bus, they hammer cheerfully on its primrose-and-brown metal plates. A friendly gesture, just high spirits. The passengers cower. The unwinding coil of militant youth suddenly storms across the Turl, forming a phalanx outside Lloyds Bank, then charges up Cyril Street into the shopping precinct, barging through crowds of shoppers, overturning racks of shoes and scattering papers from newsstands as they sweep into Broadway.

'We want Shaytan Rahman!'

White shoppers huddle in doorways. 'Where's bloody police, then? Keeping a low profile I shouldn't wonder.'

Tariq's mob whirls erratically like refuse caught in a gale, devoid of all sense of direction and purpose, breaking, smashing, chanting, steaming. Gazing down from the fourth floor of the *Echo*, Joe Reddaway remembers something about a seven-headed satanic beast out of the Book of Revelation. The streets below are thick with hideous effigies of Gamal Rahman, daubed in black and red, beaten and scourged with sticks: 'Kill the Pig', 'Devil', 'Apostate'. A thousand placards bear the identical portraits of a stern, merciless Ayatollah.

Douglas Blunt looks down from the Lord Mayor's window. 'This one's a proper riot.'

'I am going down among them,' Zaheed announces. But makes no move.

Tariq catches the plaintive voice of Hassan Hassani trying to shepherd the Youth League back to the square, back to City Hall, but now the enemy shows its face: mounted police in visors are corralling the lads, pinning them back, sealing off Cyril Street to prevent a repeat invasion. The police begin to pounce into the crowd, seizing and dragging the lads to the waiting vans. This is it! Bottles, cans and stones are seized and thrown.

A young white is shouting racist taunts from a taxi; Tariq is one of fifteen, twenty, who hurl themselves upon it, trying to drag the bastard out. The mounted police scythe in. A brick goes through the window of a double-decker bus. The rear window of a car carrying two small children is smashed. The children cower, terrified, at the sight of dark alien faces, large noses, blazing eyes, terrible chants, moustaches, curls of oily black hair, hideous; the car shakes. The children will never forget or forgive.

Tariq is now squatting in the middle of the road with a thousand others. The traffic is blocked by a carpet of seated youths in head-bands. The city centre is paralysed.

'Twenty years of community relations down the drain,' Zaheed declares.

Photographers dart in and out of the storm like overloaded ballet dancers, dodging the cans and wooden staves. Drifting serenely through the carpet of Muslim youths, undisturbed by the fracas, sane as toast, is the pharmacist Iqbal, scattering his leaflets and pondering where to plant his Koranic bomb, thus elevating the faithful to martryrdom. Reaching out to the bearded messenger for a leaflet, Tariq momentarily glimpses two faces uncannily framed in one.

EMIT AND EVADE LABOUR PARTY

VOTE for Ishmail Haqq and Karamat Khan and Abdul Ayub Khan in Council Election coming up. VOTE for Islamic Party. DO NOT VOTE for Infidel Labour Party. Muslims who support Labour are enemies of Islam. Allah will not forgive those who support the Allah Antagonist.

Labour Party Leader Lucas and Housing Chairman Malik are taking bribes for Housing and Improvement Grants.

DO NOT VOTE for Trevor Lucas and DO NOT VOTE for Hani Malik. Both callous men in the Party. Both antagonists of Islam. These devils calling the Muslims the mad people. This is Satanic Labour Party/Zionist Plot to promote the Rahman Libel against Islam and the Holy Prophet, peace be upon him!

Trevor Lucas (Labour Leader Corruption)
Hani Malik (Housing Chairman Corruption)
Harry Flowers (MP Conspiracy)
Zulfikar Zaheed (Lord Mayor Corruption Conspiracy)
S. Perlman (Education Chair – Jew/Zionist Conspiracy)

New cordons of mounted police in riot gear are forming round City Hall and Central Police Station. Bottles, cans, stones, parking cones and the occasional purloined police helmet hurtle through the air. Inspired by the thud and thwack of projectiles, Tariq finds himself penetrating a broken police cordon and charging up Claygate into Goodwin Street. Shoppers, pensioners, children, scuttle for cover, terrified. A policeman goes down and twenty pairs of boots kick him senseless. The plate-glass window of a pizzeria shatters. Tariq himself smashes the window of the Burnside Clinic.

Wreaths at the War Memorial are scattered, defiled.

ॐ

Nasreen has been sitting on the alien hotel bed for one hour, twenty-two minutes. For eighty-two minutes she has been listening for a confident, virile footfall on the creaking boards of the corridor, a strong tap on the locked door. Workmen, carpenters, are working desultorily on the floor above: each outbreak of hammering she mistakes for Tariq. Her head aches from sleeplessness, shame and a sense of unreality. She no longer recognizes herself. Yet she does! I am Nasreen Hassani, mother of Imran.

Perhaps Tariq has confided in his father or his uncle, Abdul Ayub Khan. Perhaps he has asked them what he should do. But Tariq is never punctual – Hassan is always complaining about his lack of discipline. He may have overslept.

She should leave now. She will be forced to scurry out under the mocking gaze of the young Hindus but she must leave.

It is Saturday morning. Somewhere, across the city, in some pleasant, tree-lined suburb, the English girl in the stolen photograph is bringing Rajiv Lal his breakfast in bed, along with two newspapers. Rajiv always reads two newspapers on Saturdays – he once told her so.

ॐ

It is now 2.45. Gangs of white youths have gathered to taunt the young Muslims. A policeman staggers as a demonstrator (perhaps trained by Tiger Siddiqi) karate-kicks him in the face. The white youths, including a scattering of black Afro-Caribbeans, are hurling

459

stones from the rockery and flower beds outside the Education Department building. Tariq is amazed to catch sight of a big black bloke holding aloft a placard, 'Revolutionary Communist Party of Bethnal Green Says No to the Ayatollah.' In Channing Way, police riot squads are leaping on Muslim and white youths alike, pinning them to the ground. Tariq goes down, his arm twisted behind his back. Handcuffs snap round his wrists. 'Fuck you, Paki bastard.'

In the police station Tariq is strip-searched, relieved of a snap-blade knife, and herded into a cell with fifteen or twenty other Muslims youths.

It is not Lord Mayor Zaheed who now arrives at the police station but Douglas Blunt. Izza Shah, who has discharged himself from hospital – more tests – after a grim tussle with his doctors, is received by the Chief Constable and offered a chair on Blunt's advice. Every Muslim politician and lawyer in the city is demanding admission. Hani Malik is finally allowed in, as a City councillor, but a raging, gesticulating Ishmail Haqq is turned away (no civic status) after being questioned about an inflammatory leaflet found scattered around the devastated city centre. Hassan Hassani is also told to go home; he stands dazed, blinking owlishly, a spectator to his own theatre.

After three hours of negotiations the police grant bail. The prisoners are released from the cells, one by one, to be separately charged in the presence of riot-squad officers offering eyewitness evidence. A woman police constable is seated behind a table covered in labelled weapons: flick-knives, screwdrivers, bicycle chains, knuckle-dusters.

Tariq comes eye to eye with WPC Rana Khan. Still handcuffed he stands before her. Her blue-and-white uniform fits her fine, the apostate bitch. Her hat is banded in a neat pattern of checks. His heart floods with shame and humiliation – but on Rana's behalf, not his own. In that instant he renounces her.

'Name?' she says.

'You know it.'

'Name?' she repeats.

'Tariq Khan. Soldier of Allah.'

She points to his snap-blade knife. It carries a label bearing his name. 'Is this weapon yours?'

But even as she speaks the duty solicitor posted at the table cuts in: 'You are within your rights to say nothing, Mr Khan. You are advised to say nothing.'

The phrase is not new to Tariq. He has learnt 'to say nothing' because silence cannot be held against you. Anything you say may be given in evidence against you, he knows all that. But is Rana now observing his silence, his hesitation, with blatant contempt? Is she inviting him to be true to himself, to be a man? What would she think if she knew what he'd done to – with – Safia Shah?

'I've nowt to say.' He spits on the floor.

႟

Joe Reddaway is thumbing through the huge pile of citizens' letters pouring into the *Echo*.

'Am I alone' (writes Fred Challenor of Binns Road) 'in thinking our police and politicians have lost their troubled minds? Last Saturday, hundreds of Fascist delinquents caused mayhem in the city centre under the benevolent gaze of senior police officers . . . I am absolutely disgusted to hear that our Lord Mayor, Zulfikar Zaheed, is trying to push the Government to invoke the Blasphemy Act against Gamal Rahman. Does this mean he condones mob rule?'

Joe ponders the logic of this, doesn't find it, picks up a letter from G.L. Holton, of Cranbourne Avenue:

'The Government and laws of this country are being defied. Islamic leaders deliberately select times and venues to intimidate peaceful weekend shoppers, many with children . . .'

Rifling through the print-offs and faxes on his cluttered desk, Joe notices a statement by Ishmail Haqq concerning a certain leaflet distributed among Saturday's crowd (the distributor has not so far been traced). 'A blatant provocation,' declares Haqq. 'I would not be surprised if it had been concocted in certain political quarters desperate to discredit genuine Muslim Independent candidates.'

Ah: Harry Flowers has reacted to the riot with a quick move. Two moves, in fact. He is demanding that the Government's new DNA Scheme (biological proof of parentage) be free of charge. Flowers also insists that over-age children, previously denied entry to Britain, who provide positive DNA tests, should be allowed to reunite with their families in the UK. Flowers will go through the motions of raising this burning issue in the Commons, begging leave to move the Adjournment of the House, under Standing Order No. 20. The Speaker will not grant leave. Harry (Joe muses) will no doubt tell his Muslim constituents of Bruddersford West that he has been stifled, gagged, throttled, choked.

Joe's fingers begin to thump his keyboard into some Plain Speaking. By the time he's finished he will know what he thinks about everything.

႟

Mustafa Jangar calls on Zulfikar Zaheed at his luxurious suburban home in the white suburb of Belmont. He arrives on his bicycle and without an appointment. Jangar does not make appointments, not even with the Lord Mayor, for whom he has never disguised his contempt. But here Mustafa is, his forehead dramatically bandaged after the demonstration.

'Tell Zaheed it is Jangar,' he instructs the white maid.

Zaheed receives him coolly. Jangar does not accept the offer of a chair. He sits cross-legged on the floor; Zaheed fully expects him to start banging his bandaged head into the expensive carpet, leaving it soaked in blood.

'Izza Shah must resign,' Jangar declares.

'Izza?'

'He has led the Islamic Council into scandal and corruption. His daughter is a prostitute. She is now fornicating with Ali Cheema, whom Izza has corruptly appointed his spokesman.'

Zaheed turns to the french window, to his beautiful rose garden. If he is to swing the Islamic Council behind his own bid to become Member of Parliament for Bruddersford West, then Izza Shah is his best, perhaps only, hope – despite that unfortunate marriage pro-posal to Wahabia some time back. Ali Cheema must be persuaded to speak the right word in Izza's ear; letters from Wahabia indicate that she is now 'very close to Ali'.

'What can I do for you, Brother Jangar?'

'You were once Chairman of the City's Housing Committee, Brother Zaheed.'

'Well?'

'But you did not heed – and your successor Hani Malik does not heed – the Ayatollah's teachings.'

'On what?'

'At the moment of urinating or defecating, a good Muslim must squat in such a way as not to face or turn his back on Mecca.'

'So?'

'Every head of household has the duty to summon a plumber of the Faith to reinstall the toilet.' Jangar pauses ominously. 'But the Council should do it. It was your sacred duty to provide all Muslim homes with toilets which do not face towards Mecca!'

'Brother Mustafa, the terraced houses of Bruddersford and their toilet seats face where they face. You can't argue with a toilet seat – though you can always wriggle a bit.'

'Brother Zulfikar, you have spent too many corrupt years "wrig-gling a bit". Now you must stop wriggling, Brother.'

Zaheed has heard that Hassan Hassani is close to collapse from Jangar's holy thunder rolling, night after night, into his desk-top

462

publishing enterprise. Poor Hassani – they say that his wife Nasreen has stopped speaking to him. A note on Hassani's pillow demanded a divorce.

'We must get rid of Izza Shah,' Jangar repeats. 'So the true doctrine of Twelver Shi'ism may advance.'

'My dear Brother, I have as much influence in the Islamic Council as Tin Tin.'

'You can gain influence – that is what I have come to tell you. You can gain influence by ridding yourself of impure substances. Eleven substances are listed by the Ayatollah as impure: urine, excrement, sperm, bones of the dead, blood, dog meat, pork, non-Muslims, wine, beer and the sweat of a camel which eats excrement.'

Zaheed is standing at the french window. Jangar is still seated on the carpet, cross-legged, hunks of hairy shin protruding from his robe.

'There are few camels in Bruddersford,' Zaheed says.

ॐ

Nasreen has gone home to her father, S.B., taking Imran, but she won't say why, not even to Latifa. She only hopes that Imran will not pick up bad habits from her brother Ishtiak, who has not been doing well in school since returning from Pakistan. Nasreen's mother, Razia, keeps stroking Imran's head and feeding him more chapatis, then falling asleep in her chair. S.B. is rarely to be seen.

He is up the hill in the hotel bar.

The giant Hindu smiles gently, rises, takes a step towards S.B. in greeting. 'My round.'

'Thank you, friend.' S.B. accepts the pint then sits down, pouring sweat. 'Cheers.'

'Cheers.'

Tonight is the monthly meeting of the Labour Party District Committee. S.B. never misses it (except when in Islamabad). S.B. has set out for the hotel bar with every intention of arriving at the Party meeting before Item 7 on the agenda: 'Resignations and Expulsions'. He knows exactly what he will say, but he will say it better after a drink or two. He will say:

'This Rahman book cannot be regarded as fiction! It's beyond endurance that our Labour Party should cower in silence! We Muslims must defend the honour of our women, and now we have been pulled six feet out of the ground to defend our identity!'

Yes, he will rub that in to the noses of bloody Lucas, bloody Flowers, bloody Perlman.

The beer crashes through his nervous system like a storm on the

463

drought-stricken veld. 'What about this Section 11 Funding which is designed to promote the English language among ethnic minorities?' he suddenly asks the Hindu. 'That Thatcher woman is slashing Section 11. She's slashing.'

The Hindu looks surprised. 'You're right, sir.'

S.B. is brooding about Item 7: Resignations, Expulsions. They are going to expel Haqq, the Khan brothers, and a dozen other Muslim defectors who are now claiming they never formally resigned.

'Are those white bastards expecting S.B. to sit on his old hands while they throw the best Muslim comrades into the gas chambers!'

'Never,' the Hindu nods affably.

'Ishmail Haqq is no saint! Between ourselves he's a man of low character. An opportunist. But I do not defame him.'

'Never defame, sir.'

'We now have a Ministry of Minorities in Pakistan. Mrs Bhutto's work. She is an Oxford graduate you know. We should have one in the UK.'

'More than one, sir. Too few Oxford graduates all round.'

The Hindu is in fact the greater drinker of the two; almost invariably he is the first to arrive, on the dot of opening time. He owns this hotel. S.B. doesn't know it. The Hindu also owns the seedy Taj Mahal hotel, 'downtown'. His sons have reported to him that S.B.'s married daughter showed up there, waiting for an adulterous rendezvous, but was stood up. The Hindu has it on the grapevine from his daughter Jyoti Devi Chand, a community teacher, that Nasreen Hassani is hopelessly in love with Rajiv Lal. Apparently this Nasreen Hassani is quite naïve, a typical Muslim woman (Jyoti thinks), and the only person in the Department of Education who does not know that Rajiv Lal lives with an English girl, a drama teacher and good friend to Jyoti Devi Chand. In truth, the Hindu no longer cares for the company of this distempered Muslim, S.B. Hussein. Other patrons are beginning to complain about his drunken shouting, his manic outbursts. His recent absence in Pakistan was very welcome – pity he had to come back. In recent months the Muslim had developed a habit of searching his pockets, opening his wallet, finding nothing. 'Thieves everywhere!' he would exclaim.

Now the Muslim stands up, swaying. 'Meeting,' he says. 'Bloody meeting.'

The Hindu nods. 'You must attend, sir.'

S.B. takes a few shaky steps – then lurches back. The giant Hindu sees the familiar hostility in his glazed eyes.

'This is Muslim business, my good sir. Too many Hindus in Labour Party. Plotting plotting scheming hatching. That bloody Equal

Opportunities Commission is dominated by Hindu mafia. Hindus in India are writing dirty books against us. They are crusading against our holy shrines – they are Fascists.'

'You should worry more about your married daughter, sir, and less about us Hindus.'

S.B. weaves unsteadily out into the night. After some ten minutes he reappears, searching for the toilet. The Hindu guesses that his friend cannot find his car, cannot even remember what it looks like. The man once confessed that his unmarried daughter Latifa regularly walks up the hill and drives it away.

The Hindu smiles and settles back into his favourite film, remembered from distant days in Calcutta, days of his youth – but vivid as yesterday, sir. The Hindu nowadays sees himself as the film's hero, a Gai-Wallah protecting sacred cows against evil cattlemen – like those British and American movie heroes who do battle with elephant-poachers in Kenya or wherever. The Gai-Wallah liberates the cows within sight of the Muslim slaughterhouse and with two thousand spectators on the edge of their seats. The Hindu remembers spilling out of the cinema in euphoric mood, only to encounter real Muslim Leaguers driving cattle to the slaughter.

Muslim Leaguers like this drunken S.B. man.

Big riot, many dead. Those were good times.

The Hindu is happy to be alone with his memories and watching the money pour into his hotel cash register: God is love and the Hindu loves blue-skinned Krishna, loves the warrior Shiva, loves Rama who can draw the bow that no man can draw. Draw? Draw a map, sir. Look at a map of India and you will see a stain on its right ear: Pakistan.

ॐ

Lord Mayor Zaheed mounts the raised dais of the Council Chamber, resplendent in his robes of office, removes his tricorn hat, bows, and takes his seat on the 'throne'. The Council is about to debate the strike at Hightown Upper School – 'not before time' in the opinion of Councillor Sir Tom Potter.

The visitors' gallery is packed. Chief Executive Douglas Blunt detects in today's gallery a Thief of Baghdad quality. Blunt occupies this same seat during every Council debate; Rajiv Lal has placed his wasting, ascetic frame within the adjoining seat reserved for the Director of the Department under discussion. Blunt knows that Lal and Samuel Perlman have finally fallen out over the scarf issue. If Perlman's report is carried today, Lal's resignation is on the cards. Blunt reckons he's the sort to walk before he's pushed.

In the 'Muslim quarter' (more like three-quarters) of the gallery the star turn is Fatima Shah, surrounded by a tight phalanx of her sisters, all attired in black burkas – 'the Ayatollah's Revenge,' Blunt is tempted to murmur to Lal, but doesn't. Proceedings have been delayed by altercations and scuffles at the street door between stewards and young Muslims carrying placards and effigies of Gamal Rahman. Arguments about freedom of expression have cut no ice. It's a rule: no banners inside the Chamber. Another white rule! Refusing to part company with their banners – honour, izzat, forbids it – Tariq Khan and his mujaheddin are ejected into the street.

Zaheed nods to the Leader of the Council. Rising, Trevor Lucas promises to confine himself to two main points. He is clear, concise and deadly boring. Lucas is the most boring Council Leader that Douglas Blunt can remember – and not yet thirty-five years of age.

1. Bruddersford prides itself on its record of harmonious community relations. (Derisive howls from the gallery. Zaheed bangs his gavel.)

2. Education lies at the heart of healthy community relations. The policy of the Council is to reconcile 'diversity with integration'.

Lucas sits down. The Chairman of the Education Committee will now present his Report. Samuel Perlman rises. Uproar in the gallery. More of Iqbal Iqbal's leaflets flutter out of burkas and down to the chamber. The stewards pretend not to notice: strip-searching Fatima Shah is not on their ideal agenda.

Lord Mayor Zaheed rises. 'Those who regard themselves as worthy citizens of this city,' he tells the gallery, 'do not prove their point by behaving like hooligans.'

Like Lucas, Perlman is a professor of pedantic boredom. Douglas Blunt finds this new breed of Labour technocrat faintly uncongenial and a lot less fun than the old workhouse donkey aldermen who told good stories and hinted that life might be worth living.

'Any citizen can inspect the Rules of the Department of Education,' Perlman is saying. 'These Rules are passed in this Chamber, by this democratically elected Council. The Rule forbidding the wearing of the hijab, or burka, or headscarf, is a long-standing one. Such headgear impedes a full range of learning activities and is divisive. We are passing through a time of communal fever. This single issue has been blown up to fanatical proportions by pressure groups whose subversive aims lie far beyond the wearing of the hijab.'

The uproar lasts five minutes, Zaheed's pounding gavel notwithstanding. Fatima and her friends are on their feet, screaming at Perlman:

'Zionist Jew Pig!'

Zaheed is banging his gavel. Eventually Perlman can make himself heard:

'I am in complete agreement with the recent statement by the Association of Metropolitan Boroughs: "We must have integration, not endless separatism and isolation." (*Interruptions.*) Lord Mayor, grant-aided schools – church schools, religious schools, sectarian schools – do exist but they are an historical anomaly and it is not progressive policy to further increase their number. (*Furious heckling from the gallery.*) Children from every community must be educated to take their place in a modern world where integration, not segregation, is the guiding principle. (*Uproar. Insults.*) Of course parents have rights, but a sound education policy makes the long-term interests of the children its priority.'

'Hypocrite!' (This is Haqq on his feet in the gallery, bellowing.)

The entire Muslim gallery is up. Zulfikar Zaheed whacks his gavel from a standing position. Haqq eventually sits down when Zaheed's crimson-robed arm shoots out to point the stewards in his direction. Samuel Perlman adopts his most pious tone:

'In the case of Fatima Shah, we have bent over backwards to oblige her. We offered her a place at Beaumont Girls' School but her father did not accept it.'

'There are male teachers at Beaumont!' Fatima shrieks.

All the girls are up again and screaming. Douglas Blunt is reminded of a scene from Arthur Miller's play, *The Crucible*. Rajiv Lal sits motionless, expressionless, his stick-legs folded. Blunt wonders whether the man's heart actually beats.

Councillor Sidney Wright leads for the Tories. The gallery falls quiet, though not exactly.

'This,' begins Councillor Wright, '*this*, ladies and gentleman, is where six years of Socialist shilly-shallying and so-called "progressive" pandering have got us!'

'And to think,' Blunt murmurs to Rajiv Lal, 'that you have to pay to get into the Alhambra.'

No response from Rajiv Lal. Inscrutable. Wrong chap for the job, Blunt is sure of it. No balls. Councillor Wright rambles on. Blunt, whose head holds a personal dossier on each of the City's hundred councillors – he gives their Christmas presents to charity – recalls that Sidney Wright has been arrested for kerb-crawling three times, but never charged. Councillor Wright's thumbs are now comfortably tucked into his waistcoat pockets:

'I'll give you a case. A Hindu girl goes out in miniskirts, gets her skin toned like Michael Jackson, she can't stand restrictions, arranged marriages, she's twenty, clerical job, then next thing she's a prostitute up Plumb Lane, to pay for the fashionable clothes, the Chelsea Girl gear, a couple of white lads pay her fifty quid, in fact it's ten pound a throw, basic.'

Bemusement in the gallery: is this a Hindu school strike or what? Councillor John Dixon (Labour) can take no more of these Tory irrelevancies. Dixon, who wears no tie – never did, never will – constantly flicks his fingers and slaps his hands together, as if summoning a dog.

'I only thank my Maker,' he begins, 'that I'm not a Tory. Someone is whipping up this scarf issue for their own ends, it's a case all over again of them that shouts loudest . . . Frankly, this scarf palaver is nowt but demagogues, Sunnis running to keep pace with the Ayatollah and the Shi'ites. It's all Saudi Arabia money, too, coming through Regent's Park Mosque in London. Then the press come up and stir the pot. You can bend over backwards, but not in all directions at once.'

The Muslim gallery is not much roused or incensed by Dixon. He's just another backbench clown from the Martian end of the city; what's his name anyway?

Zaheed says: 'Councillor Malik.' The whole Chamber is instantly alert. Is the Labour Group now about to crack wide open? In the gallery Ishmail Haqq is nose-to-nose with destiny.

'Frankly, Lord Mayor, listening to this so-called debate,' Hani Malik begins, 'I've wondered whether I was in the Council Chamber of a great city or visiting the zoo.'

Mild protests from the Tory side, a few shouts of 'Withdraw!'

Zaheed bangs his gavel. 'The councillor has made no personal remarks and is perfectly entitled to wonder where he is.'

Laughter. But Malik means business. He always does, Labour's Housing Chairman, the hottest spot in Bruddersford politics, not excluding education. With unqualified pleasure, Douglas Blunt waits for Hani to crank up the temperature.

'I take it, Lord Mayor, that "withdraw" is Tory language for "Go back to Pakistan and take the voters of Tanner Ward with you." '

At this the entire Labour Group, regardless of faction, drum their desks in approval. Blunt sighs with sheer, undiluted admiration. At a stroke Malik has plucked the deepest of cords not merely in Bruddersford politics, not merely in British politics, but now – with the French National Front on the march – in European politics, too.

Malik scoring, Haqq scowling in the gallery.

Malik waits. 'I'd like to ask Councillor Wright why he told us his cock-and-bull story of a Hindu girl who becomes a prostitute – a story which I, as a friend of the Hindu community, regard, frankly, as rubbish (*drumming of Labour desks*), as racist (*drumming*), as shame-fully prejudiced. (*Drumming!*) Let me ask Councillor Wright how he knows so much about this case and his so-called "ten pound basic".'

Uproar. Councillor Wright is shouting: 'I demand, I demand . . . I demand . . . I demand.'

Zaheed nods at Malik to continue: 'If Councillor Wright is demanding a free ticket to White South Africa, I move we pass the hat.'

Even seen-it-all Douglas Blunt is lost in admiration. Zaheed the peacock and Malik the pikestaff make a formidable team. But the canniest mind in the chamber, Sir Tom Potter, has been biding his time. He's up:

'Will the councillor kindly yield?'

Malik nods, sits. To be seen to engage in a duel with the Tory leader is good for votes: local hero. Blunt begins to pray for Malik. Potter is testing his chin for stray hairs, the only politician in Bruddersford whom Blunt truly fears – and the wealthiest – because without ambition. Tom could have been sitting on the Tory backbenches in the Commons aeons ago – he has all the connections, all the clout – but he cares about two things only: making money and Bruddersford.

So here he goes:

'Councillor Malik's approach to this issue reminds me of the bear's approach to Charlie Chaplin in that great film, *The Gold Rush.*' (Anticipatory Tory laughter.) 'The two of 'em go round in circles but never quite meet. And your heart's in your mouth, because if the bear meets Charlie he'll surely eat him. And if the real issues at stake here ever meet Councillor Malik, it'd be a halal dinner.'

The Tory ranks are rolling with joy.

Zaheed stands: 'When Councillor Malik graciously yielded, he may have anticipated a serious question. Perhaps Councillor Potter can think of one in the nick of time.'

Douglas Blunt's bushy eyebrows rise a fraction. Zaheed is sailing close to the wind of 'abuse of the chair', but, as Blunt anticipates, Potter is too clever to say so. It's all water off a duck's back to him.

'Thank you, Lord Mayor, I never argue with the umpire, even when he's holding his light-meter under his armpit.'

Another roar of delight from the Tory benches. Blunt knows that the Labour whites are struggling to suppress their own smiles (and he his – a smile now could cost him fifty thousand a year). Every disputed catch or appeal for lbw or run-out or complaint about bad light during the current Pakistani cricket tour is firmly etched on Tory and Labour memories alike. There have been – let's face it –

many cross-party pints bought and drunk during the Test series. Potter is scratching his head like the dunce in the corner:

'Lord Mayor, the only serious question I can think of putting to Councillor Malik, whose closest colleagues are busy cutting his throat in Tanner Ward, is this: does he support Councillor Perlman or does he support Miss Fatima Shah? Does he support Mrs Patricia Newman or does he support Mr Rajiv Lal? Does he support Perlman or Lal? Newman or Fatima? The Labour Party or the Islamic Council? In other words, if I may revert to my frivolous intervention, Lord Mayor, which part of the bear does Councillor Malik prefer to get eaten by?'

Delirium in the gallery. 'Answer!' shouts Haqq. 'Answer! Answer!'

'That must be your election agent up there, Councillor Malik,' Potter says, pointing to Haqq and resuming his seat.

Malik rises. 'Councillor Potter has certainly asked the longest question of all time. My advice to him is to visit Scarborough beach on a nice hot day. There he may observe some ladies sunning themselves topless, and other ladies who'd rather preserve what they regard as a traditional modesty and decency.'

Malik pauses, sure of the whole Chamber's topless attention.

'Well! Lord Mayor, it can't have been many summers ago that topless ladies were turned away from Scarborough beach. Odd thing is, closer to hand, right here in Bruddersford, it's the young ladies with the stricter sense of decorum who are being turned away from our City Schools!'

Uneasy laughter from the Labour benches, silence in the gallery.

'And who in this Chamber would insist that the more modest young ladies should be compelled to dishonour themselves, dishonour their own standards – by Topless Fundamentalists?'

Shrieks of joy from Fatima and the burkas. Grim silence from Haqq's Muslim Independents. High tension in the Labour ranks. Perlman boiling.

Malik: 'I now address my Labour colleagues, whom experience indicates to be the thinking sheep in the pen. I ask them this: If a group of liberated women – I mean absolutely kosher, Greenham Common, CND, anti-harassment women – steps forward and demands a "women-only" hour in the municipal swimming pool, would my respected fellow-councillors say no? Would they? Not likely! Isn't it odd – comrades – that separatism is so acceptable among *modern-minded* feminists, but absolutely medieval-fundamentalist when asked-for by an intelligent young Muslim girl who simply demands to respect the tenets of her religion by covering her head?'

The gallery is on its feet, waving, yelling, chanting. Lord Mayor

470

Zaheed, who seems to have forgotten his threat of expulsion, waits indulgently for the bedlam to subside. Languidly he raises a hand.

Malik resumes: 'What we're talking about – comrades – is individual human rights. They wanted, you may remember, to force Sikh bus drivers and conductors to remove their sacred turbans – because a "British" bus driver wears a cap. And what do we think of that now? Nowt. Not a voice in this Chamber to defend it. Why and wherefore, Comrade Perlman, this passion for uniformity? As if all the separate ingredients in the larder can only be digested if boiled in the same stew.

'Now no one respects Comrade Perlman more than I do.' (Laughter.) 'After all, he arrived among us in his prime – from the South – to enlighten the natives – having been schooled, I'm informed, in the great University of 1968. At that time he'd never actually met a Muslim but he'd been told that they could be found on their knees in certain quarters of this city towards dusk. Quite harmless if not disturbed. So that was all right.

'But then! What happens next? An outbreak of Koranic fever among the Muslims. That crazy Ayatollah flies over our city on his magic carpet and whispers in the ear of every sleeping Muslim. "Don't take any more of it," he says, "you've taken enough."

'And we have taken enough. That's why I want Muslims to stay with the Labour Party because one thing's for sure – they'll get nowt out of the Tories except "Go home". As for so called "Muslim Independents", why scatter our precious seed to the passing wind of futile opportunism?'

As soon as Malik sits down, a grim-faced Trevor Lucas moves a formal Motion endorsing the Education Committee's report.

'Those in favour?' Zaheed calls.

The ballot is on a show of hands; the tellers walk in pairs among the raised arms. All eyes are on the four Muslim Labour councillors (the fifth being Lord Mayor Zaheed). Will they follow the party whip after all?

Douglas Blunt is betting ten-to-one on abstention – it's a safe ticket.

One hundred-and-one councillors are, by a statistical freak, actually in their seats (no one attending his mother's funeral, or his own, no one in jail for fraud).

Hani Malik and his three fellow-Muslims are sitting on their hands. Finally the tellers report to Zaheed.

'Forty-eight in favour,' he announces. 'Those against?'

Every Tory arm is raised. The tellers repeat their slow, painstaking count.

'Forty-eight against,' Zaheed announces. 'Abstentions?'

Hani Malik and his three Muslim colleagues raise their hands high. Pandemonium in the chamber and gallery. Lord Mayor Zulfikar Zaheed is now the sole focus of attention – a situation to which he is never averse. The casting vote is his.

'The Chair abstains,' Zaheed announces – as if this were the most honourable, self-denying gesture in the City's history. 'The Council Leader's Motion is therefore not carried,' he adds with studied langour. Blunt has won his bet and owes himself ten quid. Lucas and Perlman are not defeated, merely humiliated. Their pal, Harry Flowers, MP, shares their chastisement. Zaheed has pointed his custom-made shoes towards the Palace of Westminster.

❧

Or has he? Zulfikar Zaheed is asleep and dreaming. Pakistan are batting with effortless grace. Panthers! England toil in the field like swine. The score is beautiful to behold.

It is obvious to Zaheed – if not to Douglas Blunt – that the source of England's relentless decline as a cricketing nation is moral: while PIA, Pakistan International, 'Great People to Fly With', decorates the balcony of the Pakistan team's dressing room, Tetley's Bitter occupies the corresponding position on the adjoining balcony of the England team. The same two words – Tetley's Bitter! – run shamelessly across their manager's anorak (although without the exclamation mark).

'Unbelievable, my dear Douglas. Alcohol.'

'I think you've already made that point, Zulfikar.'

Of course you can't be surprised if old Doug's temper is on a short fuse: 358 for 5 is a humiliation, if not a downright castration. The famous Yorkshire batsman, Jack Bounder, now retired and confined to the commentary box, is chiding the England bowlers on the transistor radios.

'On this wicket it's no use delivering a few good 'uns then a few loose ones. You have to groove in on line and length all the time.'

'Wisely put,' Zaheed remarks to Blunt.

'Shithead!'

Zaheed turns, amazed, and is outraged to observe that Harry Flowers and Trevor Lucas have insolently seated themselves the other side of Douglas Blunt, having abandoned their privileged seats in the Members' stand in order to spoil Zaheed's day and assassinate him. Flowers's beer-flushed features are snarling at the Lord Mayor (who has refused to strip off his ermine-fringed robes of office, despite the heat and the half-naked condition of the natives).

'Shithead!' Flowers repeats while Lucas guffaws, his parchment-pale torso (rounded shoulders, hollow chest, nascent paunch) bared to the sun and already reddening.

Harry Flowers is drunk. 'There was a young whore of Lahore who firebombed a store and – '

Zaheed is just about to kill the man with a look when the two umpires, both English of course, decide that Pakistan has scored too many runs. They are examining the ball suspiciously. Like gypsy bagmen they produce several square, oblong and octagonal balls out of their apron pockets. Zaheed knows that these same pockets contain coins for counting an over, light meters and – by rumour – one or two spare England players.

Choosing an alternative ball, the umpires toss it to the England bowler with a wink you could see in Islamabad. Flowers and Lucas are chortling. Immediately a Pakistani batsman is clean-bowled by England's paceman, Chris Lawson.

The crowd are up and crowing, beer bellies raw and red.

'At any time during the past half-hour,' Zaheed informs Blunt, 'your umpires could have issued a warning to Lawson about his follow-through. Oh yes, my dear Douglas, Law 42.11 is quite clear about Unfair Play. And why have *your* umpires declined to issue a warning?'

Five minutes later the great batsman Kaliq is struck in 'the box' which guards his genitals. Kaliq collapses in pain. 'Gotcha!' yells Harry Flowers, Em Pee. To their credit most of the Yorkshiremen on the terraces offer the traditional silence for such misfortune – though Pakistani testicles have a lot to answer for, some 60,000 in Brudders-ford alone.

Harry Flowers beckons to a pair of beer waitresses in sexy little black dresses with frilly aprons who are touring the notoriously drunken Western Terraces. The Em Pee slaps their pert behinds, belches, and opens another beer.

'There was an old bore of Lahore who wanted more and more. He rogered a tart and began to fart, that incontinent old – Out!'

Kaliq has been run out!

'Not out!' cries Zaheed. 'Monstrous!'

No decent umpire, even an Englishman, could give Kaliq out while he's still staggering around in agony. But the umpire's finger is raised! The crowd roars!

'You are an adulterer, sir!' Zaheed tells Flowers.

The jubilant Yorkshire beer bellies are in full throttle now, sporting Viking helmets and Mickey Mouse (copyright) hats. Flowers and Lucas are braising themselves like shirtless hams.

'Out!'

Another diabolical decision by the umpires brings Pakistan's innings to a close. Even as the players walk in to the Pavilion, the radios are broadcasting a statement by Pakistan's manager protesting about the condition of the pitch – gremlins, monkeys and general rigging 'to order'!

THIRTY

ॐ

Wahabia Zaheed arrives in Bruddersford. Few of the locals have set eyes on this elegant young lady since she turned down Izza Shah with a giggle and headed south, there to be subsumed in a world of wonderment which carried her, during vacations, to Alpine ski resorts, Bermudan beaches, villas on the Côte d'Azur, and a plucky teaching stint in a dustbowl village north of Bulawayo. Now she's back. A thin black chiffon scarf covers Wahabia's head in this, the city of her birth, but her eyelids no longer dip in the presence of male strangers. Her eyes are now inhabited by fireflies; they belong to someone twice her age. Gamal Rahman's description of the downfall of the Sharaf women has merely caused the fireflies to dance.

'I am here to project Zaheed as the potential saviour of a divided city,' she tells a sceptical but totally charmed Joe Reddaway during a sweep-in, sweep-out visit to the *Echo*.

Gamal has turned sour on her since Jasmin mischievously confided to him that Wahabia shared a bed with Ali Cheema. Gamal's old contempt for her father has flared into print:

'I am familiar with oriental dynastic politics,' he told *The Times*. 'We have the Bhuttos and the Sharafs as models. Observe Wahabia Zaheed's ambitions carefully. If Daddy can snaffle Bruddersford West from the incumbent Flowerpot, Wahabia will inherit the seat after Zaheed grows bored and sulky because he's not Foreign Secretary.'

Wahabia has no objection to being likened to Benazir Bhutto by Gamal Rahman. Whatever Rahman says is news and his mockery guarantees the Muslim vote.

Wahabia had instructed Ali to meet her train at Bruddersford Central, but at the last minute there has been what she called a 'media hullabaloo' about 'the whole thing' and she had driven north in a cortège of cars, accompanied by Jasmin, Inigo Lorraine, and a camera crew. Ali was summoned to present himself at the Zaheed residence for tea. A BBC car was sent to collect him, Wahabia inside it.

'Just in case you were in one of your Sufi moods.'

Zaheed offers his hand to Ali. 'I'm delighted to have your support. I'd like you to know that I'm backing Izza Shah against Mustafa Jangar. To the hilt, old boy.'

Zaheed leads the way into the drawing room where a handsome lurcher is guarding the open french windows and the suburban Versailles gardens beyond. An English maid in uniform has entered behind them.

'Iced lemonade?' Wahabia asks Ali.

'Thank you.'

'Three iced lemonades, Ethel.'

Zaheed sighs, settling the long creases of his beautiful suit into a chintzy chair. 'It seems that the mosques wish to endorse my candidacy for Parliament but they are waiting for Izza Shah to declare himself.'

Ali clears his throat. 'Izza Shah is not well.'

'We are all deeply concerned for his health,' Zaheed says.

Ali finds it hard to conceal his aversion for Zaheed. Even Mustafa Jangar, who lives off modest donations from the faithful, is preferable to this sleek cat.

'Ali, I have many enemies,' Zaheed says. 'It seems that you are similarly honoured.'

'Oh?'

'The Bishop rang me – an old friend. He solicited my view on your candidacy for this Oxford fellowship you're after.' Zaheed pauses. Wahabia observes keenly. 'The Bishop asked whether I could shed light on your relationship with Izza Shah's daughter, Safia. I'm afraid I had to pass on that one – obviously I told him I would speak to you . . . as one Muslim to another.'

'Thank you. I believe my life has been blameless – except in the eyes of God.'

'Unfortunately provincial and peasant attitudes will prevail in our community for some years to come. Frankly, people have been talking. If you could persuade Izza Shah to receive me, we might clear the whole thing up. I know the Bishop would be grateful. I realize that there have been little difficulties between Izza Shah and myself in the past, but – '

'But the world moves on,' Wahabia cuts in.

'Exactly. I hope you will stay to dinner, Ali.'

Jasmin and Inigo are the other dinner guests. Mrs Zaheed does not appear and is never mentioned. Wahabia takes her place. Seated at Zaheed's right hand, Jasmin fizzes and foams like a bottle of champagne roughly shaken before uncorked. She lights cigarettes between courses. Zaheed, who neither smokes nor drinks, asks

Wahabia to fetch an ashtray. The telephone rings for Jasmin throughout the meal. 'I simply don't belieeeve it!' she can be heard exclaiming from the hall. She hardly touches her food (a tactfully chosen vegetarian dish). She pecks, she smokes.

'I really feel,' she tells Zaheed, 'that what has occurred in Bruddersford is nothing less than tragic. Don't you agree, Inigo?'

Inigo smiles. 'Worthy of Shakespeare.'

'Zulfikar,' Jasmin announces, 'I've decided that you should be interviewed by Inigo in your full robes of office.'

Ali cannot belieeeve that Inigo will ever marry Jasmin. The debt is too obvious – she had 'discovered' him – but now Inigo has rather thoroughly discovered himself. Gamal Rahman had once remarked to Ali that 'debts are never repaid, except in bile. The debtor is driven to expel his moral obligation to the creditor by a twist of aggression. This constant motion is fascinating to observe because it is almost invariably subconscious.'

(That was the evening Gamal, clutching a vast box of fattening Swiss chocolates, had led Ali to Susan Gainsborough's dressing room at the Royal Court Theatre after the first night of Rory McKenzie's new play, *The God-Eaters*.

'Susie, you were superb. Clearly you didn't understand a line you spoke but that's a positive advantage when performing Rory.'

'Oh Gamal, you're so sweet!')

The conversation in Zaheed's dining room turns to Bruddersford's Muslim women. Jasmin, Inigo and the 'Final Call' camera crew want to meet women. 'I'm looking,' Jasmin explains, 'for a Muslim woman who is the ideal bridge between the traditional and the modern.'

'What's wrong with Wahabia?' Zaheed smiles.

'Too modern,' Jasmin snaps.

'I suggest Nasreen Hassani,' the Lord Mayor muses. 'I ran into her only the other day when I visited Rajiv Lal at the Department of Education – to discuss the scarf crisis.'

'You shouldn't be seen talking to Rajiv Lal, Daddy,' Wahabia says.

ରଚ

Jasmin Patel and Inigo Lorraine are out on recce patrol. Their assignment is a tough one: to find an 'ordinary Muslim'. To ensure the utmost authenticity, they are wired up from head to toe with hidden mikes; a camera crew disguised as traffic wardens shadows them from a discreet distance, slapping tickets on windscreens.

Sleuthing up Bellingham Road, Jasmin and Inigo come upon a typical corner shop. A tall, super-lean young man is serving at the counter. He wears a T-shirt loudly splashed with a scene from Waikiki

Beach, Hawaii, and his hair rises, and goes on rising, in a disco swirl. Inigo and Jasmin present two tabloid newspapers for purchase.

'So how are things in Bruddersford?' Lorraine asks casually.

The Waikiki Beach Rasta snaps his fingers. 'I have three versions for journalists. The usual rubbish; the unusual rubbish; and the inside story, exclusive, if you happen to be interested in a reconditioned in-car compact disc player, one hundred per cent Nippon, I'm giving it away at sixty quid.'

'If Gamal Rahman walked in here, what would you do?'

'I wouldn't serve him. You can quote that.'

'Suppose he offered to buy your compact disc player?' Inigo asks.

'I'd charge him sixty-five.' Waikiki Beach's eyes are constantly darting round the shop, monitoring the small boys and what's happening at the freezer. 'Want to buy a Japanese mountain bike, 12-lever gears, good as new?'

'Do you regard yourself as a fundamentalist?' Jasmin asks.

The Rasta nods solemnly. 'A fanatic.'

Ten minutes later the investigators venture into a small but smartly decorated establishment selling insurance, 'home credit', driving lessons, fax and photocopying. The young man behind the counter is wearing a crisp white shirt and psychedelic tie.

'Good morning, sir.'

'I'd like a course of twelve driving lessons,' Inigo says. 'My name is Gamal Rahman. What do you say?'

'Do you have a provisional license, sir?'

Out on the street, Inigo and Jasmin catch sight of two old men shuffling along in prayer caps.

'Excuse me, sir.'

The old men politely pause in their shuffle, leaning on their sticks, their gaze firmly averted from the uncovered Hindu-type lady, waiting for the strangers to ask about Gamal Rahman,

'What is your view of the Gamal Rahman affair, sir?'

'English no good.'

'Ah. Aaah. You don't feel he writes well, is that it? Do you mean the form or content of his novel?'

'English no good.'

ৎ

Muhammad Porridge carefully puts his VOTE PORRIDGE poster in the Rolls, drives five yards down the road, on the wrong side as it happens, leans the poster against ISLAM 1, hands Haqq a thick wad of leaflets, and thumps on the next door.

Haqq, Shasti and Tiger Siddiqi are studying the leaflets with mounting incredulity:

THE BANKING SWINDLE

The whole Western Banking System works on fraud and monetary swindle. It's simply modern debt slavery. I have warned succesive British Prime Ministers that manipulation of interest rates is not the way to fight inflation. In a truly Islamic banking system the Bank's profit comes out of a share of the borrower's profit. The ISLAMIC PARTY OF EUROPE will abolish Mortgage Payments and Hire Purchase . . .

Finding no one at home, Porridge stuffs a leaflet through the letterbox, then moves on regally to the next household, where the door is eventually answered by a sleepy young man in bare feet.

'Good morning! Muhammad Porridge, Islamic Party of Europe, your next Member of Parliament.'

From a discreet distance Haqq, Shasti and Siddiqi watch the young man rubbing his eyes.

'May I ask, sir,' booms Porridge, 'whether you are currently employed.'

'Naw.'

'And I'll tell you why. You'll never get a job until we abolish the Banks and print our own local currency.'

The young man moves to close the door.

'Did you know, sir, that in 1932 the Austrian town of Woergl managed to reduce its unemployment and build a bridge by issuing 5000 Free Schillings, non interest-bearing, Islamically Zakat. This local currency was subject to a monthly devaluation, a kind of negative interest, to encourage people to spend it.'

The young man nods with increasing rapidity. Yes, yes, he knows all about it.

'The negative interest was collected in the form of stamp duties which had to be glued to the back of notes. People even paid their taxes in advance to get rid of the Free Schillings in their possession. Then three hundred other Austrian towns decided to follow the example of Woergl. But the Austrian National Bank cracked down. The Zionists, you know.'

'Aye.'

Porridge adjusts his regimental tie. 'So Vote Porridge for Parliament.' He moves on to a house whose owner loves fuchsias.

'Good morning, madam. Muhammad Porridge, Islamic Party of

Europe. Did you know that the Zionists got the United States into two world wars and they are now plotting a third?'

She did know. 'Excuse me but I hear the kettle boiling. It makes the wallpaper peel.'

Porridge has reached a house plastered in red-and-yellow VOTE HANI MALIK stickers. He doesn't seem to notice or care. The middle-aged man who answers the door folds his arms, Labour written all over him, man and boy.

'National currencies are the work of the devil, don't you agree?' Porridge begins.

The Labour man guffaws. 'That's pie in the sky, mate.'

'Bruddersford should issue its own local currency, don't you agree? It worked in Austria in the 1930s, you know.'

'In Australia? Yer must be bonkers.'

'Austria. The only solution is the Islamic one: circular banking, my dear sir. A system of continuous contracts, shared rents and profits.'

The man is grinning at Haqq. 'Thought you was the loony candidate, mate.' He studies Porridge mischievously. 'I'll tell yer summat. It was the Rahman affair that brought these characters out of the woodwork. Where were they all before Gamal Rahman?'

'Couldn't agree more,' Porridge says. 'Storm in a teacup.'

Haqq, Shasti and Siddiqi exchange astonished glances.

'Perhaps you don't understand Rahman's real crime,' Porridge instructs the Labour man. 'Are you aware, sir, that this Egyptian has insulted our Queen and Mrs Thatcher? And such is the oppressive rule of the usurious banks that neither of these ladies can set foot in the City of London without their permission. So we know who put Rahman up to it.'

The Labour man laughs. Then laughs some more. He winks at Haqq. The door closes on Porridge but he seems delighted with his progress:

'Well this street seems pretty well in the bag. Better move on. No need for you chaps to hang around. I'm relying on you to tie up the Indian sub-continent and the Urdu vote.'

An hour later ISLAM 1 glides to a halt outside Hightown Upper School, where Mustafa Jangar is delivering his daily sermon, reading at random from the Ayatollah's 'The Kingdom of the Doctrine', 'The Key of Mysteries' and 'The Explanation of Problems':

'And what about these halls of immorality which call themselves theatres, cinemas, dance, music . . . young women with bare arms, breasts, thighs . . . in streets and swimming pools?'

The constant megaphonic uproar outside the school has more or less brought effective teaching to a standstill. Every casually dressed white girl entering the school is likely to be defamed. Scuffles, fights, are common. Scarcely a day passes without flashing blue lights screaming down Hightown Road. Muhammad Porridge unfurls the flag of the 'Islamic Party of Europe': a half moon and wheatsheaf at the centre of an eight-pointed star. Abdul Ayub Khan has been patiently waiting for his new leader, who's an hour late. As a former corporal, BAOR, he can only admire and follow an officer born and bred like Mr Porridge. Mr Porridge has assured him that he can clear up the prosecution he faces over his halal slaughterhouse. 'It's all a matter of the right word at the right time in the right ear, old boy.' Abdul Ayub Khan has shown Mr Porridge his photograph album and his letters of congratulation to Mrs Thatcher; Mr Porridge confided that Mrs T. would soon convert to Islam. Indeed he had it from the Prime Minister, in strict confidence, that she would bring the Tory Party into the Islamic Party of Europe 'at the first opportunity'.

Abdul Ayub Khan had then showed Mr Porridge a photograph of Rana in her police uniform.

'She is an-up-to-date girl, my daughter. But not modern, you know.'

Now Porridge is muscling in on Mustafa Jangar's terrain, the picket line outside Hightown Upper School. Jangar despises these strangers. 'They have no roots here,' he has complained to Tariq und the mujaheddin of the Muslim Youth League. 'They are not Punjabis, Mirpuris or Kashmiris. These people are converts. So why did Izza Shah invite them here?'

Izzah Shah didn't. Though dying, Izza Shah retains complete authority among Bruddersford's Muslims.

ᘒ

Wahabia and Jasmin have decided that Nasreen Hassani is their ideal interviewee, the Muslim woman who perfectly bridges the traditional and the modern. But tracking her down is proving difficult. Wahabia calls the Department of Education, but is told that Nasreen is 'off, sick'. When Wahabia tries the Hassani home number, Nasreen's husband, Hassan Hassani, answers the phone:

'Mrs Hassani is not here.'

'When will she be home, please?'

'Mrs Hassani is not available,' he says frostily, a clear tremor in his throat.

Wahabia whips through the address section of her filofax and tries the residence of S.B. Hussein. A woman answers.

'Is that Nasreen Hassani, please?'

'No, it's Latifa. Hold on. Nas!'

By the time the television van – bearing the awesome logo of the

BBC – draws up outside S.B. Hussein's delapidated terraced house, Latifa Hussein is in a high state of excitement, a coiled spring of anticipation. Her elder sister Nasreen, by contrast, is dreading the whole thing. Cautiously she pulls the net curtain of an upper window back a fraction to observe the technicians running heavy cables all over the street (or so it seems). Nasreen feels ashamed of her father's threadbare, no-money home. And supposing the rats want to be on television? Nasreen has double reason to dread the whole occasion – these smart, urbane women, Jasmin Patel and Wahabia Zaheed, will know at a glance that she has parted from her husband. She imagines their painted eyes searching for the telltale bruises.

Their car has arrived. Nasreen can hear loud, confident female voices in the street.

'Nas! They're here!' Latifa shouts from the bottom hallway. Nasreen descends the stairs. Shyly she takes Jasmin Patel's proferred hand; Wahabia Zaheed merely smiles sweetly – one 'old girl' of Hightown Upper School to another.

'Well it's simply lovely you were all at the same school at one time or another,' Jasmin exclaims as Latifa leads the way into the sitting room where an elaborate tray of tea cups, biscuits and 'English' supermarket cakes has been laid out.

'We're racing against the clock,' Jasmin explains, 'to finish a film exposing the Hudood laws in Pakistan. We want to record the views of British Muslim women.'

Feeling faintly relieved, Nasreen pours the tea. She can profess complete ignorance about Pakistan. Latifa eagerly proffers the plate of cakes but both visitors politely decline.

'Don't tell me these Hudood laws are still going strong under Benazir Bhutto,' she protests to Jasmin.

'The Bhutto Government has made precious little difference. The prevailing law is the Zina Ordinance of 1979, enforcing the Hudood. This involves, for example, the Rajam, or Stoning, for a woman convicted of adultery.'

Nasreen sits with her arms wrapped tight across her breast.

'Lashes is an alternative to stoning,' Jasmin adds crisply, very matter of fact and petite in her tight jeans, flipping through notes on her lap. 'Now: if you can both give us a feel of where you stand on the Hudood laws, we can then bring the cameras in.'

Latifa glances at her elder sister. Both of S.B. Hussein's daughters know his unquestioning loyalty to the Bhuttos.

'I don't know,' Latifa says softly.

Nasreen sighs. 'My father told me once that the Rajam punishment applies only when four males have witnessed the woman's adultery.'

Jasmin smiles patiently. Patience is not in her nature but it's in her job. She invites Wahabia to explain: 'After all, you're a Muslim, darling.'

Wahabia addresses Nasreen respectfully. 'The rule you have described, Nasreen, applies to rape. Four males must witness the rape of a woman before she can be believed.'

Latifa leaps up. 'That's it, isn't it – the bloody patriarchy. Even Nas's husband Hassan believes that a woman should be stoned for adultery.'

Nasreen stares at her sister, appalled. From the expressions on their faces, Jasmin Patel and Wahabia Zaheed are inches from a scoop. Jasmin is leaning towards Nasreen with an expression of deep consideration.

'Is that why you've left your husband, Nasreen?'

'Are you a Hindu?' Nasreen asks Jasmin fiercely.

Jasmin stiffens. 'By origin.'

'My father told me once that in Pakistan, Hindus and other non-Muslims are not subject to the Shari'a. They are not beaten severely. The jailer does not raise his hand above his head. It is simply to bring the offender to shame before the community.'

Jasmin and Wahabia exchange glances.

'You are not married, Latifa?' Jasmin asks.

'No.'

'Would you be willing to take part in our film?'

'Me! Well . . . my dad wouldn't like it. But why not? I could tell you some things, too. Like those missing birth certificates from Pakistan. At Hightown Upper School they suddenly claimed that I was seventeen not fifteen, you see. They sent me to the Royal Infirmary for a bone X-ray. My dad went mad! He took the case to the Race Relations Board. Two years later they ruled that I was seventeen. Well of course I was! Two bloody years later I was seventeen! And I was bright, wasn't I, Nas? LRSC in Chemistry, no problem, but when I applied for teaching jobs they said I needed the Certificate of Education. Dad was livid! – he's itemized every penny he's spent on my education and Nas's – hasn't he, Nas? So now I'm studying computer science . . .'

Abruptly Latifa seems to wither into despondency. Jasmin looks at her watch and pulls back the net curtains to convey some coded signal to the camera crew in the street. Wahabia takes her opportunity:

'Nasreen, I believe you have been closely involved in the case of Fatima Shah and her scarf?'

'Well . . .'

'What's your personal view on that?'

'You really should interview Mrs Newman, not me.'

483

'It's Muslim women's views we want. Are you afraid to speak, Nasreen? The Department of Education told me that you're off, sick. Have you suffered harassment from the fundamentalists – is that it?'

Nasreen refolds her trembling hands. 'My contract of employment forbids me to speak to the press.'

'But that's a scandal!' Jasmin cries. 'How can Rajiv Lal allow it? I know him well.'

Wahabia probes again. 'Any chance, Nasreen, that you could arrange for us to interview Fatima herself? You probably know why I can't venture near Izza Shah's house.'

'Perhaps Ali Cheema can help us,' Jasmin cuts in impatiently. 'Isn't he supposed to be Fatima's adopted brother or something?'

'Fatima will no longer speak to Ali,' Latifa gaily announces.

'My God,' cries Jasmin, 'have relationships broken down entirely in this town?'

'Why won't Fatima speak to Ali?' Wahabia asks Latifa anxiously.

'Oh that's easy! Fatima imagines he's having . . . that he fancies her sister Safia. Now *she's* the one you want to talk to! She's longing to be on the telly. She'll tell you *everything*.'

'Latifa,' Nasreen says severely. 'That's enough.'

But the sharp knives of Latifa's fast-thinking, frustrated life are edging towards the smooth-fitting skin and pampered hands of the princess Zaheed. When it comes to sussing out sexual sub-plots, Nasreen is an infant compared to her virgin sister.

'I reckon Safia's the only truly liberated Muslim girl in Bruddersford,' Latifa announces. 'I told her you'd want to see her.'

The ladies' attention is now diverted by strange sounds from the street beyond the lace curtains – male wolf whistles can be heard, and hoots, and wows. Latifa scurries to the front door, proudly returning with Safia Shah. Dressed up to the nines and wearing enough make-up to blow all the city's generators, Safia stands in the doorway, flouncing her long, lustrous hair and swinging a tiny, sequinned handbag. King Rat himself would be silenced by the sight of her.

'Well, I've come, haven't I,' she declares defiantly. 'And I'm sixteen now,' she addresses Nasreen, 'not that anyone remembered my bloody birthday. As matter of fact, I spent that evening watching your famous Ali Cheema on telly – and got raped.' Safia slides her tightly skirted bottom into the chair previously occupied by Latifa. 'Well,' she rolls her eyes, 'you're interested in Muslim rape, aren't you?'

Jasmin is very interested, Wahabia very pale.

Nasreen offers Safia a cup of tea.

'No thanks.' A blob of chewing gum appears on the tip of her tongue. She stares insolently at Wahabia. 'Ali fancies you, I'm told.'

'We are just good friends, Safia.'

'Yeah?'

'Please tell us what happened to you,' Jasmin says gently, as if addressing a small child.

'So where's the cameras, then?' Safia gives Latifa a punishing look. 'I thought I were to be on telly.'

'We always have a chat first,' Jasmin says. 'A chat among women. Do please tell us what happened.'

'I told you – I was raped on my birthday.'

'Where did this happen?'

'At Ali's place.'

Safia is swinging her little handbag. When seated, her skirt barely covers her crotch. An elaborate design runs up the side of her black tights.

'What happened?' Jasmin repeats.

'Bloke just walks in and does me. They was showing that Rahman video. Reckon that fired him up.'

'How did the man get in?'

'I let him in, didn't I?'

'Someone you know?'

'Just about.'

Nasreen shudders: it all comes to her. That was why Tariq Khan had stood her up. That was why she'd sat alone in that wretched hotel room.

Jasmin sighs gravely. 'That's how it goes – the victim knows her violator in eight cases out of ten.'

'Oh *reelly*,' Safia bridles. 'I'm a statistic, then.'

'Who was the man?' Wahabia asks coldly.

'What's it to you, my lady?' Safia has forced her vowels into posh. Then she turns to Nasreen, as if to a mother. 'You know the lad. He's just a mixed-up boy and not bad-looking either. I've known worse. I'm not bringing trouble on him. Anyways, that i'n't point o'story.'

Jasmin waits for Nasreen. Evidently this disgusting tart trusts Nasreen. But Nasreen sits quietly, her trembling hands folded in the flowered frock she has worn for television.

'Please tell us the point of the story, Safia,' Jasmin says with heroic patience.

'Point o'story is our famous hypocrite and holy man, Ali Cheema, walking in off the London train just as this lad's zipping 'isself up. He knew who the lad was, too. But you won't get nowt out of Ali Cheema – too many guilty secrets.'

Wahabia stands up, trembling. 'I don't believe a word of it.'

485

'Fancy him, don't you.' Safia winks at Latifa. 'Reckon I blowed it. I read in some mag, you should never talk till the cameras are rolling.'

'Do you really mean,' Wahabia explodes, 'that you would gladly go on television and . . . and say these things about Ali, a young man who your father regards as a son?'

'Fancy him, don't you!' Safia's tears are now turning her make-up into mud pies. King Rat springs to life behind the skirting, besotted no longer. Jasmin and Wahabia recoil, shudder.

'Oh stuff it, all of you!' Latifa yells, dashing upstairs.

જી

Swathed in black, stick-thin, Fatima is huddled in the sofa normally reserved for Izza Shah's male guests. Her father seems to shrink in his armchair as he sleeps, mouth open, behind blinds which now remain drawn day and night. Fatima no longer attends the Muslim Girls' School – her father is too ill to ask why or to forbid her to watch television at all hours. A casual caller might fear that the daughter will die before the father. Constantly she sips from a glass of tepid tap water.

There are few visitors. The sofa is hers. Fatima cannot recall when Nasreen Hassani last came; Ali Cheema occasionally holds the old man's pulse, murmurs in his ear, glances at his watch, departs. Fatima sees more of him on television than in the flesh. She also sees – cannot help watching – his scarlet woman, Wahabia Zaheed, parading her make-up and whorish clothes and fast southern voice before the cameras. Safia once told Fatima that their father had proposed marriage to Wahabia, but Fatima cannot believe such a libel as she glances from the shrunken face in the armchair to the dipping firefly eyes on the television screen a few feet away.

She changes channels to BBC I's Network East. Mustafa Jangar is talking in a very excited manner. She knows him as a brave Believer, very loyal to her father.

'Are we going to allow Muslim girls to spread their legs across showroom motor cars? This so-called "integration" means one British marriage in three divorced; one-parent children and no-parent children. It means prostitution and Aids! We must plug into the global grid of the power of Islam. The Rahman affair has closed the gutter and trapped the vermin. No one can insult Islam and live to tell the tale.'

'Allah-o akhbar,' Fatima murmurs. She changes channel, bored.

That blonde writer woman, Jilly Jumpers, is on again. She reminds Fatima of Mrs Newman, though Mrs Newman is not blonde and does not squeak like a baby. Jumpers is telling her that if Muslim women

486

were allowed to express their views about Gamal Rahman, they would be right behind him. Then she says that something called the Equal Opportunities Commission should condemn the treatment of women in mosques.

Fatima frowns, baffled. She begins brooding about Mrs Newman and the school trip to Paris fifteen months ago, during the spring holiday. Mrs Newman (who insisted on saying 'Easter holiday') had taken six pupils to Paris, four girls and two boys. Having forced them to read the disgusting short stories of Guy de Maupassant, Mrs Newman insisted on showing them Maupassant's 'habitat', the suburbs he described, the stretches of the Seine where he went boating. One Maupassant story began: 'The last act of a man facing execution, be it by guillotine or the firing squad, is to defecate. In short, the bowels have the last say in our lives.'

Only a Christian could have written that.

Jilly Jumpers is on and on about mosques. Why are girls over the age of twelve no longer allowed to attend mosque classes after school? Fatima's eyes are stretched in hatred as she listens: what business of yours? Fatima seethes in her chair like a black mamba, her dry tongue flicking at her glass of water. So Mrs Newman had taken them to Paris. They stayed at the Collège Franco-Britannique in the Cité Universitaire, Boulevard Jourdan. After dragging hot feet for miles in pursuit of Maupassant, they were taken to the Louvre, Versailles and other places whose names Fatima can no longer remember. Mrs Newman seemed quite a different woman in France, younger, laughing at everything and nothing, and dolled up in a wardrobe of vulgar clothes, like a tart.

Jilly Jumpers has now turned her searchlight on the Koran. In her tinkling baby-voice she calls it 'the frightening voice of desert patriarchy' – or something like that, Fatima does not get all the lies.

Mrs Newman had occupied a room at the end of a corridor in the Collège Franco-Britannique. Whenever she came out of her room in a new change of clothes the hemline was cut shorter above the knee. Fatima began keeping a diary: not about Maupassant, the Louvre or Versailles, but recording the tart's hemlines. One night, sleepless and homesick, Fatima had wandered soft-footed down the corridor. An evil light glowed under Mrs Newman's door. Fatima could hear two voices, one a man's, talking in low murmurs. Terrified but driven, Fatima pressed her ear to the door. 'Jean-Pierre,' she heard, then 'Jean-Pierre' again. They were talking softly in French. Fatima couldn't understand what they were saying but she knew they were naked behind the door.

Jilly Jumpers is smiling her sugary smile and saying something

487

about the women of the Koran. What benefit can they get from entering Heaven if Heaven is a place full of beautiful virgins bringing glasses of wine to the men seated beneath palm trees?

Fatima fumes: doesn't the silly bitch know that alcohol is forbidden under Islam?

Izza Shah groans in his sleep.

Fatima had not told the other girls about Mrs Newman and 'Jean-Pierre'. She could not tell Ali because he was a man. It remained her secret. But now her large eyes are deep-set in calculation; her stick legs twist restlessly on the sofa; she sips from the glass at twice the pace; she pictures a suburban house in Belmont, an open toilet window at the rear, a thick wastepipe running to the ground – the whore's home.

൭

Harry Flowers is not listening to Jilly Jumpers. Shoes off, he bows and offers a chain of flowers to Pandit Morari Bapu, the honoured guest of a splendid gathering of Bruddersford's prosperous Gujarati Hindus, many of whom had sought sanctuary in Britain after expulsion from Idi Amin's Uganda. Since that time the Shri Vallabh Trust has held an annual Festival. The marquee is 175 yards long.

The Pandit sits cross-legged on a raised pink-and-white dais, under a canopy, wearing sunglasses and a black shawl over one shoulder. His attendant monks wear saffron robes.

Harry Flowers presents his flowers, content in the knowledge that Zulfikar Zaheed has not been invited. Better, was turned down. No Muslims here. Harry gives the short speech expected of him.

'Honoured Friends, I am gratified to discover that I retain some influence with the Home Office. It was surely my obligation to ensure that Pandit Bapu received a multiple-entry visa. I am glad to report that the Holy Pandit suffered no difficulties or indignities at the airport.'

Gentle applause, nothing vulgar. *Fuck you, Zaheed.*

Harry then quotes from the Ramayana, which tells how the Lord Rama came down to earth to reveal the divine principles. A giant of a man with the physique of a former wrestler is beaming; a bald dome crowns the gentle Buddha-smile of S.B. Hussein's drinking companion. His daughter, Jyoti Devi Chand, who works at the Department of Education, and who taught Nasreen not to say 'Rajivlal', sits beside him. She is happy, too. Harry Flowers is reliable, a good friend, you know where you are with him. We don't need a Muslim Em Pee or a Muslim anything.

488

That evening Councillor Sir Tom Potter raises the temperature at the annual dinner-dance of the North Welton cricket club. Even Douglas Blunt's presence in black tie and winged collar does not deter him:

'Frankly, we're sick and tired of it all,' declares Potter. 'Sick and tired to the gills. If they don't like it here, they're free to leave. What has happened to our once-green-and-pleasant land? Every year that passes we're being battered into submission in our own country. If we're not careful, the England we know will be lost for ever.'

THIRTY-ONE

෨෮

Zulfikar Zaheed makes his third appearance on the picket line outside Hightown Upper School, attended by Hani Malik, Wahabia, Joe Reddaway and what Mrs Newman now calls the Zaheeda Meedja. Zaheed emerges from his official limousine wearing his chain of office, robe and tricorn hat. The regular picket of incensed Muslim parents and politicians crowd forward with their placards.

'I am here,' Zaheed explains to the microphones, 'as a gesture of reconciliation. I believe it is now time for the Department of Education to put people before prejudice.'

(This evokes cries of approval from the parents, though Jangar, Haqq, Karamat Khan and the Freikorps of Islamic militants maintain scowls of scepticism.)

'Those Muslim girls who wish to cover their heads in school are not rebels or delinquents. They are observing ancient traditions. We have not made provision for publicly funded Muslim schools. We have not listened to the legitimate demands of the Muslim community. We have cooked up all manner of excuses to delay the provision of halal meat for school dinners. I want to see our Muslim girls back in all of our City's schools tomorrow morning! We can no longer imperil the education of our children! Our children are our future!'

On that note, Zaheed offers a graceful gesture towards the future, a young lady dressed in sombre colours and long skirts, her face scrubbed of cosmetics, her hair tied up beneath her hijab. Wahabia waits modestly until assured of the full attention of the cameras and microphones:

'My name is Wahabia Zaheed. I was born in this wonderful city, you know. I grew up here very happy. I had young friends from all the communities. Christian girls and Hindu girls and Sikh girls used to come to my house. When I was sent to this school, to Hightown Upper, I was told that I must not cover my head once I stepped inside the door. This was very painful to me. There are boys here and male teachers. I know it was a great grief to my father, Zulfikar Zaheed, that I could not modestly cover my head. But my father always said, "Wahabia, in a multicultural society we must give as well as take." I believe that we Muslims urgently need a voice in London to express our grief, our pain, our legitimate demands. That is why I feel sure that my Muslim brothers and sisters will join with all traditional Labour Party voters to ensure that Zulfikar Zaheed is nominated as our parliamentary candidate.'

Joe Reddaway appraises the camera crew from 'Final Call'. Jasmin Patel and Inigo Lorraine have been filming Zaheed and his daughter. The Patel woman is looking less than over-the-moon. Joe makes his move:

'Any comment, Mr Lorraine?'

Inigo's earnest, handsome features register bemusement. 'I'm not here to comment,' he murmurs. 'I'm here to report.'

Lord Mayor Zaheed and his entourage depart. Joe scribbles in his notebook: 'Zaheed: the amber light of Bruddersford politics. Wahabia: the green light heading for an accident.'

ᏚᎦ

Fatima remembers the house in Belmont where the prostitute lives because Mrs Newman likes to invite her favourite pupils for Saturday tea parties and make them talk French to real French people who are staying as her guests. If you remain silent Mrs Newman flushes you out of your corner with her nasty smile. Fatima is now possessed by her secret knowledge, by her unique power to strike down Satan's whore – she can already hear the jubilant muezzins chanting her praises from the minarets. Fatima has not eaten properly for weeks.

She takes the mid-morning bus. Consumed by cunning, she has discarded her hijab and borrowed from Safia's wardrobe a pair of jeans, a frilly blouse, a flashy headscarf and a pair of mirrored sun glasses. She has rubbed Safia's foundation make-up into her face until her skin is almost white. For the first time in her life she reddens her mouth – like a slut.

She takes the precaution of alighting from the bus two stops early, completing the journey on foot, wobbling on a pair of Safia's high heels. A milk float is doing its rounds in this quiet white suburb. She never sees milk floats in her own neighbourhood – there are corner shops. Mrs Newman's garden is packed with roses and fuchsia but she doesn't notice. She presses the front door bell, hears the chime, waits, her heart thudding against her ribcage. She walks to the back door. A pint of milk has been placed on the doorstep, shielded from the sun. Behind Safia's mirrored sunglasses she nervously scans the neighbouring properties (she has heard her father advocating something called 'Neighbourhood Watch'). She studies the first-floor windows. The small toilet window with mottled glass is fractionally open, just as she'd remembered. Fatima used to hide in the toilet to escape the real French people. A dog has begun barking – she's not sure where. She wants to run away but God would not forgive her. All night long her head has ached with loneliness and the call of jihad. Hiding Safia's high heels behind a dustbin, she fastens hands and knees round the thick waste pipe which runs down from the toilet, and braces herself. She scrambles upwards, moaning for strength, all fear banished by elation – Allah akhbar! – unaware of the streaks of menstrual fluid seeping through Safia's jeans on to the waste pipe and, later, on to the rather nice French chair behind the desk where Patricia Newman keeps her (French) letters. The aces of the West Yorkshire CID, when called in by the distraught owner of the purloined letters, will duly conclude that 'the boy who did this job' had cut himself badly while negotiating the toilet window. But here I go again, Dad, time-hopping.

ᕲᕧ

'Final Call' comes up on the late-night TV screens.

'What?' Inigo Lorraine engagingly asks the camera, 'did I expect to find up here?' Bruddersford railway station hangs obligingly behind him, like a smudged stage backdrop from the Age of Steam. Lorraine (who has actually been staying at the Crown Hotel for three days) carries a soft canvas shoulder bag, the collar of his raincoat raised expectantly.

'I imagined an Asian community living in a kind of belljar – I expected otherness.'

The driver of his taxi is (obligingly) a Muslim. Lorraine leans forward from the back seat: 'Would you give a lift to Gamal Rahman?'

'He should repent.'

Cut to Ali Cheema's living room, mugs of tea on the table. Lorraine wears his most attentive expression.

'Frankly,' Ali is saying, 'it is not death that Gamal Rahman has to fear but the life after death assigned to him by the Almighty.'

'But that is outrageous! – to speak so calmly of another man's death.'

'To carry out the fatwa would be illegal under British law but nevertheless a principled act of conscience and duty.' Ali shrugs coolly. 'Rahman himself is no longer the issue.'

'No longer the issue! It's not an idea that is living in hiding, under sentence of death, it's a man, a British citizen!'

'I believe his fate lies in his own hands.'

'You mean he must renounce his own beliefs, his own artistic freedom, in order to earn *your* permission to enjoy the life of a free man?'

Cut. Lorraine is found with a group of pretty Muslim girls squashed gaily together on a park bench. They wear headscarves and talk in broad Yorkshire about Gamal Rahman claiming that the Prophet took a thirteenth wife, Huda, 'very conveniently for her in the nick of time'. Insulting the famous martyr and her unborn son!

'We were born here, you know.'

Lorraine smiles genially beneath windswept hair. Now he is crossing the park, pausing within longshot of a disused mill:

'Living up to the conflicting demands of their own culture and of the West is not easy for these youngsters. And yet most of them achieve a modus vivendi with less psychic and moral tension than one might expect. Religion is the anchoring force.'

Cut. 'Don't you agree?' Lorraine is asking Ali, two tea mugs and a copy of *The Devil: an Interview* between them: 'Religion serves as the immigrant's anchor. He fears the drift of the unknown. He starts burning books. And then where does he stop?'

'Shall I explain what the Liberal Inquisition is? The Liberal Inquisition brings *you* to interrogate *me* in my home. The cameras ensure that the audience identifies with *your* Caucasian journey to the oriental "belljar" – these alien, marginal, dark-skinned Believers who speak funny English. Why doesn't your producer send me and my canvas travel bag from Bruddersford to the South, questing and probing among all these exotic media people and famous liberal writers? Why am I not allowed to drink tea in your pinewood-fitted kitchen and then comment direct-to-camera? Why not turn the lens around?'

Cut. Lorraine is found in the office of the Headmistress of High-town Upper School.

'Separate faith schools are divisive,' Mrs Newman is saying. Such is her composure that one would not guess that every day, arriving and leaving, she has to run the gauntlet of pickets yelling abuse. 'Look at Northern Ireland. We need togetherness. Here in the schools and playgrounds we should begin the struggle against prejudice and sectarianism.'

Lorraine nods with that engaging concern of his. 'But isn't it for the parents to decide?' he asks. 'Are we not in danger of turning our progressive principles into a form of cultural imperialism?'

'Is it for a parent to decide that his daughter may not take part in games because appropriate games attire is "immodest"? Should he be able to forbid his children to learn about music, because music is "wicked"? Should he be free to take his son to Pakistan for six months without a day in school? The longer I have been in this profession, the more I have cared about children and the less about parents.' She smiles. 'Some parents.'

'Yet the upshot of the scarf affair is that a whole lot of Muslim girls are now missing school entirely.'

'That is deeply disturbing.'

Cut.

Inigo Lorraine emerges from a narrow stairway into a first-floor restaurant. 'Named,' he explains dreamily, 'after the great poet Omar Khayyam.' He has cornered a handsome young waiter.

'Tariq Khan, you have lived all your life in Bruddersford. Are you proud to be British?'

'At the end of the day we are being called immigrants all over again. That's not so great. We all pay taxes but they want to put me on a boat. We're all legal you know.'

'But is it not your own reaction to the Rahman book which has generated this new outbreak of racism and prejudice?'

'Modern Christianity no longer believes in itself. People give their lives for Islam. You don't change the laws of God to suit the tabloids.'

Cut to Lorraine, carrying a soft canvas shoulder bag on the platform of Bruddersford Central Station. He addresses the camera, hair ruffled by the breeze:

'So what would I give my life for? I believe I'd do it to resist the Islamic theocratic state. Hitler, Stalin and the Ayatollah threaten everything I believe in.'

৶

Fatima is not watching television. Far into the night she toils in her room to translate the whore's collection of letters from the immoral Frenchman whom she had overheard fornicating and adultering, or adulterating, with the scarlet woman in the Collège Franco-Britannique. But this filthy Jean-Pierre's handwriting is difficult and Fatima's French isn't up to it. She frowns, and screws up her eyes, and turns the pages of her dictionary, but she can't make much sense.

All the letters are handwritten on notepaper headed:

Université de Paris III – Sorbonne Nouvelle
Institut du Monde Anglophone
5, rue de l'Ecole de Médecine, 75006 Paris

And they all begin: 'Patricia, Love of my life . . .' Fatima can translate that. She finds a letter written shortly before her own visit to Paris with Mrs Newman's school party. She understands a few phrases but the rest eludes her. This is what she would read if she could (translation courtesy of G. Rahman):

Darling, I am so delighted that you will be bringing the party of brats next week. I have rearranged my lecture schedule, deferred a couple of sessions with my agrégation students, in short, I have cleared my desk (and my bed) for you. Sweetheart, make sure that you shake off the brats as soon as you arrive. Don't waste a minute with them! Surely the usual alibi will do – profound research in the BN . . .

Fatima peers at 'BN' – what is it? [Bibliothèque Nationale, or National Library.] She hides the letters in her bottom drawer and falls exhausted into bed. Allah has entrusted her with this sacred task and she must not fail Him. The only adult Muslims she knows who understand French are Ali and his immoral bitch-friend, Wahabia Zaheed. She dare not confess to Ali what she has done. At a level too deep for recognition she knows that he does not believe in an inconvenient God. After they are married he will.

Retreating to the bathroom, Fatima wrestles with another of Safia's tampons, licking the blood from her fingers.

౼

Joe Reddaway is enjoying Zulfikar Zaheed's hospitality. 'The Lord Mayor Speaks – Exclusive to the *Echo*.' Reddaway reckons this must be his fortieth exclusive with the only Muslim in Bruddersford known by name to virtually every white citizen, the languid, laid-back commander of the headlines.

—Zaheed refused membership by golf club.

—Zaheed demands a seat in Members' Stand of Yorkshire County Cricket Club.

—White wedding guests spit on Zaheed's limo.

Zaheed, Zaheed! The summons came from Wahabia. Joe would go to the North Pole just to set eyes on her. Radioactive! A strange bloke, calling himself Iqbal Iqbal, has phoned the *Echo* to tell Joe that he had just sold a packet of 'Better Safe than Sorry' birth-control pills to Wahabia Zaheed. Joe would like to explain to Wahabia that a reporter's life is not an easy one.

Zulfikar Zaheed rises from his armchair and offers his hand. 'This is a difficult time for our city,' he says.

'Lemonade or Scotch or beer?' Wahabia asks.

'Scotch, please, on the rocks.' Joe's face is a heated-up plum pudding.

'My father is going to tell you about Ishmail Haqq,' Wahabia says, folding herself into a chair close to Joe's.

'Ishmail Haqq, alias Marshak Pirbai, could have been the hero of an R.K. Narayan novel,' Zaheed begins. 'From a village in Bangladesh he set out with dreams of glory in UK journalism and/or politics. Very much an and/or person, all options open, periscope up.'

Wahabia laughs appreciatively. 'An illegal immigrant, don't forget, Daddy.'

'Quite so, Wahabia. After taking stock of the scene, London village life, Haqq moved into Tower Hamlets, focussed his sights on the Inner London Education Authority, and became the scourge of councillors, teachers, governors, everyone.'

'Everyone,' Wahabia confirms. 'Haqq then elected himself Chairman of the London Collective of Black School Governors.'

'So-called,' Zaheed comments. 'Haqq constantly disrupted ILEA meetings by chanting "Racist!". He also developed a nervous habit of snapping cameras at people. "You'll be sorry!" '

'Everyone else was out of step,' Wahabia tells Joe.

'Haqq made several bids to become a Labour councillor in Tower Hamlets,' Zaheed continues. 'The scourge of corruption. He was nominated but never shortlisted. "I don't need the Labour Party or any party," he declared as he set out for the North. Arriving in Bruddersford, he put it about that he was the Messiah returned to earth in the guise of a Bangladeshi. When no one took any notice he rejoined the Labour Party.'

'Changing his name from Marshak Pirbai to Ishmail Haqq,' Wahabia adds. She rises. 'Now you must excuse us, so much to do.'

Joe Reddaway's clumsy, note-taking paw rests. 'That's it?'

'Check it out,' Zaheed says smoothly. 'Make it your own story, strictly non-attributable.'

'You haven't heard a word from us about Haqq,' Wahabia adds.

ॐ

Patricia Newman is Joe Reddaway's guest for dinner at the Stag's Head. It's a long time since he picked up the bill for two at the Stag's Head. He hopes she understands the codes of restaurant-selection. He has even taken himself home for a bath and a clean shirt without too many buttons missing. He notices that she is wearing a fetching dress and a string of pearls for the occasion.

'Before this Rahman affair turned nasty,' Joe chuckles, 'I thought it was a bad joke, like Papa Doc Duvalier putting a voodoo curse on Graham Greene for writing *The Comedians.*'

'This joke has degenerated into vicious flatulence. What can one expect of a civilization where every building project has to be submitted to the ulama to ensure that no toilet faces Mecca?'

'A culture where Miss Piggy mugs and toys are seized from shops by the religious police and destroyed!'

'Where if you break wind during prayers you to have start all over again!'

Patricia notices that Joe burps frequently and tends to leave bits of his meal clinging to his chin. By the main course he is eagerly quoting – pathetically eager – all the supportive things he has written about her during the school crisis.

'You've been a brick, Joe – much appreciated.'

'I've always had a thing about you, Patricia.'

'Well, I'm flattered.'

'Usually I come here to eat, sickened by all the happy couples around me. I always bring along my best intentions in the shape of Blake's "Marriage of Heaven and Hell", but after a couple of glasses I mutter, very wittily, what the hell, and abandon myself to brooding about the high salaries paid on Fleet Street (as one still calls it ha bloody ha) to young squirts who know nowt of life.' Joe belches. 'I love the theatre, Patricia, but I hate to go alone.'

'I rather like it – perhaps I'm happy with my own thoughts. The University French Faculty is doing quite a good *Bérénice*, if you're interested.'

'I'm not selling myself to you as a highbrow, Patricia. Occasionally you'll find me in the gaily oriental Alhambra, which looks as if it has wandered inland from a seaside resort.'

Joe refills their glasses – mainly his.

'So why aren't you married?' she asks him.

'My feet smell.'

'Perhaps you've trodden in too many dustbins.'

This he does not appreciate. It's a remark he wouldn't mind making about himself but he detected naked disdain poking through her ladyship's distant smile. The proposal of marriage he has rehearsed and revised recedes – it's that gut-thumping moment when the self-evident becomes the bloody obvious. He assumes an expression of the utmost gravity.

'Bloody depressing for you, Patricia,' he sighs.

'What is?'

'I don't mean to intrude, of course.'

'Are you talking about the stolen letters? Actually, this little burglary has turned out to be a blessing in disguise.'

'Oh?'

'Oh certainly. Jean-Pierre rang to say that his wife had found out about our affair. She isn't taking it well.'

'How did she find out?'

'Someone sent her photocopies of two letters from Jean-Pierre to myself. Postmarked Bruddersford. There was an accompanying note in a childish hand – littered with spelling mistakes. "Retched wife of adultrer, learn the truth about the prosatoot Madam Newman." '

'So now you're free to marry your French bloke?'

'Jean-Pierre's wife is throwing him out. Their children are grown up, there's nothing left to bind them.'

'You'd go and live in France?'

'With the greatest pleasure. I feel at home in France. I'm due a little happiness.'

'And Hightown Upper School?'

'I'll switch out the lights as I leave.'

Joe's mood turns. Another notch on his baton of rejections. How smug she is about the happy, fulfilled, erotic, love-packed life ahead of her. Oh yes, she takes his support for granted! Never mind that her purblind stubbornness has paralysed the City's education system! What does she care about the girls who are missing school?

'Patricia I have to tell you something. Only this morning a photocopy of one of Jean-Pierre's letters hurtled on to my desk through the post. Here, take a look.'

Patricia scans the letter rapidly. 'Can you read French, Joe?'

'I can say "parlez vous". I got the general gist, not the exciting details. Frankly, I ought to publish this.'

'A private letter!'

He flushes scarlet. 'This is a matter of acute public interest. I mean a Headmistress who does it right under the noses of the pupils she takes to France.'

Silence.

'*What* did you say?'

'I happened to recall a piece in the *Echo* last year by one of our cub reporters, describing the wonderful time enjoyed by six pupils from Hightown Upper who stayed in Paris at the Collège Franco-Britannique – forgive my peasant pronunciation.'

'So?'

'So I looked up the report. It listed the six happy pupils.'

'Well?'

498

'I phoned their homes – in fact I needed only one shot at the apple. It's bloody obvious, isn't it?'

'Is it?' Patricia Newman has abandoned her food. From her expression Joe might be an undercooked suet pudding discarded on her plate.

'Fatima Shah.'

'Fatima? Fatima did this? But who got into my house?'

'Fatima.'

'You mean she confessed?'

'Denied everything – hardened little bitch. But she did tell me – in a voice close to hysteria – that you used to entertain your Jean-Pierre at night in a room just down the corridor from the one occupied by Fatima and three other girls.'

'Rubbish! Lies! Do you imagine I'd ever do something so . . . so silly? You're not naïve, are you?'

'No.'

'Yet you believe her! You *want* to believe her. Thank you for dinner, Joe.' Patricia Newman throws her screwed-up napkin on the tablecloth.

'You're taking this the wrong way, Patricia.'

She is on her feet, pearls glinting. 'Your editor will be hearing from my lawyers.'

ᔕᐤ

The Governors of Hightown Upper School have invited all parents and pupils to attend a Special Meeting. The school hall is packed and festooned with banners putting Gamal Rahman to death. Not a few of the more muscular 'parents' in attendance look to be about twenty years old, wear mujaheddin headbands, and could be mistaken for Tariq Khan. But the prize exhibit is Fatima Shah and a cluster of sisters in black burkas.

Driving into the school parking lot for the meeting, Patricia Newman has found the sacred space clearly marked 'Head Teacher' occupied by a car whose rear window urged her to 'Vote HAQQ'. The affront made her tremble. Finding all the reserved spaces filled by vehicles bearing Islamic Party stickers, she was forced to reverse out into the street, amidst derisive jeers from the pickets, and to drive two blocks to find a place to park. She encounters Haqq at the door, 'checking credentials'.

'Mr Haqq, your car is parked in my reserved space.'

'Mrs Newman, you will not speak to me in that tone when I am the elected councillor for Tanner Ward.'

'I certainly will. And you're not. Now move your car.'

499

His face is suffused with rage (hers also, nothing to choose between them – they had always got on perfectly well before the Rahman business, indeed Haqq had been one of the few Muslim fathers to allow his daughter to wear an ordinary swimming costume). 'If you were not a lady I would strike you.'

'You're a gangster, Haqq, and I am bringing a legal action against you in the High Court for constant abuse and harassment. It will be an expensive action and my union will pay my legal fees. Now move your car.'

She seeks out the recently elected Chairman of the Governors, Hassan Hassani, who merely offers a nervous twitch of his wet lips.

'Half the people in this hall have no right to attend this meeting, Mr Hassani. They are not Hightown Upper parents or pupils.'

Mustafa Jangar looms up at Hassani's side.

'They are invited by the parents and Governors belonging to the Parents' Action Group,' Jangar booms.

'They cannot be invited under the Regulations. And the so-called Parents' Action Group has no status whatsoever.'

'I have granted the status, Mrs Newman,' says Hassani. 'Kindly remember I am the Chairman of the Governors now. Please remember.'

Patricia Newman approaches Rajiv Lal, whose passive posture reminds her of a bunch of damp faggots.

'I believe that Mr Hassani has the majority of the Governors behind him on this,' Rajiv says softly. 'Really this is all therapy, bleeding a wound, and it is better to let it bleed.'

An altercation at the door looks like turning into a scuffle. Haqq, who has appointed himself steward, is blocking the path of two trade union officials representing the Headteacher and the teaching staff respectively. Both unions have not only demanded an end to the violent picketing and the harassment of staff, they have also come out publicly in support of the ban on 'the scarf'.

Samuel Perlman arrives. Brushing past Haqq, he leads the union officials to their seats alongside the teachers (not a few of whom have chosen to stay away, some on sick-leave).

'You Zionist Fascist!' Haqq is pursuing Perlman, jabbing his finger in the face of the City's Education Chairman. Tariq and his muja-heddin are swarming around Perlman, yelling and jostling him.

On the platform Hassan Hassani is fitfully banging his gavel, sweat pouring from his high, domed brow.

As the white parents enter the hall, Haqq demands to examine their 'credentials'. 'On behalf of the School Governors,' Haqq repeats each time he's challenged. Asian parents meanwhile enter unimpeded, unless they look like Hindus, and there are few of those around this evening.

Perlman mounts the platform to speak to Hassan Hassani.

'The scene at the door is a disgrace,' he tells him. 'Who are these young thugs you've imported?'

'Stewards, not "thugs", Mr Perlman.'

Perlman brandishes his mobile telephone. 'Get Haqq and your "stewards" off the door or I'll call the police.'

Nothing much happens, either way. When the first pair of police constables amble through the door, the mujaheddin drift away. Confronting indignant white matrons hasn't turned out to be much fun. The white parents, meanwhile, search anxiously through the veils of the Orient for their own kind. The Muslim parents are seated in sexually segregated blocs. Haqq is trying to impose this arrangement on the white parents as well.

S.B. Hussein enters the hall, swaying majestically, as if staying upright is a triumph over gravity, and surveys the scene before mounting the platform, Hightown Upper's longest-serving Governor. He seats himself several places along from his estranged son-in-law, Hassan Hassani. If a husband loses all the arrows in his quiver, if a husband lets his tyres be punctured, then he deserves to be treated like a used condom. Hassan had been elected Chairman despite his own opposition, the puppet of the Zia-ite Jamiyat, the enemies of Benazir.

S.B.'s daughter Nasreen Hassani does not arrive with her father. They are barely on speaking terms because of the drinking and her mother still toiling in the mill. She took the bus. Nasreen sits huddled in misery among the Muslim women. She hadn't wanted to come but Rajiv Lal had instructed her to do so. 'You will bring some fitra, some common sense,' he told her. Does he know that she has left her husband? Does he know that Hassan had turned up at S.B. Hussein's house to demand the return of his son, Imran, choosing a time in the evening when S.B. was invariably at the pub?

'I divorce you! I divorce you! I divorce you!' Hassani had pointed a rigid, shaking arm at Nasreen on the doorstep. But Imran had locked himself in his room and Latifa had threatened to call the police, though inwardly she trembled at this affront to the pride and status of a husband, a father, who had done nothing wrong.

Hassan didn't have the temerity to try and force his way in.

'We're not in Pakistan now,' Latifa had hissed at him.

So Nasreen sits in the hall, with the women, head covered, eyes averted from her husband, from Rajiv Lal, from everyone.

Joe Reddaway is standing at the back of the hall. At the door Haqq had attempted to refuse him entry. 'No press tonight!'

Haqq may have had a point but it was not one that Joe was willing to entertain.

'Should I be describing you as Marshak Pirbai in tomorrow's *Echo*?' Passing Haqq, Joe's wispy carrot top had moved on into the hall among the many darker heads.

Samuel Perlman is exercising his constitutional right to address any Parent-Governor meeting. Mounting the platform, he endeavours to explain the Council's policy on what he calls 'the scarf issue'. But is it the Council's policy? Everyone in the hall knows about the tied vote in the Council Chamber. The jeering, howling and whistling is continuous. Each time Perlman says 'Muslim girls', Fatima Shah and her burka'd sisters scream hysterically, as if violated by Perlman's Zionist tongue. Ishmail Haqq is shouting 'Racist!' and 'Bullshit' at intervals so regular as to seem regulated by a metronome.

Joe Reddaway composes a plain-speaking sentence about 'the posturing of political piranhas demanding their pound of flesh' – but then wonders whether piranhas spend much time 'posturing'.

'Racist! Bullshit!' Haqq yells.

Reddaway's gaze momentarily meets Patricia Newman's. She looks right through him. He scribbles in his notebook: 'One must agree with Harry Flowers, MP, that "racist" has become the icon-word of those committed to the "race game". It is applied with the same mindless zeal as "heretic" or "Commie" in earlier times of hysteria.'

Enter now the tall, patrician figure of Muhammad Porridge, the only prominent British Muslim to have landed by parachute on Port Said in 1956: a lieutenant in the Parachute Regiment, schooled at Wellington, his father a friend of T. E. Lawrence. Joe Reddaway pushes towards him.

'Reddaway, Bruddersford *Echo*,' he says.

Porridge looks him over as if they'd never met before.

'All this scarf agitation is complete twaddle,' Porridge loudly informs Joe. 'Like all the Rahman twaddle. Total diversion from the real issues.'

'I gather you don't believe Darwinism should be taught in schools, Mr Porridge.' Joe's pen is poised.

'It's no longer accepted by scientists. I don't know if you're up-to-date with gene research, but it is now definitely pointing away from the theory that man evolved from primates.'

'Can you quote any recent authorities on that?'

'Certainly. Professor René Lapont of the University of Rennes. R-e-n-'

'Yes, I've got that. I can spell "Paris", too.'

'Darwinism, you see, is primarily an ideological doctrine designed to justify Europe's colonization of the Third World. The Koran is the last word in science.'

Porridge looks bored. Joe guesses there are no votes in Charles Darwin, for or against. Local municipal currencies is where the votes are. Print your own money. Tons of votes.

The bearded Iqbal Iqbal glides into the group, his wire-rimmed glasses gleaming. He has just placed a Koranic bomb in Samuel Perlman's briefcase – disguised as the Torah.

'Modern science is fully anticipated in the Koran,' Iqbal smiles at Joe. 'I can show you a verse about invisible small things residing in larger visible things – precisely Louis Pasteur's microbes.'

Joe is scribbling. 'What is your name, sir?'

'Iqbal. Iqbal Iqbal, B.Sc. in Pharmacology.'

'Ah – you phoned me to report the sale of contraceptives to a certain young lady.'

Iqbal's glasses glint happily. 'I have been personally responsible for all the illegal leaflets distributed in Bruddersford. It was I who fire-bombed the bookshops in the Charing Cross Road. Various other bombs concealed in Korans have failed to explode – for example at the Royal Court Theatre and during the most recent demonstration in this city.'

'You want me to quote you on all that?' Joe asks.

'Most certainly. I have already written many letters to your news-paper describing my activities but none has been published.'

Porridge, overhearing this, has begun to drift away from Iqbal.

'Racist bullshit!' Ishmail Haqq is heard to yell at Samuel Perlman. 'When you are kicked out of office we will put you on trial for spiritual genocide!'

'And when will you publicize Mrs Patricia Newman's adultery?' Iqbal asks Joe.

Porridge's lacquered head flicks back into view. 'What was that?'

'A proven adulteress is regulating the morals of our girls. There she sits. You can see her.' Iqbal is still smiling. Joe wonders whether he smiles in his sleep.

'Mrs Newman is divorced,' Joe says. 'She cannot commit "adultery".'

'She is fornicating. She is a hypocrite. A loose woman.'

'How do you know?'

'I know.'

'Be careful of slander, Brother,' Porridge rebukes him from a height worthy of a parachute jump. 'What does the Holy Koran teach us about evil tongues?'

Joe observes a cloud of insensate hatred pass across Iqbal's countenance: to be lectured on the Koran by an Englishman!

'Racist! Bullshit!' yells Haqq from the door as Samuel Perlman finishes his interminable oration. At a word from Mustafa Jangar, Hassan Hassani allows a motion of No Confidence in Samuel Perlman. The vote is by a show of hands. It is carried, overwhelmingly.

'Now get out!' Haqq shouts at Perlman, who merely folds his arms.

Mustafa Jangar is granted, or grants himself, the floor. As far as Joe can follow it, the gist of Mustafa's message is that Hightown Upper School is, this very night, to be rescued from purgatory by the Hidden Imam.

'Twaddle,' Porridge says.

'Cervical cancer is almost unknown among practising Muslim women,' roars Mustafa, 'and therefore we know that this disease is God's punishment for the promiscuity of white women! Yet this is what Mrs Newman demands of our good Muslim girls!'

Fatima and her band scream, shake, tear at their faces. Mustafa repeatedly jabs his finger in the direction of the motionless Headmistress, as if sticking needles into the devil.

'Mrs Newman's staff here are teaching our girls this so-called Biology, which means "free sex", abortion, immorality! And I say that Mrs Newman is herself a scarlet woman!'

A cohort of white parents are now on their feet and won't sit down until they're heard. Patricia Newman recognizes them all and notices that liberals and racists are huddled together like diverse animals joined in the ark by tempest and flood. She observes Lannion, a surveyor working for the Halifax Building Society, and in her experience always very reasonable, wildly waving his arm, trying to catch the Chairman's attention. But Hassan Hassani sees only the nods and negatives of Haqq and Jangar, the ringmasters of the Hightown Parents' Action Group.

'This is like a political meeting in Pakistan!' Lannion shouts.

'Racist!' yells Haqq. 'Sit down or get out!'

Lannion is doing neither. 'How do you think we feel sending our children to this oriental bazaar? How can we have a Chairman of the Governors who is himself seen on the picket line, disrupting classes through a megaphone?'

Uproar. Fatima's claque emits an orchestrated shriek. Hassani blinks uncomfortably; against his better judgment he had on one occasion joined Mustafa Jangar on the picket line.

Lannion is still on his feet, announcing a High Court action challenging 'this so-called Board of Governors'.

Hassan Hassani catches sight of his wife's head bowed in shame. She has dishonoured him. He will not allow Rajiv Lal to address the meeting – though Rajiv Lal shows no sign of wanting to do so. Hassan offers the floor to Ishmail Haqq. Despite his suffering, his bewilderment, Hassan has been loyally labouring through lonely evenings in an empty house shared only by his old father, for whom he must now cook a meal – loyally labouring with the famous Muslim barrister, Ashtiak, on a legal brief proving that Gamal Rahman's insults are punishable under the Blasphemy Act, which clearly describes as blasphemous any 'contemptuous, reviling, scurrilous or ludicrous matter relating to God, Jesus Christ, the Bible, or the formularies of the Church of England as by law established.'

Fitting Islam into that is not easy.

But when was God's work easy? Hassan is deeply impressed by the brilliant legal mind of Ashtiak, who aims to prove – conclusively! – that Islam and the English Church worship the same, unique God and revere the same prophet, Ibrahim/Abraham. Ashtiak has also spotted that the restriction of the Blasphemy Act to Christianity breaches the European Convention on Human Rights. Better still, Gamal Rahman is guilty of a seditious libel because his book has raised widespread disaffection among Her Majesty's subjects. Hassan's thoughts race ahead to Bow Street Magistrates' Court. He has requested leave of absence from work and booked his seat to London for the first hearing before the Chief Metropolitan Magistrate. Ashtiak does not expect this 'mere stipendiary' to issue a summons to Rahman and his publishers. 'The real game,' Ashtiak explains, 'is judicial review before three judges of the Queen's Bench Divisional Court. Then we'll have them by the tail.'

Haqq, meanwhile, is excoriating Mrs Patricia Newman as a scarlet woman, a prostitute and an adulteress. The hall heaves with violent emotion. White fathers are clenching their fists. 'All right,' Haqq yells at Mrs Newman's trade union representative, 'take notes, sue me for slander, Islam will not be intimidated by your racist laws and your racist legal system!'

S.B. Hussein can take no more of it. He has kept his peace and held his temper until now, but Haqq and the distance separating S.B. from his saloon bar are too much. He rises grandly.

'Now you quieten down, Brother Haqq. Patricia Newman is the finest headteacher this school has ever had. To slander a woman is ignoble.'

Haqq quietens. He nods, but sarcastically. 'Very well, Brother Hussein, let us hear the evidence.'

From the platform Haqq gestures towards Fatima Shah, huddled in black among the Muslim women. She rises immediately, on cue, stick-thin, her ashen face peeping through her burka.

'The most famous schoolgirl in the land,' Joe Reddaway tells Porridge.

'Peasants.'

Ishmail Haqq assumes his gentlest, fatherly tone: 'Tell us, Sister Fatima, did you accompany Mrs Newman on a school trip to Paris last year?'

'I did,' Fatima says.

'And did you all stay in a French college?'

'We did.'

'And did you find yourself sleepless one night – and did you take a walk along the corridor, passing Mrs Newman's room?'

'I did.'

'And did you see a light under Mrs Newman's door, and hear voices, one a man's voice?'

'I did.'

'And were you, as a modest young woman, a child, horrified and ashamed of what you heard passing between them?'

'I was.'

'And have you recently been shown some letters written by this Frenchman to Mrs Newman?'

'Yes.'

'Did you find it shaming that your Headmistress should engage in such correspondence?'

'Shaming, yes.'

All this has been heard in fascinated silence. But Joe Reddaway is now standing close to Fatima, offering her a sheet of paper.

'This is one of the letters, Mr Chairman,' he addresses Hassani. 'I'm inviting Miss Fatima Shah to translate it for us – if she can.'

Fatima keeps her gaze fixed on Haqq.

Haqq scowls at Reddaway. 'Do not attempt to harass or intimidate this young girl.'

'I don't believe she can read the letters – or be shamed by them. I don't believe any Muslim in this hall can translate this letter.'

This is too much for Muhammad Porridge, who had liaised with French forces during the 1956 Suez operation. Joe feels the letter lifted from his hand. All eyes are on the vastly tall and vastly alien white leader of the Islamic Party of Europe as he scrutinizes the letter. The hall holds its breath as if supported by a single pair of lungs.

506

Patricia Newman's hands are folded in her lap.

Nasreen Hassani's, likewise. Every megaphonic sounding of the word 'adultery' stabs her. She had never suspected that Mrs Newman would or could do something like that. She wonders whether Mrs Newman has been happy with her shameful secret.

'The gist,' Porridge finally announces, 'is this. Mrs Newman and the French professor are engaged in a joint research project. In the Bibliothèque Nationale. The professor requests further information from an English library. He sends news of his wife and children, hoping that Mrs Newman's duties as Headmistress of Hightown Upper School are not exhausting her. The letter ends: "I have the honour to be, Madame, your respectful friend and colleague." '

Porridge hands the letter back, not to Joe Reddaway, but to Mrs Newman – with an officer's gallant bow. He then reaches up to the platform to shake S.B. Hussein's astonished hand.

'You're out of order, Brother Haqq,' Porridge announces. 'That will do. Stand down.'

The hall is silent. Fatima has melted back into the burkas. Joe Reddaway is eyeing Porridge with mounting resentment, his own act of gallantry completely submerged by a display of mendacity practised only by officers and gentlemen accountable to no one.

Lounging at the back of the hall with his mujaheddin, a bewildered Tariq Khan senses that something has gone badly wrong. Even Mustafa Jangar has been reduced to muttering in Hassan Hassani's ear. Haqq has disappeared – vanished! At this juncture the Halifax Building Society surveyor, Lannion, resolves Tariq's problem by rising to propose a motion deploring the personal slanders against Mrs Newman.

'Frankly,' says Lannion, 'I hope never to witness another display of mob hysteria like this one in my lifetime.'

Tariq Khan throws a chair in the direction of Lannion's head. The white women seated in Lannion's row scream; the leg of the chair has caught one of them in the face.

As the meeting breaks up in pandemonium, the police arrive in strength. They have been waiting, not only outside the hall but inside, disguised as parents. The mujaheddin gape in astonishment as WPC Rana Khan emerges, veiled, from the ranks of Muslim women to snap handcuffs on Tariq Khan. Rana Khan is wearing the full burka.

THIRTY-TWO

ᴓ

The telephone rings in the Zaheed residence.

'You betrayed my friendship, Wahabia. I am really very upset by your political opportunism.'

'Jasmin, darling, I shall always be fond of you.'

'Gamal is very disappointed in you.'

'Send him my love.'

'Gamal blames Ali Cheema. I told him how you said "sorry" after Ali slapped you. In my flat! And I don't forget your diatribe against the Royal Court play. As for your performance outside that wretched school, whatever it's called, it amounted to rank appeasement of the fundamentalists.'

'I'm sorry you're so upset, Jasmin.'

'Upset! First your friend Ali Cheema denounces me in the press and then that swine Inigo Lorraine announces that "Final Call" needs a new producer!'

'Jasmin, you *did* censor Ali's interview with Inigo before transmission.'

'I did not! I am utterly opposed to censorship. The Channel Controller insisted that I re-edit the roughcut. The BBC cannot broadcast incitements to murder. Don't forget that Gamal's life is at stake.'

'Ali says the Liberal Inquisition is open to any idea except the idea of a Liberal Inquisition. I gather that Inigo now agrees with him. It must be very sad for you at a personal level, Jasmin.'

'Don't you dare presume to – '

'I remember Gamal once saying that media relationships can be measured on egg timers. The loser traditionally commits suttee.'

ᴓ

Entering the magistrates' entrance of Hill Street Court on a stick, Izza Shah is supported by his veiled daughter Fatima. Here she must leave him, to spend the day in the public gallery, packed in with

508

the families of the defendants and surrounded by police officers expecting trouble. At the entrance to the public gallery WPC Rana Khan is searching the women's bags and bodies; she runs professional hands down the rigid, skeletal limbs beneath Fatima's burka.

By seniority Izza Shah is chairman of the three lay magistrates whenever he is sitting. His two colleagues are invariably white; at least one must by rule be female. The Senior Clerk, who would have applauded Tom Potter's speech to the cricket club dinner had not discretion forbade it, takes some comfort that Izza Shah will be flanked by two long-serving JPs: Simms, from the National Westminster Bank, and Mrs Patricia Newman, Headmistress of Hightown Upper School.

In the magistrates' retiring room Izza Shah is studying the register of charges dating from the riot in the city centre. He can identify most of the Muslim defendants, or their families. His heart is heavy, his hands tremble. Simms and Mrs Newman exchange glances with the Senior Clerk: there is no way that an old man as ill as this can endure what lies ahead – predictably the most difficult day in the recent history of Hill Street Court.

The court rises for the magistrates. 'The court will stand!' shouts the usher. Leaning heavily on his stick, Izza Shah returns the Senior Clerk's bow – another stab of pain and fire – says 'Good morning,' then takes the centre chair on the raised dais. The Clerk rapidly runs through a series of minor cases, all expedited by summary trial on a plea of guilty.

Now to the street rioters. The Muslim Defence League has brought the famous barrister, Ahmed Ashtiak, from London to defend them all. Where legal aid has not been available, the League has covered Ashtiak's fee. Ashtiak is supported by two juniors, one of them a woman whose short skirt Izza Shah considers a disgrace. All the defendants have made previous appearances and pleaded Not Guilty. All have been advised by Ashtiak to accept the magistrates' jurisdiction, waiving their right to a jury trial in the Crown Court (where the sentences on conviction are invariably higher). Now Ashtiak tosses his grenade:

'With respect, sir, I am instructed by my clients that they object to the composition of the Bench today. Regarding Mr Simms, he is I believe the manager of a Bank whose plate glass window was broken during the recent disorders. Secondly, sir, I am instructed that my clients object to Mrs Patricia Newman on the ground that her role as Headmistress of Hightown Upper School has put her in conflict with sections of the Muslim community, and all the defendants whom I represent are Muslims.'

'The Court will retire,' Izza Shah intones.

Struggling out of his chair is a terrible effort. Everyone – his fellow-magistrates, the clerks, the lawyers, the defendants, the reporters, the probation officers, the jailer, the usher, the people in the gallery, his own daughter – stand and watch while he makes the effort.

❧

Jasmin receives the most ridiculous telephone call an hour after getting Inigo's awful letter. She is chain-smoking her way through devastation when some female calling herself Lindy Short with an Estuary accent calls Jasmin on behalf of Westminster Youth Court Justice Team – or something absurd. Jasmin has only the vaguest idea of what a Youth Court is and none at all what a 'Justice Team' is. Today isn't the day for finding out, either.

She lights another cigarette. The ashtray beside the phone is a smouldering graveyard.

'No,' she yells 'I *don't* know anyone called Marilyn Monroe who says she's nineteen but may be sixteen and whose real name is probably not Marilyn Monroe.'

'She gave us your name,' Lindy Short pleads.

'There are hundreds of Patels in London. No, thousands.'

'But she gave us your address and telephone number, Ms Patel.'

My dear Jasmin, I have enjoyed working with you, and sleeping with you, but profound philosophical differences divide us and I cannot see us happily spending a lifetime together. This is to tell you that Susie Gainsborough and I are to be married. I am happy and I only want you to be happy – if not today, then tomorrow. Your loving Inigo

Ha! Happy! Philosophical differences! First that jumped-up, over-rated Gainsborough bitch hooks Gamal, then drops him at the first sign of trouble, and now she walks off with Inigo!

'I don't care whether your girl was picked up for loitering in Leicester Square,' Jasmin snaps at Lindy Short. 'I don't care whether she was back at it only an hour after being cautioned and released. I don't care whether she sounds Yorkshire. I don't care whether you do or don't keep her in the cells because she won't give her parents' name to the court. She is *nothing* to do with *me*!'

Lindy Short is stunned. Hers is a caring profession – caring for young people! – and she has never heard so many 'don't cares' in the entire course of her career as a social worker.

. . . cannot imagine us happily spending a lifetime together.

510

'No, I can't possibly "hop in a taxi" and come to Seymour Place. I'm busy. I work, you know. I am a professional woman.'

❧

Simms and Mrs Newman are not sure whether they should assist Izza Shah along the corridor to the retiring room. On the way he has to negotiate two sets of steps. In the event they merely shuffle after him.

The Senior Clerk joins them. He advises that Simms's position would give grounds for appeal. 'Appeal' is the most dreaded word in a lower court.

'I have absolutely no clue who broke our plate glass window,' Simms protests. He chuckles uneasily. 'The NatWest can afford a window, you know.'

'I can only advise,' repeats the Senior Clerk. Poor Simms: he'd been looking forward to today's agenda, which promises to be a damned sight more lively than unpaid TV licenses or driving without insurance, but now he will be back at his desk within half an hour, staring bleakly at the boarded-up window.

He smiles bravely. 'Well, I seem to be the one in disgrace. Odd, really.'

'Regarding Mrs Newman,' the Senior Clerk opines, 'I advise that the defence's objection is more dubious – but might be sustained on appeal. On the face of it, Mrs Newman has no direct interest or involvement in the charges. On the other hand, I would like to ask her whether she knows any of the defendants, and whether she has found herself in any kind of conflict with them.'

'Mr Ashtiak did not allege that,' Patricia Newman says.

'But he may do so if his more general challenge is not sustained.'

Patricia Newman is already angrier than a Justice should be. She had expected the Senior Clerk to dismiss Ashtiak's objection as twaddle.

'Some of these lads may be former pupils of Hightown Upper School. So what?' Then she hears herself say: 'If they hate my guts, they should say so.'

She shouldn't have said that. The Senior Clerk is looking at her. Izza Shah clears his throat. Haltingly, groping his way through personal embarrassment as well as cancer of the prostate, he points out that no Bruddersford Muslim is currently in more acute contention with Mrs Newman than he himself. But he has sat with her on the Bench for several years and has never detected the faintest bias against any section of the community.

Izza Shah and Patricia Newman return to the court without Simms.

511

A muted cheer comes from the public gallery, then a chorus of hoots. It's Patricia Newman they hate.

On Izza Shah's instructions, the Senior Clerk reads the riot act:

'Persons causing disorder in court may be ejected. If their conduct amounts to a criminal offence, they may be charged accordingly. Any person who wilfully insults a Magistrate or a witness or an officer of the Court, may be ordered to be taken into custody. The Court may also commit such a person to prison.'

The Senior Clerk then informs Ashtiak that Mr Simms has stood down. 'No other objection was sustained on the grounds given.'

Ashtiak's response is much as the Senior Clerk has anticipated. The barrister names three defendants who had been punished by Mrs Newman for disorderly behaviour at school or on the way to school. 'No claim is made that the punishments were unfounded,' Ashtiak continues smoothly. 'My claim is that no magistrate can adjudicate in a trial when aware of the defendant's previous convictions.'

'A school punishment is not a "previous conviction",' the Senior Clerk corrects him.

'In the individual Justice's mind it may have the same effect,' Ashtiak says.

Izza Shah is not going to retire yet again. Whatever his personal feelings about Mrs Newman, he has always acknowledged that in sending Fatima home she was abiding by the rule book. It would take a written directive from Rajiv Lal to bring hijabs into Hightown Upper School – and any such directive would be overruled by Samuel Perlman.

'The objections to my colleague are not sustained,' Izza Shah drones angrily.

The court then stands down until a replacement for the (disgraced) bank manager can be found. Patricia Newman expects the Senior Clerk to produce a replica of Simms, a middle-aged, middle-class white male whose window did not happen to have been broken during the riot. After the slow shuffle to the retiring room, she is astonished to find a resplendent Zulfikar Zaheed at his ease, reading a newspaper.

'Spot of bother, I hear,' Zaheed says.

The Senior Clerk, who knows the city's politics like the back of his proverbial hand, allows himself the trace of a smile. He had seen the writing on the wall for Simms and pre-alerted Zaheed over the weekend. How can Ashtiak later lodge an appeal when offered two Muslims out of three? The Senior Clerk plays golf with Sir Tom

Potter, who has advised him that Zaheed cannot unseat Harry Flowers without carrying the white majority within the District Labour Party.

'Zulfikar will be leaning over backwards every which way.'

Only this morning the Senior Clerk has read Joe Reddaway's latest sardonic column on Zaheed in the *Echo*: 'the amber light of Bruddersford politics'.

Patricia Newman has also been reading Joe Reddaway.

The Bench returns to its raised dais. 'The Court will stand!' Zaheed's arrival brings hoots of triumph from the gallery, but Ashtiak betrays no emotion behind his Old Bailey mask.

The charges are brought under the Public Order Act, 1986. Possession of offensive weapon; assault; assaulting police; obstructing police; criminal damage; affray; riot. Almost all of the charges are supported by the evidence of a single, arresting police officer, a single shopkeeper, a single bystander; in very few cases is there corroboration. Ashtiak's line of defence – mistaken or unproven identity – repeats itself case after case: in the swirling confusion of a riot, mistaken identification is likely, nay probable, nay downright certain.

'All Chinese look alike to me,' Ashtiak says. 'Almost all Asians look alike to white people. He was male? Yes. He was young? Yes? He was wearing some kind of headband? Yes. He was shouting angrily? Yes. He was carrying the Ayatollah's image on a placard or banner? Yes. And that description, your Worships, could cover practically two thousand young Muslims – I am merely quoting the police's estimate – who took part in the demonstration. Time and again the police simply grabbed the nearest youth to hand.'

Ashtiak pauses dramatically.

'The Crown has not produced a single Muslim witness for the prosecution.'

Ashtiak's oratory is whipping the public gallery into a state of continuous excitement. Ishmail Haqq's presence in the gallery, seated between Karamat Khan and Abdul Ayub Khan, heightens the fever. So do Ashtiak's riveting cross-examinations of the police officers called as witnesses by the Crown.

'Officer, have you any reason to feel prejudice against Muslims?'

'No, sir. When I arrest someone I am generally not aware of his religion.'

'Please confine yourself to answering the question, Officer. Tell me, did you observe the burning by Muslims of Gamal Rahman's book in front of City Hall?'

'I was on duty that day but I did not personally observe that event.'

'What did you think when you read about it or saw it on TV?'

The witness hesitates: 'I thought it was an unfortunate thing to happen.'

'Hm. The work of religious fanatics, would you say?'

'I have no view on that, sir.'

'Did you ever discuss it with your colleagues at the police station?'

'I believe it did come up in conversation, yes.'

'So what was the general opinion?'

The Crown Prosecutor leaps up. 'I object, sir: hearsay.'

'Objection sustained,' drones Izza Shah.

Ashtiak looks at the witness: 'Are you aware that almost all of the defendants here in court today were present in front of City Hall when the Rahman book was burnt?'

The Prosecutor is again on his feet. 'Objection, sir. The officer is being asked to respond to a hypothetical claim unrelated to his evidence against an individual.'

'Objection sustained.'

Patricia Newman becomes aware that she is hearing only Ashtiak's questions and disregarding the replies of the police witnesses. It's a 'performance'; it's like flashing dry flies across a pond full of worm-eating carp; in the absence of a bleeding-heart jury, Ashtiak's target audience must be (she reckons) the public gallery:

—Are you aware that thousands of Asian letter boxes in this city remain sealed?

—Has it occurred to you that the police force in this city does not even perceive its own racism?

—Have you read the Home Office report on racial violence in West Yorkshire? Are you aware that the report finds that Asians in Bruddersford are fifty times more likely to be subjected to assault than whites?

—Were you not a prosecution witness, five years ago, during the so-called 'petrol bomb' trial? Do you recall that the jury acquitted all the Asian defendants?

—Does not the law of self-defence allow for the urgency of the moment?

And so it continues, through a steady drizzle of almost languid prosecution objections – the Crown's tone of weary resignation hinting strongly that Ashtiak, like his clients, has settled in the wrong corner of the planet. Mrs Newman fingers her bracelet and ponders the vastly histrionic irrelevance of the oriental mind. Ninety per cent of Ashtiak's experience, she assumes, has been confined to jury trials in the Crown Courts.

Does Ashtiak read her thoughts? Unlikely. But suddenly he is playing direct to Zulfikar Zaheed's wounds.

'Are you keen on cricket?' he asks a police witness.

'I play on Sundays. I sometimes watch the county side.'

'There are no Asians or Muslims in the current County side, correct?'

'Not that I know of.'

'What do you feel about that – given the tremendous enthusiasm of young Asians for the sport? Is it a fair deal, a level playing field – or is it discrimination?'

The Crown Prosecutor objects: irrelevant.

Ashtiak offers the Bench an exasperated flourish – it is for him alone to determine the relevance of a question during cross-examination.

Izza Shah turns to the Senior Clerk for advice.

'My advice is that the question posed is irrelevant but it is safer in law to allow the question.'

'The objection is not sustained,' Izza Shah sighs. 'Continue, Mr Ashtiak, though I must advise you that your line (*lahn*) of questions to the witness is not, as we say in Yorkshire, "cricket".'

The police officer tells Ashtiak that he is not privy to Yorkshire CCC's selection procedures.

Izza Shah is in terrible pain. The courtroom is blurred. He is brooding. When was a Muslim ever charged at Hill Street Court in the old days? Once in a blue moon. Muslims did not steal, or shoplift, they paid their car licenses, their TV licenses, their bus fares, and they were not dragged from pubs in a condition of alcoholic stupor. They stayed safely at home at night unless attending evening classes or working night-shift. These virtues have far from vanished but increasingly the so-called liberation of girls is leading young men into trouble. The izzat, the honour, of the family has to be protected: which meant fights, stabbings, cases so serious that they have to be referred to the Crown Court. Brothers and cousins cannot allow Muslim girls to consort with young Sikhs or Hindus who have no respect for them – but the girls should not be out, 'naked', consorting. Too many defendants plead 'Not Guilty' nowadays, opting for trial by jury in the Crown Court, wasting everyone's time, instead of accepting the fatherly punishment of the magistrates. Rights, rights, rights! But no duties, no obligations! Izza Shah has no patience with the tortuous quibbles of lawyers.

The verdicts come thick and fast, no dissension among the three magistrates, no need to retire. Proven, proven, proven. In not one case has the Bench doubted the word of policemen and bystanders. A riot took place, the city was disgraced, and the verdict is collective in spirit.

On the crowded press bench, Joe Reddaway is trying to work out why Zaheed has put himself in this position: to prove to white voters that he's a law-and-order man?

Rising, Ashtiak accepts the sentences without endorsing them, without forfeiting his right to appeal. 'The Court in its wisdom has found . . .' he begins.

'We don't need sarcasm,' Mrs Newman says loudly to Izza Shah. Now frequently a Bench Chairman herself – the masculine title is still applied to women magistrates, mainly because most of them don't object – she has mastered the winger's art of addressing the Chair loudly enough to carry to the farthest corner of the court.

Izza Shah mops his brow with a handkerchief washed, ironed and neatly folded by Fatima. For years Muslims, parents and children, have been slapped down by white headteachers in this idiom: 'We don't need sarcasm . . . we don't need lectures on the Koran . . .'

Ashtiak has paused. He waits. Izza Shah nods to him.

'Continue.'

'The Court in its wisdom has found all of my clients Guilty. To have done otherwise would no doubt have undermined the credibility of the Bruddersford police force – which of course we would all regret.'

'That remark should be withdrawn,' Patricia Newman addresses Izza Shah loudly. 'It impugns the integrity of the Court.'

Izza Shah is silent. Zulfikar Zaheed is stirring restlessly. He wishes Doug Blunt were at his side, to cool him down. Of course the Newman woman is right; of course Ashtiak has gone too far; but doesn't she realize that a Bench can think its own thoughts, and reach its own conclusions, without haughty displays of authority?

It's her tone of voice!

Ashtiak continues. 'I ask the Court to consider the circumstances in which these very serious misdemeanours took place. The young men before you today are not criminals.'

'In thirteen out of thirty cases,' Patricia Newman snaps at Izza Shah, 'there have been previous convictions.'

Ashtiak ignores this.

'What we have to consider, sir, is whether these young men have been driven to desperation, against all their natural instincts, against all the codes of a law-abiding community, by a challenge to their very existence.'

'What is meant by "existence"?' Mrs Newman asks. She is no longer pretending to address her Chairman. She is asking questions without her Chairman's leave, but Izza Shah is not rebuking her and Ashtiak is in difficulty. He decides to change tactics: he will accept her on her

516

own terms, as the prejudiced white Justice to whom he'd objected. Let her run amok – let her give grounds for appeal.

'Madam,' says Ashtiak, 'I refer to the sense of izzat, of honour, without which a Muslim loses his identity. A Muslim's identity is his existence.'

'Thank you,' Mrs Newman snaps – perhaps the two most punishing words of the day. Ashtiak's eyes flash towards Zulfikar Zaheed: Are you going to allow this white bitch to take charge of the trial? – this menopausal, divorced, adulterous, immoral white bitch who slaps down good Muslims from her bigoted perch, then sneaks off to France and opens her legs.

'Sir,' he addresses Izza Shah, 'I suggest that your lady colleague's incomprehension of Muslim culture is grounds for an appeal.'

But Izza Shah is sagging over the bench, half-awake, half-conscious, half-dead.

Zaheed's rising irritation is abruptly transferred from Patricia Newman to Ashtiak. Time to take over.

'Mr Ashtiak, please get on with it.'

A huge intake of breath in the public gallery.

'Proceed, Mr Ashtiak,' Izza Shah murmurs.

'Sir, I submit that all the defendants deserve a conditional discharge. All of them, without exception, are "good boys, honest boys", driven to despair by the hostility of the "host community". I ask the Court to consider, by way of parallel, the predicament of young black South Africans who break the law to protest against an intolerable oppression.'

'A question to you, Mr Ashtiak,' says Mrs Newman. 'Do black South Africans enjoy the franchise? Do they make the laws they must obey? Do the defendants we have convicted today not enjoy the full civil and political rights due to any British citizen?'

'Well, madam, that is of course a lot of questions. To grant a minority the vote may be like granting a dog the right to wander as far as the bone beneath the tree.'

Laughter from the gallery. But not much. The English brought us here, to toil in the mills, to undertake menial work no longer worthy of the English, and to despise us. They are deaf to izzat. They are notorious adulteresses, they are scarlet women – it is unnatural for a woman to sit in judgment on men.

Ashtiak is now into a mighty oration; he concludes his case with a warning against the creation of 'martyrs'.

The Bench retires.

Izza Shah is asleep throughout the deliberations in the retiring room. Technically, two magistrates provide a quorum and Ashtiak could not appeal on the grounds of the Chairman's incapacity. The Senior Clerk has slipped away to call a doctor – every action he takes at work, at home, on the golf course, is occasioned by a well remembered precedent.

From the word go, case by case, Zaheed leans towards fines, whereas Patricia Newman argues strongly for 'community service' if the list of previous convictions does not justify outright imprisonment.

'The most serious case, by far, is that of Tariq Khan. Two recent convictions for affray, assaulting a policeman, carrying an offensive weapon. The second offence committed while on bail. Now convicted of serious offences in two riots, including attempting to set a public house on fire with the occupants inside. And I may add that he was re-arrested only two nights ago at my school for throwing a chair at a public meeting, causing actual bodily harm.'

'No charge has yet been brought, still less a conviction.'

'But I saw it happen! I was there!'

Zaheed stands up, his fingers tucked into his waistcoat pocket. Playing with his gold watch chain. He walks to the window, which enjoys a fine view of the brick wall and iron window-bars of the cells.

The Senior Clerk returns. 'The doctor is on his way.'

'Tariq Khan deserves six months in custody for each offence,' Patricia Newman insists. 'To run consecutively.'

But Zaheed isn't having it. 'One hundred hours of Community Service will suffice. Tariq Khan is not a common criminal; he always believes himself to be fighting for Allah.'

'The entire city centre was wrecked and we haven't sent one of them to prison!'

The doctor arrives. It takes him only a moment to rule that Izza Shah is not merely asleep but semi-conscious and therefore unfit to serve.

'You should notify Mr Shah's daughter Fatima,' Zaheed advises the Senior Clerk. 'She is sitting in the gallery. Please bring the girl here. I am a close friend of the family.'

Mrs Newman's cheeks are burning. She is in disgrace, confined to the classroom, no breaks, no afternoon games for a month. Zaheed has his back to her, twirling his fob watch.

෨

Jasmin has never been inside a Youth Court, whatever it is. The taxi drops her off at a stately but shabby building in Seymour Place, Marylebone. *Does he imagine he's going to work for me when the 'Final Call' contract expires!* Entering the main door she sees lawyers moving between disconsolate or truculent groups of chain-smoking youths, a few of whom seem to have gloomy parents in tow. The security guard directs her to a crowded office. Lindy Short bounces cheerily across from her computer.

'It's *really* good of you to come,' she says. 'They'll bring Marilyn Monroe up.'

'Or Greta Garbo,' Jasmin snaps. There is nowhere to sit. Lindy Short fills in time by repeating the whole story but Jasmin isn't listening. She's breaking pencils over Inigo Lorraine. '*Susie*'! Ha! Not *a brain in her head.*

A policewoman in one of those perky, check-banded hats brings 'Marilyn' into the office, then remains on guard by the door. Jasmin distinctly recognizes the girl from somewhere, but where, when? As tarts go, she certainly looks the part.

'Don't give 'em my dad's name!' Marilyn pleads.

I've enjoyed working with you and I've enjoyed sleeping with you . . .

'Who are you and what do you want of me?' Jasmin demands.

'Look, I'm really sorry – ' Lindy Short begins.

'She knows me!' Marilyn cries. 'I'm Safia – remember?'

Jasmin remembers. This was the creature who claimed she'd been raped in Ali Cheema's house.

'How did you find my address?' she asks Safia severely.

'I saw it in Ali's address book. I don't want my dad to find out!' (This hits Jasmin's ear as *fahn'aht.*) It'd kill him.'

On the way back to Knightsbridge Jasmin lets Safia have it in words of lengthening syllables. It so happens that Susan Gainsborough's long and famous legs could have been exchanged with Safia's unfamous ones without anyone – including that shit Inigo! – noticing.

෨

By placing herself prominently in the public gallery of Hill Street Magistrates' Court, modestly attired in dull colours, her head covered, Wahabia hopes to protect her father from insult and ill-feeling. And on such a day of trauma for the Muslim community, Wahabia is anxious to be seen to be caring. As each fine is announced the families in the gallery gasp and moan, unaware that but for Daddy the Newman woman would have sent their sons to jail. Prison bars are etched into her sour features.

Wahabia is particularly struck by the defendant called Tariq Khan, a finely built young man, quite handsome, with an attractive air of innocent bewilderment. She can imagine his large, calloused hands running across her skin – the fantasy known to the girls at her private school as 'yobbing'. Ali Cheema's hands are as soft as a woman's — they have softened further since Wahabia heard Safia describe how Ali behaved when he came upon a rapist in his own home. This noble young lion of the desert, Tariq Khan, is subjected to such a bollocking by her father, such a moral pounding, that Wahabia feels sure he will be led straight to the cells. Then Daddy produces his coup.

'One hundred hours of Community Service.'

'Sir, I'm sorry about what's happened,' Tariq murmurs.

Leaving the court, Wahabia hears a menacingly polite voice addressing her in English.

'Miss Zaheed, a word with you, please.'

She turns. The face seems familiar but she cannot place it. He carries a bushy beard, wears wire-rimmed glasses, and conveys the hungry, abstracted air of a dog dreaming of hares. She had seen Gamal Rahman drift into the same expression at one of Jasmin's parties when Ali had remarked, 'Once a Muslim, always a Muslim.'

'You must feel proud of your father today,' the man says. The rictus begins at the mouth and doesn't reach the eyes.

'I am always proud of my father, sir.'

'As a Muslim he must have been pained to inflict such severe sentences on the faithful.'

'No one went to jail,' she says defensively. 'I did not hear your name, sir.'

'Such severe sentences,' the man repeats. 'They must surely merit death.' Iqbal Iqbal vanishes into the crowd. Wahabia will see him again one day, in another court.

☙

Zaheed is sleeping, England are toiling, most of their best (if that's the word) batsmen dismissed by Pakistan's bouncing, jubilant — sublime! — pace bowlers. Young Aqib Salah is scything through them! It's a rout. Seated beside Zaheed in the Northern Enclosure, Douglas Blunt broods. Not a word out of him. No Yorkshire pudding today.

—Oooo, sighs the anxious crowd. Graham Bat, England's captain and last hope, edges one from Aqib Salah towards slip — a near miss.

'That was off the pad,' Blunt observes.

'An inside edge,' Zaheed corrects him.

A melancholic Jack Bounder is on the radio. 'Judging from the flags and the cloud cover, these are perfect conditions for Pakistan's quicker bowlers. They're getting swing and movement off the seam. When it clouds over this is a wicket which broods and pouts. The England batsmen need to play like sticking plaster.'

'Get on your front foot, lad!' Douglas Blunt shouts to Graham Bat, a 'lad' of thirty-nine. The derisive Yorkshire chorus opens up:

—It's not washing day, son! Yer not 'anging yer bat out to dry!

—That's rubbish, lad!

The crowd are praying for rain – Zaheed is sure of it; praying to their Christian-Anglican-Methodist God (not that they can remember the words of any Prayer Book). And here they come, dark clouds, spot on time. The umpires whip off the bails and the England batsmen gallop for the Pavilion like two shire horses; the Pakistani players reluctantly leave the field, the covers are wheeled out, the terraces hum with relief.

—That rain's comin' from Lancashire.

—Well, it allus does.'S t'only thing those lads are generous with, rain.

But the rain is brief. Wrong God. The Pakistanis bounce back on to the field, skipping in anticipation. Aqib Salah races in. Almost every delivery is followed by a loud appeal, the fielders leaping high, arms raised.

'Blatant intimidation of the umpires,' Blunt complains.

—Eh, that's some number o' shouts 'e done. Make 'is name in t'opera, that Salah.

—Like bloody gymnasts, that lot.

(Zaheed is tense in his seat, waiting for 'monkeys'.)

Graham Bat finally makes firm contact with the ball:

—Nice stroke! Four all the way! *Fower!*

But the baby-faced Aqib Salah is stung by Bat's four. Only twenty years old, hair flopping, a good-luck amulet round his neck, he delivers a fierce bouncer at Bat. Bat ducks. Aqib Salah immediately delivers another bouncer.

The crowd stills. The umpire at the bowler's end is now speaking to Aqib Salah. Only one bouncer per over is allowed. But something more sinister is afoot: the ball is in the umpire's hand. He shows it to the bowler. He points. No spectator can hear what is being said out there but the implication is obvious to Jack Bounder in the commentary box:

'The bowler is being accused of tampering with the ball while walking back to his mark before each delivery. In plain English, it's called cheating.'

Down on the field, Aqib Salah's body-language conveys indignation, outrage.

'It's a warning,' Douglas Blunt kindly informs Zaheed. 'He's a real prima donna, young Aqib Salah.'

'You mean he's taken too many wickets.'

Aqib Salah roars in. Graham Bat ducks as the ball flicks past his helmeted head. Another bouncer, despite the warning. Abruptly the umpire hands Aqib Salah his sweater: Salah must cease to bowl! The Pakistani players swarm round the offending umpire, protesting vehemently, shaking their fists under his nose.

Harry Flowers and Trevor Lucas suddenly surface the other side of Douglas Blunt. Flowers is directing his beer-foul breath towards Zaheed.

'Here we go, Zulfy, intimidation, the usual bazaar.'

Lucas nods: 'Neil and Roy send you this message: "Forget it." '

Zaheed's back is a ramrod of dignity. 'Forget what?'

'You'd be a liability,' Flowers says. 'The voters of Bruddersford West want England to win. They've been watching your antics on television.'

'Neil and Roy advise you to support Harry,' Lucas adds.

Zaheed allows himself a bitter smile. 'Then let them put it in writing. Liars! Neil and Roy are both honourable men!'

Now some bloody fool is running from the terraces, across the pitch, heading for the umpire and pursued by stewards in luminous blue tops. Through his binoculars Zaheed recognizes the wildest of Bruddersford's Muslim youths, Tariq Khan. The Pakistani players calmly move to intercept and restrain him.

'Full marks for that,' Blunt generously concedes.

Tariq Khan is led from the field in an armlock. Things simmer down. But no more wickets fall: the umpires have saved England's bacon. Zaheed addresses Blunt:

'The demand, Douglas, is simply for neutral umpires. I admit that such an innovation represents a defeat for something unique in cricket – the view that men are capable of sufficient honour to adjudicate without bias.'

'That Salah lad was tampering with the ball,' Harry Flowers says (snarls). 'It was blatant. You're all cheats, the lot of you.'

Zulfikar Zaheed stands up. 'Harry, I demand an apology!'

'You Muslims are great ones for apologies,' Trevor Lucas says. 'I suppose Harry here is a stand-in for Gamal Rahman. Maybe Rahman's out on the field, disguised as one of the umpires. Have you thought of that, Zulfy?'

'Whereas,' responds Zaheed, painfully aware that passion is eroding logic, 'the English do their cheating then ask to shake hands. "Forgive and forget, old chap." '

Harry Flowers digs Lucas in his sunburnt ribs. 'Asking a Muslim to forgive and forget is like asking a turkey to vote for Christmas.'

Douglas Blunt pulls Zaheed down into his seat. 'Let's face it, Zulfikar, you people are excitable.'

Et tu Doug. Enraged, the Lord Mayor of Bruddersford leaves his seat, storms down the aisles, leaps the low barrier and, robes of office streaming behind him, gallops across the field of play pursued by stewards. Zulfikar's wife taps him on the shoulder; the light of day is squeezing through the bedroom curtains.

THIRTY-THREE

ॐ

Jasmin has taken pity on Safia – any enemy of Wahabia's is worth a brief shelf-life – and let her stay. The street-walking had been a cry for help, all of Jasmin's progressive friends are agreed about that. The girl passionately wants to be a model or an 'actress'. Jasmin is not hugely fond of actresses just now, and has no intention of becoming Henry Higgins in an effort to sort out the girl's atrocious, smog-thick accent, but she has wide contacts in TV and knows her way around the weekend peak-time rubbish shows which employ bimbos who can wear a fixed smile. She examines Safia's teeth like a horse vet, then phones Terry Conroy.

'Dreadful for you about Inigo, darling,' Terry drawls.

Terry agrees to audition Safia, probably in bed, and soon she's on his Saturday show, a smiling vase of flowers with shimmering legs and gorgeous bosom.

Wahabia calls Jasmin. Her tone is guarded. She and Jasmin are supposed to have fallen out.

'Jasmin, a lot of Bruddersford Muslims watch the Terry Conroy Show.'

'How naughty of them.'

'Jasmin, Izza Shah doesn't know yet about Safia. It would kill him. I've had a terrible struggle dissuading Joe Reddaway from writing a sardonic column. We all want you to get Safia off the show if you possibly can – to spare Izza Shah's feelings during his dying days.'

'Tell Ali Cheema that his "sister" was picked up by the police soliciting in Leicester Square.'

'Jasmin, the Muslim community here is prepared to raise five thousand pounds for Safia if she – '

'Wahabia, I well understand why the Zaheeds don't want Izza Shah resigning and Mustafa Jangar running amok – just yet. Safia has escaped the cage. You were released from it through sheer privilege. If you choose to go back and play keeper to the animals, that's your affair.'

Slamming down the phone, Jasmin picks up the elaborately decorated card inviting her to the wedding reception of Susan Gainsborough and Inigo Lorraine. It is to be held on a river boat, starting from Henley-on-Thames – a grand splash. RSVP.

ॐ

Zulfikar Zaheed has retired to bed early. He is content with his day's work in Hope Street Magistrates' Court – firm but fair and likely to appeal to Muslim and white voters alike: in short, a triumph. A pity that Izza Shah is so ill. Zaheed has looked forward to walking beside the President of the Islamic Council at the head of the Bruddersford contingent during the coming demo in London. Zaheed still awaits Izza Shah's formal endorsement as Labour candidate for Bruddersford West. Get Wahabia to put pressure on that brat, Ali Cheema. Hm.

Zulfikar Zaheed falls asleep, his window wide open. He enjoys the summer breeze. He dreams of cricket.

Joe Reddaway strides into the Crown Hotel.

Iqbal Iqbal turns out the lights in his pharmacy. He has not been home since his two female assistants departed and he closed up the shop. He has secluded himself in prayer.

Zaheed is smiling in his sleep as England collapse.

Muhammad Porridge keeps Joe waiting in the lounge of the Crown Hotel. Eventually he consents to descend from his suite.

'Frankly, Mr Hathaway, these Mirpur peasants will never understand the British. Take this mass demo in London they've set their thick heads on. Bound to be another fiasco. Strictly between ourselves, the usurers are behind it. The banking system can't survive without bloodshed. Zaheed's on their payroll.'

Iqbal Iqbal's car is parked at the back of the pharmacy. He slips a Koranic sura into the cassette deck. He remembers that his mother is a brain surgeon and his father a High Court judge – somewhere. Did he tell Haqq Singapore, Senegal or . . . ? He touches his smooth chin; this is not the night for beards.

Joe Reddaway is gazing bleakly at a glass of mineral water.

Iqbal picking up speed. Readings from the Holy Koran fill the car. 'Corrupt women for corrupt men, and corrupt men for corrupt women . . .'

Porridge stretches his long legs. 'I'll tell you something, Mr Faraway. The Marquis of Newcastle, on the eve of the battle to sack this city in 1643, had a dream. He was asleep in Bolling Old Hall when a Bruddersford woman came and pleaded with him not to destroy the city. I am the Marquis of Newcastle.'

525

'Yes,' says Joe, 'I believe the *Echo* reported the incident in 1643. I remember writing a "Plain Speaking" column congratulating the Marquis of Newcastle. It seemed prudent.'

Zaheed smiling. A swift throw-in at the stumps from that panther, Salem Javed! Run out!

Iqbal courteously dips his headlamps at oncoming cars, the infidels. 'Say to the believers, that they cast down their eyes and guard their private parts . . .'

Zaheed not smiling. The English umpires are refusing to confirm the run-out. Incredible! Typical! Just look at the replay on the big screen! Out by a mile!

Iqbal Iqbal slows as he enters the suburbs of Bruddersford. Keep to the speed limit, no hitches. A Sagittarian – the ninth and highest sign of the zodiac – does not stumble out of carelessness. 'O believers, follow not the steps of Satan . . .'

'Shall I tell you, Reddaway, when I converted to Islam? Allah spoke to me as I came down by parachute on Port Said.'

Joe summons a waiter and orders himself a double whisky.

Iqbal is asking himself where he acquired his Bs.C. And where his qualification in pharmacology. Harare? Tokyo? Cairo? Who am I? This question seems to be presented to some obscure and strictly secular authority, as if he, Iqbal, with beard or without, were merely some casual doodle in an author's scrapbook. As Iqbal drives past Belmont police station he lowers the volume on his Koran cassette to a murmur. He knows the words anyway. 'But for God's bounty to you and His mercy . . .'

The whisky eases Joe's rising temper. Why did this clown summon him here at this time of night? 'Do you expect Haqq to win Tanner Ward?' he asks.

'Who?'

'Ishmail Haqq.'

'Oh you mean Kaqq. No hope at all. Another peasant. Just like Zaheed.'

'Hardly.'

'They're all the same under the skin. I'll give you a thousand pounds if you publish an account of Wahabia Zaheed's fornication with Gamal Rahman.'

Zaheed smiling, England collapsing, the Pakistani players leaping and rolling around like puppies.

Iqbal Iqbal knows that Haqq and his cronies are no use at all, not serious, cowards. Louis Pasteur cannot tell us how . . . Yes, what's needed is 'here and now'. Zaheed is here and now. Iqbal parks one hundreds yards from the Zaheed residence. He knows the house and the garden by heart – months of patient study. 'And as for the unbelievers, their works are a mirage in a spacious plain . . .'

'The Zaheed girl's affair with Rahman will finish Zaheed,' Porridge says. 'In fact it will finish off the entire peasant mafia. The problems facing Bruddersford today are precisely those which faced Guernsey in 1815 and Woergl in 1932. When bankrupt, issue your own money. It's the only way.'

One light on the upper floor is still on. Iqbal's wire-rimmed glasses glint under a street lamp. He knows Wahabia's bedroom, he knows every window and door in the Zaheed residence. 'Here and now' is, at long last, here and now.

Zaheed is happy in his dreaming. Only one England wicket to fall! His wife sleeps beside him, pleased to have her Wahabia at home again.

Iqbal Iqbal observes Wahabia's bedroom light extinguished. The Zaheed residence is now in darkness . . . The night is warm. 'As for the unbelievers, they are as shadows upon a sea obscure . . .'

'Mr Porridge, do you seriously expect to become the next MP for Bruddersford West?'

'We will sweep the country, Mr Takeaway. I spoke to Thatcher only last night. She's under no illusions. "Muhammad," she said, "I'll serve in any capacity that Allah, in His infinite wisdom, bestows upon me." '

Yes, yes, out! It's all over. Zaheed's sleeping face is alight with joy, deep in its pillow, as he strides across the sacred turf of Headingley to embrace the heroes.

Two bullets smash into his skull.

Wahabia wakes up trembling and soaked in sweat. Someone – her mother – is screaming in the corridor. Fearfully Wahabia ventures out; her mother is on her knees, gasping for air, soaked in blood. Wahabia advances towards the open door of her parents' room, terrified. Then Benazir Bhutto and Hamida Sharaf speak to her: 'Go on, Wahabia Zaheed, what are you made of?'

She bends over her father. The curtains drift gently at the wide-open window. Wahabia's foot presses on something smooth – Daddy's gold watch, presented to him by General Zia. As she bends to retrieve it she feels the blood running down on the carpet presented to Daddy by Benazir Bhutto, whose father General Zia had hanged.

'Oh my beloved Daddy,' she whispers.

Zulfikar Zaheed, 1934–1989.

ॐ

—LORD MAYOR ZAHEED ASSASSINATED AT HOME. City in Shock.

—Fundamentalist Pharmacist Iqbal Iqbal Arrested. Claims to be Gamal Rahman. Bomb-store Discovered in Knightley Chemist's Shop.

—Tory Leader Potter Pays Tribute to Zaheed: 'An Honourable Man. When Will This Un-British Madness End?'

—Harry Flowers MP: 'I Have Lost a Friend. Bruddersford Has Lost a Leader. The Labour Party Will Not Bow to Terror.'

—Wahabia Zaheed: 'I Will Bear My Slaughtered Father's Burden.' Ms Zaheed Announces Bid to Become First Muslim Woman in Commons.

♬

Across the city, the mosques are packed tight. It is always so, but more so this Friday evening. The streets are thick with Muslims striding to worship Allah. The call of the muezzins reverberates across a pale, neutral sky.

Hassan Hassani squats cross-legged on the prayer mats of the Maududi Mosque, the ailing Izza Shah beside him. Izza's daughter Fatima has brought him to the door, but she may not enter – that was decided, more than 1,300 years ago. Ali Cheema helps the old man to remove his shoes and wash himself, a token ablution. Izza Shah's ravaged features seem to have been torn (to Ali's errant eye) from a pagan painting, 'Guernica' – Islamic art has almost always eschewed the human form. Izza's constant physical pain is now compounded by the vast shame which descended the morning he read Joe Redda-way's column, 'A Tale of Two Sisters'. The following day Safia and her father were plastered over the front pages of the London tabloids. The *Sun* boasted exclusive rights to Safia's life story: 'My Lucky Escape'. All of infidel Britain was laughing.

Izza has resolved to make the long journey to London, determined to take his place at the head of the Bruddersford Muslims. 'I intend to die on my feet,' he tells Ali.

Covered in a bright cloth, the pulpit has three tiers: no one but the Prophet may stand on the top tier. While some choose to sit after their devotions, others sway on their knees in prayer. Standing, kneeling, kissing the ground, the faithful resemble the infracting tides, currents, undertows of the sea breaking on the shore called Allah. The Qari is chanting his recitation, his Qirat; sparkling paper chains drift across the ceilings; pots of flowers too bright to be nature's.

Now everyone is seated. Mustafa Jangar is collecting names, monies, more names for tomorrow's buses. The national newspapers

528

have already nominated the book-burning fanatic not merely as the ailing Izza Shah's successor but also as 'Britain's Ayatollah'. Mustafa's father (it now emerged) had been a 'notorious' religious 'zealot' who fought and died as the war of partition swept through the Punjab. Destitute and fatherless, Mustafa had wandered through Kashmir, joined a band of Muslim guerrillas, and finally sought refuge in London with a shadowy Islamic 'college' which – it could now be revealed – was all along a 'school for terrorism'. Joe Reddaway knows that there is very little truth in any of this but the truth is as good as it sounds, and television cameras are now permanently banked up outside the 'terrorist's' modest, two-up, two-down, home in Benfield Road. Mustafa is clearly enjoying every moment of it and periodically emerges to oblige with a new anathema: 'We will keep Rahman in his rabbit hole for the rest of his short life! The penalties for corrupting the earth are in the Koran, 5:33. The penalty for blasphemy is in Leviticus, 24:11.' Mustafa is in first-strike mood, the world of the Powers is bubbling through his head. 'The Iranian Revolution will spread to Europe, to Russia, to China. A revolution must exterminate its opponents. It cannot show mercy.'

From the pockets of jackets worn over knee-length white cloaks, thick wads of banknotes are tossed into a red-and-white check kaffir cloth. Hassan Hassani donates sixty pounds – no one will be too poor to take part in this jihad. Tomorrow the buses.

The Hafiz is ritually called to the pulpit by an intoning voice which belongs to Mustafa Jangar. The Hafiz can recite the whole of the Koran by heart. His sermon is spoken in Arabic but not spoken; it is chanted, intoned, praising the Prophet, very rapid in its cadences. The men kneel now, then stand, then kneel, then kiss the ground, these motions again and again, hands cupped in front of the face as if catching and husbanding water in the desert.

Later, the elders of the mosque cross the square to the home of the Hafiz, Pir (Holy Person) Ishmail, a descendant of one of the Prophet's disciples. Floor after floor is lined with books, with sacred poetry and Koranic commentaries. Toiling as a poor mill worker when he first arrived in Bruddersford, Pir Ishmail had spent every spare penny on acquiring this treasury. Again they pray. Mecca lies at 129 degrees from Bruddersford.

❧

The morning is good: clear sky, gentle laughter. Slanting over the rooftops, the early sun burnishes the faces of the young men gathering at the assembly points around their crude banners and placards. With them travels Shaytan Rahman, red-eyed, fanged,

529

horned, a forked tail riding up (amateurishly) behind his shoulder and over his head. Tongues of fire in orange and yellow leap up to engulf him.

The hired buses make two stops at motorway service stations. A poster in one of the bus windows urges 'Punch Gamal Rahman!' and crudely depicts a boxing glove aimed at a startled young man. The Muslims disembark, debouch, models of decorum, quietly joining the cafeteria queues or waiting their moment in the toilets, taking no advantage of their numbers, not pushing or shoving. The white Saturday travellers are managing not to look surprised at all this Paki business, managing not to look at all. The English people are not noticing that three thousand men with dark faces and funny clothes have just turned up.

The buses of the jihad move on. S.B. Hussein's daughters, Nasreen and Latifa, are unaware that their father has been left behind at the service station, attempting to fight his way out of a locked toilet which insisted on turning somersaults.

Idle between the holy recitations on the bus, Tariq is vaguely regretting how lazy he'd been as a boy: too much TV, and now too many video films. Out of work again. Arrested by his own 'fiancée'. One hundred hours of Community Service – beginning today. His father, Karamat, has forbidden him to go on the buses, ordered him to attend the Community Service place. But how can he obey? Allah calls, always. The Hafiz at the front of the bus, Pir Ishmail, is again chanting the Prophet's praises in Punjabi – how the Prophet was neither too tall nor too short, a beautiful man.

Fleets of buses from every part of the North, the Midlands, are converging on Hyde Park. As the Muslims disgorge themselves, they kneel at once to pray on the grass, close to the railings. Ali Cheema shepherds Izza Shah into his wheelchair. The old man has slept throughout most of the journey, a groaning, fitful sleep; at the last motorway service station Ali had to help him relieve himself. Now the elders cluster round him in concern, begging him to go no further, insisting that he has already done what honour requires. But he is adamant: he will march to 'Parlhahment'.

The small contingent of women have travelled in a separate bus. They will walk behind the men. Ali gestures to Fatima, a slender black ghost lost among the broad, motherly spreads of the matrons. Her burka flits across Hyde Park, unintimidated by the Hilton Hotel rising like a pagan obelisk in Park Lane.

'You will walk with your father,' Ali instructs.

She nods and bends over the wheelchair.

Unlike the men, the women demonstrators have no structure of authority; they hold no office, they have not been elected or chosen. But by common consent, not least her own, young Wahabia Zaheed is the leader of the contingent, clothed from head to toe in black, in deepest mourning for her father. A woman reporter from the BBC's 'World at One' has interviewed her during the journey south; the photographers roaming Hyde Park, lensing burkas and beards against the Park Lane skyline, are waiting for her.

'My father was of course a martyr for honour, justice and fair play,' Wahabia told the BBC woman. 'He was the progressive face of Islam in Britain, a Socialist all his life, a true peasant of Mirpur and an English gentleman. So they killed him.'

'You say "they", Miss Zaheed. Does this imply a conspiracy?'

'Of course.'

'Is it true that you are engaged to be married to Ali Cheema?'

'I can have no thought of that during the period of mourning. There can be no joys at such a time.'

'And what do you hope to achieve today?'

'Simply justice and dignity for the Muslim citizens of this country. The Rahman book is not a single issue, you know; it is symbolic of our status as second-class citizens.'

'It's said that you once attended meetings in defence of Gamal Rahman at the University of Sussex and in London.'

'I was misled by certain manipulative people. Entering the modern world is not easy for a Muslim woman, and I was foolishly seduced by these so-called progressive people. But I have all my anchors and mooring ropes back in place now, believe me.'

'And you hope to enter Parliament at the age of . . . what will it be?'

'Well you must ask Mrs Thatcher when she will hold an election.'

'Can you talk about the night your father was murdered?'

'The police say I must not. You can prejudice a trial, you know.'

The police have erected lines of portable steel gates to pen the grand bazaar of the Orient – the turbans, white prayer caps and burkas – into the most easterly strip of the park.

Tariq joins the mujaheddin in their red and white headbands, their pledge of blood. They follow no stewards, observe no directives, they are bored with the park, with tame grey squirrels, and itching to get into the real 'London'. Tariq is increasingly obsessed by the suspicion that Shaytan Rahman himself is here, somewhere right here, deeply disguised, maybe carrying an effigy of himself, the apostate among his own kind – watching. Watching.

The trees are in full leaf,

Rounding Hyde Park Corner, the Muslims are soon passing down

531

the long empty corridor of Grosvenor Place, with the faceless wall of Buckingham Palace to the left. Most of them do not know what lies beyond the wall. There are no pedestrians here, no spectators, and Tariq's guerrillas run forward towards the crowded streets of Victoria where the traffic is already at a standstill and frightened drivers are locking their doors and silently cursing the police for their complacency. Even the wittiest banner does not amuse them:

'Islam: the Only Suitable Creed for Europe. Bernard Shaw.'

In Victoria Street the temperature rises, the police presence thickens. Ultra-relaxed in shirt sleeves, the police make no attempt to contain the spread of demonstrators or to clear a path for the traffic. Here, dwarfed by gleaming glass façades, the procession slows, halts and the speeches begin to pour from the megaphones.

Ali recognizes the tall and stately figure of Muhammad Porridge standing on the roof of ISLAM 1, microphone in hand, the half-moon flag of the Islamic Party of Europe draped across the bonnet. Ali smiles to himself: to risk such a car in such a situation is indeed proof of devotion.

'Of course this Rahman book was a plot,' Porridge declares. 'Would you or I be allowed to write a book defaming the Queen or Mrs Thatcher? All the City of London's horses and all the City of London's media have not managed to blow or blackmail me away from my position!'

A 'Rahman Wanted Dead or Alive' poster passes Porridge.

The Muslims gathered round ISLAM 1 have merely halted provisionally, as if viewing a street clown. Twenty yards away Mustafa Jangar is attracting a more fervent audience with a diatribe against the Saudi royal family.

'Those with hook noses speak loudest of betrayal.' The familiar voice comes from behind Ali's shoulder. Inigo Lorraine is smiling at him cautiously. Then he bends in consternation towards the figure in the wheelchair.

'Is this Izza Shah? He doesn't look well at all.'

'He's sleeping.'

Lorraine hesitates to address Fatima, not sure whether she would turn her back on a male stranger.

'Congratulations on your engagement,' Ali says.

'Thank you! Yes, Susie and I are very happy. And you, Ali, are you destined to remain a Sufi, celibate in everything but deed?

Mustafa Jangar's voice is booming through a megaphone: 'Man is corrupt. Adam and Eve were the first apostates. Salvation history commences with the apostasy of our first parents.' A moment later

Mustafa announces the creation of a 'non-territorial Islamic state in Britain' – and a Muslim Parliament.

'Aha,' says Lorraine. 'To be handpicked by Jangar himself, doubtless.'

'By the Archangel Gibreel,' Ali says.

'I shall be issuing imperatives in lists of nine,' declares Mustafa. 'We must establish the entire ummah in Britain!'

Urine is running out of Izza Shah's trousers on to his shoes.

Lorraine touches Ali's sleeve. 'Let's meet soon, Ali. And don't forget my wedding. I'm negotiating a surprise guest.'

Izza Shah's wheelchair has reached Westminster City Hall: Welcome to the Heart of London.

'I think Father has fainted,' Fatima says.

Passing Scotland Yard, Izza Shah's head lolls; any moment he may pitch right out of the chair. Fatima clasps him silently. Ali shepherds the chair towards two summer-shirted policemen with folded arms. One of the constables squats down to bring his eyes level with the old man's while the other calls for an ambulance on his lapel radio. They carry Izza Shah a few yards into shadow, out of the sun, lay him on the pavement, and begin to massage his heart. Ali and Fatima watch.

Tariq and the mujaheddin are running and thumping on the roofs and bonnets of stationary cars, willing something to happen, the something which will trigger their jihad, unwrap their wrath. The Bruddersford group has already merged with a vast crowd of urban youths, police haters, system haters, young men reared in confrontation with skinheads in Whitechapel and Bermondsey, all running free towards Westminster Abbey and the Houses of Parliament: the cockpit.

In Parliament Square police cordons are finally drawing the line: so far but no further. The mujaheddin have no aim except not to be halted or controlled. All the way down Victoria Street not a window has been broken, not a bystander assaulted, but now the bottles, cans and bricks from contractors' tips begin to fly. In Bridge Street the young Muslims are climbing railings and traffic lights and scattering tourists who have not been warned that a weekend in London, among the souvenir shops and Union Jack cups and junk and ripoff currency exchange shops and silly hats and balloons – have not been warned that an American Express weekend may include a sudden plunge into the Ayatollah's Orient.

The flashpoint emerges: a counter-demonstration by friends of Rahman. These are not skinheads of the BNP or the National Front, but a small group of Southall Black Sisters and young Asian women in Western clothes who have positioned themselves opposite

Westminster tube station, carrying banners denouncing male chauvinist fundamentalism. Jasmin Patel holds aloft the only friendly portrait of Gamal Rahman within a square mile, a serene, thoughtful Gamal.

The high screeching of these women gets on Tariq's nerves. He spits at a woman he identifies as a Hindu. 'Prostitutes!' he shouts, raising his hand. But a voice from behind him stills it.

'No Tariq!'

Wahabia Zaheed has arrived in her black robes of mourning, at the head of the Bruddersford women's contingent, which in truth has grown to absorb almost all the Muslim women on the march.

'That is not the way, Tariq. Now take your brothers away.'

The mujaheddin seethe, itching to slap the screaming harlots.

'It is against the Koran to move among strange women!' Wahabia shouts. 'I am the daughter of Zulfikar Zaheed. Now go!'

The mujaheddin obey.

Wahabia is face to face with a trembling Jasmin.

'How are you, Jasmin?' she says gently.

'He spat at me – your friend!'

'You are lucky. Soon it would have been worse.'

Small and quivering, Jasmin glowers with furious hostility as Wahabia moves regally among the Southall Black Sisters, many of whom she knows.

'Sisters, we only serve male oppression if we quarrel among ourselves. Women should talk to each other, not hurl abuse.'

She is challenged: 'Why are you marching at the head of the fundamentalists, Sister? Why are you making common cause with males calling for Gamal Rahman's death? Why are you showing solidarity with the oppressors of women?'

Wahabia is not unhappy with these questions. Parliament is only yards away. Its famous clock is ticking and chiming for her. 'I have to understand my own community, Sisters. I have to hear their pain and anger. A Muslim does not choose to be a Muslim. She is exactly like a black person or a gay person – her religion is her heart and her skin. If she is abused and defamed, she weeps. She mingles her tears with those of her brothers. Only then will they listen to her and begin to question their own patriarchal attitudes.'

'And you will become their slave, Sister.'

'No!'

'Benazir Bhutto is already their slave in Pakistan!'

'No! These things take time, Sisters!'

'We are living now! We wish to be free of beatings and rape and purdah now! We want to finish with arranged marriages now!'

'I, too, Sisters! When I am elected I shall carry your aspirations, your demands, your grief in there – ' She extends her arm towards Parliament. 'But first I must be elected by men and by women who traditionally obey their husbands and fathers.'

The mujaheddin have regrouped on Westminster Bridge. More stones fly, the tourists scatter, shop windows shatter, the snatch squads go in. Police helmets roll in the road, heads are smashed into pavements. Red lights are flashing and the wail of the sirens can be heard in Lambeth, Trafalgar Square, Charing Cross. The ambulances edge forward while the cameras turn, instantly conveying to millions of homes that the natives of this once-green, once-pleasant land have been too hospitable, too easy-going, too tolerant for too long.

໑

Ali Cheema leaves St Thomas's Hospital as soon as the staff wheel away Izza Shah's body from Casualty to the Morgue. Half-dragging Fatima from the building, he grips her arm and pulls her through empty, debris-littered streets – Satan's avenues – towards the buses waiting to carry them north. 'I am your father now,' he repeats, 'you must obey.'

Reaching the buses, he gratefully deposits her in the arms of the women.

When the convoy finally sets off for Bruddersford at ten that night, half the seats occupied by males on the journey south are empty. A trembling Hassan Hassani is on the bus, and Hani Malik, and Abdul Ayub Khan, and Yaqub Quddus, and Ali Cheema, but not Mustafa Jangar, not Karamat Khan, not Ishmail Haqq, Imtiaz Shasti, Tiger Siddiqi – not Tariq Khan.

Not Izza Shah.

Fatima sits huddled on the long rear-seat of the women's bus, cradled between Nasreen and Latifa, but wide awake, her eyes saucers of anguish, her cracking lips moving in silent prayer for her father's soul. Finally, as they pass Watford, she falls asleep in Nasreen's lap, her precious scarf slipping from her head.

THIRTY-FOUR

⁊

Tariq Khan boards the Intercity express from Leeds to London. The bus would be cheaper but he enjoys the power of fast trains – you become part of that power, you can stroll about, head for the bar, chat up a white girl or bump some Sikh in the corridor. No need to buy a ticket if you know the ropes. Two hours later he's gliding into King's Cross with Safia's letter in his pocket – it came on posh notepaper with an address in flash print and the name 'Terry Conroy' all across the top, and stinking of scent.

A sheathed carving knife from the Omar Khayyam, one of Uncle Abdul's best, is tucked beneath Tariq's shoulder. Safia had enclosed a fifty-pound note. It sits in his pocket with the scented letter which claimed she knew how, when and where he could kill Gamal Rahman. 'I've been thinking about you,' she said.

Even as he speeds south he should be attending the Community Service place in Bread Street. The Probation Officer in charge is a proven soft touch, a Christian, and reluctant to 'alienate a client' by reporting him to the Hill Street magistrates for non-attendance. Who cares anyway? They all come down like a ton of bricks on a young Muslim who's only defending his faith. He hadn't minded being done by Mr Zaheed so much as being arrested in full view of everyone by WPC Rana Khan, his own cousin who he wasn't good enough to marry, the bitch. Tariq is shrugging off Bruddersford. Rana will think again when he becomes world-famous by putting Gamal Rahman to death with Uncle Abdul's carving knife.

If he feels bad about anything, it's for walking out on Ishmail Haqq, Shasti and Tiger Siddiqi during the run-in to that election business – not that elections ever did any good.

⁊

'Boys, my confidence is touching infinity,' Haqq tells his campaign team in the basement of Imtiaz Shasti's Snooker Centre. Previously a video-cassette hire-shop, the basement is bleakly lined with now-

536

empty racks. The staircase up to the street smells pungently of new breeze-blocks and raw plaster.

Imtiaz Shasti lifts his fist in a victory salute. 'Those Labour people are wetting their pants.' Shasti has brought cruising and kerb-crawling to a fine art: he's convinced that forcing rush-hour traffic to a standstill wins votes because it's a display of power. 'The only thing people understand is power,' Haqq tells the boys. 'To be a winner you've got to look like one.' Shasti's newest Toyota carries a trendy iron bar in front, specially fitted in Japan to cattle-prod stray Labour voters off the streets. Politics is a lot of fun.

'Vote HAQQ! Vote tomorrow!'

This is reiterated so incessantly through Shasti's state-of-the-art public address system that if a candidate called 'Tomorrow' appeared on the ballot paper, he'd sweep home.

'Hani Malik is blackening my name to my face!' Haqq yells at bemused shoppers emerging from the Waitrose supermarket. 'Lucas and Perlman are sending all Muslims to the gas chambers!' Haqq is on the telephone to Joe Reddaway nonstop. He now claims to know exactly the sums paid by the Jewish supermarkets to Malik, Lucas and Perlman in order to 'corner the school-dinner market'.

'How much?' Reddaway asks.

'Frankly, that's confidential at this moment in time. I shall reveal the true facts and figures when I take my seat in the Council Chamber.'

The evening before the polls open Ishmail Haqq hurtles down the steps of Shasti's Snooker Centre, brandishing a mobile telephone and a copy of the *Echo* hot off the press. HAQQ CHARGES LABOUR AND CRC BOSS WITH JOB THREAT. STRONG DENIAL FROM LUCAS AND QUDDUS. The 'boys' are eating chipatis and halal samosas dipped in chilli sauce; idly they pass the front page from hand to hand.

'Where is Tariq Khan?' Haqq snaps.

ॐ

The taxi delivers Tariq to a vast mansion block somewhere posh, he's not sure where. He's seen Safia on the Terry Conroy show looking a million dollars. A posh lift carries him to the third floor; he combs his hair in the mirror and touches his knife just in case she's setting him up, some kind of revenge or the like. Safia opens the door. She still looks a million, spilling out of her dress. Gilded mirrors and chandeliers in the hallway dazzle him. The walls are lined with photos of the famous TV comedian Terry Conroy. Safia swings and sways into the most fabulous fitted kitchen he's ever seen, even in mags, and pours him a beer. She's done up to the nines, real class, you can see she's dripping with money.

'Pleased to see me, Tariq?'

'Maybe I am and maybe I'm not. So what's it all about?'

'The wedding's on Saturday.'

'What wedding?'

'Inigo Lorraine's. He's invited Terry and me.'

'So?'

'They're having a river-boat party – on the river.'

'What river?'

'How do I know what river – it's a place called Henley.'

'So?'

'Inigo Lorraine's a pal of Gamal Rahman, i'n't he? Terry says he is.'

'So?'

'So they'll likely make a splash and invite him.'

'Invite who?'

'Gamal Rahman, stupid!'

'Call me stupid and I'll thump yer. Anyways, that devil Rahman i'n't going to no weddings.'

'Terry says he is – it's a secret. You want to come or you don't? I told Terry you're my brother.'

'He'll soon see through that.'

'Give him two whiskies and Terry can't see through a window.'

'Anyways, what's it to you – killing Rahman?'

'I'm a Muslim, aren't I?'

'You! Just look at you! Just *lewk* at all this!' Tariq gestures expansively to the leather armchairs, the long velvet curtains, the glittering chandelier, the carpet woven by a hundred slaving hands.

Safia perches on his knee. 'We can buy a smashing wedding suit for you. Kit you out real lovely.'

'Yeah.'

'Another beer?'

'Yeah.' Tariq hands her his empty glass, his legs spread grandly in empty contemplation. Beer foam flecks his moustache.

She pauses – or poses – in the doorway. 'Terry won't be home tonight.'

'Yeah?'

ଢ

Joe Reddaway is in a vile mood (he reckons). Hadn't he deserved better from her than this? Hadn't he proved himself a true friend throughout the 'scarf crisis'? Has he published a single French-kiss from her stolen love letters? Yet here it is! on his desk! without a word of warning!: the leading article in this week's *Times Educational Supplement*:

'Scarf Fever in Muslim Bruddersford,' by Patricia Newman.

Joe jots down a few of her key phrases for tomorrow's 'Plain Speaking' column. But tomorrow is no good in journalism. The London papers are running big features on Mrs Patricia Newman *today*! The story is dynamite!

—pandering to the fundamentalists . . .

—playing politics with children's education . . .

—in England we speak English . . .

—what hope, what future, for Muslim girls subjected to patriarchal domination? . . .

—a city trapped in election fever, a Labour Party divided by religious schism . . .

—a Director of Education better fitted to be Professor of Cultural Meditation and Pluralistic Piety in the Hindu University of the Loving Universe.

Joe glowers at a half-eaten toasted sandwich. He's been scooped. Humiliated. A local hack. Perhaps you've trodden in too many dust-bins, she'd said. She'd looked at him as if he were an undercooked suet pudding. The woman's a bigot!

He dials the Hightown Upper School number. A secretary answers. 'Mrs Newman is unavailable, I'm afraid.'

'Ask her to call me back with answers to the following questions. One: did she clear her *TES* article in advance with the Department of Education? Two: does she anticipate disciplinary proceedings against her? Three – '

'Two is enough, Mr Reddaway. I'll give her your message. Thanks for calling.'

By mid-afternoon the incoming calls to the *Echo* are ten-to-one in favour of Patricia Newman. She is the city's heroine; she has drawn the line against foreign fanaticism where others have dithered; she has put education above politics; she has stood up to the vilest campaign of personal abuse and intimidation ever suffered by a headteacher in Bruddersford; any move to discipline her would cost Labour control of the Council in tomorrow's poll.

And Rajiv Lal must go. Joe notes that the collective fury of the citizenry has now focussed on the Hindu Director of Education.

At four in the afternoon the City's Education Committee suspends Rajiv Lal from his duties. Perlman orders him to clear his desk and be out of the D of E by four-thirty. Simultaneously the police arrest some thirty Muslim pickets, including Mustafa Jangar, outside High-town Upper School and charge them under the Public Order Act.

৩

Early on polling day Haqq is already in trouble with the Returning Officer. At 6.45 a.m. he places his car, covered with green-and-yellow stickers, inside the small yard of a primary school which is serving as a polling station. When he returns from door-knocking half an hour later the polling station officials have covered his car with a sheet and threaten him with prosecution.

Nice start! That's the system for you! Haqq is worried, even despondent. Already at this early hour he has observed white women making their way to the polls – whereas the Muslim women will vote only in the company of their husbands. Knocking the women up, urging them to turn out, is futile.

'Sister, I come for Haqq voting.'

'You come when husband waking up.'

He is short of tellers. The eight polling stations in Tanner Ward are open for thirteen hours and he needs someone on duty at all eight to write down the electoral number of each voter as he or she leaves the polling station. Half the lads he was depending on are still held on remand in London prison cells after the demos. No sign of Tariq Khan – according to Shasti he's heading south again. Problems, problems. The big parties can easily draft women and pensioners to sit as tellers while the 'crack troops' do the door-to-door stuff. But here again Muslim women won't, can't do it, alone; as for the old men, they would be confused, they wouldn't understand English, they wouldn't write down the numbers right. The Labour and Tory tellers would hoodwink them.

He passes a knot of Muslim women, constantly reaching to adjust their headscarves, a habit like flicking long hair from the eyes. He knows better than to shout at them, though he's tempted. 'Go for voting!' he yells. 'Vote Haqq. Vote Number 3!'

Haqq, Shasti and Tiger Siddiqi visit the polling station known as the 'village hall', a mix of nonconformist chapel and primary school in stained brown brick. The new utility entrance door has been painted tomato-red. He finds no Muslim Independent teller at the door, just the inevitable red, blue and yellow rosettes of the big parties. Furious, Haqq examines his rota of tellers:

'Your son, Salman!' he accuses Shasti. 'Where is he?'

'I'll kill him!'

Haqq places Tiger Siddiqi on teller-duty (there's no chair for him) while Shasti roars off to kill his son.

Reaching the Community Centre (of which Haqq is chairman), he is gratified to see the janitor's dog running up and down the pavement chasing away Labour voters. But again no Muslim Independent teller! Voters who brave the janitor's dog are arrowed to the empty sports hall where Tiger Siddiqi teaches karate, keep-fit, yoga, tennis, badminton, basketball, volleyball. As a candidate, Haqq is permitted entry. It's uncannily quiet in the sports hall. Ballot boxes create their own awe and hush.

Haqq notices that the Labour agent, Ted Francis, is talking to the Returning Officer. Haqq nods genially to the polling staff:

'Any problems?'

The Returning Office takes him aside. 'There have been complaints about the conduct of your tellers and helpers outside this polling station. It is alleged that they have been approaching voters. You know this is strictly forbidden.'

Ted Francis is sporting the largest red rosette in the world. He doesn't deign to look at Haqq while repeating his complaint to the Returning Officer: 'His people have been addressing voters in Muslim as they arrive.'

'There is no such language as "Muslim",' Haqq says.

The old Latvian SS man and his Yorkshire wife enter the polling station.

'It's that Labour Asian man,' she says, pointing at Haqq.

'Ayshun? Vot say?'

Ted Francis expands his protests to the Returning Officer: 'Mr Haqq's people have been instructing voters, in English, "Vote Number 3". Number 3 on the list is Mr Haqq here. In addition a Labour car transporting sick and disabled voters has been trailed by a Toyota all morning. This is the registration number. The clear intention is intimidation.'

Haqq glances at the written-down registration number – clearly Shasti's son Salman, a reckless lad, no discipline, too much money.

'Don't believe a word of this,' Haqq tells the Returning Officer. 'I know this man to be a proven liar.'

☙

LABOUR RETAINS CONTROL OF COUNCIL

—Malik holds Tanner against Tory by 117 votes

—Haqq wiped out: alleges foul play

—Hani Malik to chair Education Committee. Perlman moves to Environment

—New rules expected to permit Muslim scarf in schools

—Hightown Upper School Head Newman resigns 'for personal reasons'

CITY PAYS TRIBUTE TO LORD MAYOR ZAHEED
   —Muslims remember Izza Shah
   —Mustafa Jangar set to lead Islamic Council

HARRY FLOWERS SET TO WIN LABOUR RENOMINATION
   —Wahabia Zaheed alleges 'fix'

ৡ

Fatima is watching the Ayatollah's funeral at Behesht Zahra, the Martyrs' cemetery, on TV. Her new guardian, the trustee of Izza Shah's estate, is standing behind her chair with the restless motions of a young man whose work calls but who remains captivated by the extraordinary scenes of mass fervour coming from Tehran. Ali is silent, always silent. Folded into a chair like a rain-shrunken rag-doll, Fatima awaits her destiny as his wife. Obligation must prevail under Islam.

Four hundred and thirty-eight days until her sixteenth birthday.

Heat and dust. Swathed in white, with the black turban of a seyyid, a descendant of the Prophet, resting on his chest, the Supreme Imam is exhibited in a refrigerated glass catafalque. Dense crowds of women are ululating and men are flagellating their chests while firemen spray the packed mass with water. The Ayatollah's will is read out to the world in English. Fatima rejoices in its righteous anger, its hatred and curses against the superstitious faith of Wahhabism, its vows of vengeance against King Fahd of Saudi Arabia for the deaths of four hundred Iranian pilgrims during the Hajj. The whole Saudi royal family is damned, 'those traitors to Allah's great shrine, may God's curse and that of His Angels and prophets be upon them.' Intently Fatima absorbs the long list of traitors: King Hassan of Morocco, King Hussein of Jordan, President Saddam Hussein of Iraq, all 'led by the Great Satan, America, and its partner, World Zionism'. She nods as she hears the Soviet Union, too, reviled as 'a Satanic force'; she understands that Satan is abroad but it does not strike her that Gamal Rahman receives no mention at all.

But it does strike Ali Cheema. Rahman is already forgotten, an incidental motion in a madness.

The Ayatollah's son and aide, Ahmad Khomeini, is addressing the vast crowd, the world:

'Hearts full of love for Khomeini will beat forever and the sun of the Imam's leadership will shine on the universe. Khomeini was Allah's spirit in the body of time – and Allah's spirit is eternal.'

Furtively, Fatima glances up at Ali. Nothing.

542

Wide eyed, she gazes at scenes of divine ecstasy as the mourners tear the remains of the shroud from the Ayatollah's holy body and climb into his grave. Sufi mystics gather bowls of earth from the bottom of the grave and pass them out to be eaten by the multitude. The half-naked corpse is pulled from its coffin and carried aloft by a heaving sea of ecstatic Hezbollahi, the Party of God. The Ayatollah's thin white legs appear briefly before he falls into the dust. Shots are fired into the air; the helicopter which has brought the body to the cemetery returns, landing among the mourners as they soar to new levels of frenzy.

'Peace be upon him,' Fatima whispers. Her hand reaches for Ali's but does not find it.

Gamal Rahman, too, has been watching television.

෴

It is one of those glorious days that settle on southern England in high summer – the grass tennis courts of Wimbledon bathed in sunshine before the umbrellas go up and the covers down, smoked salmon sandwiches with cucumber, buck's fizz, barbecues in spacious private gardens, black tie evenings at Glyndebourne, the humming piazza at Covent Garden, lazing cricket matches on village greens, picnics in Richmond Park within sight of grazing deer.

Wahabia is driving Daddy's BMW to Henley, Ali beside her. Wahabia is shrouded in the black of mourning. Their relationship has cooled. She no longer touches him. Her role as Daughter-Widow Rampant has gathered her scattered fires into a single furnace of unflickering heat beneath the ashes. Ali finds himself in limbo. Finally rejected by the College – there had been no interview and no expression of regret from the Bishop, merely the most formal of dismissals from the College Secretary – Ali is perplexed and irritated by his new duties as executor of Izza Shah's estate and Fatima's guardian. For the first time in years he has seen fit to write to his parents' relatives in Pakistan, proposing that they settle in Bruddersford to look after the girl: 'Izza Shah left more money than anticipated. Fatima and I have both inherited very useful legacies.'

In the meanwhile, Nasreen Hassani has offered to take Fatima under her daily care.

Ali is a good navigator, even in unfamiliar terrain. He concentrates on the map spread across his knee. He observes the road signs keenly and misses nothing. Wahabia's pretty foot presses hard on the throttle of the car Daddy loved so much.

Jasmin is also driving to Henley, alone, a tense, nervy little person, beset by worries and heartache. She has braced herself to come.

Word has filtered down from her BBC Controller that her 'Final Call' contract will not be renewed unless she can guarantee the continued participation of Inigo Lorraine. He's the star. Audiences like him – *and how brilliantly he has handled the whole Gamal Rahman affair.* Jasmin keeps glancing at her watch. This bloody Saturday traffic! Everyone is heading for Henley in midsummer! Why don't they build some decent roads!

The celebrated TV comedian Terry Conroy glides his Rolls towards Henley, one hand on the wheel, the other busy with his cigar. He's crimson-drunk but can drive blindfold. Safia sits beside him, reclining in ivory-coloured leather, dressed to kill and chewing gum. (Jasmin had instructed her to kick the gum habit, and Safia intends to jettison her blob before arrival – her window will purr down at the touch of a button.) In the back seat her 'brother', Tariq, lounges in his splendid new white suit, his silk tie, his red carnation, silently gazing upon Satan's pastures, the lawns, perfumed gardens, the vines and roses climbing their trellises, the labradors and lurchers, the verandah tables laden with wine.

Wahabia parks by the river.

'That must be the boat,' Ali says.

'Are we too early?'

'No, dead on time.'

Clutching wedding presents wrapped in pink and white tissue paper, they walk back along the towpath to the jetty where the deck of the waiting boat is already thick with chattering guests. Heads turn slightly – Wahabia is wearing the full burka and no make-up; Ali wears a black tie – two in fact, one for Izza Shah, one for Zulfikar Zaheed.

He hears the throb of 'Darling darling' even before he follows Wahabia up the gangway on to the main deck of the decorative river boat. Inigo greets them hugely, introducing his beautiful bride.

'We've met,' Ali says.

The bride looks blank, the groom puzzled.

Between them bride and groom seem to possess five or six parents whom Ali makes no attempt to sort out. Waiters bear silver trays loaded with champagne glasses; Ali asks for orange juice, Wahabia for nothing. She will neither drink nor eat, she is in mourning. She stands alone, but not for long: coloured butterflies are soon flapping round her motionless black presence – she is news, she is drama, she's the stuff of headlines. Jasmin is eyeing Wahabia from a circumspect distance. Jasmin has arrived early, too early, almost the first guest, embarrassing for Inigo and Susie, and now everyone seems to be avoiding her, even people she knows well, as if she carried some contagion.

'We're off! Hooray!'

The engines are making a more serious sound now and there is motion in the decks. Guests clutching glasses and plates of quiche are making for the upper deck, where the view is.

'Hullo, Jasmin.'

'Hullo, Ali.'

He nods and passes on – Inigo has just confided that he has signed up for a new 'Final Call' series, with a new producer.

'We'll make the film we wanted to make, Ali. We'll bring you south, among the infidels.' That serene, unfolding smile. That alert, probing, considerate scrutiny. Then a further confidence (Inigo shunting him aside, bending to his ear): 'Up river there is to be a surprise guest, Ali. You will behave yourself, won't you?'

Ali merely nods. 'Of course.' He takes a plate of fresh salmon to the upper deck, feeling grim and provincial (as so often at Gamal's parties) among the colourful blazers and straw boaters. The boat is gliding between huge riverside mansions, gleaming cars stacked up in sweeping gravel driveways, lovely girls dangling their legs in hammocks under spreading yew trees, willows gracefully praying to their ponds, fly-fishers on the banks of reserved stretches of river. There are no Blasphemy laws here.

Jasmin collides with Jilly Jumpers.

'Darling, I'm so sorry,' the famous author says.

'About what, Jilly?'

'About *everything*, darling. Misfortunes never come singly, they say.'

'How's your son Jamie?' Jasmin asks frigidly.

'Jamie has gone to India! He's making a documentary for Spielberg.'

'Wonderful! For how long?'

'I wish I knew! No, I'm a liar, I don't wish I knew. Uncertainty is strangely comforting – especially where Jamie is concerned. My God, who's that?'

Jasmin follows Jumpers's astonished gaze – Safia! Safia looking like a knickerbocker glory from Forte's.

'She's Terry Conroy's latest,' Jasmin says. 'Izza Shah's delinquent daughter.'

'*Oh*. Yes, I've read about the scandal. Isn't she absolutely gorgeous in a terribly vulgar way?'

Darling, I'm so sorry . . . about everything.

'And who's that big, muscular fellow looking extremely ill at ease just behind her?' Jilly asks. 'The one in the *very new* white suit.'

Jasmin examines the dark-skinned young man from a distance. She could swear that Inigo had interviewed him in Bruddersford.

'I don't recognize him.' His restless and resentful gaze momentarily locks into hers. 'God!' she exclaims. 'He spat at me in Parliament Square!'

Hot-air balloons float overhead, below the confident purr of small private aircraft. Families are picnicking off chicken and strawberries along the banks. The boat drifts through leisurely locks, past dreaming weirs. Three ladies pass on horseback.

When he first spotted Safia and Tariq on the upper deck, Ali felt a twinge of panic. His two worlds were colliding unpleasantly, the blood was running into the cream. Had they seen him? He moves away in search of Wahabia, but Wahabia, the magnetic black stone of the Kaaba, is blocked off by a tight ring of the chattering classes, notably Jilly Jumpers.

'Oh, my dear, I'm so very, very sorry,' Jumpers is saying. 'In my view your father was the very best hope for the Muslims of your tormented city.'

'Thank you. For the whole city.'

Ali feels a tap on his shoulder. It's Safia.

'Thought you'd ignore me, did you?'

'Yes.'

'Well, yer can't.'

'What's that delinquent rapist doing with you?'

'Fuck you, Ali Cheema.'

Ali turns away, inserting himself between Wahabia and Jilly Jumpers.

'Trouble,' he murmurs to Wahabia in Punjabi. 'Safia's brought Tariq Khan on board.'

Wahabia nods. 'I remember him in Hill Street Court. Mrs Newman wanted him inside.'

'It might have been a good idea.'

'Daddy didn't think so.'

'Tariq Khan is dangerous. I'd better inform Inigo.'

'*What* exotic language are you two talking?' Jilly Jumpers cuts in.

'Don't say anything,' Wahabia commands Ali, still in Punjabi. 'Let history take its course. But for Gamal Rahman, Daddy would still be alive.'

'You have more conviction than I, Sister.'

'Obviously.'

Wahabia turns to Jumpers. 'Would you like to meet a genuine, working-class Bruddersford Muslim?'

'Oh, marvellous! Lead the way, dear!'

Wahabia leads the way. Safia backs off as they approach but Tariq stands his ground.

'Hullo, Tariq. I'm Wahabia Zaheed.'

'Aye. I know.'

'I'd like you to meet Mrs Jilly Jumpers, the famous writer.'

'Well you *are* a handsome fellow, Tariq.' Jumpers offers her hand while balancing a glass of wine and a paper plate of strawberry gateau in the other. 'So you're from that exciting, in-the-news city?'

'Aye, Bruddersford.'

'Oh perfect Yorkshire, I do love to hear it.'

'Saw you on telly,' Tariq says.

'Tell me exactly what you thought. Don't spare me!'

'Not much – no offence.'

'None taken! Too many people are running around being offended and insulted! Let me not join them.'

'Aye.'

'Ali should take you to see Oxford, his *alma mater.* I can see you're quite sweet, quite docile. And I can guess what is happening in your ear on this boat. The female voices you hear in Bruddersford are soft, muted, caring. Even the young girls are proto-mothers. Their role towards the male is bounded by duty and morality. But here in the South, the predominant pitch of these social gatherings is like crushed ice – women laugh, scream and voice opinions with a bewildering brashness. Isn't that so, Tariq?'

'I don't rightly know.'

'You see, I was right. A good novelist is always right.'

Wahabia says something clear and forceful to Tariq in Punjabi. Tariq murmurs in response, stranded by the regal force of Zaheed's daughter. Safia is watching them, a blob of chewing gum hanging on her tongue. No one has attempted to make conversation with her since the wedding party left Henley. The houseboat is passing the mansions, stables and paddocks of film moguls. The wedding guests are talking of TV franchises, the film industry, the Net Book Agreement.

Jilly Jumpers has decided that Wahabia is the most intriguing person on board, totally *different*, ruthlessly ambitious of course – and how many young women have cradled their murdered father in their arms? (It was all in the papers.) Jumpers buttonholes Wahabia again – or whatever you do to someone shrouded in a burka.

'Of course Ali and I are ideologically at daggers drawn,' Jumpers says.

'I was confused to hear a professed atheist like yourself demanding a muscular Christianity.'

'Oh yes! Unfortunately Islam has no respect for secular liberalism, which is regarded as a moral void, a black hole waiting to be filled with some version of God. So I filled it.'

'Do you really believe that all Muslim women are so subjugated and depressed as you said?'

'Not at all! Heavens! Women like yourself and poor, dear Jasmin will lead the way.'

'Jasmin isn't a Muslim.'

'Of course she isn't. I simply meant – '

'Many of my sisters who wear dark shawls and hijabs in Bruddersford hold university degrees in chemistry or physics – did you know that?'

'It doesn't surprise me *at all*, dear. I have always said there are two Islams, the patriarchal *nightmare* of the mullahs and the – '

'Some of us who heard your TV lecture missed the distinction, Mrs Jumpers.'

Jilly Jumpers now wears a fixed, still-life smile. This Wahabia Zaheed creature may be too much of a good thing – such latent animosity! But what a character for a book!

Jasmin joins them, quivering with excitement. 'Have you heard the news, Jilly?'

'No need to whisper, darling. Do you mean the huge bonanza "surprise" in store for us? I'm told he's due to embark at the next lock – apparently his minders didn't fancy the crowds at Henley.'

Jasmin is deflated. 'Did Inigo tell you?'

'Karl did. He's downstairs in the buffet guzzling strawberry gateau because it's the Jewish Sabbath or something.'

'Who's Karl?' Wahabia asks.

'Why, Gamal's publisher, of course,' Jumpers says. 'And mine. Frankly, dear, Karl publishes everyone who's anyone. He's the most *wonderful* man – he had the courage and the vision to back Gamal when that awful Tony Trevelyan was trying to get rid of him.'

Jasmin's eyes blaze at Wahabia. 'Karl was condemned to death in the Ayatollah's fatwa – if you recall.'

Wahabia glances across towards Tariq. He has heard it all. She observes a thickening in his throat, the piston-like motion of his Adam's apple. Does he realize that Daddy saved him from prison? How finely built he is! Why does he consort with that spray-painted slut Safia? Wahabia imagines a knife in its tooled leather sheath, decorated with Koranic motifs in gold, his jihad knife, strapped to his shoulder beneath his left arm. Tariq must surely have divined the hand that fate was to deal him!

Ali reappears and plucks at Wahabia's sleeve. 'Have you heard? he murmurs.

From beneath her burka Wahabia appraises him coolly. Sweat is running into his collar. Detaching herself from Jumpers, she edges through the crowd towards Tariq Khan. Ali follows her.

'Have courage, Brother,' she tells Tariq, according Safia not a glance. 'Allah has brought you to your destiny.'

Tariq stares at Zulfikar Zaheed's daughter, mute.

'It was me who brought Tariq,' Safia tells anyone who will listen. 'I knew the scenario a week ago.' But Safia is unworthy of anyone's attention.

'This is not a matter for women,' Ali mutters to Wahabia in Punjabi.

'Women know who are the real men. Is that not so, Tariq?'

'Aye.'

'A true Muslim never betrays hospitality,' Ali tells Tariq in Punjabi. 'You are a guest on this boat.'

'What a pathetic little petty-bourgeois you are,' Wahabia says.

Ali hurriedly descends to the main deck in search of Inigo Lorraine.

The legendary publisher, Karl, has now come up to the top deck, a tall man with a mid-Atlantic ease of manner and more than a faint resemblance to Gregory Peck. Or James Stewart. Or Clark Gable even – Karl has published biographies of all three. He stoops towards Jilly Jumpers and Jasmin with a fine blend of gallantry and condescension, his jacket falling open around a comfortable stomach and a vast annual turnover.

'You really cannot delay the paperback edition of Gamal's book any longer,' Jumpers is chiding him.

'I agree,' Jasmin says.

'That's something I can't discuss, Jilly. I have to consider the security of my warehouse staff. But the paperback edition is really a red herring. A book as complex as this was never intended for the mass market display racks.'

'Gamal told me on the phone the other day that if you'd grasped the nettle and brought out the paperback three months ago the furore would be dying down by now.'

'I agree,' Jasmin says.

'Who knows?' Karl says. 'Gamal doesn't. His doctors have warned him to give up making predictions. This book was the greatest disaster ever to have hit us. I'm not at liberty to tell you how much our security operation has cost but I *can* tell you it has wiped out our legendary profits from Gamal's book. From a strictly business angle the only sensible decision would have been to withdraw the book – I mean long ago. But we didn't. We thought a principle was at stake. We still do. And we all remain at risk.'

Motions of excitement palpitate among the guests who have crowded forward to the bow, scanning upriver towards the lock, where two identical black cars are growing larger by the minute. Jilly Jumpers and Jasmin are waving gaily to the unmistakably pear-shaped figure standing on the bank – 'the Louis Philippe of modern letters, and equally doomed' (Gamal Rahman, 'Unbelievable Memoirs,' *Prospero*, No 16). Sporting a blazer and boater, and flanked by short-haired minders in tight suits, Gamal salutes the approaching wedding party with comic, Chaplinesque gestures indicating helplessness – what an absurd way for a writer to be forced to live! His bulging eyes roll expressively.

'And I should have been the bridegroom!' he calls. 'Susie, Susie, where art thou Susie! Don't forget your adoring Ubu Roi!'

'What will you do, Brother?' Wahabia whispers to Tariq.

'Sister, I will do what honour dictates. Izzat!'

Fragments of what he takes to be Arabic reach the publisher Karl. He turns cautiously. Jilly Jumpers monitors his alarm.

'Tariq's really a very nice boy,' she assures Karl. 'I had a perfectly cosy little chat with him.'

'He may be a very nice boy but I can see a copy of the fatwa sticking out of his pocket.'

'Heavens! – you don't imagine . . .'

'I do imagine, Jilly.' Karl is edging towards the stairs.

The boat is now almost at rest, manoeuvring into the lock. It rocks gently. Wahabia has folded her arm through Tariq's.

'I spit upon Shaytan Rahman,' she murmurs. 'All true Muslim women, daughters of our Prophet's wives, spit upon him, Brother Tariq.'

Tariq is staring down, transfixed, at the river bank. Gamal Rahman can be heard bantering with the bride and groom across the small divide of water. (Inigo has laughed off Ali's frantic warnings – 'Not at *my* wedding, Ali, this is a celebration of life!')

'Allah akhbar, Brother!' Wahabia's hand slides inside Tariq's new-white jacket to feel the knife. She caresses it like a penis then pushes him forward sharply. 'Hurry, Brother. Now! Now!'

'Allah akhbar, Sister!' Tariq leaps for the rail, balances, then jumps for the shore. Now he's running up the river bank towards the fat, jovial, eye-rolling, boater-waving author, who sports a red carnation and a broad, chuckling smile.

Unsheathed, Uncle Abdul's carving knife flashes in the sun. A wave of horror ripples through the guests gathered on the deck. Ali Cheema observes the calculating hesitation of Gamal's minders. It could be a prank, a party turn. Manufacturing martyrs does not figure on the Government's agenda.

'Oh *my God*,' Jasmin cries. 'Gamal!'

Inigo Lorraine seizes his bride's head and pulls her face into his chest. This is something Susie mustn't see on her wedding day.

'Go on, Tareeq!' Safia shrieks from the upper deck. 'Finish the bastard!'

That does it. Wheeling birds are hurled across the summer sky by the single gun-shot. Safia is sobbing now but she's also laughing.

ൟ

Nasreen has discovered Rajiv Lal's private address by way of an envelope – a telephone bill – left lying on his desk in the Department of Education. She notices well-tended trees, a secret adventure playground which her son Imran would love, even a small duck pond with helpful little ramps. (She remembers that ducks need ramps when breeding.) Rajiv dwells in a magic garden graced by miniature Hindu temples and exquisite little figurines of copulating deities (she supposes).

Nasreen is carrying a modest bunch of roses, yellow and white.

'Nice roses,' she hears.

She hadn't noticed the fat man sitting on the bench in the sunshine. He is beaming and nodding at her while scattering breadcrumbs from a paper bag in his lap. Birds are gathering at his feet without a trace of fear.

'Lovely morning,' he adds.

'Yes,' she murmurs.

It's an educated voice though he doesn't exactly look like he sounds. Not English. More Arab or something. His eyes constantly bulge and swivel and roll like huge, oiled marbles – she shudders.

'Rajiv lives on the third floor,' the man says. 'Good luck, Nasreen, you deserve it.'

Her heart hammers in fright: has he escaped from the local hospital? She notices that the bolder birds are now perching on the two small horns protruding from the fat man's high, domed forehead.

She climbs the stairs to the third floor. A long vertical panel of glass runs all the way down the stairwell. She hesitates, then presses the bell. Rajiv can hardly accept the roses without inviting her in. She notices a spy-hole. Is he even now studying her through the magnifying lens? Has she come too early in the day? People who have lost their jobs – even ultra-dedicated people like Rajiv – often sink into apathy. They lie in bed, remembering the bustling life of the office they will never see again. She knows quite a lot of Muslim wives whose husbands have fallen into torpor after losing their jobs.

The door opens. Rajiv is wearing a Krishna-blue, open-neck shirt, fawn summer slacks – no shoes. He adjusts his glasses as if the woman standing at his door is out of focus.

'Good morning, Mr Lal . . . Forgive me, I just wanted to bring you . . . to express my support and sympathy.'

'Very kind. How did you find my address?'

His tone is almost accusatory – no welcome. She chokes with embarrassment. 'A man outside told me you live on the third floor.'

'A man?'

'Yes, he's sitting on the bench feeding the birds.'

'Bench? There's no bench.'

'I assure you – ' She breaks off. 'You have suffered an injustice . . . I've bought some silly roses.'

'Please come in.'

'Should I remove my shoes?'

'No need.'

She removes her shoes. Reluctantly he steps aside. She passes very close to him, almost touching, into the sweetly scented aroma – the holy incense of the Hindus? – pervading his sanctum.

'You must excuse the mess,' he says. 'We had some friends to dinner last night.'

We! Her heart freezes. So it's as she's always feared: there's a 'we'. Her eyes search the modern, functional furniture of the sitting room for signs of a female occupant.

'Who is that?' she asks, indicating a painting.

'Siva.'

A big, plate-glass window overlooks a balcony rich in exotic potted flowers and ferns.

'You have a lovely view here,' she says.

'Yes. The duck pond was my idea. I am very fond of ducks.'

'I never knew!'

'However, as you can see, there is no bench down there. We did have one but it attracted undesirables, drunks, people who kept the residents awake at night. So we had the bench removed.'

'What a beautiful rocking chair you have,' she murmurs. It is indeed beautiful: green leather on a burnished steel frame whose curves convey taste, style, modernity.

'Please sit down,' he says, adding, 'wherever you can.'

The chairs and sofa are piled with books, magazines, half-opened brown envelopes from important people and institutions. He makes no effort to clear a space for her. Shyly she prods some papers to one side; perches herself on the edge of the sofa; rises again.

'You should perhaps put these flowers in water.'

He takes the flowers, stiffly, then lays them down.

'I hope you are well,' he says.

'How I am is of no account, Mr Lal. I have come to express my sympathy. It was always a great honour to work for you. An inspiration, I assure you.'

'I hear you have been off work, sick. Nothing serious, I hope.'

Rajiv had still been at his Director's desk when she had requested leave of absence. A note from her doctor had passed from her hand to his. Their fingers had touched. Has he forgotten?

'I have left my husband,' Nasreen hears herself say. She has read in a magazine that once you are in love you cannot see straight because your hormones become seriously disturbed. 'Beauty,' the writer had concluded, in what struck Nasreen as a wonderful phrase, 'lies in the eye of the beholder.'

'I am sorry that you are not well,' Rajiv says.

'Yes. I can no longer love my husband. I sometimes think it's somehow to do with this Rahman book . . . somehow.'

'Shall I make you some tea?'

Why does he say 'make *you*' – to indicate that he doesn't need any himself – that he would be putting himself to trouble for her sake alone?

'No thank you, really no need.'

Rajiv silent.

'I am asking myself what you will do next in your life, Mr Lal. Many people here in Bruddersford are most concerned for you.'

'We all make our own storms.'

'Oh – no. You did nothing wrong . . .'

'I am applying for a post in India.'

'India!'

'In New Delhi.'

'But you have lived all your life in Britain!'

'Would you not be happier living in Pakistan, Nasreen?'

'What are you saying, Mr Lal?'

'I am saying that multiculturalism has failed. People don't want it. People are not by nature tolerant. By nature they are racist and bigoted. They take pleasure in what divides them.'

'You sound very bitter, Mr Lal. You have been shamefully treated.'

'Yes.'

Nasreen knows she should leave.

'I have brought you my love, my personal love, Rajiv.'

He adjusts his glasses. 'I am indebted.'

She cries now. Her long-suppressed emotions rise like vomit, spilling out into an ugly puddle which does not belong to her.

'You are a cold man. You love the world but not anyone in it. You love children but you do not have a child of your own. You – '

She hears the sudden closing of the front door. Rajiv raises his voice abruptly, discarding his usual Sufi-murmur.

'I wish,' he says loudly, 'I could intercede in your domestic difficulties, Mrs Hassani, which are causing you so much distress.'

Nasreen hears the bedroom door close on the young white woman in the stolen photograph.

'I must go now,' she says. 'My husband is expecting me.'

EPILOGUE

∽

London, 12 August

Dear Dad,

As you say, enough is enough. My Bruddersford characters have probably done themselves as much damage by now as the devil my master could have wished. I'm sorry Nasreen had no luck but she was born into the wrong religion for luck. As for Tariq, I shed no tears – it was either him or me. I did, however, hesitate over Zaheed's assassination – but once I'd enrolled as an honorary citizen of Muslim Bruddersford in the guise of Iqbal Iqbal, the djinn was pretty well bound to make a murderous exit from the toilet bowl. (I hear that Iqbal's defence will be based on a plea of 'false identity' – in short, the pharmacist is claiming to be a character in a book with no control over his own destiny.)

Rumours predicting my conversion to Islam can be discounted. I was four and three-quarters when you first recommended the principle of compromise. While gathering ripe pears in the garden, you quoted the Holy Koran: 'If you take one step towards me I will take ten steps towards you.' I remember applying this beguiling formula to the Great Pyramid; even when I'd taken a dozen steps towards it across the garden, it didn't budge.

Your statement condemning the fatwa reached me like a lifeline: let's say a Dadline. It could have come sooner – your measured silence sounded like thunder to your boy – but you are not without your own difficulties. The spitback against you is painful to read. Have these sweating, sex-obsessed, bullyboy mullahs no shame at all? Frankly, things are even worse in Egypt than when I left. Any writer condemned for 'scorning religions' (whatever that may mean) is heading straight for the Tora prison. Only last month a dozen books were seized by Islamic censors at the Cairo Bookfair – not least your own. It's not encouraging.

Am I lonely, your recent letter asks. It's a pertinent question and one that I was often tempted to put to you, a widower of so many years. I am fascinated by my Secret Service minders. They're almost as intelligent as London taxi drivers – that piquant blend of know-all and know-nothing. A boundless cynicism about the way the world really works masks a boundless naïvety. I had one massive thug, a Soho bouncer by appearance, who talked me the whole way through *The Children of Mustafa*. His shrewd views on the prophets could have been those of an Oxbridge prof. had he not prefaced every comment with 'Don't get me wrong, sir.'

You never allowed me to bespoil Oxford but I gather that 'Don't get me wrong' is not the recommended tutorial style.

Am I writing, you ask. Nothing much, nothing of consequence. I enclose a little jeu d'ésprit, which I recently tossed off in a morning. It will appear in next month's issue of *Prospero*. I have called it 'Rahman Lost'. Isaac likes it – or says he does. But he also admits he could currently get me a thousand dollars if I copied out a page of the London telephone directory.

Please write again soon.

Your devoted son Gamal

RAHMAN LOST

The world-infamous author Gamal Rahman, first reported lost a month ago, is still lost. It is not yet clear whether lost means 'dead' (as with 'lost in battle') or simply lost like a purse. Either way, there have been no substantiated sightings of the controversial writer during the four weeks since he secretly took a British Airways flight from Heathrow to Copenhagen for an International PEN Congress, and failed to walk into the expectant embrace of his host, Preben Kaarlsrot.

'I shall never forget seeing this significant writer not step off the plane,' Mr Kaarlsrot told journalists in the pine-furnished offices of Danepen, over a smorgasbord and Carlsberg-export. For its part, British Airways continues to insist that the plane definitely not did not break up over the North Sea, nor did any of its passengers tumble from the heavens without benefit of parachutes or wings.

'You'd notice that sort of thing,' a BA spokeswoman said.

The stewardesses who attended the flight are adamant that the journey passed normally. A Mr Gamal Rahman had boarded the flight under the pseudonym 'Shaytan Rahman', carrying a laptop word processor, a file of newspaper cuttings about himself, and several signed copies of his novel, *The Devil: an Interview*, which he offered to the stewardesses with 'lewd winks and slobbery chuckles' while they were demonstrating the life-jacket and oxygen routine. A male steward quieted him down, fastened his seat belt and extinguished his cigarette. Mr Rahman sounded his buzzer even as the plane sped down the runway, calling for a Johnnie Walker on the rocks.

Stewardess Greta Garbo recalls: 'He asked me whether I knew who he was. I said, "No, sir, but I can check the passenger list if you're not sure." About five minutes later he asked me where I was spending the night in Copenhagen, then invited me to change places with his laptop computer. I called the chief steward. By the time we returned Mr Rahman's seat was empty. We concluded that he had taken himself to the toilet.'

An hour later, approaching Copenhagen, the staff began to hammer on the locked toilet door but got no audible response. When the door was finally forced the tiny facility was found to be empty. 'There was no evidence of a struggle.' Aeronautical experts from Boeing insist that the chances of an overweight passenger with a 42-inch waistband being accidentally flushed down the toilet and out into the sky are put at 'one-in-a-trillion'.

From the Arabian Gulf to Morocco it is perfectly understood that the Angel Gibreel had come on behalf of Allah to claim the infamous sinner, Gamal Rahman. In Egypt you won't find a fellah, a docker, a street-sweeper, a sheikh, a paratrooper, a shopkeeper, an unemployed medical graduate or a paid-up Muslim assassin who will not give you an instantaneous response to the question: what happened to Gamal Rahman?

'Gibreel got him.'

However, Boeing's aeronautical engineers put the chances of the Angel Gibreel coming to claim a passenger travelling first-class in a 747 as 'one-in-a-zillion'.

No one in Cairo admits to having read: *The Devil: an Interview.* 'And let's face it,' says the Deputy Minister of Culture, Rahman's Auntie Lulu, 'it's unreadable.' The editor of *Misr,* Mr Anis Hussein, has advised Egyptians to 'hand in' the 'arrogant degenerate' if they spot him flitting about his 'old haunts'. To date, more than five hundred Gamal Rahmans have been handed in, many the worse for wear.

In the Western capitals Gamal Rahman temporarily enjoys a cult-following, and his sales are impressive, although few readers claim to have 'finished him'. Many of those who have not finished him are sure that someone has finished him off. The KGB, CIA, MI5, Mossad and Islamic Jihad are mentioned more or less at random. No one points the finger at the Angel Gibreel.

Egyptian tourist guides, meanwhile, are promising hard-currency visitors to the pyramids an infra-red sighting of a spectral, haunted-tormented Rahman flitting about among the great monuments to seven thousand years of Egyptian civilization. Greek graffiti, found in the Valley of the Tombs, and originally ascribed to lazing soldiers of Alexander the Great, have now been redeciphered as definitely Rahman's work.

The new deluxe tour of Giza, 'Rahman by Night', leaves the Sheraton and the Nile Hilton shortly after midnight. But the air-conditioned coach is invariably empty. Islamic terrorists have struck at the tourist trade. Only one passenger can be counted on. There he is, hunched and swaddled at the back, shrouded in a galabiyeh, two short goat-horns protruding from his brow. Is he journeying to the desert of Giza to commune with the Sphinx? Which of them talks and which listens?

Afterword & Acknowledgments

Fatima's Scarf is a work of fiction but its genesis is to be found in a real event. In 1988 Salman Rushdie published his novel, *The Satanic Verses.* Early in 1989 copies of the book were publicly burned by irate British Muslims. During the months following, there were repeated demands by Muslim leaders, and Muslim street demonstrators, that the book should be banned or prosecuted under an ancient Blasphemy Act. This campaign was given added propulsion after the Ayatollah Khomeini issued his notorious 'fatwa', or Islamic edict, in which the Iranian imam 'sentenced' the British writer to death.

So much is history. *Fatima's Scarf* owes its obvious debt to history, but it is a work of fiction and its central character, the writer Gamal Rahman, is fictitious. His biography and personality are simply his own. The only parallels between invention and reality concern his 'fate' and the intellectual trajectories which may (or may not) be involved in challenging a holy book, whether the Koran or the Christian Bible. Rahman is not Rushdie's doppelgänger.

The same applies to the Muslim fictional characters in *Fatima's Scarf.* None of them represents a real person or family. Bruddersford is a composite city put together from Bolton, Bradford, Huddersfield, Blackburn, surrounding territories and – not least – invention. The invention was originally J.B. Priestley's in his celebrated comedy, *The Good Companions,* published some sixty years before the events recounted here. But that was another Bruddersford – not a mosque in sight.

Gamal Rahman's Egypt is a different kind of fictional space from Bruddersford. It occupies the same terrain as the real Egypt but the human beings populating that terrain are never real unless named as such. History yields to invention. Gamal merely asks, like Shakespeare's Fool, '*May not an ass know when the cart draws the horse?*'

Gamal Rahman's earliest images of the world are moulded by reading. His 'Egypt' owes as much to libraries as to life. The 'real' events he reports as a journalist are filtered through literature into his own fiction. Among authors still or recently living, the following deserve particular acknowledgment:

By Isabel Allende, *The House of the Spirits,* trans. by Magda Bogin (London, 1985)

By Albert Camus, *La Peste (The Plague)* (Paris, 1947)

By Laurence Durrell, *Justine* (London, 1957, 1961); *Balthazar* (London, 1958, 1961) – these being the first volumes of *The Alexandria Quartet*

By Naguib Mahfouz, *Respected Sir*, trans. by Rasheed El-Enany (London, 1986); *The Children of Gebelawi*, trans. by Patrick Stewart (London, 1982); *Midaq Alley*, trans. by Trevor Le Gassick (London, 1992);

By Salman Rushdie, *Midnight's Children* (London, 1981); *Shame* (London, 1983); and *The Satanic Verses* (London, 1988). *Fatima's Scarf* is replete with implicit allusions to these three novels by Rushdie and to the public debates following publication of *The Satanic Verses*.

Regarding the Muslim.'intifada' in Britain, I would like to acknowledge a debt to the following works:

Shabbir Akhtar, *Be Careful With Muhammad!* (London, 1989); Tariq Ali & Howard Brenton, *Iranian Nights* (London, 1989); Lisa Appignanesi & Sara Maitland (editors), *The Rushdie File* (London, 1989); Bhikhu Parekh & others, *Law, Blasphemy & the Multi-Faith Society* (London, 1990); Salman Rushdie, *Is Nothing Sacred?* (London, 1990); Malise Ruthven, *A Satanic Affair. Salman Rushdie & the Rage of Islam* (London, 1990); Nicolas Walter, *Blasphemy Ancient & Modern* (London, 1990); Richard Webster, *A Brief History of Blasphemy* (Southwold, 1990).

On the doctrines of the Ayatollah Khomeini: Ayatollah Khomeiny [sic], *Principes politiques, philosophiques, sociaux & religieux*, textes choisis et traduits du persan par Jean-Marie Xavière (Paris, 1979);

Ayatollah Seyyed Ruhollah Khomeyni [sic], *Pour un gouvernement islamique*, traduction M. Kotobi et B. Simon avec le concours de Ozra Banisadre (Paris, 1979).

For historical background on modern Egypt, I am indebted to: Mohamed Heikal, *The Road to Ramadan* (London, 1975) and *Autumn of Fury. The Assassination of Sadat* (London, 1983); Dilip Hiro, *Islamic Fundamentalism* (London, 1989); P.J. Vatikiotis, *Nasser and His Generation* (London, 1978); David Hirst & Irene Beeson, *Sadat* (London, 1981); Jean Lacouture, *Nasser* (Paris, 1971); Edward Mortimer, *Faith and Power. The Politics of Islam* (London, 1982); Anwar el-Sadat, *In Search of Identity* (London, 1978) and *Those I Have Known* (London, 1985); *Anwar Sadat. The Last Hundred Days*, photographs by Konrad B. Muller, text by Mark Willem Blaisse (London, 1981); Jehan Sadat, *A Woman of Egypt* (London, 1987).

Verses from The Koran are from Arthur Arberry's version (1955).

Finally, I would like to thank those friends who kindly read this novel in earlier drafts, and offered me valuable comments: Martha Caute, Catherine Devons, Jane O'Grady, Malise Ruthven, Angela and Nicolas Tredell, and Nancy Webber. My greatest debt is to my wife Martha, sustainer, editor, copy editor, proof reader and much else besides during a period of eight years, culminating in the uphill task of self-publication. Without her love and professional expertise it could never have been done.